A TALE OF THE TIME OF NERO

QUO VADIS

HENRYK SIENKIEWICZ

Translated by
Jeremiah Curtin

D0869546

DOVER PUBLICATIONS, INC.
MINEOLA, NEW YORK

Bibliographical Note

This Dover edition, first published in 2011, is an unabridged republication of the English edition of *Quo Vadis: A Narrative of the Time of Nero,* originally published by Little, Brown & Company, Boston, in 1896.

International Standard Book Number

ISBN-13: 978-0-486-47686-5
ISBN-10: 0-486-47686-3

Manufactured in the United States by LSC Communications
47686307   2022
www.doverpublications.com

TO

AUGUSTE COMTE,

Of San Francisco, Cal.,

MY DEAR FRIEND AND CLASSMATE,

I BEG TO DEDICATE THIS VOLUME

JEREMIAH CURTIN

INTRODUCTORY

In the trilogy "With Fire and Sword," "The Deluge," and "Pan Michael," Sienkiewicz has given pictures of a great and decisive epoch in modern history. The results of the struggle begun under Bogdan Hmelnitski have been felt for more than two centuries, and they are growing daily in importance. The Russia which rose out of that struggle has become a power not only of European but of world-wide significance, and, to all human seeming, she is yet in an early stage of her career.

In "Quo Vadis" the author gives us pictures of opening scenes in the conflict of moral ideas with the Roman Empire, — a conflict from which Christianity issued as the leading force in history.

The Slavs are not so well known to Western Europe or to us as they are sure to be in the near future; hence the trilogy, with all its popularity and merit, is not appreciated yet as it will be.

The conflict described in "Quo Vadis" is of supreme interest to a vast number of persons reading English; and this book will rouse, I think, more attention at first than anything written by Sienkiewicz hitherto.

JEREMIAH CURTIN

ILOM, NORTHERN GUATEMALA,
June, 1896

QUO
VADIS

CHAPTER I

Petronius woke only about midday, and as usual greatly wearied. The evening before he had been at one of Nero's feasts, which was prolonged till late at night. For some time his health had been failing. He said himself that he woke up benumbed, as it were, and without power of collecting his thoughts. But the morning bath and careful kneading of the body by trained slaves hastened gradually the course of his slothful blood, roused him, quickened him, restored his strength, so that he issued from the elæothesium, that is, the last division of the bath, as if he had risen from the dead, with eyes gleaming from wit and gladness, rejuvenated, filled with life, exquisite, so unapproachable that Otho himself could not compare with him, and was really that which he had been called, — *arbiter elegantiarum.*

He visited the public baths rarely, only when some rhetor happened there who roused admiration and who was spoken of in the city, or when in the ephebias there were combats of exceptional interest. Moreover, he had in his own "insula" private baths which Celer, the famous contemporary of Severus, had extended for him, reconstructed and arranged with such uncommon taste that Nero himself acknowledged their excellence over those of the Emperor, though the imperial baths were more extensive and finished with incomparably greater luxury.

After that feast, at which he was bored by the jesting of Vatinius with Nero, Lucan, and Seneca, he took part in a diatribe as to whether woman has a soul. Rising late, he used, as was his custom, the baths. Two enormous balneatores laid him on a cypress table covered with snow-white Egyptian byssus, and with hands dipped in perfumed olive oil began to rub his shapely body; and he waited with closed eyes till the heat of the laconicum and the heat of their hands passed through him and expelled weariness.

But after a certain time he spoke, and opened his eyes; he inquired about the weather, and then about gems which the jeweller Idomeneus had promised to send him for examination that day. It appeared that the weather was beautiful, with a light breeze from the Alban hills, and that the gems had not been brought. Petronius closed his eyes again, and had given command to bear him to the tepidarium, when from behind the curtain the nomenclator looked in, announcing that young Marcus Vinicius, recently returned from Asia Minor, had come to visit him.

Petronius ordered to admit the guest to the tepidarium, to which he was borne himself. Vinicius was the son of his oldest sister, who years before had married Marcus Vinicius, a man of consular dignity from the time of Tiberius. The young man was serving then under Corbulo against the

Parthians, and at the close of the war had returned to the city. Petronius had for him a certain weakness bordering on attachment, for Marcus was beautiful and athletic, a young man who knew how to preserve a certain æsthetic measure in his profligacy; this, Petronius prized above everything.

"A greeting to Petronius," said the young man, entering the tepidarium with a springy step. "May all the gods grant thee success, but especially Asklepios and Kypris, for under their double protection nothing evil can meet one."

"I greet thee in Rome, and may thy rest be sweet after war," replied Petronius, extending his hand from between the folds of soft karbas stuff in which he was wrapped. "What's to be heard in Armenia; or since thou wert in Asia, didst thou not stumble into Bithynia?"

Petronius on a time had been proconsul in Bithynia, and, what is more, he had governed with energy and justice. This was a marvellous contrast in the character of a man noted for effeminacy and love of luxury; hence he was fond of mentioning those times, as they were a proof of what he had been, and of what he might have become had it pleased him.

"I happened to visit Heraklea," answered Vinicius. "Corbulo sent me there with an order to assemble reinforcements."

"Ah, Heraklea! I knew at Heraklea a certain maiden from Colchis, for whom I would have given all the divorced women of this city, not excluding Poppæa. But these are old stories. Tell me now, rather, what is to be heard from the Parthian boundary. It is true that they weary me every Vologeses of them, and Tiridates and Tigranes, — those barbarians who, as young Arulenus insists, walk on all fours at home, and pretend to be human only when in our presence. But now people in Rome speak much of them, if only for the reason that it is dangerous to speak of aught else."

"The war is going badly, and but for Corbulo might be turned to defeat."

"Corbulo! by Bacchus! a real god of war, a genuine Mars, a great leader, at the same time quick-tempered, honest, and dull. I love him, even for this, — that Nero is afraid of him."

"Corbulo is not a dull man."

"Perhaps thou art right, but for that matter it is all one. Dulness, as Pyrrho says, is in no way worse than wisdom, and differs from it in nothing."

Vinicius began to talk of the war; but when Petronius closed his eyes again, the young man, seeing his uncle's tired and somewhat emaciated face, changed the conversation, and inquired with a certain interest about his health.

Petronius opened his eyes again.

Health! — No. He did not feel well. He had not gone so far yet, it is true, as young Sissena, who had lost sensation to such a degree that when he was brought to the bath in the morning he inquired, "Am I sitting?" But he was not well. Vinicius had just committed him to the care of Asklepios and Kypris. But he, Petronius, did not believe in Asklepios. It was not known even whose son that Asklepios was, the son of Arsinoe or Koronis; and if the mother was doubtful, what was to be said of the father? Who, in that time, could be sure who his own father was?

Hereupon Petronius began to laugh; then he continued, —

"Two years ago, it is true, I sent to Epidaurus three dozen live blackbirds and a goblet of gold; but dost thou know why? I said to myself, 'Whether this helps or not, it will do me no harm.' Though people make offerings to the gods yet, I believe that all think as I do, — all, with the exception, perhaps, of muledrivers hired at the Porta Capena by travellers. Besides Asklepios, I have had dealings with sons of Asklepios. When I was troubled a little last year in the bladder, they performed an incubation for me. I saw that they were tricksters, but I said to myself: 'What harm! The world stands on deceit, and life is an illusion. The soul is an illusion too. But one must have reason enough to distinguish pleasant from painful illusions.' I shall give command to burn in my hypocaustum, cedar-wood sprinkled with ambergris, for during life I prefer perfumes to stenches. As to Kypris, to whom thou hast also confided me, I have known her guardianship to the extent that I have twinges in my right foot. But as to the rest she is a good goddess! I suppose that thou wilt bear sooner or later white doves to her altar."

"True," answered Vinicius. "The arrows of the Parthians have not reached my body, but a dart of Amor has struck me — unexpectedly, a few stadia from a gate of this city."

"By the white knees of the Graces! thou wilt tell me of this at a leisure hour."

"I have come purposely to get thy advice," answered Marcus.

But at that moment the epilatores came, and occupied themselves with Petronius. Marcus, throwing aside his tunic, entered a bath of tepid water, for Petronius invited him to a plunge bath.

"Ah, I have not even asked whether thy feeling is reciprocated," said Petronius, looking at the youthful body of Marcus, which was as if cut out of marble. "Had Lysippos seen thee, thou wouldst be ornamenting now the gate leading to the Palatine, as a statue of Hercules in youth."

The young man smiled with satisfaction, and began to sink in the bath, splashing warm water abundantly on the mosaic which represented Hera at the moment when she was imploring Sleep to lull Zeus to rest. Petronius looked at him with the satisfied eye of an artist.

When Vinicius had finished and yielded himself in turn to the epilatores, a lector came in with a bronze tube at his breast and rolls of paper in the tube.

"Dost wish to listen?" asked Petronius.

"If it is thy creation, gladly!" answered the young tribune; "if not, I prefer conversation. Poets seize people at present on every street corner."

"Of course they do. Thou wilt not pass any basilica, bath, library, or bookshop without seeing a poet gesticulating like a monkey. Agrippa, on coming here from the East, mistook them for madmen. And it is just such a time now. Cæsar writes verses; hence all follow in his steps. Only it is not permitted to write better verses than Cæsar, and for that reason I fear a little for Lucan. But I write prose, with which, however, I do not honor myself or others. What the lector has to read are codicilli of that poor Fabricius Veiento."

"Why 'poor'?"

"Because it has been communicated to him that he must dwell in Odyssa and not return to his domestic hearth till he receives a new command. That Odyssey will be easier for him than for Ulysses, since his wife is no Penelope. I need not tell thee, for that matter, that he acted stupidly. But here no one takes things otherwise than superficially. His is rather a wretched and dull little book, which people have begun to read passionately only when the author is banished. Now one hears on every side, 'Scandala! scandala!' and it may be that Veiento invented some things; but I, who know the city, know our patres and our women, assure thee that it is all paler than reality. Meanwhile every man is searching in the book, — for himself with alarm, for his acquaintances with delight. At the book-shop of Avirnus a hundred copyists are writing at dictation, and its success is assured."

"Are not thy affairs in it?"

"They are; but the author is mistaken, for I am at once worse and less flat than he represents me. Seest thou we have lost long since the feeling of what is worthy or unworthy, — and to me even it seems that in real truth there is no difference between them, though Seneca, Musonius, and Trasca pretend that they see it. To me it is all one! By Hercules, I say what I think! I have preserved loftiness, however, because I know what is deformed and what is beautiful; but our poet, Bronzebeard, for example, the charioteer, the singer, the actor, does not understand this."

"I am sorry, however, for Fabricius! He is a good companion."

"Vanity ruined the man. Every one suspected him, no one knew certainly; but he could not contain himself, and told the secret on all sides in confidence. Hast heard the history of Rufinus?"

"No."

"Then come to the frigidarium to cool; there I will tell thee."

They passed to the frigidarium, in the middle of which played a fountain of bright rose-color, emitting the odor of violets. There they sat in niches which were covered with velvet, and began to cool themselves. Silence reigned for a time. Vinicius looked awhile thoughtfully at a bronze faun which, bending over the arm of a nymph, was seeking her lips eagerly with his lips.

"He is right," said the young man. "That is what is best in life."

"More or less! But besides this thou lovest war, for which I have no liking, since under tents one's finger-nails break and cease to be rosy. For that matter, every man has his preferences. Bronzebeard loves song, especially his own; and old Scaurus his Corinthian vase, which stands near his bed at night, and which he kisses when he cannot sleep. He has kissed the edge off already. Tell me, dost thou not write verses?"

"No; I have never composed a single hexameter."

"And dost thou not play on the lute and sing?"

"No."

"And dost thou drive a chariot?"

"I tried once in Antioch, but unsuccessfully."

"Then I am at rest concerning thee. And to what party in the hippodrome dost thou belong?"

"To the Greens."

"Now I am perfectly at rest, especially since thou hast a large property indeed, though thou art not so rich as Pallas or Seneca. For seest thou, with us at present it is well to write verses, to sing to a lute, to declaim, and to compete in the Circus; but better, and especially safer, not to write verses, not to play, not to sing, and not to compete in the Circus. Best of all, is it to know how to admire when Bronzebeard admires. Thou art a comely young man; hence Poppæa may fall in love with thee. This is thy only peril. But no, she is too experienced; she cares for something else. She has had enough of love with her two husbands; with the third she has other views. Dost thou know that that stupid Otho loves her yet to distraction? He walks on the cliffs of Spain, and sighs; he has so lost his former habits, and so ceased to care for his person, that three hours each day suffice him to dress his hair. Who could have expected this of Otho?"

"I understand him," answered Vinicius; "but in his place I should have done something else."

"What, namely?"

"I should have enrolled faithful legions of mountaineers of that country. They are good soldiers, — those Iberians."

"Vinicius! Vinicius! I almost wish to tell thee that thou wouldst not have been capable of that. And knowest why? Such things are done, but they are not mentioned even conditionally. As to me, in his place, I should have laughed at Poppæa, laughed at Bronzebeard, and formed for myself legions, not of Iberian men, however, but Iberian women. And what is more, I should have written epigrams which I should not have read to any one, — not like that poor Rufinus."

"Thou wert to tell me his history."

"I will tell it in the unctorium."

But in the unctorium the attention of Vinicius was turned to other objects; namely, to wonderful slave women who were waiting for the bathers. Two of them, Africans, resembling noble statues of ebony, began to anoint their bodies with delicate perfumes from Arabia; others, Phrygians, skilled in hair-dressing, held in their hands, which were bending and flexible as serpents, combs and mirrors of polished steel; two Grecian maidens from Kos, who were simply like deities, waited as vestiplicæ, till the moment should come to put statuesque folds in the togas of the lords.

"By the cloud-scattering Zeus!" said Marcus Vinicius, "what a choice thou hast!"

"I prefer choice to numbers," answered Petronius. "My whole 'familia' [1] in Rome does not exceed four hundred, and I judge that for personal attendance only upstarts need a greater number of people."

---

[1] Household servants.

"More beautiful bodies even Bronzebeard does not possess," said Vinicius, distending his nostrils.

"Thou art my relative," answered Petronius, with a certain friendly indifference, "and I am neither so misanthropic as Barsus nor such a pedant as Aulus Plautius."

When Vinicius heard this last name, he forgot the maidens from Kos for a moment, and, raising his head vivaciously, inquired, —

"Whence did Aulus Plautius come to thy mind? Dost thou know that after I had disjointed my arm outside the city, I passed a number of days in his house? It happened that Plautius came up at the moment when the accident happened, and, seeing that I was suffering greatly, he took me to his house; there a slave of his, the physician Merion, restored me to health. I wished to speak with thee touching this very matter."

"Why? Is it because thou hast fallen in love with Pomponia perchance? In that case I pity thee; she is not young, and she is virtuous! I cannot imagine a worse combination. Brr!"

"Not with Pomponia — eheu!" answered Vinicius.

"With whom, then?"

"If I knew myself with whom? But I do not know to a certainty her name even, — Lygia or Callina? They call her Lygia in the house, for she comes of the Lygian nation; but she has her own barbarian name, Callina. It is a wonderful house, — that of those Plautiuses. There are many people in it; but it is quiet there as in the groves of Subiacum. For a number of days I did not know that a divinity dwelt in the house. Once about daybreak I saw her bathing in the garden fountain; and I swear to thee by that foam from which Aphrodite rose, that the rays of the dawn passed right through her body. I thought that when the sun rose she would vanish before me in the light, as the twilight of morning does. Since then, I have seen her twice; and since then, too, I know not what rest is, I know not what other desires are, I have no wish to know what the city can give me. I want neither women, nor gold, nor Corinthian bronze, nor amber, nor pearls, nor wine, nor feasts; I want only Lygia. I am yearning for her, in sincerity I tell thee, Petronius, as that Dream who is imaged on the Mosaic of thy tepidarium yearned for Paisythea, — whole days and night do I yearn."

"If she is a slave, then purchase her."

"She is not a slave."

"What is she? A freed woman of Plautius?"

"Never having been a slave, she could not be a freed woman."

"Who is she?"

"I know not, — a king's daughter, or something of that sort."

"Thou dost rouse my curiosity, Vinicius."

"But if thou wish to listen, I will satisfy thy curiosity straightway. Her story is not a long one. Thou art acquainted, perhaps personally, with Vannius, king of the Suevi, who, expelled from his country, spent a long time here in Rome, and became even famous for his skilful play with dice, and his good driving of chariots. Drusus put him on the throne again. Vannius, who was really a strong man, ruled well at first, and warred with success; afterward, however, he began to skin not only his neighbors, but his own Suevi, too much. Thereupon Vangio and Sido, two sister's sons of his, and the sons of Vibilius, king of the Hermunduri, determined to force him to Rome again — to try his luck there at dice.''

"I remember; that is of recent Claudian times."

"Yes! War broke out. Vannius summoned to his aid the Yazygi; his dear nephews called in the Lygians, who, hearing of the riches of Vannius, and enticed by the hope of booty, came in such numbers that Cæsar himself, Claudius, began to fear for the safety of the boundary. Claudius did not wish to interfere in a war among barbarians, but he wrote to Atelius Hister, who commanded the legions of the Danube, to turn a watchful eye on the course of the war, and not permit them to disturb our peace. Hister required, then, of the Lygians a promise not to cross the boundary; to this they not only agreed, but gave hostages, among whom were the wife and daughter of their leader. It is known to thee that barbarians take their wives and children to war with them. My Lygia is the daughter of that leader."

"Whence dost thou know all this?"

"Aulus Plautius told it himself. The Lygians did not cross the boundary, indeed; but barbarians come and go like a tempest. So did the Lygians vanish with their wild-ox horns on their heads. They killed Vannius's Suevi and Yazygi; but their own king fell. They disappeared with their booty then, and the hostages remained in Hister's hands. The mother died soon after, and Hister, not knowing what to do with the daughter, sent her to Pomponius, the governor of all Germany. He, at the close of the war with the Catti, returned to Rome, where Claudius, as is known to thee, permitted him to have a triumph. The maiden on that occasion walked after the car of the conqueror; but, at the end of the solemnity, — since hostages cannot be considered captives, and since Pomponius did not know what to do with her definitely — he gave her to his sister Pomponia Græcina, the wife of Plautius. In that house where all — beginning with the masters and ending with the poultry in the hen-house — are virtuous, that maiden grew up as virtuous, alas! as Græcina herself, and so beautiful that even Poppæa, if near her, would seem like an autumn fig near an apple of the Hesperides."

"And what?"

"And I repeat to thee that from the moment when I saw how the sun-rays at that fountain passed through her body, I fell in love to distraction."

"She is as transparent as a lamprey eel, then, or a youthful sardine?"

"Jest not, Petronius; but if the freedom with which I speak of my desire misleads thee, know this, — that bright garments frequently cover deep wounds. I must tell thee, too, that, while returning from Asia, I slept one night in the temple of Mopsus to have a prophetic dream. Well, Mopsus appeared in a dream to me, and declared that, through love, a great change in my life would take place."

"Pliny declares, as I hear, that he does not believe in the gods, but he believes in dreams; and perhaps he is right. My jests do not prevent me from thinking at times that in truth there is only one deity, eternal, creative, all-powerful, Venus Genetrix. She brings souls together; she unites bodies and things. Eros called the world out of chaos. Whether he did well is another question; but, since he did so, we should recognize his might, though we are free not to bless it."

"Alas! Petronius, it is easier to find philosophy in the world than wise counsel."

"Tell me, what is thy wish specially?"

"I wish to have Lygia. I wish that these arms of mine, which now embrace only air, might embrace Lygia and press her to my bosom. I wish to breathe with her breath. Were she a slave, I would give Aulus for her one hundred maidens with feet whitened with lime as a sign that they were exhibited on sale for the first time. I wish to have her in my house till my head is as white as the top of Soracte in winter."

"She is not a slave, but she belongs to the 'family' of Plautius; and since she is a deserted maiden, she may be considered an 'alumna.' Plautius might yield her to thee if he wished."

"Then it seems that thou knowest not Pomponia Græcina. Both have become as much attached to her as if she were their own daughter."

"Pomponia I know, — a real cypress. If she were not the wife of Aulus, she might be engaged as a mourner. Since the death of Julius she has not thrown aside dark robes; and in general she looks as if, while still alive, she were walking on the asphodel meadow. She is, moreover, a 'one-man woman'; hence, among our ladies of four and five divorces, she is straightway a phœnix. But! hast thou heard that in Upper Egypt the phœnix has just been hatched out, as 'tis said? — an event which happens not oftener than once in five centuries."

"Petronius! Petronius! Let us talk of the phœnix some other time."

"What shall I tell thee, my Marcus? I know Aulus Plautius, who, though he blames my mode of life, has for me a certain weakness, and even respects me, perhaps, more than others, for he knows that I have never been an informer like Domitius Afer, Tigellinus, and a whole rabble of Ahenobarbus's intimates.[1] Without pretending to be a stoic, I have been offended more than once at acts of Nero, which Seneca and Burrus looked at through their fingers. If it is thy thought that I might do something for thee with Aulus, I am at thy command."

"I judge that thou hast the power. Thou hast influence over him; and, besides, thy mind possesses inexhaustible resources. If thou wert to survey the position and speak with Plautius."

"Thou hast too great an idea of my influence and wit; but if that is the only question, I will talk with Plautius as soon as they return to the city."

"They returned two days since."

"In that case let us go to the triclinium, where a meal is now ready, and when we have refreshed ourselves, let us give command to bear us to Plautius."

---

[1] Nero's name was originally I. Domitius Ahenobarbus.

"Thou hast ever been kind to me," answered Vinicius, with vivacity; "but now I shall give command to rear thy statue among my lares, — just such a beauty as this one, — and I will place offerings before it."

Then he turned toward the statues which ornamented one entire wall of the perfumed chamber, and pointing to the one which represented Petronius as Hermes with a staff in his hand, he added, —

"By the light of Helios! if the 'godlike' Alexander resembled thee, I do not wonder at Helen."

And in that exclamation there was as much sincerity as flattery; for Petronius, though older and less athletic, was more beautiful than even Vinicius. The women of Rome admired not only his pliant mind and his taste, which gained for him the title *Arbiter elegantiæ*, but also his body. This admiration was evident even on the faces of those maidens from Kos who were arranging the folds of his toga; and one of whom, whose name was Eunice, loving him in secret, looked him in the eyes with submission and rapture. But he did not even notice this; and, smiling at Vinicius, he quoted in answer an expression of Seneca about woman, — *Animal impudens*, etc. And then, placing an arm on the shoulders of his nephew, he conducted him to the triclinium.

In the unctorium the two Grecian maidens, the Phrygians, and the two Ethiopians began to put away the vessels with perfumes. But at that moment, and beyond the curtain of the frigidarium, appeared the heads of the balneatores, and a low "Psst!" was heard. At that call one of the Grecians, the Phrygians, and the Ethiopians sprang up quickly, and vanished in a twinkle behind the curtain. In the baths began a moment of license which the inspector did not prevent, for he took frequent part in such frolics himself. Petronius suspected that they took place; but, as a prudent man, and one who did not like to punish, he looked at them through his fingers.

In the unctorium only Eunice remained. She listened for a short time to the voices and laughter which retreated in the direction of the laconicum. At last she took the stool inlaid with amber and ivory, on which Petronius had been sitting a short time before, and put it carefully at his statue. The unctorium was full of sunlight and the hues which came from the many-colored marbles with which the wall was faced. Eunice stood on the stool, and, finding herself at the level of the statue, cast her arms suddenly around its neck; then, throwing back her golden hair, and pressing her rosy body to the white marble, she pressed her lips with ecstasy to the cold lips of Petronius.

CHAPTER II

AFTER a refreshment, which was called the morning meal and to which the two friends sat down at an hour when common mortals were already long past their midday prandium, Petronius proposed a light doze. According to him, it was too early for visits yet. "There are, it is true," said he, "people who begin to visit their acquaintances about sunrise, thinking that custom an old Roman one, but I look on this as barbarous. The afternoon hours are most proper, — not earlier, however, than that one when the sun passes to the side of Jove's temple on the Capitol and begins to look slantwise on the Forum. In autumn it is still hot, and people are glad to sleep after eating. At the same time it is pleasant to hear the noise of the fountain in the atrium, and, after the obligatory thousand steps, to doze in the red light which filters in through the purple half-drawn velarium."

Vinicius recognized the justice of these words; and the two men began to walk, speaking in a careless manner of what was to be heard on the Palatine and in the city, and philosophizing a little upon life. Petronius withdrew then to the cubiculum, but did not sleep long. In half an hour he came out, and, having given command to bring verbena, he inhaled the perfume and rubbed his hands and temples with it.

"Thou wilt not believe," said he, "how it enlivens and freshens one. Now I am ready."

The litter was waiting long since; hence they took their places, and Petronius gave command to bear them to the Vicus Patricius, to the house of Aulus. Petronius's "insula" lay on the southern slope of the Palatine, near the so-called Carinæ; their nearest way, therefore, was below the Forum; but since Petronius wished to step in on the way to see the jeweller Idomeneus, he gave the direction to carry them along the Vicus Apollinis and the Forum in the direction of the Vicus Sceleratus, on the corner of which were many tabernæ of every kind.

Gigantic Africans bore the litter and moved on, preceded by slaves called pedisequii. Petronius, after some time, raised to his nostrils in silence his palm odorous with verbena, and seemed to be meditating on something.

"It occurs to me," said he after a while, "that if thy forest goddess is not a slave she might leave the house of Plautius, and transfer herself to thine. Thou wouldst surround her with love and cover her with wealth, as I do my adored Chrysothemis, of whom, speaking between us, I have quite as nearly enough as she has of me."

Marcus shook his head.

"No?" inquired Petronius. "In the worst event, the case would be left with Cæsar, and thou mayst be certain that, thanks even to my influence, our Bronzebeard would be on thy side."

"Thou knowest not Lygia," replied Vinicius.

"Then permit me to ask if thou know her otherwise than by sight? Hast spoken with her? hast confessed thy love to her?"

"I saw her first at the fountain, since then I have met her twice. Remember that during my stay in the house of Aulus, I dwelt in a separate villa, intended for guests, and, having a disjointed arm, I could not sit at the common table. Only on the eve of the day for which I announced my departure did I meet Lygia at supper, but I could not say a word to her. I had to listen to Aulus and his account of victories gained by him in Britain, and then of the fall of small states in Italy, which Licinius Stolo strove to prevent. In general I do not know whether Aulus will be able to speak of aught else, and do not think that we shall escape this history unless it be thy wish to hear about the effeminacy of these days. They have pheasants in their preserves, but they do not eat them, setting out from the principle that every pheasant eaten brings nearer the end of Roman power. I met her a second time at the garden cistern, with a freshly plucked reed in her hand, the top of which she dipped in the water and sprinkled the irises growing around. Look at my knees. By the shield of Hercules, I tell thee that they did not tremble when clouds of Parthians advanced on our maniples with howls, but they trembled before the cistern. And, confused as a youth who still wears a bulla on his neck, I merely begged pity with my eyes, not being able to utter a word for a long time."

Petronius looked at him, as if with a certain envy. "Happy man," said he, "though the world and life were the worst possible, one thing in them will remain eternally good, — youth!"

After a while he inquired: "And hast thou not spoken to her?"

"When I had recovered somewhat, I told her that I was returning from Asia, that I had disjointed my arm near the city, and had suffered severely, but at the moment of leaving that hospitable house I saw that suffering in it was more to be wished for than delight in another place, that sickness there was better than health somewhere else. Confused too on her part, she listened to my words with bent head while drawing something with the reed on the saffron-colored sand. Afterward she raised her eyes, then looked down at the marks drawn already; once more she looked at me, as if to ask about something, and then fled on a sudden like a hamadryad before a dull faun."

"She must have beautiful eyes."

"As the sea — and I was drowned in them, as in the sea. Believe me that the archipelago is less blue. After a while a little son of Plautius ran up with a question. But I did not understand what he wanted."

"O Athene!" exclaimed Petronius, "remove from the eyes of this youth the bandage with which Eros has bound them; if not, he will break his head against the columns of Venus's temple.

"O thou spring bud on the tree of life," said he, turning to Vinicius, "thou first green shoot of the vine! Instead of taking thee to the Plautiuses, I ought to give command to bear thee to the house of Gelocius, where there is a school for youths unacquainted with life."

"What dost thou wish in particular?"

"But what did she write on the sand? Was it not the name of Amor, or a heart pierced with his dart, or something of such sort, that one might know from it that the satyrs had whispered to the ear of that nymph various secrets of life? How couldst thou help looking on those marks?"

"It is longer since I have put on the toga than seems to thee," said Vinicius, "and before little Aulus ran up, I looked carefully at those marks, for I know that frequently maidens in Greece and in Rome draw on the sand a confession which their lips will not utter. But guess what she drew!"

"If it is other than I supposed, I shall not guess."

"A fish."

"What dost thou say?"

"I say, a fish. What did that mean, — that cold blood is flowing in her veins? So far I do not know; but thou, who hast called me a spring bud on the tree of life, wilt be able to understand the sign certainly."

"Carissime! ask such a thing of Pliny. He knows fish. If old Apicius were alive, he could tell thee something, for in the course of his life he ate more fish than could find place at one time in the bay of Naples."

Further conversation was interrupted, since they were borne into crowded streets where the noise of people hindered them.

From the Vicus Apollinis they turned to the Boarium, and then entered the Forum Romanum, where on clear days, before sunset, crowds of idle people assembled to stroll among the columns, to tell and hear news, to see noted people borne past in litters, and finally to look in at the jewellery-shops, the book-shops, the arches where coin was changed, shops for silk, bronze, and all other articles with which the buildings covering that part of the market placed opposite the Capitol were filled.

One-half of the Forum, immediately under the rock of the Capitol, was buried already in shade; but the columns of the temples, placed higher, seemed golden in the sunshine and the blue. Those lying lower cast lengthened shadows on marble slabs. The place was so filled with columns everywhere that the eye was lost in them as in a forest.

Those buildings and columns seemed huddled together. They towered some above others, they stretched toward the right and the left, they climbed toward the height, and they clung to the wall of the Capitol, or some of them clung to others, like greater and smaller, thicker and thinner, white or gold colored tree-trunks, now blooming under architraves, flowers of the acanthus, now surrounded with Ionic corners, now finished with a simple Doric quadrangle. Above that forest gleamed colored triglyphs; from tympans stood forth the sculptured forms of gods; from the summits winged golden quadrigæ seemed ready to fly away through space into the blue dome, fixed serenely above that crowded place of temples. Through the middle of the market and along the edges of it flowed a river of people; crowds passed under the arches of the basilica of Julius Cæsar; crowds were sitting on the steps of

Castor and Pollux, or walking around the temple of Vesta, resembling on that great marble background many-colored swarms of butterflies or beetles. Down immense steps, from the side of the temple on the Capitol dedicated to Jupiter Optimus Maximus, came new waves; at the rostra people listened to chance orators; in one place and another rose the shouts of hawkers selling fruit, wine, or water mixed with fig-juice; of tricksters; of venders of marvellous medicines; of soothsayers; of discoverers of hidden treasures; of interpreters of dreams. Here and there, in the tumult of conversations and cries, were mingled sounds of the Egyptian sistra, of the sambuké, or of Grecian flutes. Here and there the sick, the pious, or the afflicted were bearing offerings to the temples. In the midst of the people, on the stone flags, gathered flocks of doves, eager for the grain given them, and like movable many-colored and dark spots, now rising for a moment with a loud sound of wings, now dropping down again to places left vacant by people. From time to time the crowds opened before litters in which were visible the affected faces of women, or the heads of senators and knights, with features, as it were, rigid and exhausted from living. The many-tongued population repeated aloud their names, with the addition of some term of praise or ridicule. Among the unordered groups pushed from time to time, advancing with measured tread, parties of soldiers, or watchers, preserving order on the streets. Around about, the Greek language was heard as often as Latin.

Vinicius, who had not been in the city for a long time, looked with a certain curiosity on that swarm of people and on that Forum Romanum, which both dominated the sea of the world and was flooded by it, so that Petronius, who divined the thoughts of his companion, called it "the nest of the Quirites — without the Quirites." In truth, the local element was well-nigh lost in that crowd, composed of all races and nations. There appeared Ethiopians, gigantic light-haired people from the distant north, Britons, Gauls, Germans, sloping-eyed dwellers of Lericum; people from the Euphrates and from the Indus, with beards dyed brick color; Syrians from the banks of the Orontes, with black and mild eyes; dwellers in the deserts of Arabia, dried up as a bone; Jews, with their flat breasts; Egyptians, with the eternal, indifferent smile on their faces; Numidians and Africans; Greeks from Hellas, who equally with the Romans commanded the city, but commanded through science, art, wisdom, and deceit; Greeks from the islands, from Asia Minor, from Egypt, from Italy, from Narbonic Gaul. In the throng of slaves, with pierced ears, were not lacking also freemen, — an idle population, which Cæsar amused, supported, even clothed, — and free visitors, whom the ease of life and the prospects of fortune enticed to the gigantic city; there was no lack of venal persons. There were priests of Serapis, with palm branches in their hands; priests of Isis, to whose altar more offerings were brought than to the temple of the Capitoline Jove; priests of Cybele, bearing in their hands golden ears of rice; and priests of nomad divinities; and dancers of the East with bright head-dresses, and dealers in amulets, and snake-tamers, and Chaldean seers; and, finally, people without any occupation whatever, who applied for grain every week at the storehouses on the Tiber, who fought for lottery-tickets to the Circus, who spent their nights in rickety houses of districts beyond the Tiber, and sunny and warm days under covered porticos, and in foul eating-houses of the Subura, on the Milvian bridge, or before the "insulæ" of the great, where from time to time remnants from the tables of slaves were thrown out to them.

Petronius was well known to those crowds. Vinicius's ears were struck continually by "Hic est!" (Here he is). They loved him for his munificence; and his peculiar popularity increased from the time when they learned that he had spoken before Cæsar in opposition to the sentence of death issued against the whole "familia," that is, against all the slaves of the prefect Pedanius Secundus, without distinction of sex or age, because one of them had killed that monster in a moment of despair. Petronius repeated in public, it is true, that it was all one to him, and that he had spoken to Cæsar only privately, as the *arbiter elegantiarum* whose æsthetic taste was offended by a barbarous slaughter befitting Scythians and not Romans. Nevertheless, people who were indignant because of the slaughter loved Petronius from that moment forth. But he did not care for their love. He remembered that that crowd of people had loved also Britannicus, poisoned by Nero; and Agrippina, killed at his command; and Octavia, smothered in hot steam at the Pandataria, after her veins had been opened previously; and Rubelius Plautus, who had been banished; and Thrasea, to whom any morning might bring a death sentence. The love of the mob might be considered rather of ill omen; and the sceptical Petronius was superstitious also. He had a two-fold contempt for the multitude, — as an aristocrat and an æsthetic person. Men with the odor of roast beans, which they carried in their bosoms, and who besides were eternally hoarse and sweating from playing *mora* on the street-corners and peristyles, did not in his eyes deserve the term "human." Hence he gave no answer whatever to the applause, or the kisses sent from lips here and there to him. He was relating to Marcus the case of Pedanius, reviling meanwhile the fickleness of that rabble which, next morning after the terrible butchery, applauded Nero on his way to the temple of Jupiter Stator. But he gave command to halt before the book-shop of Avirnus, and, descending from the litter, purchased an ornamented manuscript, which he gave to Vinicius.

"Here is a gift for thee," said he.

"Thanks!" answered Vinicius. Then, looking at the title, he inquired, " 'Satyricon'? Is this something new? Whose is it?"

"Mine. But I do not wish to go in the road of Rufinus, whose history I was to tell thee, nor of Fabricius Veiento; hence no one knows of this, and do thou mention it to no man."

"Thou hast said that thou art no writer of verses," said Vinicius, looking at the middle of the manuscript; "but here I see prose thickly interwoven with them."

"When thou art reading, turn attention to Trimalchion's feast. As to verses, they have disgusted me, since Nero is writing an epic. Vitelius, when he wishes to relieve himself, uses ivory fingers to thrust down his throat; others serve themselves with flamingo feathers steeped in olive oil or in a decoction of wild thyme. I read Nero's poetry, and the result is immediate. Straightway I am able to praise it, if not with a clear conscience, at least with a clear stomach."

When he had said this, he stopped the litter again before the shop of Idomeneus the goldsmith, and, having settled the affair of the gems, gave command to bear the litter directly to Aulus's mansion.

"On the road I will tell thee the story of Ruñnus," said he, "as proof of what vanity in an author may be."

But before he had begun, they turned in to the Vicus Patricius, and soon found themselves before the dwelling of Aulus. A young and sturdy "janitor" opened the door leading to the ostium, over which a magpie confined in a cage greeted them noisily with the word, "Salve!"

On the way from the second antechamber, called the ostium, to the atrium itself, Vinicius said, —

"Hast noticed that the doorkeepers are without chains!"

"This is a wonderful house," answered Petronius, in an undertone. "Of course it is known to thee that Pomponia Græcina is suspected of entertaining that Eastern superstition which consists in honoring a certain Chrestos. It seems that Crispinilla rendered her this service, — she who cannot forgive Pomponia because one husband has sufficed her for a lifetime. A one-man woman! To-day, in Rome, it is easier to get a half-plate of fresh mushrooms from Noricum than to find such. They tried her before a domestic court — "

"To thy judgment this is a wonderful house. Later on I will tell thee what I heard and saw in it."

Meanwhile they had entered the atrium. The slave appointed to it, called atriensis, sent a nomenclator to announce the guests; and Petronius, who, imagining that eternal sadness reigned in this severe house, had never been in it, looked around with astonishment, and as it were with a feeling of disappointment, for the atrium produced rather an impression of cheerfulness. A sheaf of bright light falling from above through a large opening broke into a thousand sparks on a fountain in a quadrangular little basin, called the impluvium, which was in the middle to receive rain falling through the opening during bad weather; this was surrounded by anemones and lilies. In that house a special love for lilies was evident, for there were whole clumps of them, both white and red; and, finally, sapphire irises, whose delicate leaves were as if silvered from the spray of the fountain. Among the moist mosses, in which lily-pots were hidden, and among the bunches of lilies were little bronze statues representing children and water-birds. In one corner a bronze fawn, as if wishing to drink, was inclining its greenish head, grizzled, too, by dampness. The floor of the atrium was of mosaic; the walls, faced partly with red marble and partly with wood, on which were painted fish, birds, and griffins, attracted the eye by the play of colors. From the door to the side chamber they were ornamented with tortoise-shell or even ivory; at the walls between the doors were statues of Aulus's ancestors. Everywhere calm plenty was evident, remote from excess, but noble and self-trusting.

Petronius, who lived with incomparably greater show and elegance, could find nothing which offended his taste; and had just turned to Vinicius with that remark, when a slave, the velarius, pushed aside the curtain separating the atrium from the tablinum, and in the depth of the building appeared Aulus Plautius approaching hurriedly.

He was a man nearing the evening of life, with a head whitened by hoar frost, but fresh, with an energetic face, a trifle too short, but still somewhat eagle-like. This time there was expressed on it a certain astonishment, and even alarm, because of the unexpected arrival of Nero's friend, companion, and suggester.

Petronius was too much a man of the world and too quick not to notice this; hence, after the first greetings, he announced with all the eloquence and ease at his command that he had come to give thanks for the care which his sister's son had found in that house, and that gratitude alone was the cause of the visit, to which, moreover, he was emboldened by his old acquaintance with Aulus.

Aulus assured him that he was a welcome guest; and as to gratitude, he declared that he had that feeling himself, though surely Petronius did not divine the cause of it.

In fact, Petronius did not divine it. In vain did he raise his hazel eyes, endeavoring to remember the least service rendered to Aulus or to any one. He recalled none, unless it might be that which he intended to show Vinicius. Some such thing, it is true, might have happened involuntarily, but only involuntarily.

"I have great love and esteem for Vespasian, whose life thou didst save," said Aulus, "when he had the misfortune to doze while listening to Nero's verses."

"He was fortunate," replied Petronius, "for he did not hear them; but I will not deny that the matter might have ended with misfortune. Bronzebeard wished absolutely to send a centurion to him with the friendly advice to open his veins."

"But thou, Petronius, laughed him out of it."

"That is true, or rather it is not true. I told Nero that if Orpheus put wild beasts to sleep with song, his triumph was equal, since he had put Vespasian to sleep. Ahenobarbus may be blamed on condition that to a small criticism a great flattery be added. Our gracious Augusta, Poppæa, understands this to perfection."

"Alas! such are the times," answered Aulus. "I lack two front teeth, knocked out by a stone from the hand of a Briton, I speak with a hiss; still my happiest days were passed in Britain."

"Because they were days of victory," added Vinicius.

But Petronius, alarmed lest the old general might begin a narrative of his former wars, changed the conversation.

"See," said he, "in the neighborhood of Præneste country people found a dead wolf whelp with two heads; and during a storm about that time lightning struck off an angle of the temple of Luna, — a thing unparalleled, because of the late autumn. A certain Cotta, too, who had told this, added, while telling it, that the priests of that temple prophesied the fall of the city or, at least, the ruin of a great house, — ruin to be averted only by uncommon sacrifices."

Aulus, when he had heard the narrative, expressed the opinion that such signs should not be neglected; that the gods might be angered by an over-measure of wickedness. In this there was nothing wonderful; and in such an event expiatory sacrifices were perfectly in order.

"Thy house, Plautius, is not too large," answered Petronius, "though a great man lives in it. Mine is indeed too large for such a wretched owner, though equally small. But if it is a question of the ruin of something as great, for example, as the domus transitoria, would it be worth while for us to bring offerings to avert that ruin?"

Plautius did not answer that question, — a carefulness which touched even Petronius somewhat, for, with ... his inability to feel the difference between good and evil, he had never been an informer; and it was possible to talk with him in perfect safety. He changed the conversation again, therefore, and began to praise Plautius's dwelling and the good taste which reigned in the house.

"It is an ancient seat," said Plautius, "in which nothing has been changed since I inherited it."

After the curtain was pushed aside which divided the atrium from the tablinum, the house was open from end to end, so that through the tablinum and the following peristyle and the hall lying beyond it which was called the œcus, the glance extended to the garden, which seemed from a distance like a bright image set in a dark frame. Joyous, childlike laughter came from it to the atrium.

"Oh, general!" said Petronius, "permit us to listen from near by to that glad laughter which is of a kind heard so rarely in these days."

"Willingly," answered Plautius, rising; "that is my little Aulus and Lygia, playing ball. But as to laughter, I think, Petronius, that our whole life is spent in it."

"Life deserves laughter, hence people laugh at it," answered Petronius, "but laughter here has another sound."

"Petronius does not laugh for days in succession," said Vinicius; "but then he laughs entire nights."

Thus conversing, they passed through the length of the house and reached the garden, where Lygia and little Aulus were playing with balls, which slaves, appointed to that game exclusively and called spheristæ, picked up and placed in their hands. Petronius cast a quick passing glance at Lygia; little Aulus, seeing Vinicius, ran to greet him; but the young tribune, going forward, bent his head before the beautiful maiden, who stood with a ball in her hand, her hair blown apart a little. She was somewhat out of breath, and flushed.

In the garden triclinium, shaded by ivy, grapes, and woodbine, sat Pomponia Græcina; hence they went to salute her. She was known to Petronius, though he did not visit Plautius, for he had seen her at the house of Antistia, the daughter of Rubelius Plautus, and besides at the house of Seneca and Polion. He could not resist a certain admiration with which he was filled by her face, pensive but mild, by the dignity of her bearing, by her movements, by her words. Pomponia disturbed his understanding of women to such a degree that that man, corrupted to the marrow of his bones, and self-confident as no one in Rome, not only felt for her a kind of esteem, but even lost his previous self-confidence. And now, thanking her for her care of Vinicius, he thrust in, as it were involuntarily, "domina," which never occurred to him when speaking, for example, to Calvia Crispinilla, Scribonia, Veleria, Solina, and other women of high society. After he had greeted her and returned thanks, he began to complain that he saw her so rarely, that it was not possible to meet her either in the Circus or the Amphitheatre; to which she answered calmly, laying her hand on the hand of her husband:

"We are growing old, and love our domestic quiet more and more, both of us."

Petronius wished to oppose; but Aulus Plautius added in his hissing voice, —

"And we feel stranger and stranger among people who give Greek names to our Roman divinities."

"The gods have become for some time mere figures of rhetoric," replied Petronius, carelessly. "But since Greek rhetoricians taught us, it is easier for me even to say Hera than Juno."

He turned his eyes then to Pomponia, as if to signify that in presence of her no other divinity could come to his mind: and then he began to contradict what she had said touching old age.

"People grow old quickly, it is true; but there are some who live another life entirely, and there are faces moreover which Saturn seems to forget."

Petronius said this with a certain sincerity even, for Pomponia Græcina, though descending from the midday of life, had preserved an uncommon freshness of face; and since she had a small head and delicate features, she produced at times, despite her dark robes, despite her solemnity and sadness, the impression of a woman quite young.

Meanwhile little Aulus, who had become uncommonly friendly with Vinicius during his former stay in the house, approached the young man and entreated him to play ball. Lygia herself entered the triclinium after the little boy. Under the climbing ivy, with the light quivering on her face, she seemed to Petronius more beautiful than at the first glance, and really like some nymph. As he had not spoken to her thus far, he rose, inclined his head, and, instead of the usual expressions of greeting, quoted the words with which Ulysses greeted Nausikaa, —

"I supplicate thee, O queen, whether thou art some goddess or a mortal! If thou art one of the daughters of men who dwell on earth, thrice blessed are thy father and thy lady mother, and thrice blessed thy brethren."

The exquisite politeness of this man of the world pleased even Pomponia. As to Lygia, she listened, confused and flushed, without boldness to raise her eyes. But a wayward smile began to quiver at the corners of her lips, and on her face a struggle was evident between the timidity of a maiden and the wish to answer; but clearly the wish was victorious, for, looking quickly at Petronius, she answered him all at once with the words of that same Nausikaa, quoting them at one breath, and a little like a lesson learned, —

"Stranger, thou seemest no evil man nor foolish."

Then she turned and ran out as a frightened bird runs.

This time the turn for astonishment came to Petronius, for he had not expected to hear verses of Homer from the lips of a maiden of whose barbarian extraction he had heard previously from Vinicius. Hence he looked with an inquiring glance at Pomponia; but she could not give him an answer, for she was looking at that moment, with a smile, at the pride reflected on the face of her husband.

He was not able to conceal that pride. First, he had become attached to Lygia as to his own daughter; and second, in spite of his old Roman prejudices, which commanded him to thunder against Greek and the spread of the language, he considered it as the summit of social polish. He himself had never been able to learn it well; over this he suffered in secret. He was glad, therefore, that an answer was given in the language and poetry of Homer to this exquisite man both of fashion and letters, who was ready to consider Plautius's house as barbarian.

"We have in the house a pedagogue, a Greek," said he, turning to Petronius, "who teaches our boy, and the maiden overhears the lessons. She is a wagtail yet, but a dear one, to which we have both grown attached."

Petronius looked through the branches of woodbine into the garden, and at the three persons who were playing there. Vinicius had thrown aside his toga, and, wearing only his tunic, was striking the ball, which Lygia, standing opposite, with raised arms was trying to catch. The maiden did not make a great impression on Petronius at the first glance; she seemed to him too slender. But from the moment when he saw her more nearly in the triclinium he thought to himself that Aurora might look like her; and as a judge he understood that in her there was something uncommon. He considered everything and estimated everything; hence her face, rosy and clear, her fresh lips, as if set for a kiss, her eyes blue as the azure of the sea, the alabaster whiteness of her forehead, the wealth of her dark hair, with the reflection of amber or Corinthian bronze gleaming in its folds, her slender neck, the divine slope of her shoulders, the whole posture, flexible, slender, young with the youth of May and of freshly opened flowers. The artist was roused in him, and the worshipper of beauty, who felt that beneath a statue of that maiden one might write "Spring." All at once he remembered Chrysothemis, and pure laughter seized him. Chrysothemis seemed to him, with golden powder on her hair and darkened brows, to be fabulously faded, — something in the nature of a yellowed rose-tree shedding its leaves. But still Rome envied him that Chrysothemis. Then he recalled Poppæa; and that most famous Poppæa also seemed to him soulless, a waxen mask. In that maiden with Tanagrian outlines there was not only spring, but a radiant soul, which shone through her rosy body as a flame through a lamp.

"Vinicius is right," thought he, "and my Chrysothemis is old, old! — as Troy!"

Then he turned to Pomponia Græcina, and, pointing to the garden, said, —

"I understand now, domina, why thou and thy husband prefer this house to the Circus and to feasts on the Palatine."

"Yes," answered she, turning her eyes in the direction of little Aulus and Lygia.

But the old general began to relate the history of the maiden, and what he had heard years before from Atelius Hister about the Lygian people who lived in the gloom of the North.

The three outside had finished playing ball, and for some time had been walking along the sand of the garden, appearing against the dark background of myrtles and cypresses like three white statues. Lygia held little Aulus by the hand. After they had walked a while they sat on a bench near the fish-pond, which occupied the middle of the garden. After a time Aulus sprang up to frighten the fish in the transparent water, but Vinicius continued the conversation begun during the walk.

"Yes," said he, in a low, quivering voice, scarcely audible; "barely had I cast aside the pretexta, when I was sent to the legions in Asia. I had not become acquainted with the city, nor with life, nor with love. I know a small bit of Anacreon by heart, and Horace; but I cannot like Petronius quote verses, when reason is dumb from admiration and unable to find its own words. While a youth I went to school to Musonius, who told me that happiness consists in wishing what the gods wish, and therefore depends on our will. I think, however, that it is something else, — something greater and more precious, which depends not on the will, for love only can give it. The gods themselves seek that happiness; hence I too, O Lygia, who have not known love thus far, follow in their footsteps. I also seek her who would give me happiness — "

He was silent — and for a time there was nothing to be heard save the light plash of the water into which little Aulus was throwing pebbles to frighten the fish; but after a while Vinicius began again in a voice still softer and lower, —

"But thou knowest of Vespasian's son Titus? They say that he had scarcely ceased to be a youth when he so loved Berenice that grief almost drew the life out of him. So could I too love, O Lygia! Riches, glory, power are mere smoke, vanity! The rich man will find a richer than himself; the greater glory of another will eclipse a man who is famous; a strong man will be conquered by a stronger. But can Cæsar himself, can any god even, experience greater delight or be happier than a simple mortal at the moment when at his breast there is breathing another dear breast, or when he kisses beloved lips? Hence love makes us equal to the gods, O Lygia."

And she listened with alarm, with astonishment, and at the same time as if she were listening to the sound of a Grecian flute or a cithara. It seemed to her at moments that Vinicius was singing a kind of wonderful song, which was instilling itself into her ears, moving the blood in her, and penetrating her heart with a faintness, a fear, and a kind of uncomprehended delight. It seemed to her also that he was telling something which was in her before, but of which she could not give account to herself. She felt that he was rousing in her something which had been sleeping hitherto, and that in that moment a hazy dream was changing into a form more and more definite, more pleasing, more beautiful.

Meanwhile the sun had passed the Tiber long since, and had sunk low over the Janiculum. On the motionless cypresses ruddy light was falling, and the whole atmosphere was filled with it. Lygia raised on Vinicius her blue eyes as if roused from sleep; and he, bending over her with a prayer quivering in his eyes, seemed on a sudden, in the reflections of evening, more beautiful than all men, than all Greek and Roman gods whose statues she had seen on the façades of temples. And with his fingers he clasped her arm lightly just above the wrist and asked, —

"Dost thou not divine what I say to thee, Lygia?"

"No," whispered she in answer, in a voice so low that Vinicius barely heard it.

But he did not believe her, and, drawing her hand toward him more vigorously, he would have drawn it to his heart, which, under the influence of desire roused by the marvellous maiden, was beating like a hammer, and would have addressed burning words to her directly had not old Aulus appeared on a path set in a frame of myrtles, who said, while approaching them, —

"The sun is setting; so beware of the evening coolness, and do not trifle with Libitina."

"No," answered Vinicius; "I have not put on my toga yet, and I do not feel the cold."

"But see, barely half the sun's shield is looking from behind the hill. That is a sweet climate of Sicily, where people gather on the square before sunset and take farewell of disappearing Phœbus with a choral song."

And, forgetting that a moment earlier he had warned them against Libitina, he began to tell about Sicily, where he had estates and large cultivated fields which he loved. He stated also that it had come to his mind more than once to remove to Sicily, and live out his life there in quietness. "He whose head winters have whitened has had enough of hoar frost. Leaves are not falling from the trees yet, and the sky smiles on the city lovingly; but when the grapevines grow yellow-leaved, when snow falls on the Alban hills, and the gods visit the Campania with piercing wind, who knows but I may remove with my entire household to my quiet country-seat?"

"Wouldst thou leave Rome?" inquired Vinicius, with sudden alarm.

"I have wished to do so this long time, for it is quieter in Sicily and safer.'

And again he fell to praising his gardens, his herds, his house hidden in green, and the hills grown over with thyme and savory, among which were swarms of buzzing bees. But Vinicius paid no heed to that bucolic note; and from thinking only of this, that he might lose Lygia, he looked toward Petronius as if expecting salvation from him alone.

Meanwhile Petronius, sitting near Pomponia, was admiring the view of the setting sun, the garden, and the people standing near the fish-pond. Their white garments on the dark background of the myrtles gleamed like gold from the evening rays. On the sky the evening light had begun to assume purple and violet hues, and to change like an opal. A strip of the sky became lily-colored. The dark silhouettes of the cypresses grew still more pronounced than during bright daylight. In the people, in the trees, in the whole garden there reigned an evening calm.

That calm struck Petronius, and it struck him especially in the people. In the faces of Pomponia, old Aulus, their son, and Lygia there was something such as he did not see in the faces which surrounded him every day, or rather every night. There was a certain light, a certain repose, a certain serenity, flowing directly from the life which all lived there. And with a species of astonishment he thought that a beauty and sweetness might exist which he, who chased after beauty and sweetness continually, had not known. He could not hide the thought in himself, and said, turning to Pomponia, —

"I am considering in my soul how different this world of yours is from the world which our Nero rules."

She raised her delicate face toward the evening light, and said with simplicity, —

"Not Nero, but God, rules the world."

A moment of silence followed. Near the triclinium were heard in the alley, the steps of the old general, Vinicius, Lygia, and little Aulus; but before they arrived, Petronius had put another question, —

"But believest thou in the gods, then, Pomponia?"

"I believe in God, who is one, just, and all-powerful," answered the wife of Aulus Plautius.

CHAPTER III

"SHE believes in God who is one, all-powerful, and just," said Petronius, when he found himself again in the litter with Vinicius. "If her God is all-powerful, He controls life and death; and if He is just, He sends death justly. Why, then, does Pomponia wear mourning for Julius? In mourning for Julius she blames her God. I must repeat this reasoning to our Bronzebeard, the monkey, since I consider that in dialectics I am the equal of Socrates. As to women, I agree that each has three or four souls, but none of them a reasoning one. Let Pomponia meditate with Seneca or Cornutus over the question of what their great Logos is. Let them summon at once the shades of Xenophanes, Parmenides, Zeno, and Plato, who are as much wearied there in Cimmerian regions as a finch in a cage. I wished to talk with her and with Plautius about something else. By the holy stomach of the Egyptian Isis! If I had told them right out directly why we came, I suppose that their virtue would have made as much noise as a bronze shield under the blow of a club. And I did not dare to tell! Wilt thou believe, Vinicius, I did not dare! Peacocks are beautiful birds, but they have too shrill a cry. I feared an outburst. But I must praise thy choice. A real 'rosy-fingered Aurora.' And knowest thou what she reminded me of too? — Spring! not our spring in Italy, where an apple-tree merely puts forth a blossom here and there, and olive groves grow gray, just as they were gray before, but the spring which I saw once in Helvetia, — young, fresh, bright green. By that pale moon, I do not wonder at thee, Marcus; but know that thou art loving Diana, because Aulus and Pomponia are ready to tear thee to pieces, as the dogs once tore Actæon."

Vinicius was silent a time without raising his head; then he began to speak with a voice broken by passion, —

"I desired her before, but now I desire her still more. When I caught her arm, flame embraced me. I must have her. Were I Zeus, I would surround her with a cloud, as he surrounded Io, or I would fall on her in rain, as he fell on Danaë; I would kiss her lips till it pained! I would hear her scream in my arms. I would kill Aulus and Pomponia, and bear her home in my arms. I will not sleep to-night. I will give command to flog one of my slaves, and listen to his groans — "

"Calm thyself," said Petronius. "Thou hast the longing of a carpenter from the Subura."

"All one to me what thou sayst. I must have her. I have turned to thee for aid; but if thou wilt not find it, I shall find it myself. Aulus considers Lygia as a daughter; why should I look on her as a slave? And since there is no other way, let her ornament the door of my house, let her anoint it with wolf's fat, and let her sit at my hearth as wife."

"Calm thyself, mad descendant of consuls. We do not lead in barbarians bound behind our cars, to make wives of their daughters. Beware of extremes. Exhaust simple, honorable methods, and give thyself and me time for meditation. Chrysothemis seemed to me too a daughter of Jove, and still I did not marry her, just as Nero did not marry Acte, though they called her a daughter of King Attalus. Calm thyself! Think that if she wishes to leave Aulus for thee, he will have no right to detain her. Know also that thou art not burning alone, for Eros has roused in her the flame too. I saw that, and it is well to believe me. Have patience. There is a way to do everything, but to-day I have thought too much already, and it tires me. But I promise that to-morrow I will think of thy love, and unless Petronius is not Petronius, he will discover some method."

They were both silent again.

"I thank thee," said Vinicius at last. "May Fortune be bountiful to thee."

"Be patient."

"Whither hast thou given command to bear us?"

"To Chrysothemis."

"Thou art happy in possessing her whom thou lovest."

"I? Dost thou know what amuses me yet in Chrysothemis? This, that she is false to me with my freedman Theokles, and thinks that I do not notice it. Once I loved her, but now she amuses me with her lying and stupidity. Come with me to her. Should she begin to flirt with thee, and write letters on the table with her fingers steeped in wine, know that I shall not be jealous."

And he gave command to bear them both to Chrysothemis.

But in the entrance Petronius put his hand on Vinicius's shoulder, and said, —

"Wait; it seems to me that I have discovered a plan."

"May all the gods reward thee!"

"I have it! I judge that this plan is infallible. Knowest what, Marcus?"

"I listen to thee, my wisdom."

"Well, in a few days the divine Lygia will partake of Demeter's grain in thy house."

"Thou art greater than Cæsar!" exclaimed Vinicius with enthusiasm.

CHAPTER IV

In fact, Petronius kept his promise. He slept all the day following his visit to Chrysothemis, it is true; but in the evening he gave command to bear him to the Palatine, where he had a confidential conversation with Nero; in consequence of this, on the third day a centurion, at the head of some tens of pretorian soldiers, appeared before the house of Plautius.

The period was uncertain and terrible. Messengers of this kind were more frequently heralds of death. So when the centurion struck the hammer at Aulus's door, and when the guard of the atrium announced that there were soldiers in the anteroom, terror rose through the whole house. The family surrounded the old general at once, for no one doubted that danger hung over him above all. Pomponia, embracing his neck with her arms, clung to him with all her strength, and her blue lips moved quickly while uttering some whispered phrase. Lygia, with a face pale as linen, kissed his hand; little Aulus clung to his toga. From the corridor, from chambers in the lower story intended for servant-women and attendants, from the bath, from the arches of lower dwellings, from the whole house, crowds of slaves began to hurry out, and the cries of "Heu! heu, me miserum!" were heard. The women broke into great weeping; some scratched their cheeks, or covered their heads with kerchiefs.

Only the old general himself, accustomed for years to look death straight in the eye, remained calm, and his short eagle face became as rigid as if chiselled from stone. After a while, when he had silenced the uproar, and commanded the attendants to disappear, he said, —

"Let me go, Pomponia. If my end has come, we shall have time to take leave."

And he pushed her aside gently; but she said, —

"God grant thy fate and mine to be one, O Aulus!"

Then, falling on her knees, she began to pray with that force which fear for some dear one alone can give.

Aulus passed out to the atrium, where the centurion was waiting for him. It was old Caius Hasta, his former subordinate and companion in British wars.

"I greet thee, general," said he. "I bring a command, and the greeting of Cæsar; here are the tablets and the signet to show that I come in his name."

"I am thankful to Cæsar for the greeting, and I shall obey the command," answered Aulus. "Be welcome, Hasta, and say what command thou hast brought."

"Aulus Plautius," began Hasta, "Cæsar has learned that in thy house is dwelling the daughter of the king of the Lygians, whom that king during the life of the divine Claudius gave into the hands of the Romans as a pledge that the boundaries of the empire would never be violated by the Lygians. The divine Nero is grateful to thee, O general, because thou hast given her hospitality in thy house for so many years; but, not wishing to burden thee longer, and considering also that the maiden as a hostage should be under the guardianship of Cæsar and the senate, he commands thee to give her into my hands."

Aulus was too much a soldier and too much a veteran to permit himself regret in view of an order, or vain words, or complaint. A slight wrinkle of sudden anger and pain, however, appeared on his forehead. Before that frown legions in Britain had trembled on a time, and even at that moment fear was evident on the face of Hasta. But in view of the order, Aulus Plautius felt defenceless. He looked for some time at the tablets and the signet; then raising his eyes to the old centurion, he said calmly, —

"Wait, Hasta, in the atrium till the hostage is delivered to thee."

After these words he passed to the other end of the house, to the hall called œcus, where Pomponia Græcina, Lygia, and little Aulus were waiting for him in fear and alarm.

"Death threatens no one, nor banishment to distant islands," said he; "still Cæsar's messenger is a herald of misfortune. It is a question of thee, Lygia."

"Of Lygia?" exclaimed Pomponia, with astonishment.

"Yes," answered Aulus.

And turning to the maiden, he began: "Lygia, thou wert reared in our house as our own child; I and Pomponia love thee as our daughter. But know this, that thou art not our daughter. Thou art a hostage, given by thy people to Rome, and guardianship over thee belongs to Cæsar. Now Cæsar takes thee from our house."

The general spoke calmly, but with a certain strange, unusual voice. Lygia listened to his words, blinking, as if not understanding what the question was. Pomponia's cheeks became pallid. In the doors leading from the corridor to the œcus, terrified faces of slaves began to show themselves a second time.

"The will of Cæsar must be accomplished," said Aulus.

"Aulus!" exclaimed Pomponia, embracing the maiden with her arms, as if wishing to defend her, "it would be better for her to die."

Lygia, nestling up to her breast, repeated, "Mother, mother!" unable in her sobbing to find other words.

On Aulus's face anger and pain were reflected again. "If I were alone in the world," said he, gloomily, "I would not surrender her alive, and my relatives might give offerings this day to 'Jupiter Liberator.' But I have not the right to kill thee and our child, who may live to happier times. I will go to Cæsar this day, and implore him to change his command. Whether he will hear me, I know not. Meanwhile, farewell, Lygia, and know that I and Pomponia ever bless the day in which thou didst take thy seat at our hearth."

Thus speaking, he placed his hand on her head; but though he strove to preserve his calmness, when Lygia turned to him eyes filled with tears, and seizing his hand pressed it to her lips, his voice was filled with deep fatherly sorrow.

"Farewell, our joy, and the light of our eyes," said he.

And he went to the atrium quickly, so as not to let himself be conquered by emotion unworthy of a Roman and a general.

Meanwhile Pomponia, when she had conducted Lygia to the cubiculum, began to comfort, console, and encourage her, uttering words meanwhile which sounded strangely in that house, where near them in an adjoining chamber the lararium remained yet, and where the hearth was on which Aulus Plautius, faithful to ancient usage, made offerings to the household divinities. Now the hour of trial had come. On a time Virginius had pierced the bosom of his own daughter to save her from the hands of Appius; still earlier Lucretia had redeemed her shame with her life. The house of Cæsar is a den of infamy, of evil, of crime. But we, Lygia, know why we have not the right to raise hands on ourselves! Yes! The law under which we both live is another, a greater, a holier, but it gives permission to defend oneself from evil and shame even should it happen to pay for that defence with life and torment. Whoso goes forth pure from the dwelling of corruption has the greater merit thereby. The earth is that dwelling; but fortunately life is one twinkle of the eye, and resurrection is only from the grave; beyond that not Nero, but Mercy bears rule, and there instead of pain is delight, there instead of tears is rejoicing.

Next she began to speak of herself. Yes! she was calm; but in her breast there was no lack of painful wounds. For example, Aulus was a cataract on her eye; the fountain of light had not flowed to him yet. Neither was it permitted her to rear her son in Truth. When she thought, therefore, that it might be thus to the end of her life, and that for them a moment of separation might come which would be a hundred times more grievous and terrible than that temporary one over which they were both suffering then, she could not so much as understand how she might be happy even in heaven without them. And she had wept many nights through already, she had passed many nights in prayer, imploring grace and mercy. But she offered her suffering to God, and waited and trusted. And now, when a new blow struck her, when the tyrant's command took from her a dear one, — the one whom Aulus had called the light of their eyes, — she trusted yet, believing that there was a power greater than Nero's and a mercy mightier than his anger.

And she pressed the maiden's head to her bosom still more firmly. Lygia dropped to her knees after a while, and, covering her eyes in the folds of Pomponia's peplus, she remained thus a long time in silence; but when she stood up again, some calmness was evident on her face.

"I grieve for thee, mother, and for father and for my brother; but I know that resistance is useless, and would destroy all of us. I promise thee that in the house of Cæsar I will never forget thy words."

Once more she threw her arms around Pomponia's neck; then both went out to the œcus, and she took farewell of little Aulus, of the old Greek their teacher, of the dressing-maid who had been her nurse, and of all the slaves.

One of these, a tall and broad-shouldered Lygian, called Ursus in the house, who with other servants had in his time gone with Lygia's mother and her to the camp of the Romans, fell now at her feet, and then bent down to the knees of Pomponia, saying, —

"O domina! permit me to go with my lady, to serve her and watch over her in the house of Cæsar."

"Thou art not our servant, but Lygia's," answered Pomponia; "but if they admit thee through Cæsar's doors, in what way wilt thou be able to watch over her?"

"I know not, domina; I know only that iron breaks in my hands just as wood does."

When Aulus, who came up at that moment, had heard what the question was, not only did he not oppose the wishes of Ursus, but he declared that he had not even the right to detain him. They were sending away Lygia as a hostage whom Cæsar had claimed, and they were obliged in the same way to send her retinue, which passed with her to the control of Cæsar. Here he whispered to Pomponia that under the form of an escort she could add as many slaves as she thought proper, for the centurion could not refuse to receive them.

There was a certain comfort for Lygia in this. Pomponia also was glad that she could surround her with servants of her own choice. Therefore, besides Ursus, she appointed to her the old tire-woman, two maidens from Cyprus well skilled in hair-dressing, and two German maidens for the bath. Her choice fell exclusively on adherents of the new faith; Ursus, too, had professed it for a number of years. Pomponia could count on the faithfulness of those servants, and at the same time consoled herself with the thought that soon grains of truth would be in Cæsar's house.

She wrote a few words also, committing care over Lygia to Nero's freed-woman, Acte. Pomponia had not seen her, it is true, at meetings of confessors of the new faith; but she had heard from them that Acte had never refused them a service, and that she read the letters of Paul of Tarsus eagerly. It was known to her also that the young freedwoman lived in melancholy, that she was a person different from all other women of Nero's house, and that in general she was the good spirit of the palace.

Hasta engaged to deliver the letter himself to Acte. Considering it natural that the daughter of a king should have a retinue of her own servants, he did not raise the least difficulty in taking them to the palace, but wondered rather that there should be so few. He begged haste, however, fearing lest he might be suspected of want of zeal in carrying out orders.

The moment of parting came. The eyes of Pomponia and Lygia were filled with fresh tears; Aulus placed his hand on her head again, and after a while the soldiers, followed by the cry of little Aulus, who in defence of his sister threatened the centurion with his small fists, conducted Lygia to Cæsar's house.

The old general gave command to prepare his litter at once; meanwhile, shutting himself up with Pomponia in the pinacotheca adjoining the œcus, he said to her, —

"Listen to me, Pomponia. I will go to Cæsar, though I judge that my visit will be useless; and though Seneca's word means nothing with Nero now, I will go also to Seneca. To-day Sophonius, Tigellinus, Petronius, or Vatinius has more influence. As to Cæsar, perhaps he has never even heard of the Lygian people; and if he has demanded the delivery of Lygia, the hostage, he has done so because some one persuaded him to it, — it is easy to guess who could do that."

She raised her eyes to him quickly.

"Is it Petronius?"

"It is."

A moment of silence followed; then the general continued, —

"See what it is to admit over the threshold any of those people without conscience or honor. Cursed be the moment in which Vinicius entered our house, for he brought Petronius. Woe to Lygia, since those men are not seeking a hostage, but a concubine."

And his speech became more hissing than usual, because of helpless rage and of sorrow for his adopted daughter. He struggled with himself some time, and only his clenched fists showed how severe was the struggle within him.

"I have revered the gods so far," said he; "but at this moment I think that not they are over the world, but one mad, malicious monster named Nero."

"Aulus," said Pomponia. "Nero is only a handful of rotten dust before God."

But Aulus began to walk with long steps over the mosaic of the pinacotheca. In his life there had been great deeds, but no great misfortunes; hence he was unused to them. The old soldier had grown more attached to Lygia than he himself had been aware of, and now he could not be reconciled to the thought that he had lost her. Besides, he felt humiliated. A hand was weighing on him which he despised, and at the same time he felt that before its power his power was as nothing.

But when at last he stifled in himself the anger which disturbed his thoughts, he said, —

"I judge that Petronius has not taken her from us for Cæsar, since he would not offend Poppæa. Therefore he took her either for himself or Vinicius. To-day I will discover this."

And after a while the litter bore him in the direction of the Palatine. Pomponia, when left alone, went to little Aulus, who did not cease crying for his sister, or threatening Cæsar.

CHAPTER V

AULUS had judged rightly that he would not be admitted to Nero's presence. They told him that Cæsar was occupied in singing with the lute-player, Terpnos, and that in general he did not receive those whom he himself had not summoned. In other words, that Aulus must not attempt in future to see him.

Seneca, though ill with a fever, received the old general with due honor; but when he had heard what the question was, he laughed bitterly, and said, —

"I can render thee only one service, noble Plautius, not to show Cæsar at any time that my heart feels thy pain, or that I should like to aid thee; for should Cæsar have the least suspicion on this head, know that he would not give thee back Lygia, though for no other reason than to spite me."

He did not advise him, either, to go to Tigellinus or Vatinius or Vitelius. It might be possible to do something with them through money; perhaps, also, they would like to do evil to Petronius, whose influence they were trying to undermine, but most likely they would disclose before Nero how dear Lygia was to Plautius, and then Nero would all the more resolve not to yield her to him. Here the old sage began to speak with a biting irony, which he turned against himself: "Thou hast been silent, Plautius, thou hast been silent for whole years, and Cæsar does not like those who are silent. How couldst thou help being carried away by his beauty, his virtue, his singing, his declamation, his chariot-driving, and his verses? Why didst thou not glorify the death of Britannicus, and repeat panegyrics in honor of the mother-slayer, and not offer congratulations after the stifling of Octavia? Thou art lacking in foresight, Aulus, which we who live happily at the court possess in proper measure."

Thus speaking, he raised a goblet which he carried at his belt, took water from a fountain at the impluvium, freshened his burning lips, and continued, —

"Ah, Nero has a grateful heart. He loves thee because thou hast served Rome and glorified its name at the ends of the earth; he loves me because I was his master in youth. Therefore, seest thou, I know that this water is not poisoned, and I drink it in peace. Wine in my own house would be less reliable. If thou art thirsty, drink boldly of this water. The aqueducts bring it from beyond the Alban hills, and any one wishing to poison it would have to poison every fountain in Rome. As thou seest, it is possible yet to be safe in this world and to have a quiet old age. I am sick, it is true, but rather in soul than in body."

This was true. Seneca lacked the strength of soul which Cornutus possessed, for example, or Thrasea; hence his life was a series of concessions to crime. He felt this himself; he understood that an adherent of the principles of Zeno, of Citium, should go by another road, and he suffered more from that cause than from the fear of death itself.

But the general interrupted these reflections full of grief.

"Noble Annæus," said he, "I know how Cæsar rewarded thee for the care with which thou didst surround his years of youth. But the author of the removal of Lygia is Petronius. Indicate to me a method against him, indicate the influences to which he yields, and use besides with him all the eloquence with which friendship for me of long standing can inspire thee."

"Petronius and I," answered Seneca, "are men of two opposite camps; I know of no method against him, he yields to no man's influence. Perhaps with all his corruption he is worthier than those scoundrels with whom Nero surrounds himself at present. But to show him that he has done an evil deed is to lose time simply. Petronius has lost long since that faculty which distinguishes good from evil. Show him that his act is ugly, he will be ashamed of it. When I see him, I will say, 'Thy act is worthy of a freedman.' If that will not help thee, nothing can."

"Thanks for that, even," answered the general.

Then he gave command to carry him to the house of Vinicius, whom he found at sword practice with his domestic trainer. Aulus was borne away by terrible anger at sight of the young man occupied calmly with fencing during the attack on Lygia; and barely had the curtain dropped behind the trainer when this anger burst forth in a torrent of bitter reproaches and injuries. But Vinicius, when he learned that Lygia had been carried away, grew so terribly pale that Aulus could not for even an instant suspect him of sharing in the deed. The young man's forehead was covered with sweat; the blood, which had rushed to his heart for a moment, returned to his face in a burning wave; his eyes began to shoot sparks, his mouth to hurl disconnected questions. Jealousy and rage tossed him in turn, like a tempest. It seemed to him that Lygia, once she had crossed the threshold of Cæsar's house, was lost to him absolutely. When Aulus pronounced the name of Petronius, suspicion flew like a lightning flash through the young soldier's mind, that Petronius had made sport of him, and either wanted to win new favor from Nero by the gift of Lygia, or keep her for himself. That any one who had seen Lygia would not desire her at once, did not find a place in his head. Impetuousness, inherited in his family, carried him away like a wild horse, and took from him presence of mind.

"General," said he, with a broken voice, "return home and wait for me. Know that if Petronius were my own father, I would avenge on him the wrong done to Lygia. Return home and wait for me. Neither Petronius nor Cæsar will have her."

Then he went with clinched fists to the waxed masks standing clothed in the atrium, and burst out, —

"By those mortal masks! I would rather kill her and myself."

When he had said this, he sent another "Wait for me" after Aulus, then ran forth like a madman from the atrium, and flew to Petronius's house, thrusting pedestrians aside on the way.

Aulus returned home with a certain encouragement. He judged that if Petronius had persuaded Cæsar to take Lygia to give her to Vinicius, Vinicius would bring her to their house. Finally, the thought was no little consolation to him, that should Lygia not be rescued she would be avenged and protected by death from disgrace. He believed that Vinicius would do everything that he had promised. He had seen his rage, and he knew the excitability innate in the whole family. He himself, though he loved Lygia as her own father, would rather kill her than give her to Cæsar; and had he not regarded his son, the last descendant of his stock, he would doubtless have done so. Aulus was a soldier; he had hardly heard of the Stoics, but in character he was not far from their ideas, — death was more acceptable to his pride than disgrace.

When he returned home, he pacified Pomponia, gave her the consolation that he had, and both began to await news from Vinicius. At moments when the steps of some of the slaves were heard in the atrium, they thought that perhaps Vinicius was bringing their beloved child to them, and they were ready in the depth of their souls to bless both. Time passed, however, and no news came. Only in the evening was the hammer heard on the gate.

After a while a slave entered and handed Aulus a letter. The old general, though he liked to show command over himself, took it with a somewhat trembling hand, and began to read as hastily as if it were a question of his whole house.

All at once his face darkened, as if a shadow from a passing cloud had fallen on it.

"Read," said he, turning to Pomponia.

Pomponia took the letter and read as follows: —

"Marcus Vinicius to Aulus Plautius greeting. What has happened, has happened by the will of Cæsar, before which incline your heads, as I and Petronius incline ours."

A long silence followed.

CHAPTER VI

PETRONIUS was at home. The doorkeeper did not dare to stop Vinicius, who burst into the atrium like a storm, and, learning that the master of the house was in the library, he rushed into the library with the same impetus. Finding Petronius writing, he snatched the reed from his hand, broke it, trampled the reed on the floor, then fixed his fingers into his shoulder, and, approaching his face to that of his uncle, asked, with a hoarse voice, —

"What hast thou done with her? Where is she?"

Suddenly an amazing thing happened. That slender and effeminate Petronius seized the hand of the youthful athlete, which was grasping his shoulder, then seized the other, and, holding them both in his one hand with the grip of an iron vice, he said, —

"I am incapable only in the morning; in the evening I regain my former strength. Try to escape. A weaver must have taught thee gymnastics, and a blacksmith thy manners."

On his face not even anger was evident, but in his eyes there was a certain pale reflection of energy and daring. After a while he let the hands of Vinicius drop. Vinicius stood before him shamefaced and enraged.

"Thou hast a steel hand," said he; "but if thou hast betrayed me, I swear, by all the infernal gods, that I will thrust a knife into thy body, though thou be in the chambers of Cæsar."

"Let us talk calmly," said Petronius. "Steel is stronger, as thou seest, than iron; hence, though out of one of thy arms two as large as mine might be made, I have no need to fear thee. On the contrary, I grieve over thy rudeness, and if the ingratitude of men could astonish me yet, I should be astonished at thy ingratitude."

"Where is Lygia?"

"In a brothel, — that is, in the house of Cæsar."

"Petronius!"

"Calm thyself, and be seated. I asked Cæsar for two things, which he promised me, — first, to take Lygia from the house of Aulus, and second to give her to thee. Hast thou not a knife there under the folds of thy toga? Perhaps thou wilt stab me! But I advise thee to wait a couple of days, for thou wouldst be taken to prison, and meanwhile Lygia would be wearied in thy house."

Silence followed. Vinicius looked for some time with astonished eyes on Petronius; then he said, —

"Pardon me; I love her, and love is disturbing my faculties."

"Look at me, Marcus. The day before yesterday I spoke to Cæsar as follows: 'My sister's son, Vinicius, has so fallen in love with a lean little girl who is being reared with the Auluses that his house is turned into a steam-bath from sighs. Neither thou, O Cæsar, nor I — we who know, each of us, what true beauty is — would give a thousand sesterces for her; but that lad has ever been as dull as a tripod, and now he has lost all the wit that was in him.' "

"Petronius!"

"If thou understand not that I said this to insure Lygia's safety, I am ready to believe that I told the truth. I persuaded Bronzebeard that a man of his æsthetic nature could not consider such a girl beautiful; and Nero, who so far has not dared to look otherwise than through my eyes, will not find in her beauty, and, not finding it, will not desire her. It was necessary to insure our-selves against the monkey and take him on a rope. Not he, but Poppæa, will value Lygia now; and Poppæa will strive, of course, to send the girl out of the palace at the earliest. I said further to Bronzebeard, in passing: 'Take Lygia and give her to Vinicius! Thou hast the right to do so, for she is a hostage; and if thou take her, thou wilt inflict pain on Aulus.' He agreed; he had not the least reason not to agree, all the more since I gave him a chance to annoy decent people. They will make thee official guardian of the hostage, and give into thy hands that Lygian treasure; thou, as a friend of the valiant Lygians, and also a faithful servant of Cæsar, wilt not waste any of the treas-ure, but wilt strive to increase it. Cæsar, to preserve appearances, will keep her a few days in his house, and then send her to thy insula. Lucky man!"

"Is this true? Does nothing threaten her there in Cæsar's house?"

"If she had to live there permanently, Poppæa would talk about her to Locusta, but for a few days there is no danger. Ten thousand people live in it. Nero will not see her, perhaps, all the more since he left everything to me, to the degree that just now the centurion was here with information that he had conducted the maiden to the palace and committed her to Acte. She is a good soul, that Acte; hence I gave command to deliver Lygia to her. Clearly Pomponia Græcina is of that opinion too, for she wrote to Acte. To-morrow there is a feast at Nero's. I have requested a place for thee at the side of Lygia."

"Pardon me, Caius, my hastiness. I judged that thou hadst given command to take her for thyself or for Cæsar."

"I can forgive thy hastiness; but it is more difficult to forgive rude gestures, vulgar shouts, and a voice reminding one of players at mora. I do not like that style, Marcus, and do thou guard against it. Know that Tigellinus is Cæsar's pander; but know also that if I wanted the girl for myself now, look-ing thee straight in the eyes, I would say, 'Vinicius! I take Lygia from thee, and I will keep her till I am tired of her.'"

Thus speaking, he began to look with his hazel eyes straight into the eyes of Vinicius with a cold and insolent stare. The young man lost himself com-pletely.

"The fault is mine," said he. "Thou art kind and worthy. I thank thee from my whole soul. Permit me only to put one more question: Why didst thou not have Lygia sent directly to my house?"

"Because Cæsar wishes to preserve appearances. People in Rome will talk about this, — that we removed Lygia as a hostage. While they are talking, she will remain in Cæsar's palace. Afterward she will be removed quietly to thy house, and that will be the end. Bronzebeard is a cowardly cur. He knows that his power is unlimited, and still he tries to give specious appearances to every act. Hast thou recovered to the degree of being able to philosophize a little? More than once have I thought, Why does crime, even when as powerful as Cæsar, and assured of being beyond punishment, strive always for the appearances of truth, justice, and virtue? Why does it take the trouble? I consider that to murder a brother, a mother, a wife, is a thing worthy of some petty Asiatic king, not a Roman Cæsar; but if that position were mine, I should not write justifying letters to the Senate. But Nero writes. Nero is looking for appearances, for Nero is a coward. But Tiberius was not a coward; still he justified every step he took. Why is this? What a marvellous, involuntary homage paid to virtue by evil! And knowest thou what strikes me? This, that it is done because transgression is ugly and virtue is beautiful. Therefore a man of genuine æsthetic feeling is also a virtuous man. Hence I am virtuous. To-day I must pour out a little wine to the shades of Protagoras, Prodicus, and Gorgias. It seems that sophists too can be of service. Listen, for I am speaking yet. I took Lygia from Aulus to give her to thee. Well. But Lysippus would have made wonderful groups of her and thee. Ye are both beautiful; therefore my act is beautiful, and being beautiful it cannot be bad. Marcus, here sitting before thee is virtue incarnate in Caius Petronius! If Aristides were living, it would be his duty to come to me and offer a hundred minæ for a short treatise on virtue."

But Vinicius, as a man more concerned with reality than with treatises on virtue, replied, —

"To-morrow I shall see Lygia, and then have her in my house daily, always, and till death."

"Thou wilt have Lygia, and I shall have Aulus on my head. He will summon the vengeance of all the infernal gods against me. And if the beast would take at least a preliminary lesson in good declamation! He will blame me, however, as my former doorkeeper blamed my clients but him I sent to prison in the country."

"Aulus has been at my house. I promised to give him news of Lygia."

"Write to him that the will of the 'divine' Cæsar is the highest law, and that thy first son will bear the name Aulus. It is necessary that the old man should have some consolation. I am ready to pray Bronzebeard to invite him to-morrow to the feast. Let him see thee in the triclinium next to Lygia."

"Do not do that. I am sorry for them, especially for Pomponia."

And he sat down to write that letter which took from the old general the remnant of his hope.

CHAPTER VII

ONCE the highest heads in Rome inclined before Acte, the former favorite of Nero. But even at that period she showed no desire to interfere in public questions, and if on any occasion she used her influence over the young ruler, it was only to implore mercy for some one. Quiet and unassuming, she won the gratitude of many, and made no one her enemy. Even Octavia was unable to hate her. To those who envied her she seemed exceedingly harmless. It was known that she continued to love Nero with a sad and pained love, which lived not in hope, but only in memories of the time in which that Nero was not only younger and loving, but better. It was known that she could not tear her thoughts and soul from those memories, but expected nothing; since there was no real fear that Nero would return to her, she was looked upon as a person wholly inoffensive, and hence was left in peace. Poppæa considered her merely as a quiet servant, so harmless that she did not even try to drive her from the palace.

But since Cæsar had loved her once and dropped her without offence in a quiet and to some extent friendly manner, a certain respect was retained for her. Nero, when he had freed her, let her live in the palace, and gave her special apartments with a few servants. And as in their time Pallas and Narcissus, though freedmen of Claudius, not only sat at feasts with Claudius, but also held places of honor as powerful ministers, so she too was invited at times to Cæsar's table. This was done perhaps because her beautiful form was a real ornament to a feast. Cæsar for that matter had long since ceased to count with any appearances in his choice of company. At his table the most varied medley of people of every position and calling found places. Among them were senators, but mainly those who were content to be jesters as well. There were patricians, old and young, eager for luxury, excess, and enjoyment. There were women with great names, who did not hesitate to put on a yellow wig of an evening and seek adventures on dark streets for amusement's sake. There were also high officials, and priests who at full goblets were willing to jeer at their own gods. At the side of these was a rabble of every sort: singers, mimes, musicians, dancers of both sexes; poets who, while declaiming, were thinking of the sesterces which might fall to them for praise of Cæsar's verses; hungry philosophers following the dishes with eager eyes; finally, noted charioteers, tricksters, miracle-wrights, tale-tellers, jesters, and the most varied adventurers brought through fashion or folly to a few days' notoriety. Among these were not lacking even men who covered with long hair their ears pierced in sign of slavery.

The most noted sat directly at the tables; the lesser served to amuse in time of eating, and waited for the moment in which the servants would permit them to rush at the remnants of food and drink. Guests of this sort were furnished by Tigellinus, Vatinius, and Vitelius; for these guests they were forced more than once to find clothing befitting the chambers of Cæsar, who, however, liked their society, through feeling most free in it. The luxury of the court gilded everything, and covered all things with glitter. High and low, the descendants of great families, and the needy from the pavements of the city, great artists, and vile scrapings of talent, thronged to the palace to sate their dazzled eyes with a splendor almost surpassing human estimate, and to approach the giver of every favor, wealth, and property, — whose single glance might abase, it is true, but might also exalt beyond measure.

That day Lygia too had to take part in such a feast. Fear, uncertainty, and a dazed feeling, not to be wondered at after the sudden change, were struggling in her with a wish to resist. She feared Nero; she feared the people and the palace whose uproar deprived her of presence of mind; she feared the feasts of whose shamelessness she had heard from Aulus, Pomponia Græcina, and their friends. Though young, she was not without knowledge, for knowledge of evil in those times reached even children's ears early. She knew, therefore, that ruin was threatening her in the palace. Pomponia, moreover, had warned her of this at the moment of parting. But having a youthful spirit, unacquainted with corruption, and confessing a lofty faith, implanted in her by her foster mother, she had promised to defend herself against that ruin; she had promised her mother, herself and also that Divine Teacher in whom she not only believed, but whom she had come to love with her half-childlike heart for the sweetness of his doctrine, the bitterness of his death, and the glory of his resurrection.

She was confident too that now neither Aulus nor Pomponia would be answerable for her actions; she was thinking therefore whether it would not be better to resist and not go to the feast. On the one hand fear and alarm spoke audibly in her soul; on the other the wish rose in her to show courage in suffering, in exposure to torture and death. The Divine Teacher had commanded to act thus. He had given the example himself. Pomponia had told her that the most earnest among the adherents desire with all their souls such a test, and pray for it. And Lygia, when still in the house of Aulus, had been mastered at moments by a similar desire. She had seen herself as a martyr, with wounds on her feet and hands, white as snow, beautiful with a beauty not of earth, and borne by equally white angels into the azure sky; and her imagination admired such a vision. There was in it much childish brooding, but there was in it also something of delight in herself, which Pomponia had reprimanded. But now, when opposition to Cæsar's will might draw after it some terrible punishment, and the martyrdom scene of imagination become a reality, there was added to the beautiful visions and to the delight a kind of curiosity mingled with dread, as to how they would punish her, and what kind of torments they would provide. And her soul, half childish yet, was hesitating on two sides. But Acte, hearing of these hesitations, looked at her with astonishment as if the maiden were talking in a fever. To oppose Cæsar's will, expose oneself from the first moment to his anger? To act thus one would need to be a child that knows not what it says. From Lygia's own words it appears that she is, properly speaking, not really a hostage, but a maiden forgotten by her own people. No law of nations protects her; and even if it did, Cæsar is powerful enough to trample on it in a moment of anger. It has pleased Cæsar to take her, and he will dispose of her. Thenceforth she is at his will, above which there is not another on earth.

"So it is," continued Acte. "I too have read the letters of Paul of Tarsus, and I know that above the earth is God, and the Son of God, who rose from the dead; but on the earth there is only Cæsar. Think of this, Lygia. I know too that thy doctrine does not permit thee to be what I was, and that to you as to the Stoics, — of whom Epictetus has told me, — when it comes to a choice between shame and death, it is permitted to choose only death. But canst thou say that death awaits thee and not shame too? Hast thou heard of the daughter of Sejanus, a young maiden, who at command of Tiberius had to pass through shame before her death, so as to respect a law which prohibits the punishment of virgins with death? Lygia, Lygia, do not irritate Cæsar. If the decisive moment comes when thou must choose between disgrace and death, thou wilt act as thy faith commands; but seek not destruction thyself, and do not irritate for a trivial cause an earthly and at the same time a cruel divinity."

Acte spoke with great compassion, and even with enthusiasm; and being a little short-sighted, she pushed her sweet face up to Lygia's as if wishing to see surely the effect of her words.

But Lygia threw her arms around Acte's neck with childish trustfulness and said, —

"Thou art kind, Acte."

Acte, pleased by the praise and confidence, pressed her to her heart; and then disengaging herself from the arms of the maiden, answered, —

"My happiness has passed and my joy is gone, but I am not wicked."

Then she began to walk with quick steps through the room and to speak to herself, as if in despair.

"No! And he was not wicked. He thought himself good at that time, and he wished to be good. I know that best. All his change came later, when he ceased to love. Others made him what he is — yes, others — and Poppæa."

Here her eyelids filled with tears. Lygia followed her for some time with her blue eyes, and asked at last, —

"Art thou sorry for him, Acte?"

"I am sorry for him!" answered the Grecian, with a low voice.

And again she began to walk, her hands clinched as if in pain, and her face without hope.

"Dost thou love him yet, Acte?" asked Lygia, timidly.

"I love him."

And after a while she added, —

"No one loves him but me."

Silence followed, during which Acte strove to recover her calmness, disturbed by memories; and when at length her face resumed its usual look of calm sorrow, she said, —

"Let us speak of thee, Lygia. Do not even think of opposing Cæsar; that would be madness. And be calm. I know this house well, and I judge that on Cæsar's part nothing threatens thee. If Nero had given command to take thee away for himself, he would not have brought thee to the Palatine. Here Poppæa rules; and Nero, since she bore him a daughter, is more than ever under her influence. No, Nero gave command, it is true, that thou shouldst be at the feast, but he has not seen thee yet; he has not inquired about thee, hence he does not care about thee. Maybe he took thee from Aulus and Pomponia only through anger at them. Petronius wrote me to have care of thee; and since Pomponia too wrote, as thou knowest, maybe they had an understanding. Maybe he did that at her request. If this be true, if he at the request of Pomponia will occupy himself with thee, nothing threatens thee; and who knows if Nero may not send thee back to Aulus at his persuasion? I know not whether Nero loves him over much, but I know that rarely has he the courage to be of an opinion opposite to his."

"Ah, Acte!" answered Lygia; "Petronius was with us before they took me, and my mother was convinced that Nero demanded my surrender at his instigation."

"That would be bad," said Acte. But she stopped for a while, and then said, —

"Perhaps Petronius only said, in Nero's presence at some supper, that he saw a hostage of the Lygians at Aulus's, and Nero, who is jealous of his own power, demanded thee only because hostages belong to Cæsar. But he does not like Aulus and Pomponia. No! it does not seem to me that if Petronius wished to take thee from Aulus he would use such a method. I do not know whether Petronius is better than others of Cæsar's court, but he is different. Maybe too thou wilt find some one else who would be willing to intercede for thee. Hast thou not seen at Aulus's some one who is near Cæsar?"

"I have seen Vespasian and Titus."

"Cæsar does not like them."

"And Seneca."

"If Seneca advised something, that would be enough to make Nero act otherwise."

The bright face of Lygia was covered with a blush.

"And Vinicius — "

"I do not know him."

"He is a relative of Petronius, and returned not long since from Armenia."

"Dost thou think that Nero likes him?"

"All like Vinicius."

"And would he intercede for thee?"

"He would."

Acte smiled tenderly, and said, "Then thou wilt see him surely at the feast. Thou must be there, first, because thou must, — only such a child as thou could think otherwise. Second, if thou wish to return to the house of

Aulus, thou wilt find means of beseeching Petronius and Vinicius to gain for thee by their influence the right to return. If they were here, both would tell thee as I do, that it would be madness and ruin to try resistance. Cæsar might not notice thy absence, it is true; but if he noticed it and thought that thou hadst the daring to oppose his will, here would be no salvation for thee. Go, Lygia! Dost thou hear the noise in the palace? The sun is near setting; guests will begin to arrive soon."

"Thou art right," answered Lygia, "and I will follow thy advice."

How much desire to see Vinicius and Petronius there was in this resolve, how much of woman's curiosity there was to see such a feast once in life, and to see at it Cæsar, the court, the renowned Poppæa and other beauties, and all that unheard-of splendor, of which wonders were narrated in Rome, Lygia could not give account to herself of a certainty. But Acte was right, and Lygia felt this distinctly. There was need to go; therefore, when necessity and simple reason supported the hidden temptation, she ceased to hesitate.

Acte conducted her to her own unctorium to anoint and dress her; and though there was no lack of slave women in Cæsar's house, and Acte had enough of them for her personal service, still, through sympathy for the maiden whose beauty and innocence had caught her heart, she resolved to dress her herself. It became clear at once that in the young Grecian, in spite of her sadness and her perusal of the letters of Paul of Tarsus, there was yet much of the ancient Hellenic spirit, to which physical beauty spoke with more eloquence than aught else on earth. When she had undressed Lygia, she could not restrain an exclamation of wonder at sight of her form, at once slender and full, created, as it were, from pearl and roses; and stepping back a few paces, she looked with delight on that matchless, spring-like form.

"Lygia," exclaimed she at last, "thou art a hundred times more beautiful than Poppæa!"

But, reared in the strict house of Pomponia, where modesty was observed, even when women were by themselves, the maiden, wonderful as a wonderful dream, harmonious as a work of Praxiteles or as a song, stood alarmed, blushing from modesty, with knees pressed together, with her hands on her bosom, and downcast eyes. At last, raising her arms with sudden movement, she removed the pins which held her hair, and in one moment, with one shake of her head, she covered herself with it as with a mantle.

Acte, approaching her and touching her dark tresses, said, —

"Oh, what hair thou hast! I will not sprinkle golden powder on it; it gleams of itself in one place and another with gold, where it waves. I will add, perhaps, barely a sprinkle here and there; but lightly, lightly, as if a sun ray had freshened it. Wonderful must thy Lygian country be where such maidens are born!"

"I do not remember it," answered Lygia; "but Ursus has told me that with us it is forests, forests, and forests."

"But flowers bloom in those forests," said Acte, dipping her hand in a vase filled with verbena, and moistening Lygia's hair with it. When she had finished this work, Acte anointed her body lightly with odoriferous oils from Arabia, and then dressed her in a soft gold-colored tunic without sleeves, over which was to be put a snow-white peplus. But since she had to dress Lygia's hair first, she put on her meanwhile a kind of roomy dress called synthesis, and, seating her in an armchair, gave her for a time into the hands of slave women, so as to stand at a distance herself and follow the hair-dressing. Two other slave women put on Lygia's feet white sandals, embroidered with purple, fastening them to her alabaster ankles with golden lacings drawn crosswise. When at last the hair-dressing was finished, they put a peplus on her in very beautiful, light folds; then Acte fastened pearls to her neck, and touching her hair at the folds with gold dust, gave command to the women to dress her, following Lygia with delighted eyes meanwhile.

But she was ready soon; and when the first litters began to appear before the main gate, both entered the side portico from which were visible the chief entrance, the interior galleries, and the courtyard surrounded by a colonnade of Numidian marble.

Gradually people passed in greater and greater numbers under the lofty arch of the entrance, over which the splendid quadrigæ of Lysias seemed to bear Apollo and Diana into space. Lygia's eyes were struck by that magnificence, of which the modest house of Aulus could not have given her the slightest idea. It was sunset; the last rays were falling on the yellow Numidian marble of the columns, which shone like gold in those gleams and changed into rose color also. Among the columns, at the side of white statues of the Danaides and others, representing gods or heroes, crowds of people flowed past, — men and women; resembling statues also, for they were draped in togas, pepluses, and robes, falling with grace and beauty toward the earth in soft folds, on which the rays of the setting sun were expiring. A gigantic Hercules, with head in the light yet, from the breast down sunk in shadow cast by the columns, looked from above on that throng. Acte showed Lygia senators in wide-bordered togas, in colored tunics, in sandals with crescents on them, and knights, and famed artists; she showed her Roman ladies, in Roman, in Grecian, in fantastic Oriental costume, with hair dressed in towers or pyramids, or dressed like that of the statues of goddesses, low on the head, and adorned with flowers. Many men and women did Acte call by name, adding to their names histories, brief and sometimes terrible, which pierced Lygia with fear, amazement, and wonder. For her this was a strange world, whose beauty intoxicated her eyes, but whose contrasts her girlish understanding could not grasp. In those twilights of the sky, in those rows of motionless columns vanishing in the distance, and in those statuesque people, there was a certain lofty repose. It seemed that in the midst of those marbles of simple lines demigods might live free of care, at peace and in happiness. Meanwhile the low voice of Acte disclosed, time after time, a new and dreadful secret of that palace and those people. See, there at a distance is the covered portico on whose columns and floor are still visible red stains from the blood with which Caligula sprinkled the white marble when he fell beneath the knife of Cassius Chærea; there his wife was slain; there his child was dashed against a stone; under that wing is the dungeon in which the younger Drusus gnawed his hands from hunger; there the elder Drusus was poisoned; there Gemellus quivered in terror, and Claudius in convulsions; there Germanicus suffered, — everywhere those walls had heard the groans and death-rattle of the dying; and those people hurrying now to the feast in togas, in colored tunics, in flowers, and in jewels, may be the condemned of to-morrow; on more than one face, perhaps, a smile conceals terror, alarm, the uncertainty of the next day; perhaps feverishness, greed, envy are gnawing at this moment into the hearts of those crowned demigods, who in appearance are free of care. Lygia's frightened thoughts could not keep pace with Acte's words; and when that wonderful world attracted her eyes with increasing force, her heart contracted within her from fear, and in her soul she struggled with an immense, inexpressible yearning for the beloved Pomponia Græcina, and the calm house of Aulus, in which love, and not crime, was the ruling power.

Meanwhile new waves of guests were flowing in from the Vicus Apollinis. From beyond the gates came the uproar and shouts of clients, escorting their patrons. The courtyard and the colonnades were swarming with the multitude of Cæsar's slaves, of both sexes, small boys, and pretorian soldiers, who kept guard in the palace. Here and there among dark or swarthy visages was the black face of a Numidian, in a feathered helmet, and with large gold rings in his ears. Some were bearing lutes and citharas, hand lamps of gold, silver, and bronze, and bunches of flowers, reared artificially despite the late autumn season. Louder and louder the sound of conversation was mingled with the plashing of the fountain, the rosy streams of which fell from above on the marble and were broken, as if in sobs.

Acte had stopped her narration; but Lygia gazed at the throng, as if searching for some one. All at once her face was covered with a blush, and from among the columns came forth Vinicius with Petronius. They went to the great triclinium, beautiful, calm, like white gods, in their togas. It seemed to Lygia, when she saw those two known and friendly faces among strange people, and especially when she saw Vinicius, that a great weight had fallen from her heart. She felt less alone. That measureless yearning for Pomponia and the house of Aulus, which had broken out in her a little while before, ceased at once to be painful. The desire to see Vinicius and to talk with him drowned in her other voices. In vain did she remember all the evil which she had heard of the house of Cæsar, the words of Acte, the warnings of Pomponia; in spite of those words and warnings, she felt all at once that not only must she be at that feast, but that she wished to be there. At the thought that soon she would hear that dear and pleasant voice, which had spoken of love to her and of happiness worthy of the gods, and which was sounding like a song in her ears yet, delight seized her straightway.

But the next moment she feared that delight. It seemed to her that she would be false to the pure teaching in which she had been reared, false to Pomponia, and false to herself. It is one thing to go by constraint, and another to delight in such a necessity. She felt guilty, unworthy, and ruined.

Despair swept her away, and she wanted to weep. Had she been alone, she would have knelt down and beaten her breast, saying, "Mea culpa! mea culpa!" Acte, taking her hand at that moment, led her through the interior apartments to the grand triclinium, where the feast was to be. Darkness was in her eyes, and a roaring in her ears from internal emotion; the beating of her heart stopped her breath. As in a dream, she saw thousands of lamps gleaming on the tables and on the walls; as in a dream, she heard the shout with which the guests greeted Cæsar; as through a mist, she saw Cæsar himself. The shout deafened her, the glitter dazzled, the odors intoxicated; and, losing the remnant of her consciousness, she was barely able to recognize Acte, who seated her at the table and took a place at her side.

But after a while a low and known voice was heard at the other side, —

"A greeting, most beautiful of maidens on earth and of stars in heaven. A greeting to thee, divine Callina!"

Lygia, having recovered somewhat, looked up; at her side was Vinicius.

He was without a toga, for convenience and custom had enjoined to cast aside the toga at feasts. His body was covered with only a sleeveless scarlet tunic embroidered in silver palms. His bare arms were ornamented in Eastern fashion with two broad golden bands fastened above the elbow; below they were carefully stripped of hair. They were smooth, but too muscular, — real arms of a soldier, they were made for the sword and the shield. On his head was a garland of roses. With brows joining above the nose, with splendid eyes and a dark complexion, he was the impersonation of youth and strength, as it were. To Lygia he seemed so beautiful that though her first amazement had passed, she was barely able to answer, —

"A greeting, Marcus."

"Happy," said he, "are my eyes, which see thee; happy my ears, which hear thy voice, dearer to me than the sound of lutes or citharas. Were it commanded me to choose who was to rest here by my side at this feast, thou, Lygia, or Venus, I would choose thee, divine one!"

And he looked at the maiden as if he wished to sate himself with the sight of her, to burn her eyes with his eyes. His glance slipped from her face to her neck and bare arms, fondled her shapely outlines, admired her, embraced her, devoured her; but besides desire, there was gleaming in him happiness, admiration, and ecstasy beyond limit.

"I knew that I should see thee in Cæsar's house," continued he; "but still, when I saw thee, such delight shook my whole soul, as if a happiness entirely unexpected had met me."

Lygia, having recovered herself and feeling that in that throng and in that house he was the only being who was near to her, began to converse with him, and ask about everything which she did not understand and which filled her with fear. Whence did he know that he would find her in Cæsar's house? Why is she there? Why did Cæsar take her from Pomponia? She is full of fear where she is, and wishes to return to Pomponia. She would die from alarm and grief were it not for the hope that Petronius and he will intercede for her before Cæsar.

Vinicius explained that he learned from Aulus himself that she had been taken. Why she is there, he knows not. Cæsar gives account to no one of his orders and commands. But let her not fear. He, Vinicius, is near her and will stay near her. He would rather lose his eyes than not see her; he would rather lose his life than desert her. She is his soul, and hence he will guard her as his soul. In his house he will build to her, as to a divinity, an altar on which he will offer myrrh and aloes, and in spring saffron and apple-blossoms; and since she has a dread of Cæsar's house, he promises that she shall not stay in it.

And though he spoke evasively and at times invented, truth was to be felt in his voice, because his feelings were real. Genuine pity possessed him, too, and her words went to his soul so thoroughly that when she began to thank him and assure him that Pomponia would love him for his goodness, and that she herself would be grateful to him all her life, he could not master his emotion, and it seemed to him that he would never be able in life to resist her prayer. The heart began to melt in him. Her beauty intoxicated his senses, and he desired her; but at the same time he felt that she was very dear to him, and that in truth he might do homage to her, as to a divinity; he felt also irresistible need of speaking of her beauty and of his own homage. As the noise at the feast increased, he drew nearer to her, whispered kind, sweet words flowing from the depth of his soul, words as resonant as music and intoxicating as wine.

And he intoxicated her. Amid those strange people he seemed to her ever nearer, ever dearer, altogether true, and devoted with his whole soul. He pacified her; he promised to rescue her from the house of Cæsar; he promised not to desert her, and said that he would serve her. Besides, he had spoken before at Aulus's only in general about love and the happiness which it can give; but now he said directly that he loved her, and that she was dear and most precious to him. Lygia heard such words from a man's lips for the first time; and as she heard them it seemed to her that something was wakening in her as from a sleep, that some species of happiness was embracing her in which immense delight was mingled with immense alarm. Her cheeks began to burn, her heart to beat, her mouth opened as if in wonder. She was seized with fear because she was listening to such things, still she did not wish for any cause on earth to lose one word. At moments she dropped her eyes; then again she raised her clear glance to Vinicius, timid and also inquiring, as if she wished to say to him, "Speak on!" The sound of the music, the odor of flowers and of Arabian perfumes, began to daze her. In Rome it was the custom to recline at banquets, but at home Lygia occupied a place between Pomponia and little Aulus. Now Vinicius was reclining near her, youthful, immense, in love, burning; and she, feeling the heat that issued from him, felt both delight and shame. A kind of sweet weakness, a kind of faintness and forgetfulness seized her; it was as if drowsiness tortured her.

But her nearness to him began to act on Vinicius also. His nostrils dilated, like those of an Eastern steed. The beating of his heart with unusual throb was evident under his scarlet tunic; his breathing grew short, and the expressions that fell from his lips were broken. For the first time, too, he was so near her. His thoughts grew disturbed; he felt a flame in his veins which he tried in vain to quench with wine. Not wine, but her marvellous face, her bare arms, her maiden breast heaving under the golden tunic, and her form hidden in the white folds of the peplus, intoxicated him more and more. Finally, he seized her arm above the wrist, as he had done once at Aulus's, and drawing her toward him whispered, with trembling lips, —

"I love thee, Callina, — divine one."

"Let me go, Marcus," said Lygia.

But he continued, his eyes mist-covered, "Love me, my goddess!"

But at that moment was heard the voice of Acte, who was reclining on the other side of Lygia.

"Cæsar is looking at you both."

Vinicius was carried away by sudden anger at Cæsar and at Acte. Her words had broken the charm of his intoxication. To the young man even a friendly voice would have seemed repulsive at such a moment, but he judged that Acte wished purposely to interrupt his conversation with Lygia. So, raising his head and looking over the shoulder of Lygia at the young freed-woman, he said with malice:

"The hour has passed, Acte, when thou didst recline near Cæsar's side at banquets, and they say that blindness is threatening thee; how then canst thou see him?"

But she answered as if in sadness: "Still I see him. He, too, has short sight, and is looking at thee through an emerald."

Everything that Nero did roused attention, even in those nearest him; hence Vinicius was alarmed. He regained self-control, and began imperceptibly to look toward Cæsar. Lygia, who, embarrassed at the beginning of the banquet, had seen Nero as in a mist, and afterward, occupied by the presence and conversation of Vinicius, had not looked at him at all, turned to him eyes at once curious and terrified.

Acte spoke truly. Cæsar had bent over the table, half-closed one eye, and holding before the other a round polished emerald, which he used, was looking at them. For a moment his glance met Lygia's eyes, and the heart of the maiden was straitened with terror. When still a child on Aulus's Sicilian estate, an old Egyptian slave had told her of dragons which occupied dens in the mountains, and it seemed to her now that all at once the greenish eye of such a monster was gazing at her. She caught at Vinicius's hand as a frightened child would, and disconnected, quick impressions pressed into her head: Was not that he, the terrible, the all-powerful? She had not seen him hitherto, and she thought that he looked differently. She had imagined some kind of ghastly face, with malignity petrified in its features; now she saw a great head, fixed on a thick neck, terrible, it is true, but almost ridiculous, for from a distance it resembled the head of a child. A tunic of amethyst color, forbidden to ordinary mortals, cast a bluish tinge on his broad and short face. He had dark hair, dressed, in the fashion introduced by Otho, in four curls.

He had no beard, because he had sacrified it recently to Jove, — for which all Rome gave him thanks, though people whispered to each other that he had sacrificed it because his beard, like that of his whole family, was red. In his forehead, projecting strongly above his brows, there remained something Olympian. In his contracted brows the consciousness of supreme power was evident; but under that forehead of a demigod was the face of a monkey, a drunkard, and a comedian, — vain, full of changing desires, swollen with fat, notwithstanding his youth; besides, it was sickly and foul. To Lygia he seemed ominous, but above all repulsive.

After a while he laid down the emerald and ceased to look at her. Then she saw his prominent blue eyes, blinking before the excess of light, glassy, without thought, resembling the eyes of the dead.

"Is that the hostage with whom Vinicius is in love?" asked he, turning to Petronius.

"That is she," answered Petronius.

"What are her people called?"

"The Lygians."

"Does Vinicius think her beautiful?"

"Array a rotten olive trunk in the peplus of a woman, and Vinicius will declare it beautiful. But on thy countenance, incomparable judge, I read her sentence already. Thou hast no need to pronounce it! The sentence is true: she is too dry, thin, a mere blossom on a slender stalk; and thou, O divine æsthete, esteemest the stalk in a woman. Thrice and four times art thou right! The face alone does not signify. I have learned much in thy company, but even now I have not a perfect cast of the eye. But I am ready to lay a wager with Tullius Senecio concerning his mistress, that, although at a feast, when all are reclining, it is difficult to judge the whole form, thou hast said in thy mind already, 'Too narrow in the hips.' "

"Too narrow in the hips," answered Nero, blinking.

On Petronius's lips appeared a scarcely perceptible smile; but Tullius Senecio, who till that moment was occupied in conversing with Vestinius, or rather in reviling dreams, while Vestinius believed in them, turned to Petronius, and though he had not the least idea touching that of which they were talking, he said, —

"Thou art mistaken! I hold with Cæsar."

"Very well," answered Petronius. "I have just maintained that thou hast a glimmer of understanding, but Cæsar insists that thou art an ass pure and simple."

"*Habet!*" said Cæsar, laughing, and turning down the thumb, as was done in the Circus, in sign that the gladiator had received a blow and was to be finished.

But Vestinius, thinking that the question was of dreams, exclaimed, —

"But I believe in dreams, and Seneca told me on a time that he believes too."

"Last night I dreamt that I had become a vestal virgin," said Calvia Crispinilla, bending over the table.

At this Nero clapped his hands, other followed, and in a moment clapping of hands was heard all around, — for Crispinilla had been divorced a number of times, and was known throughout Rome for her fabulous debauchery.

But she, not disconcerted in the least, said, —

"Well! They are all old and ugly. Rubria alone has a human semblance, and so there would be two of us, though Rubria gets freckles in summer."

"But admit, purest Calvia," said Petronius, "that thou couldst become a vestal only in dreams."

"But if Cæsar commanded?"

"I should believe that even the most impossible dreams might come true."

"But they do come true," said Vestinius. "I understand those who do not believe in the gods, but how is it possible not to believe in dreams?"

"But predictions?" inquired Nero. "It was predicted once to me, that Rome would cease to exist, and that I should rule the whole Orient."

"Predictions and dreams are connected," said Vestinius. "Once a certain proconsul, a great disbeliever, sent a slave to the temple of Mopsus with a sealed letter which he would not let any one open; he did this to try if the god could answer the question contained in the letter. The slave slept a night in the temple to have a prophetic dream; he returned then and said: 'I saw a youth in my dreams; he was as bright as the sun, and spoke only one word, "Black."' The proconsul, when he heard this, grew pale, and turning to his guests, disbelievers like himself, said: 'Do ye know what was in the letter?'"

Here Vestinius stopped, and, raising his goblet with wine, began to drink.

"What was in the letter?" asked Senecio.

"In the letter was the question: 'What is the color of the bull which I am to sacrifice: white or black?'"

But the interest roused by the narrative was interrupted by Vitelius, who, drunk when he came to the feast, burst forth on a sudden and without cause in senseless laughter.

"What is that keg of tallow laughing at?" asked Nero.

"Laughter distinguishes men from animals," said Petronius, "and he has no other proof that he is not a wild boar."

Vitelius stopped half-way in his laughter, and smacking his lips, shining from fat and sauces, looked at those present with as much astonishment as if he had never seen them before; then he raised his two hands, which were like cushions, and said in a hoarse voice, —

"The ring of a knight has fallen from my finger, and it was inherited from my father."

"Who was a tailor," added Nero.

But Vitelius burst forth again in unexpected laughter, and began to search for his ring in the peplus of Calvia Crispinilla.

Hereupon Vestinius fell to imitating the cries of a frightened woman. Nigidia, a friend of Calvia, — a young widow with the face of a child and the eyes of a wanton, — said aloud, —

"He is seeking what he has not lost."

"And which will be useless to him if he finds it," finished the poet Lucan.

The feast grew more animated. Crowds of slaves bore around successive courses; from great vases filled with snow and garlanded with ivy, smaller vessels with various kinds of wine were brought forth unceasingly. All drank freely. On the guests, roses fell from the ceiling at intervals.

Petronius entreated Nero to dignify the feast with his song before the guests drank too deeply. A chorus of voices supported his words, but Nero refused at first. It was not a question of courage alone, he said, though that failed him always. The gods knew what efforts every success cost him. He did not avoid them, however, for it was needful to do something for art; and besides, if Apollo had gifted him with a certain voice, it was not proper to let divine gifts be wasted. He understood, even, that it was his duty to the State not to let them be wasted. But that day he was really hoarse. In the night he had placed leaden weights on his chest, but that had not helped in any way. He was thinking even to go to Antium, to breathe the sea air.

Lucan implored him in the name of art and humanity. All knew that the divine poet and singer had composed a new hymn to Venus, compared with which Lucretius's hymn was as the howl of a yearling wolf. Let that feast be a genuine feast. So kind a ruler should not cause such tortures to his subjects. "Be not cruel, O Cæsar!"

"Be not cruel!" repeated all who were sitting near.

Nero spread his hands in sign that he had to yield. All faces assumed then an expression of gratitude, and all eyes were turned to him; but he gave command first to announce to Poppæa that he would sing; he informed those present that she had not come to the feast, because she did not feel in good health; but since no medicine gave her such relief as his singing, he would be sorry to deprive her of this opportunity.

In fact, Poppæa came soon. Hitherto she had ruled Nero as if he had been her subject, but she knew that when his vanity as a singer, a charioteer, or a poet was involved, there was danger in provoking it. She came in therefore, beautiful as a divinity, arrayed, like Nero, in robes of amethyst color, and wearing a necklace of immense pearls, stolen on a time from Massinissa; she was golden-haired, sweet, and though divorced from two husbands she had the face and the look of a virgin.

She was greeted with shouts, and the appellation "Divine Augusta." Lygia had never seen any one so beautiful, and she could not believe her own eyes, for she knew that Poppæa Sabina was one of the vilest women on earth. She knew from Pomponia that she had brought Cæsar to murder his mother and his wife; she knew her from accounts given by Aulus's guests and the servants; she had heard that statues to her had been thrown down at night in the city; she had heard of inscriptions, the writers of which had been condemned to severest punishment, but which still appeared on the city walls every morning. Yet at sight of the notorious Poppæa, considered by the confessors of Christ as crime and evil incarnate, it seemed to her that angels or spirits of heaven might look like her. She was unable simply to take her eyes from Poppæa; and from her lips was wrested involuntarily the question, —

"Ah, Marcus, can it be possible?"

But he, roused by wine, and as it were impatient that so many things

had scattered her attention, and taken her from him and his words, said, —
"Yes, she is beautiful, but thou art a hundred times more beautiful. Thou
dost not know thyself, or thou wouldst be in love with thyself, as Narcissus
was; she bathes in asses' milk, but Venus bathed thee in her own milk. Thou
dost not know thyself, Ocelle mi! Look not at her. Turn thy eyes to me,
Ocelle mi! Touch this goblet of wine with thy lips, and I will put mine on
the same place."

And he pushed up nearer and nearer, and she began to withdraw toward
Acte. But at that moment silence was enjoined because Cæsar had risen.
The singer Diodorus had given him a lute of the kind called delta; another
singer named Terpnos, who had to accompany him in playing, approached
with an instrument called the nablium. Nero, resting the delta on the table,
raised his eyes; and for a moment silence reigned in the triclinium, broken
only by a rustle, as roses fell from the ceiling.

Then he began to chant, or rather to declaim, singingly and rhythmically,
to the accompaniment of the two lutes, his own hymn to Venus. Neither the
voice, though somewhat injured, nor the verses were bad, so that reproaches
of conscience took possession of Lygia again; for the hymn, though glorifying
the impure pagan Venus, seemed to her more than beautiful, and Cæsar himself, with a laurel crown on his head and uplifted eyes, nobler, much less
terrible, and less repulsive than at the beginning of the feast.

The guests answered with a thunder of applause. Cries of, "Oh, heavenly
voice!" were heard round about; some of the women raised their hands, and
held them thus, as a sign of delight, even after the end of the hymn; others
wiped their tearful eyes; the whole hall was seething as in a beehive. Poppæa,
bending her golden-haired head, raised Nero's hand to her lips, and held it
long in silence. Pythagoras, a young Greek of marvellous beauty, — the same
to whom later the half-insane Nero commanded the flamens to marry him,
with the observance of all rites, — knelt now at his feet.

But Nero looked carefully at Petronius, whose praises were desired by
him always before every other, and who said, —

"If it is a question of music, Orpheus must at this moment be as yellow from
envy as Lucan, who is here present; and as to the verses, I am sorry that they
are not worse; if they were I might find proper words to praise them."

Lucan did not take the mention of envy evil of him; on the contrary,
he looked at Petronius with gratitude, and, affecting ill-humor, began to
murmur, —

"Cursed fate, which commanded me to live contemporary with such a
poet. One might have a place in the memory of man, and on Parnassus; but
now one will quench, as a candle in sunlight."

Petronius, who had an amazing memory, began to repeat extracts from
the hymn and cite single verses, exalt, and analyze the more beautiful expressions. Lucan, forgetting as it were his envy before the charm of the
poetry, joined his ecstasy to Petronius's words. On Nero's face were reflected
delight and fathomless vanity, not only nearing stupidity, but reaching it
perfectly. He indicated to them verses which he considered the most beauti-

ful; and finally he began to comfort Lucan, and tell him not to lose heart, for though whatever a man is born that he is, the honor which people give Jove does not exclude respect for other divinities.

Then he rose to conduct Poppæa, who, being really in ill health, wished to withdraw. But he commanded the guests who remained to occupy their places anew, and promised to return. In fact, he returned a little later, to stupefy himself with the smoke of incense, and gaze at further spectacles which he himself, Petronius, or Tigellinus had prepared for the feast.

Again verses were read or dialogues listened to in which extravagance took the place of wit. After that Paris, the celebrated mime, represented the adventures of Io, the daughter of Inachus. To the guests, and especially to Lygia, unaccustomed to such scenes, it seemed that they were gazing at miracles and enchantment. Paris, with motions of his hands and body, was able to express things apparently impossible in a dance. His hands dimmed the air, creating a cloud, bright, living, quivering, voluptuous, surrounding the half-fainting form of a maiden shaken by a spasm of delight. That was a picture, not a dance; an expressive picture, disclosing the secrets of love, bewitching and shameless; and when at the end of it Corybantes rushed in and began a bacchic dance with girls of Syria to the sounds of cithara, lutes, drums, and cymbals, — a dance filled with wild shouts and still wilder license, — it seemed to Lygia that living fire was burning her, and that a thunderbolt ought to strike that house, or the ceiling fall on the heads of those feasting there.

But from the golden net fastened to the ceiling only roses fell, and the now half-drunken Vinicius said to her, —

"I saw thee in the house of Aulus, at the fountain. It was daylight, and thou didst think that no one saw thee; but I saw thee. And I see thee thus yet, though that peplus hides thee. Cast aside the peplus, like Crispinilla. See, gods and men seek love. There is nothing in the world but love. Lay thy head on my breast and close thy eyes."

The pulse beat oppressively in Lygia's hands and temples. A feeling seized her that she was flying into some abyss, and that Vinicius, who before had seemed so near and so trustworthy, instead of saving was drawing her toward it. And she felt sorry for him. She began again to dread the feast and him and herself. Some voice, like that of Pomponia, was calling yet in her soul, "O Lygia, save thyself!" But something told her also that it was too late; that the one whom such a flame had embraced as that which had embraced her, the one who had seen what was done at that feast and whose heart had beaten as hers had on hearing the words of Vinicius, the one through whom such a shiver had passed as had passed through her when he approached, was lost beyond recovery. She grew weak. It seemed at moments to her that she would faint, and then something terrible would happen. She knew that, under penalty of Cæsar's anger, it was not permitted any one to rise till Cæsar rose; but even were that not the case, she had not strength now to rise.

Meanwhile it was far to the end of the feast yet. Slaves brought new courses, and filled the goblets unceasingly with wine; before the table, on a platform open at one side, appeared two athletes to give the guests a spectacle of wrestling.

They began the struggle at once, and the powerful bodies, shining from olive oil, formed one mass; bones cracked in their iron arms, and from their set jaws came an ominous gritting of teeth. At moments was heard the quick, dull thump of their feet on the platform strewn with saffron; again they were motionless, silent, and it seemed to the spectators that they had before them a group chiselled out of stone. Roman eyes followed with delight the movement of tremendously exerted backs, thighs, and arms. But the struggle was not too prolonged; for Croton, a master, and the founder of a school of gladiators, did not pass in vain for the strongest man in the empire. His opponent began to breathe more and more quickly: next a rattle was heard in his throat; then his face grew blue; finally he threw blood from his mouth and fell.

A thunder of applause greeted the end of the struggle, and Croton, resting his foot on the breast of his opponent, crossed his gigantic arms on his breast, and cast the eyes of a victor around the hall.

Next appeared men who mimicked beasts and their voices, ball-players and buffoons. Only a few persons looked at them, however, since wine had darkened the eyes of the audience. The feast passed by degrees into a drunken revel and a dissolute orgy. The Syrian damsels, who appeared at first in the bacchic dance, mingled now with the guests. The music changed into a disordered and wild outburst of citharas, lutes, Armenian cymbals, Egyptian sistra, trumpets, and horns. As some of the guests wished to talk, they shouted at the musicians to disappear. The air, filled with the odor of flowers and the perfume of oils with which beautiful boys had sprinkled the feet of the guests during the feast, permeated with saffron and the exhalations of people, became stifling; lamps burned with a dim flame; the wreaths dropped sidewise on the heads of guests; faces grew pale and were covered with sweat. Vitelius rolled under the table. Nigidia, stripping herself to the waist, dropped her drunken childlike head on the breast of Lucan, who, drunk in like degree, fell to blowing the golden powder from her hair, and raising his eyes with immense delight. Vestinius, with the stubbornness of intoxication, repeated for the tenth time the answer of Mopsus to the sealed letter of the proconsul. Tullius, who reviled the gods, said, with a drawling voice broken by hiccoughs, —

"If the spheros of Xenophanes is round, then consider, such a god might be pushed along before one with the foot, like a barrel."

But Domitius Afer, a hardened criminal and informer, was indignant at the discourse, and through indignation spilled Falernian over his whole tunic. He had always believed in the gods. People say that Rome will perish, and there are some even who contend that it is perishing already. And surely! But if that should come, it is because the youth are without faith, and without faith there can be no virtue. People have abandoned also the strict habits of former days, and it never occurs to them that Epicureans will not stand against barbarians. As for him, he — As for him, he was sorry that he had lived to such times, and that he must seek in pleasures a refuge against griefs which, if not met, would soon kill him.

When he had said this, he drew toward him a Syrian dancer, and kissed her neck and shoulders with his toothless mouth. Seeing this, the consul Memnius Regulus laughed, and, raising his bald head with wreath awry, exclaimed, —

"Who says that Rome is perishing? What folly! I, a consul, know better. *Videant consules!* Thirty legions are guarding our *pax romana!*"

Here he put his fists to his temples and shouted, in a voice heard throughout the triclinium, —

"Thirty legions! thirty legions! from Britain to the Parthian boundaries!"

But he stopped on a sudden, and, putting a finger to his forehead, said, — "As I live, I think there are thirty-two."

He rolled under the table, and began soon to send forth flamingo tongues, roast and chilled mushrooms, locusts in honey, fish, meat, and everything which he had eaten or drunk.

But the number of the legions guarding Roman peace did not pacify Domitius.

No, no! Rome must perish; for faith in the gods was lost, and so were strict habits! Rome must perish; and it was a pity, for still life was pleasant there. Cæsar was gracious, wine was good! Oh, what a pity!

And hiding his head on the arm of a Syrian bacchanal, he burst into tears.

"What is a future life! Achilles was right, — better be a slave in the world beneath the sun than a king in Cimmerian regions. And still the question whether there are any gods — since it is unbelief — is destroying the youth."

Lucan meanwhile had blown all the gold powder from Nigidia's hair, and she being drunk had fallen asleep. Next he took wreaths of ivy from the vase before him, put them on the sleeping woman, and when he had finished looked at those present with a delighted and inquiring glance. He arrayed himself in ivy too, repeating, in a voice of deep conviction, "I am not a man at all, but a faun."

Petronius was not drunk; but Nero, who drank little at first, out of regard for his "heavenly" voice, emptied goblet after goblet toward the end, and was drunk. He wanted even to sing more of his verses, — this time in Greek, — but he had forgotten them, and by mistake sang an ode of Anacreon. Pythagoras, Diodorus, and Terpnos accompanied him; but failing to keep time, they stopped. Nero as a judge and an æsthete was enchanted with the beauty of Pythagoras, and fell to kissing his hands in ecstasy. "Such beautiful hands I have seen only once, and whose were they?" Then placing his palm on his moist forehead, he tried to remember. After a while terror was reflected on his face.

Ah! His mother's — Agrippina's!

And a gloomy vision seized him forthwith.

"They say," said he, "that she wanders by moonlight on the sea around Baiæ and Bauli. She merely walks, — walks as if seeking for something. When she comes near a boat, she looks at it and goes away; but the fisherman on whom she has fixed her eye dies."

"Not a bad theme," said Petronius.

But Vestinius, stretching his neck like a stork, whispered mysteriously, — "I do not believe in the gods; but I believe in spirits — Oi!"

Nero paid no attention to their words, and continued, —

"I celebrated the Lemuria, and have no wish to see her. This is the fifth year — I had to condemn her, for she sent assassins against me; and, had I not been quicker than she, ye would not be listening to-night to my song."

"Thanks be to Cæsar, in the name of the city and the world!" cried Domitius Afer.

"Wine! and let them strike the tympans!"

The uproar began anew. Lucan, all in ivy, wishing to outshout him, rose and cried, —

"I am not a man, but a faun; and I dwell in the forest. Eho-o-o-oo!"

Cæsar drank himself drunk at last; men were drunk, and women were drunk. Vinicius was not less drunk than others; and in addition there was roused in him, besides desire, a wish to quarrel, which happened always when he passed the measure. His dark face became paler, and his tongue stuttered when he spoke, in a voice now loud and commanding, —

"Give me thy lips! To-day, to-morrow, it is all one! Enough of this! Cæsar took thee from Aulus to give thee to me, dost understand? To-morrow, about dusk, I will send for thee, dost understand? Cæsar promised thee to me before he took thee. Thou must be mine! Give me thy lips! I will not wait for to-morrow, — give thy lips quickly."

And he moved to embrace her; but Acte began to defend her, and she defended herself with the remnant of her strength, for she felt that she was perishing. But in vain did she struggle with both hands to remove his hairless arm; in vain, with a voice in which terror and grief were quivering, did she implore him not to be what he was, and to have pity on her. Sated with wine, his breath blew around her nearer and nearer, and his face was there near her face. He was no longer the former kind Vinicius, almost dear to her soul; he was a drunken, wicked satyr, who filled her with repulsion and terror. But her strength deserted her more and more. In vain did she bend and turn away her face to escape his kisses. He rose to his feet, caught her in both arms, and drawing her head to his breast, began, panting, to press her pale lips with his.

But at this instant a tremendous power removed his arms from her neck with as much ease as if they had been the arms of a child, and pushed him aside, like a dried limb or a withered leaf. What had happened? Vinicius rubbed his astonished eyes, and saw before him the gigantic figure of the Lygian, called Ursus, whom he had seen at the house of Aulus.

Ursus stood calmly, but looked at Vinicius so strangely with his blue eyes that the blood stiffened in the veins of the young man; then the giant took his queen on his arm, and walked out of the triclinium with an even, quiet step.

Acte in that moment went after him.

Vinicius sat for the twinkle of an eye as if petrified; then he sprang up and ran toward the entrance crying, —

"Lygia! Lygia!"

But desire, astonishment, rage, and wine cut the legs from under him. He staggered once and a second time, seized the naked arm of one of the bacchanals, and began to inquire, with blinking eyes, what had happened. She, taking a goblet of wine, gave it to him with a smile in her mist-covered eyes.

"Drink!" said she.

Vinicius drank, and fell to the floor.

The greater number of the guests were lying under the table; others were walking with tottering tread through the triclinium, while others were sleeping on couches at the table, snoring, or giving forth the excess of wine. Meanwhile, from the golden network, roses were dropping and dropping on those drunken consuls and senators, on those drunken knights, philosophers, and poets, on those drunken dancing damsels and patrician ladies, on that society all dominant as yet but with the soul gone from it, on that society garlanded and ungirdled but perishing.

Dawn had begun out of doors.

CHAPTER VIII

No one stopped Ursus, no one inquired even what he was doing. Those guests who were not under the table had not kept their own places; hence the servants, seeing a giant carrying a guest on his arm, thought him some slave bearing out his intoxicated mistress. Moreover, Acte was with them, and her presence removed all suspicion.

In this way they went from the triclinium to the adjoining chamber, and thence to the gallery leading to Acte's apartments. To such a degree had her strength deserted Lygia, that she hung as if dead on the arm of Ursus. But when the cool, pure breeze of morning beat around her, she opened her eyes. It was growing clearer and clearer in the open air. After they had passed along the colonnade awhile, they turned to a side portico, coming out, not in the courtyard, but the palace gardens, where the tops of the pines and cypresses were growing ruddy from the light of morning. That part of the building was empty, so that echoes of music and sounds of the feast came with decreasing distinctness. It seemed to Lygia that she had been rescued from hell, and borne into God's bright world outside. There was something, then, besides that disgusting triclinium. There was the sky, the dawn, light, and peace. Sudden weeping seized the maiden, and, taking shelter on the arm of the giant, she repeated, with sobbing, —

"Let us go home, Ursus! home, to the house of Aulus."

"Let us go!" answered Ursus.

They found themselves now in the small atrium of Acte's apartments. Ursus placed Lygia on a marble bench at a distance from the fountain. Acte strove to pacify her; she urged her to sleep, and declared that for the moment there was no danger, — after the feast the drunken guests would sleep till evening. For a long time Lygia could not calm herself, and, pressing her temples with both hands, she repeated like a child, —

"Let us go home, to the house of Aulus!"

Ursus was ready. At the gates stood pretorians, it is true, but he would pass them. The soldiers would not stop out-going people. The space before the arch was crowded with litters. Guests were beginning to go forth in throngs. No one would detain them. They would pass with the crowd and go home directly. For that matter, what does he care? As the queen commands, so must it be. He is there to carry out her orders.

"Yes, Ursus," said Lygia, "let us go."

Acte was forced to find reason for both. They would pass out, true; no one would stop them. But it is not permitted to flee from the house of Cæsar; whoso does that offends Cæsar's majesty. They may go; but in the evening a centurion at the head of soldiers will take a death sentence to Aulus and Pomponia Græcina; they will bring Lygia to the palace again, and then there will be no rescue for her. Should Aulus and his wife receive her under their roof, death awaits them to a certainty.

Lygia's arms dropped. There was no other outcome. She must choose her own ruin or that of Plautius. In going to the feast, she had hoped that Vinicius and Petronius would win her from Cæsar, and return her to Pomponia; now she knew that it was they who had brought Cæsar to remove her from the house of Aulus. There was no help. Only a miracle could save her from the abyss, — a miracle and the might of God.

"Acte," said she, in despair, "didst thou hear Vinicius say that Cæsar had given me to him, and that he will send slaves here this evening to take me to his house?"

"I did," answered Acte; and, raising her arms from her side, she was silent. The despair with which Lygia spoke found in her no echo. She herself had been Nero's favorite. Her heart, though good, could not feel clearly the shame of such a relation. A former slave, she had grown too much inured to the law of slavery; and, besides, she loved Nero yet. If he returned to her, she would stretch her arms to him, as to happiness. Comprehending clearly that Lygia must become the mistress of the youthful and stately Vinicius, or expose Aulus and Pomponia to ruin, she failed to understand how the girl could hesitate.

"In Cæsar's house," said she, after a while, "it would not be safer for thee than in that of Vinicius."

And it did not occur to her that, though she told the truth, her words meant, "Be resigned to fate and become the concubine of Vinicius."

As to Lygia, who felt on her lips yet his kisses, burning as coals and full of beastly desire, the blood rushed to her face with shame at the mere thought of them.

"Never," cried she, with an outburst, "will I remain here, or at the house of Vinicius, — never!"

"But," inquired Acte, "is Vinicius hateful to thee?"

Lygia was unable to answer, for weeping seized her anew. Acte gathered the maiden to her bosom, and strove to calm her excitement. Ursus breathed heavily, and balled his giant fists; for, loving his queen with the devotion of a dog, he could not bear the sight of her tears. In his half-wild Lygian heart was the wish to return to the triclinium, choke Vinicius, and, should the need come, Cæsar himself; but he feared to sacrifice thereby his mistress, and was not certain that such an act, which to him seemed very simple, would befit a confessor of the Crucified Lamb.

But Acte, while caressing Lygia, asked again, "Is he so hateful to thee?"

"No," said Lygia; "it is not permitted me to hate, for I am a Christian."

"I know, Lygia. I know also from the letters of Paul of Tarsus, that it is not permitted to defile one's self, nor to fear death more than sin; but tell me if thy teaching permits one person to cause the death of others?"

"No."

"Then how canst thou bring Cæsar's vengeance on the house of Aulus?"
A moment of silence followed. A bottomless abyss yawned before Lygia again.

"I ask," continued the young freedwoman, "for I have compassion on thee
— and I have compassion on the good Pomponia and Aulus, and on their
child. It is long since I began to live in this house, and I know what Cæsar's
anger is. No! thou art not at liberty to flee from here. One way remains to
thee: implore Vinicius to return thee to Pomponia."

But Lygia dropped on her knees to implore some one else. Ursus knelt
down after a while, too, and both began to pray in Cæsar's house at the morning dawn.

Acte witnessed such a prayer for the first time, and could not take her
eyes from Lygia, who, seen by her in profile, with raised hands, and face
turned heavenward, seemed to implore rescue. The dawn, casting light on
her dark hair and white peplus, was reflected in her eyes. Entirely in the
light, she seemed herself like light. In that pale face, in those parted lips, in
those raised hands and eyes, a kind of superhuman exaltation was evident.
Acte understood then why Lygia could not become the concubine of any
man. Before the face of Nero's former favorite was drawn aside, as it were,
a corner of that veil which hides a world altogether different from that to
which she was accustomed. She was astonished by prayer in that abode of
crime and infamy. A moment earlier it had seemed to her that there was
no rescue for Lygia; now she began to think that something uncommon
would happen, that some aid would come, — aid so mighty that Cæsar himself would be powerless to resist it; that some winged army would descend
from the sky to help that maiden, or that the sun would spread its rays
beneath her feet and draw her up to itself. She had heard of many miracles
among Christians, and she thought now that everything said of them was
true, since Lygia was praying.

Lygia rose at last, with a face serene with hope. Ursus rose too, and, holding to the bench, looked at his mistress, waiting for her words.

But it grew dark in her eyes, and after a time two great tears rolled down
her cheeks slowly.

"May God bless Pomponia and Aulus," said she. "It is not permitted me
to bring ruin on them; therefore I shall never see them again."

Then turning to Ursus she said that he alone remained to her in the world;
that he must be to her as a protector and a father. They could not seek refuge
in the house of Aulus, for they would bring on it the anger of Cæsar. But
neither could she remain in the house of Cæsar or that of Vinicius. Let Ursus
take her then; let him conduct her out of the city; let him conceal her in
some place where neither Vinicius nor his servants could find her. She would
follow Ursus anywhere, even beyond the sea, even beyond the mountains,
to the barbarians, where the Roman name was not heard, and whither the
power of Cæsar did not reach. Let him take her and save her, for he alone
had remained to her.

The Lygian was ready, and in sign of obedience he bent to her feet and embraced them. But on the face of Acte, who had been expecting a miracle, disappointment was evident. Had the prayer effected only that much? To flee from the house of Cæsar is to commit an offence against majesty which must be avenged; and even if Lygia succeeded in hiding, Cæsar would avenge himself on Aulus and Pomponia. If she wishes to escape, let her escape from the house of Vinicius. Then Cæsar, who does not like to occupy himself with the affairs of others, may not wish even to aid Vinicius in the pursuit; in every case it will not be a crime against majesty.

But Lygia's thoughts were just the following: Aulus would not even know where she was; Pomponia herself would not know. She would escape not from the house of Vinicius, however, but while on the way to it. When drunk, Vinicius had said that he would send his slaves for her in the evening. Beyond doubt he had told the truth, which he would not have done had he been sober. Evidently he himself, or perhaps he and Petronius, had seen Cæsar before the feast, and won from him the promise to give her on the following evening. And if they forgot that day, they would send for her on the morrow. But Ursus will save her. He will come; he will bear her out of the litter as he bore her out of the triclinium, and they will go into the world. No one could resist Ursus, not even that terrible athlete who wrestled at the feast yesterday. But as Vinicius might send a great number of slaves, Ursus would go at once to Bishop Linus for aid and counsel. The bishop will take compassion on her, will not leave her in the hands of Vinicius; he will command Christians to go with Ursus to rescue her. They will seize her and bear her away; then Ursus can take her out of the city and hide her from the power of Rome.

And her face began to flush and smile. Consolation entered her anew, as if the hope of rescue had turned to reality. She threw herself on Acte's neck suddenly, and, putting her beautiful lips to Acte's cheek, she whispered:

"Thou wilt not betray, Acte, wilt thou?"

"By the shade of my mother," answered the freedwoman, "I will not; but pray to thy God that Ursus be able to bear thee away."

The blue, childlike eyes of the giant were gleaming with happiness. He had not been able to frame any plan, though he had been breaking his poor head; but a thing like this he could do, — and whether in the day or in the night it was all one to him! He would go to the bishop, for the bishop can read in the sky what is needed and what is not. Besides, he could assemble Christians himself. Are his acquaintances few among slaves, gladiators, and free people, both in the Subura and beyond the bridges? He can collect a couple of thousand of them. He will rescue his lady, and take her outside the city, and he can go with her. They will go to the end of the world, even to that place from which they had come, where no one has heard of Rome.

Here he began to look forward, as if to see things in the future and very distant.

"To the forest? Ai, what a forest, what a forest!"

But after a while he shook himself out of his visions. Well, he will go to the bishop at once, and in the evening will wait with something like a hundred men for the litter. And let not slaves, but even pretorians, take her from him! Better for any man not to come under his fist, even though in iron armor, — for is iron so strong? When he strikes iron earnestly, the head underneath will not survive.

But Lygia raised her finger with great and also childlike seriousness.

"Ursus, do not kill," said she.

Ursus put his fist, which was like a maul, to the back of his head, and, rubbing his neck with great seriousness, began to mutter. But he must rescue "his light." She herself had said that his turn had come. He will try all he can. But if something happens in spite of him? In every case he must save her. But should anything happen, he will repent, and so entreat the Innocent Lamb that the Crucified Lamb will have mercy on him, poor fellow. He has no wish to offend the Lamb; but then his hands are so heavy.

Great tenderness was expressed on his face; but wishing to hide it, he bowed and said, —

"Now I will go to the holy bishop."

Acte put her arms around Lygia's neck, and began to weep. Once more the freedwoman understood that there was a world in which greater happiness existed, even in suffering, than in all the excesses and luxury of Cæsar's house. Once more a kind of door to the light was opened a little before her, but she felt at once that she was unworthy to pass through it.

CHAPTER IX

LYGIA was grieved to lose Pomponia Græcina, whom she loved with her whole soul, and she grieved for the household of Aulus; still her despair passed away. She felt a certain delight even in the thought that she was sacrificing plenty and comfort for her Truth, and was entering on an unknown and wandering existence. Perhaps there was in this a little also of childish curiosity as to what that life would be, off somewhere in remote regions, among wild beasts and barbarians. But there was still more a deep and trusting faith, that by acting thus she was doing as the Divine Master had commanded, and that henceforth He Himself would watch over her, as over an obedient and faithful child. In such a case what harm could meet her? If sufferings come, she will endure them in His name. If sudden death comes, He will take her; and some time, when Pomponia dies, they will be together for all eternity. More than once when she was in the house of Aulus, she tortured her childish head because she, a Christian, could do nothing for that Crucified, of whom Ursus spoke with such tenderness. But now the moment had come. Lygia felt almost happy, and began to speak of her happiness to Acte, who could not understand her, however. To leave everything, — to leave house, wealth, the city, gardens, temples, porticos, everything that is beautiful; leave a sunny land and people near to one — and for what purpose? To hide from the love of a young and stately knight. In Acte's head these things could not find place. At times she felt that Lygia's action was right, that there must be some immense mysterious happiness in it; but she could not give a clear account to herself of the matter, especially since an adventure was before Lygia which might have an evil ending, — an adventure in which she might lose her life simply. Acte was timid by nature, and she thought with dread of what the coming evening might bring. But she was loath to mention her fears to Lygia; meanwhile, as the day was clear and the sun looked into the atrium, she began to persuade her to take the rest needed after a night without sleep. Lygia did not refuse; and both went to the cubiculum, which was spacious and furnished with luxury because of Acte's former relations with Cæsar. There they lay down side by side, but in spite of her weariness Acte could not sleep. For a long time she had been sad and unhappy, but now she was seized by a certain uneasiness which she had never felt before. So far life had seemed to her simply grievous and deprived of a morrow; now all at once it seemed to her dishonorable.

Increasing chaos rose in her head. Again the door to light began to open and close. But in the moment when it opened, that light so dazzled her that she could see nothing distinctly. She divined, merely, that in that light there was happiness of some kind, happiness beyond measure, in presence of which every other was nothing, to such a degree that if Cæsar, for example, were to set aside Poppæa, and love her, Acte, again, it would be vanity. Suddenly the thought came to her that that Cæsar whom she loved, whom she held involuntarily as a kind of demigod, was as pitiful as any slave, and that palace, with columns of Numidian marble, no better than a heap of stones. At last, however, those feelings which she had not power to define began to torment her; she wanted to sleep, but being tortured by alarm she could not.

Thinking that Lygia, threatened by so many perils and uncertainties, was not sleeping either, she turned to her to speak of her flight in the evening. But Lygia was sleeping calmly. Into the dark cubiculum, past the curtain which was not closely drawn, came a few bright rays, in which golden dust-motes were playing. By the light of these rays Acte saw her delicate face, resting on her bare arm, her closed eyes, and her mouth slightly open. She was breathing regularly, but as people breathe while asleep.

"She sleeps, — she is able to sleep," thought Acte. "She is a child yet."

Still, after a while it came to her mind that that child chose to flee rather than remain the beloved of Vinicius; she preferred want to shame, wandering to a lordly house, to robes, jewels, and feasts, to the sound of lutes and citharas. "Why?"

And she gazed at Lygia, as if to find an answer in her sleeping face. She looked at her clear forehead, at the calm arch of her brows, at her dark tresses, at her parted lips, at her virgin bosom moved by calm breathing; then she thought again, —

"How different from me!"

Lygia seemed to her a miracle, a sort of divine vision, something beloved of the gods, a hundred times more beautiful than all the flowers in Cæsar's garden, than all the statues in his palace. But in the Greek woman's heart there was no envy. On the contrary, at thought of the dangers which threatened the girl, great pity seized her. A certain motherly feeling rose in the woman. Lygia seemed to her not only as beautiful as a beautiful vision, but also very dear, and, putting her lips to her dark hair, she kissed it.

But Lygia slept on calmly, as if at home, under the care of Pomponia Græcina. And she slept rather long. Midday had passed when she opened her blue eyes and looked around the cubiculum in astonishment. Evidently she wondered that she was not in the house of Aulus.

"That is thou, Acte?" said she at last, seeing in the darkness the face of the Greek.

"I, Lygia."

"Is it evening?"

"No, child; but midday has passed."

"And has Ursus not returned?"

"Ursus did not say that he would return; he said that he would watch in the evening, with Christians, for the litter."

"True."

Then they left the cubiculum and went to the bath, where Acte bathed

Lygia; then she took her to breakfast and afterward to the gardens of the palace, in which no dangerous meeting might be feared, since Cæsar and his principal courtiers were sleeping yet. For the first time in her life Lygia saw those magnificent gardens, full of pines, cypresses, oaks, olives, and myrtles, among which appeared white here and there a whole population of statues. The mirror of ponds gleamed quietly; groves of roses were blooming, watered with the spray of fountains; entrances to charming grottos were encircled with a growth of ivy or woodbine; silver-colored swans were sailing on the water; amidst statues and trees wandered tame gazelles from the deserts of Africa, and rich-colored birds from all known countries on earth.

The gardens were empty; but here and there slaves were working, spade in hand, singing in an undertone; others, to whom was granted a moment of rest, were sitting by ponds or in the shade of groves, in trembling light produced by sun-rays breaking in between leaves; others were watering roses or the pale lily-colored blossoms of the saffron. Acte and Lygia walked rather long, looking at all the wonders of the gardens; and though Lygia's mind was not at rest, she was too much a child yet to resist pleasure, curiosity, and wonder. It occurred to her, even, that if Cæsar were good, he might be very happy in such a palace, in such gardens.

But at last, tired somewhat, the two women sat down on a bench hidden almost entirely by dense cypresses and began to talk of that which weighed on their hearts most, — that is, of Lygia's escape in the evening. Acte was far less at rest than Lygia touching its success. At times it seemed to her even a mad project, which could not succeed. She felt a growing pity for Lygia. It seemed to her that it would be a hundred times safer to try to act on Vinicius. After a while she inquired of Lygia how long she had known him, and whether she did not think that he would let himself be persuaded to return her to Pomponia.

But Lygia shook her dark head in sadness. "No. In Aulus's house, Vinicius had been different, he had been very kind, but since yesterday's feast she feared him, and would rather flee to the Lygians."

"But in Aulus's house," inquired Acte, "he was dear to thee, was he not?"

"He was," answered Lygia, inclining her head.

"And thou wert not a slave, as I was," said Acte, after a moment's thought. "Vinicius might marry thee. Thou art a hostage, and a daughter of the Lygian king. Aulus and Pomponia love thee as their own child; I am sure that they are ready to adopt thee. Vinicius might marry thee, Lygia."

But Lygia answered calmly, and with still greater sadness, "I would rather flee to the Lygians."

"Lygia, dost thou wish me to go directly to Vinicius, rouse him, if he is sleeping, and tell him what I have told thee? Yes, my precious one, I will go to him and say, 'Vinicius, this is a king's daughter, and a dear child of the famous Aulus; if thou love her, return her to Aulus and Pomponia, and take her as wife from their house.'"

But the maiden answered with a voice so low that Acte could barely hear it, —

"I would rather flee to the Lygians." And two tears were hanging on her drooping lids.

Further conversation was stopped by the rustle of approaching steps, and before Acte had time to see who was coming, Poppæa Sabina appeared in front of the bench with a small retinue of slave women. Two of them held over her head bunches of ostrich feathers fixed to golden wires; with these they fanned her lightly, and at the same time protected her from the autumn sun, which was hot yet. Before her a woman from Egypt, black as ebony, and with bosom swollen as if from milk, bore in her arms an infant wrapped in purple fringed with gold. Acte and Lygia rose, thinking that Poppæa would pass the bench without turning attention to either; but she halted before them and said, —

"Acte, the bells sent by thee for the doll were badly fastened; the child tore off one and put it to her mouth; luckily Lilith saw it in season."

"Pardon, divinity," answered Acte, crossing her arms on her breast and bending her head.

But Poppæa began to gaze at Lygia.

"What slave is this?" asked she, after a pause.

"She is not a slave, divine Augusta, but a foster child of Pomponia Græcina, and a daughter of the Lygian king given by him as hostage to Rome."

"And has she come to visit thee?"

"No, Augusta. She is dwelling in the palace since the day before yesterday."

"Was she at the feast last night?"

"She was, Augusta."

"At whose command?"

"At Cæsar's command."

Poppæa looked still more attentively at Lygia, who stood with bowed head, now raising her bright eyes to her with curiosity, now covering them with their lids. Suddenly a frown appeared between the brows of the Augusta. Jealous of her own beauty and power, she lived in continual alarm lest at some time a fortunate rival might ruin her, as she had ruined Octavia. Hence every beautiful face in the palace roused her suspicion. With the eye of a critic she took in at once every part of Lygia's form, estimated every detail of her face, and was frightened. "That is simply a nymph," thought she, "and 'twas Venus who gave birth to her." On a sudden this came to her mind which had never come before at sight of any beauty, — that she herself had grown notably older! Wounded vanity quivered in Poppæa, alarm seized her, and various fears shot through her head. "Perhaps Nero has not seen the girl, or, seeing her through the emerald, has not appreciated her. But what would happen should he meet such a marvel in the daytime, in sunlight? Moreover she is not a slave, she is the daughter of a king, — a king of barbarians, it is true, but a king. Immortal gods! she is as beautiful as I am, but younger!" The wrinkle between her brows increased, and her eyes began to shine under their golden lashes with a cold gleam.

"Hast thou spoken with Cæsar?"

"No, Augusta."

"Why dost thou choose to be here rather than in the house of Aulus?"

"I do not choose, lady. Petronius persuaded Cæsar to take me from Pomponia. I am here against my will."

"And wouldst thou return to Pomponia?"

This last question Poppæa gave with a softer and milder voice; hence a sudden hope rose in Lygia's heart.

"Lady," said she, extending her hand to her, "Cæsar promised to give me as a slave to Vinicius, but do thou intercede and return me to Pomponia."

"Then Petronius persuaded Cæsar to take thee from Aulus, and give thee to Vinicius?"

"True, lady. Vinicius is to send for me to-day, but thou art good, have compassion on me." When she had said this, she inclined, and, seizing the border of Poppæa's robe, waited for her word with beating heart. Poppæa looked at her for a while, with a face lighted by an evil smile, and said, —

"Then I promise that thou wilt become the slave of Vinicius this day."

And she went on, beautiful as a vision, but evil. To the ears of Lygia and Acte came only the wail of the infant, which began to cry, it was unknown for what reason.

Lygia's eyes too were filled with tears; but after a while she took Acte's hand and said, —

"Let us return. Help is to be looked for only whence it can come."

And they returned to the atrium, which they did not leave till evening. When darkness had come and slaves brought in tapers with great flames, both women were very pale. Their conversation failed every moment. Both were listening to hear if some one were coming. Lygia repeated again and again that, though grieved to leave Acte, she preferred that all should take place that day, as Ursus must be waiting in the dark for her then. But her breathing grew quicker from emotion, and louder. Acte collected feverishly such jewels as she could, and, fastening them in a corner of Lygia's peplus, implored her not to reject that gift and means of escape. At moments came a deep silence full of deceptions for the ear. It seemed to both that they heard at one time a whisper beyond the curtain, at another the distant weeping of a child, at another the barking of dogs.

Suddenly the curtain of the entrance moved without noise, and a tall, dark man, his face marked with small-pox, appeared like a spirit in the atrium. In one moment Lygia recognized Atacinus, a freedman of Vinicius, who had visited the house of Aulus.

Acte screamed; but Atacinus bent low and said, —

"A greeting, divine Lygia, from Marcus Vinicius, who awaits thee with a feast in his house which is decked in green."

The lips of the maiden grew pale.

"I go," said she.

Then she threw her arms around Acte's neck in farewell.

CHAPTER X

THE house of Vinicius was indeed decked in the green of myrtle and ivy, which had been hung on the walls and over the doors. The columns were wreathed with grape vine. In the atrium, which was closed above by a purple woollen cloth as protection from the night cold, it was as clear as in daylight. Eight and twelve flamed lamps were burning; these were like vessels, trees, animals, birds, or statues, holding cups filled with perfumed olive oil, lamps of alabaster, marble, or gilded Corinthian bronze, not so wonderful as that famed candlestick used by Nero and taken from the temple of Apollo, but beautiful and made by famous masters. Some of the lights were shaded by Alexandrian glass, or transparent stuffs from the Indus, of red, blue, yellow, or violet color, so that the whole atrium was filled with many colored rays. Everywhere was given out the odor of nard, to which Vinicius had grown used, and which he had learned to love in the Orient. The depths of the house, in which the forms of male and female slaves were moving, gleamed also with light. In the triclinium a table was laid for four persons. At the feast were to sit, besides Vinicius and Lygia, Petronius and Chrysothemis. Vinicius had followed in everything the words of Petronius, who advised him not to go for Lygia, but to send Atacinus with the permission obtained from Cæsar, to receive her himself in the house, receive her with friendliness and even with marks of honor.

"Thou wert drunk yesterday," said he; "I saw thee. Thou didst act with her like a quarryman from the Alban Hills. Be not over-insistent, and remember that one should drink good wine slowly. Know too that it is sweet to desire, but sweeter to be desired."

Chrysothemis had her own and a somewhat different opinion on this point; but Petronius, calling her his vestal and his dove, began to explain the difference which must exist between a trained charioteer of the Circus and the youth who sits on the quadriga for the first time. Then, turning to Vinicius, he continued, —

"Win her confidence, make her joyful, be magnanimous. I have no wish to see a gloomy feast. Swear to her, by Hades even, that thou wilt return her to Pomponia, and it will be thy affair that to-morrow she prefers to stay with thee."

Then pointing to Chrysothemis, he added, —

"For five years I have acted thus more or less with this timid dove, and I cannot complain of her harshness."

Chrysothemis struck him with her fan of peacock feathers, and said, —

"But I did not resist, thou satyr!"

"Out of consideration for my predecessor — "

"But wert thou not at my feet?"

"Yes; to put rings on thy toes."

Chrysothemis looked involuntarily at her feet, on the toes of which diamonds were really glittering; and she and Petronius began to laugh. But Vinicius did not give ear to their bantering. His heart was beating unquietly under the robes of a Syrian priest, in which he had arrayed himself to receive Lygia.

"They must have left the palace," said he, as if in a monologue.

"They must," answered Petronius. "Meanwhile I may mention the predictions of Apollonius of Tyana, or that history of Rufinus which I have not finished, I do not remember why."

But Vinicius cared no more for Apollonius of Tyana than for the history of Rufinus. His mind was with Lygia; and though he felt that it was more appropriate to receive her at home than to go in the rôle of a myrmidon to the palace, he was sorry at moments that he had not gone, for the single reason that he might have seen her sooner, and sat near her in the dark, in the double litter.

Meanwhile slaves brought in a tripod ornamented with rams' heads, bronze dishes with coals, on which they sprinkled bits of myrrh and nard.

"Now they are turning toward the Carinæ," said Vinicius, again.

"He cannot wait; he will run to meet the litter, and is likely to miss them!" exclaimed Chrysothemis.

Vinicius smiled without thinking, and said, —

"On the contrary, I will wait."

But he distended his nostrils and panted; seeing which, Petronius shrugged his shoulders, and said, —

"There is not in him a philosopher to the value of one sestertium, and I shall never make a man of that son of Mars."

"They are now in the Carinæ."

In fact, they were turning toward the Carinæ. The slaves called lampadarii were in front; others called pedisequii, were on both sides of the litter. Atacinus was right behind, overseeing the advance. But they moved slowly, for lamps showed the way badly in a place not lighted at all. The streets near the palace were empty; here and there only some man moved forward with a lantern, but farther on the place was uncommonly crowded. From almost every alley people were pushing out in threes and fours, all without lamps, all in dark mantles. Some walked on with the procession, mingling with the slaves; others in greater numbers came from the opposite direction. Some staggered as if drunk. At moments the advance grew so difficult that the lampadarii cried, —

"Give way to the noble tribune, Marcus Vinicius!"

Lygia saw those dark crowds through the curtains which were pushed aside, and trembled with emotion. She was carried away at one moment by hope, at another by fear.

"That is he! — that is Ursus and the Christians! Now it will happen quickly," said she, with trembling lips. "O Christ, aid! O Christ, save!"

Atacinus himself, who at first did not notice the uncommon animation of the street, began at last to be alarmed. There was something strange in this. The lampadarii had to cry oftener and oftener, "Give way to the litter of the noble tribune!" From the sides unknown people crowded up to the litter so much that Atacinus commanded the slaves to repulse them with clubs.

Suddenly a cry was heard in front of the procession. In one instant all the lights were extinguished. Around the litter came a rush, an uproar, a struggle.

Atacinus saw that this was simply an attack; and when he saw it he was frightened. It was known to all that Cæsar with a crowd of attendants made attacks frequently for amusement in the Subura and in other parts of the city. It was known that even at times he brought out of these night adventures black and blue spots; but whoso defended himself went to his death, even if a senator. The house of the guards, whose duty it was to watch over the city, was not very far; but during such attacks the guards feigned to be deaf and blind.

Meanwhile there was an uproar around the litter; people struck, struggled, threw, and trampled one another. The thought flashed on Atacinus to save Lygia and himself, above all, and leave the rest to their fate. So, drawing her out of the litter, he took her in his arms and strove to escape in the darkness.

But Lygia called, "Ursus! Ursus!"

She was dressed in white; hence it was easy to see her. Atacinus, with his other arm, which was free, was throwing his own mantle over her hastily, when terrible claws seized his neck, and on his head a gigantic, crushing mass fell like a stone.

He dropped in one instant, as an ox felled by the back of an axe before the altar of Jove.

The slaves for the greater part were either lying on the ground, or had saved themselves by scattering in the thick darkness, around the turns of the walls. On the spot remained only the litter, broken in the onset. Ursus bore away Lygia to the Subura; his comrades followed him, dispersing gradually along the way.

The slaves assembled before the house of Vinicius, and took counsel. They had not courage to enter. After a short deliberation they returned to the place of conflict, where they found a few corpses, and among them Atacinus. He was quivering yet; but, after a moment of more violent convulsion, he stretched and was motionless.

They took him then, and, returning, stopped before the gate a second time. But they must declare to their lord what had happened.

"Let Gulo declare it," whispered some voices; "blood is flowing from his face as from ours; and the master loves him; it is safer for Gulo than for others."

Gulo, a German, an old slave, who had nursed Vinicius, and was inherited by him from his mother, the sister of Petronius, said, —

"I will tell him; but do ye all come. Do not let his anger fall on my head alone."

Vinicius was growing thoroughly impatient. Petronius and Chrysothemis were laughing; but he walked with quick step up and down the atrium.

"They ought to be here! They ought to be here!"

He wished to go out to meet the litter, but Petronius and Chrysothemis detained him.

Steps were heard suddenly in the entrance; the slaves rushed into the atrium in a crowd, and, halting quickly at the wall, raised their hands, and began to repeat with groaning, —

"Aaaa! — aa!"

Vinicius sprang toward them.

"Where is Lygia?" cried he, with a terrible and changed voice.

"Aaaa!"

Then Gulo pushed forward with his bloody face, and exclaimed, in haste and pitifully,

"See our blood, lord! We fought! See our blood! See our blood!"

But he had not finished when Vinicius seized a bronze lamp, and with one blow shattered the skull of the slave; then, seizing his own head with both hands, he drove his fingers into his hair, repeating hoarsely, —

"Me miserum! me miserum!"

His face became blue, his eyes turned in his head, foam came out on his lips.

"Whips!" roared he at last, with an unearthly voice.

"Lord! Aaaa! Take pity!" groaned the slaves.

Petronius stood up with an expression of disgust on his face. "Come, Chrysothemis!" said he. "If 'tis thy wish to look on raw flesh, I will give command to open a butcher's stall on the Carinæ!"

And he walked out of the atrium. But through the whole house, ornamented in the green of ivy and prepared for a feast, were heard, from moment to moment, groans and the whistling of whips, which lasted almost till morning.

CHAPTER XI

VINICIUS did not lie down that night. Some time after the departure of Petronius, when the groans of his flogged slaves could allay neither his rage nor his pain, he collected a crowd of other servants, and, though the night was far advanced, rushed forth at the head of these to look for Lygia. He visited the district of the Esquiline, then the Subura, Vicus Sceleratus, and all the adjoining alleys. Passing next around the Capitol, he went to the island over the bridge of Fabricius; after that he passed through a part of the Trans-Tiber. But that was a pursuit without object, for he himself had no hope of finding Lygia, and if he sought her it was mainly to fill out with something a terrible night. In fact he returned home about daybreak, when the carts and mules of dealers in vegetables began to appear in the city, and when bakers were opening their shops.

On returning he gave command to put away Gulo's corpse, which no one had ventured to touch. The slaves from whom Lygia had been taken he sent to rural prisons, — a punishment almost more dreadful than death. Throwing himself at last on a couch in the atrium, he began to think confusedly of how he was to find and seize Lygia.

To resign her, to lose her, not to see her again, seemed to him impossible; and at this thought alone frenzy took hold of him. For the first time in life the imperious nature of the youthful soldier met resistance, met another unbending will, and he could not understand simply how any one could have the daring to thwart his wishes. Vinicius would have chosen to see the world and the city sink in ruins rather than fail of his purpose. The cup of delight had been snatched from before his lips almost; hence it seemed to him that something unheard of had happened, something crying to divine and human laws for vengeance.

But, first of all, he was unwilling and unable to be reconciled with fate, for never in life had he so desired anything as Lygia. It seemed to him that he could not exist without her. He could not tell himself what he was to do without her on the morrow, how he was to survive the days following. At moments he was transported by a rage against her, which approached madness. He wanted to have her, to beat her, to drag her by the hair to the cubiculum, and gloat over her; then, again, he was carried away by a terrible yearning for her voice, her form, her eyes, and he felt that he would be ready to lie at her feet. He called to her, gnawed his fingers, clasped his head with his hands. He strove with all his might to think calmly about searching for her, — and was unable. A thousand methods and means flew through his head, but one wilder than another. At last the thought flashed on him that no one else had intercepted her but Aulus, that in every case Aulus must know where she was hiding. And he sprang up to run to the house of Aulus.

If they will not yield her to him, if they have no fear of his threats, he will go to Cæsar, accuse the old general of disobedience, and obtain a sentence of death against him; but before that, he will gain from them a confession of where Lygia is. If they give her, even willingly, he will be revenged. They received him, it is true, in their house and nursed him, — but that is nothing! With this one injustice they have freed him from every debt of gratitude. Here his vengeful and stubborn soul began to take pleasure at the despair of Pomponia Græcina, when the centurion would bring the death sentence to old Aulus. He was almost certain that he would get it. Petronius would assist him. Moreover, Cæsar never denies anything to his intimates, the Augustians, unless personal dislike or desire enjoins a refusal.

Suddenly his heart almost died within him, under the influence of this terrible supposition, —

"But if Cæsar himself has taken Lygia?"

All knew that Nero from tedium sought recreation in night attacks. Even Petronius took part in these amusements. Their main object was to seize women and toss each on a soldier's mantle till she fainted. Even Nero himself on occasions called these expeditions "pearl hunts," for it happened that in the depth of districts occupied by a numerous and needy population they caught a real pearl of youth and beauty sometimes. Then the "sagatio," as they termed the tossing, was changed into a genuine carrying away, and the pearl was sent either to the Palatine or to one of Cæsar's numberless villas, or finally Cæsar yielded it to one of his intimates. So might it happen also with Lygia. Cæsar had seen her during the feast; and Vinicius doubted not for an instant that she must have seemed to him the most beautiful woman he had seen yet. How could it be otherwise? It is true that Lygia had been in Nero's own house on the Palatine, and he might have kept her openly. But, as Petronius said truly, Cæsar had no courage in crime, and, with power to act openly, he chose to act always in secret. This time fear of Poppæa might incline him also to secrecy. It occurred now to the young soldier that Aulus would not have dared, perhaps, to carry off forcibly a girl given him, Vinicius, by Cæsar. Besides, who would dare? Would that gigantic blue-eyed Lygian, who had the courage to enter the triclinium and carry her from the feast on his arm? But where could he hide with her; whither could he take her? No! a slave would not have ventured that far. Hence no one had done the deed except Cæsar.

At this thought it grew dark in his eyes, and drops of sweat covered his forehead. In that case Lygia was lost to him forever. It was possible to wrest her from the hands of any one else, but not from the hands of Cæsar. Now, with greater truth than ever, could he exclaim, "Væ misere mihi!" His imagination represented Lygia in Nero's arms, and, for the first time in life, he understood that there are thoughts which are simply beyond man's endurance. He knew then, for the first time, how he loved her. As his whole life flashes through the memory of a drowning man, so Lygia began to pass through his. He saw her, heard every word of hers, — saw her at the fountain, saw her at the house of Aulus, and at the feast; felt her near him, felt the odor of her hair, the warmth of her body, the delight of the kisses which at the feast he had pressed on her innocent lips. She seemed to him a hundred times sweeter, more beautiful, more desired than ever, — a hundred times more the only one, the one chosen from among all mortals and divinities. And when he thought that all this which had become so fixed in his heart, which had become his blood and life, might be possessed by Nero, a pain seized him, which was purely physical, and so piercing that he wanted to beat his head against the wall of the atrium, until he should break it. He felt that he might go mad; and he would have gone mad beyond doubt, had not vengeance remained to him. But as hitherto he had thought that he could not live unless he got Lygia, he thought now that he would not die till he had avenged her. This gave him a certain kind of comfort. "I will be thy Cassius Chærea!" [1] said he to himself in thinking of Nero. After a while, seizing earth in his hands from the flower vases surrounding the impluvium, he made a dreadful vow to Erebus, Hecate, and his own household lares, that he would have vengeance.

And he received a sort of consolation. He had at least something to live for and something with which to fill his nights and days. Then, dropping his idea of visiting Aulus, he gave command to bear him to the Palatine. Along the way he concluded that if they would not admit him to Cæsar, or if they should try to find weapons on his person, it would be a proof that Cæsar had taken Lygia. He had no weapons with him. He had lost presence of mind in general; but as is usual with persons possessed by a single idea, he preserved it in that which concerned his revenge. He did not wish his desire of revenge to fall away prematurely. He wished above all to see Acte, for he expected to learn the truth from her. At moments the hope flashed on him that he might see Lygia also, and at that thought he began to tremble. For if Cæsar had carried her away without knowledge of whom he was taking, he might return her that day. But after a while he cast aside this supposition. Had there been a wish to return her to him, she would have been sent yesterday. Acte was the only person who could explain everything, and there was need to see her before others.

Convinced of this, he commanded the slaves to hasten; and along the road he thought without order, now of Lygia, now of revenge. He had heard that Egyptian priests of the goddess Pasht could bring disease on whomever they wished, and he determined to learn the means of doing this. In the Orient they had told him, too, that Jews have certain invocations by which they cover their enemies' bodies with ulcers. He had a number of Jews among his domestic slaves; hence he promised himself to torture them on his return till they divulged the secret. He found most delight, however, in thinking of the short Roman sword which lets out a stream of blood such as had gushed from Caius Caligula and made ineffaceable stains on the columns of the por-

[1] The slayer of Caligula.

tico. He was ready to exterminate all Rome; and had vengeful gods promised that all people should die except him and Lygia, he would have accepted the promise.

In front of the arch he regained presence of mind, and thought when he saw the pretorian guard, "If they make the least difficulty in admitting me, they will prove that Lygia is in the palace by the will of Cæsar."

But the chief centurion smiled at him in a friendly manner, then advanced a number of steps, and said, —

"A greeting, noble tribune. If thou desire to give an obeisance to Cæsar, thou hast found an unfortunate moment. I do not think that thou wilt be able to see him."

"What has happened?" inquired Vinicius.

"The infant Augusta fell ill yesterday on a sudden. Cæsar and the august Poppæa are attending her, with physicians whom they have summoned from the whole city."

This was an important event. When that daughter was born to him, Cæsar was simply wild from delight, and received her with *extra humanum gaudium*. Previously the senate had committed the womb of Poppæa to the gods with the utmost solemnity. A votive offering was made at Antium, where the delivery took place; splendid games were celebrated, and besides a temple was erected to the two Fortunes. Nero, unable to be moderate in anything, loved the infant beyond measure; to Poppæa the child was dear also, even for this, that it strengthened her position and made her influence irresistible.

The fate of the whole empire might depend on the health and life of the infant Augusta; but Vinicius was so occupied with himself, his own case and his love, that without paying attention to the news of the centurion he answered, "I only wish to see Acte." And he passed in.

But Acte was occupied also near the child, and he had to wait a long time to see her. She came only about midday, with a face pale and wearied, which grew paler still at sight of Vinicius.

"Acte!" cried Vinicius, seizing her hand and drawing her to the middle of the atrium, "where is Lygia?"

"I wanted to ask thee touching that," answered she, looking him in the eyes with reproach.

But though he had promised himself to inquire of her calmly, he pressed his head with his hands again, and said, with a face distorted by pain and anger, —

"She is gone. She was taken from me on the way!"

After a while, however, he recovered, and thrusting his face up to Acte's, said through his set teeth, —

"Acte! If life be dear to thee, if thou wish not to cause misfortunes which thou are unable even to imagine, answer me truly. Did Cæsar take her?"

"Cæsar did not leave the palace yesterday."

"By the shade of thy mother, by all the gods, is she not in the palace?"

"By the shade of my mother, Marcus, she is not in the palace, and Cæsar did not intercept her. The infant Augusta is ill since yesterday, and Nero has not left her cradle."

Vinicius drew breath. That which had seemed the most terrible ceased to threaten him.

"Ah, then," said he, sitting on the bench and clinching his fists, "Aulus intercepted her, and in that case woe to him!"

"Aulus Plautius was here this morning. He could not see me, for I was occupied with the child; but he inquired of Epaphroditus, and others of Cæsar's servants, touching Lygia, and told them that he would come again to see me."

"He wished to turn suspicion from himself. If he knew not what happened, he would have come to seek Lygia in my house."

"He left a few words on a tablet, from which thou wilt see that, knowing Lygia to have been taken from his house by Cæsar, at thy request and that of Petronius, he expected that she would be sent to thee, and this morning early he was at thy house, where they told him what had happened."

When she had said this, she went to the cubiculum and returned soon with the tablet which Aulus had left.

Vinicius read the tablet, and was silent; Acte seemed to read the thoughts on his gloomy face, for she said after a while, —

"No, Marcus. That has happened which Lygia herself wished."

"It was known to thee that she wished to flee!" burst out Vinicius.

"I knew that she would not become thy concubine."

And she looked at him with her misty eyes almost sternly.

"And thou, — what hast thou been all thy life?"

"I was a slave, first of all."

But Vinicius did not cease to be enraged. Cæsar had given him Lygia; hence he had no need to inquire what she had been before. He would find her, even under the earth, and he would do what he liked with her. He would indeed! She should be his concubine. He would give command to flog her as often as he pleased. If she grew distasteful to him, he would give her to the lowest of his slaves, or he would command her to turn a handmill on his lands in Africa. He would seek her out now, and find her only to bend her, to trample on her, and conquer her.

And, growing more and more excited, he lost every sense of measure, to the degree that even Acte saw that he was promising more than he could execute; that he was talking because of pain and anger. She might have had even compassion on him, but his extravagance exhausted her patience, and at last she inquired why he had come to her.

Vinicius did not find an answer immediately. He had come to her because he wished to come, because he judged that she would give him information; but really he had come to Cæsar, and, not being able to see him, he came to her. Lygia, by fleeing, opposed the will of Cæsar; hence he would implore him to give an order to search for her throughout the city and the empire, even if it came to using for that purpose all the legions, and to ransacking in turn every house within Roman dominion. Petronius would support his prayer, and the search would begin from that day.

"Have a care," answered Acte, "lest thou lose her forever the moment she is found, at command of Cæsar."

Vinicius wrinkled his brows. "What does that mean?" inquired he.

"Listen to me, Marcus. Yesterday Lygia and I were in the gardens here, and we met Poppæa, with the infant Augusta, borne by an African woman, Lilith. In the evening the child fell ill, and Lilith insists that she was bewitched; that that foreign woman whom they met in the garden bewitched her. Should the child recover, they will forget this, but in the opposite case Poppæa will be the first to accuse Lygia of witchcraft, and wherever she is found there will be no rescue for her."

A moment of silence followed; then Vinicius said, —

"But perhaps she did bewitch her, and has bewitched me."

"Lilith repeats that the child began to cry the moment she carried her past us. And really the child did begin to cry. It is certain that she was sick when they took her out of the garden. Marcus, seek for Lygia whenever it may please thee, but till the infant Augusta recovers, speak not of her to Cæsar, or thou wilt bring on her Poppæa's vengeance. Her eyes have wept enough because of thee already, and may all the gods guard her poor head."

"Dost thou love her, Acte?" inquired Vinicius, gloomily.

"Yes, I love her." And tears glittered in the eyes of the freedwoman.

"Thou lovest her because she has not repaid thee with hatred, as she has me."

Acte looked at him for a time as if hesitating, or as if wishing to learn if he spoke sincerely; then she said, —

"O blind and passionate man — she loved thee."

Vinicius sprang up under the influence of those words, as if possessed.

"It is not true."

She hated him. How could Acte know? Would Lygia make a confession to her after one day's acquaintance? What love is that which prefers wandering, the disgrace of poverty, the uncertainty of to-morrow, or a shameful death even, to a wreath-bedecked house, in which a lover is waiting with a feast? It is better for him not to hear such things, for he is ready to go mad. He would not have given that girl for all Cæsar's treasures, and she fled. What kind of love is that which dreads delight and gives pain? Who can understand it? Who can fathom it? Were it not for the hope that he should find her, he would sink a sword in himself. Love surrenders; it does not take away. There were moments at the house of Aulus when he himself believed in near happiness, but now he knows that she hated him, that she hates him, and will die with hatred in her heart.

But Acte, usually mild and timid, burst forth in her turn with indignation. How had he tried to win Lygia? Instead of bowing before Aulus and Pomponia to get her, he took the child away from her parents by stratagem. He wanted to make, not a wife, but a concubine of her, the foster daughter of an honorable house, and the daughter of a king. He had her brought to this abode of crime and infamy; he defiled her innocent eyes with the sight of a shameful feast; he acted with her as with a wanton. Had he forgotten the house of Aulus and Pomponia Græcina, who had reared Lygia? Had he not sense enough to understand that there are women different from Nigidia or Calvia Crispinilla or Poppæa, and from all those whom he meets in Cæsar's house? Did he not understand at once on seeing Lygia that she is an honest maiden, who prefers death to infamy? Whence does he know what kind of gods she worships, and whether they are not purer and better than the wanton Venus, or than Isis, worshipped by the profligate women of Rome? No! Lygia had made no confession to her, but she had said that she looked for rescue to him, to Vinicius: she had hoped that he would obtain for her permission from Cæsar to return home, that he would restore her to Pomponia. And while speaking of this, Lygia blushed like a maiden who loves and trusts. Lygia's heart beat for him; but he, Vinicius, had terrified and offended her; had made her indignant; let him seek her now with the aid of Cæsar's soldiers, but let him know that should Poppæa's child die, suspicion will fall on Lygia, whose destruction will then be inevitable.

Emotion began to force its way through the anger and pain of Vinicius. The information that he was loved by Lygia shook him to the depth of his soul. He remembered her in Aulus's garden, when she was listening to his words with blushes on her face and her eyes full of light. It seemed to him then that she had begun to love him; and all at once, at that thought, a feeling of certain happiness embraced him, a hundred times greater than that which he desired. He thought that he might have won her gradually, and besides as one loving him. She would have wreathed his door, rubbed it with wolf's fat, and then sat as his wife by his hearth on the sheepskin. He would have heard from her mouth the sacramental: "Where thou art, Caius, there am I, Caia." And she would have been his forever. Why did he not act thus? True, he had been ready so to act. But now she is gone, and it may be impossible to find her; and should he find her, perhaps he will cause her death, and should he not cause her death, neither she nor Aulus nor Pomponia Græcina will favor him. Here anger raised the hair on his head again; but his anger turned now, not against the house of Aulus, or Lygia, but against Petronius. Petronius was to blame for everything. Had it not been for him Lygia would not have been forced to wander; she would be his betrothed, and no danger would be hanging over her dear head. But now all is past, and it is too late to correct the evil which will not yield to correction.

"Too late!" And it seemed to him that a gulf had opened before his feet. He did not know what to begin, how to proceed, whither to betake himself. Acte repeated as an echo the words, "Too late," which from another's mouth sounded like a death sentence. He understood one thing, however, that he must find Lygia, or something evil would happen to him.

And wrapping himself mechanically in his toga, he was about to depart without taking farewell even of Acte, when suddenly the curtain separating the entrance from the atrium was pushed aside, and he saw before him the pensive figure of Pomponia Græcina.

Evidently she too had heard of the disappearance of Lygia, and, judging that she could see Acte more easily than Aulus, had come for news to her.

But, seeing Vinicius, she turned her pale, delicate face to him, and said, after a pause, —

"May God forgive thee the wrong, Marcus, which thou hast done to us and to Lygia."

He stood with drooping head, with a feeling of misfortune and guilt, not understanding what God was to forgive him or could forgive him. Pomponia had no cause to mention forgiveness; she ought to have spoken of revenge.

At last he went out with a head devoid of counsel, full of grievous thoughts, immense care, and amazement.

In the court and under the gallery were crowds of anxious people. Among slaves of the palace were knights and senators who had come to inquire about the health of the infant, and at the same time to show themselves in the palace, and exhibit a proof of their anxiety, even in presence of Nero's slaves. News of the illness of the "divine" had spread quickly it was evident, for new forms appeared in the gateway every moment, and through the opening of the arcade whole crowds were visible. Some of the newly arrived, seeing that Vinicius was coming from the palace, attacked him for news; but he hurried on without answering their questions, till Petronius, who had come for news too, almost struck his breast and stopped him.

Beyond doubt Vinicius would have become enraged at sight of Petronius, and let himself do some lawless act in Cæsar's palace, had it not been that when he had left Acte he was so crushed, so weighed down and exhausted, that for the moment even his innate irascibility had left him. He pushed Petronius aside and wished to pass; but the other detained him, by force almost.

"How is the divine infant?" asked he.

But this constraint angered Vinicius a second time, and roused his indignation in an instant.

"May Hades swallow her and all this house!" said he, gritting his teeth.

"Silence, hapless man!" said Petronius, and looking around he added hurriedly, —

"If thou wish to know something of Lygia, come with me; I will tell nothing here! Come with me; I will tell my thoughts in the litter."

And putting his arm around the young tribune, he conducted him from the palace as quickly as possible. That was his main concern, for he had no news whatever; but being a man of resources, and having, in spite of his indignation of yesterday, much sympathy for Vinicius, and finally feeling responsible for all that had happened, he had undertaken something already, and when they entered the litter he said, —

"I have commanded my slaves to watch at every gate. I gave them an accurate description of the girl, and that giant who bore her from the feast at Cæsar's, — for he is the man, beyond doubt, who intercepted her. Listen to me: Perhaps Aulus and Pomponia wish to secrete her in some estate of theirs; in that case we shall learn the direction in which they took her. If my slaves do not see her at some gate, we shall know that she is in the city yet, and shall begin this very day to search in Rome for her."

"Aulus does not know where she is," answered Vinicius.

"Art thou sure of that?"

"I saw Pomponia. She too is looking for her."

"She could not leave the city yesterday, for the gates are closed at night.

Two of my people are watching at each gate. One is to follow Lygia and the giant, the other to return at once and inform me. If she is in the city, we shall find her, for that Lygian is easily recognized, even by his stature and his shoulders. Thou art lucky that it was not Cæsar who took her, and I can assure thee that he did not, for there are no secrets from me on the Palatine."

But Vinicius burst forth in sorrow still more than in anger, and in a voice broken by emotion told Petronius what he had heard from Acte, and what new dangers were threatening Lygia, — dangers so dreadful that because of them there would be need to hide her from Poppæa most carefully, in case they discovered her. Then he reproached Petronius bitterly for his counsel. Had it not been for him, everything would have gone differently. Lygia would have been at the house of Aulus, and he, Vinicius, might have seen her every day, and he would have been happier at that moment than Cæsar. And carried away as he went on with his narrative, he yielded more and more to emotion, till at last tears of sorrow and rage began to fall from his eyes.

Petronius, who had not even thought that the young man could love and desire to such a degree, when he saw the tears of despair said to himself, with a certain astonishment, —

"O mighty Lady of Cyprus, thou alone art ruler of gods and men!"

CHAPTER XII

WHEN they alighted in front of the arbiter's house, the chief of the atrium answered them that of slaves sent to the gates none had returned yet. The atriensis had given orders to take food to them, and a new command, that under penalty of rods they were to watch carefully all who left the city.

"Thou seest," said Petronius, "that they are in Rome, beyond doubt, and in that case we shall find them. But command thy people also to watch at the gates, — those, namely, who were sent for Lygia, as they will recognize her easily."

"I have given orders to send them to rural prisons," said Vinicius, "but I will recall the orders at once, and let them go to the gates."

And writing a few words on a wax-covered tablet, he handed it to Petronius, who gave directions to send it at once to the house of Vinicius. Then they passed into the interior portico, and, sitting on a marble bench, began to talk. The golden-haired Eunice and Iras pushed bronze footstools under their feet, and poured wine for them into goblets, out of wonderful narrow-necked pitchers from Volaterræ and Cæcina.

"Hast thou among thy people any one who knows that giant Lygian?" asked Petronius.

"Atacinus and Gulo knew him; but Atacinus fell yesterday at the litter, and Gulo I killed."

"I am sorry for him," said Petronius. "He carried not only thee, but me, in his arms."

"I intended to free him," answered Vinicius; "but do not mention him. Let us speak of Lygia. Rome is a sea — "

"A sea is just the place where men fish for pearls. Of course we shall not find her to-day, or to-morrow, but we shall find her surely. Thou hast accused me just now of giving thee this method; but the method was good in itself, and became bad only when turned to bad. Thou hast heard from Aulus himself, that he intends to go to Sicily with his whole family. In that case the girl would be far from thee."

"I should follow them," said Vinicius, "and in every case she would be out of danger; but now, if that child dies, Poppæa will believe, and will persuade Cæsar, that she died because of Lygia."

"True; that alarmed me, too. But that little doll may recover. Should she die, we shall find some way of escape."

Here Petronius meditated a while and added, —

"Poppæa, it is said, follows the religion of the Jews, and believes in evil spirits. Cæsar is superstitious. If we spread the report that evil spirits carried off Lygia, the news will find belief, especially as neither Cæsar nor Aulus Plautius intercepted her; her escape was really mysterious. The Lygian could not have effected it alone; he must have had help. And where could a slave find so many people in the course of one day?"

"Slaves help one another in Rome."

"Some person pays for that with blood at times. True, they support one another, but not some against others. In this case it was known that responsibility and punishment would fall on thy people. If thou give thy people the idea of evil spirits, they will say at once that they saw such with their own eyes, because that will justify them in thy sight. Ask one of them, as a test, if he did not see spirits carrying off Lygia through the air, he will swear at once by the ægis of Zeus that he saw them."

Vinicius, who was superstitious also, looked at Petronius with sudden and great fear.

"If Ursus could not have men to help him, and was not able to take her alone, who could take her?"

Petronius began to laugh.

"See," said he, "they will believe, since thou art half a believer thyself. Such is our society, which ridicules the gods. They, too, will believe, and they will not look for her. Meanwhile we shall put her away somewhere far off from the city, in some villa of mine or thine."

"But who could help her?"

"Her co-religionists," answered Petronius.

"Who are they? What deity does she worship? I ought to know that better than thou."

"Nearly every woman in Rome honors a different one. It is almost beyond doubt that Pomponia reared her in the religion of that deity which she herself worships; what one she worships I know not. One thing is certain, that no person has seen her make an offering to our gods in any temple. They have accused her even of being a Christian; but that is not possible; a domestic tribunal cleared her of the charge. They say that Christians not only worship an ass's head, but are enemies of the human race, and permit the foulest crimes. Pomponia cannot be a Christian, as her virtue is known, and an enemy of the human race could not treat slaves as she does."

"In no house are they treated as at Aulus's," interrupted Vinicius.

"Ah! Pomponia mentioned to me some god, who must be one powerful and merciful. Where she has put away all the others is her affair; it is enough that that Logos of hers cannot be very mighty, or rather he must be a very weak god, since he has had only two adherents, — Pomponia and Lygia, — and Ursus in addition. It must be that there are more of those adherents, and that they assisted Lygia."

"That faith commands forgiveness," said Vinicius. "At Acte's I met Pomponia, who said to me: 'May God forgive thee the evil which thou hast done to us and to Lygia.'"

"Evidently their God is some *curator* who is very mild. Ha! let him forgive thee, and in sign of forgiveness return thee the maiden."

"I would offer him a hecatomb to-morrow! I have no wish for food, or the bath, or sleep. I will take a dark lantern and wander through the city. Perhaps I shall find her in disguise. I am sick."

Petronius looked at him with commiseration. In fact, there was blue under his eyes, his pupils were gleaming with fever, his unshaven beard indicated a dark strip on his firmly outlined jaws, his hair was in disorder, and he was really like a sick man. Iras and the golden-haired Eunice looked at him also with sympathy; but he seemed not to see them, and he and Petronius took no notice whatever of the slave women, just as they would not have noticed dogs moving around them.

"Fever is tormenting thee," said Petronius.

"It is."

"Then listen to me. I know not what the doctor has prescribed to thee, but I know how I should act in thy place. Till this lost one is found I should seek in another that which for the moment has gone from me with her. I saw splendid forms at thy villa. Do not contradict me. I know what love is; and I know that when one is desired another cannot take her place. But in a beautiful slave it is possible to find even momentary distraction."

"I do not need it," said Vinicius.

But Petronius, who had for him a real weakness, and who wished to soften his pain, began to meditate how he might do so.

"Perhaps thine have not for thee the charm of novelty," said he, after a while (and here he began to look in turn at Iras and Eunice, and finally he placed his palm on the hip of the golden-haired Eunice). "Look at this grace! for whom some days since Fonteius Capiton the younger offered three wonderful boys from Clazomene. A more beautiful figure than hers even Skopas himself has not chiselled. I myself cannot tell why I have remained indifferent to her thus far, since thoughts of Chrysothemis have not restrained me. Well, I give her to thee; take her for thyself!"

When the golden-haired Eunice heard this, she grew pale in one moment, and, looking with frightened eyes on Vinicius, seemed to wait for his answer without breath in her breast.

But he sprang up suddenly, and, pressing his temples with his hands, said quickly, like a man who is tortured by disease, and will not hear anything, —

"No, no! I care not for her! I care not for others! I thank thee, but I do not want her. I will seek that one through the city. Give command to bring me a Gallic cloak with a hood. I will go beyond the Tiber — if I could see even Ursus."

And he hurried away. Petronius, seeing that he could not remain in one place, did not try to detain him. Taking, however, his refusal as a temporary dislike for all women save Lygia, and not wishing his own magnanimity to go for naught, he said, turning to the slave, —

"Eunice, thou wilt bathe and anoint thyself, then dress: after that thou wilt go to the house of Vinicius."

But she dropped before him on her knees, and with joined palms implored him not to remove her from the house. She would not go to Vinicius, she said. She would rather carry fuel to the hypocaustum in his house than be chief servant in that of Vinicius. She would not, she could not go; and she begged him to have pity on her. Let him give command to flog her daily, only not send her away.

And trembling like a leaf with fear and excitement, she stretched her hands to him, while he listened with amazement. A slave who ventured to beg relief from the fulfilment of a command, who said "I will not and I cannot," was something so unheard-of in Rome that Petronius could not believe his own ears at first. Finally he frowned. He was too refined to be cruel. His slaves, especially in the department of pleasure, were freer than others, on condition of performing their service in an exemplary manner, and honoring the will of their master, like that of a god. In case they failed in these two respects, he was able not to spare punishment, to which, according to general custom, they were subject. Since, besides this, he could not endure opposition, nor anything which ruffled his calmness, he looked for a while at the kneeling girl, and then said, —

"Call Tiresias, and return with him."

Eunice rose, trembling, with tears in her eyes, and went out; after a time she returned with the chief of the atrium, Tiresias, a Cretan.

"Thou wilt take Eunice," said Petronius, "and give her five-and-twenty lashes, in such fashion, however, as not to harm her skin."

When he had said this, he passed into the library, and, sitting down at a table of rose-colored marble, began to work on his "Feast of Trimalchion." But the flight of Lygia and the illness of the infant Augusta had disturbed his mind so much that he could not work long. That illness, above all, was important. It occurred to Petronius that were Cæsar to believe that Lygia had cast spells on the infant, the responsibility might fall on him also, for the girl had been brought at his request to the palace. But he could reckon on this, that at the first interview with Cæsar he would be able in some way to show the utter absurdity of such an idea; he counted a little, too, on a certain weakness which Poppæa had for him, — a weakness hidden carefully, it is true, but not so carefully that he could not divine it. After a while he shrugged his shoulders at these fears, and decided to go to the triclinium to strengthen himself, and then order the litter to bear him once more to the palace, after that to the Campus Martius, and then to Chrysothemis.

But on the way to the triclinium at the entrance to the corridor assigned to servants, he saw unexpectedly the slender form of Eunice standing, among other slaves, at the wall; and forgetting that he had given Tiresias no order beyond flogging her, he wrinkled his brow again, and looked around for the atriensis. Not seeing him among the servants, he turned to Eunice.

"Hast thou received the lashes?"

She cast herself at his feet a second time, pressed the border of his toga to her lips, and said, —

"Oh, yes, lord, I have received them! Oh, yes, lord!"

In her voice were heard, as it were, joy and gratitude. It was clear that she looked on the lashes as a substitute for her removal from the house, and that now she might stay there. Petronius, who understood this, wondered at the passionate resistance of the girl; but he was too deeply versed in human nature not to know that love alone could call forth such resistance.

"Dost thou love some one in this house?" asked he.

She raised her blue, tearful eyes to him, and answered, in a voice so low that it was hardly possible to hear her, —

"Yes, lord."

And with those eyes, with that golden hair thrown back, with fear and hope in her face, she was so beautiful, she looked at him so entreatingly, that Petronius, who, as a philosopher, had proclaimed the might of love, and who, as a man of æsthetic nature, had given homage to all beauty, felt for her a certain species of compassion.

"Whom of those dost thou love?" inquired he, indicating the servants with his head.

There was no answer to that question. Eunice inclined her head to his feet and remained motionless.

Petronius looked at the slaves, among whom were beautiful and stately youths. He could read nothing on any face; on the contrary, all had certain strange smiles. He looked then for a while on Eunice lying at his feet, and went in silence to the triclinium.

After he had eaten, he gave command to bear him to the palace, and then to Chrysothemis, with whom he remained till late at night. But when he returned, he gave command to call Tiresias.

"Did Eunice receive the flogging?" inquired he.

"She did, lord. Thou didst not let the skin be cut, however."

"Did I give no other command touching her?"

"No, lord," answered the atriensis with alarm.

"That is well. Whom of the slaves does she love?"

"No one, lord."

"What dost thou know of her?"

Tiresias began to speak in a somewhat uncertain voice:

"At night Eunice never leaves the cubiculum in which she lives with old Acrisiona and Ifida; after thou art dressed she never goes to the bath-rooms. Other slaves ridicule her, and call her Diana."

"Enough," said Petronius. "My relative, Vinicius, to whom I offered her to-day, did not accept her; hence she may stay in the house. Thou art free to go."

"Is it permitted me to speak more of Eunice, lord?"

"I have commanded thee to say all thou knowest."

"The whole familia are speaking of the flight of the maiden who was to dwell in the house of the noble Vinicius. After thy departure, Eunice came to me and said that she knew a man who could find her."

"Ah! What kind of man is he?"

"I know not, lord; but I thought that I ought to inform thee of this matter."

"That is well. Let that man wait to-morrow in my house for the arrival of the tribune, whom thou wilt request in my name to meet me here."

The atriensis bowed and went out. But Petronius began to think of Eunice. At first it seemed clear to him that the young slave wished Vinicius to find Lygia for this reason only, that she would not be forced from his house. Afterward, however, it occurred to him that the man whom Eunice was pushing forward might be her lover, and all at once that thought seemed to him disagreeable. There was, it is true, a simple way of learning the truth, for it was enough to summon Eunice; but the hour was late, Petronius felt tired after his long visit with Chrysothemis, and was in a hurry to sleep. But on the way to the cubiculum he remembered — it is unknown why — that he had noticed wrinkles, that day, in the corners of Chrysothemis's eyes. He thought, also, that her beauty was more celebrated in Rome than it deserved; and that Fonteius Capiton, who had offered him three boys from Clazomene for Eunice, wanted to buy her too cheaply.

CHAPTER XIII

NEXT morning, Petronius had barely finished dressing in the unctorium when Vinicius came, called by Tiresias. He knew that no news had come from the gates. This information, instead of comforting him, as a proof that Lygia was still in Rome, weighed him down still more, for he began to think that Ursus might have conducted her out of the city immediately after her seizure, and hence before Petronius's slaves had begun to keep watch at the gates. It is true that in autumn, when the days become shorter, the gates are closed rather early; but it is true, also, that they are opened for persons going out, and the number of these is considerable. It was possible, also, to pass the walls by other ways, well known, for instance, to slaves who wish to escape from the city. Vinicius had sent out his people to all roads leading to the provinces, to watchmen in the smaller towns, proclaiming a pair of fugitive slaves, with a detailed description of Ursus and Lygia, coupled with the offer of a reward for seizing them. But it was doubtful whether that pursuit would reach the fugitives; and even should it reach them, whether the local authorities would feel justified in making the arrest at the private instance of Vinicius, without the support of a pretor. Indeed, there had not been time to obtain such support. Vinicius himself, disguised as a slave, had sought Lygia the whole day before, through every corner of the city, but had been unable to find the least indication or trace of her. He had seen Aulus's servants, it is true; but they seemed to be seeking something also, and that confirmed him in the belief that it was not Aulus who had intercepted the maiden, and that the old general did not know what had happened to her.

When Tiresias announced to him, then, that there was a man who would undertake to find Lygia, he hurried with all speed to the house of Petronius; and barely had he finished saluting his uncle, when he inquired for the man.

"We shall see him at once, Eunice knows him," said Petronius. "She will come this moment to arrange the folds of my toga, and will give nearer information concerning him."

"Oh! she whom thou hadst the wish to bestow on me yesterday?"

"The one whom thou didst reject; for which I am grateful, for she is the best vestiplica in the whole city."

In fact, the vestiplica came in before he had finished speaking, and taking the toga, laid on a chair inlaid with pearl, she opened the garment to throw it on Petronius's shoulder. Her face was clear and calm; joy was in her eyes.

Petronius looked at her. She seemed to him very beautiful. After a while, when she had covered him with the toga, she began to arrange it, bending at times to lengthen the folds. He noticed that her arms had a marvellous pale rose-color, and her bosom and shoulders the transparent reflections of pearl or alabaster.

"Eunice," said he, "has the man come to Tiresias whom thou didst mention yesterday?"

"He has, lord."

"What is his name?"

"Chilo Chilonides."

"Who is he?"

"A physician, a sage, a soothsayer, who knows how to read people's fates and predict the future."

"Has he predicted the future to thee?"

Eunice was covered with a blush which gave a rosy color to her ears and her neck even.

"Yes, lord."

"What has he predicted?"

"That pain and happiness would meet me."

"Pain met thee yesterday at the hands of Tiresias; hence happiness also should come."

"It has come, lord, already."

"What?"

"I remain," said she in a whisper.

Petronius put his hand on her golden head.

"Thou hast arranged the folds well to-day, and I am satisfied with thee, Eunice."

Under that touch her eyes were mist-covered in one instant from happiness, and her bosom began to heave quickly.

Petronius and Vinicius passed into the atrium, where Chilo Chilonides was waiting. When he saw them, he made a low bow. A smile came to the lips of Petronius at thought of his suspicion of yesterday, that this man might be Eunice's lover. The man who was standing before him could not be any one's lover. In that marvellous figure there was something both foul and ridiculous. He was not old; in his dirty beard and curly locks a gray hair shone here and there. He had a lank stomach and stooping shoulders, so that at the first cast of the eye he appeared to be hunchbacked; above that hump rose a large head, with the face of a monkey and also of a fox; the eye was penetrating. His yellowish complexion was varied with pimples; and his nose, covered with them completely, might indicate too great a love for the bottle. His neglected apparel, composed of a dark tunic of goat's wool and a mantle of similar material with holes in it, showed real or simulated poverty. At sight of him, Homer's Thersites came to the mind of Petronius. Hence, answering with a wave of the hand to his bow, he said, —

"A greeting, divine Thersites! How are the lumps which Ulysses gave thee at Troy, and what is he doing himself in the Elysian Fields?"

"Noble lord," answered Chilo Chilonides, "Ulysses, the wisest of the dead, sends a greeting through me to Petronius, the wisest of the living, and the request to cover my lumps with a new mantle."

"By Hecate Triformis!" exclaimed Petronius, "the answer deserves a new mantle."

But further conversation was interrupted by the impatient Vinicius, who inquired directly, —

"Dost thou know clearly what thou art undertaking?"

"When two households in two lordly mansions speak of naught else, and when half Rome is repeating the news, it is not difficult to know," answered Chilo. "The night before last a maiden named Lygia, but specially Callina, and reared in the house of Aulus Plautius, was intercepted. Thy slaves were conducting her, O lord, from Cæsar's palace to thy 'insula,' and I undertake to find her in the city, or, if she has left the city — which is little likely — to indicate to thee, noble tribune, whither she has fled and where she has hidden."

"That is well," said Vinicius, who was pleased with the precision of the answer. "What means hast thou to do this?"

Chilo smiled cunningly. "Thou hast the means, lord; I have the wit only."

Petronius smiled also, for he was perfectly satisfied with his guest.

"That man can find the maiden," thought he.

Meanwhile Vinicius wrinkled his joined brows, and said, —

"Wretch, in case thou deceive me for gain, I will give command to beat thee with clubs."

"I am a philosopher, lord, and a philosopher cannot be greedy of gain, especially of such as thou hast just offered magnanimously."

"Oh, art thou a philosopher?" inquired Petronius. "Eunice told me that thou art a physician and a soothsayer. Whence knowest thou Eunice?"

"She came to me for aid, for my fame struck her ears."

"What aid did she want?"

"Aid in love, lord. She wanted to be cured of unrequited love."

"Didst thou cure her?"

"I did more, lord. I gave her an amulet which secures mutuality. In Paphos, on the island of Cyprus, is a temple, O lord, in which is preserved a zone of Venus. I gave her two threads from that zone, enclosed in an almond shell."

"And didst thou make her pay well for them?"

"One can never pay enough for mutuality, and I, who lack two fingers on my right hand, am collecting money to buy a slave copyist to write down my thoughts, and preserve my wisdom for mankind."

"Of what school art thou, divine sage?"

"I am a Cynic, lord, because I wear a tattered mantle; I am a Stoic, because I bear poverty patiently; I am a Peripatetic, for, not owning a litter, I go on foot from one wine-shop to another, and on the way teach those who promise to pay for a pitcher of wine."

"And at the pitcher thou dost become a rhetor?"

"Heraclitus declares that 'all is fluid,' and canst thou deny, lord, that wine is fluid?"

"And he declared that fire is a divinity; divinity, therefore, is blushing in thy nose."

"But the divine Diogenes from Apollonia declared that air is the essence of things, and the warmer the air the more perfect the beings it makes, and from the warmest come the souls of sages. And since the autumns are cold, a genuine sage should warm his soul with wine; and wouldst thou hinder, O lord, a pitcher of even the stuff produced in Capua or Telesia from bearing heat to all the bones of a perishable human body?"

"Chilo Chilonides, where is thy birthplace?"

"On the Euxine Pontus. I come from Mesembria."

"Oh, Chilo, thou art great!"

"And unrecognized," said the sage, pensively.

But Vinicius was impatient again. In view of the hope which had gleamed before him, he wished Chilo to set out at once on his work; hence the whole conversation seemed to him simply a vain loss of time, and he was angry at Petronius.

"When wilt thou begin the search?" asked he, turning to the Greek.

"I have begun it already," answered Chilo. "And since I am here, and answering thy affable question, I am searching yet. Only have confidence, honored tribune, and know that if thou wert to lose the string of thy sandal I should find it, or him who picked it up on the street."

"Hast thou been employed in similar services?" asked Petronius.

The Greek raised his eyes. "To-day men esteem virtue and wisdom too low, for a philosopher not to be forced to seek other means of living."

"What are thy means?"

"To know everything, and to serve those with news who are in need of it."

"And who pay for it?"

"Ah, lord, I need to buy a copyist. Otherwise my wisdom will perish with me."

"If thou hast not collected enough yet to buy a sound mantle, thy services cannot be very famous."

"Modesty hinders me. But remember, lord, that to-day there are not such benefactors as were numerous formerly; and for whom it was as pleasant to cover service with gold as to swallow an oyster from Puteoli. No; my services are not small, but the gratitude of mankind is small. At times, when a valued slave escapes, who will find him, if not the only son of my father? When on the walls there are inscriptions against the divine Poppæa, who will indicate those who composed them? Who will discover at the book-stalls verses against Cæsar? Who will declare what is said in the houses of knights and senators? Who will carry letters which the writers will not intrust to slaves? Who will listen to news at the doors of barbers? For whom have wine-shops and bake-shops no secret? In whom do slaves trust? Who can see through every house, from the atrium to the garden? Who knows every street, every alley and hiding-place? Who knows what they say in the baths, in the Circus, in the markets, in the fencing-schools, in slave-dealers' sheds, and even in the arenas?"

"By the gods! enough, noble sage!" cried Petronius; "we are drowning

in thy services, thy virtue, thy wisdom, and thy eloquence. Enough! We
wanted to know who thou art, and we know!"

But Vinicius was glad, for he thought that this man, like a hound, once
put on the trail, would not stop till he had found out the hiding-place.

"Well," said he, "dost thou need indications?"

"I need arms."

"Of what kind?" asked Vinicius, with astonishment.

The Greek stretched out one hand; with the other he made the gesture of
counting money.

"Such are the times, lord," said he, with a sigh.

"Thou wilt be the ass, then," said Petronius, "to win the fortress with bags
of gold?"

"I am only a poor philosopher," answered Chilo, with humility; "ye have
the gold."

Vinicius tossed him a purse, which the Greek caught in the air, though
two fingers were lacking on his right hand.

He raised his head then, and said: "I know more than thou thinkest. I have
not come empty-handed. I know that Aulus did not intercept the maiden, for
I have spoken with his slaves. I know that she is not on the Palatine, for all
are occupied with the infant Augusta; and perhaps I may even divine why ye
prefer to search for the maiden with my help rather than that of the city
guards and Cæsar's soldiers. I know that her escape was effected by a servant,
— a slave coming from the same country as she. He could not find assistance
among slaves, for slaves all stand together, and would not act against thy
slaves. Only a co-religionist would help him."

"Dost hear, Vinicius?" broke in Petronius. "Have I not said the same,
word for word, to thee?"

"That is an honor for me," said Chilo. "The maiden, lord," continued he,
turning again to Vinicius, "worships beyond a doubt the same divinity as
that most virtuous of Roman ladies, that genuine matron, Pomponia. I have
heard this, too, that Pomponia was tried in her own house for worshipping
some kind of foreign god, but I could not learn from her slaves what god
that is, or what his worshippers are called. If I could learn that, I should
go to them, become the most devoted among them, and gain their confidence.
But thou, lord, who hast passed, as I know too, a number of days in the
house of the noble Aulus, canst thou not give me some information thereon?"

"I cannot," said Vinicius.

"Ye have asked me long about various things, noble lords, and I have answered the questions; permit me now to give one. Hast thou not seen,
honored tribune, some statuette, some offering, some token, some amulet
on Pomponia or thy divine Lygia? Hast thou not seen them making signs
to each other, intelligible to them alone?"

"Signs? Wait! Yes; I saw once that Lygia made a fish on the sand."

"A fish? A-a! O-o-o! Did she do that once, or a number of times?"

"Only once."

"And art thou certain, lord, that she outlined a fish? O-o?"

"Yes," answered Vinicius, with roused curiosity. "Dost thou divine what that means?"

"Do I divine!" exclaimed Chilo. And bowing in sign of farewell, he added: "May Fortune scatter on you both equally all gifts, worthy lords!"

"Give command to bring thee a mantle," said Petronius to him at parting.

"Ulysses gives thee thanks for Thersites," said the Greek; and bowing a second time, he walked out.

"What wilt thou say of that noble sage?" inquired Petronius.

"This, that he will find Lygia," answered Vinicius, with delight; "but I will say, too, that were there a kingdom of rogues he might be the king of it."

"Most certainly. I shall make a nearer acquaintance with this stoic; meanwhile I must give command to perfume the atrium."

But Chilo Chilonides, wrapping his new mantle about him, threw up on his palm, under its folds, the purse received from Vinicius, and admired both its weight and its jingle. Walking on slowly, and looking around to see if they were not looking at him from the house, he passed the portico of Livia, and, reaching the corner of the Clivus Virbius, turned toward the Subura.

"I must go to Sporus," said he to himself, "and pour out a little wine to Fortuna. I have found at last what I have been seeking this long time. He is young, irascible, bounteous as mines in Cyprus, and ready to give half his fortune for that Lygian linnet. Just such a man have I been seeking this long time. It is needful, however, to be on one's guard with him, for the wrinkling of his brow forebodes no good. Ah! the wolf-whelps lord it over the world to-day! I should fear that Petronius less. O gods! but the trade of procurer pays better at present than virtue. Ah! she drew a fish on the sand! If I know what that means, may I choke myself with a piece of goat's cheese! But I shall know. Fish live under water, and searching under water is more difficult than on land, *ergo* he will pay me separately for this fish. Another such purse and I might cast aside the beggar's wallet and buy myself a slave. But what wouldst thou say, Chilo, were I to advise thee to buy not a male but a female slave? I know thee; I know that thou wouldst consent. If she were beautiful, like Eunice, for instance, thou thyself wouldst grow young near her, and at the same time wouldst have from her a good and certain income. I sold to that poor Eunice two threads from my old mantle. She is dull; but if Petronius were to give her to me, I would take her. Yes, yes, Chilo Chilonides, thou hast lost father and mother, thou art an orphan; therefore buy to console thee even a female slave. She must indeed live somewhere, therefore Vinicius will hire her a dwelling, in which thou too mayest find shelter; she must dress, hence Vinicius will pay for the dress; and must eat, hence he will support her. Och! what a hard life! Where are the times in which for an obolus a man could buy as much pork and beans as he could hold in both hands, or a piece of goat's entrails as long as the arm of a boy twelve years old, and filled with blood? But here is that villain Sporus! In the wine-shop it will be easier to learn something."

Thus conversing, he entered the wine-shop and ordered a pitcher of "dark" for himself. Seeing the sceptical look of the shopkeeper, he took a gold coin from his purse, and, putting it on the table, said, —

"Sporus, I toiled to-day with Seneca from dawn till midday, and this is what my friend gave me at parting."

The plump eyes of Sporus became plumper still at this sight, and the wine was soon before Chilo. Moistening his fingers in it, he drew a fish on the table, and said, —

"Knowest what that means?"

"A fish? Well, a fish, — yes, that's a fish."

"Thou art dull; though thou dost add so much water to the wine that thou mightst find a fish in it. This is a symbol which, in the language of philosophers, means 'the smile of fortune.' If thou hadst divined it, thou too mightst have made a fortune. Honor philosophy, I tell thee, or I shall change my wine-shop, — an act to which Petronius, my personal friend, has been urging me this long time."

CHAPTER XIV

For a number of days after the interview, Chilo did not show himself any-where. Vinicius, since he had learned from Acte that Lygia loved him, was a hundred times more eager to find her, and began himself to search. He was unwilling, and also unable, to ask aid of Cæsar, who was in great fear because of the illness of the infant Augusta.

Sacrifices in the temples did not help, neither did prayers and offerings, nor the art of physicians, nor all the means of enchantment to which they turned finally. In a week the child died. Mourning fell upon the court and Rome. Cæsar, who at the birth of the infant was wild with delight, was wild now from despair, and, confining himself in his apartments, refused food for two days; and though the palace was swarming with senators and Augustians, who hastened with marks of sorrow and sympathy, he denied audience to every one. The senate assembled in an extraordinary session, at which the dead child was pronounced divine. It was decided to rear to her a temple and appoint a special priest to her service. New sacrifices were offered in other temples in honor of the deceased; statues of her were cast from precious metals; and her funeral was one immense solemnity, during which the people wondered at the unrestrained marks of grief which Cæsar exhibited; they wept with him, stretched out their hands for gifts, and above all amused themselves with the unparalleled spectacle.

That death alarmed Petronius. All knew in Rome that Poppæa ascribed it to enchantment. The physicians, who were thus enabled to explain the vanity of their efforts, supported her; the priests, whose sacrifices proved powerless, did the same, as well as the sorcerers, who were trembling for their lives, and also the people. Petronius was glad now that Lygia had fled; for he wished no evil to Aulus and Pomponia, and he wished good to him-self and Vinicius; therefore when the cypress, set out before the Palatine as a sign of mourning, was removed, he went to the reception appointed for the senators and Augustians to learn how far Nero had lent ear to reports of spells, and to neutralize results which might come from his belief.

Knowing Nero, he thought, too, that though he did not believe in charms, he would feign belief, so as to magnify his own suffering, and take vengeance on some one, finally, to escape the suspicion that the gods had begun to punish him for crimes. Petronius did not think that Cæsar could love really and deeply even his own child; though he loved her passionately, he felt certain, however, that he would exaggerate his suffering. He was not mis-taken. Nero listened, with stony face and fixed eyes, to the consolation offered by knights and senators. It was evident that, even if he suffered, he was

thinking of this: What impression would his suffering make upon others?
He was posing as a Niobe, and giving an exhibition of parental sorrow, as
an actor would give it on the stage. He had not the power even then to endure
in his silent and as it were petrified sorrow, for at moments he made a gesture
as if to cast the dust of the earth on his head, and at moments he groaned
deeply; but seeing Petronius, he sprang up and cried in a tragic voice, so
that all present could hear him, —

"Eheu! And thou art guilty of her death! At thy advice the evil spirit
entered these walls, — the evil spirit which, with one look, drew the life
from her breast! Woe is me! Would that my eyes had not seen the light of
Helios! Woe is me! Eheu! eheu!"

And raising his voice still more, he passed into a despairing shout; but
Petronius resolved at that moment to put everything on one cast of the
dice; hence, stretching out his hand, he seized the silk kerchief which Nero
wore around his neck always, and, placing it on the mouth of the Imperator,
said solemnly, —

"Lord, Rome and the world are benumbed with pain; but do thou preserve thy voice for us!"

Those present were amazed; Nero himself was amazed for a moment.
Petronius alone was unmoved; he knew too well what he was doing. He
remembered, besides, that Terpnos and Diodorus had a direct order to close
Cæsar's mouth whenever he raised his voice too much and exposed it to danger.

"O Cæsar!" continued he, with the same seriousness and sorrow, "we have
suffered an immeasurable loss; let even this treasure of consolation remain
to us!"

Nero's face quivered, and after a while tears came from his eyes. All at once
he rested his hands on Petronius's shoulders, and, dropping his head on his
breast, began to repeat, amid sobs, —

"Thou alone of all thought of this, — thou alone, O Petronius! thou alone!"
Tigellinus grew yellow from envy; but Petronius continued, —

"Go to Antium! there she came to the world, there joy flowed in on thee,
there solace will come to thee. Let the sea air freshen thy divine throat; let
thy breast breathe the salt dampness. We, thy devoted ones, will follow thee
everywhere; and when we assuage thy pain with friendship, thou wilt comfort us with song."

"True!" answered Nero, sadly, "I will write a hymn in her honor, and
compose music for it."

"And then thou wilt find the warm sun in Baiæ."

"And afterward — forgetfulness in Greece."

"In the birthplace of poetry and song."

And his stony, gloomy state of mind passed away gradually, as clouds pass
that are covering the sun; and then a conversation began which, though full
of sadness, yet was full of plans for the future, — touching a journey, artistic
exhibitions, and even the receptions required at the promised coming of
Tiridates, King of Armenia. Tigellinus tried, it is true, to bring forward

again the enchantment; but Petronius, sure now of victory, took up the challenge directly.

"Tigellinus," said he, "dost thou think that enchantments can injure the gods?"

"Cæsar himself has mentioned them," answered the courtier.

"Pain was speaking, not Cæsar; but thou — what is thy opinion of the matter?"

"The gods are too mighty to be subject to charms."

"Then wouldst thou deny divinity to Cæsar and his family?"

"Peractum est!" muttered Eprius Marcellus, standing near, repeating that shout which the people gave always when a gladiator in the arena received such a blow that he needed no other.

Tigellinus gnawed his own anger. Between him and Petronius there had long existed a rivalry touching Nero. Tigellinus had this superiority, that Nero acted with less ceremony, or rather with none whatever in his presence; while thus far Petronius overcame Tigellinus at every encounter with wit and intellect.

So it happened now. Tigellinus was silent, and simply recorded in his memory those senators and knights who, when Petronius withdrew to the depth of the chamber, surrounded him straightway, supposing that after this incident he would surely be Cæsar's first favorite.

Petronius, on leaving the palace, betook himself to Vinicius, and described his encounter with Cæsar and Tigellinus.

"Not only have I turned away danger," said he, "from Aulus Plautius, Pomponia, and us, but even from Lygia, whom they will not seek, even for this reason, that I have persuaded Bronzebeard, the monkey, to go to Antium, and thence to Naples or Baiæ; and he will go. I know that he has not ventured yet to appear in the theatre publicly; I have known this long time that he intends to do so at Naples. He is dreaming, moreover, of Greece, where he wants to sing in all the more prominent cities, and then make a triumphal entry into Rome, with all the crowns which the 'Græculi' will bestow on him. During that time we shall be able to seek Lygia unhindered and secrete her in safety. But has not our noble philosopher been here yet?"

"Thy noble philosopher is a cheat. No; he has not shown himself, and he will not show himself again!"

"But I have a better understanding, if not of his honesty, of his wit. He has drawn blood once from thy purse, and will come even for this, to draw it a second time."

"Let him beware lest I draw his own blood."

"Draw it not; have patience till thou art convinced surely of his deceit. Do not give him more money, but promise a liberal reward if he brings thee certain information. Wilt thou thyself undertake something?"

"My two freedmen, Nymphidius and Demas, are searching for her with sixty men. Freedom is promised the slave who finds her. Besides I have sent out special persons by all roads leading from Rome to inquire at every inn for the Lygian and the maiden. I course through the city myself day and night, counting on a chance meeting."

"Whenever thou hast tidings let me know, for I must go to Antium."

"I will do so."

"And if thou wake up some morning and say, 'It is not worth while to torment myself for one girl, and take so much trouble because of her,' come to Antium. There will be no lack of women there, or amusement."

Vinicius began to walk with quick steps. Petronius looked for some time at him, and said at last, —

"Tell me sincerely, not as a mad head, who talks something into his brain and excites himself, but as a man of judgment who is answering a friend: Art thou concerned as much as ever about this Lygia?"

Vinicius stopped a moment, and looked at Petronius as if he had not seen him before; then he began to walk again. It was evident that he was restraining an outburst. At last, from a feeling of helplessness, sorrow, anger, and invincible yearning, two tears gathered in his eyes, which spoke with greater power to Petronius than the most eloquent words.

Then, meditating for a moment, he said, —

"It is not Atlas who carries the world on his shoulders, but woman; and sometimes she plays with it as with a ball."

"True," said Vinicius.

And they began to take farewell of each other. But at that moment a slave announced that Chilo Chilonides was waiting in the antechamber, and begged to be admitted to the presence of the lord.

Vinicius gave command to admit him immediately, and Petronius said, —

"Ha! have I not told thee? By Hercules! keep thy calmness; or he will command thee, not thou him."

"A greeting and honor to the noble tribune of the army, and to thee, lord," said Chilo, entering. "May your happiness be equal to your fame, and may your fame course through the world from the pillars of Hercules to the boundaries of the Arsacidæ."

"A greeting, O lawgiver of virtue and wisdom," answered Petronius.

But Vinicius inquired with affected calmness, "What dost thou bring?"

"The first time I came I brought thee hope, O lord; at present, I bring certainty that the maiden will be found."

"That means that thou hast not found her yet?"

"Yes, lord; but I have found what that sign means which she made. I know who the people are who rescued her, and I know the God among whose worshippers to seek her."

Vinicius wished to spring from the chair in which he was sitting; but Petronius placed his hand on his shoulder, and turning to Chilo said, —

"Speak on!"

"Art thou perfectly certain, lord, that she drew a fish on the sand?"

"Yes," burst out Vinicius.

"Then she is a Christian and Christians carried her away."

A moment of silence followed.

"Listen, Chilo," said Petronius. "My relative has predestined to thee a considerable sum of money for finding the girl, but a no less considerable number of rods if thou deceive him. In the first case thou wilt purchase not one, but three scribes; in the second, the philosophy of all the seven sages, with the addition of thy own, will not suffice to get thee ointment."

"The maiden is a Christian, lord," cried the Greek.

"Stop, Chilo. Thou art not a dull man. We know that Junia and Calvia Crispinilla accused Pomponia Græcina of confessing the Christian superstition; but we know too, that a domestic court acquitted her. Wouldst thou raise this again? Wouldst thou persuade us that Pomponia, and with her Lygia, could belong to the enemies of the human race, to the poisoners of wells and fountains, to the worshippers of an ass's head, to people who murder infants and give themselves up to the foulest license? Think, Chilo, if that thesis which thou art announcing to us will not rebound as an antithesis on thy own back."

Chilo spread out his arms in sign that that was not his fault, and then said, —

"Lord, utter in Greek the following sentence: Jesus Christ, Son of God, Saviour." [1]

"Well, I have uttered it. What comes of that?"

"Now take the first letters of each of those words and put them into one word."

"Fish!" said Petronius with astonishment. [2]

"There, that is why fish has become the watchword of the Christians," answered Chilo, proudly.

A moment of silence followed. But there was something so striking in the conclusions of the Greek that the two friends could not guard themselves from amazement.

"Vinicius, art thou not mistaken?" asked Petronius. "Did Lygia really draw a fish for thee?"

"By all the infernal gods, one might go mad!" cried the young man, with excitement. "If she had drawn a bird for me, I should have said a bird."

"Therefore she is a Christian," repeated Chilo.

"This signifies," said Petronius, "that Pomponia and Lygia poison wells, murder children caught on the street, and give themselves up to dissoluteness! Folly! Thou, Vinicius, wert at their house for a time, I was there a little while; but I know Pomponia and Aulus enough, I know even Lygia enough, to say monstrous and foolish! If a fish is the symbol of the Christians, which it is difficult really to deny, and if those women are Christians, then, by Proserpina! evidently Christians are not what we hold them to be."

"Thou speakest like Socrates, lord," answered Chilo. "Who has ever examined a Christian? Who has learned their religion? When I was travelling three years ago from Naples hither to Rome (oh, why did I not stay in Naples!), a man joined me, whose name was Glaucus, of whom people said

---

[1] Ἰησοῦς Χριστός, Θεοῦ Υἱός, Σωτήρ (Iēsous Christos, Theou Uios, Sōtēr).

[2] ΙΧΘΥΣ (Ichthus), the Greek word for "fish."

that he was a Christian; but in spite of that I convinced myself that he was a good and virtuous man."

"Was it not from that virtuous man that thou hast learned now what the fish means?"

"Unfortunately, lord, on the way, at an inn, some one thrust a knife into that honorable old man; and his wife and child were carried away by slave-dealers. I lost in their defence these two fingers; since, as people say, there is no lack among Christians of miracles, I hope that the fingers will grow out on my hand again."

"How is that? Hast thou become a Christian?"

"Since yesterday, lord, since yesterday! The fish made me a Christian. But see what a power there is in it. For some days I shall be the most zealous of the zealous, so that they may admit me to all their secrets; and when they admit me to their secrets, I shall know where the maiden is hiding. Perhaps then my Christianity will pay me better than my philosophy. I have made a vow also to Mercury, that if he helps me to find the maiden, I will sacrifice to him two heifers of the same size and color and will gild their horns."

"Then thy Christianity of yesterday and thy philosophy of long standing permit thee to believe in Mercury?"

"I believe always in that in which I need to believe; that is my philosophy, which ought to please Mercury. Unfortunately (ye know, worthy lords, what a suspicious god he is), he does not trust the promises even of blameless philosophers, and prefers the heifers in advance; meanwhile this outlay is immense. Not every one is a Seneca, and I cannot afford the sacrifice; should the noble Vinicius, however, wish to give something, on account of that sum which he promised — "

"Not an obolus, Chilo!" said Petronius, "not an obolus. The bounty of Vinicius will surpass thy expectations, but only when Lygia is found, — that is, when thou shalt indicate to us her hiding-place. Mercury must trust thee for the two heifers, though I am not astonished at him for not wishing to do so; in this I recognize his acuteness."

"Listen to me, worthy lords. The discovery which I have made is great; for though I have not found the maiden yet, I have found the way in which I must seek her. Ye have sent freedmen and slaves throughout the city and into the country; has any one given you a clew? No! I alone have given one. I tell you more. Among your slaves there may be Christians, of whom ye have no knowledge, for this superstition has spread everywhere; and they, instead of aiding, will betray you. It is unfortunate that they see me here; do thou therefore, noble Petronius, enjoin silence on Eunice; and thou too, noble Vinicius, spread a report that I sell thee an ointment which insures victory in the Circus to horses rubbed with it. I alone will search for her, and single-handed I will find the fugitives; and do ye trust in me, and know that whatever I receive in advance will be for me simply an encouragement, for I shall hope always for more, and shall feel the greater certainty that the promised reward will not fail me. Ah, it is true! As a philosopher I despise money, though neither Seneca, nor even Musonius, nor Cornutus despises it, though they have not lost fingers in any one's defence, and are able themselves to write and leave their names to posterity. But, aside from the slave, whom I intend to buy, and besides Mercury, to whom I have promised the heifers, — and ye know how dear cattle have become in these times, — the searching itself involves much outlay. Only listen to me patiently. Well, for the last few days my feet are wounded from continual walking. I have gone to wine-shops to talk with people, to bakeries, to butcher-shops, to dealers in olive oil, and to fishermen. I have run through every street and alley; I have been in the hiding-places of fugitive slaves; I have lost money, nearly a hundred ases, in playing mora; I have been in laundries, in drying-sheds, in cheap kitchens; I have seen mule-drivers and carvers; I have seen people who cure bladder complaints and pull teeth; I have talked with dealers in dried figs; I have been at cemeteries; and do ye know why? This is why; so as to outline a fish everywhere, look people in the eyes, and hear what they would say of that sign. For a long time I was unable to learn anything, till at last I saw an old slave at a fountain. He was drawing water with a bucket, and weeping. Approaching him, I asked the cause of his tears. When we had sat down on the steps of the fountain, he answered that all his life he had been collecting sestertium after sestertium, to redeem his beloved son; but his master, a certain Pansa, when the money was delivered to him, took it, but kept the son in slavery. 'And so I am weeping,' said the old man, 'for though I repeat, Let the will of God be done, I, poor sinner, am not able to keep down my tears.' Then, as if penetrated by a forewarning, I moistened my finger in the water and drew a fish for him. To this he answered, 'My hope, too, is in Christ.' I asked him then, 'Hast thou confessed to me by that sign?' 'I have,' said he; 'and peace be with thee.' I began then to draw him out, and the honest old man told me everything. His master, that Pansa, is himself a freedman of the great Pansa; and he brings stones by the Tiber to Rome, where slaves and hired persons unload them from the boats, and carry them to buildings in the night time, so as not to obstruct movement in the streets during daylight. Among these people many Christians work, and also his son; as the work is beyond his son's strength, he wished to redeem him. But Pansa preferred to keep both the money and the slave. While telling me this, he began again to weep; and I mingled my tears with his, — tears came to me easily because of my kind heart, and the pain in my feet, which I got from walking excessively. I began also to lament that as I had come from Naples only a few days since, I knew no one of the brotherhood, and did not know where they assembled for prayer. He wondered that Christians in Naples had not given me letters to their brethren in Rome; but I explained to him that the letters were stolen from me on the road. Then he told me to come to the river at night, and he would acquaint me with brethren who would conduct me to houses of prayer and to elders who govern the Christian community. When I heard this, I was so delighted that I gave him the sum needed to redeem his son, in the hope that the lordly Vinicius would return it to me twofold."

"Chilo," interrupted Petronius, "in thy narrative falsehood appears on the surface of truth, as oil does on water. Thou hast brought important information; I do not deny that. I assert, even, that a great step is made toward finding Lygia; but do not cover thy news with falsehood. What is the name of that old man from whom thou hast learned that the Christians recognize each other through the sign of a fish?"

"Euricius. A poor, unfortunate old man! He reminded me of Glaucus, whom I defended from murderers, and he touched me mainly by this."

"I believe that thou didst discover him, and wilt be able to make use of the acquaintance; but thou hast given him no money. Thou hast not given him an as; dost understand me? Thou hast not given anything."

"But I helped him to lift the bucket, and I spoke of his son with the greatest sympathy. Yes, lord, what can hide before the penetration of Petronius? Well, I did not give him money, or rather, I gave it to him, but only in spirit, in intention, which, had he been a real philosopher, should have sufficed him. I gave it to him because I saw that such an act was indispensable and useful; for think, lord, how this act has won all the Christians at once to me, what access to them it has opened, and what confidence it has roused in them."

"True," said Petronius, "and it was thy duty to do it."

"For this very reason I have come to get the means to do it."

Petronius turned to Vinicius, —

"Give command to count out to him five thousand sestertia, but in spirit, in intention."

"I will give thee a young man," said Vinicius, "who will take the sum necessary; thou wilt say to Euricius that the youth is thy slave, and thou wilt count out to the old man, in the youth's presence, this money. Since thou hast brought important tidings, thou wilt receive the same amount for thyself. Come for the youth and the money this evening."

"Thou art a real Cæsar!" said Chilo. "Permit me, lord, to dedicate my work to thee; but permit also that this evening I come only for the money, since Euricius told me that all the boats had been unloaded, and that new ones would come from Ostia only after some days. Peace be with you! Thus do Christians take farewell of one another. I will buy myself a slave woman, — that is, I wanted to say a slave man. Fish are caught with a bait, and Christians with fish. *Pax vobiscum! pax! pax! pax!*"

CHAPTER XV

PETRONIUS to VINICIUS:

"I send to thee from Antium, by a trusty slave, this letter, to which, though thy hand is more accustomed to the sword and the javelin than the pen, I think that thou wilt answer through the same messenger without needless delay. I left thee on a good trail, and full of hope; hence I trust that thou hast either satisfied thy pleasant desires in the embraces of Lygia, or wilt satisfy them before the real wintry wind from the summits of Soracte shall blow on the Campania. Oh, my Vinicius! may thy preceptress be the golden goddess of Cyprus; be thou, on thy part, the preceptor of that Lygian Aurora, who is fleeing before the sun of love. And remember always that marble, though most precious, is nothing of itself, and acquires real value only when the sculptor's hand turns it into a masterpiece. Be thou such a sculptor, carissime! To love is not sufficient; one must know how to love; one must know how to teach love. Though the plebs, too, and even animals, experience pleasure, a genuine man differs from them in this especially, that he makes love in some way a noble art, and, admiring it, knows all its divine value, makes it present in his mind, thus satisfying not his body merely, but his soul. More than once, when I think here of the emptiness, the uncertainty, the dreariness of life, it occurs to me that perhaps thou hast chosen better, and that not Cæsar's court, but war and love, are the only objects for which it is worth while to be born and to live.

"Thou wert fortunate in war, be fortunate also in love; and if thou art curious as to what men are doing at the court of Cæsar, I will inform thee from time to time. We are living here at Antium, and nursing our heavenly voice; we continue to cherish the same hatred of Rome, and think of betaking ourselves to Baiæ for the winter, to appear in public at Naples, whose inhabitants, being Greeks, will appreciate us better than that wolf brood on the banks of the Tiber. People will hasten thither from Baiæ, from Pompeii, Puteoli, Cumæ, and Stabia; neither applause nor crowns will be lacking, and that will be an encouragement for the proposed expedition to Achæa.

"But the memory of the infant Augusta? Yes! we are bewailing her yet. We are singing hymns of our own composition, so wonderful that the sirens have been hiding from envy in Amphitrite's deepest caves. But the dolphins would listen to us, were they not prevented by the sound of the sea. Our suffering is not allayed yet; hence we will exhibit it to the world in every form which sculpture can employ, and observe carefully if we are beautiful in our suffering and if people recognize this beauty. Oh, my dear! we shall die buffoons and comedians!

"All the Augustians are here, male and female, not counting ten thousand servants, and five hundred she asses, in whose milk Poppæa bathes. At times even it is cheerful here. Calvia Crispinilla is growing old. It is said that she has begged Poppæa to let her take the bath immediately after herself. Lucan slapped Nigidia on the face, because he suspected her of relations with a gladiator. Sporus lost his wife at dice to Senecio. Torquatus Silanus has offered me for Eunice four chestnut horses, which this year will win the prize beyond doubt. I would not accept! Thanks to thee, also, that thou didst not take her. As to Torquatus Silanus, the poor man does not even suspect that he is already more a shade than a man. His death is decided. And knowest what his crime is? He is the great-grandson of the deified Augustus. There is no rescue for him. Such is our world.

"As is known to thee, we have been expecting Tiridates here; meanwhile Vologeses has written an offensive letter. Because he has conquered Armenia, he asks that it be left to him for Tiridates; if not, he will not yield it in any case. Pure comedy! So we have decided on war. Corbulo will receive power such as Pompeius Magnus received in the war with pirates. There was a moment, however, when Nero hesitated. He seems afraid of the glory which Corbulo will win in case of victory. It was even thought to offer the chief command to our Aulus. This was opposed by Poppæa, for whom evidently Pomponia's virtue is as salt in the eye.

"Vatinius described to us a remarkable fight of gladiators, which is to take place in Beneventum. See to what cobblers rise in our time, in spite of the saying, 'Ne sutor ultra crepidam!' Vitelius is the descendant of a cobbler; but Vatinius is the son of one! Perhaps he drew thread himself! The actor Aliturus represented Œdipus yesterday wonderfully. I asked him, by the way, as a Jew, if Christians and Jews were the same. He answered that the Jews have an eternal religion, but that Christians are a new sect risen recently in Judea; that in the time of Tiberius the Jews crucified a certain man, whose adherents increase daily, and that the Christians consider him as God. They refuse, it seems, to recognize other gods, ours especially. I cannot understand what harm it would do them to recognize these gods.

"Tigellinus shows me open enmity now. So far he is unequal to me; but he is superior in this, that he cares more for life, and is at the same time a greater scoundrel, which brings him nearer Ahenobarbus. These two will understand each other earlier or later, and then my turn will come. I know not when it will come; but I know this, that as things are it must come; hence let time pass. Meanwhile we must amuse ourselves. Life of itself would not be bad were it not for Bronzebeard. Thanks to him, a man at times is disgusted with himself. It is not correct to consider the struggle for his favor as a kind of rivalry in a circus, — as a kind of game, as a struggle, in which victory flatters vanity. True, I explain it to myself in that way frequently; but still it seems to me sometimes that I am like Chilo, and better in nothing than he. When he ceases to be needful to thee, send him to me. I have taken a fancy to his edifying conversation. A greeting from me to thy divine Christian, or rather beg her in my name not to be a fish to thee. Inform me of thy health, inform me of thy love, know how to love, teach how to love, and farewell."

Vinicius to Petronius:

"Lygia is not found yet! Were it not for the hope that I shall find her soon, thou wouldst not receive an answer; for when a man is disgusted with life, he has no wish to write letters. I wanted to learn whether Chilo was not deceiving me; and at night when he came to get the money for Euricius, I threw on a military mantle, and unobserved followed him and the slave whom I sent with him. When they reached the place, I watched from a distance, hidden behind a portico pillar, and convinced myself that Euricius was not invented. Below, a number of tens of people were unloading stones from a spacious barge, and piling them up on the bank. I saw Chilo approach them, and begin to talk with some old man, who after a while fell at his feet. Others surrounded them with shouts of admiration. Before my eyes the boy gave a purse to Euricius, who on seizing it began to pray with upraised hands, while at his side some second person was kneeling, evidently his son. Chilo said something which I could not hear, and blessed the two who were kneeling, as well as others, making in the air signs in the form of a cross, which they honor apparently, for all bent their knees. The desire seized me to go among them, and promise three such purses to him who would deliver to me Lygia; but I feared to spoil Chilo's work, and after hesitating a moment went home.

"This happened at least twelve days after thy departure. Since then Chilo has been a number of times with me. He says that he has gained great significance among the Christians; that if he has not found Lygia so far, it is because the Christians in Rome are innumerable, hence all are not acquainted with each person in their community, and cannot know everything that is done in it. They are cautious, too, and in general reticent. He gives assurance, however, that when he reaches the elders, who are called presbyters, he will learn every secret. He has made the acquaintance of a number of these already, and has begun to inquire of them, though carefully, so as not to rouse suspicion by haste, and not to make the work still more difficult. Though it is hard to wait, though patience fails, I feel that he is right, and I wait.

"He learned, too, that they have places of meeting for prayer, frequently outside the city, in empty houses and even in sandpits. There they worship Christ, sing hymns, and have feasts. There are many such places. Chilo supposes that Lygia goes purposely to different ones from Pomponia, so that the latter, in case of legal proceedings or an examination, might swear boldly that she knew nothing of Lygia's hiding-place. It may be that the presbyters have advised caution. When Chilo discovers those places, I will go with him; and if the gods let me see Lygia, I swear to thee by Jupiter that she will not escape my hands this time.

"I am thinking continually of those places of prayer. Chilo is unwilling that I should go with him; he is afraid. But I cannot stay at home. I should know her at once, even in disguise or if veiled. They assemble in the night, but I should recognize her in the night even. I should know her voice and motions anywhere. I will go myself in disguise, and look at every person who goes in or out. I am thinking of her always, and shall recognize her. Chilo is to come to-morrow, and we shall go. I will take arms. Some of my slaves sent to the provinces have returned empty-handed. But I am certain now that she is in the city, — perhaps not far away even. I myself have visited many houses under pretext of renting them. She will fare better with me a hundred times; where she is, whole legions of poor people dwell. Besides, I shall spare nothing for her sake. Thou writest that I have chosen well. I have chosen suffering and sorrow. We shall go first to those houses which are in the city, then beyond the gates. Hope looks for something every morning, otherwise life would be impossible. Thou sayest that one should know how to love. I knew how to talk of love to Lygia. But now I only yearn; I do nothing but wait for Chilo. Life to me is unendurable in my own house. Farewell!"

CHAPTER XVI

BUT Chilo did not appear for some time, and Vinicius knew not at last what to think of his absence. In vain he repeated to himself that searching, if continued to a certain and successful issue, must be gradual. His blood and impulsive nature rebelled against the voice of judgment. To do nothing, to wait, to sit with folded arms, was so repulsive to him that he could not be reconciled to it in any way. To search the alleys of the city in the dark garb of a slave, through this alone, that it was useless, seemed to him merely a mask for his own inefficiency, and could give no satisfaction. His freedmen, persons of experience, whom he commanded to search independently, turned out a hundred times less expert than Chilo. Meanwhile there rose in him, besides his love for Lygia, the stubbornness of a player resolved to win. Vinicius had been always a person of this kind. From earliest youth he had accomplished what he desired with the passionateness of one who does not understand failure, or the need of yielding something. For a time military discipline had put his self-will within bounds, but also it had engrafted into him the conviction that every command of his to subordinates must be fulfilled; his prolonged stay in the Orient, among people pliant and inured to slavish obedience, confirmed in him the faith that for his "I wish" there were no limits. At present his vanity, too, was wounded painfully. There was, besides, in Lygia's opposition and resistance, and in her flight itself, which was to him incomprehensible, a kind of riddle. In trying to solve this riddle he racked his head terribly. He felt that Acte had told the truth, and that Lygia was not indifferent. But if this were true, why had she preferred wandering and misery to his love, his tenderness, and a residence in his splendid mansion? To this question he found no answer, and arrived only at a kind of dim understanding that between him and Lygia, between their ideas, between the world which belonged to him and Petronius, and the world of Lygia and Pomponia, there existed some sort of difference, some kind of misunderstanding as deep as an abyss, which nothing could fill up or make even. It seemed to him, then, that he must lose Lygia; and at this thought he lost the remnant of balance which Petronius wished to preserve in him. There were moments in which he did not know whether he loved Lygia or hated her; he understood only that he must find her, and he would rather that the earth swallowed her than that he should not see and possess her. By the power of imagination he saw her as clearly at times as if she had been before his face. He recalled every word which he had spoken to her; every word which he had heard from her. He felt her near; felt her on his bosom, in his arms; and then desire embraced him like a flame. He loved her and called to her.

And when he thought that he was loved, that she might do with willingness all that he wished of her, sore and endless sorrow seized him, and a kind of deep tenderness flooded his heart, like a mighty wave. But there were moments, too, in which he grew pale from rage, and delighted in thoughts of the humiliation and tortures which he would inflict on Lygia when he found her. He wanted not only to have her, but to have her as a trampled slave. At the same time he felt that if the choice were left him, to be her slave or not to see her in life again, he would rather be her slave. There were days in which he thought of the marks which the lash would leave on her rosy body, and at the same time he wanted to kiss those marks. It came to his head also that he would be happy if he could kill her.

In this torture, torment, uncertainty, and suffering, he lost health, and even beauty. He became a cruel and incomprehensible master. His slaves, and even his freedmen, approached him with trembling; and when punishments fell on them causelessly, — punishments as merciless as undeserved, — they began to hate him in secret; while he, feeling this, and feeling his own isolation, took revenge all the more on them. He restrained himself with Chilo alone, fearing lest he might cease his searches; the Greek, noting this, began to gain control of him, and grew more and more exacting. At first he assured Vinicius at each visit that the affair would proceed easily and quickly; now he began to discover difficulties, and without ceasing, it is true, to guarantee the undoubted success of the searches, he did not hide the fact that they must continue yet for a good while.

At last he came, after long days of waiting, with a face so gloomy that the young man grew pale at sight of him, and springing up had barely strength to ask, —

"Is she not among the Christians?"

"She is, lord," answered Chilo; "but I found Glaucus among them."

"Of what art thou speaking, and who is Glaucus?"

"Thou hast forgotten, lord, it seems, that old man with whom I journeyed from Naples to Rome, and in whose defence I lost these two fingers, — a loss which prevents me from writing. Robbers, who bore away his wife and child, stabbed him with a knife. I left him dying at an inn in Minturna, and bewailed him long. Alas! I have convinced myself that he is alive yet, and belongs in Rome to the Christian community."

Vinicius, who could not understand what the question was, understood only that Glaucus was becoming a hindrance to the discovery of Lygia; hence he suppressed his rising anger, and said, —

"If thou didst defend him, he should be thankful and help thee."

"Ah! worthy tribune, even gods are not always grateful, and what must the case be with men? True, he should be thankful. But, unhappily, he is an old man, of a mind weak and darkened by age and disappointment; for which reason, not only is he not grateful, but, as I learned from his co-religionists, he accuses me of having conspired with the robbers, and says that I am the cause of his misfortunes. That is the recompense for my fingers!"

"Scoundrel! I am certain that it was as he says," replied Vinicius.

"Then thou knowest more than he does, lord, for he only surmises that it was so; which, however, would not prevent him from summoning the Christians, and from revenging himself on me cruelly. He would have done that undoubtedly, and others, with equal certainty, would have helped him; but fortunately he does not know my name, and in the house of prayer where we met, he did not notice me. I, however, knew him at once, and at the first moment wished to throw myself on his neck. Wisdom, however, and the habit of thinking before every step which I intend to take, restrained me. Therefore, on issuing from the house of prayer, I inquired concerning him, and those who knew him declared that he was the man who had been betrayed by his comrade on the journey from Naples. Otherwise I should not have known that he gives out such a story."

"How does this concern me? Tell what thou sawest in the house of prayer."

"It does not concern thee, lord, but it concerns me just as much as my life. Since I wish that my wisdom should survive me, I would rather renounce the reward which thou hast offered, than expose my life for empty lucre; without which, I as a true philosopher shall be able to live and seek divine wisdom."

But Vinicius approached him with an ominous countenance, and began in a suppressed voice, —

"Who told thee that death would meet thee sooner at the hands of Glaucus than at mine? Whence knowest thou, dog, that I will not have thee buried right away in my garden?"

Chilo, who was a coward, looked at Vinicius, and in the twinkle of an eye understood that one more unguarded word and he was lost beyond redemption.

"I will search for her, lord, and I will find her!" cried he, hurriedly.

Silence followed, during which were heard the quick breathing of Vinicius, and the distant song of slaves at work in the garden.

Only after a while did the Greek resume his speech, when he noticed that the young patrician was somewhat pacified.

"Death passed me, but I looked on it with the calmness of Socrates. No, lord, I have not said that I refuse to search for the maiden; I desired merely to tell thee that search for her is connected now with great peril to me. On a time thou didst doubt that there was a certain Euricius in the world, and though thou wert convinced by thine own eyes that the son of my father told the truth to thee, thou hast suspicions now that I have invented Glaucus. Ah! would that he were only a fiction, that I might go among the Christians with perfect safety, as I went some time since; I would give up for that the poor old slave woman whom I bought, three days since, to care for my advanced age and maimed condition. But Glaucus is living, lord; and if he had seen me once, thou wouldst not have seen me again, and in that case who would find the maiden?"

Here he was silent again, and began to dry his tears.

"But while Glaucus lives," continued he, "how can I search for her? — for I may meet him at any step; and if I meet him I shall perish, and with me will cease all my searching."

"What art thou aiming at? What help is there? What dost thou wish to undertake?" inquired Vinicius.

"Aristotle teaches us, lord, that less things should be sacrificed for greater, and King Priam said frequently that old age was a grievous burden. Indeed, the burden of old age and misfortune weighs upon Glaucus this long time, and so heavily that death would be to him a benefit. For what is death, according to Seneca, but liberation?"

"Play the fool with Petronius, not with me! Tell what thy desire is."

"If virtue is folly, may the gods permit me to be a fool all my life. I desire, lord, to set aside Glaucus, for while he is living my life and searches are in continual peril."

"Hire men to beat him to death with clubs; I will pay them."

"They will rob thee, lord, and afterward make profit of the secret. There are as many ruffians in Rome as grains of sand in the arena, but thou wilt not believe how dear they are when an honest man needs to employ their villainy. No, worthy tribune! But if watchmen catch the murderers in the act? They would tell, beyond doubt, who hired them, and then thou wouldst have trouble. They will not point to me, for I shall not give my name. Thou art doing ill not to trust in me, for, setting aside my keenness, remember that there is a question of two other things, — of my life, and the reward which thou has promised me."

"How much dost thou need?"

"A thousand sestertia, for turn attention to this, that I must find honest ruffians, men who when they have received earnest money, will not take it off without a trace. For good work there must be good pay! Something might be added, too, for my sake, to wipe away the tears which I shall shed out of pity for Glaucus. I take the gods to witness how I love him. If I receive a thousand sestertia to-day, two days hence his soul will be in Hades; and then, if souls preserve memory and the gift of thought, he will know for the first time how I loved him. I will find people this very day, and tell them that for each day of the life of Glaucus I will withhold one hundred sestertia. I have, besides, a certain idea, which seems to me infallible."

Vinicius promised him once more the desired sum, forbidding him to mention Glaucus again; but asked what other news he brought, where he had been all the time, what he had seen, and what he had discovered. But Chilo was not able to tell much. He had been in two more houses of prayer, — had observed each person carefully, especially the women, — but had seen no one who resembled Lygia: the Christians, however, looked on him as one of their own sect, and, since he redeemed the son of Euricius, they honored him as a man following in the steps of "Christ." He had learned from them, also, that a great lawgiver of theirs, a certain Paul of Tarsus, was in Rome, imprisoned because of charges preferred by the Jews, and with this man he had resolved to become acquainted. But most of all was he pleased by this,

— that the supreme priest of the whole sect, who had been Christ's disciple, and to whom Christ had confided government over the whole world of Christians, might arrive in Rome any moment. All the Christians desired evidently to see him, and hear his teachings. Some great meetings would follow, at which he, Chilo, would be present; and what is more, since it is easy to hide in the crowd, he would take Vinicius to those meetings. Then they would find Lygia certainly. If Glaucus were once set aside, it would not be connected even with great danger. As to revenge, the Christians, too, would revenge; but in general they were peaceful people.

Here Chilo began to relate, with a certain surprise, that he had never seen that they gave themselves up to debauchery, that they poisoned wells or fountains, that they were enemies of the human race, worshipped an ass, or ate the flesh of children. No; he had seen nothing of that sort. Certainly he would find among them even people who would hide away Glaucus for money; but their religion, as far as he knew, did not incite to crime, — on the contrary, it enjoined forgiveness of offences.

Vinicius remembered what Pomponia had said to him at Acte's, and in general he listened to Chilo's words with pleasure. Though his feeling for Lygia assumed at times the seeming of hatred, he felt a relief when he heard that the religion which she and Pomponia confessed was neither criminal nor repulsive. But a species of undefined feeling rose in him that it was just that reverence for Christ, unknown and mysterious, which created the difference between himself and Lygia; hence he began at once to fear that religion and to hate it.

CHAPTER XVII

For Chilo, it was really important to set aside Glaucus, who, though advanced in years, was by no means decrepit. There was considerable truth in what Chilo had narrated to Vinicius. He had known Glaucus on a time, he had betrayed him, sold him to robbers, deprived him of family, of property, and delivered him to murder. But he bore the memory of these events easily, for he had thrown the man aside dying, not at an inn, but in a field near Minturna. This one thing he had not foreseen, that Glaucus would be cured of his wounds and come to Rome. When he saw him, therefore, in the house of prayer, he was in truth terrified, and at the first moment wished to discontinue the search for Lygia. But on the other hand, Vinicius terrified him still more. He understood that he must choose between the fear of Glaucus, and the pursuit and vengeance of a powerful patrician, to whose aid would come, beyond doubt, another and still greater, Petronius. In view of this, Chilo ceased to hesitate. He thought it better to have small enemies than great ones, and, though his cowardly nature trembled somewhat at bloody methods, he saw the need of killing Glaucus through the aid of other hands.

At present the only question with him was the choice of people, and to this he was turning that thought of which he had made mention to Vinicius. Spending his nights in wine-shops most frequently, and lodging in them, among men without a roof, without faith or honor, he could find persons easily to undertake any task, and still more easily others who, if they sniffed coin on his person, would begin, but when they had received earnest money, would extort the whole sum by threatening to deliver him to justice. Besides, for a certain time past Chilo had felt a repulsion for nakedness, for those disgusting and terrible figures lurking about suspected houses in the Subura or in the Trans-Tiber. Measuring everything with his own measure, and not having fathomed sufficiently the Christians or their religion, he judged that among them, too, he could find willing tools. Since they seemed more reliable than others, he resolved to turn to them and present the affair in such fashion that they would undertake it, not for money's sake merely, but through devotion.

In view of this, he went in the evening to Euricius, whom he knew as devoted with whole soul to his person, and who, he was sure, would do all in his power to assist him. Naturally cautious, Chilo did not even dream of revealing his real intentions, which would be in clear opposition, moreover, to the faith which the old man had in his piety and virtue. He wished to find people who were ready for anything, and to talk with them of the affair only in such a way that, out of regard to themselves, they would guard it as an eternal secret.

The old man Euricius, after the redemption of his son, hired one of those little shops so numerous near the Circus Maximus, in which were sold olives, beans, unleavened paste, and water sweetened with honey, to spectators coming to the Circus. Chilo found him at home arranging his shop; and when he had greeted him in Christ's name, he began to speak of the affair which had brought him. Since he had rendered them a service, he considered that they would pay him with gratitude. He needed two or three strong and courageous men, to ward off danger threatening not only him, but all Christians. He was poor, it was true, since he had given to Euricius almost all that he owned; still he would pay such men for their services if they would trust him and perform faithfully what he commanded.

Euricius and his son Quartus listened to him as their benefactor almost on their knees. Both declared that they were ready themselves to do all that he asked of them, believing that a man so holy could not ask for deeds inconsistent with the teaching of Christ.

Chilo assured them that that was true, and, raising his eyes to heaven, he seemed to be praying; in fact, he was thinking whether it would not be well to accept their proposal, which might save him a thousand sestertia. But after a moment of thought he rejected it. Euricius was an old man, perhaps not so much weighted by years as weakened by care and disease. Quartus was sixteen years of age. Chilo needed dexterous, and, above all, stalwart men. As to the thousand sestertia, he considered that — thanks to the plan which he had invented — he would be able in every case to spare a large part of it.

They insisted for some time, but when he refused decisively they yielded. "I know the baker Demas," said Quartus, "in whose mills slaves and hired men are employed. One of those hired men is so strong that he would take the place, not of two, but of four. I myself have seen him lift stones from the ground which four men could not stir."

"If that is a God-fearing man, who can sacrifice himself for the brotherhood, make me acquainted with him," said Chilo.

"He is a Christian, lord," answered Quartus; "nearly all who work for Demas are Christians. He has night as well as day laborers; this man is of the night laborers. Were we to go now to the mill, we should find them at supper, and thou mightest speak to him freely. Demas lives near the Emporium."

Chilo consented most willingly. The Emporium was at the foot of the Aventine, hence not very far from the Circus Maximus. It was possible, without going around the hill, to pass along the river through the Porticus Æmilia, which would shorten the road considerably.

"I am old," said Chilo, when they went under the Colonnade; "at times I suffer effacement of memory. Yes, though our Christ was betrayed by one of his disciples, the name of the traitor I cannot recall at this moment —"

"Judas, lord, who hanged himself," answered Quartus, wondering a little in his soul how it was possible to forget that name.

"Oh, yes — Judas! I thank thee," said Chilo.

And they went on some time in silence. When they came to the Emporium, which was closed, they passed it, and going around the storehouse, from which grain was distributed to the populace, they turned toward the left, to houses which stretched along the Via Ostiensis, up to the Mons Testaceus and the Forum Pistorium. There they halted before a wooden building, from the interior of which came the noise of millstones. Quartus went in; but Chilo, who did not like to show himself to large numbers of people, and was in continual dread that some fate might bring him to meet Glaucus, remained outside.

"I am curious about that Hercules who serves in a mill," said he to himself, looking at the brightly shining moon. "If he is a scoundrel and a wise man, he will cost me something; if a virtuous Christian and dull, he will do what I want without money."

Further meditation was interrupted by the return of Quartus, who issued from the building with a second man, wearing only a tunic called "exomis," cut in such fashion that the right arm and right breast were exposed. Such garments, since they left perfect freedom of movement, were used especially by laborers. Chilo, when he saw the man coming, drew a breath of satisfaction, for he had not seen in his life such an arm and such a breast.

"Here, lord," said Quartus, "is the brother whom it was thy wish to see."

"May the peace of Christ be with thee!" answered Chilo. "Do thou, Quartus, tell this brother whether I deserve faith and trust, and then return in the name of God; for there is no need that thy gray-haired father should be left in loneliness."

"This is a holy man," said Quartus, "who gave all his property to redeem me from slavery, — me, a man unknown to him. May our Lord the Saviour prepare him a heavenly reward therefor!"

The gigantic laborer, hearing this, bent down and kissed Chilo's hand.

"What is thy name, brother?" inquired the Greek.

"At holy baptism, father, the name Urban was given me."

"Urban, my brother, hast thou time to talk with me freely?"

"Our work begins at midnight, and only now are they preparing our supper."

"Then there is time sufficient. Let us go to the river; there thou wilt hear my words."

They went, and sat on the embankment, in a silence broken only by the distant sound of the millstones and the plash of the onflowing river. Chilo looked into the face of the laborer, which, notwithstanding a somewhat severe and sad expression, such as was usual on faces of barbarians living in Rome, seemed to him kind and honest.

"This is a good-natured, dull man who will kill Glaucus for nothing," thought Chilo.

"Urban," inquired he then, "dost thou love Christ?"

"I love him from the soul of my heart," said the laborer.

"And thy brethren and sisters, and those who taught thee truth and faith in Christ?"

"I love them, too, father."

"Then may peace be with thee!"

"And with thee, father!"

Again silence set in, but in the distance the millstones were roaring, and the river was plashing below the two men.

Chilo looked with fixed gaze into the clear moonlight, and with a slow, restrained voice began to speak of Christ's death. He seemed not as speaking to Urban, but as if recalling to himself that death, or some secret which he was confiding to the drowsy city. There was in this, too, something touching as well as impressive. The laborer wept; and when Chilo began to groan and complain that in the moment of the Saviour's passion there was no one to defend him, if not from crucifixion, at least from the insults of Jews and soldiers, the gigantic fists of the barbarian began to squeeze from pity and suppressed rage. The death only moved him; but at thought of that rabble reviling the Lamb nailed to the cross, the simple soul in him was indignant, and a wild desire of vengeance seized the man.

"Urban, dost thou know who Judas was?" asked Chilo, suddenly.

"I know, I know! — but he hanged himself!" exclaimed the laborer.

And in his voice there was a kind of sorrow that the traitor had meted out punishment to himself, and that Judas could not fall into his hands.

"But if he had not hanged himself," continued Chilo, "and if some Christian were to meet him on land or on sea, would it not be the duty of that Christian to take revenge for the torment, the blood, and the death of the Saviour?"

"Who is there who would not take revenge, father?"

"Peace be with thee, faithful servant of the Lamb! True, it is permitted to forgive wrongs done ourselves; but who has the right to forgive a wrong done to God? But as a serpent engenders a serpent, as malice breeds malice, and treason breeds treason, so from the poison of Judas another traitor has come; and as that one delivered to Jews and Roman soldiers the Saviour, so this man who lives among us intends to give Christ's sheep to the wolves; and if no one will anticipate the treason, if no one will crush the head of the serpent in time, destruction is waiting for us all, and with us will perish the honor of the Lamb."

The laborer looked at Chilo with immense alarm, as if not understanding what he had heard. But the Greek, covering his head with a corner of his mantle, began to repeat, with a voice coming as if from beneath the earth, —

"Woe to you, servants of the true God! woe to you, Christian men and Christian women!"

And again came silence, again were heard only the roar of the millstones, the deep song of the millers, and the sound of the river.

"Father," asked the laborer at last, "what kind of traitor is that?"

Chilo dropped his head. "What kind of traitor? A son of Judas, a son of his poison, a man who pretends to be a Christian, and goes to houses of prayer only to complain of the brotherhood to Cæsar, — declaring that they will not recognize Cæsar as a god; that they poison fountains, murder children, and wish to destroy the city, so that one stone may not remain on another. Behold! in a few days a command will be given to the pretorians to cast old men, women, and children into prison, and lead them to death, just as they led to death the slaves of Pedanius Secundus. All this has been done by that second Judas. But if no one punished the first Judas, if no one took vengeance on him, if no one defended Christ in the hour of torment, who will punish this one, who will destroy the serpent before Cæsar hears him, who will destroy him, who will defend from destruction our brothers in the faith of Christ?"

Urban, who had been sitting thus far on a stone, stood up on a sudden, and said, —

"I will, father."

Chilo rose also; he looked for a while on the face of the laborer, lighted up by the shining of the moon, then, stretching his arm, he put his hand slowly on his head.

"Go among Christians," said he, with solemnity; "go to the houses of prayer, and ask the brethren about Glaucus; and when they show him to thee, slay him at once in Christ's name!"

"About Glaucus?" repeated the laborer, as if wishing to fix that name in his memory.

"Dost thou know him?"

"No, I do not. There are thousands of Christians in Rome, and they are not all known to one another. But to-morrow, in Ostrianum, brethren and sisters will assemble in the night to the last soul, because a great apostle of Christ has come, who will teach them, and the brethren will point out to me Glaucus."

"In Ostrianum?" inquired Chilo. "But that is outside the city gates! The brethren and all the sisters, — at night? Outside the city gates, in Ostrianum?"

"Yes, father; that is our cemetery, between the Viæ Salaria and Nomentana. Is it not known to thee that the Great Apostle will teach there?"

"I have been two days from home, hence I did not receive his epistle; and I do not know where Ostrianum is, for I came here not long since from Corinth, where I govern a Christian community. But it is as thou sayest, — there thou wilt find Glaucus among the brethren, and thou wilt slay him on the way home to the city. For this all thy sins will be forgiven. And now peace be with thee — "

"Father — "

"I listen to thee, servant of the Lamb."

On the laborer's face perplexity was evident. Not long before he had killed a man, and perhaps two, but the teaching of Christ forbids killing. He had not killed them in his own defence, for even that is not permitted. He had not killed them, Christ preserve! for profit. The bishop himself had given him brethren to assist, but had not permitted him to kill; he had killed inadvertently, for God had punished him with too much strength. And now he was doing grievous penance. Others sing when the millstones are grinding; but he, hapless man, is thinking of his sin, of his offence against the Lamb. How much has he prayed already and wept? How much has he implored the Lamb? And he feels that he has not done penance enough yet! But now he has promised again to kill a traitor, — and done well! He is permitted to pardon only offences against himself; hence he will kill Glaucus, even before the eyes of all the brethren and sisters, in Ostrianum to-morrow. But let

Glaucus be condemned previously by the elders among the brethren, by the bishop, or by the Apostle. To kill is not a great thing; to kill a traitor is even as pleasant as to kill a bear or a wolf. But suppose Glaucus to perish innocently? How take on his conscience a new murder, a new sin, a new offence against the Lamb?

"There is no time for a trial, my son," said Chilo. "The traitor will hurry from Ostrianum straightway to Cæsar in Antium, or hide in the house of a certain patrician whom he is serving. I will give thee a sign; if thou show it after the death of Glaucus, the bishop and the Great Apostle will bless thy deed."

Saying this, he took out a small coin, and began to search for a knife at his belt; having found it, he scratched with the point on the sestertium the sign of the cross; this coin he gave to the laborer.

"Here is the sentence of Glaucus, and a sign for thee. If thou show this to the bishop after the death of Glaucus, he will forgive thee the killing which thou hast done without wishing it."

The laborer stretched out his hand involuntarily for the coin; but having the first murder too freshly in his memory just then, he experienced a feeling of terror.

"Father," said he with a voice almost of entreaty, "dost thou take this deed on thy conscience, and hast thou thyself heard Glaucus betraying his brethren?"

Chilo understood that he must give proofs, mention names, otherwise doubt might creep into the heart of the giant. All at once a happy thought flashed through his head.

"Listen, Urban," said he, "I dwell in Corinth, but I came from Kos; and here in Rome I instruct in the religion of Christ a certain serving maiden named Eunice. She serves as vestiplica in the house of a friend of Cæsar, a certain Petronius. In that house I have heard how Glaucus has undertaken to betray all the Christians; and, besides, he has promised another informer of Cæsar's, Vinicius, to find a certain maiden for him among the Christians."

Here he stopped and looked with amazement at the laborer, whose eyes blazed suddenly like the eyes of a wild beast, and his face took on an expression of mad rage and threat.

"What is the matter with thee?" asked Chilo, almost in fear.

"Nothing, father; to-morrow I will kill Glaucus."

The Greek was silent. After a while he took the arm of the laborer, turned him so that the light of the moon struck his face squarely, and examined him with care. It was evident that he was wavering in spirit whether to inquire further and bring everything out with clearness, or for that time to stop with what he had learned or surmised.

At last, however, his innate caution prevailed. He breathed deeply once and a second time; then, placing his hand on the laborer's head again, he asked, in an emphatic and solemn voice, —

"But in holy baptism the name Urban was given thee?"

"It was, father."

"Then peace be with thee, Urban!"

CHAPTER XVIII

PETRONIUS to VINICIUS:

"Thy case is a bad one, carissime. It is clear that Venus has disturbed thy mind, deprived thee of reason and memory, as well as the power to think of aught else except love. Read some time thy answer to my letter, and thou wilt see how indifferent thy mind is to all except Lygia; how exclusively it is occupied with her, how it returns to her always, and circles above her, as a falcon above chosen prey. By Pollux! find her quickly, or that of thee which fire has not turned into ashes will become an Egyptian sphinx, which, enamored, as 'tis said, of pale Isis, grew deaf and indifferent to all things, waiting only for night, so as to gaze with stony eyes at the loved one.

"Run disguised through the city in the evening, even honor Christian houses of prayer in thy philosopher's company. Whatever excites hope and kills time is praiseworthy. But for my friendship's sake do this one thing: Ursus, Lygia's slave, is a man of uncommon strength very likely; hire Croton, and go out three together; that will be safer and wiser. The Christians, since Pomponia and Lygia belong to them, are surely not such scoundrels as most people imagine. But when a lamb of their flock is in question they are no triflers, as they have shown by carrying away Lygia. When thou seest Lygia thou wilt not restrain thyself, I am sure, and wilt try to bear her away on the spot. But how wilt thou and Chilonides do it? Croton would take care of himself, even though ten like Ursus defended the maiden. Be not plundered by Chilo, but be not sparing of money on Croton. Of all counsels which I can give this is the best one.

"Here they have ceased to speak of the infant Augusta, or to say that she perished through witchcraft. Poppæa mentions her at times yet; but Cæsar's mind is stuffed with something else. Moreover, if it be true that the divine Augusta is in a changed state again, the memory of that child will be blown away without trace. We have been in Naples for some days, or rather in Baiæ. If thou art capable of any thought, echoes of our life must strike thy ear, for surely Rome talks of naught else. We went directly to Baiæ, where at first memories of the mother attacked us, and reproaches of conscience. But dost thou know to what Ahenobarbus has gone already? To this, that for him even the murder of his mother is a mere theme for verses, and a reason for buffoonish tragic scenes. Formerly he felt real reproaches only in so far as he was a coward; now, when he is convinced that the earth is under his feet as before, and that no god is taking vengeance, he feigns them only to move people by his fate. He springs up at night sometimes declaring that the Furies are hunting him; he rouses us, looks around, assumes the posture of an actor playing the rôle of Orestes, and the posture of a bad actor too; he declaims Greek verses, and looks to see if we are admiring him. We admire him apparently; and instead of saying to him, Go to sleep, thou buffoon! we bring ourselves also to the tone of tragedy, and protect the great artist from the Furies. By Castor! this news at least must have reached thee, that he has appeared in public at Naples. They drove in from the city and the surrounding towns all the Greek ruffians, who filled the arena with such a vile odor of sweat and garlic that I thank the gods that, instead of sitting in the first rows with the Augustians, I was behind the scenes with Ahenobarbus. And wilt thou believe it, he was afraid really! He took my hand and put it to his heart, which was beating with increased pulsation; his breath was short; and at the moment when he had to appear he grew as pale as a parchment, and his forehead was covered with drops of sweat. Still he saw that in every row of seats were pretorians, armed with clubs, to rouse enthusiasm if the need came. But there was no need. No herd of monkeys from the environs of Carthage could howl as did this rabble. I tell thee that the smell of garlic came to the stage; but Nero bowed, pressed his hand to his heart, sent kisses from his lips, and shed tears. Then he rushed in among us, who were waiting behind the scenes, like a drunken man, crying, 'What were the triumphs of Julius compared with this triumph of mine?' But the rabble was howling yet and applauding, knowing that it would applaud to itself favors, gifts, banquets, lottery tickets, and a fresh exhibition by the Imperial buffoon. I do not wonder that they applauded, for such a sight had not been seen till that evening. And every moment he repeated: 'See what the Greeks are! see what the Greeks are!' From that evening it has seemed to me that his hatred for Rome is increasing. Meanwhile special couriers were hurried to Rome announcing the triumph, and we expect thanks from the Senate one of these days. Immediately after Nero's first exhibition, a strange event happened here. The theatre fell in on a sudden, but just after the audience had gone. I was there, and did not see even one corpse taken from the ruins. Many, even among the Greeks, see in this event the anger of the gods, because the dignity of Cæsar was disgraced; he, on the contrary, finds in it favor of the gods, who have his song, and those who listen to it, under their evident protection. Hence there are offerings in all the temples, and great thanks. For Nero it is a great encouragement to make the journey to Achæa. A few days since he told me, however, that he had doubts as to what the Roman people might say; that they might revolt out of love for him, and fear touching the distribution of grain and touching the games, which might fail them in case of his prolonged absence.

"We are going, however, to Beneventum to look at the cobbler magnificence which Vatinius will exhibit, and thence to Greece, under the protection of the divine brothers of Helen. As to me, I have noted one thing, that when a man is among the mad he grows mad himself, and, what is more, finds a certain charm in mad pranks. Greece and the journey in a thousand ships; a kind of triumphal advance of Bacchus among nymphs and bacchantes crowned with myrtle, vine, and honeysuckle; there will be women in tiger skins harnessed to chariots; flowers, thyrses, garlands, shouts of 'Evoe!' music, poetry, and applauding Hellas. All this is well; but we cherish besides more daring projects. We wish to create a species of Oriental Imperium, — an empire of palm-trees, sunshine, poetry, and reality turned into a dream, reality turned into the delight of life only. We want to forget Rome; to fix the balancing point of the world somewhere between Greece, Asia, and Egypt; to live the life not of men but of gods; not to know what commonness is; to wander in golden galleys under the shadow of purple sails along the Archipelago; to be Apollo, Osiris, and Baal in one person; to be rosy with the dawn, golden with the sun, silver with the moon; to command, to sing, to dream. And wilt thou believe that I, who have still sound judgment to the value of a sestertium, and sense to the value of an as, let myself be borne away by these fantasies, and I do this for the reason that, if they are not possible, they are at least grandiose and uncommon? Such a fabulous empire would be a thing which, some time or other, after long ages, would seem a dream to mankind. Except when Venus takes the form of Lygia, or even of a slave Eunice, or when art beautifies it, life itself is empty, and many a time it has the face of a monkey. But Bronzebeard will not realize his plans, even for this cause, that in his fabulous kingdom of poetry and the Orient no place is given to treason, meanness, and death; and that in him with the poses of a poet sits a wretched comedian, a dull charioteer, and a frivolous tyrant. Meanwhile we are killing people whenever they displease us in any way. Poor Torquatus Silanus is now a shade; he opened his veins a few days since. Lecanius and Licinus will enter on the consulate with teror. Old Thrasea will not escape death, for he dares to be honest. Tigellinus is not able yet to frame a command for me to open my veins. I am still needed not only as *elegantiæ arbiter*, but as a man without whose counsel and taste the expedition to Achæa might fail. More than once, however, I think that sooner or later it must end in opening my veins; and knowest thou what the question will be then with me? — that Bronzebeard should not get my goblet, which thou knowest and admirest. Shouldst thou be near at the moment of my death, I will give it to thee; shouldst thou be at a distance, I will break it. But meanwhile I have before me yet Beneventum of the cobblers and Olympian Greece; I have Fate too, which, unknown and unforeseen, points out the road to every one.

"Be well, and engage Croton; otherwise they will snatch Lygia from thee a second time. When Chilonides ceases to be needful, send him to me wherever I may be. Perhaps I shall make him a second Vatinius, and consuls and senators may tremble before him yet, as they trembled before that knight Dratevka. It would be worth while to live to see such a spectacle. When thou hast found Lygia, let me know, so that I may offer for you both a pair of swans and a pair of doves in the round temple of Venus here. Once I saw Lygia in a dream, sitting on thy knee, seeking thy kisses. Try to make that dream prophetic. May there be no clouds on thy sky; or if there be, let them have the color and the odor of roses! Be in good health, and farewell!"

CHAPTER XIX

BARELY had Vinicius finished reading when Chilo pushed quietly into his library, unannounced by any one, for the servants had the order to admit him at every hour of the day or night.

"May the divine mother of thy magnanimous ancestor Æneas be full of favor to thee, as the son of Maia was kind to me."

"What dost thou mean?" asked Vinicius, springing from the table at which he was sitting.

Chilo raised his head and said, "Eureka!"

The young patrician was so excited that for a long time he could not utter a word.

"Hast thou seen her?" asked he, at last.

"I have seen Ursus, lord, and have spoken with him."

"Dost thou know where they are secreted?"

"No, lord. Another, through boastfulness, would have let the Lygian know that he divined who he was; another would have tried to extort from him the knowledge of where he lived, and would have received either a stroke of the fist, — after which all earthly affairs would have become indifferent to him, — or he would have roused the suspicion of the giant and caused this, — that a new hiding-place would be found for the girl, this very night perhaps. I did not act thus. It suffices me to know that Ursus works near the Emporium, for a miller named Demas, the same name as that borne by thy freedman; now any trusted slave of thine may go in the morning on his track, and discover their hiding place. I bring thee merely the assurance that, since Ursus is here, the divine Lygia also is in Rome, and a second news that she will be in Ostrianum to-night, almost certainly — "

"In Ostrianum? Where is that?" interrupted Vinicius, wishing evidently to run to the place indicated.

"An old hypogeum between the Viæ Salaria and Nomentana. That pontifex maximus of the Christians, of whom I spoke to thee, and whom they expected somewhat later, has come, and to-night he will teach and baptize in that cemetery. They hide their religion, for, though there are no edicts to prohibit it as yet, the people hate them, so they must be careful. Ursus himself told me that all, to the last soul, would be in Ostrianum to-night, for every one wishes to see and hear him who was the foremost disciple of Christ, and whom they call Apostle. Since among them women hear instruction as well as men, Pomponia alone perhaps of women will not be there; she could not explain to Aulus, a worshipper of the ancient gods, her absence from home at night. But Lygia, lord, who is under the care of Ursus and the Christian elders, will go undoubtedly with other women."

Vinicius, who had lived hitherto in a fever, and upheld as it were, by hope alone, now that his hope seemed fulfilled felt all at once the weakness that a man feels after a journey which has proved beyond his strength. Chilo noticed this, and resolved to make use of it.

"The gates are watched, it is true, by thy people, and the Christians must know that. But they do not need gates. The Tiber, too, does not need them; and though it is far from the river to those roads, it is worth while to walk one road more to see the 'Great Apostle.' Moreover they may have a thousand ways of going beyond the walls, and I know that they have. In Ostrianum thou wilt find Lygia; and even should she not be there, which I will not admit, Ursus will be there, for he has promised to kill Glaucus. He told me himself that he would be ¬here, and that he would kill him. Dost hear, noble tribune? Either thou wilt follow Ursus and learn where Lygia dwells, or thou wilt command thy people to seize him as a murderer, and, having him in thy hand, thou wilt make him confess where he has hidden Lygia. I have done my best! Another would have told thee that he had drunk ten cantars of the best wine with Ursus before he wormed the secret out of him; another would have told thee that he had lost a thousand sestertia to him in *scriptæ duodecim*, or that he had bought the intelligence for two thousand; I know that thou wouldst repay me doubly, but in spite of that, once in my life — I mean, as always in my life — I shall be honest, for I think, as the magnanimous Petronius says, that thy bounty exceeds all my hopes and expectations."

Vinicius, who was a soldier and accustomed not only to take counsel of himself in all cases, but to act, was overcome by a momentary weakness and said, —

"Thou wilt not deceive thyself as to my liberality, but first thou wilt go with me to Ostrianum."

"I, to Ostrianum?" inquired Chilo, who had not the least wish to go there. "I, noble tribune, promised thee to point out Lygia, but I did not promise to take her away for thee. Think, lord, what would happen to me if that Lygian bear, when he had torn Glaucus to pieces, should convince himself straightway that he had torn him not altogether justly? Would he not look on me (of course without reason) as the cause of the accomplished murder? Remember, lord, that the greater philosopher a man is, the more difficult it is for him to answer the foolish questions of common people; what should I answer him were he to ask me why I calumniated Glaucus? But if thou suspect that I deceive thee, I say, pay me only when I point out the house in which Lygia lives, show me to-day only a part of thy liberality, so that if thou, lord (which may all the gods ward from thee), succumb to some accident, I shall not be entirely without recompense. Thy heart could not endure that."

Vinicius went to a casket called "arca," standing on a marble pedestal, and, taking out a purse, threw it to Chilo.

"There are scrupula," said he; "when Lygia shall be in my house, thou wilt get the same full of aurei."

"Thou art Jove!" exclaimed Chilo.

But Vinicius frowned.

"Thou wilt receive food here," said he; "then thou mayest rest. Thou wilt not leave this house till evening, and when night falls thou wilt go with me to Ostrianum."

Fear and hesitation were reflected on the Greek's face for a time; but afterward he grew calm, and said, —

"Who can oppose thee, lord! Receive these my words as of good omen, just as our great hero received words like them in the temple of Ammon. As to me, these 'scruples'" (here he shook the purse) "have outweighed mine, not to mention thy society, which for me is delight and happiness."

Vinicius interrupted him impatiently, and asked for details of his conversation with Ursus. From them it seemed clear that either Lygia's hiding-place would be discovered that night, or he would be able to seize her on the road back from Ostrianum. At thought of this, Vinicius was borne away by wild delight. Now, when he felt clearly sure of finding Lygia, his anger against her, and his feeling of offence almost vanished. In return for that delight he forgave her every fault. He thought of her only as dear and desired, and he had the same impression as if she were returning after a long journey. He wished to summon his slaves and command them to deck the house with garlands. In that hour he had not a complaint against Ursus, even. He was ready to forgive all people everything. Chilo, for whom, in spite of his services, he had felt hitherto a certain repulsion, seemed to him for the first time an amusing and also an uncommon person. His house grew radiant; his eyes and his face became bright. He began again to feel youth and the pleasure of life. His former gloomy suffering had not given him yet a sufficient measure of how he loved Lygia. He understood this now for the first time, when he hoped to possess her. His desires woke in him, as the earth, warmed by the sun, wakes in spring; but his desires this time were less blind and wild, as it were, and more joyous and tender. He felt also within himself energy without bounds, and was convinced that should he but see Lygia with his own eyes, all the Christians on earth could not take her from him, nor could Cæsar himself.

Chilo, emboldened by the young tribune's delight, regained power of speech and began to give advice. According to him, it behooved Vinicius not to look on the affair as won, and to observe the greatest caution, without which all their work might end in nothing. He implored Vinicius not to carry off Lygia from Ostrianum. They ought to go there with hoods on their heads, with their faces hidden, and restrict themselves to looking at all who were present from some dark corner. When they saw Lygia, it would be safest to follow her at a distance, see what house she entered, surround it next morning at daybreak, and take her away in open daylight. Since she was a hostage and belonged specially to Cæsar, they might do that without fear of law. In the event of not finding her in Ostrianum they could follow Ursus, and the result would be the same. To go to the cemetery with a crowd of attendants was impracticable, — that might draw attention to them easily; then the Christians need only put out the lights, as they did when she was intercepted, and scatter in the darkness, or betake themselves to places known to them only. But Vinicius and he should arm, and, still better, take a couple of strong, trusty men to defend them in case of need.

Vinicius saw the perfect truth of what he said, and, recalling Petronius's counsel, commanded his slaves to bring Croton. Chilo, who knew every one in Rome, was set at rest notably when he heard the name of the famous athlete, whose superhuman strength in the arena he had wondered at more than once, and he declared that he would go to Ostrianum. The purse filled with great aurei seemed to him much easier of acquisition through the aid of Croton.

Hence he sat down in good spirits at the table to which, after a time, he was called by the chief of the atrium.

While eating, he told the slaves that he had obtained for their master a miraculous ointment. The worst horse, if rubbed on the hoofs with it, would leave every other far behind. A certain Christian had taught him how to prepare that ointment, for the Christian elders were far more skilled in enchantment and miracles than even the Thessalians, though Thessaly was renowned for its witches. The Christians had immense confidence in him — why, any one easily understands who knows what a fish means. While speaking he looked sharply at the eyes of the slaves, in the hope of discovering a Christian among them and informing Vinicius. But when the hope failed him, he fell to eating and drinking uncommon quantities, not sparing praises on the cook, and declaring that he would endeavor to buy him of Vinicius. His joyfulness was dimmed only by the thought that at night he must go to Ostrianum. He comforted himself, however, as he would go in disguise, in darkness, and in the company of two men, one of whom was so strong that he was the idol of Rome; the other a patrician, a man of high dignity in the army. "Even should they discover Vinicius," said he to himself, "they will not dare to raise a hand on him; as to me, they will be wise if they see the tip of my nose even."

He fell then to recalling his conversation with the laborer; and the recollection of that filled him again with delight. He had not the least doubt that that laborer was Ursus. He knew of the uncommon strength of the man, from the narratives of Vinicius, and those who had brought Lygia from Cæsar's palace. When he inquired of Euricius touching men of exceptional strength, there was nothing remarkable in this, that they pointed out Ursus. Then the confusion and rage of the laborer at mention of Vinicius and Lygia left him no doubt that those persons concerned him particularly; the laborer had mentioned also his penance for killing a man, — Ursus had killed Atacinus; finally, the appearance of the laborer answered perfectly to the account which Vinicius had given of the Lygian. The change of name was all that could provoke doubt, but Chilo knew that frequently Christians took new names at baptism.

"Should Ursus kill Glaucus," said Chilo to himself, "that will be better still; but should he not kill him, that will be a good sign, for it will show how difficult it is for Christians to murder. I described Glaucus as a real son of Judas, and a traitor to all Christians; I was so eloquent that a stone would have been moved, and would have promised to fall on the head of Glaucus. Still I hardly moved that Lygian bear to put his paw on him. He hesitated, was unwilling, spoke of his penance and compunction. Evidently murder is not common among them. Offences against one's self must be forgiven, and there is not much freedom in taking revenge for others. *Ergo,* stop! think, Chilo, what can threaten thee? Glaucus is not free to avenge himself on thee. If Ursus will not kill Glaucus for such a great crime as the betrayal of all Christians, so much the more will he not kill thee for the small offence of betraying one Christian. Moreover, when I have once pointed out to this ardent wood-pigeon the nest of that turtle-dove, I will wash my hands of everything, and transfer myself to Naples. The Christians talk, also, of a kind of washing of the hands; that is evidently a method by which, if a man has an affair with them, he may finish it decisively. What good people these Christians are, and how ill men speak of them! O God! such is the justice of this world. But I love that religion, since it does not permit killing; but if it does not permit killing, it certainly does not permit stealing, deceit, or false testimony; hence I will not say that it is easy. It teaches, evidently, not only to die honestly, as the Stoics teach, but to live honestly also. If ever I have property and a house, like this, and slaves in such numbers as Vinicius, perhaps I shall be a Christian as long as may be convenient. For a rich man can permit himself everything, even virtue. This is a religion for the rich; hence I do not understand how there are so many poor among its adherents. What good is it for them, and why do they let virtue tie their hands? I must think over this sometime. Meanwhile praise to thee, Hermes! for helping me discover this badger. But if thou hast done so for the two white yearling heifers with gilded horns, I know thee not. Be ashamed, O slayer of Argos! such a wise god as thou, and not foresee that thou wilt get nothing! I will offer thee my gratitude; and if thou prefer two beasts to it, thou art the third beast thyself, and in the best event thou shouldst be a shepherd, not a god. Have a care, too, lest I, as a philosopher, prove to men that thou art non-existent, and then all will cease to bring thee offerings. It is safer to be on good terms with philosophers."

Speaking thus to himself and to Hermes, he stretched on the sofa, put his mantle under his head, and was sleeping when the slave removed the dishes. He woke, — or rather they roused him, — only at the coming of Croton. He went to the atrium, then, and began to examine with pleasure the form of the trainer, an ex-gladiator, who seemed to fill the whole place with his immensity. Croton had stipulated as to the price of the trip, and was just speaking to Vinicius.

"By Hercules! it is well, lord," said he, "that thou hast sent to-day for me, since I shall start to-morrow for Beneventum, whither the noble Vatinius has summoned me to make a trial, in presence of Cæsar, of a certain Syphax, the most powerful negro that Africa has ever produced. Dost thou imagine, lord, how his spinal column will crack in my arms, or how besides I shall break his black jaw with my fist?"

"By Pollux! Croton, I am sure that thou wilt do that," answered Vinicius.

"And thou wilt act excellently," added Chilo. "Yes, to break his jaw, besides! That's a good idea and a deed which befits thee. But rub thy limbs with olive oil to-day, my Hercules, and gird thyself, for know this, you mayst meet a real Cacus. The man who is guarding that girl in whom the worthy Vinicius takes interest, has exceptional strength very likely."

Chilo spoke thus only to rouse Croton's ambition.

"That is true," said Vinicius; "I have not seen him, but they tell me that he can take a bull by the horns and drag him wherever he pleases."

"Oi!" exclaimed Chilo, who had not imagined that Ursus was so strong.

But Croton laughed, from contempt. "I undertake, worthy lord," said he, "to bear away with this hand whomever thou shalt point out to me, and with this other defend myself against seven such Lygians, and bring the maiden to thy dwelling though all the Christians in Rome were pursuing me like Calabrian wolves. If not, I will let myself be beaten with clubs in this impluvium."

"Do not permit that, lord," cried Chilo. "They will hurl stones at us, and what could his strength effect? Is it not better to take the girl from the house, — not expose thyself or her to destruction?"

"This is true, Croton," said Vinicius.

"I receive thy money, I do thy will! But remember, lord, that to-morrow I go to Beneventum."

"I have five hundred slaves in the city," answered Vinicius.

He gave them a sign to withdraw, went to the library himself, and sitting down wrote the following words to Petronius, —

"The Lygian has been found by Chilo. I go this evening with him and Croton to Ostrianum, and shall carry her off from the house to-night or to-morrow. May the gods pour down on thee everything favorable. Be well, O carissime! for joy will not let me write further."

Laying aside the reed then, he began to walk with quick step; for besides delight, which was overflowing his soul, he was tormented with fever. He said to himself that to-morrow Lygia would be in that house. He did not know how to act with her, but felt that if she would love him he would be her servant. He recalled Acte's assurance that he had been loved, and that moved him to the uttermost. Hence it would be merely a question of conquering a certain maiden modesty, and a question of certain ceremonies which Christian teaching evidently commanded. But if that were true, Lygia, when once in his house, would yield to persuasion of superior force; she would have to say to herself, "It has happened!" and then she would be amiable and loving.

But Chilo appeared and interrupted the course of these pleasant thoughts.

"Lord," said the Greek, "this is what has come to my head. Have not the Christians signs, 'passwords,' without which no one will be admitted to Ostrianum? I know that it is so in houses of prayer, and I have received those passwords from Euricius; permit me then to go to him, lord, to ask precisely, and receive the needful signs."

"Well, noble sage," answered Vinicius, gladly; "thou speakest as a man of forethought, and for that praise belongs to thee. Thou wilt go, then, to Euricius, or whithersoever it may please thee; but as security thou wilt leave on this table here that purse which thou hast received from me."

Chilo, who always parted with money unwillingly, squirmed; still he obeyed the command and went out. From the Carinæ to the Circus, near which was the little shop of Euricius, it was not very far; hence he returned considerably before evening.

"Here are the signs, lord. Without them they would not admit us. I have inquired carefully about the road. I told Euricius that I needed the signs only for my friends; that I would not go myself, since it was too far for my advanced age; that, moreover, I should see the Great Apostle myself to-morrow, and he would repeat to me the choicest parts of his sermon."

"How! Thou wilt not be there? Thou must go!" said Vinicius.

"I know that I must; but I will go well hooded, and I advise thee to go in like manner, or we may frighten the birds."

In fact they began soon to prepare, for darkness had come on the world. They put on Gallic cloaks with hoods, and took lanterns; Vinicius, besides, armed himself and his companions with short, curved knives; Chilo put on a wig, which he obtained on the way from the old man's shop, and they went out, hurrying so as to reach the distant Nomentan Gate before it was closed.

CHAPTER XX

THEY went through the Vicus Patricius, along the Viminal to the former Viminal gate, near the plain on which Diocletian afterward built splendid baths. They passed the remains of the wall of Servius Tullius, and through places more and more deserted they reached the Via Nomentana; there, turning to the left, towards the Via Salaria, they found themselves among hills full of sand-pits, and here and there they found graveyards.

Meanwhile it had grown dark completely, and since the moon had not risen yet, it would have been rather difficult for them to find the road were it not that the Christians themselves indicated it, as Chilo foresaw.

In fact, on the right, on the left, and in front, dark forms were evident, making their way carefully toward sandy hollows. Some of these people carried lanterns, — covering them, however, as far as possible with mantles; others, knowing the road better, went in the dark. The trained military eye of Vinicius distinguished, by their movements, younger men from old ones, who walked with canes, and from women, wrapped carefully in long mantles. The highway police, and villagers leaving the city, took those night wanderers, evidently, for laborers, going to sand-pits; or grave-diggers, who at times celebrated ceremonies of their own in the night-time. In proportion, however, as the young patrician and his attendants pushed forward, more and more lanterns gleamed, and the number of persons grew greater. Some of them sang songs in low voices, which to Vinicius seemed filled with sadness. At moments a separate word or a phrase of the song struck his ear, as, for instance, "Awake, thou that sleepest," or "Rise from the dead"; at times, again, the name of Christ was repeated by men and women.

But Vinicius turned slight attention to the words, for it came to his head that one of those dark forms might be Lygia. Some, passing near, said, "Peace be with thee!" or "Glory be to Christ!" but disquiet seized him, and his heart began to beat with more life, for it seemed to him that he heard Lygia's voice. Forms or movements like hers deceived him in the darkness every moment, and only when he had corrected mistakes made repeatedly did he begin to distrust his own eyes.

The way seemed long to him. He knew the neighborhood exactly, but could not fix places in the darkness. Every moment they came to some narrow passage, or piece of wall, or booths, which he did not remember as being in the vicinity of the city. Finally the edge of the moon appeared from behind a mass of clouds, and lighted the place better than dim lanterns. Something from afar began at last to glimmer like a fire, or the flame of a torch. Vinicius turned to Chilo.

"Is that Ostrianum?" asked he.

Chilo, on whom night, distance from the city, and those ghostlike forms made a deep impression, replied in a voice somewhat uncertain, —

"I know not, lord; I have never been in Ostrianum. But they might praise God in some spot nearer the city."

After a while, feeling the need of conversation, and of strengthening his courage, he added, —

"They come together like murderers; still they are not permitted to murder, unless that Lygian has deceived me shamefully."

Vinicius, who was thinking of Lygia, was astonished also by the caution and mysteriousness with which her co-religionists assembled to hear their highest priest; hence he said, —

"Like all religions, this has its adherents in the midst of us; but the Christians are a Jewish sect. Why do they assemble here, when in the Trans-Tiber there are temples to which the Jews take their offerings in daylight?"

"The Jews, lord, are their bitterest enemies. I have heard that, before the present Cæsar's time, it came to war, almost, between Jews and Christians. Those outbreaks forced Claudius Cæsar to expell all the Jews, but at present that edict is abolished. The Christians, however, hide themselves from Jews, and from the populace, who, as is known to thee, accuse them of crimes and hate them."

They walked on some time in silence, till Chilo, whose fear increased as he receded from the gates, said, —

"When returning from the shop of Euricius, I borrowed a wig from a barber, and have put two beans in my nostrils. They must not recognize me; but if they do, they will not kill me. They are not malignant! They are even very honest. I esteem and love them."

"Do not win them to thyself by premature praises," retorted Vinicius.

They went now into a narrow depression, closed, as it were, by two ditches on the side, over which an aqueduct was thrown in one place. The moon came out from behind clouds, and at the end of the depression they saw a wall, covered thickly with ivy, which looked silvery in the moonlight. That was Ostrianum.

Vinicius's heart began to beat now with more vigor. At the gate two quarrymen took the signs from them. In a moment Vinicius and his attendants were in a rather spacious place enclosed on all sides by a wall. Here and there were separate monuments, and in the centre was the entrance to the hypogeum itself, or crypt. In the lower part of the crypt, beneath the earth, were graves; before the entrance a fountain was playing. But it was evident that no very large number of persons could find room in the hypogeum; hence Vinicius divined without difficulty that the ceremony would take place outside, in the space where a very numerous throng was soon gathered.

As far as the eye could reach, lantern gleamed near lantern, but many of those who came had no light whatever. With the exception of a few uncovered heads, all were hooded, from fear of treason or the cold; and the young patrician thought with alarm that, should they remain thus, he would not be able to recognize Lygia in that crowd and in the dim light.

But all at once, near the crypt, some pitch torches were ignited and put into a little pile. There was more light. After a while the crowd began to sing a certain strange hymn, at first in a low voice, and then louder. Vinicius had never heard such a hymn before. The same yearning which had struck him in the hymns murmured by separate persons on the way to the cemetery, was heard now in that, but with far more distinctness and power; and at last it became as penetrating and immense as if together with the people, the whole cemetery, the hills, the pits, and the region about, had begun to yearn. It might seem, also, that there was in it a certain calling in the night, a certain humble prayer for rescue in wandering and darkness.

Eyes turned upward seemed to see some one far above, there on high, and outstretched hands seemed to implore him to descend. When the hymn ceased, there followed a moment as it were of suspense, — so impressive that Vinicius and his companions looked unwittingly toward the stars, as if in dread that something uncommon would happen, and that some one would really descend to them.

Vinicius had seen a multitude of temples of most various structure in Asia Minor, in Egypt, and in Rome itself; he had become acquainted with a multitude of religions, most varied in character, and had heard many hymns; but here, for the first time, he saw people calling on a divinity with hymns, — not to carry out a fixed ritual, but calling from the bottom of the heart, with the genuine yearning which children might feel for a father or a mother. One had to be blind not to see that those people not merely honored their God, but loved him with the whole soul. Vinicius had not seen the like, so far, in any land, during any ceremony, in any sanctuary; for in Rome and in Greece those who still rendered honor to the gods did so to gain aid for themselves or through fear; but it had not even entered any one's head to love those divinities.

Though his mind was occupied with Lygia, and his attention with seeking her in the crowd, he could not avoid seeing those uncommon and wonderful things which were happening around him. Meanwhile a few more torches were thrown on the fire, which filled the cemetery with ruddy light and darkened the gleam of the lanterns. That moment an old man, wearing a hooded mantle but with a bare head, issued from the hypogeum. This man mounted a stone which lay near the fire.

The crowd swayed before him. Voices near Vinicius whispered, "Peter! Peter!" Some knelt, others extended their hands toward him. There followed a silence so deep that one heard every charred particle that dropped from the torches, the distant rattle of wheels on the Via Nomentana, and the sound of wind through the few pines which grew close to the cemetery.

Chilo bent toward Vinicius and whispered, —

"This is he! The foremost disciple of Christ — a fisherman!"

The old man raised his hand, and with the sign of the cross blessed those present, who fell on their knees simultaneously. Vinicius and his attendants, not wishing to betray themselves, followed the example of others. The young man could not seize his impressions immediately, for it seemed to him that the form which he saw there before him was both simple and uncommon, and, what was more, the uncommonness flowed just from the simplicity. The old man had no mitre on his head, no garland of oak-leaves on his temples, no palm in his hand, no golden tablet on his breast, he wore no white robe embroidered with stars; in a word, he bore no insignia of the kind worn by priests — Oriental, Egyptian, or Greek — or by Roman flamens. And Vinicius was struck by that same difference again which he felt when listening to the Christian hymns; for that "fisherman," too, seemed to him, not like some high priest skilled in ceremonial, but as it were a witness, simple, aged, and immensely venerable, who had journeyed from afar to relate a truth which he had seen, which he had touched, which he believed as he believed in existence, and he had come to love this truth precisely because he believed it. There was in his face, therefore, such a power of convincing as truth itself has. And Vinicius, who had been a sceptic, who did not wish to yield to the charm of the old man, yielded, however, to a certain feverish curiosity to know what would flow from the lips of that companion of the mysterious "Christus," and what that teaching was of which Lygia and Pomponia Græcina were followers.

Meanwhile Peter began to speak, and he spoke from the beginning like a father instructing his children and teaching them how to live. He enjoined on them to renounce excess and luxury, to love poverty, purity of life, and truth, to endure wrongs and persecutions patiently, to obey the government and those placed above them, to guard against treason, deceit, and calumny; finally, to give an example in their own society to each other, and even to pagans.

Vinicius, for whom good was only that which could bring back to him Lygia, and evil everything which stood as a barrier between them, was touched and angered by certain of those counsels. It seemed to him that by enjoining purity and a struggle with desires the old man dared, not only to condemn his love, but to rouse Lygia against him and confirm her in opposition. He understood that if she were in the assembly listening to those words, and if she took them to heart, she must think of him as an enemy of that teaching and an outcast.

Anger seized him at this thought. "What have I heard that is new?" thought he. "Is this the new religion? Every one knows this, every one has heard it. The Cynics enjoined poverty and a restriction of necessities; Socrates enjoined virtue as an old thing and a good one; the first Stoic one meets, even such a one as Seneca, who has five hundred tables of lemon-wood, praises moderation, enjoins truth, patience in adversity, endurance in misfortune, — and all that is like stale, mouse-eaten grain; but people do not wish to eat it because it smells of age."

And besides anger, he had a feeling of disappointment, for he expected the discovery of unknown, magic secrets of some kind, and thought that at least he would hear a rhetor astonishing by his eloquence; meanwhile he heard only words which were immensely simple, devoid of every ornament He was astonished only by the mute attention with which the crowd listened

But the old man spoke on to those people sunk in listening, — told them to be kind, poor, peaceful, just, and pure; not that they might have peace during life, but that they might live eternally with Christ after death, in such joy and such glory, in such health and delight, as no one on earth had attained at any time. And here Vinicius, though predisposed unfavorably, could not but notice that still there was a difference between the teaching of the old man and that of the Cynics, Stoics, and other philosophers; for they enjoin good and virtue as reasonable, and the only thing practical in life, while he promised immortality, and that not some kind of hapless immortality beneath the earth, in wretchednes, emptiness, and want, but a magnificent life, equal to that of the gods almost. He spoke meanwhile of it as of a thing perfectly certain; hence, in view of such a faith, virtue acquired a value simply measureless, and the misfortunes of this life became incomparably trivial. To suffer temporally for inexhaustible happiness is a thing absolutely different from suffering because such is the order of nature. But the old man said further that virtue and truth should be loved for themselves, since the highest eternal good and the virtue existing before ages is God; whoso therefore loves them loves God, and by that same becomes a cherished child of His.

Vinicius did not understand this well, but he knew previously, from words spoken by Pomponia Græcina to Petronius, that, according to the belief of Christians, God was one and almighty; when, therefore, he heard now again that He is all good and all just, he thought involuntarily that, in presence of such a demiurge, Jupiter, Saturn, Apollo, Juno, Vesta, and Venus would seem like some vain and noisy rabble, in which all were interfering at once, and each on his or her own account.

But the greatest astonishment seized him when the old man declared that God was universal love also; hence he who loves man fulfils God's supreme command. But it is not enough to love men of one's own nation, for the God-man shed his blood for all, and found among pagans such elect of his as Cornelius the Centurion; it is not enough either to love those who do good to us, for Christ forgave the Jews who delivered him to death, and the Roman soldiers who nailed him to the cross; we should not only forgive but love those who injure us, and return them good for evil; it is not enough to love the good, we must love the wicked also, since by love alone is it possible to expel from them evil.

Chilo at these words thought to himself that his work had gone for nothing, that never in the world would Ursus dare to kill Glaucus, either that night or any other night. But he comforted himself at once by another inference from the teaching of the old man; namely, that neither would Glaucus kill him, though he should discover and recognize him.

Vinicius did not think now that there was nothing new in the words of the old man, but with amazement he asked himself: "What kind of God is this, what kind of religion is this, and what kind of people are these?" All that he had just heard could not find place in his head simply. For him all was an unheard-of medley of ideas. He felt that if he wished, for example, to follow that teaching, he would have to place on a burning pile all his thoughts, habits, and character, his whole nature up to that moment, burn them into ashes, and then fill himself with a life altogether different, and an entirely new soul. To him the science or the religion which commanded a Roman to love Parthians, Syrians, Greeks, Egyptians, Gauls, and Britons, to forgive enemies, to return them good for evil, and to love them, seemed madness. At the same time he had a feeling that in that madness itself there was something mightier than all philosophies so far. He thought that because of its madness it was impracticable, but because of its impracticability it was divine. In his soul he rejected it; but he felt that he was parting as if from a field full of spikenard, a kind of intoxicating incense; when a man has once breathed of this he must, as in the land of the lotus-eaters, forget all things else ever after, and yearn for it only.

It seemed to him that there was nothing real in that religion, but that reality in presence of it was so paltry that it deserved not the time for thought. Expanses of some kind, of which hitherto he had not had a suspicion, surrounded him, — certain immensities, certain clouds. That cemetery began to produce on him the impression of a meeting-place for madmen, but also of a place mysterious and awful, in which, as on a mystic bed, something was in progress of birth the like of which had not been in the world so far. He brought before his mind all that, which from the first moment of his speech, the old man had said touching life, truth, love, God; and his thoughts were dazed from the brightness, as the eyes are blinded from lightning flashes which follow each other unceasingly.

As is usual with people for whom life has been turned into one single passion, Vinicius thought of all this through the medium of his love for Lygia; and in the light of those flashes he saw one thing distinctly, that if Lygia was in the cemetery, if she confessed that religion, obeyed and felt it, she never could and never would be his mistress.

For the first time, then, since he had made her acquaintance at Aulus's, Vinicius felt that though now he had found her he would not get her. Nothing similar had come to his head so far, and he could not explain it to himself then, for that was not so much an express understanding as a dim feeling of irreparable loss and misfortune. There rose in him an alarm, which was turned soon into a storm of anger against the Christians in general, and against the old man in particular. That fisherman, whom at the first cast of the eye he considered a peasant, now filled him with fear almost, and seemed some mysterious power deciding his fate inexorably and therefore tragically.

The quarrymen again, unobserved, added torches to the fire; the wind ceased to sound in the pines; the flame rose evenly, with a slender point toward the stars, which were twinkling in a clear sky. Having mentioned the death of Christ, the old man talked now of Him only. All held the breath in their breasts, and a silence set in which was deeper than the preceding one, so that it was possible almost to hear the beating of hearts. That man had seen! and he narrated as one in whose memory every moment had been fixed in such a way that were he to close his eyes he would see yet. He told, therefore, how on their return from the Cross he and John had sat two days and nights in the supper-chamber, neither sleeping nor eating, in suffering, in sorrow, in doubt, in alarm, holding their heads in their hands, and thinking that He had died. Oh, how grievous, how grievous that was! The third day had dawned and the light whitened the walls, but he and John were sitting in the chamber, without hope or comfort. How desire for sleep tortured them (for they had spent the night before the Passion without sleep)! They roused themselves then, and began again to lament. But barely had the sun risen when Mary of Magdala, panting, her hair dishevelled, rushed in with the cry, "They have taken away the Lord!" When they heard this, he and John sprang up and ran toward the sepulchre. But John, being younger, arrived first; he saw the place empty, and dared not enter. Only when there were three at the entrance did he, the person now speaking to them, enter, and find on the stone a shirt with a winding sheet; but the body he found not.

Fear fell on them then, because they thought that the priests had borne away Christ, and both returned home in greater grief still. Other disciples came later and raised a lament, now in company, so that the Lord of Hosts might hear them more easily, and now separately and in turn. The spirit died within them, for they had hoped that the Master would redeem Israel, and it was now the third day since his death; hence they did not understand why the Father had deserted the Son, and they preferred not to look at the daylight, but to die, so grievous was the burden.

The remembrance of those terrible moments pressed even then from the eyes of the old man two tears, which were visible by the light of the fire, coursing down his gray beard. His hairless and aged head was shaking, and the voice died in his breast.

"That man is speaking the truth and is weeping over it," said Vinicius in his soul. Sorrow seized by the throat the simple-hearted listeners also. They had heard more than once of Christ's sufferings, and it was known to them that joy succeeded sorrow; but since an apostle who had seen it told this, they wrung their hands under the impression, and sobbed or beat their breasts.

But they calmed themselves gradually, for the wish to hear more gained the mastery. The old man closed his eyes, as if to see distant things more distinctly in his soul, and continued, —

"When the disciples had lamented in this way, Mary of Magdala rushed in a second time, crying that she had seen the Lord. Unable to recognize him, she thought him the gardener: but He said, 'Mary!' She cried 'Rabboni!' and fell at his feet. He commanded her to go to the disciples, and vanished. But they, the disciples, did not believe her; and when she wept for joy, some upbraided her, some thought that sorrow had disturbed her mind, for she said, too, that she had seen angels at the grave, but they, running thither a second time, saw the grave empty. Later in the evening appeared Cleopas, who had come with another from Emmaus, and they returned quickly, saying: 'The Lord has indeed risen!' And they discussed with closed doors, out of fear of the Jews. Meanwhile He stood among them, though the doors had made no sound, and when they feared, He said, 'Peace be with you!'

·   ·   ·   ·   ·   ·   ·   ·   ·   ·   ·   ·

"And I saw Him, as did all, and He was like light, and like the happiness of our hearts, for we believed that He had risen from the dead, and that the seas will dry and the mountains turn to dust, but His glory will not pass.

.   .   .   .

"After eight days Thomas Didymus put his finger in the Lord's wounds and touched His side; Thomas fell at His feet then, and cried, 'My Lord and my God!' 'Because thou hast seen me thou hast believed; blessed are they who have not seen and have believed!' said the Lord. And we heard those words, and our eyes looked at Him, for He was among us."

Vinicius listened, and something wonderful took place in him. He forgot for a moment where he was; he began to lose the feeling of reality, of measure, of judgment. He stood in the presence of two impossibilities. He could not believe what the old man said; and he felt that it would be necessary either to be blind or renounce one's own reason, to admit that that man who said "I saw" was lying. There was something in his movements, in his tears, in his whole figure, and in the details of the events which he narrated, which made every suspicion impossible. To Vinicius it seemed at moments that he was dreaming. But round about he saw the silent throng; the odor of lanterns came to his nostrils; at a distance the torches were blazing; and before him on the stone stood an aged man near the grave, with a head trembling somewhat, who, while bearing witness, repeated, "I saw!"

And he narrated to them everything up to the Ascension into heaven. At moments he rested, for he spoke very circumstantially; but it could be felt that each minute detail had fixed itself in his memory, as a thing is fixed in a stone into which it has been engraved. Those who listened to him were seized by ecstasy. They threw back their hoods to hear him better, and not lose a word of those which for them were priceless. It seemed to them that some superhuman power had borne them to Galilee; that they were walking with the disciples through those groves and on those waters; that the cemetery was turned into the lake of Tiberius; that on the bank, in the mist of morning, stood Christ, as he stood when John, looking from the boat, said, "It is the Lord," and Peter cast himself in to swim, so as to fall the more quickly at the beloved feet. In the faces of those present were evident enthusiasm beyond bounds, oblivion of life, happiness, and love immeasurable. It was clear that during Peter's long narrative some of them had visions. When he began to tell how, at the moment of Ascension, the clouds closed in under the feet of the Saviour, covered Him, and hid Him from the eyes of the Apostles, all heads were raised toward the sky unconsciously, and a moment followed as it were of expectation, as if those people hoped to see Him or as if they hoped that He would descend again from the fields of heaven, and see how the old Apostle was feeding the sheep confided to him, and bless both the flock and him.

Rome did not exist for those people, nor did the man Cæsar; there were no temples of pagan gods; there was only Christ, who filled the land, the sea, the heavens, and the world.

At the houses scattered here and there along the Via Nomentana, the cocks began to crow, announcing midnight. At that moment Chilo pulled the corner of Vinicius's mantle and whispered, —

"Lord, I see Urban over there, not far from the old man, and with him is a maiden."

Vinicius shook himself, as if out of a dream, and, turning in the direction indicated by the Greek, he saw Lygia.

CHAPTER XXI

EVERY drop of blood quivered in the young patrician at sight of her. He forgot the crowd, the old man, his own astonishment at the incomprehensible things which he had heard, — he saw only her. At last, after all his efforts, after long days of alarm, trouble, and suffering, he had found her! For the first time he realized that joy might rush at the heart, like a wild beast, and squeeze it till breath was lost. He, who had supposed hitherto that on "Fortuna" had been imposed a kind of duty to accomplish all his wishes, hardly believed his own eyes now and his own happiness. Were it not for that disbelief, his passionate nature might have urged him to some unconsidered step; but he wished to convince himself first that that was not the continuation of those miracles with which his head was filled, and that he was not dreaming. But there was no doubt, — he saw Lygia, and an interval of barely a few steps divided them. She stood in perfect light, so that he could rejoice in the sight of her as much as he liked. The hood had fallen from her head and dishevelled her hair; her mouth was open slightly, her eyes raised toward the Apostle, her face fixed in listening and delighted. She was dressed in a dark woollen mantle, like a daughter of the people, but never had Vinicius seen her more beautiful; and notwithstanding all the disorder which had risen in him, he was struck by the nobility of that wonderful patrician head in distinction to the dress, almost that of a slave. Love flew over him like a flame, immense, mixed with a marvellous feeling of yearning, homage, honor, and desire. He felt the delight which the sight of her caused him; he drank of her as of life-giving water after long thirst. Standing near the gigantic Lygian, she seemed to him smaller than before, almost a child; he noticed, too, that she had grown more slender. Her complexion had become almost transparent; she made on him the impression of a flower, and a spirit. But all the more did he desire to possess that woman, so different from all women whom he had seen or possessed in Rome or the Orient. He felt that for her he would have given them all, and with them Rome and the world in addition.

He would have lost himself in gazing, and forgotten himself altogether, had it not been for Chilo, who pulled the corner of his mantle, out of fear that he might do something to expose them to danger. Meanwhile the Christians began to pray and sing. After a while Maranatha thundered forth, and then the Great Apostle baptized with water from the fountain those whom the presbyters presented as ready for baptism. It seemed to Vinicius that that night would never end. He wished now to follow Lygia as soon as possible, and seize her on the road or at her house.

At last some began to leave the cemetery, and Chilo whispered, —

"Let us go out before the gate, lord, we have not removed our hoods, and people look at us."

Such was the case, for during the discourse of the Apostle all had cast aside their hoods so as to hear better, and they had not followed the general example. Chilo's advice seemed wise, therefore. Standing before the gate, they could look at all who passed; Ursus it was easy to recognize by his form and size.

"Let us follow them," said Chilo; "we shall see to what house they go. To-morrow, or rather to-day, thou wilt surround the entrances with slaves and take her."

"No!" said Vinicius.

"What dost thou wish to do, lord?"

"We will follow her to the house and take her now, if thou wilt undertake that task, Croton?"

"I will," replied Croton, "and I will give myself to thee as a slave if I do not break the back of that bison who is guarding her."

But Chilo fell to dissuading and entreating them by all the gods not to do so. Croton was taken only for defence against attack in case they were recognized, not to carry off the girl. To take her when there were only two of them was to expose themselves to death, and, what was worse, they might let her out of their hands, and then she would hide in another place or leave Rome. And what could they do? Why not act with certainty? Why expose themselves to destruction and the whole undertaking to failure?

Though Vinicius restrained himself with the greatest effort from seizing Lygia in his arms at once, right there in the cemetery, he felt that the Greek was right, and would have lent ear, perhaps, to his counsels, had it not been for Croton, to whom reward was the question.

"Lord, command that old goat to be silent," said he, "or let me drop my fist on his head. Once in Buxentum, whither Lucius Saturnius took me to a play, seven drunken gladiators fell on me at an inn, and none of them escaped with sound ribs. I do not say to take the girl now from the crowd, for they might throw stones before our feet, but once she is at home I will seize her, carry her away, and take her whithersoever thou shalt indicate."

Vinicius was pleased to hear those words, and answered, —

"Thus let it be, by Hercules! To-morrow we may not find her at home; if we surprise them they will remove the girl surely."

"This Lygian seems tremendously strong!" groaned Chilo.

"No one will ask thee to hold his hands," answered Croton.

But they had to wait long yet, and the cocks had begun to crow before dawn when they saw Ursus coming through the gate, and with him Lygia. They were accompanied by a number of other persons. It seemed to Chilo that he recognized among them the Great Apostle; next to him walked another old man, considerably lower in stature, two women who were not young, and a boy, who lighted the way with a lantern. After that handful followed a crowd, about two hundred in number; Vinicius, Chilo, and Croton walked with these people.

"Yes, lord," said Chilo, "thy maiden is under powerful protection. That is the Great Apostle with her, for see how passing people kneel to him."

People did in fact kneel before him, but Vinicius did not look at them. He did not lose Lygia from his eyes for a moment; he thought only of bearing her away and, accustomed as he had been in wars to stratagems of all sorts, he arranged in his head the whole plan of seizure with soldierly precision. He felt that the step on which he had decided was bold, but he knew well that bold attacks give success generally.

The way was long; hence at moments he thought too of the gulf which that wonderful religion had dug between him and Lygia. Now he understood everything that had happened in the past, and why it had happened. He was sufficiently penetrating for that. Lygia he had not known hitherto. He had seen in her a maiden wonderful beyond others, a maiden toward whom his feelings were inflamed: he knew now that her religion made her different from other women, and his hope that feeling, desire, wealth, luxury, would attract her he knew now to be a vain illusion. Finally he understood this, which he and Petronius had not understood, that the new religion ingrafted into the soul something unknown to that world in which he lived, and that Lygia, even if she loved him, would not sacrifice any of her Christian truths for his sake, and that, if pleasure existed for her, it was a pleasure different altogether from that which he and Petronius and Cæsar's court and all Rome were pursuing. Every other woman whom he knew might become his mistress, but that Christian would become only his victim. And when he thought of this, he felt anger and burning pain, for he felt that his anger was powerless. To carry off Lygia seemed to him possible; he was almost sure that he could take her, but he was equally sure that, in view of her religion, he himself with his bravery was nothing, that his power was nothing, and that through it he could effect nothing. That Roman military tribune, convinced that the power of the sword and the fist which had conquered the world, would command it forever, saw for the first time in life that beyond that power there might be something else; hence he asked himself with amazement what it was. And he could not answer distinctly; through his head flew merely pictures of the cemetery, the assembled crowd, and Lygia, listening with her whole soul to the words of the old man, as he narrated the passion, death, and resurrection of the God-man, who had redeemed the world, and promised it happiness on the other shore of the Styx.

When he thought of this, chaos rose in his head. But he was brought out of this chaos by Chilo, who fell to lamenting his own fate. He had agreed to find Lygia. He had sought for her in peril of his life, and he had pointed her out. But what more do they want? Had he offered to carry the maiden away? Who could ask anything like this of a maimed man deprived of two fingers, an old man, devoted to meditation, to science, and virtue? What would happen were a lord of such dignity as Vinicius to meet some mishap while bearing the maiden away? It is true that the gods are bound to watch over their chosen ones, — but have not such things happened more than once, as if the gods were playing games instead of watching what was passing in the world? Fortune is blindfold, as is well known, and does not see even in daylight; what must the case be at night? Let something happen, — let that Lygian bear hurl a millstone at the noble Vinicius, or a keg of wine, or, still worse, water, — who will give assurance that instead of a reward blame will not fall on the hapless Chilo? He, the poor sage, has attached himself to the noble Vinicius as Aristotle to Alexander of Macedon. If the noble lord should give him at least that purse which he had thrust into his girdle before leaving home, there would be something with which to invoke aid in case of need, or to influence the Christians. Oh, why not listen to the counsels of an old man, counsels dictated by experience and prudence?"

Vinicius, hearing this, took the purse from his belt, and threw it to the fingers of Chilo.

"Thou hast it; be silent!"

The Greek felt that it was unusually heavy, and gained confidence.

"My whole hope is in this," said he, "that Hercules or Theseus performed deeds still more arduous; what is my personal, nearest friend, Croton, if not Hercules? Thee, worthy lord, I will not call a demigod, for thou art a full god, and in future thou wilt not forget a poor, faithful servant, whose needs it will be necessary to provide for from time to time, for once he is sunk in books, he thinks of nothing else; some few stadia of garden land and a little house, even with the smallest portico, for coolness in summer, would befit such a donor. Meanwhile I shall admire thy heroic deeds from afar, and invoke Jove to befriend thee, and if need be I will make such an outcry that half Rome will be roused to thy assistance. What a wretched, rough road! The olive oil is burned out in the lantern; and if Croton, who is as noble as he is strong, would bear me to the gate in his arms, he would learn, to begin with, whether he will carry the maiden easily; second, he would act like Æneas, and win all the good gods to such a degree that touching the result of the enterprise I should be thoroughly satisfied."

"I should rather carry a sheep which died of mange a month ago," answered the gladiator; "but give that purse, bestowed by the worthy tribune, and I will bear thee to the gate."

"Mayst thou knock the great toe from thy foot," replied the Greek; "what profit hast thou from the teachings of that worthy old man, who described poverty and charity as the two foremost virtues? Has he not commanded thee expressly to love me? Never shall I make thee, I see, even a poor Christian; it would be easier for the sun to pierce the walls of the Mamertine prison than for truth to penetrate thy skull of a hippopotamus."

"Never fear!" said Croton, who with the strength of a beast had no human feeling. "I shall not be a Christian! I have no wish to lose my bread."

"But if thou knew even the rudiments of philosophy, thou wouldst know that gold is vanity."

"Come to me with thy philosophy. I will give thee one blow of my head in the stomach; we shall see then who wins."

"An ox might have said the same to Aristotle," retorted Chilo.

It was growing gray in the world. The dawn covered with pale light the outlines of the walls. The trees along the wayside, the buildings, and the gravestones scattered here and there began to issue from the shade. The road was no longer quite empty. Marketmen were moving toward the gates, leading asses and mules laden with vegetables; here and there moved creaking carts in which game was conveyed. On the road and along both sides of it was a light mist at the very earth, which promised good weather. People at some distance seemed like apparitions in that mist. Vinicius stared at the slender form of Lygia, which became more silvery as the light increased.

"Lord," said Chilo, "I should offend thee were I to foresee the end of thy bounty, but now, when thou hast paid me, I may not be suspected of speaking for my own interest only. I advise thee once more to go home for slaves and a litter, when thou hast learned in what house the divine Lygia dwells; listen not to that elephant trunk, Croton, who undertakes to carry off the maiden only to squeeze thy purse as if it were a bag of curds."

"I have a blow of the fist to be struck between the shoulders, which means that thou wilt perish," said Croton.

"I have a cask of Cephalonian wine, which means that I shall be well," answered Chilo.

Vinicius made no answer, for he approached the gate, at which a wonderful sight struck his eyes. Two soldiers knelt when the Apostle was passing; Peter placed his hand on their iron helmets for a moment, and then made the sign of the cross on them. It had never occurred to the patrician before that there could be Christians in the army; with astonishment he thought that as fire in a burning city takes in more and more houses, so to all appearances that doctrine embraces new souls every day, and extends itself over all human understandings. This struck him also with reference to Lygia, for he was convinced that, had she wished to flee from the city, there would be guards willing to facilitate her flight. He thanked the gods then that this had not happened.

After they had passed vacant places beyond the wall, the Christians began to scatter. There was need, therefore, to follow Lygia more from a distance, and more carefully, so as not to rouse attention. Chilo fell to complaining of wounds, of pains in his legs, and dropped more and more to the rear. Vinicius did not oppose this, judging that the cowardly and incompetent Greek would not be needed. He would even have permitted him to depart, had he wished; but the worthy sage was detained by circumspection. Curiosity pressed him evidently, since he continued behind, and at moments even approached with his previous counsels; he thought too that the old man accompanying the Apostle might be Glaucus, were it not for his rather low stature.

They walked a good while before reaching the Trans-Tiber, and the sun was near rising when the group surrounding Lygia dispersed. The Apostle, an old woman, and a boy went up the river; the old man of lower stature, Ursus, and Lygia entered a narrow vicus, and, advancing still about a hundred yards, went into a house in which were two shops,—one for the sale of olives, the other for poultry.

Chilo, who walked about fifty yards behind Vinicius and Croton, halted all at once, as if fixed to the earth, and, squeezing up to the wall, began to hiss at them to turn.

They did so, for they needed to take counsel.

"Go, Chilo," said Vinicius, "and see if this house fronts on another street."

Chilo, though he had complained of wounds in his feet, sprang away as quickly as if he had had the wings of Mercury on his ankles, and returned in a moment.

"No," said he, "there is but one entrance."

Then, putting his hands together, he said, "I implore thee, lord, by Jupiter, Apollo, Vesta, Cybele, Isis, Osiris, Mithra Baal, and all the gods of the Orient and the Occident to drop this plan. Listen to me—"

But he stopped on a sudden, for he saw that Vinicius's face was pale from emotion, and that his eyes were glittering like the eyes of a wolf. It was enough to look at him to understand that nothing in the world would restrain him from the undertaking. Croton began to draw air into his herculean breast, and to sway his undeveloped skull from side to side as bears do when confined in a cage, but on his face not the least fear was evident.

"I will go in first," said he.

"Thou wilt follow me," said Vinicius, in commanding tones.

And after a while both vanished in the dark entrance.

Chilo sprang to the corner of the nearest alley and watched from behind it, waiting for what would happen.

CHAPTER XXII

Only inside the entrance did Vinicius comprehend the whole difficulty of the undertaking. The house was large, of several stories, one of the kind of which thousands were built in Rome, in view of profit from rent; hence, as a rule, they were built so hurriedly and badly that scarcely a year passed in which numbers of them did not fall on the heads of tenants. Real hives, too high and too narrow, full of chambers and little dens, in which poor people fixed themselves too numerously. In a city where many streets had no names, those houses had no numbers; the owners committed the collection of rent to slaves, who, not obliged by the city government to give names of occupants, were ignorant themselves of them frequently. To find some one by inquiry in such a house was often very difficult, especially when there was no gate-keeper.

Vinicius and Croton came to a narrow, corridor-like passage walled in on four sides, forming a kind of common atrium for the whole house, with a fountain in the middle whose stream fell into a stone basin fixed in the ground. At all the walls were internal stairways, some of stone, some of wood, leading to galleries from which there were entrances to lodgings. There were lodgings on the ground, also; some provided with wooden doors, others separated from the yard by woollen screens only. These, for the greater part, were worn, rent, or patched.

The hour was early, and there was not a living soul in the yard. It was evident that all were asleep in the house except those who had returned from Ostrianum.

"What shall we do, lord?" asked Croton, halting.

"Let us wait here; some one may appear," replied Vinicius. "We should not be seen in the yard."

At this moment, he thought Chilo's counsel practical. If there were some tens of slaves present, it would be easy to occupy the gate, which seemed the only exit, search all the lodgings simultaneously, and thus come to Lygia's; otherwise Christians, who surely were not lacking in that house, might give notice that people were seeking her. In view of this, there was risk in inquiring of strangers. Vinicius stopped to think whether it would not be better to go for his slaves. Just then, from behind a screen hiding a remoter lodging, came a man with a sieve in his hand, and approached the fountain.

At the first glance the young tribune recognized Ursus.

"That is the Lygian!" whispered Vinicius.

"Am I to break his bones now?"

"Wait awhile!"

Ursus did not notice the two men, as they were in the shadow of the entrance, and he began quietly to sink in water vegetables which filled the sieve. It was evident that, after a whole night spent in the cemetery, he intended to prepare a meal. After a while the washing was finished; he took the wet sieve and disappeared behind the screen. Croton and Vinicius followed him, thinking that they would come directly to Lygia's lodgings. Their astonishment was great when they saw that the screen divided from the court, not lodgings, but another dark corridor, at the end of which was a little garden containing a few cypresses, some myrtle bushes, and a small house fixed to the windowless stone wall of another stone building.

Both understood at once that this was for them a favoring circumstance. In the courtyard all the tenants might assemble; the seclusion of the little house facilitated the enterprise. They would set aside defenders, or rather Ursus, quickly, and would reach the street just as quickly with the captured Lygia; and there they would help themselves. It was likely that no one would attack them; if attacked, they would say that a hostage was fleeing from Cæsar. Vinicius would declare himself then to the guards, and summon their assistance.

Ursus was almost entering the little house, when the sound of steps attracted his attention; he halted, and, seeing two persons, put his sieve on the balustrade and turned to them.

"What do ye want here?" asked he.

"Thee!" said Vinicius.

Then, turning to Croton, he said in a low, hurried voice:

"Kill!"

Croton rushed at him like a tiger, and in one moment, before the Lygian was able to think or to recognize his enemies, Croton had caught him in his arms of steel.

Vinicius was too confident in the man's preternatural strength to wait for the end of the struggle. He passed the two, sprang to the door of the little house, pushed it open and found himself in a room a trifle dark, lighted, however, by a fire burning in the chimney. A gleam of this fire fell on Lygia's face directly. A second person, sitting at the fire, was that old man who had accompanied the young girl and Ursus on the road from Ostrianum.

Vinicius rushed in so suddenly that before Lygia could recognize him he had seized her by the waist, and, raising her, rushed toward the door again. The old man barred the way, it is true; but pressing the girl with one arm to his breast, Vinicius pushed him aside with the other, which was free. The hood fell from his head, and at sight of that face, which was known to her and which at that moment was terrible, the blood grew cold in Lygia from fright, and the voice died in her throat. She wished to summon aid, but had not the power. Equally vain was her wish to grasp the door, to resist. Her fingers slipped along the stone, and she would have fainted but for the terrible picture which struck her eyes when Vinicius rushed into the garden.

Ursus was holding in his arms some man doubled back completely, with hanging head and mouth filled with blood. When he saw them, he struck the head once more with his fist, and in the twinkle of an eye sprang toward Vinicius like a raging wild beast.

"Death!" thought the young patrician.

Then he heard, as through a dream, the scream of Lygia, "Kill not!" He felt that something, as it were a thunderbolt, opened the arms with which he held Lygia; then the earth turned round with him, and the light of day died in his eyes.

.   .   .   .

Chilo, hidden behind the angle of the corner house, was waiting for what would happen, since curiosity was struggling with fear in him. He thought that if they succeeded in carrying off Lygia, he would fare well near Vinicius. He feared Urban no longer, for he also felt certain that Croton would kill him. And he calculated that in case a gathering should begin on the streets, which so far were empty, — if Christians, or people of any kind, should offer resistance, — he, Chilo, would speak to them as one representing authority, as an executor of Cæsar's will, and if need came, call the guards to aid the young patrician against the street rabble — thus winning to himself fresh favor. In his soul he judged yet that the young tribune's method was unwise; considering, however, Croton's terrible strength, he admitted that it might succeed, and thought, "If it go hard with him, Vinicius can carry the girl, and Croton clear the way." Delay grew wearisome, however; the silence of the entrance which he watched alarmed him.

"If they do not hit upon her hiding-place, and make an uproar, they will frighten her."

But this thought was not disagreeable; for Chilo understood that in that event he would be necessary again to Vinicius, and could squeeze afresh a goodly number of sestertia from the tribune.

"Whatever they do," said he to himself, "they will work for me, though no one divines that. O gods! O gods! only permit me — "

And he stopped suddenly, for it seemed to him that some one was bending forward through the entrance; then, squeezing up to the wall, he began to look, holding the breath in his breast.

And he had not deceived himself, for a head thrust itself half out of the entrance and looked around. After a while, however, it vanished.

"That is Vinicius, or Croton," thought Chilo; "but if they have taken the girl, why does she not scream, and why are they looking out to the street? They must meet people anyhow, for before they reach the Carinæ there will be movement in the city — What is that? By the immortal gods!"

And suddenly the remnant of his hair stood on end.

In the door appeared Ursus, with the body of Croton hanging on his arm, and looking around once more, he began to run, bearing it along the empty street toward the river.

Chilo made himself as flat against the wall as a bit of mud.

"I am lost if he sees me!" thought he.

But Ursus ran past the corner quickly, and disappeared beyond the neighboring house. Chilo, without further waiting, his teeth chattering from terror, ran along the cross street with a speed which even in a young man might have roused admiration.

"If he sees me from a distance when he is returning, he will catch and kill me," said he to himself. "Save me, Zeus; save me, Apollo; save me, Hermes; save me, O God of the Christians! I will leave Rome, I will return to Mesembria, but save me from the hands of that demon!"

And that Lygian who had killed Croton seemed to him at that moment some superhuman being. While running, he thought that he might be some god who had taken the form of a barbarian. At that moment he believed in all the gods of the world, and in all myths, at which he jeered usually. It flew through his head, too, that it might be the God of the Christians who had killed Croton; and his hair stood on end again at the thought that he was in conflict with such a power.

Only when he had run through a number of alleys, and saw some workmen coming toward him from a distance, was he calmed somewhat. Breath failed in his breast; so he sat on the threshold of a house and began to wipe, with a corner of his mantle, his sweat-covered forehead.

"I am old, and need calm," said he.

The people coming toward him turned into some little side street, and again the place round about was empty. The city was sleeping yet. In the morning movement began earlier in the wealthier parts of the city, where the slaves of rich houses were forced to rise before daylight; in portions inhabited by a free population, supported at the cost of the State, hence unoccupied, they woke rather late, especially in winter. Chilo, after he had sat some time on the threshold, felt a piercing cold; so he rose, and, convincing himself that he had not lost the purse received from Vinicius, turned toward the river with a step now much slower.

"I may see Croton's body somewhere," said he to himself. "O gods! that Lygian, if he is a man, might make millions of sestertia in the course of one year; for if he choked Croton, like a whelp, who can resist him? They would give for his every appearance in the arena as much gold as he himself weighs. He guards that maiden better than Cerberus does Hades. But may Hades swallow him, for all that! I will have nothing to do with him. He is too bony. But where shall I begin in this case? A dreadful thing has happened. If he has broken the bones of such a man as Croton, beyond a doubt the soul of Vinicius is puling above that cursed house now, awaiting his burial. By Castor! but he is a patrician, a friend of Cæsar, a relative of Petronius, a man known in all Rome, a military tribune. His death cannot pass without punishment. Suppose I were to go to the pretorian camp, or the guards of the city, for instance?"

Here he stopped and began to think, but said after a while, —

"Woe is me! Who took him to that house if not I? His freedmen and his slaves know that I came to his house, and some of them know with what object. What will happen if they suspect me of having pointed out to him purposely the house in which his death met him? Though it appear afterward, in the court, that I did not wish his death, they will say that I was the cause of it. Besides, he is a patrician; hence in no event can I avoid punishment. But if I leave Rome in silence, and go far away somewhere, I shall place myself under still greater suspicion."

It was bad in every case. The only question was to choose the less evil. Rome was immense; still Chilo felt that it might become too small for him. Any other man might go directly to the prefect of the city guards and tell what had happened, and, though some suspicion might fall on him, await the issue calmly. But Chilo's whole past was of such character that every closer acquaintance with the prefect of the city or the prefect of the guard must cause him very serious trouble, and confirm also every suspicion which might enter the heads of officials.

On the other hand, to flee would be to confirm Petronius in the opinion that Vinicius had been betrayed and murdered through conspiracy. Petronius was a powerful man, who could command the police of the whole Empire, and who beyond doubt would try to find the guilty parties even at the ends of the earth. Still, Chilo thought to go straight to him, and tell what had happened. Yes; that was the best plan. Petronius was calm, and Chilo might be sure of this, at least, that he would hear him to the end. Petronius, who knew the affair from its inception, would believe in Chilo's innocence more easily than would the prefects.

But to go to him, it was needful to know with certainty what had happened to Vinicius. Chilo did not know that. He had seen, it is true, the Lygian stealing with Croton's body to the river, but nothing more. Vinicius might be killed; but he might be wounded or detained. Now it occurred to Chilo for the first time, that surely the Christians would not dare to kill a man so powerful, — a friend of Cæsar, and a high military official, — for that kind of act might draw on them a general persecution. It was more likely that they had detained him by superior force, to give Lygia means to hide herself a second time.

This thought filled Chilo with hope.

"If that Lygian dragon has not torn him to pieces at the first attack, he is alive, and if he is alive he himself will testify that I have not betrayed him; and then not only does nothing threaten me, but — O Hermes, count again on two heifers — a fresh field is opening. I can inform one of the freedmen where to seek his lord; and whether he goes to the prefect or not is his affair, the only point being that I should not go. Also, I can go to Petronius, and count on a reward. I have found Lygia; now I shall find Vinicius, and then again Lygia. It is needful to know first whether Vinicius is dead or living."

Here it occurred to him that he might go in the night to the baker Demas and inquire about Ursus. But he rejected that thought immediately. He preferred to have nothing to do with Ursus. He might suppose, justly, that if Ursus had not killed Glaucus he had been warned, evidently, by the Christian elder to whom he had confessed his design, — warned that the affair was an unclean one, to which some traitor had persuaded him. In every case, at the mere recollection of Ursus, a shiver ran through Chilo's whole body. But he thought that in the evening he would send Euricius for news to that house in which the thing had happened. Meanwhile he needed refreshment, a bath, and rest. The sleepless night, the journey to Ostrianum, the flight from the Trans-Tiber, had wearied him exceedingly.

One thing gave him permanent comfort: he had on his person two purses, — that which Vinicius had given him at home, and that which he had thrown him on the way from the cemetery. In view of this happy circumstance, and of all the excitement through which he had passed, he resolved to eat abundantly, and drink better wine than he drank usually.

When the hour for opening the wine-shop came at last, he did so in such a marked measure that he forgot the bath; he wished to sleep, above all, and drowsiness overcame his strength so that he returned with tottering step to his dwelling in the Subura, where a slave woman, purchased with money obtained from Vinicius, was waiting for him.

When he had entered a sleeping-room, as dark as the den of a fox, he threw himself on the bed, and fell asleep in one instant. He woke only in the evening, or rather he was roused by the slave woman, who called him to rise, for some one was inquiring, and wished to see him on urgent business.

The watchful Chilo came to himself in one moment, threw on his hooded mantle hastily, and, commanding the slave woman to stand aside, looked out cautiously.

And he was benumbed! for he saw before the door of the sleeping-room the gigantic form of Ursus.

At that sight he felt his feet and head grow icy-cold, the heart ceased to beat in his bosom, and shivers were creeping along his back. For a time he was unable to speak; then with chattering teeth he said, or rather groaned, —

"Syra — I am not at home — I don't know that — good man — "

"I told him that thou wert at home, but asleep, lord," answered the girl; "he asked to rouse thee."

"O gods! I will command that thou — "

But Ursus, as if impatient of delay, approached the door of the sleeping-room, and, bending, thrust in his head.

"O Chilo Chilonides!" said he.

"*Pax tecum! pax! pax!*" answered Chilo. "O best of Christians! Yes, I am Chilo; but this is a mistake, — I do not know thee!"

"Chilo Chilonides," repeated Ursus, "thy lord, Vinicius, summons thee to go with me to him."

CHAPTER XXIII

A PIERCING pain roused Vinicius. At the first moment he could not understand where he was, nor what was happening. He felt a roaring in his head, and his eyes were covered as if with mist. Gradually, however, his consciousness returned, and at last he beheld through that mist three persons bending over him. Two he recognized: one was Ursus, the other the old man whom he had thrust aside when carrying off Lygia. The third, an utter stranger, was holding his left arm, and feeling it from the elbow upward as far as the shoulder-blade. This caused so terrible a pain that Vinicius, thinking it a kind of revenge which they were taking, said through his set teeth, "Kill me!" But they paid no apparent heed to his words, just as though they heard them not, or considered them the usual groans of suffering. Ursus, with his anxious and also threatening face of a barbarian, held a bundle of white cloth torn in long strips. The old man spoke to the person who was pressing the arm of Vinicius, —

"Glaucus, art thou certain that the wound in the head is not mortal?"

"Yes, worthy Crispus," answered Glaucus. "While serving in the fleet as a slave, and afterward while living at Naples, I cured many wounds, and with the pay which came to me from that occupation I freed myself and my relatives at last. The wound in the head is slight. When this one [here he pointed to Ursus with his head] took the girl from the young man, he pushed him against the wall; the young man while falling put out his arm, evidently to save himself; he broke and disjointed it, but by so doing saved his head and his life."

"Thou hast had more than one of the brotherhood in thy care," added Crispus, "and hast the repute of a skilful physician; therefore I sent Ursus to bring thee."

"Ursus, who on the road confessed that yesterday he was ready to kill me!"

"He confessed his intention earlier to me than to thee; but I, who know thee and thy love for Christ, explained to him that the traitor is not thou, but the unknown, who tried to persuade him to murder."

"That was an evil spirit, but I took him for an angel," said Ursus, with a sigh.

"Some other time thou wilt tell me, but now we must think of this wounded man." Thus speaking, he began to set the arm. Though Crispus sprinkled water on his face, Vinicius fainted repeatedly from suffering; that was, however, a fortunate circumstance, since he did not feel the pain of putting his arm into joint, nor of setting it. Glaucus fixed the limb between two strips of wood, which he bound quickly and firmly, so as to keep the arm motionless. When the operation was over, Vinicius recovered consciousness again and saw

Lygia above him. She stood there at the bed holding a brass basin with water, in which from time to time Glaucus dipped a sponge and moistened the head of his patient.

Vinicius gazed and could not believe his eyes. What he saw seemed a dream, or the pleasant vision brought by fever, and only after a long time could he whisper, —

"Lygia!"

The basin trembled in her hand at that sound, but she turned on him eyes full of sadness.

"Peace be with thee!" answered she, in a low voice.

She stood there with extended arms, her face full of pity and sorrow. But he gazed, as if to fill his sight with her, so that after his lids were closed the picture might remain under them. He looked at her face, paler and smaller than it had been, at the tresses of dark hair, at the poor dress of a laboring woman; he looked so intently that her snowy forehead began to grow rose-colored under the influence of his look. And first he thought that he would love her always; and second, that that paleness of hers and that poverty were his work, — that it was he who had driven her from a house where she was loved, and surrounded with plenty and comfort, and thrust her into that squalid room, and clothed her in that poor robe of dark wool.

He would have arrayed her in the costliest brocade, in all the jewels of the earth; hence astonishment, alarm, and pity seized him, and sorrow so great that he would have fallen at her feet had he been able to move.

"Lygia," said he, "thou didst not permit my death."

"May God return health to thee," she answered, with sweetness.

For Vinicius, who had a feeling both of those wrongs which he had inflicted on her formerly, and those which he had wished to inflict on her recently, there was a real balsam in Lygia's words. He forgot at the moment that through her mouth Christian teaching might speak; he felt only that a beloved woman was speaking, and that in her answer there was a special tenderness, a goodness simply preterhuman, which shook him to the depth of his soul. As just before he had grown weak from pain, so now he grew weak from emotion. A certain faintness came on him, at once immense and agreeable. He felt as if falling into some abyss, but he felt that to fall was pleasant, and that he was happy. He thought at that moment of weakness that a divinity was standing above him.

Meanwhile Glaucus had finished washing the wound in his head, and had applied a healing ointment. Ursus took the brass basin from Lygia's hands; she brought a cup of water and wine which stood ready on the table, and put it to the wounded man's lips. Vinicius drank eagerly, and felt great relief. After the operation the pain had almost passed; the wound and contusion began to grow firm; perfect consciousness returned to him.

"Give me another drink," said he.

Lygia took the empty cup to the next room; meanwhile Crispus, after a few words with Glaucus, approached the bed saying, —

"God has not permitted thee, Vinicius, to accomplish an evil deed, and has preserved thee in life so that thou shouldst come to thy mind. He, before whom man is but dust, delivered thee defenceless into our hands; but Christ, in whom we believe, commanded us to love even our enemies. Therefore we have dressed thy wounds, and, as Lygia has said, we will implore God to restore thy health, but we cannot watch over thee longer. Be in peace, then, and think whether it beseems thee to continue thy pursuit of Lygia. Thou hast deprived her of guardians, and us of a roof, though we return thee good for evil."

"Do ye wish to leave me?" inquired Vinicius.

"We wish to leave this house, in which prosecution by the prefect of the city may reach us. Thy companion was killed; thou, who art powerful among thy own people, art wounded. This did not happen through our fault, but the anger of the law might fall on us."

"Have no fear of prosecution," replied Vinicius; "I will protect you."

Crispus did not like to tell him that with them it was not only a question of the prefect and the police, but of him; they wished to secure Lygia from his further pursuit.

"Lord," said he, "thy right arm is well. Here are tablets and a stilus; write to thy servants to bring a litter this evening and bear thee to thy own house, where thou wilt have more comfort than in our poverty. We dwell here with a poor widow, who will return soon with her son, and this youth will take thy letter; as to us, we must all find another hiding-place."

Vinicius grew pale, for he understood that they wished to separate him from Lygia, and that if he lost her now he might never see her in life again. He knew indeed that things of great import had come between him and her, in virtue of which, if he wished to possess her, he must seek some new methods which he had not had time yet to think over. He understood too that whatever he might tell these people, though he should swear that he would return Lygia to Pomponia Græcina, they would not believe him, and were justified in refusing belief. Moreover, he might have done that before. Instead of hunting for Lygia, he might have gone to Pomponia and sworn to her that he renounced pursuit, and in that case Pomponia herself would have found Lygia and brought her home. No; he felt that such promises would not restrain them, and no solemn oath would be received, the more since, not being a Christian, he could swear only by the immortal gods, in whom he did not himself believe greatly, and whom they considered evil spirits.

He desired desperately to influence Lygia and her guardians in some way, but for that there was need of time. For him it was all-important to see her, to look at her for a few days even. As every fragment of a plank or an oar seems salvation to a drowning man, so to him it seemed that during those few days he might say something to bring him nearer to her, that he might think out something, that something favorable might happen. Hence he collected his thoughts and said, —

"Listen to me, Christians. Yesterday I was with you in Ostrianum, and I heard your teaching; but though I did not know it, your deeds have convinced me that you are honest and good people. Tell that widow who occupies this house to stay in it, stay in it yourselves, and let me stay. Let this man [here he turned to Glaucus], who is a physician, or at least understands the care of wounds, tell whether it is possible to carry me from here to-day. I am sick, I have a broken arm, which must remain immovable for a few days even; therefore I declare to you that I will not leave this house unless you bear me hence by force!"

Here he stopped, for breath failed in his breast, and Crispus said, —

"We will use no force against thee, lord; we will only take away our own heads."

At this the young man, unused to resistance, frowned and said, —

"Permit me to recover breath"; and after a time he began again to speak, —

"Of Croton, whom Ursus killed, no one will inquire. He had to go to-day to Beneventum, whither he was summoned by Vatinius, therefore all will think that he has gone there. When I entered this house in company with Croton, no one saw us except a Greek who was with us in Ostrianum. I will indicate to you his lodgings; bring that man to me. On him I will enjoin silence; he is paid by me. I will send a letter to my own house stating that I too went to Beneventum. If the Greek has informed the prefect already, I will declare that I myself killed Croton, and that it was he who broke my arm. I will do this, by my father's shade and by my mother's! Ye may remain in safety here; not a hair will fall from the head of one of you. Bring hither, and bring in haste, the Greek whose name is Chilo Chilonides!"

"Then Glaucus will remain with thee," said Crispus, "and the widow will nurse thee."

"Consider, old man, what I say," said Vinicius, who frowned still more. "I owe thee gratitude, and thou seemest good and honest; but thou dost not tell me what thou hast in the bottom of thy soul. Thou art afraid lest I summon my slaves and command them to take Lygia. Is this true?"

"It is," said Crispus, with sternness.

"Then remember this, I shall speak before all to Chilo, and write a letter home that I have gone to Beneventum. I shall have no messengers hereafter but you. Remember this, and do not irritate me longer."

Here he was indignant, and his face was contorted with anger. Afterward he began to speak excitedly, —

"Hast thou thought that I would deny that I wish to stay here to see her? A fool would have divined that, even had I denied it. But I will not try to take her by force any longer. I will tell thee more: if she will not stay here, I will tear the bandages with this sound hand from my arm, will take neither food nor drink; let my death fall on thee and thy brethren. Why hast thou nursed me? Why hast thou not commanded to kill me?"

He grew pale from weakness and anger.

Lygia, who had heard all from the other room and who was certain that Vinicius would do what he promised, was terrified. She would not have him die for anything. Wounded and defenceless, he roused in her compassion, not fear. Living from the time of her flight among people in continual religious enthusiasm, thinking only of sacrifices, offerings, and boundless charity, she had grown so excited herself through that new inspiration, that for her it took the place of house, family, lost happiness, and made her one of those Christian maidens who, later on, changed the former soul of the world. Vinicius had been too important in her fate, had been thrust too much on her, to let her forget him. She had thought of him whole days, and more than once had begged God for the moment in which, following the inspiration of religion, she might return good for his evil, mercy for his persecution, break him, win him to Christ, save him. And now it seemed to her that precisely that moment had come, and that her prayers had been heard.

She approached Crispus therefore with a face as if inspired, and addressed him as though some other voice spoke through her, —

"Let him stay among us, Crispus, and we will stay with him till Christ gives him health."

The old presbyter, accustomed to seek in all things the inspiration of God, beholding her exaltation, thought at once that perhaps a higher power was speaking through her, and, fearing in his heart, he bent his gray head, saying, —

"Let it be as thou sayest."

On Vinicius, who the whole time had not taken his eyes from her, this ready obedience of Crispus produced a wonderful and pervading impression. It seemed to him that among the Christians Lygia was a kind of sibyl or priestess whom they surrounded with obedience and honor; and he yielded himself also to that honor. To the love which he felt was joined now a certain awe, in presence of which love itself became something almost insolent. He could not familiarize himself, however, with the thought that their relations had changed: that now not she was dependent on his will, but he on hers; that he was lying there sick and broken; that he had ceased to be an attacking, a conquering force; that he was like a defenceless child in her care. For his proud and commanding nature such relations with any other person would have been humiliating; now, however, not only did he not feel humiliated, but he was thankful to her as to his sovereign. In him those were feelings unheard-of, feelings which he could not have entertained the day before, and which would have amazed him even on that day had he been able to analyze them clearly. But he did not inquire at the moment why it was so, just as if the position had been perfectly natural; he merely felt happy because he remained there.

And he wished to thank her with gratefulness, and still with a kind of feeling unknown to him in such a degree that he knew not what to call it, for it was simply submission. His previous excitement had so exhausted him that he could not speak, and he thanked her only with his eyes, which were gleaming from delight because he remained near her, and would be able to see her — to-morrow, next day, perhaps a long time. That delight was diminished only by the dread that he might lose what he had gained. So great was this dread that when Lygia gave him water a second time, and the wish seized him to take her hand, he feared to do so. He feared! — he, that Vinicius who at Cæsar's feast had kissed her lips in spite of her! he, that Vinicius who after her flight had promised himself to drag her by the hair to the cubiculum, or give command to flog her!

CHAPTER XXIV

But he began also to fear that some outside force might disturb his delight. Chilo might give notice of his disappearance to the prefect of the city, or to his freedmen at home; and in such an event an invasion of the house by the city guards was likely. Through his head flew the thought, it is true, that in that event he might give command to seize Lygia and shut her up in his house, but he felt that he ought not to do so, and he was not capable of acting thus. He was tyrannical, insolent, and corrupt enough, if need be he was inexorable, but he was not Tigellinus or Nero. Military life had left in him a certain feeling of justice, and religion, and a conscience to understand that such a deed would be monstrously mean. He would have been capable, perhaps, of committing such a deed during an access of anger and while in possession of his strength, but at that moment he was filled with tenderness, and was sick. The only question for Vinicius at that time was that no one should stand between him and Lygia.

He noticed, too, with astonishment, that from the moment when Lygia had taken his part, neither she herself nor Crispus asked from him any assurances, just as if they felt confident that, in case of need, some superhuman power would defend them. The young tribune, in whose head the distinction between things possible and impossible had grown involved and faint since the discourse of the Apostle in Ostrianum, was also not too far from supposing that that might take place. But considering things more soberly, he remembered what he had said of the Greek, and asked again that Chilo be brought to him.

Crispus agreed, and they decided to send Ursus. Vinicius, who in recent days, before his visit to Ostrianum, had sent slaves frequently to Chilo, though without result, indicated his lodgings accurately to the Lygian; then writing a few words on the tablet, he said, turning to Crispus, —

"I give a tablet, for this man is suspicious and cunning. Frequently when summoned by me, he gave directions to answer my people that he was not at home; he did so always when he had no good news for me, and feared my anger."

"If I find him, I will bring him, willing or unwilling," said Ursus. Then, taking his mantle, he went out hurriedly.

To find any one in Rome was not easy, even with the most accurate directions; but in those cases the instinct of a hunter aided Ursus, and also his great knowledge of the city. After a certain time, therefore, he found himself at Chilo's lodgings.

He did not recognize Chilo, however. He had seen him but once in his life before, and moreover, in the night. Besides, that lofty and confident old man who had persuaded him to murder Glaucus was so unlike the Greek, bent double from terror, that no one could suppose the two to be one person. Chilo, noticing that Ursus looked at him as a perfect stranger, recovered from his first fear. The sight of the tablet, with the writing of Vinicius, calmed him still more. At least the suspicion that he would take him into an ambush purposely did not trouble him. He thought, besides, that the Christians had not killed Vinicius, evidently because they had not dared to raise hands on so noted a person.

"And then Vinicius will protect me in case of need," thought he; "of course he does not send to deliver me to death."

Summoning some courage, therefore, he said: "My good man, has not my friend the noble Vinicius sent a litter? My feet are swollen; I cannot walk so far."

"He has not," answered Ursus; "we shall go on foot."

"But if I refuse?"

"Do not, for thou wilt have to go."

"And I will go, but of my own will. No one could force me, for I am a free man, and a friend of the prefect of the city. As a sage, I have also means to overcome others, and I know how to turn people into trees and wild beasts. But I will go, I will go! I will only put on a mantle somewhat warmer, and a hood, lest the slaves of that quarter might recognize me; they would stop me every moment to kiss my hands."

He put on a new mantle then, and let down a broad Gallic hood, lest Ursus might recognize his features on coming into clearer light.

"Where wilt thou take me?" asked he on the road.

"To the Trans-Tiber."

"I am not long in Rome, and I have never been there, but there too, of course, live men who love virtue."

But Ursus, who was a simple man, and had heard Vinicius say that the Greek had been with him in Ostrianum, and had seen him with Croton enter the house in which Lygia lived, stopped for a moment and said, —

"Speak no untruth, old man, for to-day thou wert with Vinicius in Ostrianum and under our gate."

"Ah!" said Chilo, "then is your house in the Trans-Tiber? I have not been long in Rome, and know not how the different parts are named. That is true, friend; I was under the gate, and implored Vinicius in the name of virtue not to enter. I was in Ostrianum, and dost thou know why? I am working for a certain time over the conversion of Vinicius, and wished him to hear the chief of the Apostles. May the light penetrate his soul and thine! But thou art a Christian, and wishest truth to overcome falsehood."

"That is true," answered Ursus, with humility.

Courage returned to Chilo completely.

"Vinicius is a powerful lord," said he, "and a friend of Cæsar. He listens often yet to the whisperings of the evil spirit; but if even a hair should fall from his head, Cæsar would take vengeance on all the Christians."

"A higher power is protecting us."

"Surely, surely! But what do ye intend to do with Vinicius?" inquired Chilo, with fresh alarm.

"I know not. Christ commands mercy."

"Thou hast answered excellently. Think of this always, or thou wilt fry in hell like a sausage in a frying-pan."

Ursus sighed, and Chilo thought that he could always do what he liked with that man, who was terrible at the moment of his first outburst. So, wishing to know what happened at the seizing of Lygia, he asked further, in the voice of a stern judge, —

"How did ye treat Croton? Speak, and do not prevaricate."

Ursus sighed a second time. "Vinicius will tell thee."

"That means that thou didst stab him with a knife, or kill him with a club."

"I was without arms."

The Greek could not resist amazement at the superhuman strength of the barbarian.

"May Pluto — that is to say, may Christ pardon thee!"

They went on for some time in silence; then Chilo said:

"I will not betray thee; but have a care of the watches."

"I fear Christ, not the watches."

"And that is proper. There is no more grievous crime than murder. I will pray for thee; but I know not if even my prayer can be effective, unless thou make a vow never to touch any one in life with a finger."

"As it is, I have not killed purposely," answered Ursus.

But Chilo, who desired to secure himself in every case, did not cease to condemn murder, and urge Ursus to make the vow. He inquired also about Vinicius; but the Lygian answered his inquiries unwillingly, repeating that from Vinicius himself he would hear what he needed. Speaking in this way, they passed at last the long road which separated the lodgings of the Greek from the Trans-Tiber, and found themselves before the house. Chilo's heart began to beat again unquietly. From dread it seemed to him that Ursus was beginning to look at him with a kind of greedy expression.

"It is small consolation to me," said he to himself, "if he kills me unwillingly. I prefer in every case that paralysis should strike him, and with him all the Lygians, — which do thou effect, O Zeus, if thou art able."

Thus meditating, he wrapped himself more closely in his Gallic mantle, repeating that he feared the cold. Finally, when they had passed the entrance and the first court, and found themselves in the corridor leading to the garden of the little house, he halted suddenly and said, —

"Let me draw breath, or I shall not be able to speak with Vinicius and give him saving advice."

He halted; for though he said to himself that no danger threatened, still his legs trembled under him at the thought that he was among those mysterious people whom he had seen in Ostrianum.

Meanwhile a hymn came to their ears from the little house.

"What is that?" inquired Chilo.

"Thou sayest that thou art a Christian, and knowest not that among us it is the custom after every meal to glorify our Saviour with singing," answered Ursus. "Miriam and her son must have returned, and perhaps the Apostle is with them, for he visits the widow and Crispus every day."

"Conduct me directly to Vinicius."

"Vinicius is in the same room with all, for that is the only large one; the others are very small chambers, to which we go only to sleep. Come in; thou wilt rest there."

They entered. It was rather dark in the room; the evening was cloudy and cold, the flames of a few candles did not dispel the darkness altogether. Vinicius divined rather than recognized Chilo in the hooded man. Chilo, seeing the bed in the corner of the room, and on it Vinicius, moved toward him directly, not looking at the others, as if with the conviction that it would be safest near him.

"Oh, lord, why didst thou not listen to my counsels?" exclaimed he, putting his hands together.

"Silence!" said Vinicius, "and listen!"

Here he looked sharply into Chilo's eyes, and spoke slowly with emphasis, as if wishing the Greek to understand every word of his as a command, and to keep it forever in memory.

"Croton threw himself on me to kill and rob me, dost understand? I killed him then, and these people dressed the wounds which I received in the struggle."

Chilo understood in a moment that if Vinicius spoke in this way it must be in virtue of some agreement with the Christians, and in that case he wished people to believe him. He saw this, too, from his face; hence in one moment, without showing doubt or astonishment, he raised his eyes and exclaimed, —

"That was a faith-breaking ruffian! But I warned thee, lord, not to trust him; my teachings bounded from his head as do peas when thrown against a wall. In all Hades there are not torments enough for him. He who cannot be honest must be a rogue; what is more difficult than for a rogue to become honest? But to fall on his benefactor, a lord so magnanimous — O gods!"

Here he remembered that he had represented himself to Ursus on the way as a Christian, and stopped.

"Were it not for the 'sica,' which I brought, he would have slain me," said Vinicius.

"I bless the moment in which I advised thee to take a knife even."

Vinicius turned an inquiring glance on the Greek, and asked, —

"What hast thou done to-day?"

"How? What! have I not told thee, lord, that I made a vow for thy health?"

"Nothing more?"

"I was just preparing to visit thee, when this good man came and said that thou hadst sent for me."

"Here is a tablet. Thou wilt go with it to my house; thou wilt find my freedman and give it to him. It is written on the tablet that I have gone to Beneventum. Thou wilt tell Demas from thyself that I went this morning, summoned by an urgent letter from Petronius." Here he repeated with emphasis: "I have gone to Beneventum, dost understand?"

"Thou has gone, lord. This morning I took leave of thee at the Porta Capena, and from the time of thy departure such sadness possesses me that if thy magnanimity will not soften it, I shall cry myself to death, like the unhappy wife of Zethos[1] in grief for Itylos."

Vinicius, though sick and accustomed to the Greek's suppleness, could not repress a smile. He was glad, moreover, that Chilo understood in a flash; hence he said, —

"Therefore I will write that thy tears be wiped away. Give me the candle." Chilo, now pacified perfectly, rose, and, advancing a few steps toward the chimney, took one of the candles which was burning at the wall. But while he was doing this, the hood slipped from his head, and the light fell directly on his face. Glaucus sprang from his seat and, coming up quickly, stood before him.

"Dost thou not recognize me, Cephas?" asked he. In his voice there was something so terrible that a shiver ran through all present.

Chilo raised the candle, and dropped it to the earth almost the same instant; then he bent nearly double and began to groan, —

"I am not he — I am not he! Mercy!"

Glaucus turned toward the faithful, and said, —

"This is the man who betrayed — who ruined me and my family!"

That history was known to all the Christians and to Vinicius, who had not guessed who that Glaucus was, — for this reason only, that he fainted repeatedly from pain during the dressing of his wound, and had not heard his name. But for Ursus that short moment, with the words of Glaucus, was like a lightning-flash in darkness. Recognizing Chilo, he was at his side with one spring, and, seizing his arm, bent it back, exclaiming, —

"This is the man who persuaded me to kill Glaucus!"

"Mercy!" groaned Chilo. "I will give you — O lord!" exclaimed he, turning his head to Vinicius, "save me! I trusted in thee, take my part. Thy letter — I will deliver it. O lord, lord!"

But Vinicius, who looked with more indifference than any one at what was passing, first because all the affairs of the Greek were more or less known to him, and second because his heart knew not what pity was, said, —

"Bury him in the garden; some one else will take the letter."

It seemed to Chilo that those words were his final sentence. His bones were shaking in the terrible hands of Ursus; his eyes were filled with tears from pain.

"By your God, pity!" cried he; "I am a Christian! *Pax vobiscum!* I am a Christian; and if ye do not believe me, baptize me again, baptize me twice, ten times! Glaucus, that is a mistake! Let me speak, make me a slave! Do not kill me! Have mercy!"

His voice, stifled with pain, was growing weaker and weaker, when the

[1] Aedon turned into a nightingale.

Apostle Peter rose at the table; for a moment his white head shook, drooping toward his breast, and his eyes were closed; but he opened them then, and said amid silence, —

"The Saviour said this to us: 'If thy brother has sinned against thee, chastise him; but if he is repentant, forgive him. And if he has offended seven times in the day against thee, and has turned to thee seven times, saying, "Have mercy on me!" forgive him.'"

Then came a still deeper silence. Glaucus remained a long time with his hands covering his face; at last he removed them and said, —

"Cephas, may God forgive thy offences, as I forgive them in the name of Christ."

Ursus, letting go the arms of the Greek, added at once:

"May the Saviour be merciful to thee as I forgive thee."

Chilo dropped to the ground, and, supported on it with his hands, turned his head like a wild beast caught in a snare, looking around to see whence death might come. He did not trust his eyes and ears yet, and dared not hope for forgiveness. Consciousness returned to him slowly; his blue lips were still trembling from terror.

"Depart in peace!" said the Apostle, meanwhile.

Chilo rose, but could not speak. He approached the bed of Vinicius, as if seeking protection in it still; for he had not time yet to think that that man, though he had used his services and was still his accomplice, condemned him, while those against whom he had acted forgave. This thought was to come to him later. At present simply astonishment and incredulity were evident in his look. Though he had seen that they forgave him, he wished to bear away his head at the earliest from among these incomprehensible people, whose kindness terrified him almost as much as their cruelty would have terrified. It seemed to him that should he remain longer, something unexpected would happen again; hence, standing above Vinicius, he said with a broken voice, —

"Give the letter, lord, — give the letter!" And snatching the tablet which Vinicius handed him, he made one obeisance to the Christians, another to the sick man, pushed along sidewise by the very wall, and hurried out through the door. In the garden, when darkness surrounded him, fear raised the hair on his head again, for he felt sure that Ursus would rush out and kill him in the night. He would have run with all his might, but his legs would not move; next moment they were perfectly uncontrollable, for Ursus stood near him really.

Chilo fell with his face to the earth, and began to groan: "Urban — in Christ's name" —

But Urban said: "Fear not. The Apostle commanded me to lead thee out beyond the gate, lest thou might go astray in the darkness, and, if strength failed thee, to conduct thee home."

"What dost thou say?" asked Chilo, raising his face. "What? Thou wilt not kill me?"

"No, I will not; and if I seized thee too roughly and harmed a bone in thee, pardon me."

"Help me to rise," said the Greek. "Thou wilt not kill me? Thou wilt not? Take me to the street; I will go farther alone."

Ursus raised him as he might a feather, and placed him on his feet; then he conducted him through the dark corridor to the second court. From there was a passage to the entrance and the street. In the corridor Chilo repeated again in his soul, "It is all over with me!" Only when he found himself on the street did he recover and say, "I can go on alone."

"Peace be with thee."

"And with thee! and with thee! Let me draw breath."

And after Ursus had gone, he breathed with a full breast. He felt his waist and hips, as if to convince himself that he was living, and then moved forward with hurried step.

"But why did they not kill me?" And in spite of all his talk with Euricius about Christian teaching, in spite of his conversation at the river with Urban, and in spite of all that he had heard in Ostrianum, he could find no answer to that question.

CHAPTER XXV

NEITHER could Vinicius discover the cause of what had happened; and in the bottom of his soul he was almost as much astonished as Chilo. That those people should treat him as they had, and, instead of avenging his attack, dress his wounds carefully, he ascribed partly to the doctrine which they confessed, more to Lygia, and a little, also, to his great significance. But their conduct with Chilo simply went beyond his understanding of man's power of forgiveness. And the question thrust itself into his mind: Why did they not kill the Greek? They might have killed him with impunity. Ursus would have buried him in the garden, or borne him in the dark to the Tiber, which during that period of night-murders, committed by Cæsar himself even, cast up human bodies so frequently in the morning that no one inquired whence they came. To his thinking, the Christians had not only the power, but the right to kill Chilo. True, pity was not entirely a stranger to that world to which the young patrician belonged. The Athenians raised an altar to pity, and opposed for a long time the introduction of gladiatorial combats into Athens. In Rome itself the conquered received pardon sometimes, as, for instance, Calicratus, king of the Britons, who, taken prisoner in the time of Claudius, and provided for by him bountifully, dwelt in the city in freedom. But vengeance for a personal wrong seemed to Vinicius, as to all, proper and justified. The neglect of it was entirely opposed to his spirit. True, he had heard in Ostrianum that one should love even enemies; that, however, he considered as a kind of theory without application in life. And now this passed through his head: that perhaps they had not killed Chilo because the day was among festivals, or was in some period of the moon during which it was not proper for Christians to kill a man. He had heard that there are days among various nations on which it is not permitted to begin war even. But why, in such a case, did they not deliver the Greek up to justice? Why did the Apostle say that if a man offended seven times, it was necessary to forgive him seven times; and why did Glaucus say to Chilo, "May God forgive thee, as I forgive thee"?

Chilo had done him the most terrible wrong that one man could do another. At the very thought of how he would act with a man who killed Lygia, for instance, the heart of Vinicius seethed up, as does water in a caldron; there were no torments which he would not inflict in his vengeance! But Glaucus had forgiven; Ursus, too, had forgiven, — Ursus, who might in fact kill whomever he wished in Rome with perfect impunity, for all he needed was to kill the king of the grove in Nemi, and take his place. Could the gladiator holding that office to which he had succeeded only by killing the previous "king," resist the man whom Croton could not resist? There was only one answer to all these questions: that they refrained from killing him through a goodness so great that the like of it had not been in the world up to that time, and through an unbounded love of man, which commands to forget one's self, one's wrongs, one's happiness and misfortune, and live for others. What reward those people were to receive for this, Vinicius heard in Ostrianum, but he could not understand it. He felt, however, that the earthly life connected with the duty of renouncing everything good and rich for the benefit of others must be wretched. So in what he thought of the Christians at that moment, besides the greatest astonishment, there was pity, and as it were a shade of contempt. It seemed to him that they were sheep which earlier or later must be eaten by wolves; his Roman nature could yield no recognition to people who let themselves be devoured. This one thing struck him, however, — that after Chilo's departure the faces of all were bright with a certain deep joy. The Apostle approached Glaucus, placed his hand on his head, and said, —

"In thee Christ has triumphed."

The other raised his eyes, which were full of hope, and as bright with joy as if some great unexpected happiness had been poured on him. Vinicius, who could understand only joy or delight born of vengeance, looked on him with eyes staring from fever, and somewhat as he would on a madman. He saw, however, and saw not without internal indignation, that Lygia pressed her lips of a queen to the hand of that man, who had the appearance of a slave; and it seemed to him that the order of the world was inverted utterly. Next Ursus told how he had conducted Chilo to the street, and had asked forgiveness for the harm which he might have done his bones; for this the Apostle blessed him also. Crispus declared that it was a day of great victory. Hearing of this victory, Vinicius lost the thread of his thought altogether.

But when Lygia gave him a cooling draught again, he held her hand for a moment, and asked, —

"Then must thou also forgive me?"

"We are Christians; it is not permitted us to keep anger in the heart."

"Lygia," said he, "whoever thy God is, I honor Him only because He is thine."

"Thou wilt honor Him in thy heart when thou lovest Him."

"Only because He is thine," repeated Vinicius, in a fainter voice; and he closed his eyes, for weakness had mastered him again.

Lygia went out, but returned after a time, and bent over him to learn if he were sleeping. Vinicius, feeling that she was near, opened his eyes and smiled. She placed her hand over them lightly, as if to incline him to slumber. A great sweetness seized him then; but soon he felt more grievously ill than before, and was very ill in reality. Night had come, and with it a more violent fever. He could not sleep, and followed Lygia with his eyes wherever she went.

At times he fell into a kind of doze, in which he saw and heard everything which happened around him, but in which reality was mingled with feverish dreams. It seemed to him that in some old, deserted cemetery stood a temple, in the form of a tower, in which Lygia was priestess. He did not take his eyes from her, but saw her on the summit of the tower, with a lute in her hands, all in the light, like those priestesses who in the night-time sing hymns in honor of the moon, and whom he had seen in the Orient. He himself was climbing up winding steps, with great effort, to bear her away with him. Behind was creeping up Chilo, with teeth chattering from terror, and repeating, "Do not do that, lord; she is a priestess, for whom He will take vengeance." Vinicius did not know who that He was, but he understood that he himself was going to commit some sacrilege, and he felt a boundless fear also. But when he went to the balustrade surrounding the summit of the tower, the Apostle with his silvery beard stood at Lygia's side on a sudden, and said: "Do not raise a hand; she belongs to me." Then he moved forward with her, on a path formed by rays from the moon, as if on a path made to heaven. He stretched his hands toward them, and begged both to take him into their company.

Here he woke, became conscious, and looked before him. The lamp on the tall staff shone more dimly, but still cast a light sufficiently clear. All were sitting in front of the fire warming themselves, for the night was chilly, and the chamber rather cold. Vinicius saw the breath coming as steam from their lips. In the midst of them sat the Apostle; at his knees, on a low footstool, was Lygia; farther on, Glaucus, Crispus, Miriam, and at the edge, on one side Ursus, on the other Miriam's son Nazarius, a youth with a handsome face, and long, dark hair reaching down to his shoulders.

Lygia listened with eyes raised to the Apostle, and every head was turned toward him, while he told something in an undertone. Vinicius gazed at Peter with a certain superstitious awe, hardly inferior to that terror which he felt during the fever dream. The thought passed through his mind that that dream had touched truth; that the gray-haired man there, freshly come from distant shores, would take Lygia from him really, and take her somewhere away by unknown paths. He felt sure also that the old man was speaking of him, perhaps telling how to separate him from Lygia, for it seemed to him impossible that any one could speak of aught else. Hence, collecting all his presence of mind, he listened to Peter's words.

But he was mistaken altogether, for the Apostle was speaking of Christ again.

"They live only through that name," thought Vinicius.

The old man was describing the seizure of Christ. "A company came, and servants of the priest to seize Him. When the Saviour asked whom they were seeking, they answered, 'Jesus of Nazareth.' But when He said to them, 'I am He,' they fell on the ground, and dared not raise a hand on Him. Only after the second inquiry did they seize Him."

Here the Apostle stopped, stretched his hands toward the fire and continued: —

"The night was cold, like this one, but the heart in me was seething; so, drawing a sword to defend Him, I cut an ear from the servant of the high-priest. I would have defended Him more than my own life had He not said to me, 'Put thy sword into the sheath: the cup which my Father has given me, shall I not drink it?' Then they seized and bound Him."

When he had spoken thus far, Peter placed his palm on his forehead, and was silent, wishing before he went further to stop the crowd of his recollections. But Ursus, unable to restrain himself, sprang to his feet, trimmed the light on the staff till the sparks scattered in golden rain and the flame shot up with more vigor. Then he sat down, and exclaimed:

"No matter what happened. I — "

He stopped suddenly, for Lygia had put her finger to her lips. But he breathed loudly, and it was clear that a storm was in his soul; and though he was ready at all times to kiss the feet of the Apostle, that act was one he could not accept; if some one in his presence had raised hands on the Redeemer, if he had been with Him on that night — Oi! splinters would have shot from the soldiers, the servants of the priest, and the officials. Tears came to his eyes at the very thought of this, and because of his sorrow and mental struggle; for on the one hand he thought that he would not only have defended the Redeemer, but would have called Lygians to his aid, — splendid fellows, — and on the other, if he had acted thus he would have disobeyed the Redeemer, and hindered the salvation of man. For this reason he could not keep back his tears.

After a while Peter took his palm from his forehead, and resumed the narrative. But Vinicius was overpowered by a new feverish, waking dream. What he heard now was in his mind mixed up with what the Apostle had told the night previous in Ostrianum, of that day in which Christ appeared on the shore of the sea of Tiberius. He saw a sheet of water broadly spread out; on it the boat of a fisherman, and in the boat Peter and Lygia. He himself was moving with all his might after that boat, but pain in his broken arm prevented him from reaching it. The wind hurled waves in his eyes, he began to sink, and called with entreating voice for rescue. Lygia knelt down then before the Apostle, who turned his boat, and reached an oar, which Vinicius seized: with their assistance he entered the boat and fell on the bottom of it.

It seemed to him, then, that he stood up, and saw a multitude of people sailing after them. Waves covered their heads with foam; in the whirl only the hands of a few could be seen; but Peter saved the drowning time after time, and gathered them into his boat, which grew larger, as if by a miracle. Soon crowds filled it, as numerous as those which were collected in Ostrianum, and then still greater crowds. Vinicius wondered how they could find place there, and he was afraid that they would sink to the bottom. But Lygia pacified him by showing him a light on the distant shore toward which they were sailing. These dream pictures of Vinicius were blended again with descriptions which he had heard in Ostrianum, from the lips of the Apostle, as to how Christ had appeared on the lake once. So that he saw now in that light on the shore a certain form toward which Peter was steering, and as he approached it the weather grew calmer, the water grew smoother, the light became greater. The crowd began to sing sweet hymns; the air was filled with the odor of nard; the play of water formed a rainbow, as if from the bottom of the lake lilies and roses were looking, and at last the boat struck its breast safely against the sand. Lygia took his hand then, and said, "Come, I will lead thee!" and she led him to the light.

Vinicius woke again; but his dreaming ceased slowly, and he did not recover at once the sense of reality. It seemed for a time to him that he was still on the lake, and surrounded by crowds, among which, not knowing the reason himself, he began to look for Petronius, and was astonished not to find him. The bright light from the chimney, at which there was no one at that time, brought him completely to his senses. Olive sticks were burning slowly under the rosy ashes; but the splinters of pine, which evidently had been put there some moments before, shot up a bright flame, and in the light of this, Vinicius saw Lygia, sitting not far from his bedside.

The sight of her touched him to the depth of his soul. He remembered that she had spent the night before in Ostrianum, and had busied herself the whole day in nursing him, and now when all had gone to rest, she was the only one watching. It was easy to divine that she must be wearied, for while sitting motionless her eyes were closed. Vinicius knew not whether she was sleeping or sunk in thought. He looked at her profile, at her drooping lashes, at her hands lying on her knees; and in his pagan head the idea began to hatch with difficulty that at the side of naked beauty, confident, and proud of Greek and Roman symmetry, there is another in the world, new, immensely pure, in which a soul has its dwelling.

He could not bring himself so far as to call it Christian, but, thinking of Lygia, he could not separate her from the religion which she confessed. He understood, even, that if all the others had gone to rest, and she alone were watching, she whom he had injured, it was because her religion commanded her to watch. But that thought, which filled him with wonder for the religion, was disagreeable to him. He would rather that Lygia acted thus out of love for him, his face, his eyes, his statuesque form, — in a word for reasons because of which more than once snow-white Grecian and Roman arms had been wound around his neck.

Still he felt all at once, that, were she like other women, something would be lacking in her. He was amazed, and knew not what was happening in him; for he saw that new feelings of some kind were rising in him, new likings, strange to the world in which he had lived hitherto.

She opened her eyes then, and, seeing that Vinicius was gazing at her, she approached him and said, —

"I am with thee."

"I saw thy soul in a dream," replied he.

CHAPTER XXVI

NEXT morning he woke up weak, but with a cool head and free of fever. It seemed to him that a whispered conversation had roused him; but when he opened his eyes, Lygia was not there. Ursus, stooping before the chimney, was raking apart the gray ashes, and seeking live coals beneath them. When he found some, he began to blow, not with his mouth, but as it were with the bellows of a blacksmith. Vinicius, remembering how that man had crushed Croton the day before, examined with attention befitting a lover of the arena his gigantic back, which resembled the back of a Cyclops, and his limbs strong as columns.

"Thanks to Mercury that my neck was not broken by him," thought Vinicius. "By Pollux! if the other Lygians are like this one, the Danubian legions will have heavy work some time!"

But aloud he said, "Hei, slave!"

Ursus drew his head out of the chimney, and, smiling in a manner almost friendly, said, —

"God give thee a good day, lord, and good health; but I am a free man, not a slave."

On Vinicius, who wished to question Ursus touching Lygia's birthplace, these words produced a certain pleasant impression; for discourse with a free though a common man was less disagreeable to his Roman and patrician pride, than with a slave, in whom neither law nor custom recognized human nature.

"Then thou dost not belong to Aulus?" asked he.

"No, lord, I serve Callina, as I served her mother, of my own will."

Here he hid his head again in the chimney, to blow the coals, on which he had placed some wood. When he had finished, he took it out and said, —

"With us there are no slaves."

"Where is Lygia?" inquired Vinicius.

"She has gone out, and I am to cook food for thee. She watched over thee the whole night."

"Why didst thou not relieve her?"

"Because she wished to watch, and it is for me to obey."

Here his eyes grew gloomy, and after a while he added:

"If I had disobeyed her, thou wouldst not be living."

"Art thou sorry for not having killed me?"

"No, lord. Christ has not commanded us to kill."

"But Atacinus and Croton?"

"I could not do otherwise," muttered Ursus. And he looked with regret on his hands, which had remained pagan evidently, though his soul had accepted the cross. Then he put a pot on the crane, and fixed his thoughtful eyes on the fire.

"That was thy fault, lord," said he at last. "Why didst thou raise thy hand against her, a king's daughter?"

Pride boiled up, at the first moment, in Vinicius, because a common man and a barbarian had not merely dared to speak to him thus familiarly, but to blame him in addition. To those uncommon and improbable things which had met him since yesterday, was added another. But being weak and without his slaves, he restrained himself, especially since a wish to learn some details of Lygia's life gained the upper hand in him.

When he had calmed himself, therefore, he inquired about the war of the Lygians against Vannius and the Suevi. Ursus was glad to converse, but could not add much that was new to what in his time Aulus Plautius had told. Ursus had not been in battle, for he had attended the hostages to the camp of Atelius Hister. He knew only that the Lygians had beaten the Suevi and the Yazygi, but that their leader and king had fallen from the arrows of the Yazygi. Immediately after they received news that the Semnones had set fire to forests on their boundaries, they returned in haste to avenge the wrong, and the hostages remained with Atelius, who ordered at first to give them kingly honors. Afterward Lygia's mother died. The Roman commander knew not what to do with the child. Ursus wished to return with her to their own country, but the road was unsafe because of wild beasts and wild tribes. When news came that an embassy of Lygians had visited Pomponius, offering him aid against the Marcomani, Hister sent him with Lygia to Pomponius. When they came to him they learned, however, that no ambassadors had been there, and in that way they remained in the camp; whence Pomponius took them to Rome, and at the conclusion of his triumph he gave the king's daughter to Pomponia Græcina.

Though only certain small details of this narrative had been unknown to Vinicius, he listened with pleasure, for his enormous pride of family was pleased that an eye-witness had confirmed Lygia's royal descent. As a king's daughter she might occupy a position at Cæsar's court equal to the daughters of the very first families, all the more since the nation whose ruler her father had been, had not warred with Rome so far, and, though barbarian, it might become terrible; for, according to Atelius Hister himself, it possessed an immense force of warriors. Ursus, moreover, confirmed this completely.

"We live in the woods," said he, in answer to Vinicius, "but we have so much land that no man knows where the end is, and there are many people on it. There are also wooden towns in the forest, in which there is great plenty; for what the Semnones, the Marcomani, the Vandals, and the Quadi plunder through the world, we take from them. They dare not come to us: but when the wind blows from their side, they burn our forests. We fear neither them nor the Roman Cæsar."

"The gods gave Rome dominion over the earth," said Vinicius severely.

"The gods are evil spirits," replied Ursus, with simplicity, "and where there are no Romans, there is no supremacy."

Here he fixed the fire, and said, as if to himself, —

"When Cæsar took Callina to the palace, and I thought that harm might meet her, I wanted to go to the forest and bring Lygians to help the king's daughter. And Lygians would have moved toward the Danube, for they are virtuous people though pagan. There I should have given them 'good tidings.' But as it is, if ever Callina returns to Pomponia Græcina I will bow down to her for permission to go to them; for Christus was born far away, and they have not even heard of Him. He knew better than I where He should be born; but if He had come to the world with us, in the forests, we would not have tortured Him to death, that is certain. We would have taken care of the Child, and guarded Him, so that never should He want for game, mushrooms, beaver-skins, or amber. And what we plundered from the Suevi and the Marcomani we would have given Him, so that He might have comfort and plenty."

Thus speaking, he put near the fire the vessel with food for Vinicius, and was silent. His thoughts wandered evidently, for a time yet, through the Lygian wildernesses, till the liquid began to boil; then he poured it into a shallow plate, and, cooling it properly, said, —

"Glaucus advises thee, lord, to move even thy sound arm as little as possible; Callina has commanded me to give thee food."

Lygia commanded! There was no answer to that. It did not even come to Vinicius's head to oppose her will, just as if she had been the daughter of Cæsar or a goddess. He uttered not a word, therefore; and Ursus, sitting near his bed, took out the liquid with a small cup, and put it to his mouth. He did this so carefully, and with such a kindly smile, that Vinicius could not believe his own eyes, could not think him the same terrible Titan who the day before had crushed Croton, and, rushing on him like a storm, would have torn him to pieces but for Lygia's pity. The young patrician, for the first time in life, began to ponder over this: What can take place in the breast of a simple man, a barbarian, and a servant?

But Ursus proved to be a nurse as awkward as painstaking; the cup was lost among his herculean fingers so completely that there was no place left for the mouth of the sick man. After a few fruitless efforts the giant was troubled greatly, and said, —

"Ei! it would be easier to lead an aurochs out of a snare."

The anxiety of the Lygian amused Vinicius, but his remark did not interest him less. He had seen in circuses the terrible urus, brought from wildernesses of the north, against which the most daring bestiarii went with dread, and which yielded only to elephants in size and strength.

"Hast thou tried to take such beasts by the horns?" inquired he, with astonishment.

"Till the twentieth winter passed over me, I was afraid," answered Ursus; "but after that it happened."

And he began to feed Vinicius still more awkwardly than before.

"I must ask Miriam or Nazarius," said he.

But now Lygia's pale face appeared from behind the curtain.

"I will assist directly," said she. And after a while she came from the cubiculum, in which she had been preparing to sleep, as it seemed, for she was in a single close tunic, called by the ancients capitium, covering the breast completely, and her hair was unbound. Vinicius, whose heart beat with more quickness at sight of her, began to upbraid her for not thinking of sleep yet; but she answered joyously, —

"I was just preparing to sleep, but first I will take the place of Ursus."

She took the cup, and, sitting on the edge of the bed, began to give food to Vinicius, who felt at once overcome and delighted. When she inclined toward him, the warmth of her body struck him, and her unbound hair fell on his breast. He grew pale from the impression; but in the confusion and impulse of desires he felt also that that was a head dear above all and magnified above all, in comparison with which the whole world was nothing. At first he had desired her; now he began to love her with a full breast. Before that, as generally in life and in feeling, he had been, like all people of that time, a blind, unconditional egotist, who thought only of himself; at present he began to think of her.

After a while, therefore, he refused further nourishment; and though he found inexhaustible delight in her presence and in looking at her, he said, —

"Enough! Go to rest, my divine one."

"Do not address me in that way," answered Lygia; "it is not proper for me to hear such words."

She smiled at him, however, and said that sleep had fled from her, that she felt no toil, that she would not go to rest till Glaucus came. He listened to her words as to music; his heart rose with increasing delight, increasing gratitude, and his thought was struggling to show her that gratitude.

"Lygia," said he, after a moment of silence, "I did not know thee hitherto. But I know now that I wished to attain thee by a false way; hence I say, return to Pomponia Græcina, and be assured that in future no hand will be raised against thee."

Her face became sad on a sudden. "I should be happy," answered she, "could I look at her, even from a distance; but I cannot return to her now."

"Why?" inquired Vinicius, with astonishment.

"We Christians know, through Acte, what is done on the Palatine. Hast thou not heard that Cæsar, soon after my flight and before his departure for Naples, summoned Aulus and Pomponia, and, thinking that they had helped me, threatened them with his anger? Fortunately Aulus was able to say to him, 'Thou knowest, lord, that a lie has never passed my lips; I swear to thee now that we did not help her to escape, and we do not know, as thou dost not, what has happened to her.' Cæsar believed, and afterward forgot. By the advice of the elders I have never written to mother where I am, so that she might take an oath boldly at all times that she has no knowledge of me. Thou wilt not understand this, perhaps, O Vinicius; but it is not permitted us to lie, even in a question involving life. Such is the religion on which we fashion our hearts; therefore I have not seen Pomponia from the hour when I left her house. From time to time distant echoes barely reach her that I am alive and not in danger."

Here a longing seized Lygia, and her eyes were moist with tears; but she calmed herself quickly, and said, —

"I know that Pomponia, too, yearns for me; but we have consolation which others have not."

"Yes," answered Vinicius, "Christ is your consolation, but I do not understand that."

"Look at us! For us there are no partings, no pains, no sufferings; or if they come they are turned into pleasure. And death itself, which for you is the end of life, is for us merely its beginning, — the exchange of a lower for a higher happiness, a happiness less calm for one calmer and eternal. Consider what must a religion be which enjoins on us love even for our enemies, forbids falsehood, purifies our souls from hatred, and promises happiness inexhaustible after death."

"I heard those teachings in Ostrianum, and I have seen how ye acted with me and with Chilo; when I remember your deeds, they are like a dream, and it seems to me that I ought not to believe my ears or eyes. But answer me this question: Art thou happy?"

"I am," answered Lygia. "One who confesses Christ cannot be unhappy."

Vinicius looked at her, as though what she said passed every measure of human understanding.

"And hast thou no wish to return to Pomponia?"

"I should like, from my whole soul, to return to her; and shall return, if such be God's will."

"I say to thee, therefore, return; and I swear by my lares that I will not raise a hand against thee."

Lygia thought for a moment, and answered, —

"No, I cannot expose those near me to danger. Cæsar does not like the Plautiuses. Should I return — thou knowest how every news is spread throughout Rome by slaves — my return would be noised about in the city. Nero would hear of it surely through his slaves, and punish Aulus and Pomponia, — at least take me from them a second time."

"True," answered Vinicius, frowning, "that would be possible. He would do so, even to show that his will must be obeyed. It is true that he only forgot thee, or would remember thee, because the loss was not his, but mine. Perhaps, if he took thee from Aulus and Pomponia, he would send thee to me and I could give thee back to them."

"Vinicius, wouldst thou see me again on the Palatine?" inquired Lygia.

He set his teeth, and answered, —

"No. Thou art right. I spoke like a fool! No!"

And all at once he saw before him a precipice, as it were without bottom. He was a patrician, a military tribune, a powerful man; but above every power of that world to which he belonged was a madman whose will and malignity it was impossible to foresee. Only such people as the Christians might cease to reckon with Nero or fear him, — people for whom this whole world, with its separations and sufferings, was as nothing; people for whom death itself was as nothing. All others had to tremble before him. The terrors of the time in which they lived showed themselves to Vinicius in all their monstrous extent. He could not return Lygia to Aulus and Pomponia, then, through fear that the monster would remember her, and turn on her his anger; for the very same reason, if he should take her as wife, he might expose her, himself, and Aulus. A moment of ill-humor was enough to ruin all. Vinicius felt, for the first time in life, that either the world must change and be transformed, or life would become impossible altogether. He understood also this, which a moment before had been dark to him, that in such times only Christians could be happy.

But above all, sorrow seized him, for he understood, too, that it was he who had so involved his own life and Lygia's that out of the complication there was scarcely an outcome. And under the influence of that sorrow he began to speak:

"Dost thou know that thou art happier than I? Thou art in poverty, and in this one chamber, among simple people, thou hast thy religion and thy Christ; but I have only thee, and when I lacked thee I was like a beggar without a roof above him and without bread. Thou art dearer to me than the whole world. I sought thee, for I could not live without thee. I wished neither feasts nor sleep. Had it not been for the hope of finding thee, I should have cast myself on a sword. But I fear death, for if dead I could not see thee. I speak the pure truth in saying that I shall not be able to live without thee. I have lived so far only in the hope of finding and beholding thee. Dost thou remember our conversations at the house of Aulus? Once thou didst draw a fish for me on the sand, and I knew not what its meaning was. Dost thou remember how we played ball? I loved thee then above life, and thou hadst begun already to divine that I loved thee. Aulus came, frightened us with Libitina, and interrupted our talk. Pomponia, at parting, told Petronius that God is one, all-mighty and all-merciful, but it did not even occur to us that Christ was thy God and hers. Let Him give thee to me and I will love Him, though He seems to me a god of slaves, foreigners, and beggars. Thou sittest near me, and thinkest of Him only. Think of me too, or I shall hate Him. For me thou alone art a divinity. Blessed be thy father and mother; blessed the land which produced thee! I should wish to embrace thy feet and pray to thee, give thee honor, homage, offerings, thou thrice divine! Thou knowest not, or canst not know, how I love thee."

Thus speaking, he placed his hand on his pale forehead and closed his eyes. His nature never knew bounds in love or anger He spoke with enthusiasm, like a man who, having lost self-control, has no wish to observe any measure in words or feelings. But he spoke from the depth of his soul, and sincerely. It was to be felt that the pain, ecstasy, desire, and homage accumulated in his breast had burst forth at last in an irresistible torrent of words. To Lygia his words appeared blasphemous, but still her heart began to beat as if it would tear the tunic enclosing her bosom. She could not resist pity for him:

and his suffering. She was moved by the homage with which he spoke to her. She felt beloved and deified without bounds; she felt that that unbending and dangerous man belonged to her now, soul and body, like a slave; and that feeling of his submission and her own power filled her with happiness. Her recollections revived in one moment. He was for her again that splendid Vinicius, beautiful as a pagan god; he, who in the house of Aulus had spoken to her of love, and roused as if from sleep her heart half childlike at that time; he from whose embraces Ursus had wrested her on the Palatine, as he might have wrested her from flames. But at present, with ecstasy, and at the same time with pain in his eagle face, with pale forehead and imploring eyes, — wounded, broken by love, loving, full of homage and submissive, — he seemed to her such as she would have wished him, and such as she would have loved with her whole soul, therefore dearer than he had ever been before.

All at once she understood that a moment might come in which his love would seize her and bear her away, as a whirlwind; and when she felt this, she had the same impression that he had a moment before, — that she was standing on the edge of a precipice. Was it for this that she had left the house of Aulus? Was it for this that she had saved herself by flight? Was it for this that she had hidden so long in wretched parts of the city? Who was that Vinicius? An Augustian, a soldier, a courtier of Nero! Moreover he took part in his profligacy and madness, as was shown by that feast, which she could not forget; and he went with others to the temples, and made offerings to vile gods, in whom he did not believe, perhaps, but still he gave them official honor. Still more he had pursued her to make her his slave and mistress, and at the same time to thrust her into that terrible world of excess, luxury, crime, and dishonor which calls for the anger and vengeance of God. He seemed changed, it is true, but still he had just said to her that if she would think more of Christ than of him, he was ready to hate Christ. It seemed to Lygia that the very idea of any other love than the love of Christ was a sin against Him and against religion. When she saw then that other feelings and desires might be roused in the depth of her soul, she was seized by alarm for her own future and her own heart.

At this moment of internal struggle appeared Glaucus, who had come to care for the patient and study his health. In the twinkle of an eye, anger and impatience were reflected on the face of Vinicius. He was angry that his conversation with Lygia had been interrupted; and when Glaucus questioned him, he answered with contempt almost. It is true that he moderated himself quickly; but if Lygia had any illusions as to this, — that what he had heard in Ostrianum might have acted on his unyielding nature, — those illusions must vanish. He had changed only for her; but beyond that single feeling there remained in his breast the former harsh and selfish heart, truly Roman and wolfish, incapable not only of the sweet sentiment of Christian teaching but even of gratitude.

She went away at last filled with internal care and anxiety. Formerly in her prayers she had offered to Christ a heart calm, and really pure as a tear. Now that calmness was disturbed. To the interior of the flower a poisonous insect had come and began to buzz. Even sleep, in spite of the two nights passed without sleep, brought her no relief. She dreamed that at Ostrianum Nero, at the head of a whole band of Augustians, bacchantes, corybantes, and gladiators, was trampling crowds of Christians with his chariot wreathed in roses; and Vinicius seized her by the arm, drew her to the quadriga, and, pressing her to his bosom, whispered "Come with us."

CHAPTER XXVII

FROM that moment Lygia showed herself more rarely in the common chamber, and approached his couch less frequently. But peace did not return to her. She saw that Vinicius followed her with imploring glance; that he was waiting for every word of hers, as for a favor; that he suffered and dared not complain, lest he might turn her away from him; that she alone was his health and delight. And then her heart swelled with compassion. Soon she observed, too, that the more she tried to avoid him, the more compassion she had for him; and by this itself the more tender were the feelings which rose in her. Peace left her. At times she said to hrself that it was her special duty to be near him always, first, because the religion of God commands return of good for evil; second, that by conversing with him, she might attract him to the faith. But at the same time conscience told her that she was tempting herself; that only love for him and the charm which he exerted were attracting her, nothing else. Thus she lived in a ceaseless struggle, which was intensified daily. At times it seemed that a kind of net surrounded her, and that in trying to break through it she entangled herself more and more. She had also to confess that for her the sight of him was becoming more needful, his voice was becoming dearer, and that she had to struggle with all her might against the wish to sit at his bedside. When she approached him, and he grew radiant, delight filled her heart. On a certain day she noticed traces of tears on his eyelids, and for the first time in life the thought came to her, to dry them with kisses. Terrified by that thought, and full of self-contempt, she wept all the night following.

He was as enduring as if he had made a vow of patience. When at moments his eyes flashed with petulance, self-will, and anger, he restrained those flashes promptly, and looked with alarm at her, as if to implore pardon. This acted still more on her. Never had she such a feeling of being greatly loved as then; and when she thought of this, she felt at once guilty and happy. Vinicius, too, had changed essentially. In his conversations with Glaucus there was less pride. It occurred to him frequently that even that poor slave physician and that foreign woman, old Miriam, who surrounded him with attention, and Crispus, whom he saw absorbed in continual prayer, were still human. He was astonished at such thoughts, but he had them. After a time he conceived a liking for Ursus, with whom he conversed entire days; for with him he could talk about Lygia. The giant, on his part, was inexhaustible in narrative, and while performing the most simple services for the sick man, he began to show him also some attachment. For Vinicius, Lygia had been at all times a being of another order, higher a hundred times than those around her: nevertheless, he began to observe simple and poor people, — a thing which he had never done before, — and he discovered in them various traits the existence of which he had never suspected.

Nazarius, however, he could not endure, for it seemed to him that the young lad had dared to fall in love with Lygia. He had restrained his aversion for a long time, it is true; but once when he brought her two quails, which he had bought in the market with his own earned money, the descendant of the Quirites spoke out in Vinicius, for whom one who had wandered in from a strange people had less worth than the meanest worm. When he heard Lygia's thanks, he grew terribly pale; and when Nazarius went out to get water for the birds, he said, —

"Lygia, canst thou endure that he should give thee gifts? Dost thou not know that the Greeks call people of his nation Jewish dogs?"

"I do not know what the Greeks call them; but I know that Nazarius is a Christian and my brother."

When she had said this she looked at Vinicius with astonishment and regret, for he had disaccustomed her to similar outbursts; and he set his teeth, so as not to tell her that he would have given command to beat such a brother with sticks, or would have sent him as a compeditus [1] to dig earth in his Sicilian vineyards. He restrained himself, however, throttled the anger within him, and only after a while did he say, —

"Pardon me, Lygia. For me thou art the daughter of a king and the adopted child of Plautius." And he subdued himself to that degree that when Nazarius appeared in the chamber again, he promised him, on returning to his villa, the gift of a pair of peacocks or flamingoes, of which he had a garden full.

Lygia understood what such victories over himself must have cost him; but the oftener he gained them the more her heart turned to him. His merit with regard to Nazarius was less, however, than she supposed. Vinicius might be indignant for a moment, but he could not be jealous of him. In fact the son of Miriam did not, in his eyes, mean much more than a dog; besides, he was a child yet, who, if he loved Lygia, loved her unconsciously and servilely. Greater struggles must the young tribune have with himself to submit, even in silence, to that honor with which among those people the name of Christ and His religion was surrounded. In this regard wonderful things took place in Vinicius. That was in every case a religion which Lygia believed; hence for that single reason he was ready to receive it. Afterward, the more he returned to health, the more he remembered the whole series of events which had happened since that night at Ostrianum, and the whole series of thoughts which had come to his head from that time, the more he was astonished at the superhuman power of that religion which changed the souls of men to their foundations. He understood that in it there was something uncommon, something which had not been on earth before, and he felt that could it embrace the whole world, could it ingraft on the world its love and charity, an epoch would come recalling that in which not Jupiter, but Saturn had

[1] A man who labors with chained feet.

ruled. He did not dare either to doubt the supernatural origin of Christ, or
His resurrection, or the other miracles. The eye-witnesses who spoke of them
were too trustworthy and despised falsehood too much to let him suppose
that they were telling things that had not happened. Finally, Roman scepticism
permitted disbelief in the gods, but believed in miracles. Vinicius, therefore,
stood before a kind of marvellous puzzle which he could not solve. On the
other hand, however, that religion seemed to him opposed to the existing
state of things, impossible of practice, and mad in a degree beyond all others.
According to him, people in Rome and in the whole world might be bad,
but the order of things was good. Had Cæsar, for example, been an honest
man, had the Senate been composed, not of insignificant libertines, but of
men like Thrasea, what more could one wish? Nay, Roman peace and supremacy were good; distinction among people just and proper. But that
religion, according to the understanding of Vinicius, would destroy all order,
all supremacy, every distinction. What would happen then to the dominion
and lordship of Rome? Could the Romans cease to rule, or could they
recognize a whole herd of conquered nations as equal to themselves? That
was a thought which could find no place in the head of a patrician. As regarded him personally, that religion was opposed to all his ideas and habits,
his whole character and understanding of life. He was simply unable to
imagine how he could exist were he to accept it. He feared and admired it;
but as to accepting it, his nature shuddered at that. He understood, finally,
that nothing save that religion separated him from Lygia; and when he
thought of this, he hated it with all the powers of his soul.

Still he acknowledged to himself that it had adorned Lygia with that
exceptional, unexplained beauty which in his heart had produced, besides
love, respect, besides desire, homage, and had made of that same Lygia a
being dear to him beyond all others in the world. And then he wished anew to
love Christ. And he understood clearly that he must either love or hate Him;
he could not remain indifferent. Meanwhile two opposing currents were
as if driving him: he hesitated in thoughts, in feelings; he knew not how to
choose, he bowed his head, however, to that God by him uncomprehended,
and paid silent honor for this sole reason, that He was Lygia's God.

. Lygia saw what was happening in him; she saw how he was breaking himself, how his nature was rejecting that religion; and though this mortified
her to the death, compassion, pity, and gratitude for the silent respect which
he showed Christ inclined her heart to him with irresistible force. She recalled Pomponia Græcina and Aulus. For Pomponia a source of ceaseless
sorrow and tears that never dried was the thought that beyond the grave
she would not find Aulus. Lygia began now to understand better that pain,
that bitterness. She too had found a being dear to her, and she was threatened
by eternal separation from this dear one.

At times, it is true, she was self-deceived, thinking that his soul would
open itself to Christ's teaching; but these illusions could not remain. She
knew and understood him too well. Vinicius a Christian! — These two ideas
could find no place together in her unenlightened head. If the thoughtful,

discreet Aulus had not become a Christian under the influence of the wise and perfect Pomponia, how could Vinicius become one? To this there was no answer, or rather there was only one, — that for him there was neither hope nor salvation.

But Lygia saw with terror that that sentence of condemnation which hung over him instead of making him repulsive made him still dearer simply through compassion. At moments the wish seized her to speak to him of his dark future; but once, when she had sat near him and told him that outside Christian truth there was no life, he, having grown stronger at that time, rose on his sound arm and placed his head on her knees suddenly. "Thou art life!" said he. And that moment breath failed in her breast, presence of mind left her, a certain quiver of ecstasy rushed over her from head to feet. Seizing his temples with her hands, she tried to raise him, but bent the while so that her lips touched his hair; and for a moment both were overcome with delight, with themselves, and with love, which urged them the one to the other.

Lygia rose at last and rushed away, with a flame in her veins and a giddiness in her head; but that was the drop which overflowed the cup filled already to the brim. Vinicius did not divine how dearly he would have to pay for that happy moment, but Lygia understood that now she herself needed rescue. She spent the night after that evening without sleep, in tears and in prayer, with the feeling that she was unworthy to pray and could not be heard. Next morning she went from the cubiculum early, and, calling Crispus to the garden summer-house, covered with ivy and withered vines, opened her whole soul to him, imploring him at the same time to let her leave Miriam's house, since she could not trust herself longer, and could not overcome her heart's love for Vinicius.

Crispus, an old man, severe and absorbed in endless enthusiasm, consented to the plan of leaving Miriam's house, but he had no words of forgiveness for that love, to his thinking sinful. His heart swelled with indignation at the very thought that Lygia, whom he had guarded since the time of her flight, whom he had loved, whom he had confirmed in the faith, and on whom he looked now as a white lily grown up on the field of Christian teaching undefiled by any earthly breath, could have found a place in her soul for love other than heavenly. He had believed hitherto that nowhere in the world did there beat a heart more purely devoted to the glory of Christ. He wanted to offer her to Him as a pearl, a jewel, the precious work of his own hands; hence the disappointment which he felt filled him with grief and amazement.

"Go and beg God to forgive thy fault," said he, gloomily. "Flee before the evil spirit who involved thee bring thee to utter fall, and before thou oppose the Saviour. God died on the cross to redeem thy soul with His blood, but thou hast preferred to love him who wished to make thee his concubine. God saved thee by a miracle of His own hands, but thou hast opened thy heart to impure desire, and hast loved the son of darkness. Who is he? The friend and servant of Antichrist, his copartner in crime and profligacy. Whither will he lead thee, if not to that abyss and to that Sodom in which he himself is living, but which God will destroy with the flame of His anger? But I say to thee, would thou hadst died, would the walls of this house had fallen on thy head before that serpent had crept into thy bosom and beslimed it with the poison of iniquity."

And he was borne away more and more, for Lygia's fault filled him not only with anger but with loathing and contempt for human nature in general, and in particular for women, whom even Christian truth could not save from Eve's weakness. To him it seemed nothing that the maiden had remained pure, that she wished to flee from that love, that she had confessed it with compunction and penitence. Crispus had wished to transform her into an angel, to raise her to heights where love for Christ alone existed, and she had fallen in love with an Augustian. The very thought of that filled his heart with horror, strengthened by a feeling of disillusion and disappointment. No, no, he could not forgive her. Words of horror burned his lips like glowing coals; he struggled still with himself not to utter them, but he shook his emaciated hands over the terrified girl. Lygia felt guilty, but not to that degree. She had judged even that withdrawal from Miriam's house would be her victory over temptation, and would lessen her fault. Crispus rubbed her into the dust; showed her all the misery and insignificance of her soul, which she had not suspected hitherto. She had judged even that the old presbyter, who from the moment of her flight from the Palatine had been to her as a father, would show some compassion, console her, give her courage, and strengthen her.

"I offer my pain and disappointment to God," said he, "but thou hast deceived the Saviour also, for thou hast gone as it were to a quagmire which has poisoned thy soul with its miasma. Thou mightst have offered it to Christ as a costly vessel, and said to Him, 'Fill it with grace, O Lord!' but thou hast preferred to offer it to the servant of the evil one. May God forgive thee and have mercy on thee; for till thou cast out the serpent, I who held thee as chosen — "

But he ceased suddenly to speak, for he saw that they were not alone. Through the withered vines and the ivy, which was green alike in summer and winter, he saw two men, one of whom was Peter the Apostle. The other he was unable to recognize at once, for a mantle of coarse woollen stuff, called cilicium, concealed a part of his face. It seemed to Crispus for a moment that that was Chilo.

They, hearing the loud voice of Crispus, entered the summer-house and sat on a stone bench. Peter's companion had an emaciated face; his head, which was growing bald, was covered at the sides with curly hair; he had reddened eyelids and a crooked nose; in the face, ugly and at the same time inspired, Crispus recognized the features of Paul of Tarsus.

Lygia, casting herself on her knees, embraced Peter's feet, as if from despair, and, sheltering her tortured head in the fold of his mantle, remained thus in silence.

"Peace to your souls!" said Peter.

And seeing the child at his feet he asked what had happened. Crispus began then to narrate all that Lygia had confessed to him, — her sinful love, her desire to flee from Miriam's house, — and his sorrow that a soul which he had thought to offer to Christ pure as a tear had defiled itself with earthly feelings for a sharer in all those crimes into which the pagan world had sunk, and which called for God's vengeance.

Lygia during his speech embraced with increasing force the feet of the Apostle, as if wishing to seek refuge near them, and to beg even a little compassion.

But the Apostle, when he had listened to the end, bent down and placed his aged hand on her head; then he raised his eyes to the old presbyter, and said, —

"Crispus, hast thou not heard that our beloved Master was in Cana, at a wedding, and blessed love between man and woman?"

Crispus's hands dropped, and he looked with astonishment on the speaker, without power to utter one word. After a moment's silence Peter asked again, —

"Crispus, dost thou think that Christ, who permitted Mary of Magdala to lie at his feet, and who forgave the public sinner, would turn from this maiden, who is as pure as a lily of the field?"

Lygia nestled up more urgently to the feet of Peter, with sobbing, understanding that she had not sought refuge in vain. The Apostle raised her face, which was covered with tears, and said to her, —

"While the eyes of him whom thou lovest are not open to the light of truth, avoid him, lest he bring thee to sin, but pray for him, and know that there is no sin in thy love. And since it is thy wish to avoid temptation, this will be accounted to thee as a merit. Do not suffer, and do not weep; for I tell thee that the grace of the Redeemer has not deserted thee, and that thy prayers will be heard; after sorrow will come days of gladness."

When he had said this, he placed both hands on her head, and, raising his eyes, blessed her. From his face there shone a goodness beyond that of earth.

The penitent Crispus began humbly to explain himself; "I have sinned against mercy," said he; "but I thought that by admitting to her heart an earthly love she had denied Christ."

"I denied Him thrice," answered Peter, "and still He forgave me, and commanded me to feed His sheep."

"And because," concluded Crispus, "Vinicius is an Augustian."

"Christ softened harder hearts than his," replied Peter.

Then Paul of Tarsus, who had been silent so far, placed his finger on his breast, pointing to himself, and said, —

"I am he who persecuted and hurried servants of Christ to their death; I am he who during the stoning of Stephen kept the garments of those who stoned him; I am he who wished to root out the truth in every part of the inhabited earth, and yet the Lord predestined me to declare it in every land. I have declared it in Judea, in Greece, on the Islands, and in this godless city, where first I resided as a prisoner. And now when Peter, my superior, has summoned me, I enter this house to bend that proud head to the feet of

Christ, and cast a grain of seed in that stony field, which the Lord will fertilize, so that it may bring forth a bountiful harvest."

And he rose. To Crispus that diminutive hunchback seemed then that which he was in reality, — a giant, who was to stir the world to its foundations and gather in lands and nations.

CHAPTER XXVIII

Petronius to Vinicius: —

"Have pity, carissime; imitate not in thy letters the Lacedemonians or Julius Cæsar! Couldst thou, like Julius, write *Veni, vidi, vici* (I came, I saw, I conquered), I might understand thy brevity. But thy letter means absolutely *Veni, vidi, fugi* (I came, I saw, I fled). Since such a conclusion of the affair is directly opposed to thy nature, since thou art wounded, and since, finally, uncommon things are happening to thee, thy letter needs explanation. I could not believe my eyes when I read that the Lygian giant killed Croton as easily as a Caledonian dog would kill a wolf in the defiles of Hibernia. That man is worth as much gold as he himself weighs, and it depends on him alone to become a favorite of Cæsar. When I return to the city, I must gain a nearer acquaintance with that Lygian, and have a bronze statue of him made for myself. Ahenobarbus will burst from curiosity, when I tell him that it is from nature. Bodies really athletic are becoming rarer in Italy and in Greece; of the Orient no mention need be made; the Germans, though large, have muscles covered with fat, and are greater in bulk than in strength. Learn from the Lygian if he is an exception, or if in his country there are more men like him. Should it happen sometime to thee or me to organize games officially, it would be well to know where to seek for the best bodies.

"But praise to the gods of the Orient and the Occident that thou hast come out of such hands alive. Thou hast escaped, of course, because thou art a patrician, and the son of a consul; but everything which has happened astonishes me in the highest degree, — that cemetery where thou wert among the Christians, they, their treatment of thee, the subsequent flight of Lygia; finally, that peculiar sadness and disquiet which breathes from thy short letter. Explain, for there are many points which I cannot understand; and if thou wish the truth, I will tell thee plainly, that I understand neither the Christians nor thee nor Lygia. Wonder not that I, who care for few things on earth except my own person, inquire of thee so eagerly. I have contributed to all this affair of thine; hence it is my affair so far. Write soon, for I cannot foresee surely when we may meet. In Bronzebeard's head plans change, as winds do in autumn. At present, while tarrying in Beneventum, he has the wish to go straightway to Greece, without returning to Rome. Tigellinus, however, advises him to visit the city even for a time, since the people, yearning overmuch for his person (read 'for games and bread') may revolt. So I cannot tell how it will be. Should Achæa overbalance, we may want to see Egypt. I should insist with all my might on thy coming, for I think that in thy state of mind travelling and our amusements would be a medicine, but thou mightst not find us. Consider, then, whether in that case respose in thy Sicilian estates would not be preferable to remaining in Rome. Write me minutely of thyself, and farewell. I add no wish this time, except health; for, by Pollux! I know not what to wish thee."

Vinicius, on receiving this letter, felt at first no desire to reply. He had a kind of feeling that it was not worth while to reply, that an answer would benefit no one in any way, that it would explain nothing. Discontent, and a feeling of the vanity of life, possessed him. He thought, moreover, that Petronius would not comprehend him in any case, and that something had happened which would remove them from each other. He could not come to an agreement with himself, even. When he returned from the Trans-Tiber to his splendid "insula," he was exhausted, and found for the first days a certain satisfaction in rest and in the comfort and abundance about him. That satisfaction lasted but a short time, however. He felt soon that he was living in vanity; that all which so far had formed the interest of his life either had ceased to exist for him or had shrunk to proportions barely perceptible. He had a feeling as if those ties which hitherto had connected him with life had been cut in his soul, and that no new ones had been formed. At the thought that he might go to Beneventum and thence to Achæa, to swim in a life of luxury and wild excess, he had a feeling of emptiness. "To what end? What shall I gain from it?" These were the first questions which passed through his head. And for the first time in life, also, he thought that if he went, the conversation of Petronius, his wit, his quickness, his exquisite outlining of thought, and his choice of apt phrases for every idea might annoy him.

But solitude, too, had begun to annoy him. All his acquaintances were with Cæsar in Beneventum; so he had to stay at home alone, with a head full of thoughts, and a heart full of feelings which he could not analyze. He had moments, however, in which he judged that if he could converse with some one about everything that took place in him, perhaps he might be able to grasp it all somehow, bring it to order, and estimate it better. Under the influence of this hope, and after some days of hesitation, he decided to answer Petronius; and, though not certain that he would send the answer, he wrote it in the following words: —

"it is thy wish that I write more minutely, agreed then; whether I shall be able to do it more clearly, I cannot tell, for there are many knots which I know not myself how to loosen. I described to thee my stay among the Christians, and their treatment of enemies, among whom they had a right to count both me and Chilo; finally, of the kindness with which they nursed me, and of the disappearance of Lygia. No, my dear friend, I was not spared because of being the son of a consul. Such considerations do not exist for them, since they forgave even Chilo, though I urged them to bury him in the garden. Those are people such as the world has not seen hitherto, and their teaching is of a kind that the world has not heard up to this time. I can say nothing else, and he errs who measures them with our measure. I tell thee that, if I had been lying with a broken arm in my own house, and if my own people, even my own family, had nursed me, I should have had more comforts, of course, but I should not have received half the care which I found among them.

"Know this, too, that Lygia is like the others. Had she been my sister or my wife, she could not have nursed me more tenderly. Delight filled my heart more than once, for I judged that love alone could inspire the like tenderness. More than once I saw love in her look, in her face; and, wilt thou believe me? among those simple people then in that poor chamber, which was at once a culina and a triclinium, I felt happier than ever before. No; she was not indifferent to me — and to-day even I cannot think that she was. Still that same Lygia left Miriam's dwelling in secret because of me. I sit now whole days with my head on my hands, and think, Why did she do so? Have I written thee that I volunteered to restore her to Aulus? True, she declared that to be impossible at present, because Aulus and Pomponia had gone to Sicily, and because news of her return going from house to house, through slaves, would reach the Palatine, and Cæsar might take her from Aulus again. But she knew that I would not pursue her longer; that I had left the way of violence; that, unable to cease loving her or to live without her, I would bring her into my house through a wreathed door, and seat her on a sacred skin at my hearth. Still she fled! Why? Nothing was threatening her. Did she not love me, she might have rejected me. The day before her flight, I made the acquaintance of a wonderful man, a certain Paul of Tarsus, who spoke to me of Christ and His teachings, and spoke with such power that every word of his, without his willing it, turns all the foundations of our society into ashes. That same man visited me after her flight, and said: 'If God open thy eyes to the light, and take the beam from them as He took it from mine, thou wilt feel that she acted properly; and then, perhaps, thou wilt find her.' And now I am breaking my head over these words, as if I had heard them from the mouth of the Pythoness at Delphi. I seem to understand something. Though they love people, the Christians are enemies of our life, our gods, and our crimes; hence she fled from me, as from a man who belongs to our society, and with whom she would have to share a life counted criminal by Christians. Thou wilt say that since she might reject me, she had no need to withdraw. But if she loved me? In that case she desired to flee from love. At the very thought of this I wish to send slaves into every alley in Rome, and command them to cry throughout the houses, 'Return, Lygia!' But I cease to understand why she fled. I should not have stopped her from believing in her Christ, and would myself have reared an altar to Him in the atrium. What harm could one more god do me? Why might I not believe in Him, — I who do not believe overmuch in the old gods? I know with full certainty that the Christians do not lie, and they say that He rose from the dead. A man cannot rise from the dead. That Paul of Tarsus, who is a Roman citizen, but who, as a Jew, knows the old Hebrew writings, told me that the coming of Christ was promised by prophets for whole thousands of years. All these are uncommon things, but does not the uncommon surround us on every side? People have not ceased talking yet of Apollonius of Tyana. Paul's statement that there is one God, not a whole assembly of them, seems sound to me. Perhaps Seneca is of this opinion, and before him many others. Christ lived, gave Himself to be crucified for the salvation of the world, and rose from the dead. All this is perfectly certain. I do not see, therefore, a reason why I should insist on an opposite opinion, or why I should not rear to Him an altar, if I am ready to rear one to Serapis, for instance. It would not be difficult for me even to renounce other gods, for no reasoning mind believes in them at present. But it seems that all this is not enough yet for the Christians. It is not enough to honor Christ, one must also live according to His teachings; and here thou art on the shore of a sea which they command thee to wade through.

"If I promised to do so, they themselves would feel that the promise was an empty sound of words. Paul told me so openly. Thou knowest how I love Lygia, and knowest that there is nothing that I would not do for her. Still, even at her wish, I cannot raise Soracte or Vesuvius on my shoulders, or place Thrasymene Lake on the palm of my hand, or from black make my eyes blue, like those of the Lygians. If she so desired, I could have the wish, but the change does not lie in my power. I am not a philosopher, but also I am not so dull as I have seemed, perhaps, more than once to thee. I will state now the following: I know not how the Christians order their own lives, but I know that where their religion begins, Roman rule ends, Rome itself ends, our mode of life ends, the distinction between conquered and conqueror, between rich and poor, lord and slave, ends, government ends, Cæsar ends, law and all the order of the world ends; and in place of these appears Christ, with a certain mercy not existent hitherto, and kindness, opposed to human and our Roman instincts. It is true that Lygia is more to me than all Rome and its lordship; and I would let society vanish could I have her in my house. But that is another thing. Agreement in words does not satisfy the Christians; a man must feel that their teaching is truth, and not have aught else in his soul. But that, the gods are my witnesses, is beyond me. Dost understand what that means? There is something in my nature which shudders at this religion; and were my lips to glorify it, were I to conform to its precepts, my soul and my reason would say that I do so through love for Lygia, and that apart from her there is to me nothing on earth more repulsive. And, a strange thing, Paul of Tarsus understands this, and so does that old theurgus Peter, who in spite of all his simplicity and low origin is the highest among them, and was the disciple of Christ. And dost thou know what they are doing? They are praying for me, and calling down something which they call grace; but nothing descends on me, save disquiet, and a greater yearning for Lygia.

"I have written thee that she went away secretly; but when going she left me a cross which she put together from twigs of boxwood. When I woke up, I found it near my bed. I have it now in the lararium, and I approach it yet, I cannot tell why, as if there were something divine in it, — that is, with awe and reverence. I love it because her hand bound it, and I hate it because it divides us. At times it seems to me that there are enchantments of some kind in all this affair, and that the theurgus, Peter, though he declares himself to be a simple shepherd, is greater than Apollonius, and all who preceded him, and that he has involved us all — Lygia, Pomponia, and me — with them.

"Thou hast written that in my previous letter disquiet and sadness are visible. Sadness there must be, for I have lost her again, and there is disquiet because something has changed in me. I tell thee sincerely, that nothing is more repugnant to my nature than that religion, and still I cannot recognize myself since I met Lygia. Is it enchantment, or love? Circe changed people's bodies by touching them, but my soul has been changed. No one but Lygia could have done that, or rather Lygia through that wonderful religion which she professes. When I returned to my house from the Christians, no one was waiting for me. The slaves thought that I was in Beneventum, and would not return soon; hence there was disorder in the house. I found the slaves drunk, and a feast, which they were giving themselves, in my triclinium. They had more thought of seeing death than me, and would have been less terrified by it. Thou knowest with what a firm hand I hold my house; all to the last one dropped on their knees, and some fainted from terror. But dost thou know how I acted? At the first moment I wished to call for rods and hot iron, but immediately a kind of shame seized me, and, wilt thou lend belief? a species of pity for those wretched people. Among them are old slaves whom my grandfather, Marcus Vinicius, brought from the Rhine in the time of Augustus. I shut myself up alone in the library, and there came stranger thoughts still to my head; namely, that after what I had heard and seen among the Christians, it did not become me to act with slaves as I had acted hitherto — that they too were people. For a number of days they moved about in mortal terror, in the belief that I was delaying so as to invent punishment the more cruel; but I did not punish, and did not punish because I was not able. Summoning them on the third day, I said, 'I forgive you; strive then with earnest service to correct your fault!' They fell on their knees, covering their faces with tears, stretching forth their hands with groans, and called me lord and father; but I — with shame do I write this — was equally moved. It seemed to me that at that moment I was looking at the sweet face of Lygia, and her eyes filled with tears, thanking me for that act. And, *proh pudor!* I felt that my lips too were moist. Dost know what I will confess to thee? This, — that I cannot do without her, that it is ill for me alone, that I am simply unhappy, and that my sadness is greater than thou wilt admit. But, as to my slaves, one thing arrested my attention. The forgiveness which they received not only did not make them insolent, not only did not weaken discipline, but never had fear roused them to such ready service as has gratitude. Not only do they serve, but they seem to vie with one another to divine my wishes. I mention this to thee because, when, the day before I left the Christians, I told Paul that society would fall apart because of his religion, as a cask without hoops, he answered, 'Love is a stronger hoop than fear.' And now I see that in certain cases his opinion may be right. I have verified it also with references to clients, who, learning of my return, hurried to salute me. Thou knowest that I have never been penurious with them; but my father acted haughtily with clients on principle, and taught me to treat them in like manner. But when I saw their worn mantles and hungry faces, I had a feeling something like compassion. I gave command to bring them food, and conversed besides with them, — called some by name, some I asked about their wives and children, — and again in the eyes before me I saw tears; again it seemed to me that Lygia saw what I was doing, that she praised and was delighted. Is my mind beginning to wander, or is love confusing my feelings? I cannot tell. But this I do know: I have a continual feeling that she is looking at me from a distance, and I am afraid to do aught that might trouble or offend her.

"So it is, Caius! but they have changed my soul, and sometimes I feel well for that reason. At times again I am tormented with the thought, for I fear that my manhood and energy are taken from me; that, perhaps, I am useless, not only for counsel, for judgment, for feasts, but for war even. These are undoubted enchantments! And to such a degree am I changed that I tell thee this, too, which came to my head when I lay wounded: that if Lygia were like Nigidia, Poppæa, Crispinilla, and our divorced women, if she were as vile, as pitiless, and as cheap as they, I should not love her as I do at present. But since I love her for that which divides us, thou wilt divine what a chaos is rising in my soul, in what darkness I live, how it is that I cannot see certain roads before me, and how far I am from knowing what to begin. If life may be compared to a spring, in my spring disquiet flows instead of water. I live through the hope that I shall see her, perhaps, and sometimes it seems to me that I shall see her surely. But what will happen to me in a year or two years, I know not, and cannot divine. I shall not leave Rome. I could not endure the society of the Augustians; and besides, the one solace in my sadness and disquiet is the thought that I am near Lygia, that through Glaucus the physician, who promised to visit me, or through Paul of Tarsus, I can learn something of her at times. No; I would not leave Rome, even were ye to offer me the government of Egypt. Know also, that I have ordered the sculptor to make a stone monument for Gulo, whom I slew in anger. Too late did it come to my mind that he had carried me in his arms, and was the first to teach me how to put an arrow on a bow. I know not why it was that a recollection of him rose in me which was sorrow and reproach. If what I write astonish thee, I reply that it astonishes me no less, but I write pure truth. — Farewell."

CHAPTER XXIX

VINICIUS received no answer to this letter. Petronius did not write, thinking evidently that Cæsar might command a return to Rome any day. In fact, news of it was spread in the city, and roused great delight in the hearts of the rabble, eager for games with gifts of grain and olives, great supplies of which had been accumulated in Ostia. Helius, Nero's freedman, announced at last the return in the Senate. But Nero, having embarked with his court on ships at Misenum, returned slowly, disembarking at coast towns for rest, or exhibitions in theatres. He remained between ten and twenty days in Minturna, and even thought to return to Naples and wait there for spring, which was earlier than usual, and warm. During all this time Vinicius lived shut up in his house, thinking of Lygia, and all those new things which occupied his soul, and brought to it ideas and feelings foreign to it thus far. He saw, from time to time, only Glaucus the physician, every one of whose visits delighted him, for he could converse with the man about Lygia. Glaucus knew not, it is true, where she had found refuge, but he gave assurance that the elders were protecting her with watchful care. Once too, when moved by the sadness of Vinicius, he told him that Peter had blamed Crispus for reproaching Lygia with her love. The young patrician, hearing this, grew pale from emotion. He had thought more than once that Lygia was not indifferent to him, but he fell into frequent doubt and uncertainty. Now for the first time he heard the confirmation of his desires and hopes from strange lips, and, besides, those of a Christian. At the first moment of gratitude he wished to run to Peter. When he learned, however, that he was not in the city, but teaching in the neighborhood, he implored Glaucus to accompany him thither, promising to make liberal gifts to the poor community. It seemed to him, too, that if Lygia loved him, all obstacles were thereby set aside, as he was ready at any moment to honor Christ. Glaucus, though he urged him persistently to receive baptism, would not venture to assure him that he would gain Lygia at once, and said that it was necessary to desire the religion for its own sake, through love of Christ, not for other objects. "One must have a Christian soul, too," said he. And Vinicius, though every obstacle angered him, had begun to understand that Glaucus, as a Christian, said what he ought to say. He had not become clearly conscious that one of the deepest changes in his nature was this, — that formerly he had measured people and things only by his own selfishness, but now he was accustoming himself gradually to the thought that other eyes might see differently, other hearts feel differently, and that justice did not mean always the same as personal profit.

He wished often to see Paul of Tarsus, whose discourse made him curious and disturbed him. He arranged in his mind arguments to overthrow his teaching, he resisted him in thought; still he wished to see him and to hear him. Paul, however, had gone to Aricium, and, since the visits of Glaucus had become rarer, Vinicius was in perfect solitude. He began again to run through back streets adjoining the Subura, and narrow lanes of the Trans-Tiber, in the hope that even from a distance he might see Lygia. When even that hope failed him, weariness and impatience began to rise in his heart. At last the time came when his former nature was felt again mightily, like that onrush of a wave to the shore from which it had receded. It seemed to him that he had been a fool to no purpose, that he had stuffed his head with things which brought sadness, that he ought to accept from life what it gives. He resolved to forget Lygia, or at least to seek pleasure and the use of things aside from her. He felt that this trial, however, was the last, and he threw himself into it with all the blind energy of impulse peculiar to him. Life itself seemed to urge him to this course.

The city, torpid and depopulated by winter, began to revive with hope of the near coming of Cæsar. A solemn reception was in waiting for him. Meanwhile spring was there; the snow on the Alban Hills had vanished under the breath of winds from Africa. Grass-plots in the gardens were covered with violets. The Forums and the Campus Martius were filled with people warmed by a sun of growing heat. Along the Appian Way, the usual place for drives outside the city, a movement of richly ornamented chariots had begun. Excursions were made to the Alban Hills. Youthful women, under pretext of worshipping Juno in Lanuvium, or Diana in Aricia, left home to seek adventures, society, meetings, and pleasure beyond the city. Here Vinicius saw one day among lordly chariots the splendid car of Chrysothemis, preceded by two Molossian dogs; it was surrounded by a crowd of young men and by old senators, whose position detained them in the city. Chrysothemis, driving four Corsican ponies herself, scattered smiles round about, and light strokes of a golden whip; but when she saw Vinicius she reined in her horses, took him into her car, and then to a feast at her house, which lasted all night. At that feast Vinicius drank so much that he did not remember when they took him home; he recollected, however, that when Chrysothemis mentioned Lygia he was offended, and, being drunk, emptied a goblet of Falernian on her head. When he thought of this in soberness, he was angrier still. But a day later Chrysothemis, forgetting evidently the injury, visited him at his house, and took him to the Appian Way a second time. Then she supped at his house, and confessed that not only Petronius, but his lute-player, had grown tedious to her long since, and that her heart was free now. They appeared together for a week, but the relation did not promise permanence. After the Falernian incident, however, Lygia's name was never mentioned, but Vinicius could not free himself from thoughts of her. He had the feeling always that her eyes were looking at his face, and that feeling filled him, as it were, with fear. He suffered, and could not escape the thought that he was saddening Lygia, or the regret which that thought roused in him. After the first scene of jealousy which Chrysothemis made because of two Syrian damsels whom he purchased, he let her go in rude fashion. He did not cease at once from pleasure and license, it is true, but he followed them out of spite, as it were, toward Lygia. At last he saw that the thought of her did not leave him for an instant; that she was the one cause of his evil activity as well as his good; and that really nothing in the world occupied him except her. Disgust, and then weariness, mastered him. Pleasure had grown loathsome, and left mere reproaches. It seemed to him that he was wretched, and this last feeling filled him with measureless astonishment, for formerly he recognized as good everything which pleased him. Finally, he lost freedom, self-confidence, and fell into perfect torpidity, from which even the news of Cæsar's coming could not rouse him. Nothing touched him, and he did not visit Petronius till the latter sent an invitation and his litter.

On seeing his uncle, though greeted with gladness, he replied to his questions unwillingly; but his feelings and thoughts, repressed for a long time, burst forth at last, and flowed from his mouth in a torrent of words. Once more he told in detail the history of his search for Lygia, his life among the Christians, everything which he had heard and seen there, everything which had passed through his head and heart; and finally he complained that he had fallen into a chaos, in which were lost composure and the gift of distinguishing and judging. Nothing, he said, attracted him, nothing was pleasing; he did not know what to hold to, nor how to act. He was ready both to honor and persecute Christ; he understood the loftiness of His teaching, but he felt also an irresistible repugnance to it. He understood that, even should he possess Lygia, he would not possess her completely, for he would have to share her with Christ. Finally, he was living as if not living, — without hope, without a morrow, without belief in happiness; around him was darkness in which he was groping for an exit, and could not find it.

Petronius, during this narrative, looked at his changed face, at his hands, which while speaking he stretched forth in a strange manner, as if actually seeking a road in the darkness, and he fell to thinking. All at once he rose, and, approaching Vinicius, caught with his fingers the hair above his ear.

"Dost know," asked he, "that thou hast gray hairs on thy temple?"

"Perhaps I have," answered Vinicius; "I should not be astonished were all my hair to grow white soon."

Silence followed. Petronius was a man of sense, and more than once he meditated on the soul of man and on life. In general, life, in the society in which they both lived, might be happy or unhappy externally, but internally it was at rest. Just as a thunderbolt or an earthquake might overturn a temple, so might misfortune crush a life. In itself, however, it was composed of simple and harmonious lines, free of complication. But there was something else in the words of Vinicius, and Petronius stood for the first time before a series of spiritual snarls which no one had straightened out hitherto. He was sufficiently a man of reason to feel their importance, but with all his quickness he could not answer the questions put to him. After a long silence, he said at last. —

"These must be enchantments."

"I too have thought so," answered Vinicius; "more than once it seemed to me that we were enchanted, both of us."

"And if thou," said Petronius, "were to go, for example, to the priests of Serapis? Among them, as among priests in general, there are many deceivers, no doubt; but there are others who have reached wonderful secrets."

He said this, however, without conviction and with an uncertain voice, for he himself felt how empty and even ridiculous that counsel must seem on his lips.

Vinicius rubbed his forehead, and said: "Enchantments! I have seen sorcerers who employed unknown and subterranean powers to their personal profit; I have seen those who used them to the harm of their enemies. But these Christians live in poverty, forgive their enemies, preach submission, virtue, and mercy; what profit could they get from enchantments, and why should they use them?"

Petronius was angry that his acuteness could find no reply; not wishing, however, to acknowledge this, he said, so as to offer an answer of some kind, —

"That is a new sect." After a while he added: "By the divine dweller in Paphian groves, how all that injures life! Thou wilt admire the goodness and virtue of those people; but I tell thee that they are bad, for they are enemies of life, as are diseases, and death itself. As things are, we have enough of these enemies; we do not need the Christians in addition. Just count them: diseases, Cæsar, Tigellinus, Cæsar's poetry, cobblers who govern the descendants of ancient Quirites, freedmen who sit in the Senate. By Castor! there is enough of this. That is a destructive and disgusting sect. Hast thou tried to shake thyself out of this sadness, and make some little use of life?"

"I have tried," answered Vinicius.

"Ah, traitor!" said Petronius, laughing; "news spreads quickly through slaves; thou hast seduced from me Chrysothemis!"

Vinicius waved his hand in disgust.

"In every case I thank thee," said Petronius. "I will send her a pair of slippers embroidered with pearls. In my language of a lover that means, 'Walk away.' I owe thee a double gratitude, — first, thou didst not accept Eunice; second, thou hast freed me from Chrysothemis. Listen to me! Thou seest before thee a man who has risen early, bathed, feasted, possessed Chrysothemis, written satires, and even at times interwoven prose with verses, but who has been as wearied as Cæsar, and often unable to unfetter himself from gloomy thoughts. And dost thou know why that was so? It was because I sought at a distance that which was near. A beautiful woman is worth her weight always in gold; but if she loves in addition, she has simply no price. Such a one thou wilt not buy with the riches of Verres. I say now to myself as follows: I will fill my life with happiness, as a goblet with the foremost wine which the earth has produced, and I will drink till my hand becomes powerless and my lips grow pale. What will come, I care not; and this is my latest philosophy."

"Thou hast proclaimed it always; there is nothing new in it."

"There is substance, which was lacking."

When he had said this, he called Eunice, who entered dressed in white drapery, — the former slave no longer, but as it were a goddess of love and happiness.

Petronius opened his arms to her, and said, —

"Come."

At this she ran up to him, and, sitting on his knee, surrounded his neck with her arms, and placed her head on his breast. Vinicius saw how a reflection of purple began to cover her cheeks, how her eyes melted gradually in mist. They formed a wonderful group of love and happiness. Petronius stretched his hand to a flat vase standing at one side on a table, and, taking a whole handful of violets, covered with them the head, bosom, and robe of Eunice; then he pushed the tunic from her arms, and said, —

"Happy he who, like me, has found love enclosed in such a form! At times it seems to me that we are a pair of gods. Look thyself! Has Praxiteles, or Miron, or Skopas, or Lysias even, created more wonderful lines? Or does there exist in Paros or in Pentelicus such marble as this, — warm, rosy, and full of love? There are people who kiss off the edges of vases, but I prefer to look for pleasure where it may be found really."

He began to pass his lips along her shoulders and neck. She was penetrated with a quivering; her eyes now closed, now opened, with an expression of unspeakable delight. Petronius after a while raised her exquisite head, and said, turning to Vinicius, —

"But think now, what are thy gloomy Christians in comparison with this? And if thou understand not the difference, go thy way to them. But this sight will cure thee."

Vinicius distended his nostrils, through which entered the odor of violets, which filled the whole chamber, and he grew pale; for he thought that if he could have passed his lips along Lygia's shoulders in that way, it would have been a kind of sacrilegious delight so great that let the world vanish afterward! But accustomed now to a quick perception of that which took place in him, he noticed that at that moment he was thinking of Lygia, and of her only.

"Eunice," said Petronius, "give command, thou divine one, to prepare garlands for our heads and a meal."

When she had gone out he turned to Vinicius.

"I offered to make her free, but knowest thou what she answered? — 'I would rather be thy slave than Cæsar's wife!' And she would not consent. I freed her then without her knowledge. The pretor favored me by not requiring her presence. But she does not know that she is free, as also she does not know that this house and all my jewels, excepting the gems, will belong to her in case of my death." He rose and walked through the room, and said: "Love changes some more, others less, but it has changed even me. Once I loved the odor of verbenas; but as Eunice prefers violets, I like them now beyond all other flowers, and since spring came we breathe only violets."

Here he stopped before Vinicius and inquired, —

"But as to thee, dost thou keep always to nard?"

"Give me peace!" answered the young man.

"I wished thee to see Eunice, and I mentioned her to thee, because thou, perhaps, art seeking also at a distance that which is near. Maybe for thee too is beating, somewhere in the chambers of thy slaves, a true and simple heart. Apply such a balsam to thy wounds. Thou sayest that Lygia loves thee? Perhaps she does. But what kind of love is that which abdicates? Is not the meaning this, — that there is another force stronger than her love? No, my dear, Lygia is not Eunice."

"All is one torment merely," answered Vinicius. "I saw thee kissing Eunice's shoulders, and I thought then that if Lygia would lay hers bare to me I should not care if the ground opened under us next moment. But at the very thought of such an act a certain dread seized me, as if I had attacked some vestal or wished to defile a divinity. Lygia is not Eunice, but I understand the difference not in thy way. Love has changed thy nostrils, and thou preferrest violets to verbenas; but it has changed my soul: hence, in spite of my misery and desire, I prefer Lygia to be what she is rather than to be like others."

"In that case no injustice is done thee. But I do not understand the position."

"True, true!" answered Vinicius, feverishly. "We understand each other no longer."

Another moment of silence followed.

"May Hades swallow thy Christians!" exclaimed Petronius. "They have filled thee with disquiet, and destroyed thy sense of life. May Hades devour them! Thou art mistaken in thinking that their religion is good, for good is what gives people happiness, namely, beauty, love, power; but these they call vanity. Thou art mistaken in this, that they are just! for if we pay good for evil, what shall we pay for good? And besides, if we pay the same for one and the other, why are people to be good?"

"No, the pay is not the same; but according to their teaching it begins in a future life, which is without limit."

"I do not enter into that question, for we shall see hereafter if it be possible to see anything without eyes. Meanwhile they are simply incompetents. Ursus strangled Croton because he has limbs of bronze; but these are mopes, and the future cannot belong to mopes."

"For them life begins with death."

"Which is as if one were to say, 'Day begins with night.' Hast thou the intent to carry off Lygia?"

"No, I cannot pay her evil for good, and I swore that I would not."

"Dost thou intend to accept the religion of Christ?"

"I wish to do so, but my nature cannot endure it."

"But wilt thou be able to forget Lygia?"

"No."

"Then travel."

At that moment the slaves announced that the repast was ready; but Petronius, to whom it seemed that he had fallen on a good thought, said, on the way to the triclinium, —

"Thou has ridden over a part of the world, but only as a soldier hastening to his place of destination, and without halting by the way. Go with us to Achæa. Cæsar has not given up the journey. He will stop everywhere on the way, sing, receive crowns, plunder temples, and return as a triumphator to Italy. That will resemble somewhat a journey of Bacchus and Apollo in one person. Augustians, male and female, a thousand citharæ. By Castor! that will be worth witnessing, for hitherto the world has not seen anything like it!"

Here he placed himself on the couch before the table, by the side of Eunice; and when the slaves put a wreath of anemones on his head, he continued, —

"What hast thou seen in Corbulo's service? Nothing. Hast thou seen the Grecian temples thoroughly, as I have, — I who was passing more than two years from the hands of one guide to those of another? Hast thou been in Rhodes to examine the site of the Colossus? Hast thou seen in Panopeus, in Phocis, the clay from which Prometheus shaped man; or in Sparta the eggs laid by Leda; or in Athens the famous Sarmatian armor made of horse-hoofs; or in Eubœa the ship of Agamemnon; or the cup for whose pattern the left breast of Helen served? Hast thou seen Alexandria, Memphis, the Pyramids, the hair which Isis tore from her head in grief for Osiris? Hast thou heard the shout of Memnon? The world is wide; everything does not end at the Trans-Tiber! I will accompany Cæsar, and when he returns I will leave him and go to Cyprus; for it is the wish of this golden-haired goddess of mine that we offer doves together to the divinity in Paphos, and thou must know that whatever she wishes must happen."

"I am thy slave," said Eunice.

He rested his garlanded head on her bosom, and said with a smile, —

"Then I am the slave of a slave. I admire thee, divine one, from feet to head!"

Then he said to Vinicius: "Come with us to Cyprus. But first remember that thou must see Cæsar. It is bad that thou hast not been with him yet; Tigellinus is ready to use this to thy disadvantage. He has no personal hatred for thee, it is true; but he cannot love thee, even because thou art my sister's son. We shall say that thou wert sick. We must think over what thou art to answer should he ask thee about Lygia. It will be best to wave thy hand and say that she was with thee till she wearied thee. He will understand that. Tell him also that sickness kept thee at home; that thy fever was increased by disappointment at not being able to visit Naples and hear his song; that thou wert assisted to health only by the hope of hearing him. Fear no exaggeration. Tigellinus promises to invent, not only something great for Cæsar, but something enormous. I am afraid that he will undermine me; I am afraid too of thy disposition."

"Dost thou know," said Vinicius, "that there are people who have no fear of Cæsar, and who live as calmly as if he were non-existent?"

"I know whom thou hast in mind — the Christians."

"Yes; they alone. But our life, — what is it if not unbroken terror?"

"Do not mention thy Christians. They fear not Cæsar, because he has not even heard of them perhaps; and in every case he knows nothing of them, and they concern him as much as withered leaves. But I tell thee that they are incompetents. Thou feelest this thyself; if thy nature is repugnant to their teaching, it is just because thou feelest their incompetence. Thou art a man of other clay; so trouble not thyself or me with them. We shall be able to live and die, and what more they will be able to do is unknown."

These words struck Vinicius; and when he returned home, he began to think that in truth, perhaps, the goodness and charity of Christians was a proof of their incompetence of soul. It seemed to him that people of strength and temper could not forgive thus. It came to his head that this must be the real cause of the repulsion which his Roman soul felt toward their teaching. "We shall be able to live and die!" said Petronius. As to them, they know only how to forgive, and understand neither true love nor true hatred.

CHAPTER XXX

CÆSAR, on returning to Rome, was angry because he had returned, and after some days was filled anew with a wish to visit Achæa. He even issued an edict in which he declared that his absence would be short, and that public affairs would not be exposed to detriment because of it. In company with Augustians, among whom was Vinicius, he repaired to the Capitol to make offerings to the gods for an auspicious journey. But on the second day, when he visited the temple of Vesta, an event took place which changed all his projects. Nero feared the gods, though he did not believe in them; he feared especially the mysterious Vesta, who filled him with such awe that at sight of the divinity and the sacred fire his hair rose on a sudden from terror, his teeth chattered, a shiver ran through his limbs, and he dropped into the arms of Vinicius, who happened there behind him. He was borne out of the temple at once, and conveyed to the Palatine, where he recovered soon, but did not leave the bed for that day. He declared, moreover, to the great astonishment of those present, that he deferred his journey, since the divinity had warned him secretly against haste. An hour later it was announced throughout Rome that Cæsar, seeing the gloomy faces of the citizens, and moved by love for them, as a father for his children, would remain to share their lot and their pleasures. The people, rejoiced at this decision, and certain also that they would not miss games and a distribution of wheat, assembled in crowds before the gates of the Palatine, and raised shouts in honor of the divine Cæsar, who interrupted the play at dice with which he was amusing himself with Augustians, and said:

"Yes, there was need to defer the journey. Egypt, and predicted dominion over the Orient, cannot escape me; hence Achæa, too, will not be lost. I will give command to cut through the isthmus of Corinth; I will rear such monuments in Egypt that the pyramids will seem childish toys in comparison; I will have a sphinx built seven times greater than that which is gazing into the desert outside Memphis; but I will command that it have my face. Coming ages will speak only of that monument and of me."

"With thy verses thou hast reared a monument to thyself already, not seven, but thrice seven, times greater than the pyramid of Cheops," said Petronius.

"But with my song?" inquired Nero.

"Ah! if men could only build for thee a statue, like that of Memnon, to call with thy voice at sunrise! For all ages to come the seas adjoining Egypt would swarm with ships in which crowds from the three parts of the world would be lost in listening to thy song."

"Alas! who can do that?" said Nero.

"But thou canst give command to cut out of basalt thyself driving a quadriga."

"True! I will do that!"

"Thou wilt bestow a gift on humanity."

"In Egypt I will marry the Moon, who is now a widow, and I shall be a god really."

"And thou wilt give us stars for wives; we will make a new constellation, which will be called the constellation of Nero. But do thou marry Vitelius to the Nile, so that he may beget hippopotamuses. Give the desert to Tigellinus, he will be king of the jackals."

"And what dost thou predestine to me?" inquired Vatinius.

"Apis bless thee! Thou didst arrange such splendid games in Beneventum that I cannot wish thee ill. Make a pair of boots for the sphinx, whose paws must grow numb during night-dews; after that thou will make sandals for the Colossi which form the alleys before the temples. Each one will find there a fitting occupation. Domitius Afer, for example, will be treasurer, since he is known for his honesty. I am glad, Cæsar, when thou art dreaming of Egypt, and I am saddened because thou hast deferred thy plan of a journey."

"Thy mortal eyes saw nothing, for the deity becomes invisible to whomever it wishes," said Nero. "Know that when I was in the temple of Vesta she herself stood near me, and whispered in my ear, 'Defer the journey.' That happened so unexpectedly that I was terrified, though for such an evident care of the gods for me I should be thankful."

"We were all terrified," said Tigellinus, "and the vestal Rubria fainted."

"Rubria!" said Nero; "what a snowy neck she has!"

"But she blushed at sight of the divine Cæsar — "

"True! I noticed that myself. That is wonderful. There is something divine in every vestal, and Rubria is very beautiful.

"Tell me," said he, after a moment's meditation, "why people fear Vesta more than other gods. What does this mean? Though I am the chief priest, fear seized me to-day. I remember only that I was falling back, and should have dropped to the ground had not some one supported me. Who was it?"

"I," answered Vinicius.

"Oh, thou 'stern Mars'! Why wert thou not in Beneventum? They told me that thou wert ill, and indeed thy face is changed. But I heard that Croton wished to kill thee? Is that true?"

"It is, and he broke my arm; but I defended myself."

"With a broken arm?"

"A certain barbarian helped me; he was stronger than Croton."

Nero looked at him with astonishment. "Stronger than Croton? Art thou jesting? Croton was the strongest of men, but now here is Syphax from Ethiopia."

"I tell thee, Cæsar, what I saw with my own eyes."

"Where is that pearl? Has he not become king of Nemi?"

"I cannot tell, Cæsar. I lost sight of him."

"Thou knowest not even of what people he is?"

"I had a broken arm, and could not inquire for him."

"Seek him, and find him for me."

"I will occupy myself with that," said Tigellinus.

But Nero spoke further to Vinicius: "I thank thee for having supported me; I might have broken my head by a fall. On a time thou wert a good companion, but campaigning and service with Corbulo have made thee wild in some way; I see thee rarely.

"How is that maiden too narrow in the hips, with whom thou wert in love," asked he after a while, "and whom I took from Aulus for thee?"

Vinicius was confused, but Petronius came to his aid at that moment.

"I will lay a wager, lord," said he, "that he has forgotten. Dost thou see his confusion? Ask him how many of them there were since that time, and I will not give assurance of his power to answer. The Vinicii are good soldiers, but still better gamecocks. They need whole flocks. Punish him for that, lord, by not inviting him to the feast which Tigellinus promises to arrange in thy honor on the pond of Agrippa."

"I will not do that. I trust, Tigellinus, that flocks of beauty will not be lacking there."

"Could the Graces be absent where Amor will be present?" answered Tigellinus.

"Weariness tortures me," said Nero. "I have remained in Rome at the will of the goddess, but I cannot endure the city. I will go to Antium. I am stifled in these narrow streets, amid these tumble-down houses, amid these alleys. Foul air flies even here to my house and my gardens. Oh, if an earthquake would destroy Rome, if some angry god would level it to the earth! I would show how a city should be built, which is the head of the world and my capital."

"Cæsar," answered Tigellinus, "thou sayest, 'If some angry god would destroy the city,' — is it so?"

"It is! What then?"

"But art thou not a god?"

Nero waved his hand with an expression of weariness, and said, —

"We shall see thy work on the pond of Agrippa. Afterward I go to Antium. Ye are all little, hence do not understand that I need immense things."

Then he closed his eyes, giving to understand in that way that he needed rest. In fact, the Augustians were beginning to depart. Petronius went out with Vinicius, and said to him, —

"Thou art invited, then, to share in the amusement. Bronzebeard has renounced the journey, but he will be madder than ever; he has fixed himself in the city as in his own house. Try thou, too, to find in these madnesses amusement and forgetfulness. Well! we have conquered the world, and have a right to amuse ourselves. Thou, Marcus, art a very comely fellow, and to that I ascribe in part the weakness which I have for thee. By the Ephesian Diana! if thou couldst see thy joined brows, and thy face in which the ancient blood of the Quirites is evident! Others near thee looked like freedmen. True! were it not for that mad religion, Lygia would be in thy house to-day. Attempt once more to prove to me that they are not enemies of life and mankind. They have acted well toward thee, hence thou mayst be grateful to them; but in thy place I should detest that religion, and seek pleasure where I could find it. Thou art a comely fellow, I repeat, and Rome is swarming with divorced women."

"I wonder only that all this does not torture thee yet?"

"Who has told thee that it does not? It tortures me this long time, but I am not of thy years. Besides, I have other attachments which are lacking thee. I love books, thou hast no love for them; I love poetry, which annoys thee; I love pottery, gems, a multitude of things, at which thou dost not look; I have a pain in my loins, which thou hast not; and, finally, I have found Eunice, but thou hast found nothing similar. For me, it is pleasant in my house, among masterpieces; of thee I can never make a man of æsthetic feeling. I know that in life I shall never find anything beyond what I have found; thou thyself knowest not that thou art hoping yet continually, and seeking. If death were to visit thee, with all thy courage and sadness, thou wouldst die with astonishment that it was necessary to leave the world; but I should accept death as a necessity, with the conviction that there is no fruit in the world which I have not tasted. I do not hurry, neither shall I loiter; I shall try merely to be joyful to the end. There are cheerful sceptics in the world. For me, the Stoics are fools; but stoicism tempers men, at least, while thy Christians bring sadness into the world, which in life is the same as rain in nature. Dost thou know what I have learned? That during the festivities which Tigellinus will arrange at the pond of Agrippa, there will be lupanaria, and in them women from the first houses of Rome. Will there be not even one sufficiently beautiful to console thee? There will be maidens, too, appearing in society for the first time — as nymphs. Such is our Roman Cæsardom! The air is mild already; the midday breeze will warm the water and not bring pimples on naked bodies. And thou, Narcissus, know this, that there will not be one to refuse thee, — not one, even though she be a vestal virgin."

Vinicius began to strike his head with his palm, like a man occupied eternally with one thought.

"I should need luck to find such a one."

"And who did this for thee, if not the Christians? But people whose standard is a cross cannot be different. Listen to me: Greece was beautiful, and created wisdom; we created power; and what, to thy thinking, can this teaching create? If thou know, explain; for, by Pollux! I cannot divine it."

"Thou art afraid, it seems, lest I become a Christian," said Vinicius, shrugging his shoulders.

"I am afraid that thou hast spoiled life for thyself. If thou canst not be a Grecian, be a Roman; possess and enjoy. Our madnesses have a certain sense, for there is in them a kind of thought of our own. I despise Bronzebeard, because he is a Greek buffoon. If he held himself a Roman, I should recognize that he was right in permitting himself madness. Promise me that if thou find some Christian on returning home, thou wilt show thy tongue to him. If he be Glaucus the physician, he will not wonder. — Till we meet on the pond of Agrippa."

CHAPTER XXXI

PRETORIANS surrounded the groves on the banks of the pond of Agrippa, lest over-numerous throngs of spectators might annoy Cæsar and his guests; though it was said that everything in Rome distinguished for wealth, beauty, or intellect was present at that feast, which had no equal in the history of the city. Tigellinus wished to recompense Cæsar for the deferred journey to Achæa, to surpass all who had ever feasted Nero, and prove that no man could entertain as he could. With this object in view, while with Cæsar in Naples, and later in Beneventum, he had made preparations and sent orders to bring from remotest regions of the earth beasts, birds, rare fish, and plants, not omitting vessels and cloths, which were to enhance the splendor of the feast. The revenues of whole provinces went to satisfy mad projects; but the powerful favorite had no need to hesitate. His influence grew daily. Tigellinus was not dearer than others to Nero yet, perhaps, but he was becoming more and more indispensable. Petronius surpassed him infinitely in polish, intellect, wit; in conversation he knew better how to amuse Cæsar: but to his misfortune he surpassed in conversation Cæsar himself, hence he roused his jealousy; moreover he could not be an obedient instrument in everything, and Cæsar feared his opinion when there were questions in matters of taste. But before Tigellinus, Nero never felt any restraint. The very title, *arbiter elegantiarum*, which had been given to Petronius, annoyed Nero's vanity, for who had the right to bear that title but himself? Tigellinus had sense enough to know his own deficiencies; and seeing that he could not compete with Petronius, Lucan, or others distinguished by birth, talents, or learning, he resolved to extinguish them by the suppleness of his services, and above all by such a magnificence that the imagination of Nero himself would be struck by it. He had arranged to give the feast on a gigantic raft, framed of gilded timbers. The borders of this raft were decked with splendid shells found in the Red Sea and the Indian Ocean, shells brilliant with the colors of pearls and the rainbow. The banks of the pond were covered with groups of palm, with groves of lotus, and blooming roses. In the midst of these were hidden fountains of perfumed water, statues of gods and goddesses, and gold or silver cages filled with birds of various colors. In the centre of the raft rose an immense tent, or rather, not to hide the feasters, only the roof of a tent, made of Syrian purple, resting on silver columns; under it were gleaming, like suns, tables prepared for the guests, loaded with Alexandrian glass, crystal, and vessels simply beyond price, — the plunder of Italy, Greece, and Asia Minor. The raft, which because of plants accumulated on it had the appearance of an island and a garden, was joined by cords of gold and purple to boats shaped like fish, swans, mews, and flamingoes, in which sat at painted oars naked rowers of both sexes, with forms and features of marvellous beauty, their hair dressed in Oriental fashion, or gathered in golden nets. When Nero arrived at the main raft with Poppæa and the Augustians, and sat beneath the purple tent-roof, the oars struck the water, the boats moved, the golden cords stretched, and the raft with the feast and the guests began to move and describe circles on the pond. Other boats surrounded it, and other smaller rafts, filled with women playing on citharæ and harps, women whose rosy bodies on the blue background of the sky and the water and in the reflections from golden instruments seemed to absorb that blue and those reflections, and to change and bloom like flowers.

From the groves at the banks, from fantastic buildings reared for that day and hidden among thickets, were heard music and song. The neighborhood resounded, the groves resounded; echoes bore around the voices of horns and trumpets. Cæsar himself, with Poppæa on one side of him, and Pythagoras on the other, was amazed; and more especially when among the boats young slave maidens appeared as sirens, and were covered with green network in imitation of scales, he did not spare praises on Tigellinus. But he looked at Petronius from habit, wishing to learn the opinion of the "arbiter," who seemed indifferent for a long time, and only when questioned outright, answered, —

"I judge, lord, that ten thousand naked maidens make less impression than one."

But the "floating feast" pleased Cæsar, for it was something new. Besides, such exquisite dishes were served that the imagination of Apicius would have failed at sight of them, and wines of so many kinds that Otho, who used to serve eighty, would have hidden under water with shame, could he have witnessed the luxury of that feast. Besides women, the Augustians sat down at the table, among whom Vinicius excelled all with his beauty. Formerly his figure and face indicated too clearly the soldier by profession; now mental suffering and the physical pain through which he had passed had chiselled his features, as if the delicate hand of a master had passed over them. His complexion had lost its former swarthiness, but the yellowish gleam of Numidian marble remained on it. His eyes had grown larger and more pensive. His body had retained its former powerful outlines, as if created for armor; but above the body of a legionary was seen the head of a Grecian god, or at least of a refined patrician, at once subtle and splendid. Petronius, in saying that none of the ladies of Cæsar's court would be able or willing to resist Vinicius, spoke like a man of experience. All gazed at him now, not excepting Poppæa, or the vestal virgin Rubria, whom Cæsar wished to see at the feast.

Wines, cooled in mountain snow, soon warmed the hearts and heads of the guests. Boats shaped as grasshoppers or butterflies shot forth from the bushes at the shore every moment. The blue surface of the pond seemed occupied by butterflies. Above the boats here and there flew doves, and other birds from India and Africa, fastened with silver and blue threads or strings. The sun had passed the greater part of the sky, but the day was warm and even hot, though in the beginning of May. The pond heaved from the strokes of oars, which beat the water in time with music; but in the air there was not the least breath of wind; the groves were motionless, as if lost in listening and in gazing at that which was happening on the water. The raft circled continually on the pond, bearing guests who were increasingly drunk and boisterous.

The feast had not run half its course yet, when the order in which all sat at the table was observed no longer. Cæsar gave the example, for, rising himself, he commanded Vinicius, who sat next to Rubria the vestal, to move. Nero occupied the place, and began to whisper something in Rubria's ear. Vinicius found himself next to Poppæa, who extended her arm and begged him to fasten her loosened bracelet. When he did so, with hands trembling somewhat, she cast at him from beneath her long lashes a glance as it were of modesty, and shook her golden head as if in resistance.

Meanwhile the sun, growing larger, ruddier, sank slowly behind the tops of the grove; the guests were for the greater part thoroughly intoxicated. The raft circled now nearer the shore, on which, among bunches of trees and flowers, were seen groups of people, disguised as fauns or satyrs, playing on flutes, bagpipes, and drums, with groups of maidens representing nymphs, dryads, and hamadryads. Darkness fell at last amid drunken shouts from the tent, shouts raised in honor of Luna. Meanwhile the groves were lighted with a thousand lamps. From the lupanaria on the shores shone swarms of lights; on the terraces appeared new naked groups, formed of the wives and daughters of the first Roman houses. These with voice and unrestrained manner began to lure partners. The raft touched the shore at last. Cæsar and the Augustians vanished in the groves, scattered in lupanaria, in tents hidden in thickets, in grottos artificially arranged among fountains and springs. Madness seized all; no one knew whither Cæsar had gone; no one knew who was a senator, who a knight, who a dancer, who a musician. Satyrs and fauns fell to chasing nymphs with shouting. They struck lamps with thyrses to quench them. Darkness covered certain parts of the grove. Everywhere, however, laughter and shouts were heard, and whispers, and panting breaths. In fact Rome had not seen anything like that before.

Vinicius was not drunk, as he had been at the feast in Nero's palace, when Lygia was present; but he was roused and intoxicated by the sight of everything done round about, and at last the fever of pleasure seized him. Rushing into the forest, he ran, with others, examining who of the dryads seemed most beautiful. New flocks of these raced around him every moment with shouts and with songs; these flocks were pursued by fauns, satyrs, senators, knights, and by sounds of music. Seeing at last a band of maidens led by one arrayed as Diana, he sprang to it, intending to examine the goddess more closely. All at once the heart sank in his bosom, for he thought that in that goddess, with the moon on her forehead, he recognized Lygia.

They encircled him with a mad whirl, and, wishing evidently to incline him to follow, rushed away the next moment like a herd of deer. But he stood on the spot with beating heart, breathless; for though he saw that the Diana was not Lygia, and that at close sight she was not even like her, the too powerful impression deprived him of strength. Straightway he was seized by such yearning as he had never felt before, and love for Lygia rushed to his breast in a new, immense wave. Never had she seemed so dear, pure, and beloved as in that forest of madness and frenzied excess. A moment before, he himself wished to drink of that cup, and share in that shameless letting loose of the senses; now disgust and repugnance possessed him. He felt that infamy was stifling him; that his breast needed air and the stars which were hidden by the thickets of that dreadful grove. He determined to flee; but barely had he moved when before him stood some veiled figure, which placed its hands on his shoulders and whispered, flooding his face with burning breath, —

"I love thee! Come! no one will see us, hasten!"

Vinicius was roused, as if from a dream.

"Who art thou?"

But she leaned her breast on him and insisted, —

"Hurry! See how lonely it is here, and I love thee! Come!"

"Who art thou?" repeated Vinicius.

"Guess!"

As she said this, she pressed her lips to his through the veil, drawing toward her his head at the same time, till at last breath failed the woman and she tore her face from him.

"Night of love! night of madness!" said she, catching the air quickly. "To-day is free! Thou hast me!"

But that kiss burned Vinicius; it filled him with disquiet. His soul and heart were elsewhere; in the whole world nothing existed for him except Lygia. So, pushing back the veiled figure, he said, —

"Whoever thou be, I love another, I do not wish thee."

"Remove the veil," said she, lowering her head toward him.

At that moment the leaves of the nearest myrtle began to rustle; the veiled woman vanished like a dream vision, but from a distance her laugh was heard, strange in some way, and ominous.

Petronius stood before Vinicius.

"I have heard and seen," said he.

"Let us go from this place," replied Vinicius.

And they went. They passed the lupanaria gleaming with light, the grove, the line of mounted pretorians, and found the litters.

"I will go with thee," said Petronius.

They sat down together. On the road both were silent, and only in the atrium of Vinicius's house did Petronius ask, —

"Dost thou know who that was?"

"Was it Rubria?" asked Vinicius, repulsed at the very thought that Rubria was a vestal.

"No."

"Who then?"

Petronius lowered his voice.

"The fire of Vesta was defiled, for Rubria was with Cæsar. But with thee was speaking" — and he finished in a still lower voice, "the divine Augusta." A moment of silence followed.

"Cæsar," said Petronius, "was unable to hide from Poppæa his desire for Rubria; therefore she wished, perhaps, to avenge herself. But I hindered you both. Hadst thou recognized the Augusta and refused her, thou wouldst have been ruined beyond rescue, — thou, Lygia, and I, perhaps."

"I have enough of Rome, Cæsar, feasts, the Augusta, Tigellinus, and all of you!" burst out Vinicius. "I am stifling. I cannot live thus; I cannot. Dost understand me?"

"Vinicius, thou art losing sense, judgment, moderation."

"I love only her in this world."

"What of that?"

"This, that I wish no other love. I have no wish for your life, your feasts, your shamelessness, your crimes!"

"What is taking place in thee? Art thou a Christian?"

The young man seized his head with both hands, and repeated, as if in despair, —

"Not yet! not yet!"

CHAPTER XXXII

PETRONIUS went home shrugging his shoulders and greatly dissatisfied. It was evident to him that he and Vinicius had ceased to understand each other, that their souls had separated entirely. Once Petronius had immense influence over the young soldier. He had been for him a model in everything, and frequently a few ironical words of his sufficed to restrain Vinicius or urge him to something. At present there remained nothing of that; such was the change that Petronius did not try his former methods, feeling that his wit and irony would slip without effect along the new principles which love and contact with the uncomprehended society of Christians had put in the soul of Vinicius. The veteran sceptic understood that he had lost the key to that soul. This knowledge filled him with dissatisfaction and even with fear, which was heightened by the events of that night. "If on the part of the Augusta it is not a passing whim but a more enduring desire," thought Petronius, "one of two things will happen, — either Vinicius will not resist her, and he may be ruined by any accident, or, what is like him to-day, he will resist, and in that event he will be ruined certainly, and perhaps I with him, even because I am his relative, and because the Augusta, having included a whole family in her hatred, will throw the weight of her influence on the side of Tigellinus. In this way and that it is bad." Petronius was a man of courage and felt no dread of death; but since he hoped nothing from it, he had no wish to invite it. After long meditation, he decided at last that it would be better and safer to send Vinicius from Rome on a journey. Ah! but if in addition he could give him Lygia for the road, he would do so with pleasure. But he hoped that it would not be too difficult to persuade him to the journey without her. He would spread a report on the Palatine then of Vinicius's illness, and remove danger as well from his nephew as himself. The Augusta did not know whether she was recognized by Vinicius; she might suppose that she was not, hence her vanity had not suffered much so far. But it might be different in the future, and it was necessary to avoid peril. Petronius wished to gain time, above all; for he understood that once Cæsar set out for Achæa, Tigellinus, who comprehended nothing in the domain of art, would descend to the second place and lose his influence. In Greece Petronius was sure of victory over every opponent.

Meanwhile he determined to watch over Vinicius, and urge him to the journey. For a number of days he was ever thinking over this, that if he obtained an edict from Cæsar expelling the Christians from Rome, Lygia would leave it with the other confessors of Christ, and after her Vinicius too. Then there would be no need to persuade him. The thing itself was possible. In fact it was not so long since, when the Jews began disturbances out of hatred to the Christians, Claudius, unable to distinguish one from the other, expelled the Jews. Why should not Nero expel the Christians? There would be more room in Rome without them. After that "floating feast" Petronius saw Nero daily, both on the Palatine and in other houses. To suggest such an idea was easy, for Nero never opposed suggestions which brought harm or ruin to any one. After mature decision Petronius framed a whole plan for himself. He would prepare a feast in his own house, and at this feast persuade Cæsar to issue an edict. He had even a hope, which was not barren, that Cæsar would confide the execution of the edict to him. He would send out Lygia with all the consideration proper to the mistress of Vinicius to Baiæ, for instance, and let them love and amuse themselves there with Christianity as much as they liked.

Meanwhile he visited Vinicius frequently, first, because he could not, despite all his Roman selfishness, rid himself of attachment to the young tribune, and second, because he wished to persuade him to the journey. Vinicius feigned sickness, and did not show himself on the Palatine, where new plans appeared every day. At last Petronius heard from Cæsar's own lips that three days from then he would go to Antium without fail. Next morning he went straightway to inform Vinicius, who showed him a list of persons invited to Antium, which list one of Cæsar's freedmen had brought him that morning.

"My name is on it; so is thine," said he. "Thou wilt find the same at thy house on returning."

"Were I not among the invited," replied Petronius, "it would mean that I must die; I do not expect that to happen before the journey to Achæa. I shall be too useful to Nero. Barely have we come to Rome," said he, on looking at the list, "when we must leave again, and drag over the road to Antium. But we must go, for this is not merely an invitation, it is a command as well."

"And if some one would not obey?"

"He would be invited in another style to go on a journey notably longer, —one from which people do not return. What a pity that thou hast not obeyed my counsel and left Rome in season! Now thou must go to Antium."

"I must go to Antium. See in what times we live and what vile slaves we are!"

"Hast thou noticed that only to-day?"

"No. but thou hast explained to me that Christian teaching is an enemy of life, since it shackles it. But can their shackles be stronger than those which we carry? Thou hast said, 'Greece created wisdom and beauty, and Rome power.' Where is our power?"

"Call Chilo and talk with him. I have no desire to-day to philosophize. By Hercules! I did not create these times, and I do not answer for them. Let us speak of Antium. Know that great danger is awaiting thee, and it would be better, perhaps, to measure strength with that Ursus who choked Croton than to go there, but still thou canst not refuse."

Vinicius waved his hand carelessly, and said, —

"Danger! We are all wandering in the shadow of death, and every moment some head sinks in its darkness."

"Am I to enumerate all who had a little sense, and therefore, in spite of the times of Tiberius, Caligula, Claudius, and Nero, lived eighty and ninety years? Let even such a man as Domitius Afer serve thee as an example. He has grown old quietly, though all his life he has been a criminal and a villain."

"Perhaps for that very reason!" answered Vinicius.

Then he began to glance over the list and read: "Tigellinus, Vatinius, Sextus Africanus, Aquilinus Regulus, Suilius Nerulinus, Eprius Marcellus, and so on! What an assembly of ruffians and scoundrels! And to say that they govern the world! Would it not become them better to exhibit an Egyptian or Syrian divinity through villages, jingle sistra, and earn their bread by telling fortunes or dancing?"

"Or exhibiting learned monkeys, calculating dogs, or a flute-playing ass," added Petronius. "That is true, but let us speak of something more important. Summon thy attention and listen. I have said on the Palatine that thou art ill, unable to leave the house; still thy name is on the list, which proves that some one does not credit my stories and has seen to this purposely. Nero cares nothing for the matter, since for him thou art a soldier, who has no conception of poetry or music, and with whom at the very highest he can talk only about races in the Circus. So Poppæa must have seen to putting down thy name, which means that her desire for thee was not a passing whim, and that she wants to win thee."

"She is a daring Augusta."

"Indeed she is daring, for she may ruin herself beyond redemption. May Venus inspire her, however, with another love as soon as possible; but since she desires thee thou must observe the very greatest caution. She has begun to weary Bronzebeard already; he prefers Rubria now, or Pythagoras, but, through consideration of self, he would wreak the most horrible vengeance on us."

"In the grove I knew not that she was speaking to me; but thou wert listening. I said that I loved another, and did not wish her. Thou knowest that."

"I implore thee, by all the infernal gods, lose not the remnant of reason which the Christians have left in thee. How is it possible to hesitate, having a choice between probable and certain destruction? Have I not said already that if thou hadst wounded the Augusta's vanity, there would have been no rescue for thee? By Hades! if life has grown hateful to thee, better open thy veins at once, or cast thyself on a sword, for shouldst thou offend Poppæa, a less easy death may meet thee. It was easier once to converse with thee. What concerns thee specially? Would this affair cause thee loss, or hinder thee from loving thy Lygia? Remember, besides, that Poppæa saw her on the Palatine. It will not be difficult for her to guess why thou art rejecting such lofty favor, and she will get Lygia even from under the earth. Thou wilt ruin not only thyself, but Lygia too. Dost understand?"

Vinicius listened as if thinking of something else, and at last he said, —

"I must see her."

"Who? Lygia?"

"Lygia."

"Dost thou know where she is?"

"No."

"Then thou wilt begin anew to search for her in old cemeteries and beyond the Tiber?"

"I know not, but I must see her."

"Well, though she is a Christian, it may turn out that she has more judgment than thou; and it will certainly, unless she wishes thy ruin."

Vinicius shrugged his shoulders. "She saved me from the hands of Ursus."

"Then hurry, for Bronzebeard will not postpone his departure. Sentences of death may be issued in Antium also."

But Vinicius did not hear. One thought alone occupied him, an interview with Lygia; hence he began to think over methods.

Meanwhile something intervened which might set aside every difficulty. Chilo came to his house unexpectedly.

He entered wretched and worn, with signs of hunger on his face and in rags; but the servants, who had the former command to admit him at all hours of the day or night, did not dare to detain him, so he went straight to the atrium, and standing before Vinicius said, —

"May the gods give thee immortality, and share with thee dominion over the world."

Vinicius at the first moment wished to give the order to throw him out of doors; but the thought came to him that the Greek perhaps knew something of Lygia, and curiosity overcame his disgust.

"Is that thou?" asked he. "What has happened to thee?"

"Evil, O son of Jove," answered Chilo. "Real virtue is a ware for which no one inquires now, and a genuine sage must be glad of this even, that once in five days he has something with which to buy from the butcher a sheep's head, to gnaw in a garret, washing it down with his tears. Ah, lord! What thou didst give me I paid Atractus for books, and afterward I was robbed and ruined. The slave who was to write down my wisdom fled, taking the remnant of what thy generosity bestowed on me. I am in misery, but I thought to myself: To whom can I go, if not to thee, O Serapis, whom I love and deify, for whom I have exposed my life?"

"Why hast thou come, and what dost thou bring?"

"I come for aid, O Baal, and I bring my misery, my tears, my love, and finally the information which through love for thee I have collected. Thou rememberest, lord, I told thee once how I had given a slave of the divine Petronius one thread from the girdle of the Paphian Venus? I know now that it helped her, and thou, O descendant of the Sun, who knowest what is happening in that house, knowest also what Eunice is there. I have another such thread. I have preserved it for thee, lord."

Here he stopped, on noticing the anger which was gathering on the brows of Vinicius, and said quickly, so as to anticipate the outburst, —

"I know where the divine Lygia is living; I will show thee the street and the house."

Vinicius repressed the emotion with which that news filled him, and said, —

"Where is she?"

"With Linus, the elder priest of the Christians. She is there with Ursus, who goes as before to the miller, a namesake of thy dispensator Demas. Yes, Demas! Ursus works in the night; so if thou surround the house at night, thou wilt not find him. Linus is old, and besides him there are only two aged women in the house."

"Whence dost thou know all this?"

"Thou rememberest, lord, that the Christians had me in their hands, and spared me. True, Glaucus was mistaken in thinking that I was the cause of his misfortunes; but he believed that I was, poor man, and he believes so yet. Still they spared me. Then be not astonished, lord, that gratitude filled my heart. I am a man of former, of better times. This was my thought: Am I to desert friends and benefactors? Would I not have been hard-hearted not to inquire about them, not to learn what was happening to them, how health was serving them, and where they were living? By the Pessinian Cybele! I am not capable of such conduct. At first I was restrained by fear that they might interpret my wishes incorrectly. But the love which I bore them proved greater than my fear, and the ease with which they forgive every injustice lent me special courage. But above all I was thinking of thee, lord. Our last attempt ended in defeat; but can such a son of Fortune be reconciled with defeat? So I prepared victory for thee. The house stands apart. Thou mayst give command to thy slaves to surround it so that not a mouse could escape. My lord, on thee alone it depends to have that magnanimous king's daughter in thy house this very night. But should that happen, remember that the cause of it is the very poor and hungry son of my father."

The blood rushed to Vinicius's head. Temptation shook all his being again. Yes; that was the method, and this time a certain one. Once he has Lygia in his house, who can take her? Once he makes Lygia his mistress, what will be left to her, unless to remain so forever? And let all religions perish! What will the Christians mean to him then, with their mercy and forbidding faith? Is it not time to shake himself free of all that? Is it not time to live as all live? What will Lygia do later, save to reconcile her fate with the religion which she professes? That, too, is a question of inferior significance. Those are matters devoid of importance. First of all, she will be his, — and his this very day. And it is a question, too, whether that religion will hold out in her soul against the world which is new to her, against luxury, and excitements to which she must yield. All may happen to-day. He needs only to detain Chilo, and give an order at dark. And then delight without end! "What has my life been?" thought Vinicius; "suffering, unsatisfied desire, and an endless propounding of problems without answer." In this way all will be cut short and ended. He recollected, it is true, that he had promised not to raise a hand against her. But by what had he sworn? Not by the gods, for he did not believe in them; not by Christ, for he did not believe in

Him yet. Finally, if she feels injured, he will marry her, and thus repair the wrong. Yes; to that he feels bound, for to her he is indebted for life. Here he recalled the day in which with Croton he had attacked her retreat; he remembered the Lygian's fist raised above him, and all that had happened later. He saw her again bent over his couch, dressed in the garb of a slave, beautiful as a divinity, a benefactress kind and glorified. His eyes passed to the lararium unconsciously, and to the little cross which she left him before going. Will he pay for all that by a new attack? Will he drag her by the hair as a slave to his cubiculum? And how will he be able to do so, since he not only desires but loves her, and he loves her specially because she is as she is? All at once he felt that it was not enough for him to have her in the house, it was not enough to seize her in his arms by superior force; he felt that his love needed something more, — her consent, her love, and her soul. Blessed that roof, if she come under it willingly; blessed the moment, blessed the day, blessed his life. Then the happiness of both will be as inexhaustible as the ocean, as the sun. But to seize her by violence would be to destroy that happiness forever, and at the same time to destroy, and defile that which is most precious and alone beloved in life. Terror seized him now at the very thought of this. He glanced at Chilo, who, while watching him, pushed his hands under his rags and scratched himself uneasily. That instant, disgust unspeakable took possession of Vinicius, and a wish to trample that former assistant of his, as he would a foul worm or venomous serpent. In an instant he knew what to do. But knowing no measure in anything, and following the impulse of his stern Roman nature, he turned toward Chilo and said, —

"I will not do what thou advisest, but, lest thou go without just reward, I will command to give thee three hundred stripes in the domestic prison."

Chilo grew pale. There was so much cold resolution in the beautiful face of Vinicius that he could not deceive himself for a moment with the hope that the promised reward was no more than a cruel jest.

Hence he threw himself on his knees in one instant, and bending double began to groan in a broken voice, —

"How, O king of Persia? Why? — O pyramid of kindness! Colossus of mercy! For what? — I am old, hungry, unfortunate — I have served thee — dost thou repay in this manner?"

"As thou didst the Christians," said Vinicius. And he called the dispensator.

But Chilo sprang toward his feet, and, embracing them convulsively, talked, while his face was covered with deathly pallor, —

"O lord, O lord! I am old! Fifty, not three hundred stripes. Fifty are enough! A hundred, not three hundred! Oh, mercy, mercy!"

Vinicius thrust him away with his foot, and gave the order. In the twinkle of an eye two powerful Quadi followed the dispensator, and, seizing Chilo by the remnant of his hair, tied his own rags around his neck and dragged him to the prison.

"In the name of Christ!" called the Greek, at the exit of the corridor.

Vinicius was left alone. The order just issued roused and enlivened him.

He endeavored to collect his scattered thoughts, and bring them to order. He felt great relief, and the victory which he had gained over himself filled him with comfort. He thought that he had made some great approach toward Lygia, and that some high reward should be given him. At the first moment it did not even occur to him that he had done a grievous wrong to Chilo, and had him flogged for the very acts for which he had rewarded him previously. He was too much of a Roman yet to be pained by another man's suffering, and to occupy his attention with one wretched Greek. Had he even thought of Chilo's suffering he would have considered that he had acted properly in giving command to punish such a villain. But he was thinking of Lygia, and said to her: I will not pay thee with evil for good; and when thou shalt learn how I acted with him who strove to persuade me to raise hands against thee, thou wilt be grateful. But here he stopped at this thought: Would Lygia praise his treatment of Chilo? The religion which she professes commands forgiveness; nay, the Christians forgave the villain, though they had greater reasons for revenge. Then for the first time was heard in his soul the cry: "In the name of Christ!" He remembered then that Chilo had ransomed himself from the hands of Ursus with such a cry, and he determined to remit the remainder of the punishment.

With that object he was going to summon the dispensator, when that person stood before him, and said, —

"Lord, the old man has fainted, and perhaps he is dead. Am I to command further flogging?"

"Revive him and bring him before me."

The chief of the atrium vanished behind the curtain, but the revival could not have been easy, for Vinicius waited a long time and was growing impatient, when the slaves brought in Chilo, and disappeared at a signal.

Chilo was as pale as linen, and down his legs threads of blood were flowing to the mosaic pavement of the atrium. He was conscious, however, and, falling on his knees, began to speak, with extended hands, —

"Thanks to thee, lord. Thou art great and merciful."

"Dog," said Vinicius, "know that I forgave thee because of that Christ to whom I owe my own life."

"O lord, I will serve Him and thee."

"Be silent and listen. Rise! Thou wilt go and show me the house in which Lygia dwells."

Chilo sprang up; but he was barely on his feet when he grew more deathly pale yet, and said in a failing voice, —

"Lord, I am really hungry — I will go, lord, I will go! but I have not the strength. Command to give me even remnants from the plate of thy dog, and I will go."

Vinicius commanded to give him food, a piece of gold, and a mantle. But Chilo, weakened by stripes and hunger, could not go to take food, though terror raised the hair on his head, lest Vinicius might mistake his weakness for stubbornness and command to flog him anew.

"Only let wine warm me," repeated he, with chattering teeth, "I shall be able to go at once, even to Magna Græcia."

He regained some strength after a time, and they went out.

The way was long, for, like the majority of Christians, Linus dwelt in the Trans-Tiber, and not far from Miriam. At last Chilo showed Vinicius a small house, standing apart, surrounded by a wall covered entirely with ivy, and said, —

"Here it is, lord."

"Well," said Vinicius, "go thy way now, but listen first to what I tell thee. Forget that thou hast served me; forget where Miriam, Peter, and Glaucus dwell; forget also this house, and all Christians. Thou wilt come every month to my house, where Demas, my freedman, will pay thee two pieces of gold. But shouldst thou spy further after Christians, I will have thee flogged, or delivered into the hands of the prefect of the city."

Chilo bowed down, and said, —

"I will forget."

But when Vinicius vanished beyond the corner of the street, he stretched his hands after him, and, threatening with his fists, exclaimed, —

"By Ate and the Furies! I will not forget!"

Then he grew faint again.

CHAPTER XXXIII

Vinicius went directly to the house in which Miriam lived. Before the gate he met Nazarius, who was confused at sight of him; but greeting the lad cordially, he asked to be conducted to his mother's lodgings.

Besides Miriam, Vinicius found Peter, Glaucus, Crispus, and Paul of Tarsus, who had returned recently from Fregellæ. At sight of the young tribune, astonishment was reflected on all faces; but he said, —

"I greet you in the name of Christ, whom ye honor."

"May His name be glorified forever!" answered they.

"I have seen your virtue and experienced your kindness, hence I come as a friend."

"And we greet thee as a friend," answered Peter. "Sit down, lord, and partake of our refreshment, as a guest."

"I will sit down and share your repast; but first listen to me, thou Peter, and thou Paul of Tarsus, so that ye may know my sincerity. I know where Lygia is. I have returned from before the house of Linus, which is near this dwelling. I have a right to her given me by Cæsar. I have at my houses in the city nearly five hundred slaves. I might surround her hiding-place and seize her; still I have not done so, and will not."

"For this reason the blessing of the Lord will be upon thee, and thy heart will be purified," said Peter.

"I thank thee. But listen to me further: I have not done so, though I am living in suffering and sadness. Before I knew you, I should have taken her undoubtedly, and held her by force; but your virtue and your religion, though I do not profess it, have changed something in my soul, so that I do not venture on violence. I know not myself why this is so, but it is so; hence I come to you, for ye take the place of Lygia's father and mother, and I say to you: Give her to me as wife, and I swear that not only will I not forbid her to confess Christ, but I will begin myself to learn His religion."

He spoke with head erect and decisively; but still he was moved, and his legs trembled beneath his mantle. When silence followed his words, he continued, as if wishing to anticipate an unfavorable answer, —

"I know what obstacles exist, but I love her as my own eyes; and though I am not a Christian yet, I am neither your enemy nor Christ's. I wish to be sincere, so that you may trust me. At this moment it is a question of life with me, still I tell you the truth. Another might say, Baptize me; I say, Enlighten me. I believe that Christ rose from the dead, for people say so who love the truth, and who saw Him after death. I believe, for I have seen myself, that your religion produces virtue, justice, and mercy, — not

crime, which is laid to your charge. I have not known your religion much
so far. A little from you, a little from your works, a little from Lygia, a little
from conversations with you. Still I repeat that it has made some change
in me. Formerly I held my servants with an iron hand; I cannot do so now.
I knew no pity; I know it now. I was fond of pleasure; the other night I fled
from the pond of Agrippa, for the breath was taken from me through disgust. Formerly I believed in superior force; now I have abandoned it. Know
ye that I do not recognize myself. I am disgusted by feasts, wine, singing,
citharæ, garlands, the court of Cæsar, naked bodies, and every crime. When
I think that Lygia is like snow in the mountains, I love her the more; and
when I think that she is what she is through your religion, I love and desire
that religion. But since I understand it not, since I know not whether I shall
be able to live according to it, nor whether my nature can endure it, I am in
uncertainty and suffering, as if I were in prison."

Here his brows met in wrinkle of pain, and a flush appeared on his cheeks;
after that he spoke on with growing haste and greater emotion, —

"As ye see, I am tortured from love and uncertainty. Men tell me that in
your religion there is no place for life, or human joy, or happiness, or law,
or order, or authority, or Roman dominion. Is this true? Men tell me that ye
are madmen; but tell me yourselves what ye bring. Is it a sin to love, a sin
to feel joy, a sin to want happiness? Are ye enemies of life? Must a Christian be wretched? Must I renounce Lygia? What is truth in your view? Your
deeds and words are like transparent water, but what is under that water?
Ye see that I am sincere. Scatter the darkness. Men say this to me also: Greece
created beauty and wisdom, Rome created power; but they — what do they
bring? Tell, then, what ye bring. If there is brightness beyond your doors,
open them."

"We bring love," said Peter.

And Paul of Tarsus added, —

"If I speak with the tongues of men and of angels, but have not love, I
am become sounding brass."

But the heart of the old Apostle was stirred by that soul in suffering,
which, like a bird in a cage, was struggling toward air and the sun; hence,
stretching his hand to Vinicius, he said, —

"Whoso knocketh, to him will be opened. The favor and grace of God is
upon thee; for this reason I bless thee, thy soul and thy love, in the name of
the Redeemer of mankind."

Vinicius, who had spoken with enthusiasm already, sprang toward Peter
on hearing this blessing, and an uncommon thing happened. That descendant
of Quirites, who till recently had not recognized humanity in a foreigner,
seized the hand of the old Galilean, and pressed it in gratitude to his lips.

Peter was pleased; for he understood that his sowing had fallen on an
additional field, that his fishing-net had gathered in a new soul.

Those present, not less pleased by that evident expression of honor for
the Apostle of God, exclaimed in one voice, —

"Praise to the Lord in the highest!"

Vinicius rose with a radiant face, and began, —

"I see that happiness may dwell among you, for I feel happy, and I think that ye can convince me of other things in the same way. But I will add that this cannot happen in Rome. Cæsar is going to Antium, and I must go with him, for I have the order. Ye know that not to obey is death. But if I have found favor in your eyes, go with me to teach your truth. It will be safer for you than for me. Even in that great throng of people, ye can announce your truth in the very court of Cæsar. They say that Acte is a Christian; and there are Christians among pretorians even, for I myself have seen soldiers kneeling before thee, Peter, at the Nomentan gate. In Antium I have a villa where we shall assemble to hear your teaching, at the side of Nero. Glaucus told me that ye are ready to go to the end of the earth for one soul; so do for me what ye have done for those for whose sake ye have come from Judea, — do it, and desert not my soul."

Hearing this, they began to take counsel, thinking with delight of the victory of their religion, and of the significance for the pagan world which the conversion of an Augustian, and a descendant of one of the oldest Roman families, would have. They were ready, indeed, to wander to the end of the earth for one human soul, and since the death of the Master they had, in fact, done nothing else; hence a negative answer did not even come to their minds. Peter was at that moment the pastor of a whole multitude, hence he could not go; but Paul of Tarsus, who had been in Aricium and Fregellæ not long before, and who was preparing for a long journey to the East to visit churches there and freshen them with a new spirit of zeal, consented to accompany the young tribune to Antium. It was easy to find a ship there going to Grecian waters.

Vinicius, though sad because Peter, to whom he owed so much, could not visit Antium, thanked him with gratitude, and then turned to the old Apostle with his last request, —

"Knowing Lygia's dwelling," said he, "I might have gone to her and asked, as is proper, whether she would take me as husband should my soul become Christian, but I prefer to ask thee, O Apostle! Permit me to see her, or take me thyself to her. I know not how long I shall be in Antium; and remember that near Cæsar no one is sure of to-morrow. Petronius himself told me that I should not be altogether safe there. Let me see her before I go; let me delight my eyes with her; and let me ask her if she will forget my evil and return good."

Peter smiled kindly and said, —

"But who could refuse thee a proper joy, my son?"

Vinicius stooped again to Peter's hands, for he could not in any way restrain his overflowing heart. The Apostle took him by the temples and said, —

"Have no fear of Cæsar, for I tell thee that a hair will not fall from thy head."

He sent Miriam for Lygia, telling her not to say who was with them, so as to give the maiden more delight.

It was not far; so after a short time those in the chamber saw among the myrtles of the garden Miriam leading Lygia by the hand.

Vinicius wished to run forth to meet her; but at sight of that beloved form happiness took his strength, and he stood with beating heart, breathless, barely able to keep his feet, a hundred times more excited than when for the first time in life he heard the Parthian arrows whizzing round his head.

She ran in, unsuspecting; but at sight of him she halted as if fixed to the earth. Her face flushed, and then became very pale; she looked with astonished and frightened eyes on those present.

But round about she saw clear glances, full of kindness. The Apostle Peter approached her and asked, —

"Lygia, dost thou love him as ever?"

A moment of silence followed. Her lips began to quiver like those of a child who is preparing to cry, who feels that it is guilty, but sees that it must confess the guilt.

"Answer," said the Apostle.

Then, with humility, obedience, and fear in her voice, she whispered, kneeling at the knees of Peter, —

"I do."

In one moment Vinicius knelt at her side. Peter placed his hands on their heads, and said, —

"Love each other in the Lord and to His glory, for there is no sin in your love."

CHAPTER XXXIV

WHILE walking with Lygia through the garden, Vinicius described briefly, in words from the depth of his heart, that which a short time before he had confessed to the Apostles, — that is, the alarm of his soul, the changes which had taken place in him, and, finally, that immense yearning which had veiled life from him, beginning with the hour when he left Miriam's dwelling. He confessed to Lygia that he had tried to forget her, but was not able. He thought whole days and nights of her. That little cross of boxwood twigs which she had left reminded him of her, — that cross, which he had placed in the lararium and revered involuntarily as something divine. And he yearned more and more every moment, for love was stronger than he, and had seized his soul altogether, even when he was at the house of Aulus. The Parcæ weave the thread of life for others; but love, yearning, and melancholy had woven it for him. His acts had been evil, but they had their origin in love. He had loved her when she was in the house of Aulus, when she was on the Palatine, when he saw her in Ostrianum listening to Peter's words, when he went with Croton to carry her away, when she watched at his bedside, and when she deserted him. Then came Chilo, who discovered her dwelling, and advised him to seize her a second time; but he chose to punish Chilo, and go to the Apostles to ask for truth and for her. And blessed be that moment in which such a thought came to his head, for now he is at her side, and she will not flee from him, as the last time she fled from the house of Miriam.

"I did not flee from thee," said Lygia.

"Then why didst thou go?"

She raised her iris-colored eyes to him, and, bending her blushing face, said, —

"Thou knowest — "

Vinicius was silent for a moment from excess of happiness, and began again to speak, as his eyes were opened gradually to this, — that she was different utterly from Roman women, and resembled Pomponia alone. Besides, he could not explain this to her clearly, for he could not define his feeling, — that beauty of a new kind altogether was coming to the world in her, such beauty as had not been in it thus far; beauty which is not merely a statue, but a spirit. He told her something, however, which filled her with delight, — that he loved her just because she had fled from him, and that she would be sacred to him at his hearth. Then, seizing her hand, he could not continue; he merely gazed on her with rapture as on his life's happiness which he had won, and repeated her name, as if to assure himself that he had found her and was near her.

"Oh, Lygia, Lygia!"

At last he inquired what had taken place in her mind, and she confessed that she had loved him while in the house of Aulus, and that if he had taken her back to them from the Palatine she would have told them of her love and tried to soften their anger against him.

"I swear to thee," said Vinicius, "that it had not even risen in my mind to take thee from Aulus. Petronius will tell thee sometime that I told him then how I loved and wished to marry thee. 'Let her anoint my door with wolf fat, and let her sit at my hearth,' said I to him. But he ridiculed me, and gave Cæsar the idea of demanding thee as a hostage and giving thee to me. How often in my sorrow have I cursed him; but perhaps fate ordained thus, for otherwise I should not have known the Christians, and should not have understood thee."

"Believe me, Marcus," replied Lygia, "it was Christ who led thee to Himself by design."

Vinicius raised his head with a certain astonishment.

"True," answered he, with animation. "Everything fixed itself so marvellously that in seeking thee I met the Christians. In Ostrianum I listened to the Apostle with wonder, for I had never heard such words. And there thou didst pray for me?"

"I did," answered Lygia.

They passed near the summer-house covered with thick ivy, and approached the place where Ursus, after stifling Croton, threw himself upon Vinicius.

"Here," said the young man, "I should have perished but for thee."

"Do not mention that," answered Lygia, "and do not speak of it to Ursus."

"Could I be revenged on him for defending thee? Had he been a slave, I should have given him freedom straightway."

"Had he been a slave, Aulus would have freed him long ago."

"Dost thou remember," asked Vinicius, "that I wished to take thee back to Aulus, but the answer was, that Cæsar might hear of it and take revenge on Aulus and Pomponia? Think of this: thou mayst see them now as often as thou wishest."

"How, Marcus?"

"I say 'now,' and I think that thou wilt be able to see them without danger, when thou art mine. For should Cæsar hear of this, and ask what I did with the hostage whom he gave me, I should say 'I married her, and she visits the house of Aulus with my consent.' He will not remain long in Antium, for he wishes to go to Achæa; and even should he remain, I shall not need to see him daily. When Paul of Tarsus teaches me your faith, I will receive baptism at once, I will come here, gain the friendship of Aulus and Pomponia, who will return to the city by that time, and there will be no further hindrance, I will seat thee at my hearth. Oh, carissima! carissima!"

And he stretched forth his hand, as if taking Heaven as witness of his love; and Lygia, raising her clear eyes to him, said, —

"And then I shall say, 'Wherever thou art, Caius, there am I, Caia.'"

"No, Lygia," cried Vinicius, "I swear to thee that never has woman been so honored in the house of her husband as thou shalt be in mine."

For a time they walked on in silence, without being able to take in with their breasts their happiness, in love with each other, like two deities, and as beautiful as if spring had given them to the world with the flowers.

They halted at last under the cypress growing near the entrance of the house. Lygia leaned against his breast, and Vinicius began to entreat again with a trembling voice, —

"Tell Ursus to go to the house of Aulus for thy furniture and playthings of childhood."

But she, blushing like a rose or like the dawn, answered, —

"Custom commands otherwise."

"I know that. The pronuba [1] usually brings them behind the bride, but do this for me. I will take them to my villa in Antium, and they will remind me of thee."

Here he placed his hands together and repeated, like a child who is begging for something, —

"It will be some days before Pomponia returns; so do this, diva, do this, carissima."

"But Pomponia will do as she likes," answered Lygia, blushing still more deeply at mention of the pronuba.

And again they were silent, for love had begun to stop the breath in their breasts. Lygia stood with shoulders leaning against the cypress, her face whitening in the shadow, like a flower, her eyes drooping, her bosom heaving with more and more life. Vinicius changed in the face, and grew pale. In the silence of the afternoon they only heard the beating of their hearts, and in their mutual ecstasy that cypress, the myrtle bushes, and the ivy of the summer-house became for them a paradise of love. But Miriam appeared in the door, and invited them to the afternoon meal. They sat down then with the Apostles, who gazed at them with pleasure, as on the young generation which after their death would preserve and sow still further the seed of the new faith. Peter broke and blessed bread. There was calm on all faces, and a certain immense happiness seemed to overflow the whole house.

"See," said Paul at last, turning to Vinicius, "are we enemies of life and happiness?"

"I know how that is," answered Vinicius, "for never have I been so happy as among you."

---

[1] The matron who accompanies the bride and explains to her the duties of a wife.

CHAPTER XXXV

On the evening of that day Vinicius, while returning home through the Forum, saw at the entrance to the Vicus Tuscus the gilded litter of Petronius, carried by eight stalwart Bithynians, and, stopping it with a sign of his hand, he approached the curtains.

"Thou hast had a pleasant dream, I trust, and a happy one!" cried he, laughing at sight of the slumbering Petronius.

"Oh, is it thou?" said Petronius, waking up. "Yes; I dropped asleep for a moment, as I passed the night at the Palatine. I have come out to buy something to read on the road to Antium. What is the news?"

"Art thou visiting the book-shops?" inquired Vinicius.

"Yes, I do not like to bring disorder into my library, so I am collecting a special supply for the journey. It is likely that some new things of Musonius and Seneca have come out. I am looking also for Persius, and a certain edition of the Eclogues of Vergilius, which I do not possess. Oh, how tired I am; and how my hands ache from covers and rings! For when a man is once in a book-shop curiosity seizes him to look here and there. I was at the shop of Avirnus, and at that of Atractus on the Argiletum, and with the Sozii on Vicus Sandalarius. By Castor! how I want to sleep!"

"Thou wert on the Palatine? Then I would ask thee what is it to be heard there? Or, knowest what? — send home the litter and the tubes with books, and come to my house. We will talk of Antium, and of something else."

"That is well," answered Petronius, coming out of the litter. "Thou must know, besides, that we start for Antium the day after to-morrow."

"Whence should I know that?"

"In what world art thou living? Well, I shall be the first to announce the news to thee. Yes; be ready for the day after to-morrow in the morning. Peas in olive oil have not helped, a cloth around his thick neck has not helped, and Bronzebeard is hoarse. In view of this, delay is not to be mentioned. He curses Rome and its atmosphere, with what the world stands on; he would be glad to level it to the earth or to destroy it with fire, and he longs for the sea at the earliest. He says that the smells which the wind brings from the narrow streets are driving him into the grave. To-day great sacrifices were offered in all the temples to restore his voice; and woe to Rome, but especially to the Senate, should it not return quickly!"

"Then there would be no reason for his visit to Achæa?"

"But is that the only talent possessed by our divine Cæsar?" asked Petronius, smiling. "He would appear in the Olympic games, as a poet, with his 'Burning of Troy'; as a charioteer, as a musician, as an athlete, — nay, even as a dancer, and would receive in every case all the crowns intended for victors.

Dost know why that monkey grew hoarse? Yesterday he wanted to equal our Paris in dancing, and danced for us the adventures of Leda, during which he sweated and caught cold. He was as wet and slippery as an eel freshly taken from water. He changed masks one after another, whirled like a spindle, waved his hands like a drunken sailor, till disgust seized me while looking at that great stomach and those slim legs. Paris taught him during two weeks; but imagine to thyself Ahenobarbus as Leda or as the divine swan. That was a swan! — there is no use in denying it. But he wants to appear before the public in that pantomime, — first in Antium, and then in Rome."

"People are offended already because he sang in public; but to think that a Roman Cæsar will appear as a mime! No; even Rome will not endure that!"

"My dear friend, Rome will endure anything; the Senate will pass a vote of thanks to the 'Father of his country.' And the rabble will be elated because Cæsar is its buffoon."

"Say thyself, is it possible to be more debased?"

Petronius shrugged his shoulders. "Thou art living by thyself at home, and meditating, now about Lygia, now about Christians, so thou knowest not, perhaps, what happened two days since. Nero married, in public, Pythagoras, who appeared as a bride. That passed the measure of madness, it would seem, would it not? And what wilt thou say? the flamens, who were summoned, came and performed the ceremony with solemnity. I was present. I can endure much; still I thought, I confess, that the gods, if there be any, should give a sign. But Cæsar does not believe in the gods, and he is right."

"So he is in one person chief priest, a god, and an atheist," said Vinicius.

"True," said Petronius, beginning to laugh. "That had not entered my head; but the combination is such as the world has not seen." Then, stopping a moment, he said: "One should add that this chief priest who does not believe in the gods, and this god who reviles the gods, fears them in his character of atheist."

"The proof of this is what happened in the temple of Vesta."

"What a society!"

"As the society is, so is Cæsar. But this will not last long."

Thus conversing, they entered the house of Vinicius, who called for supper joyously; then, turning to Petronius he said, —

"No, my dear, society must be renewed."

"We shall not renew it," answered Petronius, "even for the reason that in Nero's time man is like a butterfly, — he lives in the sunshine of favor, and at the first cold wind he perishes, even against his will. By the son of Maia! more than once have I given myself this question: By what miracle has such a man as Lucius Saturninus been able to reach the age of ninety-three, to survive Tiberius, Caligula, Claudius? But never mind. Wilt thou permit me to send thy litter for Eunice? My wish to sleep has gone, somehow, and I should like to be joyous. Give command to cithara players to come to the supper, and afterward we will talk of Antium. It is needful to think of it, especially for thee."

Vinicius gave the order to send for Eunice, but declared that he had no thought of breaking his head over the stay in Antium.

"Let those break their heads who cannot live otherwise than in the rays of Cæsar's favor. The world does not end on the Palatine, especially for those who have something else in their hearts and souls."

He said this so carelessly and with such animation and gladness that his whole manner struck Petronius; hence, looking for a time at him, he asked, —

"What is taking place in thee? Thou art to-day as thou wert when wearing the golden bulla on thy neck."

"I am happy," answered Vinicius. "I have invited thee purposely to tell thee so."

"What has happened?"

"Something which I would not give for the Roman Empire."

Then he sat down, and, leaning on the arm of the chair, rested his head on his hand, and asked, —

"Dost remember how we were at the house of Aulus Plautius, and there thou didst see for the first time the godlike maiden called by thee 'the dawn and the spring'? Dost remember that Psyche, that incomparable, that one more beautiful than our maidens and our goddesses?"

Petronius looked at him with astonishment, as if he wished to make sure that his head was right.

"Of whom art thou speaking?" asked he at last. "Evidently I remember Lygia."

"I am her betrothed."

"What!"

But Vinicius sprang up and called his dispensator.

"Let the slaves stand before me to the last soul, quickly!"

"Art thou her betrothed?" repeated Petronius.

But before he recovered from his astonishment the immense atrium was swarming with people. Panting old men ran in, men in the vigor of life, women, boys, and girls. With each moment the atrium was filled more and more; in corridors, called "fauces," voices were heard calling in various languages. Finally, all took their places in rows at the walls and among the columns. Vinicius, standing near the impluvium, turned to Demas, the freedman, and said, —

"Those who have served twenty years in my house are to appear to-morrow before the pretor, where they will receive freedom; those who have not served out the time will receive three pieces of gold and double rations for a week. Send an order to the village prisons to remit punishment, strike the fetters from people's feet, and feed them sufficiently. Know that a happy day has come to me, and I wish rejoicing in the house."

For a moment they stood in silence, as if not believing their ears; then all hands were raised at once, and all mouths cried, —

"A-a! lord! a-a-a!"

Vinicius dismissed them with a wave of his hand. Though they desired to thank him and to fall at his feet, they went away hurriedly, filling the house with happiness from cellar to roof.

"To-morrow," said Vinicius, "I will command them to meet again in the garden, and to make such signs on the ground as they choose. Lygia will free those who draw a fish."

Petronius, who never wondered long at anything, had grown indifferent, and asked, —

"A fish, is it? Ah, ha! According to Chilo, that is the sign of a Christian, I remember." Then he extended his hand to Vinicius, and said: "Happiness is always where a man sees it. May Flora strew flowers under thy feet for long years. I wish thee everything which thou wishest thyself."

"I thank thee, for I thought that thou wouldst dissuade me, and that, as thou seest, would be time lost."

"I? Dissuade? By no means. On the contrary, I tell thee that thou art doing well."

"Ha, traitor!" answered Vinicius, joyfully; "hast forgotten what thou didst tell me once when we were leaving the house of Pomponia Græcina?"

"No," answered Petronius, with cool blood; "but I have changed my opinion. My dear," added he after a while, "in Rome everything changes. Husbands change wives, wives change husbands; why should not I change opinions? It lacked little of Nero's marrying Acte, whom for his sake they represented as the descendant of a kingly line. Well, he would have had an honest wife, and we an honest Augusta. By Proteus and his barren spaces in the sea! I shall change my opinion as often as I find it appropriate or profitable. As to Lygia, her royal descent is more certain than Acte's. But in Antium be on thy guard against Poppæa, who is revengeful."

"I do not think of doing so. A hair will not fall from my head in Antium."

"If thou think to astonish me a second time, thou art mistaken; but whence hast thou that certainty?"

"The Apostle Peter told me so."

"Ah, the Apostle Peter told thee! Against that there is no argument; permit me, however, to take certain measures of precaution even to this end, that the Apostle Peter may not turn out a false phophet; for, should the Apostle be mistaken, perchance he might lose thy confidence, which certainly will be of use to him in the future."

"Do what may please thee, but I believe him. And if thou think to turn me against him by repeating his name with irony, thou art mistaken."

"But one question more. Hast thou become a Christian?"

"Not yet; but Paul of Tarsus will travel with me to explain the teachings of Christ, and afterward I will receive baptism; for thy statement that they are enemies of life and pleasantness is not true."

"All the better for thee and Lygia," answered Petronius; then, shrugging his shoulders, he said, as if to himself, "But it is astonishing how skilled those people are in gaining adherents, and how that sect is extending."

"Yes," answered Vinicius, with as much warmth as if he had been baptized already; "there are thousands and tens of thousands of them in Rome, in the cities of Italy, in Greece and Asia. There are Christians among the legions and among the pretorians; they are in the palace of Cæsar itself. Slaves and citizens, poor and rich, plebeian and patrician, confess that faith. Dost thou know that the Cornelii are Christians, that Pomponia Græcina is a Christian, that likely Octavia was, and Acte is? Yes, that teaching will embrace the world, and it alone is able to renew it. Do not shrug thy shoulders, for who knows whether in a month or a year thou wilt not receive it thyself?"

"I?" said Petronius. "No, by the son of Leto! I will not receive it; even if the truth and wisdom of gods and men were contained in it. That would require labor, and I have no fondness for labor. Labor demands self-denial, and I will not deny myself anything. With thy nature, which is like fire and boiling water, something like this may happen any time. But I? I have my gems, my cameos, my vases, my Eunice. I do not believe in Olympus, but I arrange it on earth for myself; and I shall flourish till the arrows of the divine archer pierce me, or till Cæsar commands me to open my veins. I love the odor of violets too much, and a comfortable triclinium. I love even our gods, as rhetorical figures, and Achæa, to which I am preparing to go with our fat, thin-legged, incomparable, godlike Cæsar, the august period-compelling Hercules, Nero."

Then he was joyous at the very supposition that he could accept the teaching of Galilean fishermen, and began to sing in an undertone, —

"I will entwine my bright sword in myrtle,
After the example of Harmodius and Aristogiton."

But he stopped, for the arrival of Eunice was announced. Immediately after her coming supper was served, during which songs were sung by the cithara players; Vinicius told of Chilo's visit, and also how that visit had given the idea of going to the Apostles directly, — an idea which came to him while they were flogging Chilo.

At mention of this, Petronius, who began to be drowsy, placed his hand on his forehead, and said, —

"The thought was good, since the object was good. But as to Chilo, I should have given him five pieces of gold; but as it was thy will to flog him, it was better to flog him, for who knows but in time senators will bow to him, as to-day they are bowing to our cobbler-knight, Vatinius. Good-night."

And, removing his wreath, he, with Eunice, prepared for home. When they had gone, Vinicius went to his library and wrote to Lygia as follows: —

"When thou openest thy beautiful eyes, I wish this letter to say Good-day! to thee. Hence I write now, though I shall see thee to-morrow. Cæsar will go to Antium after to-morrow, — and I, eheu! must go with him. I have told thee already that not to obey would be to risk life — and at present I could not find courage to die. But if thou wish me not to go, write one word, and I will stay. Petronius will turn away danger from me with a speech. To-day, in the hour of my delight, I gave rewards to all my slaves; those who have served in the house twenty years I shall take to the pretor to-morrow and free. Thou, my dear, shouldst praise me, since this act as I think will be in accord with that mild religion of thine; secondly, I do this for thy sake. They are to thank thee for their freedom. I shall tell them so to-morrow, so that they may be grateful to thee and praise thy name. I give myself in bondage to happiness and thee. God grant that I never see liberation. May Antium be cursed, and the journey of Ahenobarbus! Thrice and four times happy am I in not being so wise as Petronius; if I were, I should be forced to go to Greece perhaps. Meanwhile the moment of separation will sweeten my memory of thee. Whenever I can tear myself away, I shall sit on a horse, and rush back to Rome, to gladden my eyes with sight of thee, and my ears with thy voice. When I cannot come I shall send a slave with a letter, and an inquiry about thee. I salute thee, divine one, and embrace thy feet. Be not angry that I call thee divine. If thou forbid, I shall obey, but to-day I cannot call thee otherwise. I congratulate thee on thy future house with my whole soul."

CHAPTER XXXVI

IT was known in Rome that Cæsar wished to see Ostia on the journey, or rather the largest ship in the world, which had brought wheat recently from Alexandria, and from Ostia to go by the Via Littoralis to Antium. Orders had been given a number of days earlier; hence at the Porta Ostiensis, from early morning, crowds made up of the local rabble and of all nations of the earth had collected to feast their eyes with the sight of Cæsar's retinue, on which the Roman population could never gaze sufficiently. The road to Antium was neither difficult nor long. In the place itself, which was composed of palaces and villas built and furnished in a lordly manner, it was possible to find everything demanded by comfort, and even the most exquisite luxury of the period. Cæsar had the habit, however, of taking with him on a journey every object in which he found delight, beginning with musical instruments and domestic furniture, and ending with statues and mosaics, which were taken even when he wished to remain on the road merely a short time for rest or recreation. He was accompanied, therefore, on every expedition by whole legions of servants, without reckoning divisions of pretorian guards, and Augustians; of the latter each had a personal retinue of slaves.

Early on the morning of that day herdsmen from the Campania, with sunburnt faces, wearing goat-skins on their legs, drove forth five hundred she-asses through the gates, so that Poppæa on the morrow of her arrival at Antium might have her bath in their milk. The rabble gazed with delight and ridicule at the long ears swaying amid clouds of dust, and listened with pleasure to the whistling of whips and the wild shouts of the herdsmen. After the asses had gone by, crowds of youth rushed forth, swept the road carefully, and covered it with flowers and needles from pine-trees. In the crowds people whispered to each other, with a certain feeling of pride, that the whole road to Antium would be strewn in that way with flowers taken from private gardens round about, or bought at high prices from dealers at the Porta Mugionis. As the morning hours passed, the throng increased every moment. Some had brought their whole families, and, lest the time might seem tedious, they spread provisions on stones intended for the new temple of Ceres, and ate their prandium beneath the open sky. Here and there were groups, in which the lead was taken by persons who had travelled; they talked of Cæsar's present trip, of his future journeys, and journeys in general. Sailors and old soldiers narrated wonders which during distant campaigns they had heard about countries which a Roman foot had never touched. Home-stayers, who had never gone beyond the Appian Way, listened with amazement to marvellous tales of India, of Arabia, of archipelagos surrounding Britain in which, on a small island inhabited by spirits, Briareus had imprisoned the sleeping Saturn. They heard of hyperborean regions of stiffened seas, of the hisses and roars which the ocean gives forth when the sun plunges into his bath. Stories of this kind found ready credence among the rabble, stories believed by such men even as Tacitus and Pliny. They spoke also of that ship which Cæsar was to look at, — a ship which had brought wheat to last for two years, without reckoning four hundred passengers, an equal number of soldiers, and a multitude of wild beasts to be used during the summer games. This produced general good feeling toward Cæsar, who not only nourished the populace, but amused it. Hence a greeting full of enthusiasm was waiting for him.

Meanwhile came a detachment of Numidian horse, who belonged to the pretorian guard. They wore yellow uniforms, red girdles, and great earrings, which cast a golden gleam on their black faces. The points of their bamboo spears glittered like flames, in the sun. After they had passed, a procession-like movement began. The throng crowded forward to look at it more nearly; but divisions of pretorian foot were there, and, forming in line on both sides of the gate, prevented approach to the road. In advance moved wagons carrying tents, purple, red, and violet, and tents of byssus woven from threads as white as snow; and oriental carpets, and tables of citrus, and pieces of mosaic, and kitchen utensils, and cages with birds from the East, North, and West, birds whose tongues or brains were to go to Cæsar's table, and vessels with wine and baskets with fruit. But objects not to be exposed to bruising or breaking in vehicles were borne by slaves. Hence hundreds of people were seen on foot, carrying vessels, and statues of Corinthian bronze. There were companies appointed specially to Etruscan vases; others to Grecian; others to golden or silver vessels, or vessels of Alexandrian glass. These were guarded by small detachments of pretorian infantry and cavalry; over each division of slaves were taskmasters, holding whips armed at the end with lumps of lead or iron, instead of snappers. The procession, formed of men bearing with importance and attention various objects, seemed like some solemn religious procession; and the resemblance grew still more striking when the musical instruments of Cæsar and the court were borne past. There were seen harps, Grecian lutes, lutes of the Hebrews and Egyptians, lyres, formingas, citharas, flutes, long, winding buffalo horns and cymbals. While looking at that sea of instruments, gleaming beneath the sun in gold, bronze, precious stones, and pearls, it might be imagined that Apollo and Bacchus had set out on a journey through the world. After the instruments came rich chariots filled with acrobats, dancers male and female, grouped artistically, with wands in their hands. After them followed slaves intended, not for service, but excess; so there were boys and little girls, selected from all Greece and Asia Minor, with long hair, or with winding curls arranged in golden nets, children resembling Cupids, with wonderful faces, but faces covered completely with a thick coating of cosmetics, lest the wind of the Campania might tan their delicate complexions.

And again appeared a pretorian cohort of gigantic Sicambrians, blue-eyed, bearded, blond and red haired. In front of them Roman eagles were carried by banner-bearers called "imaginarii," tablets with inscriptions, statues of German and Roman gods, and finally statues and busts of Cæsar. From under the skins and armor of the soldier appeared limbs sunburnt and mighty, looking like military engines capable of wielding the heavy weapons with which guards of that kind were furnished. The earth seemed to bend beneath their measured and weighty tread. As if conscious of strength which they could use against Cæsar himself, they looked with contempt on the rabble of the street, forgetting, it was evident, that many of themselves had come to that city in manacles. But they were insignificant in numbers, for the pretorian force had remained in camp specially to guard the city and hold it within bounds. When they had marched past, Nero's chained lions and tigers were led by, so that, should the wish come to him of imitating Dionysus, he would have them to attach to his chariots. They were led in chains of steel by Arabs and Hindoos, but the chains were so entwined with garlands that the beasts seemed led with flowers. The lions and tigers, tamed by skilled trainers, looked at the crowds with green and seemingly sleepy eyes; but at moments they raised their giant heads, and breathed through wheezing nostrils the exhalations of the multitude, licking their jaws the while with spiny tongues.

Now came Cæsar's vehicles and litters, great and small, gold or purple, inlaid with ivory or pearls, or glittering with diamonds; after them came another small cohort of pretorians in Roman armor, pretorians composed of Italian volunteers only; [1] then crowds of select slave servants, and boys; and at last came Cæsar himself, whose approach was heralded from afar by the shouts of thousands.

In the crowd was the Apostle Peter, who wished to see Cæsar once in life. He was accompanied by Lygia, whose face was hidden by a thick veil, and Ursus, whose strength formed the surest defence of the young girl in the wild and boisterous crowd. The Lygian seized a stone to be used in building the temple, and brought it to the Apostle, so that by standing on it he might see better than others.

The crowd muttered when Ursus pushed it apart, as a ship pushes waves; but when he carried the stone, which four of the strongest men could not raise, the muttering was turned into wonderment, and cries of "Macte!" were heard round about.

Meanwhile Cæsar appeared. He was sitting in a chariot drawn by six white Idumean stallions shod with gold. The chariot had the form of a tent with sides open, purposely, so that the crowds could see Cæsar. A number of persons might have found place in the chariot; but Nero, desiring that attention should be fixed on him exclusively, passed through the city alone, having at his feet merely two deformed dwarfs. He wore a white tunic, and a toga of amethyst color, which cast a bluish tinge on his face. On his head was a laurel

---

[1] The inhabitants of Italy were freed from military service by Augustus, in consequence of which the so-called *cohors Italica*, stationed generally in Asia, was composed of volunteers. The pretorian guards, in so far as they were not composed of foreigners, were made up of volunteers.

wreath. Since his departure from Naples he had increased notably in body. His face had grown wide; under his lower jaw hung a double chin, by which his mouth, always too near his nose, seemed to touch his nostrils. His bulky neck was protected, as usual, by a silk kerchief, which he arranged from moment to moment with a white and fat hand grown over with red hair, forming as it were bloody stains; he would not permit epilatores to pluck out this hair, since he had been told that to do so would bring trembling of the fingers and injure his lute-playing. Measureless vanity was depicted then, as at all times, on his face, together with tedium and suffering. On the whole, it was a face both terrible and trivial. While advancing he turned his head from side to side, blinking at times, and listening carefully to the manner in which the multitude greeted him. He was met by a storm of shouts and applause: "Hail, divine Cæsar! Imperator, hail, conqueror! hail, incomparable! — Son of Apollo, Apollo himself!"

When he heard these words, he smiled; but at moments a cloud, as it were, passed over his face, for the Roman rabble was satirical and keen in reckoning, and let itself criticise even great triumphators, even men whom it loved and respected. It was known that on a time they shouted during the entrance to Rome of Julius Cæsar: "Citizens, hide your wives; the old libertine is coming!" But Nero's monstrous vanity could not endure the least blame or criticism; meanwhile in the throng, amid shouts of applause were heard cries of "Ahenobarbus, Ahenobarbus! Where hast thou put thy flaming beard? Dost thou fear that Rome might catch fire from it?" And those who cried out in that fashion knew not that their jest concealed a dreadful prophecy.

These voices did not anger Cæsar overmuch, since he did not wear a beard, for long before he had devoted it in a golden cylinder to Jupiter Capitolinus. But other persons, hidden behind piles of stones and the corners of temples, shouted: "Matricide! Nero! Orestes! Alcmæon!" and still others: "Where is Octavia?" "Surrender the purple!" At Poppæa, who came directly after him, they shouted, "Flava coma (yellow hair)!!" with which name they indicated a street-walker. Cæsar's musical ear caught these exclamations also, and he raised the polished emerald to his eyes as if to see and remember those who uttered them. While looking thus, his glance rested on the Apostle standing on the stone.

For a while those two men looked at each other. It occurred to no one in that brilliant retinue, and to no one in that immense throng, that at that moment two powers of the earth were looking at each other, one of which would vanish quickly as a bloody dream, and the other, dressed in simple garments, would seize in eternal possession the world and the city.

Meanwhile Cæsar had passed; and immediately after him eight Africans bore a magnificent litter, in which sat Poppæa, who was detested by the people. Arrayed, as was Nero, in amethyst color, with a thick application of cosmetics on her face, immovable, thoughtful, indifferent, she looked like some beautiful and wicked divinity carried in procession. In her wake followed a whole court of servants, male and female, next a line of wagons bearing materials of dress and use. The sun had sunk sensibly from midday when the passage of Augustians began, — a brilliant glittering line gleaming like an endless serpent. The indolent Petronius, greeted kindly by the multitude, had given command to bear him and his godlike slave in a litter. Tigellinus went in a chariot drawn by ponies ornamented with white and purple feathers. They saw him as he rose in the chariot repeatedly, and stretched his neck to see if Cæsar was preparing to give him the sign to pass to his chariot. Among others the crowd greeted Licinianus with applause, Vitelius with laughter, Vatinius with hissing. Toward Licinus and Lecanius the consuls they were indifferent, but Tullius Senecio they loved, it was unknown why, and Vestinius received applause.

The court was innumerable. It seemed that all that was richest, most brilliant and noted in Rome, was migrating to Antium. Nero never travelled otherwise than with thousands of vehicles; the society which acompanied him almost always exceeded the number of soldiers in a legion.[1] Hence Domitius Afer appeared, and the decrepit Lucius Saturninus; and Vespasian, who had not gone yet on his expedition to Judea, from which he returned for the crown of Cæsar, and his sons, and young Nerva, and Lucan, and Annius Gallo, and Quintianus, and a multitude of women renowned for wealth, beauty, luxury, and vice.

The eyes of the multitude were turned to the harness, the chariots, the horses, the strange livery of the servants, made up of all peoples of the earth. In that procession of pride and grandeur one hardly knew what to look at; and not only the eye, but the mind, was dazzled by such gleaming of gold, purple, and violet, by the flashing of precious stones, the glitter of brocade, pearls, and ivory. It seemed that the very rays of the sun were dissolving in that abyss of brilliancy. And though wretched people were not lacking in that throng, people with sunken stomachs, and with hunger in their eyes, that spectacle inflamed not only their desire of enjoyment and their envy, but filled them with delight and pride, because it gave a feeling of the might and invincibility of Rome, to which the world contributed, and before which the world knelt. Indeed there was not on earth any one who ventured to think that that power would not endure through all ages, and outlive all nations, or that there was anything in existence that had strength to oppose it.

Vinicius, riding at the end of the retinue, sprang out of his chariot at sight of the Apostle and Lygia, whom he had not expected to see, and, greeting them with a radiant face, spoke with hurried voice, like a man who has no time to spare, —

"Hast thou come? I know not how to thank thee, O Lygia! God could not have sent me a better omen. I greet thee even while taking farewell, but not farewell for a long time. On the road I shall dispose relays of horses, and every free day I shall come to thee till I get leave to return. — Farewell!"

"Farewell, Marcus!" answered Lygia; then she added in a lower voice: "May Christ go with thee, and open thy soul to Paul's word."

He was glad at heart that she was concerned about his becoming a Christian soon; hence he answered, —

"Ocelle mi! let it be as thou sayest. Paul prefers to travel with my people,

---

[1] In the time of the Cæsars a legion was always 12,000 men.

but he is with me, and will be to me a companion and master. Draw aside thy veil, my delight, let me see thee before my journey. Why art thou thus hidden?"

She raised the veil, and showed him her bright face and her wonderfully smiling eyes, inquiring, —

"Is the veil bad?"

And her smile had in it a little of maiden opposition; but Vinicius, while looking at her with delight, answered, —

"Bad for my eyes, which till death would look on thee only."

Then he turned to Ursus and said, —

"Ursus, guard her as the sight in thy eye, for she is my domina as well as thine."

Seizing her hand then, he pressed it with his lips, to the great astonishment of the crowd, who could not understand signs of such honor from a brilliant Augustian to a maiden arrayed in simple garments, almost those of a slave.

"Farewell!"

Then he departed quickly, for Cæsar's whole retinue had pushed forward considerably. The Apostle Peter blessed him with a slight sign of the cross; but the kindly Ursus began at once to glorify him, glad that his young mistress listened eagerly and was grateful to him for those praises.

The retinue moved on and hid itself in clouds of golden dust; they gazed long after it, however, till Demas the miller approached, he for whom Ursus worked in the night-time. When he had kissed the Apostle's hand, he entreated them to enter his dwelling for refreshment, saying that it was near the Emporium, that they must be hungry and wearied since they had spent the greater part of the day at the gate.

They went with him, and, after rest and refreshment in his house, returned to the Trans-Tiber only toward evening. Intending to cross the river by the Æmilian bridge, they passed through the Clivus Publicus, going over the Aventine, between the temples of Diana and Mercury. From that height the Apostle looked on the edifices about him, and on those vanishing in the distance. Sunk in silence he meditated on the immensity and dominion of that city, to which he had come to announce the word of God. Hitherto he had seen the rule of Rome and its legions in various lands through which he had wandered, but they were single members as it were of the power, which that day for the first time he had seen impersonated in the form of Nero. That city, immense, predatory, ravenous, unrestrained, rotten to the marrow of its bones, and unassailable in its preterhuman power; that Cæsar, a fratricide, a matricide, a wife-slayer, after him dragged a retinue of bloody spectres no less in number than his court. That profligate, that buffoon, but also lord of thirty legions, and through them of the whole earth; those courtiers covered with gold and scarlet, uncertain of the morrow, but mightier meanwhile than kings, — all this together seemed a species of hellish kingdom of wrong and evil. In his simple heart he marvelled that God could give such inconceivable almightiness to Satan, that He could yield the earth to him to knead, overturn, and trample it, to squeeze blood and tears from it, to twist it like a whirlwind, to storm it like a tempest, to consume it like a flame. And his Apostle-heart was alarmed by those thoughts, and in spirit he spoke to the Master: "O Lord, how shall I begin in this city, to which Thou hast sent me? To it belong seas and lands, the beasts of the field, and the creatures of the water; it owns other kingdoms and cities, and thirty legions which guard them; but I, O Lord, am a fisherman from a lake! How shall I begin, and how shall I conquer its malice?"

Thus speaking, he raised his gray, trembling head toward heaven, praying and exclaiming from the depth of his heart to his Divine Master, himself full of sadness and fear.

Meanwhile his prayer was interrupted by Lygia.

"The whole city is as if on fire," said she.

In fact the sun went down that day in a marvellous manner. Its immense shield had sunk half-way behind the Janiculum, the whole expanse of heaven was filled with a red gleam. From the place on which they were standing, Peter's glance embraced large expanses. Somewhat to the right they saw the long extending walls of the Circus Maximus; above it the towering palaces of the Palatine; and directly in front of them, beyond the Forum Boarium and the Velabrum, the summit of the Capitol, with the temple of Jupiter. But the walls and the columns and the summits of the temples were as if sunk in that golden and purple gleam. The parts of the river visible from afar flowed as if in blood; and as the sun sank moment after moment behind the mountain, the gleam became redder and redder, more and more like a conflagration, and it increased and extended till finally it embraced the seven hills, from which it extended to the whole region about.

"The whole city seems on fire!" repeated Lygia.

Peter shaded his eyes with his hand, and said, —

"The wrath of God is upon it."

CHAPTER XXXVII

Vinicius to Lygia:

"The slave Phlegon, by whom I send this letter, is a Christian; hence he will be one of those to receive freedom from thy hands, my dearest. He is an old servant of our house; so I can write to thee with full confidence, and without fear that the letter will fall into other hands than thine. I write from Laurentum, where we have halted because of heat. Otho owned here a lordly villa, which on a time he presented to Poppæa; and she, though divorced from him, saw fit to retain the magnificent present. When I think of the women who surround me now and of thee, it seems to me that from the stones hurled by Deucalion there must have risen people of various kinds, altogether unlike one another, and that thou art of those born of crystal.

"I admire and love thee from my whole soul, and wish to speak only of thee; hence I am forced to constrain myself to write of our journey, of that which happens to me, and of news of the court. Well, Cæsar was the guest of Poppæa, who prepared for him secretly a magnificent reception. She invited only a few of his favorites, but Petronius and I were among them. After dinner we sailed in golden boats over the sea, which was as calm as if it had been sleeping, and as blue as thy eyes, O divine one. We ourselves rowed, for evidently it flattered the Augusta that men of consular dignity, or their sons, were rowing for her. Cæsar, sitting at the rudder in a purple toga, sang a hymn in honor of the sea; this hymn he had composed the night before, and with Diodorus had arranged music to it. In other boats he was accompanied by slaves from India who knew how to play on sea-shells while round about appeared numerous dolphins, as if really enticed from Amphitrite's depths by music. Dost thou know what I was doing? I was thinking of thee, and yearning. I wanted to gather in that sea, that calm, and that music, and give the whole to thee.

"Dost thou wish that we should live in some place at the seashore far from Rome, my Augusta? I have land in Sicily, on which there is an almond forest which has rose-colored blossoms in spring, and this forest goes down so near the sea that the tips of the branches almost touch the water. There I will love thee and magnify Paul's teaching, for I know now that it will not be opposed to love and happiness. Dost thou wish? — But before I hear thy answer I will write further of what happened on the boat.

"Soon the shore was far behind. We saw a sail before us in the distance, and all at once a dispute rose as to whether it was a common fishing-boat or a great ship from Ostia. I was the first to discover what it was, and then the Augusta said that for my eyes evidently nothing was hidden, and, dropping the veil over her face on a sudden, she inquired if I could recognize her thus.

Petronius answered immediately that it was not possible to see even the sun behind a cloud; but she said, as if in jest, that love alone could blind such a piercing glance as mine, and, naming various women of the court, she fell to inquiring and guessing which one I loved. I answered calmly, but at last she mentioned thy name. Speaking of thee, she uncovered her face again, and looked at me with evil and inquiring eyes.

"I feel real gratitude to Petronius, who turned the boat at that moment, through which general attention was taken from me; for had I heard hostile or sneering words touching thee, I should not have been able to hide my anger, and should have had to struggle with the wish to break the head of that wicked, malicious woman with my oar. Thou rememberest the incident at the pond of Agrippa about which I told thee at the house of Linus on the eve of my departure. Petronius is alarmed on my account, and to-day again he implored me not to offend the Augusta's vanity. But Petronius does not understand me, and does not realize that, apart from thee, I know no pleasure or beauty or love, and that for Poppæa I feel only disgust and contempt. Thou hast changed my soul greatly, — so greatly that I should not wish now to return to my former life. But have no fear that harm may reach me here. Poppæa does not love me, for she cannot love any one, and her desires arise only from anger at Cæsar, who is under her influence yet, and who is even capable of loving her yet; still, he does not spare her, and does not hide from her his transgressions and shamelessness.

"I will tell thee, besides, something which should pacify thee. Peter told me in parting not to fear Cæsar, since a hair would not fall from my head; and I believe him. Some voice in my soul says that every word of his must be accomplished; that since he blessed our love, neither Cæsar, nor all the powers of Hades, nor predestination itself, could take thee from me, O Lygia. When I think of this I am as happy as if I were in heaven, which alone is calm and happy. But what I say of heaven and predestination may offend thee, a Christian. Christ has not washed me yet, but my heart is like an empty chalice, which Paul of Tarsus is to fill with the sweet doctrine professed by thee, — the sweeter for me that it is thine. Thou, divine one, count even this as a merit to me that I have emptied it of the liquid with which I had filled it before, and that I do not withdraw it, but hold it forth as a thirsty man standing at a pure spring. Let me find favor in thy eyes.

"In Antium my days and nights will pass in listening to Paul, who acquired such influence among my people on the first day that they surround him continually, seeing in him not only a wonder-worker, but a being almost supernatural. Yesterday I saw gladness on his face, and when I asked what he was doing, he answered, 'I am sowing.' Petronius knows that he is among my people, and wishes to see him, as does Seneca also, who heard of him from Gallo.

"But the stars are growing pale, O Lygia, and 'Lucifer' of the morning is bright with growing force. Soon the dawn will make the sea ruddy; all is sleeping round about, but I am thinking of thee and loving thee. Be greeted together with the morning dawn, sponsa mea!"

CHAPTER XXXVIII

Vinicius to Lygia:

"Hast thou ever been in Antium, my dear one, with Aulus and Pomponia? If not, I shall be happy when I show this place to thee. All the way from Laurentum there is a line of villas along the seashore; and Antium itself is an endless succession of palaces and porticos, whose columns in fair weather see themselves in the water. I, too, have a residence here right over the sea, with an olive garden and a forest of cypresses behind the villa, and when I think that the place will sometime be thine, its marble seems whiter to me, its groves more shady, and the sea bluer. Oh, Lygia, how good it is to live and love! Old Menikles, who manages the villa, planted irises on the ground under myrtles, and at sight of them the house of Aulus, the impluvium, and the garden in which I sat near thee, came to my mind. The irises will remind thee, too, of thy childhood's home; therefore I am certain that thou wilt love Antium and this villa.

"Immediately after our arrival I talked long with Paul at dinner. We spoke of thee, and afterward he taught. I listened long, and I say only this, that even could I write like Petronius, I should not have power to explain everything which passed through my soul and my mind. I had not supposed that there could be such happiness in this world, such beauty and peace of which hitherto people had no knowledge. But I retain all this for conversation with thee, for at the first free moment I shall be in Rome.

"How could the earth find place at once for the Apostle Peter, Paul of Tarsus, and Cæsar? Tell me this. I ask because I passed the evening after Paul's teaching with Nero, and dost thou know what I heard there? Well, to begin with, he read his poem on the destruction of Troy, and complained that never had he seen a burning city. He envied Priam, and called him happy just for this, that he saw the conflagration and ruin of his birthplace. Whereupon Tigellinus said, 'Speak a word, O divinity, I will take a torch, and before the night passes thou shalt see blazing Antium.' But Cæsar called him a fool. 'Where,' asked he, 'should I go to breathe the sea air, and preserve the voice with which the gods have gifted me, and which men say I should preserve for the benefit of mankind? Is it not Rome that injures me; is it not the exhalations of the Subura and the Esquiline which add to my hoarseness? Would not the palaces of Rome present a spectacle a hundredfold more tragic and magnificent than Antium?' Here all began to talk, and to say what an unheard tragedy the picture of a city like that would be, a city which had conquered the world turned now into a heap of gray ashes. Cæsar declared that then his poem would surpass the songs of Homer, and he began to describe how he would rebuild the city, and how coming ages would admire his achievements, in presence of which all other human works would be petty. 'Do that! do that!' exclaimed the drunken company. 'I must have more faithful and more devoted friends,' answered he. I confess that I was alarmed at once when I heard this, for thou art in Rome, carissima. I laugh now at that alarm, and I think that Cæsar and his friends, though mad, would not dare to permit such insanity. Still, see how a man fears for his love; I should prefer that the house of Linus were not in that narrow Trans-Tiber alley, and in a part occupied by common people, who are less considered in such a case. For me, the very palaces on the Palatine would not be a residence fit for thee; hence I should wish also that nothing were lacking thee of those ornaments and comforts to which thou art accustomed from childhood.

"Go to the house of Aulus, my Lygia. I have thought much here over this matter. If Cæsar were in Rome, news of thy return might reach the Palatine through slaves, turn attention to thee, and bring persecution, because thou didst dare to act against the will of Cæsar. But he will remain long in Antium, and before he returns slaves will have ceased to speak of thee. Linus and Ursus can be with thee. Besides, I live in hope that before Palatine sees Cæsar, thou, my goddess, shalt be dwelling in thy own house on the Carinæ. Blessed be the day, hour, and moment in which thou shalt cross my threshold; and if Christ, whom I am learning to accept, effects this, may His name be blessed also. I shall serve Him, and give life and blood for Him. I speak incorrectly; we shall serve Him, both of us, as long as the threads of life hold.

"I love thee and salute thee with my whole soul."

CHAPTER XXXIX

Ursus was taking water from a cistern, and while drawing up a double amphora, with a rope, was singing a strange Lygian song in an undertone, looking meanwhile with delighted eyes at Lygia and Vinicius, who, among the cypresses in Linus's garden, seemed as white as two statues. Their clothing was not moved by the least breeze. A golden and lily-colored twilight was sinking on the world while they were conversing in the calm of evening, each holding the other by the hand.

"May not some evil meet thee, Marcus, because thou hast left Antium without Cæsar's knowledge?" asked Lygia.

"No, my dear," answered Vinicius. "Cæsar announced that he would shut himself in for two days with Terpnos, and compose new songs. He acts thus frequently, and at such times neither knows nor remembers aught else. Moreover, what is Cæsar to me since I am near thee and am looking at thee? I have yearned too much already, and these last nights sleep has left me. More than once, when I dozed from weariness, I woke on a sudden, with a feeling that danger was hanging over thee; at times I dreamed that the relays of horses which were to bear me from Antium to Rome were stolen, — horses with which I passed that road more swiftly than any of Cæsar's couriers. Besides, I could not live longer without thee; I love thee too much for that, my dearest."

"I knew that thou wert coming. Twice Ursus ran out, at my request, to the Carinæ, and inquired for thee at thy house. Linus laughed at me, and Ursus also."

It was, indeed, evident that she had expected him; for instead of her usual dark dress, she wore a soft white stola, out of whose beautiful folds her arms and head emerged like primroses out of snow. A few ruddy anemones ornamented her hair.

Vinicius pressed his lips to her hands; then they sat on the stone bench amidst wild grape-vines, and inclining toward each other, were silent, looking at the twilight whose last gleams were reflected in their eyes.

The charm of the quiet evening mastered them completely.

"How calm it is here, and how beautiful the world is," said Vinicius, in a lowered voice. "The night is wonderfully still. I feel happier than ever in life before. Tell me, Lygia, what is this? Never have I thought that there could be such love. I thought that love was merely fire in the blood and desire; but now for the first time I see that it is possible to love with every drop of one's blood and every breath, and feel therewith such sweet and immeasurable calm as if Sleep and Death had put the soul to rest. For me this is something new. I look on this calmness of the trees, and it seems to be within me. Now I understand for the first time that there may be happiness of which people have not known thus far. Now I begin to understand why thou and Pomponia Græcina have such peace. Yes! Christ gives it."

At that moment Lygia placed her beautiful face on his shoulder and said, — "My dear Marcus — " But she was unable to continue. Joy, gratitude, and the feeling that at last she was free to love deprived her of voice, and her eyes were filled with tears of emotion.

Vinicius, embracing her slender form with his arm, drew her toward him and said, —

"Lygia! May the moment be blessed in which I heard His name for the first time."

"I love thee, Marcus," said she then in a low voice.

Both were silent again, unable to bring words from their overcharged breasts. The last lily reflections had died on the cypresses, and the garden began to be silver-like from the crescent of the moon. After a while Vinicius said, —

"I know. Barely had I entered here, barely had I kissed thy dear hands, when I read in thy eyes the question whether I had received the divine doctrine to which thou art attached, and whether I was baptized. No, I am not baptized yet; but knowest thou, my flower, why? Paul said to me: 'I have convinced thee that God came into the world and gave Himself to be crucified for its salvation; but let Peter wash thee in the fountain of grace, he who first stretched his hands over thee and blessed thee.' And I, my dearest, wish thee to witness my baptism, and I wish Pomponia to be my godmother. This is why I am not baptized yet, though I believe in the Saviour and in His teaching. Paul has convinced me, has converted me; and could it be otherwise? How was I not to believe that Christ came into the world, since he, who was His disciple, says so, and Paul, to whom He appeared? How was I not to believe that He was God, since He rose from the dead? Others saw Him in the city and on the lake and on the mountain; people saw Him whose lips have not known a lie. I began to believe this the first time I heard Peter in Ostrianum, for I said to myself even then: In the whole world any other man might lie rather than this one who says, 'I saw.' But I feared thy religion. It seemed to me that thy religion would take thee from me. I thought that there was neither wisdom nor beauty nor happiness in it. But to-day, when I know it, what kind of man should I be were I not to wish truth to rule the world instead of falsehood, love instead of hatred, virtue instead of crime, faithfulness instead of unfaithfulness, mercy instead of vengeance? What sort of man would he be who would not choose and wish the same? But your religion teaches this. Others desire justice also; but thy religion is the only one which makes man's heart just, and besides makes it pure, like thine and Pomponia's, makes it faithful, like thine and Pomponia's. I should be blind were I not to see this. But if in addition Christ God has promised eternal life, and has promised happiness as immeasurable as the all-might of God can give, what more can one wish? Were I to ask Seneca why he enjoins virtue, if wickedness brings more happiness, he would not be able to say anything sensible. But I know now that I ought to be virtuous, because virtue and love flow from Christ, and because, when death closes my eyes, I shall find life and happiness, I shall find myself and thee. Why not love and accept a religion which both speaks the truth and destroys death? Who would not prefer good to evil? I thought thy religion opposed to happiness; meanwhile Paul has convinced me that not only does it not take away, but that it gives. All this hardly finds a place in my head; but I feel that it is true, for I have never been so happy, neither could I be, had I taken thee by force and possessed thee in my house. Just see, thou hast said a moment since, 'I love thee,' and I could not have won these words from thy lips with all the might of Rome. O Lygia! Reason declares this religion divine, and the best; the heart feels it, and who can resist two such forces?"

Lygia listened, fixing on him her blue eyes, which in the light of the moon were like mystic flowers, and bedewed like flowers.

"Yes, Marcus, that is true!" said she, nestling her head more closely to his shoulder.

And at that moment they felt immensely happy, for they understood that besides love they were united by another power, at once sweet and irresistible, by which love itself becomes endless, not subject to change, deceit, treason, or even death. Their hearts were filled with perfect certainty that, no matter what might happen, they would not cease to love and belong to each other. For that reason an unspeakable repose flowed in on their souls. Vinicius felt, besides, that that love was not merely profound and pure, but altogether new, — such as the world had not known and could not give. In his head all was combined in this love, — Lygia, the teaching of Christ, the light of the moon resting calmly on the cypresses, and the still night, — so that to him the whole universe seemed filled with it.

After a while he said with a lowered and quivering voice: "Thou wilt be the soul of my soul, and the dearest in the world to me. Our hearts will beat together, we shall have one prayer and one gratitude to Christ. O my dear! To live together, to honor together the sweet God, and to know that when death comes our eyes will open again, as after a pleasant sleep, to a new light, — what better could be imagined? I only marvel that I did not understand this at first. And knowest thou what occurs to me now? That no one can resist this religion. In two hundred or three hundred years the whole world will accept it. People will forget Jupiter, and there will be no God except Christ, and no other temples but Christian. Who would not wish his own happiness? Ah! but I heard Paul's conversation with Petronius and dost thou know what Petronius said at the end? 'That is not for me'; but he could give no other answer."

"Repeat Paul's words to me," said Lygia.

"It was at my house one evening. Petronius began to speak playfully and to banter, as he does usually, whereupon Paul said to him: 'How canst thou deny, O wise Petronius, that Christ existed and rose from the dead, since thou wert not in the world at that time, but Peter and John saw Him, and I saw Him on the road to Damascus? Let thy wisdom show, first of all, then, that we are liars, and then only deny our testimony.' Petronius answered that he had no thought of denying, for he knew that many incomprehensible things were done, which trustworthy people affirmed. 'But the discovery of some new foreign god is one thing,' said he, 'and the reception of his teaching another. I have no wish to know anything which may deform life and mar its beauty. Never mind whether our gods are true or not; they are beautiful, their rule is pleasant for us, and we live without care.' 'Thou art willing to reject the religion of love, justice, and mercy through dread of the cares of life,' replied Paul; 'but think, Petronius, is thy life really free from anxieties? Behold, neither thou nor any man among the richest and most powerful knows when he falls asleep at night that he may not wake to a death sentence. But tell me, if Cæsar professed this religion, which enjoins love and justice, would not thy happiness be more assured? Thou art alarmed about thy delight, but would not life be more joyous then? As to life's beauty and ornaments, if ye have reared so many beautiful temples and statues to evil, revengeful, adulterous, and faithless divinities, what would ye not do in honor of one God of truth and mercy? Thou art ready to praise thy lot, because thou art wealthy and living in luxury; but it was possible even in thy case to be poor and deserted, though coming of a great house, and then in truth it would have been better for thee if people confessed Christ. In Rome even wealthy parents, unwilling to toil at rearing children, cast them out of the house frequently; those children are called alumni. And chance might have made thee an alumnus, like one of those. But if parents live according to our religion, this cannot happen. And hadst thou, at manhood's years, married a woman of thy love, thy wish would be to see her faithful till death. Meanwhile look around, what happens among you, what vileness, what shame, what bartering in the faith of wives! Nay, ye yourselves are astonished when a woman appears whom ye call "univira" (of one husband). But I tell thee that those women who carry Christ in their hearts will not break faith with their husbands, just as Christian husbands will keep faith with their wives. But ye are neither sure of rulers nor fathers nor wives nor children nor servants. The whole world is trembling before you, and ye are trembling before your own slaves, for ye know that any hour may raise an awful war against your oppression, such a war as has been raised more than once. Though rich, thou art not sure that the command may not come to thee to-morrow to leave thy wealth; thou art young, but to-morrow it may be necessary for thee to die. Thou lovest, but treason is in wait for thee; thou art enamoured of villas and statues, but to-morrow power may thrust thee forth into the empty places of the Pandataria; thou hast thousands of servants, but to-morrow these servants may let thy blood flow. And if that be the case, how canst thou be calm and happy, how canst thou live in delight? But I proclaim love, and I proclaim a religion which commands rulers to love their subjects, masters their slaves, slaves to serve with love, to do justice and be merciful; and at last it promises happiness boundless as a sea without end. How, then,

Petronius, canst thou say that that religion spoils life, since it corrects, and since thou thyself wouldst be a hundred times happier and more secure were it to embrace the world as Rome's dominion has embraced it?'

"Thus discussed Paul, and then Petronius said, 'That is not for me.' Feigning drowsiness, he went out, and when going added: 'I prefer my Eunice, O little Jew, but I should not wish to struggle with thee on the platform.' I listened to Paul's words with my whole soul, and when he spoke of our women, I magnified with all my heart that religion from which thou hast sprung as a lily from a rich field in springtime. And I thought then: There is Poppæa, who cast aside two husbands for Nero, there is Calvia Crispinilla, there is Nigidia, there are almost all whom I know, save only Pomponia; they trafficked with faith and with oaths, but she and my own one will not desert, will not deceive, and will not quench the fire, even though all in whom I place trust should desert and deceive me. Hence I said to thee in my soul, How can I show gratitude to thee, if not with love and honor? Didst thou feel that in Antium I spoke and conversed with thee all the time as if thou hadst been at my side? I love thee a hundred times more for having escaped me from Cæsar's house. Neither do I care for Cæsar's house any longer; I wish not its luxury and music, I wish only thee. Say a word, we will leave Rome to settle somewhere at a distance."

Without removing her head from his shoulder, Lygia, as if meditating, raised her eyes to the silver tops of the cypresses, and answered, —

"Very well, Marcus. Thou hast written to me of Sicily, where Aulus wishes to settle in old age." And Vinicius interrupted her with delight.

"True, my dear! Our lands are adjacent. That is a wonderful coast, where the climate is sweeter and the nights still brighter than in Rome, odoriferous and transparent. There life and happiness are almost one and the same."

And he began then to dream of the future.

"There we may forget anxieties. In groves, among olive-trees, we shall walk and rest in the shade. O Lygia! what a life to love and cherish each other, to look at the sea together, to look at the sky together, to honor together a kind God, to do in peace what is just and true."

Both were silent, looking into the future; only he drew her more firmly toward him, and the knight's ring on his finger glittered meanwhile in the rays of the moon. In the part occupied by the poor toiling people, all were sleeping; no murmur broke the silence.

"Wilt thou permit me to see Pomponia?" asked Lygia.

"Yes, dear one. We will invite them to our house, or go to them ourselves. If thou wish, we can take Peter the Apostle. He is bowed down with age and work. Paul will visit us also, — he will convert Aulus Plautius; and as soldiers found colonies in distant lands, so we will found a colony of Christians."

Lygia raised her hand and, taking his palm, wished to press it to her lips; but he whispered, as if fearing to frighten happiness, —

"No, Lygia, no! It is I who honor thee and exalt thee; give me thy hands."

"I love thee."

He had pressed his lips to her hands, white as jessamine, and for a time they heard only the beating of their own hearts. There was not the slightest movement in the air; the cypresses stood as motionless as if they too were holding breath in their breasts.

All at once the silence was broken by an unexpected thunder, deep, and as if coming from under the earth. A shiver ran through Lygia's body. Vinicius stood up, and said, —

"Lions are roaring in the vivarium."

Both began to listen. Now the first thunder was answered by a second, a third, a tenth, from all sides and divisions of the city. In Rome several thousand lions were quartered at times in various arenas, and frequently in the night-time they approached the grating, and, leaning their gigantic heads against it, gave utterance to their yearning for freedom and the desert. Thus they began on this occasion, and, answering one another in the stillness of night, they filled the whole city with roaring. There was something so indescribably gloomy and terrible in those roars that Lygia, whose bright and calm visions of the future were scattered, listened with a straitened heart and with wonderful fear and sadness.

But Vinicius encircled her with his arm, and said, —

"Fear not, dear one. The games are at hand, and all the vivaria are crowded."

Then both entered the house of Linus, accompanied by the thunder of lions, growing louder and louder.

CHAPTER XL

In Antium, meanwhile, Petronius gained new victories almost daily over courtiers vying with him for the favor of Cæsar. The influence of Tigellinus had fallen completely. In Rome, when there was occasion to set aside men who seemed dangerous, to plunder their property or to settle political cases, to give spectacles astounding by their luxury and bad taste, or finally to satisfy the monstrous whims of Cæsar, Tigellinus, as adroit, as he was ready for anything, became indispensable. But in Antium, among palaces reflected in the azure of the sea, Cæsar led a Hellenic existence. From morning till evening Nero and his attendants read verses, discoursed on their structure and finish, were delighted with happy turns of expression, were occupied with music, the theatre, — in a word, exclusively with that which Grecian genius had invented, and with which it had beautified life. Under these conditions Petronius, incomparably more refined than Tigellinus and the other courtiers, — witty, eloquent, full of subtile feelings and tastes, — obtained pre-eminence of necessity. Cæsar sought his society, took his opinion, asked for advice when he composed, and showed a more lively friendship than at any other time whatever. It seemed to courtiers that his influence had won a supreme triumph at last, that friendship between him and Cæsar had entered on a period of certainty which would last for years. Even those who had shown dislike previously to the exquisite Epicurean, began now to crowd around him and vie for his favor. More than one was even sincerely glad in his soul that preponderance had come to a man who knew really what to think of a given person, who received with a sceptical smile the flattery of his enemies of yesterday, but who, either through indolence or culture, was not vengeful, and did not use his power to the detriment or destruction of others. There were moments when he might have destroyed even Tigellinus, but he preferred to ridicule him, and expose his vulgarity and want of refinement. In Rome the Senate drew breath, for no death sentence had been issued for a month and a half. It is true that in Antium and the city people told wonders of the refinement which the profligacy of Cæsar and his favorite had reached, but every one preferred a refined Cæsar to one brutalized in the hands of Tigellinus. Tigellinus himself lost his head, and hesitated whether or not to yield as conquered, for Cæsar had said repeatedly that in all Rome and in his court there were only two spirits capable of understanding each other, two real Hellenes, — he and Petronius.

The amazing dexterity of Petronius confirmed people in the conviction that his influence would outlive every other. They did not see how Cæsar could dispense with him, — with whom could he converse touching poetry, music, and comparative excellence; in whose eyes could he look to learn whether his creation was indeed perfect? Petronius, with his habitual indifference, seemed to attach no importance to his position. As usual, he was remiss, slothful, sceptical, and witty. He produced on people frequently the impression of a man who made light of them, of himself, of Cæsar, of the whole world. At moments he ventured to criticise Cæsar to his face, and when others judged that he was going too far, or simply preparing his own ruin, he was able to turn the criticism suddenly in such a way that it came out to his profit; he roused amazement in those present, and the conviction that there was no position from which he could not issue in triumph.

About a week after the return of Vinicius from Rome, Cæsar read in a small circle an extract from his Troyad; when he had finished and the shouts of rapture had ended, Petronius, interrogated by a glance from Cæsar, replied, —

"Common verses, fit for the fire."

The hearts of those present stopped beating from terror. Since the years of his childhood Nero had never heard such a sentence from any man. The face of Tigellinus was radiant with delight. But Vinicius grew pale, thinking that Petronius, who thus far had never been drunk, was drunk this time.

Nero, however, inquired in a honeyed voice, in which more or less deeply wounded vanity was quivering, —

"What defect dost thou find in them?"

"Do not believe them," said Petronius, attacking him, and pointing to those present; "they understand nothing. Thou hast asked what defect there is in thy verses. If thou desire truth, I will tell thee. Thy verses would be worthy of Virgil, of Ovid, even of Homer, but they are not worthy of thee. Thou art not free to write such. The conflagration described by thee does not blaze enough; thy fire is not hot enough. Listen not to Lucan's flatteries. Had he written those verses, I should acknowledge him a genius, but thy case is different. And knowest thou why? Thou art greater than they. From him who is gifted of the gods as thou art, more is demanded. But thou art slothful, — thou wouldst rather sleep after dinner than sit to wrinkles. Thou canst create a work such as the world has not heard of to this day; hence I tell thee to thy eyes, write better!"

And he said this carelessly, as if bantering and also chiding; but Cæsar's eyes were mist-covered from delight.

"The gods have given me a little talent," said he, "but they have given me something greater, — a true judge and friend, the only man able to speak the truth to my eyes."

Then he stretched his fat hand, grown over with reddish hair, to a golden candelabrum plundered from Delphi, to burn the verses. But Petronius seized them before the flame touched the paper.

"No, no!" said he; "even thus they belong to mankind. Leave them to me."

"In such case let me send them to thee in a cylinder of my own invention," answered Nero, embracing Petronius.

"True; thou art right," said he, after a while. "My conflagration of Troy does not blaze enough; my fire is not hot enough. But I thought it sufficient

to equal Homer. A certain timidity and low estimate of my power have
fettered me always. Thou hast opened my eyes. But knowest why it is, as
thou sayest? When a sculptor makes the statue of a god, he seeks a model;
but never have I had a model. I never have seen a burning city; hence there
is a lack of truth in my description."

"Then I will say that only a great artist understands this."

Nero grew thoughtful, and after a while he said, —

"Answer one question, Petronius. Dost thou regret the burning of Troy?"

"Do I regret? By the lame consort of Venus, not in the least! And I will tell
thee the reason. Troy would not have been consumed if Prometheus had not
given fire to man, and the Greeks made war on Priam. Æschylus would not
have written his Prometheus had there been no fire, just as Homer would
not have written the Iliad had there been no Trojan war. I think it better to
have Prometheus and the Iliad than a small and shabby city, which was unclean, I think, and wretched, and in which at best there would be now some
procurator annoying thee through quarrels with the local areopagus."

"That is what we call speaking with sound reason," said Nero. "For art
and poetry it is permitted, and it is right, to sacrifice everything. Happy
were the Achæans who furnished Homer with the substance of the Iliad,
and happy Priam who beheld the ruin of his birthplace. As to me, I have
never seen a burning city."

A time of silence followed, which was broken at last by Tigellinus, —

"But I have said to thee, Cæsar, already, command and I will burn Antium;
or dost thou know what? If thou art sorry for these villas and palaces, give
command to burn the ships in Ostia; or I will build a wooden city on the
Alban Hills, into which thou shalt hurl the fire thyself. Dost thou wish?"

"Am I to gaze on the burning of wooden sheds?" asked Nero, casting a
look of contempt on him. "Thy mind has grown utterly barren, Tigellinus.
And I see, besides, that thou dost set no great value on my talent or my
Troyad, since thou judgest that any sacrifice would be too great for it."

Tigellinus was confused; but Nero, as if wishing to change the conversation, added after a while, —

"Summer is passing. Oh, what a stench there must be in that Rome now!
And still we must return for the summer games."

"When thou dismissest the Augustians, O Cæsar, permit me to remain
with thee a moment," said Tigellinus.

An hour later Vinicius, returning with Petronius from Cæsar's villa, said, —

"I was a trifle alarmed for thee. I judged that while drunk thou hadst ruined
thyself beyond redemption. Remember that thou art playing with death."

"That is my arena," answered Petronius, carelessly; "and the feeling that
I am the best gladiator in it amuses me. See how it ended. My influence has
increased this evening. He will send me his verses in a cylinder which —
dost wish to lay a wager? — will be immensely rich and in immensely bad
taste. I shall command my physician to keep physic in it. I did this for another reason, — because Tigellinus, seeing how such things succeed, will wish
surely to imitate me, and I imagine what will happen. The moment he starts a
witticism, it will be as if a bear of the Pyrenees were rope-walking. I shall

laugh like Democritus. If I wished I could destroy Tigellinus perhaps, and become pretorian prefect in his place, and have Ahenobarbus himself in my hands. But I am indolent; I prefer my present life and even Cæsar's verses to trouble."

"What dexterity to be able to turn even blame into flattery! But are those verses really so bad? I am no judge in those matters."

"The verses are not worse than others. Lucan has more talent in one finger, but in Bronzebeard too there is something. He has, above all, an immense love for poetry and music. In two days we are to be with him to hear the music of his hymn to Aphrodite, which he will finish to-day or to-morrow. We shall be in a small circle, — only I, thou, Tullius Senecio, and young Nerva. But as to what I said touching Nero's verses, that I use them after feasting as Vitelius does flamingo feathers, is not true. At times they are eloquent. Hecuba's words are touching. She complains of the pangs of birth, and Nero was able to find happy expressions, — for this reason, perhaps, that he gives birth to every verse in torment. At times I am sorry for him. By Pollux, what a marvellous mixture! The fifth stave was lacking in Caligula, but still he never did such strange things."

"Who can foresee to what the madness of Ahenobarbus will go?" asked Vinicius.

"No man whatever. Such things may happen yet that the hair will stand on men's heads for whole centuries at thought of them. But it is that precisely which interests me; and though I am bored more than once, like Jupiter Ammon in the desert, I believe that under another Cæsar I should be bored a hundred times more. Paul, thy little Jew, is eloquent, — that I accord to him; and if people like him proclaim that religion, our gods must defend themselves seriously, lest in time they be led away captive. It is true that if Cæsar, for example, were a Christian, all would feel safer. But thy prophet of Tarsus, in applying proofs to me, did not think, seest thou, that for me this uncertainty becomes the charm of life. Whoso does not play at dice will not lose property, but still people play at dice. There is in that a certain delight and destruction of the present. I have known sons of knights and senators to become gladiators of their own will. I play with life, thou sayest, and that is true, but I play because it pleases me; while Christian virtues would bore me in a day, as do the discourses of Seneca. Because of this, Paul's eloquence is exerted in vain. He should understand that people like me will never accept his religion. With thy disposition thou mightst either hate the name Christian, or become a Christian immediately. I recognize, while yawning, the truth of what they say. We are mad. We are hastening to the precipice, something unknown is coming toward us out of the future, something is breaking beneath us, something is dying around us, — agreed! But we shall succeed in dying; meanwhile we have no wish to burden life, and serve death before it takes us. Life exists for itself alone, not for death."

"But I pity thee, Petronius."

"Do not pity me more than I pity myself. Formerly thou wert glad among us; while campaigning in Armenia, thou wert longing for Rome."

"And now I am longing for Rome."

"True; for thou art in love with a Christian vestal, who sits in the Trans-Tiber. I neither wonder at this, nor do I blame thee. I wonder more, that in spite of a religion described by thee as a sea of happiness, and in spite of a love which is soon to be crowned, sadness has not left thy face. Pomponia Græcina is eternally pensive; from the time of thy becoming a Christian thou hast ceased to laugh. Do not try to persuade me that this religion is cheerful. Thou hast returned from Rome sadder than ever. If Christians love in this way, by the bright curls of Bacchus! I shall not imitate them!"

"That is another thing," answered Vinicius. "I swear to thee, not by the curls of Bacchus, but by the soul of my father, that never in times past have I experienced even a foretaste of such happiness as I breathe to-day. But I yearn greatly; and what is stranger, when I am far from Lygia, I think that danger is threatening her. I know not what danger, nor whence it may come; but I feel it, as one feels a coming tempest."

"In two days I will try to obtain for thee permission to leave Antium, for as long a time as may please thee. Poppæa is somewhat more quiet; and, as far as I know, no danger from her threatens thee or Lygia."

"This very day she asked me what I was doing in Rome, though my departure was secret."

"Perhaps she gave command to set spies on thee. Now, however, even she must count with me."

"Paul told me," said Vinicius, "that God forewarns sometimes, but does not permit us to believe in omens; hence I guard myself against this belief, but I cannot ward it off. I will tell thee what happened, so as to cast the weight from my heart. Lygia and I were sitting side by side on a night as calm as this, and planning our future. I cannot tell thee how happy and calm we were. All at once lions began to roar. That is common in Rome, but since then I have no rest. It seems to me that in that roaring there was a threat, an announcement as it were of misfortune. Thou knowest that I am not frightened easily; that night, however, something happened which filled all the darkness with terror. It came so strangely and unexpectedly that I have those sounds in my ears yet, and unbroken fear in my heart, as if Lygia were asking my protection from something dreadful, — even from those same lions. I am in torture. Obtain for me permission to leave Antium, or I shall go without it. I cannot remain. I repeat to thee, I cannot!"

"Sons of consuls or their wives are not given to lions yet in the arenas," said Petronius, laughing. "Any other death may meet thee but that. Who knows, besides, that they were lions? German bisons roar with no less gentleness than lions. As to me, I ridicule omens and fates. Last night was warm and I saw stars falling like rain. Many a man has an evil foreboding at such a sight; but I thought, 'If among these is my star too, I shall not lack society at least!'" Then he was silent, but added after a moment's thought, —

"If your Christ has risen from the dead, He may perhaps protect you both from death."

"He may," answered Vinicius, looking at the heavens filled with stars.

CHAPTER XLI

NERO played and sang, in honor of the "Lady of Cyprus," a hymn the verses and music of which were composed by himself. That day he was in voice, and felt that his music really captivated those present. That feeling added such power to the sounds produced and roused his own soul so much that he seemed inspired. At last he grew pale from genuine emotion. This was surely the first time that he had no desire to hear praises from others. He sat for a time with his hands on the cithara and with bowed head; then, rising suddenly, he said, —

"I am tired and need air. Meanwhile ye will tune the citharæ."

He covered his throat then with a silk kerchief.

"Ye will go with me," said he, turning to Petronius and Vinicius, who were sitting in a corner of the hall. "Give me thy arm, Vinicius, for strength fails me; Petronius will talk to me of music."

They went out on the terrace, which was paved with alabaster and sprinkled with saffron.

"Here one can breathe more freely," said Nero. "My soul is moved and sad, though I see that with what I have sung to thee on trial just now I may appear in public, and my triumph will be such as no Roman has ever achieved."

"Thou mayst appear here, in Rome, in Achæa. I admire thee with my whole heart and mind, divinity," answered Petronius.

"I know. Thou art too slothful to force thyself to flattery, and thou art as sincere as Tullius Senecio, but thou hast more knowledge than he. Tell me, what is thy judgment on music?"

"When I listen to poetry, when I look at a quadriga directed by thee in the Circus, when I look at a beautiful statue, temple, or picture, I feel that I comprehend perfectly what I see, that my enthusiasm takes in all that these can give. But when I listen to music, especially thy music, new delights and beauties open before me every instant. I pursue them, I try to seize them; but before I can take them to myself, new and newer ones flow in, just like waves of the sea, which roll on from infinity. Hence I tell thee that music is like the sea. We stand on one shore and gaze at remoteness, but we cannot see the other shore."

"Ah, what deep knowledge thou hast!" said Nero; and they walked on for a moment, only the slight sound of the saffron leaves under their feet being heard.

"Thou hast expressed my idea," said Nero at last; "hence I say now, as ever, in all Rome thou art the only man able to understand me. Thus it is, my judgment of music is the same as thine. When I play and sing, I see things which I did not know as existing in my dominions or in the world. I am Cæsar, and the world is mine. I can do everything. But music opens new kingdoms to me, new mountains, new seas, new delights unknown before. Most frequently I cannot name them or grasp them; I only feel them. I feel the gods, I see Olympus. Some kind of breeze from beyond the earth blows in on me; I behold, as in a mist, certain immeasurable greatnesses, but calm and bright as sunshine. The whole Spheros plays around me; and I declare to thee" (here Nero's voice quivered with genuine wonder) "that I, Cæsar and god, feel at such times as diminutive as dust. Wilt thou believe this?"

"I will. Only great artists have power to feel small in the presence of art."

"This is a night of sincerity; hence I open my soul to thee as to a friend, and I will say more: dost thou consider that I am blind or deprived of reason? Dost thou think that I am ignorant of this, that people in Rome write insults on the walls against me, call me a matricide, a wife-murderer, hold me a monster and a tyrant, because Tigellinus obtained a few sentences of death against my enemies? Yes, my dear, they hold me a monster, and I know it. They have talked cruelty on me to that degree that at times I put the question to myself, 'Am I not cruel?' But they do not understand this, that a man's deeds may be cruel at times while he himself is not cruel. Ah, no one will believe, and perhaps even thou, my dear, wilt not believe, that at moments when music caresses my soul I feel as kind as a child in the cradle. I swear by those stars which shine above us, that I speak the pure truth to thee. People do not know how much goodness lies in this heart, and what treasures I see in it when music opens the door to them."

Petronius, who had not the least doubt that Nero was speaking sincerely at that moment, and that music might bring out various more noble inclinations of his soul, which were overwhelmed by mountains of egotism, profligacy, and crime, said, —

"Men should know thee as nearly as I do; Rome has never been able to appreciate thee."

Cæsar leaned more heavily on Vinicius's arm, as if he were bending under the weight of injustice, and answered, —

"Tigellinus has told me that in the Senate they whisper into one another's ears that Diodorus and Terpnos play on the cithara better than I. They refuse me even that! But tell me, thou who art truthful always, do they play better, or as well?"

"By no means. Thy touch is finer, and has greater power. In thee the artist is evident, in them the expert. The man who hears their music first understands better what thou art."

"If that be true, let them live. They will never imagine what a service thou hast rendered them in this moment. For that matter, if I had condemned those two, I should have had to take others in place of them."

"And people would say, besides, that out of love for music thou destroyest music in thy dominions. Never kill art for art's sake, O divinity."

"How different thou art from Tigellinus!" answered Nero. "But seest thou, I am an artist in everything; and since music opens for me spaces the existence of which I had not divined, regions which I do not possess, delight and happiness which I do not know, I cannot live a common life. Music tells me that the uncommon exists, so I seek it with all the power of dominion which the gods have placed in my hands. At times it seems to me that to reach those Olympian worlds I must do something which no man has done hitherto, — I must surpass the stature of man in good or evil. I know that people declare me mad. But I am not mad, I am only seeking. And if I am going mad, it is out of disgust and impatience that I cannot find. I am seeking! Dost understand me? And therefore I wish to be greater than man, for only in that way can I be the greatest as an artist."

Here he lowered his voice so that Vinicius could not hear him, and, putting his mouth to the ear of Petronius, he whispered, —

"Dost know that I condemned my mother and wife to death mainly because I wished to lay at the gate of an unknown world the greatest sacrifice that man could put there? I thought that afterward something would happen, that doors would be opened beyond which I should see something unknown. Let it be wonderful or awful, surpassing human conception, if only great and uncommon. But that sacrifice was not sufficient. To open the empyrean doors it is evident that something greater is needed, and let it be given as the Fates desire."

"What dost thou intend to do?"

"Thou shalt see sooner than thou thinkest. Meanwhile be assured that there are two Neros, — one such as people know, the other an artist, whom thou alone knowest, and if he slays as does death, or is in frenzy like Bacchus, it is only because the flatness and misery of common life stifle him; and I should like to destroy them, though I had to use fire or iron. Oh, how flat this world will be when I am gone from it! No man has suspected yet, not thou even, what an artist I am. But precisely because of this I suffer, and sincerely do I tell thee that the soul in me is as gloomy as those cypresses which stand dark there in front of us. It is grievous for a man to bear at once the weight of supreme power and the highest talents."

"I sympathize with thee, O Cæsar; and with me earth and sea, not counting Vinicius, who deifies thee in his soul."

"He, too, has always been dear to me," said Cæsar, "though he serves Mars, not the Muses."

"He serves Aphrodite first of all," answered Petronius. And suddenly he determined to settle the affair of his nephew at a blow, and at the same time to eliminate every danger which might threaten him. "He is in love, as was Troilus with Cressida. Permit him, lord, to visit Rome, for he is dying on my hands. Dost thou know that that Lygian hostage whom thou gavest him has been found, and Vinicius, when leaving for Antium, left her in care of a certain Linus? I did not mention this to thee, for thou wert composing thy hymn, and that was more important than all besides. Vinicius wanted her as a mistress; but when she turned out to be as virtuous as Lucretia, he fell in love with her virtue, and now his desire is to marry her. She is a king's daughter, hence she will cause him no detriment; but he is a real soldier: he sighs and withers and groans, but he is waiting for the permission of his Imperator."

"The Imperator does not choose wives for his soldiers. What good is my permission to Vinicius?"

"I have told thee, O lord, that he deifies thee."

"All the more may he be certain of permission. That is a comely maiden, but too narrow in the hips. The Augusta Poppæa has complained to me that she enchanted our child in the gardens of the Palatine."

"But I told Tigellinus that the gods are not subject to evil charms. Thou rememberest, divinity, his confusion and thy exclamation, 'Habet!'"

"I remember."

Here he turned to Vinicius, —

"Dost thou love her, as Petronius says?"

"I love her, lord," replied Vinicius.

"Then I command thee to set out for Rome to-morrow, and marry her. Appear not again before my eyes without the marriage ring."

"Thanks to thee, lord, from my heart and soul."

"Oh, how pleasant it is to make people happy!" said Nero. "Would that I might do nothing else all my life!"

"Grant us one favor more, O divinity," said Petronius: "declare thy will in this matter before the Augusta. Vinicius would never venture to wed a woman displeasing to the Augusta; thou wilt dissipate her prejudice, O lord, with a word, by declaring that thou hast commanded this marriage."

"I am willing," said Cæsar. "I could refuse nothing to thee or Vinicius."

He turned toward the villa, and they followed. Their hearts were filled with delight over the victory; and Vinicius had to use self-restraint to avoid throwing himself on the neck of Petronius, for it seemed now that all dangers and obstacles were removed.

In the atrium of the villa young Nerva and Tullius Senecio were entertaining the Augusta with conversation. Terpnos and Diodorus were tuning citharæ.

Nero entered, sat in an armchair inlaid with tortoise-shell, whispered something in the ear of a Greek slave near his side, and waited.

The page returned soon with a golden casket. Nero opened it and took out a necklace of great opals.

"These are jewels worthy of this evening," said he.

"The light of Aurora is playing in them," answered Poppæa, convinced that the necklace was for her.

Cæsar, now raising, now lowering the rosy stones, said at last, —

"Vinicius, thou wilt give, from me, this necklace to her whom I command thee to marry, the youthful daughter of the Lygian king."

Poppæa's glance, filled with anger and sudden amazement, passed from Cæsar to Vinicius. At last it rested on Petronius. But he, leaning carelessly over the arm of the chair, passed his hand along the back of the harp as if to fix its form firmly in his mind.

Vinicius gave thanks for the gift, approached Petronius, and asked, —
"How shall I thank thee for what thou hast done this day for me?"

"Sacrifice a pair of swans to Euterpe," replied Petronius, "praise Cæsar's songs, and laugh at omens. Henceforth the roaring of lions will not disturb thy sleep, I trust, nor that of thy Lygian lily."

"No," said Vinicius; "now I am perfectly at rest."

"May Fortune favor thee! But be careful, for Cæsar is taking his lute again. Hold thy breath, listen, and shed tears."

In fact Cæsar had taken the lute and raised his eyes. In the hall conversation had stopped, and people were as still as if petrified. Terpnos and Diodorus, who had to accompany Cæsar, were on the alert, looking now at each other and now at his lips, waiting for the first tones of the song.

Just then a movement and noise began in the entrance; and after a moment Cæsar's freedman, Phaon, appeared from beyond the curtain. Close behind him was the consul Lecanius.

Nero frowned.

"Pardon, divine Imperator," said Phaon, with panting voice, "there is a conflagration in Rome! The greater part of the city is in flames!"

At this news all sprang from their seats.

"O gods! I shall see a burning city and finish the Troyad," said Nero, setting aside his lute.

Then he turned to the consul, —

"If I go at once, shall I see the fire?"

"Lord," answered Lecanius, as pale as a wall, "the whole city is one sea of flame; smoke is suffocating the inhabitants, and people faint, or cast themselves into the fire from delirium. Rome is perishing, lord."

A moment of silence followed, which was broken by the cry of Vinicius, —
"*Væ misero mihi!*"

And the young man, casting his toga aside, rushed forth in his tunic.

Nero raised his hands and exclaimed, —

"Woe to thee, sacred city of Priam!"

CHAPTER XLII

VINICIUS had barely time to command a few slaves to follow him; then, springing on his horse, he rushed forth in the deep night along the empty streets toward Laurentum. Through the influence of the dreadful news he had fallen as it were into frenzy and mental distraction. At moments he did not know clearly what was happening in his mind; he had merely the feeling that misfortune was on the horse with him, sitting behind his shoulders, and shouting in his ears, "Rome is burning!" that it was lashing his horse and him, urging them toward the fire. Laying his bare head on the beast's neck, he rushed on, in his single tunic, alone, at random, not looking ahead, and taking no note of obstacles against which he might perchance dash himself.

In silence and in that calm night, the rider and the horse, covered with gleams of the moon, seemed like dream visions. The Idumean stallion, dropping his ears and stretching his neck, shot on like an arrow past the motionless cypresses and the white villas hidden among them. The sound of hoofs on the stone flags roused dogs here and there; these followed the strange vision with their barking; afterward, excited by its suddenness, they fell to howling, and raised their jaws toward the moon. The slaves hastening after Vinicius soon dropped behind, as their horses were greatly inferior. When he had rushed like a storm through sleeping Laurentum, he turned toward Ardea, in which, as in Aricia, Bovillæ, and Ustrinum, he had kept relays of horses from the day of his coming to Antium, so as to pass in the shortest time possible the interval between Rome and him. Remembering these relays, he forced all the strength from his horse.

Beyond Ardea it seemed to him that the sky on the northeast was covered with a rosy reflection. That might be the dawn, for the hour was late, and in July daybreak came early. But Vinicius could not keep down a cry of rage and despair, for it seemed to him that that was the glare of the conflagration. He remembered the consul's words, "The whole city is one sea of flame," and for a while he felt that madness was threatening him really, for he had lost utterly all hope that he could save Lygia, or even reach the city before it was turned into one heap of ashes. His thoughts were quicker now than the rush of the stallion, they flew on ahead like a flock of birds, black, monstrous, and rousing despair. He knew not, it is true, in what part of the city the fire had begun; but he supposed that the Trans-Tiber division, as it was packed with tenements, timber-yards, storehouses, and wooden sheds serving as slave marts, might have become the first food of the flames.

In Rome fires happened frequently enough; during these fires, as frequently, deeds of violence and robbery were committed, especially in the parts occupied by a needy and half-barbarous population. What might happen, therefore, in a place like the Trans-Tiber, which was the retreat of a rabble collected from all parts of the earth? Here the thought of Ursus with his preterhuman power flashed into Vinicius's head; but what could be done by a man, even were he a Titan, against the destructive force of fire?

The fear of servile rebellion was like a nightmare, which had stifled Rome for whole years. It was said that hundreds of thousands of those people were thinking of the times of Spartacus, and merely waiting for a favorable moment to seize arms against their oppressors and Rome. Now the moment had come! Perhaps war and slaughter were raging in the city together with fire. It was possible even that the pretorians had hurled themselves on the city, and were slaughtering at command of Cæsar.

And that moment the hair rose from terror on his head. He recalled all the conversations about burning cities, which for some time had been repeated at Cæsar's court with wonderful persistence; he recalled Cæsar's complaints that he was forced to describe a burning city without having seen a real fire; his contemptuous answer to Tigellinus, who offered to burn Antium or an artificial wooden city; finally, his complaints against Rome, and the pestilential alleys of the Subura. Yes; Cæsar has commanded the burning of the city! He alone could give such a command, as Tigellinus alone could accomplish it. But if Rome is burning at command of Cæsar, who can be sure that the population will not be slaughtered at his command also? The monster is capable even of such a deed. Conflagration, a servile revolt, and slaughter! What a horrible chaos, what a letting loose of destructive elements and popular frenzy! And in all this is Lygia.

The groans of Vinicius were mingled with the snorting and groans of his horse; the beast, running on a road which rose continually toward Aricia, was using the last of its breath. Who will snatch her from the burning city; who can save her? Here Vinicius, stretching himself entirely on the horse, thrust his fingers into his own hair, ready to gnaw the beast's neck from pain.

At that moment a horseman, rushing also like a whirlwind, but in the opposite direction, toward Antium, shouted as he raced past, "Rome is perishing!" and on he went. To the ears of Vinicius came only one more expression: "Gods!" the rest was drowned by the thunder of hoofs. But that expression sobered him, — "Gods!"

Vinicius raised his head suddenly, and, stretching his arms toward the sky filled with stars, began to pray.

"Not to you do I call whose temples are burning, but to Thee! Thou Thyself hast suffered. Thou alone art merciful! Thou alone hast understood people's pain; Thou didst come to this world to teach pity to mankind; then show it now. If Thou art what Peter and Paul declare, save for me Lygia, take her in Thy arms, bear her out of the flames. Thou hast the power to do that! Give her to me, and I will give Thee my blood. But if Thou art unwilling to do this for me, do it for her. She loves Thee and trusts in Thee.

Thou dost promise life and happiness after death, but happiness after death will not pass away, and she does not wish to die yet. Let her live. Take her in Thy arms, bear her out of Rome. Thou canst do so, unless Thou art unwilling."

And he stopped, for he felt that further prayer might turn to a threat; he feared to offend Divinity at the moment when he needed favor and mercy most. He was terrified at the very thought of that, and, so as not to admit to his head a shade even of threat, he began to lash his horse again, especially since the white walls of Aricia, which lay midway to Rome, gleamed up before him in the moonlight.

After a time he rushed at full speed past the temple of Mercury, which stood in a grove before the city. Evidently people knew of the catastrophe, for there was an uncommon movement in front of the temple. While passing, Vinicius saw crowds on the steps and between the columns. These people holding torches were hastening to put themselves under protection of the deity. Moreover the road was not so empty or free as beyond Ardea. Crowds were hurrying, it is true, to the grove by side-paths, but on the main road were groups which pushed aside hurriedly before the on-rushing horseman. From the town came the sound of voices. Vinicius rode into Aricia like a whirlwind, overturning and trampling a number of persons on the way. He was surrounded by shouts of "Rome is burning!" "Rome is on fire!" "May the gods rescue Rome!"

The horse stumbled, but, reined in by a powerful hand, rose on his haunches before the inn, where Vinicius had another beast in relay. Slaves, as if waiting for the arrival of their master, stood before the inn, and at his command ran one before the other to lead out a fresh horse. Vinicius, seeing a detachment of ten mounted pretorians, going evidently with news from the city to Antium, sprang toward them.

"What part of the city is on fire?" inquired he.

"Who art thou?" asked the decurion.

"Vinicius, a tribune of the army, an Augustian. Answer on thy head!"

"The fire broke out in the shops near the Circus Maximus. When we were despatched, the centre of the city was on fire."

"And the Trans-Tiber?"

"The fire has not reached the Trans-Tiber yet, but it is seizing new parts every moment with a force which nothing can stop. People are perishing from heat and smoke; all rescue is impossible."

At this moment they brought the fresh horse. The young tribune sprang to his back and rushed on. He was riding now toward Albanum, leaving Alba Longa and its splendid lake on the right. The road from Aricia lay at the foot of the mountain, which hid the horizon completely, and Albanum lying on the other side of it. But Vinicius knew that on reaching the top he should see, not only Bovillæ and Ustrinum, where fresh horses were ready for him, but Rome as well: for beyond Albanum the low level Campania stretched on both sides of the Appian Way, along which only the arches of the aqueducts ran toward the city, and nothing obstructed the view.

"From the top I shall see the flames," said he; and he began to lash his horse anew. But before he had reached the top of the mountain he felt the wind on his face, and with it came the odor of smoke to his nostrils. At the same time the summit of the height was becoming gilded.

"The fire!" thought Vinicius.

The night had paled long since, the dawn had passed into light, and on all the nearer summits golden and rosy gleams were shining, which might come either from burning Rome or the rising daylight. Vinicius touched the summit at last, and then a terrible sight struck his eyes.

The whole lower region was covered with smoke, forming as it were one gigantic cloud lying close to the earth. In this cloud towns, aqueducts, villas, trees, disappeared; but beyond this gray ghastly plain the city was burning on the hills.

The conflagration had not the form of a pillar of fire, as happens when a single building is burning, even when of the greatest size. That was a long belt, rather, shaped like the belt of dawn. Above this belt rose a wave of smoke, in places entirely black, in places looking rose-colored, in places like blood, in places turning in on itself, in some places inflated, in others squeezed and squirming, like a serpent which is unwinding and extending. That monstrous wave seemed at times to cover even the belt of fire, which became then as narrow as a ribbon; but later this ribbon illuminated the smoke from beneath, changing its lower rolls into waves of flame. The two extended from one side of the sky to the other, hiding its lower part, as at times a stretch of forest hides the horizon. The Sabine hills were not visible in the least.

To Vinicius it seemed at the first glance of the eye that not only the city was burning, but the whole world, and that no living being could save itself from that ocean of flame and smoke.

The wind blew with growing strength from the region of the fire, bringing the smell of burnt things and of smoke, which began to hide even nearer objects. Clear daylight had come, and the sun lighted up the summits surrounding the Alban Lake. But the bright golden rays of the morning appeared as it were reddish and sickly through the haze. Vinicius, while descending toward Albanum, entered smoke which was denser, less and less transparent. The town itself was buried in it thoroughly. The alarmed citizens had moved out to the street. It was a terror to think of what might be in Rome, when it was difficult to breathe in Albanum.

Despair seized Vinicius anew, and terror began to raise the hair on his head. But he tried to fortify himself as best he might. "It is impossible," thought he, "that a city should begin to burn in all places at once. The wind is blowing from the north and bears smoke in this direction only. On the other side there is none. But in every case it will be enough for Ursus to go through the Janiculum gate with Lygia, to save himself and her. It is equally impossible that a whole population should perish, and the world-ruling city be swept from the face of the earth with its inhabitants. Even in captured places, where fire and slaughter rage together, some people survive in all cases; why, then, should Lygia perish of a certainty? On the contrary, God watches over her, He who Himself, conquered death." Thus reasoning, he began to pray again, and, yielding to fixed habit, he made great vows to Christ, with promises of gifts and sacrifices. After he had hurried through Albanum, nearly all of whose inhabitants were on roofs and on trees to look at Rome, he grew somewhat calm, and regained his cool blood. He remembered, too, that Lygia was protected not only by Ursus and Linus, but by the Apostle Peter. At the mere remembrance of this, fresh solace entered his heart. For him Peter was an incomprehensible, an almost superhuman being. From the time when he heard him at Ostrianum, a wonderful impression clung to him, touching which he had written to Lygia at the beginning of his stay in Antium, — that every word of the old man was true, or would show its truth hereafter. The nearer acquaintance which during his illness he had formed with the Apostle heightened the impression, which was turned afterward into fixed faith. Since Peter had blessed his love and promised him Lygia, Lygia could not perish in the flames. The city might burn, but no spark from the fire would fall on her garments. Under the influence of a sleepless night, mad riding, and impressions, a wonderful exaltation possessed the young tribune; in this exaltation all things seemed possible: Peter speaks to the flame, opens it with a word, and they pass uninjured through an alley of fire. Moreover, Peter saw future events; hence, beyond doubt, he foresaw the fire, and in that case how could he fail to warn and lead forth the Christians from the city, and among others Lygia, whom he loved, as he might his own child? And a hope, which was strengthening every moment, entered the heart of Vinicius. If they were fleeing from the city, he might find them in Bovillæ, or meet them on the road. The beloved face might appear any moment from out the smoke, which was stretching more widely over all the Campania.

This seemed to him more likely, since he met increasing numbers of people, who had deserted the city and were going to the Alban Hills; they had escaped the fire, and wished to go beyond the line of smoke. Before he had reached Ustrinum he had to slacken his pace because of the throng. Besides pedestrians with bundles on their backs, he met horses with packs, mules and vehicles laden with effects, and finally litters in which slaves were bearing the wealthier citizens. Ustrinum was so thronged with fugitives from Rome that it was difficult to push through the crowd. On the market square, under temple porticos, and on the streets were swarms of fugitives. Here and there people were erecting tents under which whole families were to find shelter. Others settled down under the naked sky, shouting, calling on the gods, or cursing the fates. In the general terror it was difficult to inquire about anything. People to whom Vinicius applied either did not answer, or with eyes half bewildered from terror answered that the city and the world were perishing. New crowds of men, women, and children arrived from the direction of Rome every moment; these increased the disorder and outcry. Some, gone astray in the throng, sought desperately those whom they had lost; others fought for a camping-place. Half-wild shepherds from the Campania crowded to the town to hear news, or find profit in plunder made easy by the uproar. Here and there crowds of slaves of every nationality and gladiators fell to robbing houses and villas in the town, and to fighting with the soldiers who appeared in defence of the citizens.

Junius, a senator, whom Vinicius saw at the inn surrounded by a detachment of Batavian slaves, was the first to give more detailed news of the conflagration. The fire had begun at the Circus Maximus, in the part which touches the Palatine and the Cæiian Hill, but extended with incomprehensible rapidity and seized the whole centre of the city. Never since the time of Brennus had such an awful catastrophe come upon Rome. "The entire Circus has burnt, as well as the shops and houses surrounding it," said Junius; "the Aventine and Cælian Hills are on fire. The flames surrounding the Palatine have reached the Carinæ."

Here Junius, who possessed on the Carinæ a magnificent "insula," filled with works of art which he loved, seized a handful of foul dust, and, scattering it on his head, began to groan despairingly.

But Vinicius shook him by the shoulder: "My house too is on the Carinæ," said he; "but when everything is perishing, let it perish also."

Then recollecting that at his advice Lygia might have gone to the house of Aulus, he inquired, —

"But the Vicus Patricius?"

"On fire!" replied Junius.

"The Trans-Tiber?"

Junius looked at him with amazement.

"Never mind the Trans-Tiber," said he, pressing his aching temples with his palms.

"The Trans-Tiber is more important to me than all other parts of Rome," cried Vinicius, with vehemence.

"The way is through the Via Portuensis, near the Aventine; but the heat will stifle thee. The Trans-Tiber? I know not. The fire had not reached it; but whether it is not there at this moment the gods alone know." Here Junius hesitated a moment, then said in a low voice: "I know that thou wilt not betray me, so I will tell thee that this is no common fire. People were not permitted to save the Circus. When houses began to burn in every direction, I myself heard thousands of voices exclaiming, 'Death to those who save!' Certain people ran through the city and hurled burning torches into buildings. On the other hand people are revolting, and crying that the city is burning at command. I can say nothing more. Woe to the city, woe to us all, and to me! The tongue of man cannot tell what is happening there. People are perishing in flames or slaying one another in the throng. This is the end of Rome!"

And again he fell to repeating, "Woe! Woe to the city and to us!" Vinicius sprang to his horse, and hurried forward along the Appian Way. But now it was rather a struggling through the midst of a river of people and vehicles, which was flowing from the city. The city, embraced by a monstrous conflagration, lay before Vinicius as a thing on the palm of his hand. From the sea of fire and smoke came a terrible heat, and the uproar of people could not drown the roar and the hissing of flames.

CHAPTER XLIII

As Vinicius approached the walls, he found it easier to reach Rome than penetrate to the middle of the city. It was difficult to push along the Appian Way, because of the throng of people. Houses, fields, cemeteries, gardens, and temples, lying on both sides of it, were turned into camping places. In the temple of Mars, which stood near the Porta Appia, the crowd had thrown down the doors, so as to find a refuge within during night-hours. In the cemeteries the larger monuments were seized, and battles fought in defence of them, which were carried to bloodshed. Ustrinum with its disorder gave barely a slight foretaste of that which was happening beneath the walls of the capital. All regard for the dignity of law, for family ties, for difference of position, had ceased. Gladiators drunk with wine seized in the Emporium gathered in crowds, ran with wild shouts through the neighboring squares, scattering, trampling, and robbing the people. A multitude of barbarians, exposed for sale in the city, escaped from the booths. For them the burning and ruin of Rome was at once the end of slavery and the hour of revenge; so that when the permanent inhabitants, who had lost all they owned in the fire, stretched their hands to the gods in despair, calling for rescue, these slaves with howls of delight scattered the crowds, dragged clothing from people's backs, and bore away the younger women. They were joined by slaves serving in the city from of old, wretches who had nothing on their bodies save woollen girdles around their hips, dreadful figures from the alleys, who were hardly ever seen on the streets in the daytime, and whose existence in Rome it was difficult to suspect. Men of this wild and unrestrained crowd, Asiatics, Africans, Greeks, Thracians, Germans, Britons, howling in every language of the earth, raged, thinking that the hour had come in which they were free to reward themselves for years of misery and suffering. In the midst of that surging throng of humanity, in the glitter of day and of fire, shone the helmets of pretorians, under whose protection the more peaceable population had taken refuge, and who in hand-to-hand battle had to meet the raging multitude in many places. Vinicius had seen captured cities, but never had his eyes beheld a spectacle in which despair, tears, pain, groans, wild delight, madness, rage, and license were mingled together in such immeasurable chaos. Above this heaving, mad human multitude roared the fire, surging up to the hill-tops of the greatest city on earth, sending into the whirling throng its fiery breath, and covering it with smoke, through which it was impossible to see the blue sky. The young tribune with supreme effort, and exposing his life every moment, forced his way at last to the Appian Gate; but there he saw that he could not reach the city through the division of the Porta Capena, not merely because of the throng, but also because of the terrible heat from which the whole atmosphere was quivering inside the gate. Besides, the bridge at the Porta Trigenia, opposite the temple of the Bona Dea, did not exist yet, hence whoso wished to go beyond the Tiber had to push through to the Pons Sublicius, that is, to pass around the Aventine through a part of the city covered now with one sea of flame. That was an impossibility. Vinicius understood that he must return toward Ustrinum, turn from the Appian Way, cross the river below the city, and go to the Via Portuensis, which led straight to the Trans-Tiber. That was not easy because of the increasing disorder on the Appian Way. He must open a passage for himself there, even with the sword. Vinicius had no weapons; he had left Antium just as the news of the fire had reached him in Cæsar's villa. At the fountain of Mercury, however, he saw a centurion who was known to him. This man, at the head of a few tens of soldiers, was defending the precinct of the temple; he commanded him to follow. Recognizing a tribune and an Augustian, the centurion did not dare to disobey the order.

Vinicius took command of the detachment himself, and, forgetting for that moment the teaching of Paul touching love for one's neighbor, he pressed and cut the throng in front with a haste that was fatal to many who could not push aside in season. He and his men were followed by curses and a shower of stones; but to these he gave no heed, caring only to reach freer spaces at the earliest. Still he advanced with the greatest effort. People who had encamped would not move, and heaped loud curses on Cæsar and the pretorians. The throng assumed in places a threatening aspect. Vinicius heard voices accusing Nero of burning the city. He and Poppæa were threatened with death. Shouts of "Sanio," "Histrio" (buffoon, actor), "Matricide!" were heard round about. Some shouted to drag him to the Tiber; others that Rome had shown patience enough. It was clear that were a leader found, these threats could be changed into open rebellion which might break out any moment. Meanwhile the rage and despair of the crowd turned against the pretorians, who for another reason could not make their way out of the crowd: the road was blocked by piles of goods, borne from the fire previously, boxes, barrels of provisions, furniture the most costly, vessels, infants' cradles, beds, carts, hand-packs. Here and there they fought hand to hand; but the pretorians conquered the weaponless multitude easily. After they had ridden with difficulty across the Viæ Latina, Numitia, Ardea, Lavinia, and Ostia, and passed around villas, gardens, cemeteries, and temples, Vinicius reached at last a village called Vicus Alexandri, beyond which he crossed the Tiber. There was more open space at this spot, and less smoke. From fugitives, of whom there was no lack even there, he learned that only certain alleys of the Trans-Tiber were burning, but that surely nothing could resist the fury of the conflagration, since people were spreading the fire purposely, and permitted no one to quench it, declaring that they acted at command. The young tribune had not the least doubt then that Cæsar had given command to burn Rome; and the vengeance which people demanded seemed to him just and proper. What more could Mithridates or any of Rome's most inveterate enemies have done? The measure had been exceeded; his madness had grown to be too enormous, and the existence of people too difficult because of him. Vinicius believed that Nero's hour had struck, that those ruins into which the city was falling should and must overwhelm the monstrous buffoon together with all those crimes of his. Should a man be found of courage sufficient to stand at the head of the despairing people, that might happen in a few hours. Here vengeful and daring thoughts began to fly through his head. But if he should do that? The house of Vinicius, which till recent times counted a whole series of consuls, was known throughout Rome. The crowds needed only a name. Once, when four hundred slaves of the prefect Pedanius Secundus were sentenced, Rome reached the verge of rebellion and civil war. What would happen to-day in view of a dreadful calamity surpassing almost everything which Rome had undergone in the course of eight centuries? Whoso calls the Quirites to arms, thought Vinicius, will overthrow Nero undoubtedly, and clothe himself in purple. And why should he not do this? He was firmer, more active, younger than other Augustians. True, Nero commanded thirty legions stationed on the borders of the Empire; but would not those legions and their leaders rise up at news of the burning of Rome and its temples? And in that case Vinicius might become Cæsar. It was even whispered among the Augustians that a soothsayer had predicted the purple to Otho. In what way was he inferior to Otho? Perhaps Christ Himself would assist him with His divine power; maybe that inspiration was His? "Oh, would that it were!" exclaimed Vinicius, in spirit. He would take vengeance on Nero for the danger of Lygia and his own fear; he would begin the reign of truth and justice, he would extend Christ's religion from the Euphrates to the misty shores of Britain; he would array Lygia in the purple, and make her mistress of the world.

But these thoughts which had burst forth in his head like a bunch of sparks from a blazing house, died away like sparks. First of all was the need to save Lygia. He looked now on the catastrophe from near by; hence fear seized him again, and before that sea of flame and smoke, before the touch of dreadful reality, that confidence with which he believed that Peter would rescue Lygia died in his heart altogether. Despair seized him a second time when he had come out on the Via Portuensis, which led directly to the Trans-Tiber. He did not recover till he came to the gate, where people repeated what fugitives had said before, that the greater part of that division of the city was not seized by the flames yet, but that fire had crossed the river in a number of places.

Still the Trans-Tiber was full of smoke, and crowds of fugitives made it more difficult to reach the interior of the place, since people, having more time there, had saved greater quantities of goods. The main street itself was in many parts filled completely, and around the Naumachia Augusta great heaps were piled up. Narrow alleys, in which smoke had collected more densely, were simply impassable. The inhabitants were fleeing in thousands. On the way Vinicius saw wonderful sights. More than once two rivers of people, flowing in opposite directions, met in a narrow passage, stopped each other, men fought hand to hand, struck and trampled one another. Families lost one another in the uproar; mothers called on their children despairingly. The young tribune's hair stood on end at thought of what must happen nearer the fire. Amid shouts and howls it was difficult to inquire about anything or understand what was said. At times new columns of smoke from beyond the river rolled toward them, smoke black and so heavy that it moved near the ground, hiding houses, people, and every object, just as night does. But the wind caused by the conflagration blew it away again, and then Vinicius pushed forward farther toward the alley in which stood the house of Linus. The fervor of a July day, increased by the heat of the burning parts of the city, became unendurable. Smoke pained the eyes; breath failed in men's breasts. Even the inhabitants who, hoping that the fire would not cross the river, had remained in their houses so far, began to leave them; and the throng increased hourly. The pretorians accompanying Vinicius remained in the rear. In the crush some one wounded his horse with a hammer; the beast threw up its bloody head, reared, and refused obedience. The crowd recognized in Vinicius an Augustian by his rich tunic, and at once cries were raised round about: "Death to Nero and his incendiaries!" This was a moment of terrible danger; hundreds of hands were stretched toward Vinicius; but his frightened horse bore him away, trampling people as he went, and the next moment a new wave of black smoke rolled in and filled the street with darkness. Vinicius, seeing that he could not ride past, sprang to the earth and rushed forward on foot, slipping along walls, and at times waiting till the fleeing multitude passed him. He said to himself in spirit that these were vain efforts. Lygia might not be in the city; she might have saved herself by flight. It was easier to find a pin on the seashore than her in that crowd and chaos. Still he wished to reach the house of Linus, even at the cost of his own life. At times he stopped and rubbed his eyes. Tearing off the edge of his tunic, he covered his nose and mouth with it and ran on. As he approached the river, the heat increased terribly. Vinicius, knowing that the fire had begun at the Circus Maximus, thought at first that that heat came from its cinders and from the Forum Boarium and the Velabrum, which, situated near by, must be also in flames. But the heat was growing unendurable. One old man on crutches and fleeing, the last whom Vinicius noticed, cried: "Go not near the bridge of Cestius! The whole island is on fire!" It was, indeed, impossible to be deceived any longer. At the turn toward the Vicus Judæorum, on which stood the house of Linus, the young tribune saw flames amid clouds of smoke. Not only the island was burning, but the Trans-Tiber, or at least the other end of the street on which Lygia dwelt.

Vinicius remembered that the house of Linus was surrounded by a garden; between the garden and the Tiber was an unoccupied field of no great size. This thought consoled him. The fire might stop at the vacant place. In that hope he ran forward, though every breeze brought not only smoke, but sparks in thousands, which might raise a fire at the other end of the alley and cut off his return.

At last he saw through the smoky curtain the cypresses in Linus's garden.

The houses beyond the unoccupied field were burning already like piles of fuel, but Linus's little "insula" stood untouched yet. Vinicius glanced heavenward with thankfulness, and sprang toward the house though the very air began to burn him. The door was closed, but he pushed it open and rushed in.

There was not a living soul in the garden, and the house seemed quite empty. "Perhaps they have fainted from smoke and heat," thought Vinicius. He began to call, —

"Lygia! Lygia!"

Silence answered him. Nothing could be heard in the stillness there save the roar of the distant fire.

"Lygia!"

Suddenly his ear was struck by that gloomy sound which he had heard before in that garden. Evidently the vivarium near the temple of Esculapius, on the neighboring island, had caught fire. In this vivarium every kind of wild beast, and among others lions, began to roar from affright. A shiver ran through Vinicius from foot to head. Now, a second time, at a moment when his whole being was concentrated in Lygia, these terrible voices answered, as a herald of misfortune, as a marvellous prophecy of an ominous future.

But this was a brief impression, for the thunder of the flames, more terrible yet than the roaring of wild beasts, commanded him to think of something else. Lygia did not answer his calls; but she might be in a faint or stifled in that threatened building. Vinicius sprang to the interior. The little atrium was empty, and dark with smoke. Feeling for the door which led to the sleeping-rooms, he saw the gleaming flame of a small lamp, and approaching it saw the lararium in which was a cross instead of lares. Under the cross a taper was burning. Through the head of the young catechumen, the thought passed with lightning speed that that cross sent him the taper with which he could find Lygia; hence he took the taper and searched for the sleeping-rooms. He found one, pushed aside the curtains, and, holding the taper, looked around.

There was no one there, either. Vinicius was sure that he had found Lygia's sleeping-room, for her clothing was on nails in the wall, and on the bed lay a capitium, or close garment worn by women next the body. Vinicius seized that, pressed it to his lips, and taking it on his arm went farther. The house was small, so that he examined every room, and even the cellar quickly. Nowhere could he find a living soul. It was evident that Lygia, Linus, and Ursus, with other inhabitants of that part, must have sought safety in flight.

"I must seek them among the crowd beyond the gates of the city," thought Vinicius.

He was not astonished greatly at not meeting them on the Via Portuensis, for they might have left the Trans-Tiber through the opposite side along the Vatican Hill. In every case they were safe from fire at least. A stone fell from his breast. He saw, it is true, the terrible danger with which the flight was connected, but he was comforted at thought of the preterhuman strength of Ursus. "I must flee now," said he, "and reach the gardens of Agrippina through the gardens of Domitius, where I shall find them. The smoke is not so terrible there, since the wind blows from the Sabine Hill."

The hour had come now in which he must think of his own safety, for the river of fire was flowing nearer and nearer from the direction of the island, and rolls of smoke covered the alley almost completely. The taper, which had lighted him in the house, was quenched from the current of air. Vinicius rushed to the street, and ran at full speed toward the Via Portuensis, whence he had come; the fire seemed to pursue him with burning breath, now surrounding him with fresh clouds of smoke, now covering him with sparks, which fell on his hair, neck, and clothing. The tunic began to smoulder on him in places; he cared not, but ran forward lest he might be stifled from smoke. He had the taste of soot and burning in his mouth; his throat and lungs were as if on fire. The blood rushed to his head, and at moments all things, even the smoke itself, seemed red to him. Then he thought: "This is living fire! Better cast myself on the ground and perish." The running tortured him more and more. His head, neck, and shoulders were streaming with sweat, which scalded like boiling water. Had it not been for Lygia's name, repeated by him in thought, had it not been for her capitium, which he wound across his mouth, he would have fallen. Some moments later he failed to recognize the street along which he ran. Consciousness was leaving him gradually; he remembered only that he must flee, for in the open field beyond waited Lygia, whom Peter had promised him. And all at once he was seized by a certain wonderful conviction, half feverish, like a vision before death, that he must see her, marry her, and then die.

But he ran on as if drunk, staggering from one side of the street to the other. Meanwhile something changed in that monstrous conflagration which had embraced the giant city. Everything which till then had only glimmered, burst forth visibly into one sea of flame; the wind had ceased to bring smoke. That smoke which had collected in the streets was borne away by a mad whirl of heated air. That whirl drove with it millions of sparks, so that Vinicius was running in a fiery cloud as it were. But he was able to see before him all the better, and in a moment, almost when he was ready to fall, he saw the end of the street. That sight gave him fresh strength. Passing the corner, he found himself in a street which led to the Via Portuensis and the Codetan Field. The sparks ceased to drive him. He understood that if he could run to the Via Portuensis he was safe, even were he to faint on it.

At the end of the street he saw again a cloud, as it seemed, which stopped the exit. "If that is smoke," thought he, "I cannot pass." He ran with the remnant of his strength. On the way he threw off his tunic, which, on fire from the sparks, was burning him like the shirt of Nessus, having only Lygia's capitium around his head and before his mouth. When he had run farther, he saw that what he had taken for smoke was dust, from which rose a multitude of cries and voices.

"The rabble are plundering houses," thought Vinicius. But he ran toward the voices. In every case people were there; they might assist him. In this hope he shouted for aid with all his might before he reached them. But this was his last effort. It grew redder still in his eyes, breath failed his lungs, strength failed his bones; he fell.

They heard him, however, or rather saw him. Two men ran with gourds full of water. Vinicius, who had fallen from exhaustion but had not lost consciousness, seized a gourd with both hands, and emptied one-half of it.

"Thanks," said he; "place me on my feet, I can walk on alone."

The other laborer poured water on his head; the two not only placed him on his feet, but raised him from the ground, and carried him to the others, who surrounded him and asked if he had suffered seriously. This tenderness astonished Vinicius.

"People, who are ye?" asked he.

"We are breaking down houses, so that the fire may not reach the Via Portuensis," answered one of the laborers.

"Ye came to my aid when I had fallen. Thanks to you."

"We are not permitted to refuse aid," answered a number of voices.

Vinicius, who from early morning had seen brutal crowds, slaying and robbing, looked with more attention on the faces around him, and said, —

"May Christ reward you."

"Praise to His name!" exclaimed a whole chorus of voices.

"Linus?" inquired Vinicius.

But he could not finish the question or hear the answer, for he fainted from emotion and over-exertion. He recovered only in the Codetan Field in a garden, surrounded by a number of men and women. The first words which he uttered were, —

"Where is Linus?"

For a while there was no answer; then some voice, known to Vinicius, said all at once, —

"He went out by the Nomentan Gate to Ostrianum two days ago. Peace be with thee, O king of Persia!"

Vinicius rose to a sitting posture, and saw Chilo before him.

"Thy house is burned surely, O lord," said the Greek, "for the Carinæ is in flames; but thou wilt be always as rich as Midas. Oh, what a misfortune! The Christians, O son of Serapis, have predicted this long time that fire would destroy the city. But Linus, with the daughter of Jove, is in Ostrianum. Oh, what a misfortune for the city!"

Vinicius became weak again.

"Hast thou seen them?" he inquired.

"I saw them, O lord. May Christ and all the gods be thanked that I am able to pay for thy benefactions with good news. But, O Cyrus, I shall pay thee still more, I swear by this burning Rome."

It was evening, but in the garden one could see as in daylight, for the conflagration had increased. It seemed that not single parts of the city were burning, but the whole city through the length and the breadth of it. The sky was red as far as the eye could see it, and that night in the world was a red night.

CHAPTER XLIV

Light from the burning city filled the sky as far as human eye could reach. The moon rose large and full from behind the mountains, and inflamed at once by the glare took on the color of heated brass. It seemed to look with amazement on the world-ruling city which was perishing. In the rose-colored abysses of heaven rose-colored stars were glittering; but in distinction from usual nights the earth was brighter than the heavens. Rome, like a giant pile, illuminated the whole Campania. In the bloody light were seen distant mountains, towns, villas, temples, mountains, and the aqueducts stretching toward the city from all the adjacent hills; on the aqueducts were swarms of people, who had gathered there for safety or to gaze at the burning.

Meanwhile the dreadful element was embracing new divisions of the city. It was impossible to doubt that criminal hands were spreading the fire, since new conflagrations were breaking out all the time in places remote from the principal fire. From the heights on which Rome was founded the flames flowed like waves of the sea into the valleys densely occupied by houses, — houses of five and six stories, full of shops, booths, movable wooden amphitheatres, built to accommodate various spectacles; and finally storehouses of wood, olives, grain, nuts, pine cones, the kernels of which nourished the more needy population, and clothing, which through Cæsar's favor was distributed from time to time among the rabble huddled into narrow alleys. In those places the fire, finding abundance of inflammable materials, became almost a series of explosions, and took possession of whole streets with unheard-of rapidity. People encamping outside the city, or standing on the aqueducts knew from the color of the flame what was burning. The furious power of the wind carried forth from the fiery gulf thousands and millions of burning shells of walnuts and almonds, which, shooting suddenly into the sky, like countless flocks of bright butterflies, burst with a crackling, or, driven by the wind, fell in other parts of the city, on aqueducts, and fields beyond Rome. All thought of rescue seemed out of place; confusion increased every moment, for on one side the population of the city was fleeing through every gate to places outside; on the other the fire had lured in thousands of people from the neighborhood, such as dwellers in small towns, peasants, and half-wild shepherds of the Campania, brought in by hope of plunder. The shout, "Rome is perishing!" did not leave the lips of the crowd; the ruin of the city seemed at that time to end every rule, and loosen all bonds which hitherto had joined people in a single integrity. The mob, in which slaves were more numerous, cared nothing for the lordship of Rome. Destruction of the city could only free them; hence here and there they assumed a threatening attitude. Violence and robbery were extending. It seemed that only the spectacle of the perishing city arrested attention, and restrained for the moment an outburst of slaughter, which would begin as soon as the city was turned into ruins. Hundreds of thousands of slaves, forgetting that Rome, besides temples and walls, possessed some tens of legions in all parts of the world, appeared merely waiting for a watchword and a leader. People began to mention the name of Spartacus, but Spartacus was not alive. Meanwhile citizens assembled, and armed themselves each with what he could. The most monstrous reports were current at all the gates. Some declared that Vulcan, commanded by Jupiter, was destroying the city with fire from beneath the earth; others that Vesta was taking vengeance for Rubria. People with these convictions did not care to save anything, but, besieging the temples, implored mercy of the gods. It was repeated most generally, however, that Cæsar had given command to burn Rome, so as to free himself from odors which rose from the Subura, and build a new city under the name of Neronia. Rage seized the populace at thought of this; and if, as Vinicius believed, a leader had taken advantage of that outburst of hatred, Nero's hour would have struck whole years before it did.

It was said also that Cæsar had gone mad, that he would command pretorians and gladiators to fall upon the people and make a general slaughter. Others swore by the gods that wild beasts had been let out of all the vivaria at Bronzebeard's command. Men had seen on the streets lions with burning manes, and mad elephants and bisons, trampling down people in crowds. There was even some truth in this; for in certain places elephants, at sight of the approaching fire, had burst the vivaria, and, gaining their freedom, rushed away from the fire in wild fright, destroying everything before them like a tempest. Public report estimated at tens of thousands the number of persons who had perished in the conflagration. In truth a great number had perished. There were people who, losing all their property, or those dearest their hearts, threw themselves willingly into the flames, from despair. Others were suffocated by smoke. In the middle of the city, between the Capitol, on one side, and the Quirinal, the Viminal, and the Esquiline on the other, as also between the Palatine and the Cælian Hill, where the streets were most densely occupied, the fire began in so many places at once that whole crowds of people, while fleeing in one direction, struck unexpectedly on a new wall of fire in front of them, and died a dreadful death in a deluge of flame.

In terror, in distraction, and bewilderment, people knew not where to flee. The streets were obstructed with goods, and in many narrow places were simply closed. Those who took refuge in those markets and squares of the city, where the Flavian Amphitheatre stood afterward, near the temple of the Earth, near the Portico of Silvia, and higher up, at the temples of Juno and Lucinia, between the Clivus Virbius and the old Esquiline Gate, perished from heat, surrounded by a sea of fire. In places not reached by the flames were found afterward hundreds of bodies burned to a crisp, though here and there unfortunates tore up flat stones and half buried themselves in defence against the heat. Hardly a family inhabiting the centre of the city survived in full; hence along the walls, at the gates, on all roads were heard howls of despairing women, calling on the dear names of those who had perished in the throng or the fire.

And so, while some were imploring the gods, others blasphemed them because of this awful catastrophe. Old men were seen coming from the temple of Jupiter Liberator, stretching forth their hands, and crying, "If thou be a liberator, save thy altars and the city!" But despair turned mainly against the old Roman gods, who, in the minds of the populace, were bound to watch over the city more carefully than others. They had proved themselves powerless; hence were insulted. On the other hand it happened on the Via Asinaria that when a company of Egyptian priests appeared conducting a statue of Isis, which they had saved from the temple near the Porta Cælimontana, a crowd of people rushed among the priests, attached themselves to the chariot, which they drew to the Appian Gate, and seizing the statue placed it in the temple of Mars, overwhelming the priests of that deity who dared to resist them. In other places people invoked Serapis, Baal, or Jehovah, whose adherents, swarming out of the alleys in the neighborhood of the Subura and the Trans-Tiber, filled with shouts and uproar the fields near the walls. In their cries were heard tones as if of triumph; when, therefore, some of the citizens joined the chorus and glorified "the Lord of the World," others, indignant at this glad shouting, strove to repress it by violence. Here and there hymns were heard, sung by men in the bloom of life, by old men, by women and children, — hymns wonderful and solemn, whose meaning they understood not, but in which were repeated from moment to moment the words, "Behold the Judge cometh in the day of wrath and disaster." Thus this deluge of restless and sleepless people encircled the burning city, like a tempest-driven sea.

But neither despair nor blasphemy nor hymn helped in any way. The destruction seemed as irresistible, perfect, and pitiless as Predestination itself. Around Pompey's Amphitheatre stores of hemp caught fire, and ropes used in circuses, arenas, and every kind of machine at the games, and with them the adjoining buildings containing barrels of pitch with which ropes were smeared. In a few hours all that part of the city, beyond which lay the Campus Martius, was so lighted by bright yellow flames that for a time it seemed to the spectators, only half conscious from terror, that in the general ruin the order of night and day had been lost, and that they were looking at sunshine. But later a monstrous bloody gleam extinguished all other colors of flame. From the sea of fire shot up to the heated sky gigantic fountains, and pillars of flame spreading at their summits into fiery branches and feathers; then the wind bore them away, turned them into golden threads, into hair, into sparks, and swept them on over the Campania toward the Alban Hills. The night became brighter; the air itself seemed penetrated, not only with light, but with flame. The Tiber flowed on as living fire. The hapless city was turned into one pandemonium. The conflagration seized more and more space, took hills by storm, flooded level places, drowned valleys, raged, roared, and thundered.

CHAPTER XLV

MACRINUS, a weaver, to whose house Vinicius was carried, washed him, and gave him clothing and food. When the young tribune had recovered his strength altogether, he declared that he would search further for Linus that very night. Macrinus, who was a Christian, confirmed Chilo's report, that Linus, with Clement the chief priest, had gone to Ostrianum, where Peter was to baptize a whole company of confessors of the new faith. In that division of the city it was known to Christians that Linus had confided the care of his house two days before to a certain Gaius. For Vinicius this was a proof that neither Lygia nor Ursus had remained in the house, and that they also must have gone to Ostrianum.

This thought gave him great comfort. Linus was an old man, for whom it would be difficult to walk daily to the distant Nomentan Gate, and back to the Trans-Tiber; hence it was likely that he lodged those few days with some co-religionist beyond the walls, and with him also Lygia and Ursus. Thus they escaped the fire, which in general had not reached the other slope of the Esquiline. Vinicius saw in all this a dispensation of Christ, whose care he felt above him, and his heart was filled more than ever with love; he swore in his soul to pay with his whole life for those clear marks of favor.

But all the more did he hurry to Ostrianum. He would find Lygia, find Linus and Peter; he would take them to a distance, to some of his lands, even to Sicily. Let Rome burn; in a few days it would be a mere heap of ashes. Why remain in the face of disaster and a mad rabble? In his lands troops of obedient slaves would protect them, they would be surrounded by the calm of the country, and live in peace under Christ's wings blessed by Peter. Oh, if he could find them!

That was no easy thing. Vinicius remembered the difficulty with which he had passed from the Appian Way to the Trans-Tiber, and how he must circle around to reach the Via Portuensis. He resolved, therefore, to go around the city this time in the opposite direction. Going by the Via Triumphatoris, it was possible to reach the Æmilian bridge by going along the river, thence passing the Pincian Hill, all the Campus Martius, outside the gardens of Pompey, Lucullus, and Sallust, to make a push forward to the Via Nomentana. That was the shortest way; but Macrinus and Chilo advised him not to take it. The fire had not touched that part of the city, it is true; but all the market squares and streets might be packed densely with people and their goods. Chilo advised him to go through the Ager Vaticanus to the Porta Flaminia, cross the river at that point, and push on outside the walls beyond the gardens of Acilius to the Porta Salaria. Vinicius, after a moment's hesitation, took this advice.

Macrinus had to remain in care of his house; but he provided two mules, which would serve Lygia also in a further journey. He wished to give a slave, too; but Vinicius refused, judging that the first detachment of pretorians he met on the road would pass under his orders.

Soon he and Chilo moved on through the Pagus Janiculensis to the Triumphal Way. There were vehicles there, too, in open places; but they pushed between them with less difficulty, as the inhabitants had fled for the greater part by the Via Portuensis toward the sea. Beyond the Septimian Gate they rode between the river and the splendid gardens of Domitius; the mighty cypresses were red from the conflagration, as if from evening sunshine. The road became freer; at times they had to struggle merely with the current of incoming rustics. Vinicius urged his mule forward as much as possible; but Chilo, riding closely in the rear, talked to himself almost the whole way.

"Well, we have left the fire behind, and now it is heating our shoulders. Never yet has there been so much light on this road in the night-time. O Zeus! if thou wilt not send torrents of rain on that fire, thou hast no love for Rome, surely. The power of man will not quench those flames. Such a city, — a city which Greece and the whole world was serving! And now the first Greek who comes along may roast beans in its ashes. Who could have looked for this? And now there will be no longer a Rome, nor Roman rulers. Whoso wants to walk on the ashes, when they grow cold, and whistle over them, may whistle without danger. O gods! to whistle over such a world-ruling city! What Greek, or even barbarian, could have hoped for this? And still one may whistle; for a heap of ashes, whether left after a shepherd's fire or a burnt city, is mere ashes, which the wind will blow away sooner or later."

Thus talking, he turned from moment to moment toward the conflagration, and looked at the waves of flame with a face filled at once with delight and malice.

"It will perish! It will perish!" continued he, "and will never be on earth again. Whither will the world send its wheat now, its olives, and its money? Who will squeeze gold and tears from it? Marble does not burn, but it crumbles in fire. The Capitol will turn into dust, and the Palatine into dust. O Zeus! Rome was like a shepherd, and other nations like sheep. When the shepherd was hungry, he slaughtered a sheep, ate the flesh, and to thee, O father of the gods, he made an offering of the skin. Who, O Cloud-compeller, will do the slaughtering now, and into whose hand wilt thou put the shepherd's whip? For Rome is burning, O father, as truly as if thou hadst fired it with thy thunderbolt."

"Hurry!" urged Vinicius; "what art thou doing there?"

"I am weeping over Rome, lord, — Jove's city!"

For a time they rode on in silence, listening to the roar of the burning, and the sound of birds' wings. Doves, a multitude of which had their nests about villas and in small towns of the Campania, and also every kind of field-bird from near the sea and the surrounding mountains, mistaking evidently the gleam of the conflagration for sunlight, were flying, whole flocks of them, blindly into the fire. Vinicius broke the silence first, —

"Where wert thou when the fire burst out?"

"I was going to my friend Euricius, lord, who kept a shop near the Circus Maximus, and I was just meditating on the teaching of Christ, when men began to shout: 'Fire!' People gathered around the Circus for safety, and through curiosity; but when the flames seized the whole Circus, and began to appear in other places also, each had to think of his own safety."

"Didst thou see people throwing torches into houses?"

"What have I not seen, O grandson of Æneas! I saw people making a way for themselves through the crowd with swords; I have seen battles, the entrails of people trampled on the pavement. Ah, if thou hadst seen that, thou wouldst have thought that barbarians had captured the city, and were putting it to the sword. People round about cried that the end of the world had come. Some lost their heads altogether, and, forgetting to flee, waited stupidly till the flames seized them. Some fell into bewilderment, others howled in despair; I saw some also who howled from delight. O lord, there are many bad people in the world who know not how to value the benefactions of your mild rule, and those just laws in virtue of which ye take from all what they have and give it to yourselves. People will not be reconciled to the will of God!"

Vinicius was too much occupied with his own thoughts to note the irony quivering in Chilo's words. A shudder of terror seized him at the simple thought that Lygia might be in the midst of that chaos on those terrible streets where people's entrails were trampled on. Hence, though he had asked at least ten times of Chilo touching all which the old man could know, he turned to him once again, —

"But hast thou seen them in Ostrianum with thy own eyes?"

"I saw them, O son of Venus; I saw the maiden, the good Lygian, holy Linus, and the Apostle Peter."

"Before the fire?"

"Before the fire, O Mithra!"

But a doubt rose in the soul of Vinicius whether Chilo was not lying; hence, reining his mule in, he looked threateningly at the old Greek and inquired, —

"What wert thou doing there?"

Chilo was confused. True, it seemed to him, as to many, that with the destruction of Rome would come the end also of Roman dominion. But he was face to face with Vinicius; he remembered that the young soldier had prohibited him, under a terrible threat, from watching the Christians, and especially Linus and Lygia.

"Lord," said he, "why dost thou not believe that I love them? I do. I was in Ostrianum, for I am half a Christian. Pyrrho has taught me to esteem virtue more than philosophy; hence I cleave more and more to virtuous people. And, besides, I am poor; and when thou, O Jove, wert at Antium, I suffered hunger frequently over my books; therefore I sat at the wall of Ostrianum, for the Christians, though poor, distribute more alms than all other inhabitants of Rome taken together."

This reason seemed sufficient to Vinicius, and he inquired less severely, —

"And dost thou not know where Linus is dwelling at this moment?"

"Thou didst punish me sharply on a time for curiosity," replied the Greek. Vinicius ceased talking and rode on.

"O lord," said Chilo, after a while, "thou wouldst not have found the maiden but for me, and if we find her now, thou wilt not forget the needy sage?"

"Thou wilt receive a house with a vineyard at Ameriola."

"Thanks to thee, O Hercules! With a vineyard? Thanks to thee! Oh, yes, with a vineyard!"

They were passing the Vatican Hill now, which was ruddy from the fire; but beyond the Naumachia they turned to the right, so that when they had passed the Vatican Field they would reach the river, and, crossing it, go to the Flaminian Gate. Suddenly Chilo reined in his mule, and said, —

"A good thought has come to my head, lord!"

"Speak!" answered Vinicius.

"Between the Janiculum and the Vatican Hill, beyond the gardens of Agrippina, are excavations from which stones and sand were taken to build the Circus of Nero. Hear me, lord. Recently the Jews, of whom, as thou knowest, there is a multitude in Trans-Tiber, have begun to persecute Christians cruelly. Thou hast in mind that in the time of the divine Claudius there were such disturbances that Cæsar was forced to expel them from Rome. Now, when they have returned, and when, thanks to the protection of the Augusta, they feel safe, they annoy Christians more insolently. I know this; I have seen it. No edict against Christians has been issued; but the Jews complain to the prefect of the city that Christians murder infants, worship an ass, and preach a religion not recognized by the Senate; they beat them, and attack their houses of prayer so fiercely that the Christians are forced to hide."

"What dost thou wish to say?" inquired Vinicius.

"This, lord, that synagogues exist openly in the Trans-Tiber; but that Christians, in their wish to avoid persecution, are forced to pray in secret and assemble in ruined sheds outside the city or in sand-pits. Those who dwell in the Trans-Tiber have chosen just that place which was excavated for the building of the Circus and various houses along the Tiber. Now, when the city is perishing, the adherents of Christ are praying. Beyond doubt we shall find a countless number of them in the excavation; so my advice is to go in there along the road."

"But thou hast said that Linus has gone to Ostrianum," cried Vinicius impatiently.

"But thou has promised me a house with a vineyard at Ameriola," answered Chilo; "for that reason I wish to seek the maiden wherever I hope to find her. They might have returned to the Trans-Tiber after the outbreak of the fire. They might have gone around outside the city, as we are doing at this moment. Linus has a house, perhaps he wished to be nearer his house to see if the fire had seized that part of the city also. If they have returned, I swear to thee, by Persephone, that we shall find them at prayer in the excavation; in the worst event, we shall get tidings of them."

"Thou art right; lead on!" said the tribune.

Chilo, without hesitation, turned to the left toward the hill.

For a while the slope of the hill concealed the conflagration, so that, though the neighboring heights were in the light, the two men were in the shade. When they had passed the Circus, they turned still to the left, and entered a kind of passage completely dark. But in that darkness Vinicius saw swarms of gleaming lanterns.

"They are there," said Chilo. "There will be more of them to-day than ever, for other houses of prayer are burnt or are filled with smoke, as is the whole Trans-Tiber."

"True!" said Vinicius, "I hear singing."

In fact, the voices of people singing reached the hill from the dark opening, and the lanterns vanished in it one after the other. But from side passages new forms appeared continually, so that after some time Vinicius and Chilo found themselves amid a whole assemblage of people.

Chilo slipped from his mule, and, beckoning to a youth who sat near, said to him, —

"I am a priest of Christ and a bishop. Hold the mules for us; thou wilt receive my blessing and forgiveness of sins."

Then, without waiting for an answer, he thrust the reins into his hands, and, in company with Vinicius, joined the advancing throng.

They entered the excavation after a while, and pushed on through the dark passage by the dim light of lanterns till they reached a spacious cave, from which stone had been taken evidently, for the walls were formed of fresh fragments.

It was brighter there than in the corridor, for, in addition to tapers and lanterns, torches were burning. By the light of these Vinicius saw a whole throng of kneeling people with upraised hands. He could not see Lygia, the Apostle Peter, or Linus, but he was surrounded by faces solemn and full of emotion. On some of them expectation or alarm was evident; on some, hope. Light was reflected in the whites of their upraised eyes; perspiration was flowing along their foreheads, pale as chalk; some were singing hymns, others were repeating feverishly the name cf Jesus, some were beating their breasts. It was apparent that they expected something uncommon at any moment.

Meanwhile the hymn ceased, and above the assembly, in a niche formed by the removal of an immense stone, appeared Crispus, the acquaintance of Vinicius, with a face as it were half delirious, pale, stern, and fanatical. All eyes were turned to him, as though waiting for words of consolation and hope. After he had blessed the assembly, he began in hurried, almost shouting tones, —

"Bewail your sins, for the hour has come! Behold the Lord has sent down destroying flames on Babylon, on the city of profligacy and crime. The hour of judgment has struck, the hour of wrath and dissolution. The Lord has promised to come, and soon you will see Him. He will not come as the Lamb, who offered His blood for your sins, but as an awful judge, who in His justice will hurl sinners and unbelievers into the pit. Woe to the world, woe to sinners! there will be no mercy for them. I see Thee, O Christ! Stars are falling to the earth in showers, the sun is darkened, the earth opens in yawning gulfs, the dead rise from their graves, but Thou art moving amid the sound of trumpets and legions of angels, amid thunders and lightnings. I see Thee, I hear Thee, O Christ!"

Then he was silent, and, raising his eyes, seemed to gaze into something distant and dreadful. That moment a dull roar was heard in the cave, — once, twice, a tenth time. In the burning city whole streets of partly consumed houses began to fall with a crash. But most Christians took those sounds as a visible sign that the dreadful hour was approaching; belief in the early second coming of Christ and in the end of the world was universal among them, now the destruction of the city had strengthened it. Terror seized the assembly. Many voices repeated, "The day of judgment! Behold, it is coming!" Some covered their faces with their hands, believing that the earth would be shaken to its foundation, that beasts of hell would rush out through its openings and hurl themselves on sinners. Others cried, "Christ have mercy on us!" "Redeemer, be pitiful!" Some confessed their sins aloud; others cast themselves into the arms of friends, so as to have some near heart with them in the hour of dismay.

But there were faces which seemed rapt into heaven, faces with smiles not of earth; these showed no fear. In some places were heard voices; those were of people who in religious excitement had begun to cry out unknown words in strange languages. Some person in a dark corner cried, "Wake thou that sleepest!" Above all rose the shout of Crispus, "Watch ye! watch ye!"

At moments, however, silence came, as if all were holding the breath in their breasts, and waiting for what would come. And then was heard the distant thunder of parts of the city falling into ruins, after which were heard again groans and cries, —

"Renounce earthly riches, for soon there will be no earth beneath your feet! Renounce earthly loves, for the Lord will condemn those who love wife or child more than Him. Woe to the one who loves the creature more than the Creator! Woe to the rich! woe to the luxurious! woe to the dissolute! woe to husband, wife, and child!"

Suddenly a roar louder than any which had preceded shook the quarry. All fell to the earth, stretching their arms in cross form to ward away evil spirits by that figure. Silence followed, in which was heard only panting breath, whispers full of terror, "Jesus, Jesus, Jesus!" and in places the weeping of children. At that moment a certain calm voice spoke above that prostrate multitude, —

"Peace be with you!"

That was the voice of Peter the Apostle, who had entered the cave a moment earlier. At the sound of his voice terror passed at once, as it passes from a flock in which the shepherd has appeared. People rose from the earth; those who were nearer gathered at his knees, as if seeking protection under his wings. He stretched his hands over them and said, —

"Why are ye troubled in heart? Who of you can tell what will happen before the hour cometh? The Lord has punished Babylon with fire; but His mercy will be on those whom baptism has purified, and ye whose sins are redeemed by the blood of the Lamb will die with His name on your lips. Peace be with you!"

After the terrible and merciless words of Crispus, those of Peter fell like a balm on all present. Instead of fear of God, the love of God took possession of their spirits. Those people found the Christ whom they had learned to love from the Apostle's narratives; hence not a merciless judge, but a mild and patient Lamb, whose mercy surpasses man's wickedness a hundredfold. A feeling of solace possessed the whole assembly; and comfort, with thankfulness to the Apostle, filled their hearts. Voices from various sides began to cry, "We are thy sheep, feed us!" Those nearer said, "Desert us not in the day of disaster!" And they knelt at his knees; seeing which Vinicius approached, seized the edge of Peter's mantle, and, inclining, said, —

"Save me, lord. I have sought her in the smoke of the burning and in the throng of people; nowhere could I find her, but I believe that thou canst restore her."

Peter placed his hand on the tribune's head.

"Have trust," said he, "and come with me."

CHAPTER XLVI

THE city burned on. The Circus Maximus had fallen in ruins. Entire streets and alleys in parts which began to burn first were falling in turn. After every fall pillars of flame rose for a time to the very sky. The wind had changed, and blew now with mighty force from the sea, bearing toward the Cælian, the Esquiline, and the Viminal rivers of flame, brands, and cinders. Still the authorities provided for rescue. At command of Tigellinus, who had hastened from Antium the third day before, houses on the Esquiline were torn down so that the fire, reaching empty spaces, died of itself. That was, however, undertaken solely to save a remnant of the city; to save that which was burning was not to be thought of. There was need also to guard against further results of the ruin. Incalculable wealth had perished in Rome; all the property of its citizens had vanished; hundreds of thousands of people were wandering in utter want outside the walls. Hunger had begun to pinch this throng the second day, for the immense stores of provisions in the city had burned with it. In the universal disorder and in the destruction of authority no one had thought of furnishing new supplies. Only after the arrival of Tigellinus were proper orders sent to Ostia; but meanwhile the people had grown more threatening.

The house at Aqua Appia, in which Tigellinus lodged for the moment, was surrounded by crowds of women, who from morning till late at night cried, "Bread and a roof!" Vainly did pretorians, brought from the great camp between the Via Salaria and the Nomentana, strive to maintain order of some kind. Here and there they were met by open, armed resistance. In places weaponless crowds pointed to the burning city, and shouted, "Kill us in view of that fire!" They abused Cæsar, the Augustians, the pretorians; excitement rose every moment, so that Tigellinus, looking at night on the thousands of fires around the city, said to himself that those were fires in hostile camps.

Besides flour, as much baked bread as possible was brought at his command, not only from Ostia, but from all towns and neighboring villages. When the first instalment came at night to the Emporium, the people broke the chief gate toward the Aventine, seized all supplies in the twinkle of an eye, and caused terrible disturbance. In the light of the conflagration they fought for loaves, and trampled many of them into the earth. Flour from torn bags whitened like snow the whole space from the granary to the arches of Drusus and Germanicus. The uproar continued till soldiers seized the building and dispersed the crowd with arrows and missiles.

Never since the invasion by the Gauls under Brennus had Rome beheld such disaster. People in despair compared the two conflagrations. But in the time of Brennus the Capitol remained. Now the Capitol was encircled by a dreadful wreath of flame. The marbles, it is true, were not blazing; but at night, when the wind swept the flames aside for a moment, rows of columns in the lofty sanctuary of Jove were visible, red as glowing coals. In the days of Brennus, moreover, Rome had a disciplined integral people, attached to the city and its altars; but now crowds of a many-tongued populace roamed nomad-like around the walls of burning Rome, — people composed for the greater part of slaves and freedmen, excited, disorderly, and ready, under the pressure of want, to turn against authority and the city.

But the very immensity of the fire, which terrified every heart, disarmed the crowd in a certain measure. After the fire might come famine and disease; and to complete the misfortune the terrible heat of July had appeared. It was impossible to breathe air inflamed both by fire and the sun. Night brought no relief, on the contrary it presented a hell. During daylight an awful and ominous spectacle met the eye. In the centre a giant city on heights was turned into a roaring volcano; round about as far as the Alban Hills was one boundless camp, formed of sheds, tents, huts, vehicles, bales, packs, stands, fires, all covered with smoke and dust, lighted by sunrays reddened by passing through smoke, — everything filled with roars, shouts, threats, hatred and terror, a monstrous swarm of men, women, and children. Mingled with Quirites were Greeks, shaggy men from the North with blue eyes, Africans, and Asiatics; among citizens were slaves, freedmen, gladiators, merchants, mechanics, servants, and soldiers, — a real sea of people, flowing around the island of fire.

Various reports moved this sea as wind does a real one. These reports were favorable and unfavorable. People told of immense supplies of wheat and clothing to be brought to the Emporium and distributed gratis. It was said, too, that provinces in Asia and Africa would be stripped of their wealth at Cæsar's command, and the treasures thus gained be given to the inhabitants of Rome, so that each man might build his own dwelling. But it was noised about also that water in the aqueducts had been poisoned; that Nero intended to annihilate the city, destroy the inhabitants to the last person, then move to Greece or to Egypt, and rule the world from a new place. Each report ran with lightning speed, and each found belief among the rabble, causing outbursts of hope, anger, terror, or rage. Finally a kind of fever mastered those nomadic thousands. The belief of Christians that the end of the world by fire was at hand, spread even among adherents of the gods, and extended daily. People fell into torpor or madness. In clouds lighted by the burning, gods were seen gazing down on the ruin; hands were stretched toward those gods then to implore pity or send them curses.

Meanwhile soldiers, aided by a certain number of inhabitants, continued to tear down houses on the Esquiline and the Cælian, as also in the Trans-Tiber; these divisions were saved therefore in considerable part. But in the city itself were destroyed incalculable treasures accumulated through centuries of conquest; priceless works of art, splendid temples, the most precious monuments of Rome's past, and Rome's glory. They foresaw that of all Rome there would remain barely a few parts on the edges, and that hundreds of thousands of people would be without a roof. Some spread reports that the soldiers were tearing down houses not to stop the fire, but to prevent any part of the city from being saved. Tigellinus sent courier after courier to Antium, imploring Cæsar in each letter to come and calm the despairing people with his presence. But Nero moved only when fire had seized the "domus transitoria," and he hurried so as not to miss the moment in which the conflagration should be at its highest.

Meanwhile fire had reached the Via Nomentana, but turned from it at once with a change of wind toward the Via Lata and the Tiber. It surrounded the Capitol, spread along the Forum Boarium, destroyed everything which it had spared before, and approached the Palatine a second time.

Tigellinus, assembling all the pretorian forces, despatched courier after courier to Cæsar with an announcement that he would lose nothing of the grandeur of the spectacle, for the fire had increased.

But Nero, who was on the road, wished to come at night, so as to sate himself all the better with a view of the perishing capital. Therefore he halted, in the neighborhood of Aqua Albana, and, summoning to his tent the tragedian Aliturus, decided with his aid on posture, look, and expression; learned fitting gestures, disputing with the actor stubbornly whether at the words "O sacred city, which seemed more enduring than Ida," he was to raise both hands, or, holding in one the forminga, drop it by his side and raise only the other. This question seemed to him then more important than all others. Starting at last about nightfall, he took counsel of Petronius also whether to the lines describing the catastrophe he might add a few magnificent blasphemies against the gods, and whether, considered from the standpoint of art, they would not have rushed spontaneously from the mouth of a man in such a position, a man who was losing his birthplace.

At length he approached the walls about midnight with his numerous court, composed of whole detachments of nobles, senators, knights, freedmen, slaves, women, and children. Sixteen thousand pretorians, arranged in line of battle along the road, guarded the peace and safety of his entrance, and held the excited populace at a proper distance. The people cursed, shouted, and hissed on seeing the retinue, but dared not attack it. In many places, however, applause was given by the rabble, which, owning nothing, had lost nothing in the fire, and which hoped for a more bountiful distribution than usual of wheat, olives, clothing, and money. Finally, shouts, hissing, and applause were drowned in the blare of horns and trumpets, which Tigellinus had caused to be sounded.

Nero, on arriving at the Ostian Gate, halted, and said, "Houseless ruler of a houseless people, where shall I lay my unfortunate head for the night?"

After he had passed the Clivus Delphini, he ascended the Appian aqueduct on steps prepared purposely. After him followed the Augustians and a choir of singers, bearing citharæ, lutes, and other musical instruments.

And all held the breath in their breasts, waiting to learn if he would say some great words, which for their own safety they ought to remember. But he stood solemn, silent, in a purple mantle, and a wreath of golden laurels, gazing at the raging might of the flames. When Terpnos gave him a golden lute, he raised his eyes to the sky, filled with the conflagration, as if he were waiting for inspiration.

The people pointed at him from afar as he stood in the bloody gleam. In the distance fiery serpents were hissing. The ancient and most sacred edifices were in flames: the temple of Hercules, reared by Evander, was burning; the temple of Jupiter Stator was burning, the temple of Luna, built by Servius Tullius, the house of Numa Pompilius, the sanctuary of Vesta with the penates of the Roman people; through waving flames the Capitol appeared at intervals; the past and the spirit of Rome was burning. But he, Cæsar, was there with a lute in his hand and a theatrical expression on his face, not thinking of his perishing country, but of his posture and the prophetic words with which he might describe best the greatness of the catastrophe, rouse most admiration, and receive the warmest plaudits. He detested that city, he detested its inhabitants, he loved only his own songs and verses; hence he rejoiced in heart that at last he saw a tragedy like that which he was writing. The versemaker was happy, the declaimer felt inspired, the seeker for emotions was delighted at the awful sight, and thought with rapture that even the destruction of Troy was as nothing if compared with the destruction of that giant city. What more could he desire? There was world-ruling Rome in flames, and he, standing on the arches of the aqueduct with a golden lute, conspicuous, purple, admired, magnificent, poetic. Down below, somewhere in the darkness, the people are muttering and storming. But let them mutter! Ages will pass, thousands of years will go by, but mankind will remember and glorify the poet, who in that night sang the fall and the burning of Troy. What was Homer compared with him? What Apollo himself with his hollowed-out lute?

Here he raised his hands and, striking the strings, pronounced the words of Priam.

"O nest of my fathers, O dear cradle!" His voice in the open air, with the roar of the conflagration, and the distant murmur of crowding thousands, seemed marvellously weak, uncertain, and low, and the sound of the accompaniment like the buzzing of insects. But senators, dignitaries, and Augustians, assembled on the aqueduct, bowed their heads and listened in silent rapture. He sang long, and his motive was ever sadder. At moments, when he stopped to catch breath, the chorus of singers repeated the last verse; then Nero cast the tragic "syrma" [1] from his shoulder with a gesture learned from Aliturus, struck the lute, and sang on. When at last he had finished the lines composed, he improvised, seeking grandiose comparisons in the spectacle unfolded before him. His face began to change. He was not moved, it is true, by the destruction of his country's capital; but he was delighted and moved

---

[1] A robe with train, worn especially by tragic actors.

with the pathos of his own words to such a degree that his eyes filled with
tears on a sudden. At last he dropped the lute to his feet with a clatter, and,
wrapping himself in the "syrma," stood as if petrified, like one of those statues
of Niobe which ornamented the courtyard of the Palatine.

Soon a storm of applause broke the silence. But in the distance this was
answered by the howling of multitudes. No one doubted then that Cæsar
had given command to burn the city, so as to afford himself a spectacle and
sing a song at it. Nero, when he heard that cry from hundreds of thousands,
turned to the Augustians with the sad, resigned smile of a man who is suffering from injustice.

"See," said he, "how the Quirites value poetry and me."

"Scoundrels!" answered Vatinius. "Command the pretorians, lord, to fall
on them."

Nero turned to Tigellinus, —

"Can I count on the loyalty of the soldiers?"

"Yes, divinity," answered the prefect.

But Petronius shrugged his shoulders, and said, —

"On their loyalty, yes, but not on their numbers. Remain meanwhile where
thou art, for here it is safest; but there is need to pacify the people."

Seneca was of this opinion also, as was Licinus the consul. Meanwhile the
excitement below was increasing. The people were arming with stones, tent-
poles, sticks from the wagons, planks, and various pieces of iron. After a
while some of the pretorian leaders came, declaring that the cohorts, pressed
by the multitude, kept the line of battle with extreme difficulty, and, being
without orders to attack, they knew not what to do.

"O gods," said Nero, "what a night!" On one side a fire, on the other a
raging sea of people. And he fell to seeking expressions the most splendid to
describe the danger of the moment, but, seeing around him alarmed looks
and pale faces, he was frightened, with the others.

"Give me my dark mantle with a hood!" cried he; "must it come really to
battle?"

"Lord," said Tigellinus, in an uncertain voice, "I have done what I could,
but danger is threatening. Speak, O lord, to the people, and make them
promises."

"Shall Cæsar speak to the rabble? Let another do that in my name. Who
will undertake it?"

"I!" answered Petronius, calmly.

"Go, my friend; thou art most faithful to me in every necessity. Go, and
spare no promises."

Petronius turned to the retinue with a careless, sarcastic expression, —

"Senators here present, also Piso, Nerva, and Senecio, follow me."

Then he descended the aqueduct slowly. Those whom he had summoned
followed, not without hesitation, but with a certain confidence which his
calmness had given them. Petronius, halting at the foot of the arches, gave
command to bring him a white horse, and, mounting, rode on, at the head

of the cavalcade, between the deep ranks of pretorians, to the black, howling multitude; he was unarmed, having only a slender ivory cane which he carried habitually.

When he had ridden up, he pushed his horse into the throng. All around, visible in the light of the burning, were upraised hands, armed with every manner of weapon, inflamed eyes, sweating faces, bellowing and foaming lips. A mad sea of people surrounded him and his attendants; round about was a sea of heads, moving, roaring, dreadful.

The outbursts increased and became an unearthly roar; poles, forks, and even swords were brandished above Petronius; grasping hands were stretched toward his horse's reins and toward him, but he rode farther; cool, indifferent, contemptuous. At moments he struck the most insolent heads with his cane, as if clearing a road for himself in an ordinary crowd; and that confidence of his, that calmness, amazed the raging rabble. They recognized him at length, and numerous voices began to shout, —

"Petronius! Arbiter Elegantiarum! Petronius! Petronius!" was heard on all sides. And as that name was repeated, the faces about became less terrible, the uproar less savage: for that exquisite patrician, though he had never striven for the favor of the populace, was still their favorite. He passed for a humane and magnanimous man; and his popularity had increased, especially since the affair of Pedanius Secundus, when he spoke in favor of mitigating the cruel sentence condemning all the slaves of that prefect to death. The slaves more especially loved him thenceforward with that unbounded love which the oppressed or unfortunate are accustomed to give those who show them even small sympathy. Besides, in that moment was added curiosity as to what Cæsar's envoy would say, for no one doubted that Cæsar had sent him.

He removed his white toga, bordered with scarlet, raised it in the air, and waved it above his head, in sign that he wished to speak.

"Silence! Silence!" cried the people on all sides.

After a while there was silence. Then he straightened himself on the horse and said in a clear, firm voice, —

"Citizens, let those who hear me repeat my words to those who are more distant, and bear yourselves, all of you, like men, not like beasts in the arena."

"We will, we will!"

"Then listen. The city will be rebuilt. The gardens of Lucullus, Mæcenas, Cæsar, and Agrippina will be opened to you. To-morrow will begin the distribution of wheat, wine, and olives, so that every man may be full to the throat. Then Cæsar will have games for you, such as the world has not seen yet; during these games banquets and gifts will be given you. Ye will be richer after the fire than before it."

A murmur answered him which spread from the centre in every direction, as a wave rises on water in which a stone has been cast. Those nearer repeated his words to those more distant. Afterward were heard here and there shouts of anger or applause, which turned at length into one universal call of "Panem et circenses!!!"

Petronius wrapped himself in his toga and listened for a time without moving, resembling in his white garment a marble statue. The uproar increased, drowned the roar of the fire, was answered from every side and from ever-increasing distances. But evidently the envoy had something to add, for he waited. Finally, commanding silence anew, he cried, —

"I promised you panem et circenses; and now give a shout in honor of Cæsar, who feeds and clothes you; then go to sleep, dear populace, for the dawn will begin before long."

He turned his horse then, and, tapping lightly with his cane the heads and faces of those who stood in his way, he rode slowly to the pretorian ranks. Soon he was under the aqueduct. He found almost a panic above, where they had not understood the shout "Panem et circenses," and supposed it to be a new outburst of rage. They had not even expected that Petronius would save himself; so Nero, when he saw him, ran to the steps, and with face pale from emotion, inquired, —

"Well, what are they doing? Is there a battle?"

Petronius drew air into his lungs, breathed deeply, and answered, —

"By Pollux! they are sweating! and such a stench! Will some one give me an epilimma? — for I am faint." Then he turned to Cæsar.

"I promised them," said he, "wheat, olives, the opening of the gardens, and games. They worship thee anew, and are howling in thy honor. Gods, what a foul odor those plebeians have!"

"I had pretorians ready," cried Tigellinus; "and hadst thou not quieted them, the shouters would have been silenced forever. It is a pity, Cæsar, that thou didst not let me use force."

Petronius looked at him, shrugged his shoulders, and added, —

"The chance is not lost. Thou mayst have to use it to-morrow."

"No, no!" cried Cæsar, "I will give command to open the gardens to them, and distribute wheat. Thanks to thee, Petronius, I will have games; and that song, which I sang to-day, I will sing publicly."

Then he placed his hands on the arbiter's shoulder, was silent a moment, and starting up at last inquired, —

"Tell me sincerely, how did I seem to thee while I was singing?"

"Thou wert worthy of the spectacle, and the spectacle was worthy of thee," said Petronius.

"But let us look at it again," said he, turning to the fire, "and bid farewell to ancient Rome."

CHAPTER XLVII

THE Apostle's words put confidence in the souls of the Christians. The end of the world seemed ever near to them, but they began to think that the day of judgment would not come immediately, that first they would see the end of Nero's reign, which they looked on as the reign of Satan, and the punishment of God for Cæsar's crimes, which were crying for vengeance. Strengthened in heart, they dispersed, after the prayer, to their temporary dwellings, and even to the Trans-Tiber; for news had come that the fire, set there in a number of places, had, with the change of wind, turned back toward the river, and, after devouring what it could here and there, had ceased to extend.

The Apostle, with Vinicius and Chilo, who followed him, left the excavation also. The young tribune did not venture to interrupt his prayers; hence he walked on in silence, merely imploring pity with his eyes, and trembling from alarm. Many approached to kiss Peter's hands, and the hem of his mantle; mothers held out their children to him; some knelt in the dark, long passage, and, holding up tapers, begged a blessing; others, going alongside, sang: so there was no chance for question or answer. Thus it was in the narrow passage. Only when they came out to broader spaces, from which the burning city was in view, did the Apostle bless them three times, and say, turning to Vinicius, —

"Fear not. The hut of the quarryman is near; in it we shall find Linus, and Lygia, with her faithful servant. Christ, who predestined her to thee, has preserved her."

Vinicius tottered, and placed his hand against the cliff. The road from Antium, the events at the wall, the search for Lygia amidst burning houses, sleeplessness, and his terrible alarm had exhausted him; and the news that the dearest person in the world was near by, and that soon he would see her, took the remnant of his strength from him. So great a weakness possessed him on a sudden that he dropped to the Apostle's feet, and, embracing his knees, remained thus, without power to say a word.

"Not to me, not to me, but to Christ," said the Apostle, who warded off thanks and honor.

"What a good God!" said the voice of Chilo from behind, "but what shall I do with the mules that are waiting down here?"

"Rise and come with me," said Peter to the young man.

Vinicius rose. By the light of the burning, tears were visible on his face, which was pale from emotion. His lips moved, as if in prayer.

"Let us go," said he.

But Chilo repeated again: "Lord, what shall I do with the mules that are waiting? Perhaps this worthy prophet prefers riding to walking."

Vinicius did not know himself what to answer; but hearing from Peter that the quarryman's hut was near by, he said, —

"Take the mules to Macrinus."

"Pardon me, lord, if I mention the house in Ameriola. In view of such an awful fire, it is easy to forget a thing so paltry."

"Thou wilt get it."

"O grandson of Numa Pompilius, I have always been sure, but now, when this magnanimous prophet also has heard the promise, I will not remind thee even of this, that thou hast promised me a vineyard. *Pax vobiscum.* I shall find thee, lord. *Pax vobiscum.*"

They answered, "And peace with thee."

Then both turned to the right toward the hills. Along the road Vinicius said, —

"Lord, wash me with the water of baptism, so that I may call myself a real confessor of Christ, for I love Him with all the power of my soul. Wash me quickly, for I am ready in heart. And what thou commandest I will do; but tell me, so that I may do it in addition."

"Love men as thy own brothers," answered the Apostle, "for only with love mayst thou serve Him."

"Yes, I understand and feel that. When a child I believed in the Roman gods, though I did not love them. But I so love Him the One God that I would give my life for Him gladly." And he looked toward the sky, repeating with exaltation: "For He is one, for He alone is kind and merciful; hence, let not only this city perish, but the whole world, Him alone will I confess and recognize."

"And He will bless thee and thy house," concluded the Apostle.

Meanwhile they turned into another ravine, at the end of which a faint light was visible. Peter pointed to it and said, —

"There is the hut of the quarryman who gave us a refuge when, on the way from Ostrianum with the sick Linus, we could not go to the Trans-Tiber."

After a while they arrived. The hut was rather a cave rounded out in an indentation of the hill, and was faced outside with a wall made of reeds. The door was closed, but through an opening, which served for a window, the interior was visible, lighted by a fire. Some dark giant figure rose up to meet them, and inquired, —

"Who are ye?"

"Servants of Christ," answered Peter. "Peace be with thee, Ursus."

Ursus bent to the Apostle's feet; then, recognizing Vinicius, seized his hand by the wrist, and raised it to his lips.

"And thou, lord," said he. "Blessed be the name of the Lamb, for the joy which thou wilt bring to Callina."

He opened the door then, and entered. Linus was lying on a bundle of straw, with an emaciated face and a forehead as yellow as ivory. Near the fire sat Lygia with a string of small fish, intended evidently for supper. Occupied in removing the fish from the string, and thinking that it was Ursus who had entered, she did not raise her eyes. But Vinicius approached, and, pronouncing her name, stretched his hand to her. She sprang up quickly then; a flash of astonishment and delight shot across her face. Without a word, like a child who after days of fear and sorrow had found father or mother, she threw herself into his open arms.

He embraced her, pressed her to his bosom for some time with such ecstasy as if she had been saved by a miracle. Then, withdrawing his arms, he took her temples between his hands, kissed her forehead and her eyes, embraced her again, repeated her name, bent to her knees, to her palms, greeted her, did her homage, honored her. His delight had no bounds; neither had his love and happiness.

At last he told her how he had rushed in from Antium; had searched for her at the walls, in the smoke at the house of Linus; how he had suffered and was terrified; how much he had endured before the Apostle had shown him her retreat.

"But now," said he, "that I have found thee, I will not leave thee near fire and raging crowds. People are slaying one another under the walls, slaves are revolting and plundering. God alone knows what miseries may fall yet on Rome. But I will save thee and all of you. Oh, my dear, let us go to Antium; we will take a ship there and sail to Sicily. My land is thy land, my houses are thy houses. Listen to me! In Sicily we shall find Aulus. I will give thee back to Pomponia, and take thee from her hands afterward. But, O carissima, have no further fear of me. Christ has not washed me yet, but ask Peter if on the way hither I have not told him my wish to be a real confessor of Christ, and begged him to baptize me, even in this hut of a quarryman. Believe, and let all believe me."

Lygia heard these words with radiant face. The Christians formerly, because of Jewish persecutions, and then because of the fire and disturbance caused by the disaster, lived in fear and uncertainty. A journey to quiet Sicily would put an end to all danger, and open a new epoch of happiness in their lives. If Vinicius had wished to take only Lygia, she would have resisted the temptation surely, as she did not wish to leave Peter and Linus; but Vinicius said to them, "Come with me; my lands are your lands, my houses your houses." At this Lygia inclined to kiss his hand, in sign of obedience, and said, —

"Where thou art, Caius, there am I, Caia."

Then confused that she had spoken words which by Roman custom were repeated only at marriage, she blushed deeply, and stood in the light of the fire, with drooping head, in doubt lest he might take them ill of her. But in his face boundless homage alone was depicted. He turned then to Peter, and continued, —

"Rome is burning at command of Cæsar. In Antium he complained that he had never seen a great fire. And if he has not hesitated at such a crime, think what may happen yet. Who knows that he may not bring in troops, and command a slaughter? Who knows what proscriptions may come; who knows whether after the fire, civil war, murder, and famine may not come?

Hide yourselves, therefore, and let us hide Lygia. There ye can wait till the storm passes, and when it is over return to sow your grain anew."

Outside, from the direction of the Vatican Field, as if to confirm his fears, distant cries were heard full of rage and terror. At that moment the quarryman entered, the master of the hut, and, shutting the door hastily, he cried, —

"People are killing one another near the Circus of Nero. Slaves and gladiators have attacked the citizens."

"Do ye hear?" said Vinicius.

"The measure is full," said the Apostle; "and disasters will come, like a boundless sea." Then he turned, and, pointing to Lygia, said, "Take the maiden, whom God has predestined to thee, and save her, and let Linus, who is sick, and Ursus go with you."

But Vinicius, who had come to love the Apostle with all the power of his impetuous soul, exclaimed: "I swear, my teacher, that I will not leave thee here to destruction."

"The Lord bless thee for thy wish," answered Peter; "but hast thou not heard that Christ repeated thrice on the lake to me, 'Feed my lambs'?"

Vinicius was silent.

"If thou, to whom no one has confided care over me, sayest that thou wilt not leave me to destruction, how canst thou wish me to leave my flock in the day of disaster? When there was a storm on the lake, and we were terrified in heart, He did not desert us; why should I, a servant, not follow my Master's example?"

Then Linus raised his emaciated face and inquired, —

"O vicegerent of the Lord, why should I not follow thy example?"

Vinicius began to pass his hand over his head, as if struggling with himself or fighting with his thoughts; then, seizing Lygia by the hand, he said, in a voice in which the energy of a Roman soldier was quivering, —

"Hear me, Peter, Linus, and thou, Lygia! I spoke as my human reason dictated; but ye have another reason, which regards, not your own danger, but the commands of the Redeemer. True, I did not understand this, and I erred, for the beam is not taken from my eyes yet, and the former nature is heard in me. But since I love Christ, and wish to be His servant, though it is a question for me of something more than my own life, I kneel here before thee, and swear that I will accomplish the command of love, and will not leave my brethren in the day of trouble."

Then he knelt, and enthusiasm possessed him; raising his hands and eyes, he cried: "Do I understand Thee, O Christ? Am I worthy of Thee?"

His hands trembled; his eyes glistened with tears; his body trembled with faith and love. Peter took an earthen vessel with water, and, bringing it near him, said with solemnity, —

"Behold, I baptize thee in the name of the Father, Son, and Holy Ghost. Amen."

Then a religious ecstasy seized all present. They thought that some light from beyond this world had filled the hut, that they heard some superhuman music, that the cliffs had opened above their heads, that choirs of angels were floating down from heaven, and far up there they saw a cross, and pierced hands blessing them.

Meanwhile the shouts of fighting were heard outside, and the roar of flames in the burning city.

CHAPTER XLVIII

CAMPS of people were disposed in the lordly gardens of Cæsar, formerly gardens of Domitius and Agrippina; they were disposed also on the Campus Martius, in the gardens of Pompey, Sallust, and Mæcenas, in porticos, tennis-courts, splendid summer-houses, and buildings erected for wild beasts. Peacocks, flamingoes, swans, ostriches, gazelles, African antelopes, and deer, which had served as ornaments to those gardens, went under the knives of the rabble. Provisions began to come in now from Ostria so abundantly that one might walk, as on a bridge, over ships, boats, and barges from one bank of the Tiber to the other. Wheat was sold at the unheard-of low price of three sestertia, and was given gratis to the indigent. Immense supplies of wine, olives, and chestnuts were brought to the city; sheep and cattle were driven in every day from the mountains. Wretches who before the fire had been hiding in alleys of the Subura, and were perishing of hunger in ordinary times, had a more pleasant life now. The danger of famine was averted completely, but it was more difficult to suppress robbery, murder, and abuses. A nomadic life insured impunity to thieves; the more easily since they proclaimed themselves admirers of Cæsar, and were unsparing of plaudits wherever he appeared. Moreover, when, by the pressure of events, the authorities were in abeyance, and there was a lack of armed force to quell insolence in a city inhabited by the dregs of contemporary mankind, deeds were done which passed human imagination. Every night there were battles and murders; every night boys and women were snatched away. At the Porta Mugionis, where there was a halting-place for herds driven in from the Campania, it come to engagements in which people perished by hundreds. Every morning the banks of the Tiber were covered with drowned bodies, which no one collected; these decayed quickly because of heat heightened by fire, and filled the air with foul odors. Sickness broke out on the camping-grounds, and the more timorous foresaw a great pestilence.

But the city burned on unceasingly. Only on the sixth day, when the fire reached empty spaces on the Esquiline, where an enormous number of houses had been demolished purposely, did it weaken. But the piles of burning cinders gave such strong light yet that people would not believe that the end of the catastrophe had come. In fact the fire burst forth with fresh force on the seventh night in the buildings of Tigellinus, but had short duration for lack of fuel. Burnt houses, however, fell here and there, and threw up towers of flame and pillars of sparks. But the glowing ruins began to grow black on the surface. After sunset the heavens ceased to gleam with bloody light, and only after dark did blue tongues quiver above the extended black waste, tongues which rose from piles of cinders.

Of the fourteen divisions of Rome there remained only four, including the Trans-Tiber. Flames had consumed all the others. When at last the piles of cinders had been turned into ashes, an immense space was visible from the Tiber to the Esquiline, gray, gloomy, dead. In this space stood rows of chimneys, like columns over graves in a cemetery. Among these columns gloomy crowds of people moved about in the daytime, some seeking for precious objects, others for the bones of those dear to them. In the night dogs howled above the ashes and ruins of former dwellings.

All the bounty and aid shown by Cæsar to the populace did not restrain evil speech and indignation. Only the herd of robbers, criminals, and homeless ruffians, who could eat, drink, and rob enough, were contented. People who had lost all their property and their nearest relatives were not won over by the opening of gardens, the distribution of bread, or the promise of games and gifts. The catastrophe had been too great and unparalleled. Others, in whom was hidden yet some spark of love for the city and their birthplace, were brought to despair by news that the old name "Roma" was to vanish, and that from the ashes of the capital Cæsar would erect a new city called Neropolis. A flood of hatred rose and swelled every day, despite the flatteries of the Augustians and the calumnies of Tigellinus. Nero, more sensitive than any former Cæsar to the favor of the populace, thought with alarm that in the sullen and mortal struggle which he was waging with patricians in the Senate, he might lack support. The Augustians themselves were not less alarmed, for any morning might bring them destruction. Tigellinus thought of summoning certain legions from Asia Minor. Vatinius, who laughed even when slapped on the face, lost his humor; Vitelius lost his appetite.

Others were taking counsel among themselves how to avert the danger, for it was no secret that were an outburst to carry off Cæsar, not one of the Augustians would escape, except, perhaps, Petronius. To their influence were ascribed the madnesses of Nero, to their suggestions all the crimes which he committed. Hatred for them almost surpassed that for Nero. Hence some began to make efforts to rid themselves of responsibility for the burning of the city. But to free themselves they must clear Cæsar also from suspicion, or no one would believe that they had not caused the catastrophe. Tigellinus took counsel on this subject with Domitius Afer, and even with Seneca, though he hated him. Poppæa, who understood that the ruin of Nero would be her own sentence, took the opinion of her confidants and of Hebrew priests, for it had been admitted for years that she held the faith of Jehovah. Nero found his own methods, which, frequently terrible, were more frequently foolish, and fell now into terror, now into childish delight, but above all he complained.

On a time a long and fruitless consultation was held in the house of Tiberius, which had survived the fire. Petronius thought it best to leave troubles, go to Greece, thence to Egypt and Asia Minor. The journey had been planned long before; why defer it, when in Rome were sadness and danger?

Cæsar accepted the counsel with eagerness; but Seneca when he had thought awhile, said, —

"It is easy to go, but it would be more difficult to return."

"By Heracles!" replied Petronius, "we may return at the head of Asiatic legions."

"This will I do!" exclaimed Nero.

But Tigellinus opposed. He could discover nothing himself, and if the arbiter's idea had come to his own head he would beyond doubt have declared it the saving one; but with him the question was that Petronius might not be a second time the only man who in difficult moments could rescue all and every one.

"Hear me, divinity," said he, "this advice is destructive! Before thou art at Ostia a civil war will break out; who knows but one of the surviving collateral descendants of the divine Augustus will declare himself Cæsar, and what shall we do if the legions take his side?"

"We shall try," answered Nero, "that there be no descendants of Augustus. There are not many now; hence it is easy to rid ourselves of them."

"It is possible to do so, but is it a question of them alone? No longer ago than yesterday my people heard in the crowd that a man like Thrasea should be Cæsar."

Nero bit his lips. After a while he raised his eyes and said: "Insatiable and thankless. They have grain enough, and they have coal on which to bake cakes; what more do they want?"

"Vengeance!" replied Tigellinus.

Silence followed. Cæsar rose on a sudden, extended his hand, and began to declaim, —

"Hearts call for vengeance, and vengeance wants a victim." Then, forgetting everything, he said, with radiant face: "Give me the tablet and stilus to write this line. Never could Lucan have composed the like. Have ye noticed that I found it in a twinkle?"

"O incomparable!" exclaimed a number of voices.

Nero wrote down the line, and said, —

"Yes, vengeance wants a victim." Then he cast a glance on those around him. "But if we spread the report that Vatinius gave command to burn the city, and devote him to the anger of the people?"

"O divinity! Who am I?" exclaimed Vatinius.

"True! One more important than thou is demanded. Is it Vitelius?"

Vitelius grew pale, but began to laugh.

"My fat," answered he, "might start the fire again."

But Nero had something else on his mind; in his soul he was looking for a victim who might really satisfy the people's anger, and he found him.

"Tigellinus," said he after a while, "it was thou who didst burn Rome!"

A shiver ran through those present. They understood that Cæsar had ceased to jest this time, and that a moment had come which was pregnant with events.

The face of Tigellinus was wrinkled, like the lips of a dog about to bite.

"I burnt Rome at thy command!" said he.

And the two glared at each other like a pair of devils. Such silence followed that the buzzing of flies was heard as they flew through the atrium.

"Tigellinus," said Nero, "dost thou love me?"

"Thou knowest, lord."

"Sacrifice thyself for me."

"O divine Cæsar," answered Tigellinus, "why present the sweet cup which I may not raise to my lips? The people are muttering and rising; dost thou wish the pretorians also to rise?"

A feeling of terror pressed the hearts of those present. Tigellinus was pretorian prefect, and his words had the direct meaning of a threat. Nero himself understood this, and his face became pallid.

At that moment Epaphroditus, Cæsar's freedman, entered, announcing that the divine Augusta wished to see Tigellinus, as there were people in her apartments whom the prefect ought to hear.

Tigellinus bowed to Cæsar, and went out with a face calm and contemptuous. Now, when they had wished to strike him, he had shown his teeth; he had made them understand who he was, and, knowing Nero's cowardice, he was confident that that ruler of the world would never dare to raise a hand against him.

Nero sat in silence for a moment; then, seeing that those present expected some answer, he said, —

"I have reared a serpent in my bosom."

Petronius shrugged his shoulders, as if to say that it was not difficult to pluck the head from such a serpent.

"What wilt thou say? Speak, advise!" exclaimed Nero, noticing this motion. "I trust in thee alone, for thou hast more sense than all of them, and thou lovest me."

Petronius had the following on his lips: "Make me pretorian prefect, I will deliver Tigellinus to the people, and pacify the city in a day." But his innate slothfulness prevailed. To be prefect meant to bear on his shoulder's Cæsar's person and also thousands of public affairs. And why should he perform that labor? Was it not better to read poetry in his splendid library, look at vases and statues, or hold to his breast the divine body of Eunice, twining her golden hair through his fingers, and inclining his lips to her coral mouth? Hence he said, —

"I advise the journey to Achæa."

"Ah!" answered Nero, "I looked for something more from thee. The Senate hates me. If I depart, who will guarantee that it will not revolt and proclaim some one else Cæsar? The people have been faithful to me so far, but now they will follow the Senate. By Hades! if that Senate and that people had one head! — "

"Permit me to say, O divinity, that if thou desire to save Rome, there is need to save even a few Romans," remarked Petronius, with a smile.

"What care I for Rome and Romans?" complained Nero. "I should be obeyed in Achæa. Here only treason surrounds me. All desert me, and ye are making ready for treason. I know it, I know it. Ye do not even imagine what future ages will say of you if ye desert such an artist as I am."

Here he tapped his forehead on a sudden, and cried, —

"True! Amid these cares even I forget who I am."

Then he turned to Petronius with a radiant face.

"Petronius," said he, "the people murmur; but if I take my lute and go to the Campus Martius, if I sing that song to them which I sang during the conflagration, dost thou not think that I will move them, as Orpheus moved wild beasts?"

To this Tullius Senecio, who was impatient to return to his slave women brought in from Antium, and who had been impatient a long time, replied, —

"Beyond doubt, O Cæsar, if they permit thee to begin."

"Let us go to Hellas!" cried Nero, with disgust.

But at that moment Poppæa appeared, and with her Tigellinus. The eyes of those present turned to him unconsciously, for never had triumphator ascended the Capitol with pride such as his when he stood before Cæsar. He began to speak slowly and with emphasis, in tones through which the bite of iron, as it were, was heard, —

"Listen, O Cæsar, for I can say: I have found! The people want vengeance, — they want not one victim, but hundreds, thousands. Hast heard, lord, who Christos was, — he who was crucified by Pontius Pilate? And knowest thou who the Christians are? Have I not told thee of their crimes and foul ceremonies, of their predictions that fire would cause the end of the world? People hate and suspect them. No one has seen them in a temple at any time, for they consider our gods evil spirits; they are not in the Stadium, for they despise horse races. Never have the hands of a Christian done thee honor with plaudits. Never has one of them recognized thee as god. They are enemies of the human race, of the city, and of thee. The people murmur against thee; but thou hast given me no command to burn Rome, and I did not burn it. The people want vengeance; let them have it. The people want blood and games; let them have them. The people suspect thee; let their suspicion turn in another direction."

Nero listened with amazement at first; but as Tigellinus proceeded, his actor's face changed, and assumed in succession expressions of anger, sorrow, sympathy, indignation. Suddenly he rose, and, casting off the toga, which dropped at his feet, he raised both hands and stood silent for a time. At last he said, in the tones of a tragedian, —

"O Zeus, Apollo, Here, Athene, Persephone, and all ye immortals! why did ye not come to aid us? What has this hapless city done to those cruel wretches that they burnt it so inhumanly?"

"They are enemies of mankind and of thee," said Poppæa.

"Do justice!" cried others. "Punish the incendiaries! The gods themselves call for vengeance!"

Nero sat down, dropped his head to his breast, and was silent a second time, as if stunned by the wickedness of which he had heard. But after a while he shook his hands, and said, —

"What punishments, what tortures befit such a crime? But the gods will inspire me, and, aided by the powers of Tartarus, I will give my poor people such a spectacle that they will remember me for ages with gratitude."

The forehead of Petronius was covered with a sudden cloud. He thought of the danger hanging over Lygia and over Vinicius, whom he loved, and over all those people whose religion he rejected, but of whose innocence he was certain. He thought also that one of those bloody orgies would begin which his eyes, those of an æsthetic man, could not suffer. But above all he thought: "I must save Vinicius, who will go mad if that maiden perishes"; and this consideration outweighed every other, for Petronius understood well that he was beginning a game far more perilous than any in his life. He began, however, to speak freely and carelessly, as his wont was when criticising or ridiculing plans of Cæsar and the Augustians that were not sufficiently æsthetic, —

"Ye have found victims! That is true. Ye may send them to the arena, or array them in 'painful tunics.' That is true also. But hear me! Ye have authority, ye have pretorians, ye have power; then be sincere, at least, when no one is listening! Deceive the people, but deceive not one another. Give the Christians to the populace, condemn them to any torture ye like; but have courage to say to yourselves that it was not they who burnt Rome. Phy! Ye call me 'arbiter elegantiarum'; hence I declare to you that I cannot endure wretched comedies! Phy! how all this reminds me of the theatrical booths near the Porta Asinaria, in which actors play the parts of gods and kings to amuse the suburban rabble, and when the play is over wash down onions with sour wine, or get blows of clubs! Be gods and kings in reality; for I say that ye can permit yourselves the position! As to thee, O Cæsar, thou hast threatened us with the sentence of coming ages; but think, those ages will utter judgment concerning thee also. By the divine Clio! Nero, ruler of the world, Nero, a god, burnt Rome, because he was as powerful on earth as Zeus on Olympus, — Nero the poet loved poetry so much that he sacrificed to it his country! From the beginning of the world no one did the like, no one ventured on the like. I beseech thee in the name of the double-crowned Libethrides, renounce not such glory, for songs of thee will sound to the end of ages! What will Priam be when compared with thee; what Agamemnon; what Achilles; what the gods themselves? We need not say that the burning of Rome was good, but it was colossal and uncommon. I tell thee, besides, that the people will raise no hand against thee! It is not true that they will. Have courage; guard thyself against acts unworthy of thee, — for this alone threatens thee, that future ages may say, 'Nero burned Rome; but as a timid Cæsar and a timid poet he denied the great deed out of fear, and cast the blame of it on the innocent!'"

The arbiter's words produced the usual deep impression on Nero; but Petronius was not deceived as to this, — that what he had said was a desperate means which in a fortunate event might save the Christians, it is true, but might still more easily destroy himself. He had not hesitated, however, for it was a question at once of Vinicius whom he loved, and of hazard with which he amused himself. "The dice are thrown," said he to himself, "and we shall see how far fear for his own life outweighs in the monkey his love of glory."

And in his soul he had no doubt that fear would outweigh.

Meanwhile silence fell after his words. Poppæa and all present were looking at Nero's eyes as at a rainbow. He began to raise his lips, drawing them to his very nostrils, as was his custom when he knew not what to do; at last disgust and trouble were evident on his features.

"Lord," cried Tigellinus, on noting this, "permit me to go; for when people wish to expose thy person to destruction, and call thee, besides, a cowardly Cæsar, a cowardly poet, an incendiary, and a comedian, my ears cannot suffer such expressions!"

"I have lost," thought Petronius. But turning to Tigellinus, he measured him with a glance in which was that contempt for a ruffian which is felt by a great lord who is an exquisite.

"Tigellinus," said he, "it was thou whom I called a comedian; for thou art one at this very moment."

"Is it because I will not listen to thy insults?"

"It is because thou art feigning boundless love for Cæsar, — thou who a short while since wert threatening him with pretorians, which we all understood as did he!"

Tigellinus, who had not thought Petronius sufficiently daring to throw dice such as those on the table, turned pale, lost his head, and was speechless. This was, however, the last victory of the arbiter over his rival, for that moment Poppæa said, —

"Lord, how permit that such a thought should even pass through the head of any one, and all the more that any one should venture to express it aloud in thy presence!"

"Punish the insolent!" exclaimed Vitelius.

Nero raised his lips again to his nostrils, and, turning his near-sighted, glassy eyes on Petronius, said, —

"Is this the way thou payest me for the friendship which I had for thee?"

"If I am mistaken, show me my error," said Petronius; "but know that I speak that which love for thee dictates."

"Punish the insolent!" repeated Vitelius.

"Punish!" called a number of voices.

In the atrium there was a murmur and a movement, for people began to withdraw from Petronius. Even Tullius Senecio, his constant companion at the court, pushed away, as did young Nerva, who had shown him hitherto the greatest friendship. After a while Petronius was alone on the left side of the atrium, with a smile on his lips; and gathering with his hands the folds of his toga, he waited yet for what Cæsar would say or do.

"Ye wish me to punish him," said Cæsar; "but he is my friend and comrade. Though he has wounded my heart, let him know that for friends this heart has naught but forgiveness."

"I have lost, and am ruined," thought Petronius.

Meanwhile Cæsar rose, and the consultation was ended.

CHAPTER XLIX

Petronius went home. Nero and Tigellinus went to Poppæa's atrium, where they were expected by people with whom the prefect had spoken already.

There were two Trans-Tiber rabbis in long solemn robes and mitred, a young copyist, their assistant, together with Chilo. At sight of Cæsar the priests grew pale from emotion, and, raising their hands an arm's length, bent their heads to his hands.

"Be greeted, O ruler of the earth, guardian of the chosen people, and Cæsar, lion among men, whose reign is like sunlight, like the cedar of Lebanon, like a spring, like a palm, like the balsam of Jericho."

"Do ye refuse to call me god?" inquired Nero.

The priests grew still paler. The chief one spoke again, —

"Thy words, O lord, are as sweet as a cluster of grapes, as a ripe fig, — for Jehovah filled thy heart with goodness! Thy father's predecessor, Cæsar Caius, was stern; still our envoys did not call him god, preferring death itself to violation of the law."

"And did not Caligula give command to throw them to the lions?"

"No, lord; Cæsar Caius feared Jehovah's anger."

And they raised their heads, for the name of the powerful Jehovah gave them courage; confident in his might, they looked into Nero's eyes with more boldness.

"Do ye accuse the Christians of burning Rome?" inquired Cæsar.

"We, lord, accuse them of this alone, — that they are enemies of the law, of the human race, of Rome, and of thee; that long since they have threatened the city and the world with fire! The rest will be told thee by this man, whose lips are unstained by a lie, for in his mother's veins flowed the blood of the chosen people."

Nero turned to Chilo: "Who art thou?"

"One who honors thee, O Cyrus; and, besides, a poor Stoic — "

"I hate the Stoics," said Nero. "I hate Thrasea; I hate Musonius and Cornutus. Their speech is repulsive to me; their contempt for art, their voluntary squalor and filth."

"O lord, thy master Seneca has one thousand tables of citrus wood. At thy wish I will have twice as many. I am a Stoic from necessity. Dress my stoicism, O Radiant One, in a garland of roses, put a pitcher of wine before it; it will sing Anacreon in such strains as to deafen every Epicurean."

Nero, who was pleased by the title "Radiant," smiled and said, —

"Thou dost please me."

"This man is worth his weight in gold!" cried Tigellinus.

"Put thy liberality with my weight," answered Chilo, "or the wind will blow my reward away."

"He would not outweigh Vitelius," put in Cæsar.

"Eheu! Silver-bowed, my wit is not of lead."

"I see that thy faith does not hinder thee from calling me a god."

"O Immortal! My faith is in thee; the Christians blaspheme against that faith, and I hate them."

"What dost thou know of the Christians?"

"Wilt thou permit me to weep, O divinity?"

"No," answered Nero; "weeping annoys me."

"Thou art triply right, for eyes that have seen thee should be free of tears forever. O lord, defend me against my enemies."

"Speak of the Christians," said Poppæa, with a shade of impatience.

"It will be at thy command, O Isis," answered Chilo. "From youth I devoted myself to philosophy, and sought truth. I sought it among the ancient divine sages, in the Academy at Athens, and in the Serapeum at Alexandria. When I heard of the Christians, I judged that they formed some new school in which I could find certain kernels of truth; and to my misfortune I made their acquaintance. The first Christian whom evil fate brought near me was one Glaucus, a physician of Naples. From him I learned in time that they worship a certain Chrestos, who promised to exterminate all people and destroy every city on earth, but to spare them if they helped him to exterminate the children of Deucalion. For this reason, O lady, they hate men, and poison fountains; for this reason in their assemblies they shower curses on Rome, and on all temples in which our gods are honored. Chrestos was crucified; but he promised that when Rome was destroyed by fire, he would come again and give Christians dominion over the world."

"People will understand now why Rome was destroyed," interrupted Tigellinus.

"Many understand that already, O lord, for I go about in the gardens, I go to the Campus Martius, and teach. But if ye listen to the end, ye will know my reasons for vengeance. Glaucus the physician did not reveal to me at first that their religion taught hatred. On the contrary, he told me that Chrestos was a good divinity, that the basis of their religion was love. My sensitive heart could not resist such a truth; hence I took to loving Glaucus, I trusted him, I shared every morsel of bread with him, every copper coin, and dost thou know, lady, how he repaid me? On the road from Naples to Rome he thrust a knife into my body, and my wife, the beautiful and youthful Berenice, he sold to a slave-merchant. If Sophocles knew my history — but what do I say? One better than Sophocles is listening."

"Poor man!" said Poppæa.

"Whoso has seen the face of Aphrodite is not poor, lady; and I see it at this moment. But then I sought consolation in philosophy. When I came to Rome, I tried to meet Christian elders to obtain justice against Glaucus. I thought that they would force him to yield up my wife. I became acquainted with their chief priest; I became acquainted with another, named Paul, who was in prison in this city, but was liberated afterward; I became acquainted with the son of Zebedee, with Linus and Clitus and many others. I know where they lived before the fire, I know where they meet. I can point out one excavation in the Vatican Hill and a cemetery beyond the Nomentan Gate, where they celebrate their shameless ceremonies. I saw the Apostle Peter. I saw how Glaucus killed children, so that the Apostle might have something to sprinkle on the heads of those present; and I saw Lygia, the foster-child of Pomponia Græcina, who boasted that though unable to bring the blood of an infant, she brought the death of an infant, for she bewitched the little Augusta, thy daughter, O Cyrus, and thine, O Isis!"

"Dost hear, Cæsar?" asked Poppæa.

"Can that be!" exclaimed Nero.

"I could forgive wrongs done myself," continued Chilo, "but when I heard of yours, I wanted to stab her. Unfortunately I was stopped by the noble Vinicius, who loves her."

"Vinicius? But did she not flee from him?"

"She fled, but he made search for her; he could not exist without her. For wretched pay I helped him in the search, and it was I who pointed out to him the house in which she lived among the Christians in the Trans-Tiber. We went there together, and with us thy wrestler Croton, whom the noble Vinicius hired to protect him. But Ursus, Lygia's slave, crushed Croton. That is a man of dreadful strength, O Lord, who can break a bull's neck as easily as another might a poppy stalk. Aulus and Pomponia loved him because of that."

"By Hercules," said Nero, "the mortal who crushed Croton deserves a statue in the Forum. But, old man, thou art mistaken or art inventing, for Vinicius killed Croton with a knife."

"That is how people calumniate the gods. O lord, I myself saw Croton's ribs breaking in the arms of Ursus, who rushed then on Vinicius and would have killed him but for Lygia. Vinicius was ill for a long time after that but they nursed him in the hope that through love he would become a Christian. In fact, he did become a Christian."

"Vinicius?"

"Yes."

"And, perhaps, Petronius too?" inquired Tigellinus, hurriedly.

Chilo squirmed, rubbed his hands, and said, —

"I admire thy penetration, O lord. He may have become one! He may very well have become one."

"Now I understand why he defended the Christians."

Nero laughed: "Petronius a Christian! Petronius an enemy of life and luxury! Be not foolish; do not ask me to believe that, since I am ready not to believe anything."

"But the noble Vinicius became a Christian, lord. I swear by that radiance which comes from thee that I speak the truth, and that nothing pierces me with such disgust as lying. Pomponia Græcina is a Christian, little Aulus is a Christian, Lygia is a Christian, and so is Vinicius. I served him faithfully, and in return, at the desire of Glaucus the physician, he gave command to flog me, though I am old and was sick and hungry. And I have sworn by Hades that I will not forget that for him. O lord, avenge my wrongs on them, and I will deliver to thee Peter the Apostle and Linus and Clitus and Glaucus and Crispus, the highest ones, and Lygia and Ursus. I will point out hundreds of them to you, thousands; I will indicate their houses of prayer, the cemeteries, — all thy prisons will not hold them! Without me ye could not find them. In misfortunes I have sought consolation, hitherto in philosophy alone, now I will find it in favors that will descend on me. I am old, and have not known life; let me begin."

"It is thy wish to be a Stoic before a full plate," said Nero.

"Whoso renders service to thee will fill it by that same."

"Thou art not mistaken, O philosopher."

But Poppæa did not forget her enemies. Her fancy for Vinicius was, indeed, rather a momentary whim, which had risen under the influence of jealousy, anger, and wounded vanity. Still the coolness of the young patrician touched her deeply, and filled her heart with a stubborn feeling of offence. This alone, that he had dared to prefer another, seemed to her a crime calling for vengeance. As to Lygia, she hated her from the first moment, when the beauty of that northern lily alarmed her. Petronius, who spoke of the too narrow hips of the girl, might talk what he pleased into Cæsar, but not into the Augusta. Poppæa the critic understood at one cast of the eye that in all Rome Lygia alone could rival and even surpass her. Thenceforth she vowed her ruin.

"Lord," said she, "avenge our child."

"Hasten!" cried Chilo, "hasten! Otherwise Vinicius will hide her. I will point out the house to which she returned after the fire."

"I will give thee ten men, and go this moment," said Tigellinus.

"O lord! thou hast not seen Croton in the arms of Ursus; if thou wilt give fifty men, I will only show the house from a distance. But if ye will not imprison Vinicius, I am lost."

Tigellinus looked at Nero. "Would it not be well, O divinity, to finish at once with the uncle and nephew?"

Nero thought a moment and answered, —

"No, not now. People would not believe us if we tried to persuade them that Petronius, Vinicius, or Pomponia Græcina had fired Rome. Their houses were too beautiful. Their turn will come later; to-day other victims are needed."

"Then, O lord, give me soldiers as a guard," said Chilo.

"See to this, Tigellinus."

"Thou wilt lodge meanwhile with me," said the prefect to Chilo.

Delight beamed from the face of the Greek.

"I will give up all! only hasten! — hasten!" cried he, with a hoarse voice.

CHAPTER L

On leaving Cæsar, Petronius had himself borne to his house on the Carinæ, which, being surrounded on three sides by a garden, and having in front the small Cecilian Forum, escaped the fire luckily. For this cause other Augustians, who had lost their houses and in them vast wealth and many works of art, called Petronius fortunate. For years it had been repeated that he was the first-born of Fortune, and Cæsar's growing friendship in recent times seemed to confirm the correctness of this statement.

But that first-born of Fortune might meditate now on the fickleness of his mother, or rather on her likeness to Chronos, who devoured his own children.

"Were my house burnt," said he to himself, "and with it my gems, Etruscan vases, Alexandrian glass, and Corinthian bronze, Nero might indeed have forgotten the offence. By Pollux! And to think that it depended on me alone to be pretorian prefect at this moment. I should proclaim Tigellinus the incendiary, which he is really; I should array him in the 'painful tunic,' and deliver him to the populace, protect the Christians, rebuild Rome. Who knows even if a better epoch would not begin thus for honest people? I ought to have taken the office, simply out of regard for Vinicius. In case of overwork I could have surrendered command to him, and Nero would not have even tried to resist. Then let Vinicius baptize all the pretorians, nay, Cæsar himself; what harm could that be to me? Nero pious, Nero virtuous and merciful, — this would be even an amusing spectacle."

And his carelessness was so great that he began to laugh. But after a time his thoughts turned in another direction. It seemed to him that he was in Antium; that Paul of Tarsus was saying to him, "Ye call us enemies of life, but answer me, Petronius: If Cæsar were a Christian, and acted according to our religion, would not life be safer and more certain?"

And remembering these words, he continued: "By Castor! No matter how many Christians they murder here, Paul will find as many new ones; for he is right, unless the world can rest on scoundrelism. But who knows that this will not be the case soon? I myself, who have learned not a little, did not learn how to be a great enough scoundrel; hence I shall have to open my veins. But in every case it must have ended thus, and if not thus, in some other way. I am sorry for Eunice and my Myrrhene vase; but Eunice is free, and the vase will go with me. Ahenobarbus will not get it, in any event! I am sorry also for Vinicius. But, though I was bored less of late than before, I am ready. In the world things are beautiful; but people are so vile for the greater part that life is not worth a regret. He who knew how to live should know how to die. Though I belong to the Augustians, I was freer than they supposed."

Here he shrugged his shoulders. "They may think that my knees are trembling at this moment, and that terror has raised the hair on my head; but on reaching home, I will take a bath in violet water, my golden-haired herself will anoint me; then after refreshment we will have sung to us that hymn to Apollo composed by Anthemios. I said once to myself that it was not worth while to think of death, for death thinks of us without our assistance. It would be a wonder if there are really Elysian fields, and in them shades of people. Eunice would come in time to me, and we should wander together over asphodel meadows. I should find, too, society better than this. What buffoons, tricksters, a vile herd without taste or polish! Tens of Arbiters Elegantiarum could not transform those Trimalchions into decent people. By Persephone! I have had enough!"

And he noted with astonishment that something separated him from those people already. He had known them well earlier, and had known what to think of them; still they seemed to him now as farther away and more deserving of contempt than usual. Indeed, he had had enough of them!

But afterward he began to think over his position. Thanks to his acuteness, he knew that destruction was not threatening him directly. Nero had seized an appropriate occasion to utter a few select, lofty phrases about friendship and forgiveness, thus binding himself for the moment. "He will have to seek pretexts, and before he finds them much time may pass. First of all, he will celebrate the games with Christians," said Petronius to himself; "only then will he think of me, and if that be true, it is not worth while to take trouble or change my course of life. Nearer danger threatens Vinicius!"

And thenceforth he thought only of Vinicius, whom he resolved to rescue. Four sturdy Bithynians bore his litter quickly through ruins, ash-heaps, and stones with which the Carinæ was filled yet; but he commanded them to run swiftly so as to be home at the earliest. Vinicius, whose "insula" had been burned, was living with him, and was at home, fortunately.

"Hast seen Lygia to-day?" were the first words of Petronius.

"I have just come from her."

"Hear what I tell thee, and lose no time in questions. It has been decided this morning at Cæsar's to lay the blame of burning Rome on the Christians. Persecutions and tortures threaten them. Pursuit may begin any instant. Take Lygia and flee at once beyond the Alps even, or to Africa. And hasten, for the Palatine is nearer the Trans-Tiber than is this place."

Vinicius was, indeed, too much of a soldier to lose time in useless queries. He listened with frowning brows, and a face intent and terrible, but fearless. Evidently the first feeling of his nature in presence of peril was a wish to defend and give battle.

"I go," said he.

"One word more. Take a purse of gold, take weapons, and a handful of thy Christians. In case of need, rescue her!"

Vinicius was in the door of the atrium already.

"Send me news by a slave!" cried Petronius.

When left alone, he began to walk by the columns which adorned the atrium, thinking of what had happened. He knew that Lygia and Linus had returned after the fire to the former house, which, like the greater part of the Trans-Tiber, had been saved; and that was an unfavorable circumstance, for otherwise it would have been difficult to find them among throngs of people. Petronius hoped, however, that as things were, no one in the Palatine knew where they lived, and therefore in every case Vinicius would anticipate the pretorians. It occurred to him also that Tigellinus, wishing to seize at one attempt as many Christians as possible, would extend his net over all Rome. "If they send no more than ten people after her," thought he, "that giant Lygian will break their bones and what will it be if Vinicius comes with assistance?" Thinking of this he was consoled. True, armed resistance to the pretorians was almost the same as war with Cæsar. Petronius knew also that if Vinicius hid from the vengeance of Nero, that vengeance might fall on himself; but he cared little. On the contrary, he rejoiced at the thought of crossing Nero's plans and those of Tigellinus, and determined to spare in the matter neither men nor money. Since in Antium Paul of Tarsus had converted most of his slaves, he, while defending Christians, might count on their zeal and devotion.

The entrance of Eunice interrupted his thoughts. At sight of her all his cares and troubles vanished without a trace. He forgot Cæsar, the disfavor into which he had fallen, the degraded Augustians, the persecution threatening the Christians, Vinicius, Lygia, and looked only at her with the eyes of an æsthetic man enamoured of marvellous forms, and of a lover for whom love breathes from those forms. She, in a transparent violet robe called "Coa vestis," through which her maiden-like form appeared, was really as beautiful as a goddess. Feeling herself admired meanwhile, and loving him with all her soul, ever eager for his fondling, she blushed with delight as if she had been an innocent maiden.

"What wilt thou say to me, Charis?" asked Petronius, stretching his hands to her.

She, inclining her golden head to him, answered, —

"Anthemios has come with his choristers, and asks if 'tis thy wish to hear him."

"Let him stay; he will sing to us during dinner the hymn to Apollo. By the groves of Paphos! when I see thee in that Coan gauze, I think that Aphrodite has veiled herself with a piece of the sky, and is standing before me."

"O lord!"

"Come hither, Eunice, embrace me with thy arms, and give thy lips to me. Dost thou love me?"

"I should not have loved Zeus more."

Then she pressed her lips to his, while quivering in his arms from happiness. After a while Petronius asked, —

"But if we should have to separate?"

Eunice looked at him with fear in her eyes.

"How is that, lord?"

"Fear not; I ask, for who knows but I may have to set out on a long journey?"

"Take me with thee —"

. Petronius changed the conversation quickly, and said, —

"Tell me, are there asphodels on the grass plot in the garden?"

"The cypresses and the grass plots are yellow from the fire, the leaves have fallen from the myrtles, and the whole garden seems dead."

"All Rome seems dead, and soon it will be a real graveyard. Dost thou know that an edict against the Christians is to be issued, and a persecution will begin during which thousands will perish?"

"Why punish the Christians, lord? They are good and peaceful."

"For that very reason."

"Let us go to the sea. Thy beautiful eyes do not like to see blood."

"Well, but meanwhile I must bathe. Come to the clæothesium to anoint my arms. By the girdle of Kypris! never hast thou seemed to me so beautiful. I will give command to make a bath for thee in the form of a shell; thou wilt be like a costly pearl in it. Come, Golden-haired!"

He went out, and an hour later both, in garlands of roses and with misty eyes, were resting before a table covered with a service of gold. They were served by boys dressed as Cupids, they drank wine from ivy-wreathed goblets, and heard the hymn to Apollo sung to the sound of harps, under direction of Anthemios. What cared they if around the villa chimneys pointed up from the ruins of houses, and gusts of wind swept the ashes of burnt Rome in every direction? They were happy thinking only of love, which had made their lives like a divine dream. But before the hymn was finished a slave, the chief of the atrium, entered the hall.

"Lord," said he, in a voice quivering with alarm, "a centurion with a detachment of pretorians is standing before the gate, and, at command of Cæsar, wishes to see thee."

The song and the sound of lutes ceased. Alarm was roused in all present; for Cæsar, in communications with friends, did not employ pretorians usually, and their arrival at such times foreboded no good. Petronius alone showed not the slightest emotion, but said, like a man annoyed by continual visits, —

"They might let me dine in peace." Then turning to the chief of the atrium, he said, "Let him enter."

The slave disappeared behind the curtain; a moment later heavy steps were heard, and an acquaintance of Petronius appeared, the centurion Aper, armed, and with an iron helmet on his head.

"Noble lord," said he, "here is a letter from Cæsar."

Petronius extended his white hand lazily, took the tablet, and, casting his eye over it, gave it, in all calmness to Eunice.

"He will read a new book of the Troyad this evening, and invites me to come."

"I have only the order to deliver the letter," said the centurion.

"Yes, there will be no answer. But, centurion, thou mightst rest a while with us and empty a goblet of wine?"

"Thanks to thee, noble lord. A goblet of wine I will drink to thy health willingly; but rest I may not, for I am on duty."

"Why was the letter given to thee, and not sent by a slave?"

"I know not, lord. Perhaps because I was sent in this direction on other duty."

"I know, against the Christians?"

"Yes, lord."

"Is it long since the pursuit was begun?"

"Some divisions were sent to the Trans-Tiber before midday." When he had said this, the centurion shook a little wine from the goblet in honor of Mars; then he emptied it, and said, —

"May the gods grant thee, lord, what thou desirest."

"Take the goblet too," said Petronius.

Then he gave a sign to Anthemios to finish the hymn to Apollo.

"Bronzebeard is beginning to play with me and Vinicius," thought he, when the harps sounded anew. "I divine his plan! He wanted to terrify me by sending the invitation through a centurion. They will ask the centurion in the evening how I received him. No, no! thou wilt not amuse thyself over-much, cruel and wicked prophet. I know that thou wilt not forget the offence, I know that my destruction will not fail; but if thou think that I shall look into thy eyes imploringly, that thou wilt see fear and humility on my face, thou art mistaken."

"Cæsar writes, lord," said Eunice, " 'Come if thou hast the wish'; wilt thou go?"

"I am in excellent health, and can listen even to his verses," answered Petronius; "hence I shall go, all the more since Vinicius cannot go."

In fact, after the dinner was finished and after the usual walk, he gave himself into the hands of hairdressers and of slaves who arranged his robes, and an hour later, beautiful as a god, he gave command to take him to the Palatine.

It was late, the evening was warm and calm; the moon shone so brightly that the lampadarii going before the litter put out their torches. On the streets and among the ruins crowds of people were pushing along, drunk with wine, in garlands of ivy and honeysuckle, bearing in their hands branches of myrtle and laurel taken from Cæsar's gardens. Abundance of grain and hopes of great games filled the hearts of all with gladness. Here and there songs were sung magnifying the "divine night" and love; here and there they were dancing by the light of the moon, and the slaves were forced repeatedly to demand space for the litter "of the noble Petronius," and then the crowd pushed apart, shouting in honor of their favorite.

He was thinking of Vinicius, and wondering why he had no news from him. He was an Epicurean and an egotist, but passing time, now with Paul of Tarsus, now with Vinicius, hearing daily of the Christians, he had changed somewhat without his own knowledge. A certain breeze from them had blown on him; this cast new seeds into his soul. Besides his own person others began to occupy him; moreover, he had been always attached to Vinicius, for in childhood he had loved greatly his sister, the mother of Vinicius; at present, therefore, when he had taken part in his affairs, he looked on them with that interest with which he would have looked on some tragedy.

Petronius did not lose hope that Vinicius had anticipated the pretorians and fled with Lygia, or, in the worse case, had rescued her. But he would have preferred to be certain, since he foresaw that he might have to answer various questions for which he would better be prepared.

Stopping before the house of Tiberius, he alighted from the litter, and after a while entered the atrium, filled already with Augustians. Yesterday's friends, though astonished that he was invited, still pushed back; but he moved on among them, beautiful, free, unconcerned, as self-confident as if he himself had the·power to distribute favors. Some, seeing him thus, were alarmed in spirit lest they had shown him indifference too early.

Cæsar, however, feigned not to see him, and did not return his obeisance, pretending to be occupied in conversation. But Tigellinus approached and said, —

"Good evening, Arbiter Elegantiarum. Dost thou assert still that it was not the Christians who burnt Rome?"

Petronius shrugged his shoulders, and, clapping Tigellinus on the back as he would a freedman, answered, —

"Thou knowest as well as I what to think of that."

"I do not dare to rival thee in wisdom."

"And thou art right, for when Cæsar reads to us a new book from the Troyad, thou, instead of crying out like a jackdaw, wouldst have to give an opinion that was not pointless."

Tigellinus bit his lips. He was not over-rejoiced that Cæsar had decided to read a new book, for that opened a field in which he could not rival Petronius. In fact, during the reading, Nero, from habit, turned his eyes involuntarily toward Petronius, looking carefully to see what he could read in his face. The latter listened, raised his brows, agreed at times, in places increased his attention as if to be sure that he heard correctly. Then he praised or criticised, demanded corrections or the smoothing of certain verses. Nero himself felt that for others in their exaggerated praises it was simply a question of themselves, that Petronius alone was occupied with poetry for its own sake; that he alone understood it, and that if he praised one could be sure that the verses deserved praise. Gradually therefore he began to discuss with him, to dispute; and when at last Petronius brought the fitness of a certain expression into doubt, he said, —

"Thou wilt see in the last book why I used it."

"Ah," thought Petronius, "then we shall wait for the last book."

More than one hearing this said in spirit: "Woe to me! Petronius with time before him may return to favor and overturn even Tigellinus." And they began again to approach him. But the end of the evening was less fortunate; for Cæsar, at the moment when Petronius was taking leave, inquired suddenly. with blinking eyes and a face at once glad and malicious, —

"But why did not Vinicius come?"

Had Petronius been sure that Vinicius and Lygia were beyond the gates of the city, he would have answered, "With thy permission he has married and gone." But seeing Nero's strange smile, he answered, —

"Thy invitation, divinity, did not find him at home."

"Say to Vinicius that I shall be glad to see him," answered Nero, "and tell him from me not to neglect the games in which Christians will appear."

These words alarmed Petronius. It seemed to him that they related to Lygia directly. Sitting in his litter, he gave command to bear him home still more quickly than in the morning. That, however, was not easy. Before the house of Tiberius stood a crowd dense and noisy, drunk as before, though not singing and dancing, but, as it were, excited. From afar came certain shouts which Petronius could not understand at once, but which rose and grew till at last they were one savage roar, —

"To the lions with Christians!"

Rich litters of courtiers pushed through the howling rabble. From the depth of burnt streets new crowds rushed forth continually; these, hearing the cry, repeated it. News passed from mouth to mouth that the pursuit had continued from the forenoon, that a multitude of incendiaries were seized; and immediately along the newly cleared and the old streets, through alleys lying among ruins around the Palatine, over all the hills and gardens were heard through the length and breadth of Rome shouts of swelling rage, —

"To the lions with Christians!"

"Herd!" repeated Petronius, with contempt; "a people worthy of Cæsar!" And he began to think that a society resting on superior force, on cruelty of which even barbarians had no conception, on crimes and mad profligacy, could not endure. Rome ruled the world, but was also its ulcer. The odor of a corpse was rising from it. Over its decaying life the shadow of death was descending. More than once this had been mentioned even among the Augustians, but never before had Petronius had a clearer view of this truth that the laurelled chariot on which Rome stood in the form of a triumphator, and which dragged behind a chained herd of nations, was going to the precipice. The life of that world-ruling city seemed to him a kind of mad dance, an orgy, which must end. He saw then that the Christians alone had a new basis of life; but he judged that soon there would not remain a trace of the Christians. And what then?

The mad dance would continue under Nero; and if Nero disappeared, another would be found of the same kind or worse, for with such a people and such patricians there was no reason to find a better leader. There would be a new orgy, and moreover a fouler and a viler one.

But the orgy could not last forever, and there would be need of sleep when it was over, even because of simple exhaustion.

While thinking of this, Petronius felt immensely wearied. Was it worth while to live, and live in uncertainty, with no purpose but to look at such a society? The genius of death was not less beautiful than the genius of sleep, and he also had wings at his shoulders.

The litter stopped before the arbiter's door, which was opened that instant by the watchful keeper.

"Has the noble Vinicius returned?" inquired Petronius.

"Yes, lord, a moment ago," replied the slave.

"He has not rescued her," thought Petronius. And casting aside his toga, he ran into the atrium. Vinicius was sitting on a stool; his head bent almost to his knees with his hands on his head; but at the sound of steps he raised his stony face, in which the eyes alone had a feverish brightness.

"Thou wert late?" asked Petronius.

"Yes; they seized her before midday."

A moment of silence followed.

"Hast thou seen her?"

"Yes."

"Where is she?"

"In the Mamertine prison."

Petronius trembled and looked at Vinicius with an inquiring glance. The latter understood.

"No," said he. "She was not thrust down to the Tullianum [1] nor even to the middle prison. I paid the guard to give her his own room. Ursus took his place at the threshold and is guarding her."

"Why did Ursus not defend her?"

"They sent fifty pretorians, and Linus forbade him."

"But Linus?"

"Linus is dying; therefore they did not seize him."

"What is thy intention?"

"To save her or die with her. I too believe in Christ."

Vinicius spoke with apparent calmness; but there was such despair in his voice that the heart of Petronius quivered from pure pity.

"I understand thee," said he; "but how dost thou think to save her?"

"I paid the guards highly, first to shield her from indignity, and second not to hinder her flight."

"When can that happen?"

"They answered that they could give her to me at once, as they feared responsibility. When the prison will be filled with a multitude of people, and when the tally of prisoners is confused, they will deliver her. But that is a desperate thing! Do thou save her, and me first! Thou art a friend of Cæsar. He himself gave her to me. Go to him and save me!"

Petronius, instead of answering, called a slave, and, commanding him to bring two dark mantles and two swords, turned to Vinicius, —

"On the way I will tell thee," said he. "Meanwhile take the mantle and weapon, and we will go to the prison. There give the guards a hundred thousand sestertia; give them twice and five times more, if they will free Lygia at once. Otherwise it will be too late."

"Let us go," said Vinicius.

After a while both were on the street.

"Now listen to me," said Petronius. "I did not wish to lose time. I am in

[1] The lowest part of the prison, lying entirely underground, with a single opening in the ceiling. Jugurtha died there of hunger.

disfavor, beginning with to-day. My own life is hanging on a hair; hence I
can do nothing with Cæsar. Worse than that, I am sure that he would act in
opposition to my request. If that were not the case, would I advise thee to
flee with Lygia or to rescue her? Besides, if thou escape, Cæsar's wrath will
turn on me. To-day he would rather do something at thy request than at
mine. Do not count on that, however. Get her out of the prison, and flee!
Nothing else is left. If that does not succeed, there will be time for other
methods. Meanwhile know that Lygia is in prison, not alone for belief in
Christ; Poppæa's anger is pursuing her and thee. Thou hast offended the
Augusta by rejecting her, dost remember? She knows that she was rejected
for Lygia, whom she hated from the first cast of the eye. Nay, she tried to
destroy Lygia before by ascribing the death of her own infant to her witchcraft. The hand of Poppæa is in this. How explain that Lygia was the first to
be imprisoned? Who could point out the house of Linus? But I tell thee that
she has been followed this long time. I know that I wring thy soul, and take
the remnant of thy hope from thee, but I tell thee this purposely, for the
reason that if thou free her not before they come at the idea that thou wilt
try, ye are both lost."

"Yes; I understand!" muttered Vinicius.

The streets were empty because of the late hour. Their further conversation was interrupted, however, by a drunken gladiator who came toward
them. He reeled against Petronius, put one hand on his shoulder, covering his
face with a breath filled with wine, and shouted in a hoarse voice, —

"To the lions with Christians!"

"Mirmillon," answered Petronius, quietly, "listen to good counsel; go thy
way."

With his other hand the drunken man seized him by the arm, —

"Shout with me, or I'll break thy neck: Christians to the lions!"

But the arbiter's nerves had had enough of those shouts. From the time that
he had left the Palatine they had been stifling him like a nightmare, and rending his ears. So when he saw the fist of the giant above him, the measure of
his patience was exceeded.

"Friend," said he, "thou hast the smell of wine, and art stopping my way."

Thus speaking, he drove into the man's breast to the hilt the short sword
which he had brought from home; then, taking the arm of Vinicius, he continued as if nothing had happened, —

"Cæsar said to-day, 'Tell Vinicius from me to be at the games in which
Christians will appear.' Dost understand what that means? They wish to make
a spectacle of thy pain. That is a settled affair. Perhaps that is why thou and I
are not imprisoned yet. If thou art not able to get her at once — I do not
know — Acte might take thy part; but can she effect anything? Thy Sicilian
lands, too, might tempt Tigellinus. Make the trial."

"I will give him all that I have," answered Vinicius.

From the Carinæ to the Forum was not very far; hence they arrived soon.
The night had begun to pale, and the walls of the castle came out definitely
from the shadow.

Suddenly, as they turned toward the Mamertine prison, Petronius stopped, and said, —

"Pretorians! Too late!"

In fact the prison was surrounded by a double rank of soldiers. The morning dawn was silvering their helmets and the points of their javelins.

Vinicius grew as pale as marble. "Let us go on," said he.

After a while they halted before the line. Gifted with an uncommon memory, Petronius knew not only the officers, but nearly all the pretorian soldiers. Soon he saw an acquaintance, a leader of a cohort, and nodded to him.

"But what is this, Niger?" asked he; "are ye commanded to watch the prison?"

"Yes, noble Petronius. The prefect feared lest they might try to rescue the incendiaries."

"Have ye the order to admit no one?" inquired Vinicius.

"We have not; acquaintances will visit the prisoners, and in that way we shall seize more Christians."

"Then let me in," said Vinicius; and pressing Petronius's hand, he said, "See Acte, I will come to learn her answer."

"Come," responded Petronius.

At that moment under the ground and beyond the thick walls was heard singing. The hymn, at first low and muffled, rose more and more. The voices of men, women, and children were mingled in one harmonious chorus. The whole prison began to sound, in the calmness of dawn, like a harp. But those were not voices of sorrow or despair; on the contrary, gladness and triumph were heard in them.

The soldiers looked at one another with amazement. The first golden and rosy gleams of the morning appeared in the sky.

CHAPTER LI

THE cry, "Christians to the lions!" was heard increasingly in every part of the city. At first not only did no one doubt that they were the real authors of the catastrophe, but no one wished to doubt, since their punishment was to be a splendid amusement for the populace. Still the opinion spread that the catastrophe would not have assumed such dreadful proportions but for the anger of the gods; for this reason "piacula," or purifying sacrifices, were commanded in the temples. By advice of the Sibylline books, the Senate ordained solemnities and public prayer to Vulcan, Ceres, and Proserpina. Matrons made offerings to Juno; a whole procession of them went to the seashore to take water and sprinkle with it the statue of the goddess. Married women prepared feasts to the gods and night watches. All Rome purified itself from sin, made offerings, and placated the Immortals. Meanwhile new broad streets were opened among the ruins. In one place and another foundations were laid for magnificent houses, palaces, and temples. But first of all they built with unheard-of haste an enormous wooden amphitheatre in which Christians were to die. Immediately after that consultation in the house of Tiberius, orders went to consuls to furnish wild beasts. Tigellinus emptied the vivaria of all Italian cities, not excepting the smaller ones. In Africa, at his command, gigantic hunts were organized, in which the entire local population was forced to take part. Elephants and tigers were brought in from Asia, crocodiles and hippopotamuses from the Nile, lions from the Atlas, wolves and bears from the Pyrenees, savage hounds from Hibernia, Molossian dogs from Epirus, bisons and the gigantic wild aurochs from Germany. Because of the number of prisoners, the games were to surpass in greatness anything seen up to that time. Cæsar wished to drown all memory of the fire in blood, and make Rome drunk with it; hence never had there been a greater promise of bloodshed.

The willing people helped guards and pretorians in hunting Christians. That was no difficult labor for whole groups of them camped with the other population in the midst of the gardens, and confessed their faith openly. When surrounded, they knelt, and while singing hymns let themselves be borne away without resistance. But their patience only increased the anger of the populace, who, not understanding its origin, considered it as rage and persistence in crime. A madness seized the persecutors. It happened that the mob wrested Christians from pretorians, and tore them to pieces; women were dragged to prison by the hair; children's heads were dashed against stones. Thousands of people rushed, howling, night and day through the streets. Victims were sought in ruins, in chimneys, in cellars. Before the prison bacchanalian feasts and dances were celebrated at fires, around casks of wine.

In the evening was heard with delight bellowing which was like thunder, and which sounded throughout the city. The prisons were overflowing with thousands of people; every day the mob and pretorians drove in new victims. Pity had died out. It seemed that people had forgotten to speak, and in their wild frenzy remembered one shout alone: "To the lions with Christians!" Wonderfully hot days came, and nights more stifling than ever before; the very air seemed filled with blood, crime, and madness.

And that surpassing measure of cruelty was answered by an equal measure of desire for martyrdom, — the confessors of Christ went to death willingly, or even sought death till they were restrained by the stern commands of superiors. By the injunction of these superiors they began to assemble only outside the city, in excavations near the Appian Way, and in vineyards belonging to patrician Christians, of whom none had been imprisoned so far. It was known perfectly on the Palatine that to the confessors of Christ belonged Flavius, Domitilla, Pomponia Græcina, Cornelius Pudens, and Vinicius. Cæsar himself, however, feared that the mob would not believe that such people had burned Rome, and since it was important beyond everything to convince the mob, punishment and vengeance were deferred till later days. Others were of the opinion, but erroneously, that those patricians were saved by the influence of Acte. Petronius, after parting with Vinicius, turned to Acte, it is true, to gain assistance for Lygia; but she could offer him only tears, for she lived in oblivion and suffering, and was endured only in so far as she hid herself from Poppæa and Cæsar.

But she had visited Lygia in prison, she had carried her clothing and food, and above all had saved her from injury on the part of the prison-guards, who, moreover, were bribed already.

Petronius, unable to forget that had it not been for him and his plan of taking Lygia from the house of Aulus, probably she would not be in prison at that moment, and, besides, wishing to win the game against Tigellinus, spared neither time nor efforts. In the course of a few days he saw Seneca, Domitius Afer, Crispinilla, and Diodorus, through whom he wished to reach Poppæa; he saw Terpnos, and the beautiful Pythagoras, and finally Aliturus and Paris, to whom Cæsar usually refused nothing. With the help of Chrysothemis, then mistress of Vatinius, he tried to gain even his aid, not sparing in this case and in others promises and money.

But all these efforts were fruitless. Seneca, uncertain of the morrow, fell to explaining to him that the Christians, even if they had not burned Rome, should be exterminated, for the good of the city, — in a word, he justified the coming slaughter for political reasons. Terpnos and Diodorus took the money, and did nothing in return for it. Vatinius reported to Cæsar that they had been trying to bribe him. Aliturus alone, who at first was hostile to the Christians, took pity on them then, and made bold to mention to Cæsar the imprisoned maiden, and to implore in her behalf. He obtained nothing, however, but the answer, —

"Dost thou think that I have a soul inferior to that of Brutus, who spared not his own sons for the good of Rome?"

When this answer was repeated to Petronius, he said, —

"Since Nero has compared himself to Brutus, there is no salvation."

But he was sorry for Vinicius, and dread seized him lest he might attempt his own life. "Now," thought the arbiter, "he is upheld by the efforts which he makes to save her, by the sight of her, and by his own suffering; but when all means fail and the last ray of hope is quenched, by Castor! he will not survive, he will throw himself on his sword." Petronius understood better how to die thus than to love and suffer like Vinicius.

Meanwhile Vinicius did all that he could think of to save Lygia. He visited Augustians; and he, once so proud, now begged their assistance. Through Vitelius he offered Tigellinus all his Sicilian estates, and whatever else the man might ask; but Tigellinus, not wishing apparently to offend the Augusta, refused. To go to Cæsar himself, embrace his knees and implore, would lead to nothing. Vinicius wished, it is true, to do this; but Petronius, hearing of his purpose, inquired, —

"But should he refuse thee, or answer with a jest or a shameless threat, what wouldst thou do?"

At this the young tribune's features contracted with pain and rage, and from his fixed jaws a gritting sound was heard.

"Yes," said Petronius, "I advise thee against this, because thou wouldst close all paths of rescue."

Vinicius restrained himself, and passing his palm over his forehead, which was covered with cold sweat, replied, —

"No, no! I am a Christian."

"But thou will forget this, as thou didst a moment ago. Thou hast the right to ruin thyself, but not her. Remember what the daughter of Sejanus passed through before death."

Speaking thus he was not altogether sincere, since he was concerned more for Vinicius than for Lygia. Still he knew that in no way could he restrain him from a dangerous step as well as by telling him that he would bring inexorable destruction on Lygia. Moreover he was right; for on the Palatine they had counted on the visit of the young tribune, and had taken needful precautions.

But the suffering of Vinicius surpassed human endurance. From the moment that Lygia was imprisoned and the glory of coming martyrdom had fallen on her, not only did he love her a hundred times more, but he began simply to give her in his soul almost religious honor, as he would a superhuman being. And now, at the thought that he must lose this being both loved and holy, that besides death torments might be inflicted on her more terrible than death itself, the blood stiffened in his veins. His soul was turned into one groan, his thoughts were confused. At times it seemed to him that his skull was filled with living fire, which would either burn or burst it. He ceased to understand what was happening; he ceased to understand why Christ, the Merciful, the Divine, did not come with aid to His adherents; why the dingy walls of the Palatine did not sink through the earth, and with them Nero, the Augustians, the pretorian camp, and all that city of crime. He thought that it could not and should not be otherwise; and all that his eyes saw, and because of which his heart was breaking, was a dream. But the roaring of wild beasts informed him that it was reality; the sound of the axes beneath which rose the arena told him that it was reality; the howling of the people and the overfilled prisons confirmed this. Then his faith in Christ was alarmed; and that alarm was a new torture, the most dreadful of all, perhaps.

"Remember what the daughter of Sejanus endured before death," said Petronius to him, meanwhile.

CHAPTER LII

AND everything had failed. Vinicius lowered himself to the degree that he sought support from freedmen and slaves, both those of Cæsar and Poppæa; he overpaid their empty promises, he won their good will with rich gifts. He found the first husband of Poppæa, Rufius Crispinus, and obtained from him a letter. He gave a villa in Antium to Rufius, her son by the first marriage; but thereby he merely angered Cæsar, who hated his step-son. By a special courier he sent a letter to Poppæa's second husband, Otho, in Spain. He sacrificed his property and himself, until he saw at last that he was simply the plaything of people; that if he had pretended that the imprisonment of Lygia concerned him little, he would have freed her sooner.

Petronius saw this, too. Meanwhile day followed day. The amphitheatre was finished. The "tesseræ" were distributed, — that is, tickets of entrance, to the ludus matutinus (morning games). But this time the morning games, because of the unheard-of number of victims, were to continue for days, weeks, and months. It was not known where to put the Christians. The prisons were crammed, and fever was raging in them. The puticuli — common pits in which slaves were kept — began to be overfilled. There was fear that diseases might spread over the whole city; hence, haste.

All these reports struck the ears of Vinicius, extinguishing in him the last hope. While there was yet time, he might delude himself with the belief that he could do something, but now there was no time. The spectacles must begin. Lygia might find herself any day in a cuniculum of the circus, whence the only exit was to the arena. Vinicius, not knowing whither fate and the cruelty of superior force might throw her, visited all the circuses, bribed guards and beast-keepers, laying before them plans which they could not execute. In time he saw that he was working for this only, — to make death less terrible to her; and just then he felt that instead of brains he had glowing coals in his head.

For the rest he had no thought of surviving her, and determined to perish at the same time. But he feared lest pain might burn his life out before the dreadful hour came. His friends and Petronius thought also that any day might open the kingdom of shadows before him. His face was black, and resembled those waxen masks kept in lararia. In his features astonishment had grown frigid, as if he had no understanding of what had happened and what might happen. When any one spoke to him, he raised his hands to his face mechanically, and, pressing his temples, looked at the speaker with an inquiring and astonished gaze. He passed whole nights with Ursus at Lygia's door in the prison; if she commanded him to go away and rest, he returned to

Petronius, and walked in the atrium till morning. The slaves found him frequently kneeling with upraised hands or lying with his face to the earth. He prayed to Christ, for Christ was his last hope. Everything had failed him. Only a miracle could save Lygia; hence he beat the stone flags with his forehead and prayed for the miracle.

But he knew enough yet to understand that Peter's prayers were more important than his own. Peter had promised him Lygia, Peter had baptized him, Peter had performed miracles, let him give aid and rescue.

And a certain night he went to seek the Apostle. The Christians, of whom not many remained, had concealed him now carefully even from other brethren, lest any of the weaker in spirit might betray him wittingly or unwittingly. Vinicius, amid the general confusion and disaster, occupied also in efforts to get Lygia out of prison, had lost sight of Peter, he had barely seen him once from the time of his own baptism till the beginning of the persecution. But betaking himself to that quarryman in whose hut he was baptized, he learned that there would be a meeting outside the Porta Salaria in a vineyard which belonged to Cornelius Pudens. The quarryman offered to guide him, and declared that he would find Peter there. They started about dusk, and, passing beyond the wall, through hollows overgrown with reeds, reached the vineyard in a wild and lonely place. The meeting was held in a wine-shed. As Vinicius drew near, the murmur of prayer reached his ears. On entering he saw by dim lamplight a few tens of kneeling figures sunk in prayer. They were saying a kind of litany; a chorus of voices, male and female, repeated every moment, "Christ have mercy on us." In those voices, deep, piercing sadness and sorrow were heard.

Peter was present. He was kneeling in front of the others, before a wooden cross nailed to the wall of the shed, and was praying. From a distance Vinicius recognized his white hair and his upraised hands. The first thought of the young patrician was to pass through the assembly, cast himself at the Apostle's feet, and cry, "Save!" but whether it was the solemnity of the prayer, or because weakness bent the knees under Vinicius, he began to repeat while he groaned and clasped his hands: "Christ have mercy!" Had he been conscious, he would have understood that his was not the only prayer in which there was a groan; that he was not the only one who had brought with him his pain, alarm, and grief. There was not in that assembly one soul which had not lost persons dear to the heart; and when the most zealous and courageous confessors were in prison already, when with every moment new tidings were borne about of insults and tortures inflicted on them in the prisons, when the greatness of the calamity exceeded every imagination, when only that handful remained, there was not one heart there which was not terrified in its faith, which did not ask doubtfully, Where is Christ? and why does He let evil be mightier than God? Meanwhile they implored Him despairingly for mercy, since in each soul there still smouldered a spark of hope that He would come, hurl Nero into the abyss, and rule the world. They looked yet toward the sky; they listened yet; they prayed yet with trembling. Vinicius, too, in proportion as they repeated, "Christ have mercy on us!" was seized by such an ecstasy as formerly in the quarryman's hut. Now from the depths they call on Him in the profoundness of their sorrow, now Peter calls on Him; so any moment the heavens may be rent, the earth tremble to its foundations, and He appear in infinite glory, with stars at His feet, merciful, but awful. He will raise up the faithful, and command the abysses to swallow the persecutors.

Vinicius covered his face with both hands, and bowed to the earth. Immediately silence was around him, as if fear had stopped further breathing on the lips of all present. And it seemed to him that something must happen surely, that a moment of miracle would follow. He felt certain that when he rose and opened his eyes he would see a light from which mortal eyes would be blinded, and hear a voice from which hearts would grow faint.

But the silence was unbroken. It was interrupted at last by the sobbing of women. Vinicius rose and looked forward with dazed eyes. In the shed, instead of glories not of earth, shone the faint gleam of lanterns, and rays of the moon, entering through an opening in the roof, filled the place with silvery light. The people kneeling around Vinicius raised their tearful eyes toward the cross in silence; here and there sobbing was heard, and from outside came the warning whistles of watchmen. Meanwhile Peter rose, and, turning to the assembly, said, —

"Children, raise your hearts to the Redeemer and offer Him your tears."

After that he was silent.

All at once was heard the voice of a woman, full of sorrowful complaint and pain, —

"I am a widow; I had one son who supported me. Give him back, O Lord!"

Silence followed again. Peter was standing before the kneeling audience, old, full of care. In that moment he seemed to them decrepitude and weakness personified. With that a second voice began to complain, —

"Executioners insulted my daughter, and Christ permitted them!"

Then a third, —

"I alone have remained to my children, and when I am taken who will give them bread and water?"

Then a fourth, —

"Linus, spared at first, they have taken now and put to torture, O Lord!"

Then a fifth, —

"When we return to our houses, pretorians will seize us. We know not where to hide."

"Woe to us! Who will protect us?"

And thus in that silence of the night complaint after complaint was heard. The old fisherman closed his eyes and shook his white head over that human pain and fear. New silence followed; the watchman merely gave out low whistles beyond the shed.

Vinicius sprang up again, so as to break through the crowd to the Apostle and demand salvation; but on a sudden he saw before him, as it were, a precipice, the sight of which took strength from his feet. What if the Apostle were to confess his own weakness, affirm that the Roman Cæsar was stronger than Christ the Nazarene? And at that thought terror raised the hair on his head, for he felt that in such a case not only the remnant of his hope would fall into that abyss, but with it he himself, and all through which he had life, and there would remain only night and death, resembling a shoreless sea.

Meanwhile Peter began to speak in a voice so low at first that it was barely possible to hear him, —

"My children, on Golgotha I saw them nail God to the cross. I heard the hammers, and I saw them raise the cross on high, so that the rabble might gaze at the death of the Son of Man. I saw them open His side, and I saw Him die. When returning from the cross, I cried in pain, as ye are crying, 'Woe! woe! O Lord, Thou art God! Why hast Thou permitted this? Why hast Thou died, and why hast Thou tormented the hearts of us who believed that Thy kingdom would come?'

"But He, our Lord and God, rose from the dead the third day, and was among us till He entered His kingdom in great glory.

"And we, seeing our little faith, became strong in heart, and from that time we are sowing His grain."

Here, turning toward the place whence the first complaint came, he began in a voice now stronger, —

"Why do ye complain? God gave Himself to torture and death, and ye wish Him to shield you from the same. People of little faith, have ye received His teaching? Has He promised you nothing but life? He comes to you and says, 'Follow in my path.' He raises you to Himself, and ye catch at this earth with your hands, crying, 'Lord, save us!' I am dust before God, but before you I am His apostle and vicegerent. I speak to you in the name of Christ. Not death is before you, but life; not tortures, but endless delights; not tears and groans, but singing; not bondage, but rule! I, God's apostle, say this: O widow, thy son will not die; he will be born into glory, into eternal life, and thou wilt rejoin him! To thee, O father, whose innocent daughter was defiled by executioners, I promise that thou shalt find her whiter than the lilies of Hebron! To you, mothers, whom they are tearing away from your orphans; to you who lose fathers; to you who complain; to you who will see the death of loved ones; to you the careworn, the unfortunate, the timid; to you who must die, — in the name of Christ I declare that ye will wake as if from sleep to a happy waking, as if from night to the light of God. In the name of Christ, let the beam fall from your eyes, and let your hearts be inflamed."

When he had said this, he raised his hand as if commanding, and they felt new blood in their veins, and also a quiver in their bones; for before them was standing, not a decrepit and careworn old man, but a potentate, who took their souls and raised them from dust and terror.

"Amen!" called a number of voices.

From the Apostle's eyes came a light ever increasing, power issued from him, majesty issued from him, and holiness. Heads bent before him, and he, when the "Amen" ceased, continued: —

"Ye sow in tears to reap in joy. Why fear ye the power of evil? Above the earth, above Rome, above the walls of cities is the Lord, who has taken His dwelling within you. The stones will be wet from tears, the sand steeped in blood, the valleys will be filled with your bodies, but I say that ye are victorious. The Lord is advancing to the conquest of this city of crime, oppression, and pride, and ye are His legions! He redeemed with His own blood and torture the sins of the world; so He wishes that ye should redeem with torture and blood this nest of injustice. This He announces to you through my lips."

And he opened his arms, and fixed his eyes upward; the hearts almost ceased to beat in their breasts, for they felt that his glance beheld something which their mortal sight could not see.

In fact, his face had changed, and was overspread with serenity; he gazed some time in silence, as if speechless from ecstasy, but after a while they heard his voice, —

"Thou art here, O Lord, and dost show Thy ways to me. True, O Christ! Not in Jerusalem, but in this city of Satan wilt Thou fix Thy capital. Here out of these tears and this blood dost Thou wish to build Thy Church. Here, where Nero rules to-day, Thy eternal kingdom is to stand. Thine, O Lord, O Lord! And Thou commandest these timid ones to form the foundation of Thy holy Zion of their bones, and Thou commandest my spirit to assume rule over it, and over peoples of the earth. And Thou art pouring the fountain of strength on the weak, so that they become strong; and now Thou commandest me to feed Thy sheep from this spot, to the end of ages. Oh, be Thou praised in Thy decrees by which Thou commandest to conquer. Hosanna! Hosanna!"

Those who were timid rose; into those who doubted streams of faith flowed. Some voices cried, "Hosanna!" others, "Pro Christo!" Then silence followed. Bright summer lightning illuminated the interior of the shed, and the pale, excited faces.

Peter, fixed in a vision, prayed a long time yet; but conscious at last, he turned his inspired face, full of light, to the assembly, and said, —

"This is how the Lord has overcome doubt in you; so ye will go to victory in His name."

And though he knew that they would conquer, though he knew what would grow out of their tears and blood, still his voice quivered with emotion when he was blessing them with the cross, and he said, —

"Now I bless you, my children, as ye go to torture, to death, to eternity."

They gathered round him and wept. "We are ready," said they; "but do thou, O holy head, guard thyself, for thou art the vicegerent who performs the office of Christ."

And thus speaking, they seized his mantle; he placed his hands on their heads, and blessed each one separately, just as a father does children whom he is sending on a long journey.

And they began at once to go out of the shed, for they were in a hurry, to their houses, and from them to the prisons and arenas. Their thoughts were separated from the earth, their souls had taken flight toward eternity, and they walked on as if in a dream, in ecstasy opposing that force which was in them to the force and the cruelty of the "Beast."

Nereus, the servant of Pudens, took the Apostle and led him by a secret path in the vineyard to his house. But Vinicius followed them in the clear night, and when they reached the cottage of Nereus at last, he threw himself suddenly at the feet of the Apostle.

"What dost thou wish, my son?" asked Peter, recognizing him.

After what he had heard in the vineyard, Vinicius dared not implore him for anything; but, embracing his feet with both hands, he pressed his forehead to them with sobbing, and called for compassion in that dumb manner.

"I know. They took the maiden whom thou lovest. Pray for her."

"Lord," groaned Vinicius, embracing his feet still more firmly, — "Lord, I am a wretched worm; but thou didst know Christ. Implore Him, — take her part."

And from pain he trembled like a leaf; and he beat the earth with his forehead, for, knowing the strength of the Apostle, he knew that he alone could rescue her.

Peter was moved by that pain. He remembered how on a time Lygia herself, when attacked by Crispus, lay at his feet in like manner imploring pity. He remembered that he had raised her and comforted her; hence now he raised Vinicius.

"My son," said he, "I will pray for her; but do thou remember that I told those doubting ones that God Himself passed through the torment of the cross, and remember that after this life begins another, —an eternal one."

"I know; I have heard!" answered Vinicius, catching the air with his pale lips; "but thou seest, lord, that I cannot! If blood is required, implore Christ to take mine, — I am a soldier. Let Him double, let Him triple, the torment intended for her, I will suffer it; but let Him spare her. She is a child yet, and He is mightier than Cæsar, I believe, mightier. Thou didst love her thyself; thou didst bless us. She is an innocent child yet."

Again he bowed, and, putting his face to Peter's knees, he repeated, —

"Thou didst know Christ, lord, — thou didst know Him. He will give ear to thee; take her part."

Peter closed his lids, and prayed earnestly. The summer lightning illuminated the sky again. Vinicius, by the light of it, looked at the lips of the Apostle, waiting sentence of life or death from them. In the silence quails were heard calling in the vineyard, and the dull, distant sound of treadmills near the Via Salaria.

"Vinicius," asked the Apostle at last, "dost thou believe?"

"Would I have come hither if I believed not?" answered Vinicius.

"Then believe to the end, for faith will remove mountains. Hence, though thou wert to see that maiden under the sword of the executioner or in the jaws of a lion, believe that Christ can save her. Believe, and pray to Him, and I will pray with thee."

Then, raising his face toward heaven, he said aloud, —

"O merciful Christ, look on this aching heart and console it! O merciful

Christ, temper the wind to the fleece of the lamb! O merciful Christ, who didst implore the Father to turn away the bitter cup from Thy mouth, turn it from the mouth of this Thy servant! Amen."

But Vinicius, stretching his hand toward the stars, said, groaning, —

"I am Thine; take me instead of her."

The sky began to grow pale in the east.

CHAPTER LIII

VINICIUS, on leaving the Apostle, went to the prison with a heart renewed by hope. Somewhere in the depth of his soul, despair and terror were still crying; but he stifled those voices. It seemed to him impossible that the intercession of the vicegerent of God and the power of his prayer should be without effect. He feared to hope; he feared to doubt. "I will believe in His mercy," said he to himself, "even though I saw her in the jaws of a lion." And at this thought, even though the soul quivered in him and cold sweat drenched his temples, he believed. Every throb of his heart was a prayer then. He began to understand that faith would move mountains, for he felt in himself a wonderful strength, which he had not felt earlier. It seemed to him that he could do things which he had not the power to do the day before. At moments he had an impression that the danger had passed. If despair was heard groaning again in his soul, he recalled that night, and that holy gray face raised to heaven in prayer. "No, Christ will not refuse His first disciple and the pastor of His flock! Christ will not refuse him! I will not doubt!" And he ran toward the prison as a herald of good news.

But there an unexpected thing awaited him.

All the pretorian guards taking turn before the Mamertine prison knew him, and generally they raised not the least difficulty; this time, however, the line did not open, but a centurion approached him and said, —

"Pardon, noble tribune, to-day we have a command to admit no one."

"A command?" repeated Vinicius, growing pale.

The soldier looked at him with pity, and answered, —

"Yes, lord, a command of Cæsar. In the prison there are many sick, and perhaps it is feared that visitors might spread infection through the city."

"But hast thou said that the order was for to-day only?"

"The guards change at noon."

Vinicius was silent and uncovered his head, for it seemed to him that the pileolus which he wore was of lead.

Meanwhile the soldier approached him, and said in a low voice, —

"Be at rest, lord, the guard and Ursus are watching over her." When he had said this, he bent and, in the twinkle of an eye, drew with his long Gallic sword on the flag stone the form of a fish.

Vinicius looked at him quickly.

"And thou art a pretorian?"

"Till I shall be there," answered the soldier, pointing to the prison.

"And I, too, worship Christ."

"May His name be praised! I know, lord, I cannot admit thee to the prison, but write a letter, I will give it to the guard."

"Thanks to thee, brother."

He pressed the soldier's hand, and went away. The pileolus ceased to weigh like lead. The morning sun rose over the walls of the prison, and with its brightness consolation began to enter his heart again. That Christian soldier was for him a new witness of the power of Christ. After a while he halted, and, fixing his glance on the rosy clouds above the Capitol and the temple of Jupiter Stator, he said, —

"I have not seen her to-day, O Lord, but I believe in Thy mercy."

At the house he found Petronius, who, making day out of night as usual, had returned not long before. He had succeeded, however, in taking his bath and anointing himself for sleep.

"I have news for thee," said he. "To-day I was with Tullius Senecio, whom Cæsar also visited. I know not whence it came to the mind of the Augusta to bring little Rufius with her, — perhaps to soften the heart of Cæsar by his beauty. Unfortunately, the child, wearied by drowsiness, fell asleep during the reading, as Vespasian did once; seeing this, Ahenobarbus hurled a goblet at his step-son, and wounded him seriously. Poppæa fainted; all heard how Cæsar said, 'I have enough of this brood!' and that, knowest thou, means as much as death."

"The punishment of God was hanging over the Augusta," answered Vinicius; "but why dost thou tell me this?"

"I tell thee because the anger of Poppæa pursued thee and Lygia; occupied now by her own misfortune, she may leave her vengeance and be more easily influenced. I will see her this evening and talk with her."

"Thanks to thee. Thou givest me good news."

"But do thou bathe and rest. Thy lips are blue, and there is not a shadow of thee left."

"Is not the time of the first 'ludus matutinus' announced?" inquired Vinicius.

"In ten days. But they will take other prisons first. The more time that remains to us the better. All is not lost yet."

But he did not believe this; for he knew perfectly that since to the request of Aliturus, Cæsar had found the splendidly sounding answer in which he compared himself to Brutus, there was no rescue for Lygia. He hid also, through pity, what he had heard at Senecio's, that Cæsar and Tigellinus had decided to select for themselves and their friends the most beautiful Christian maidens, and defile them before the torture; the others were to be given, on the day of the games, to pretorians and beast-keepers.

Knowing that Vinicius would not survive Lygia in any case, he strengthened hope in his heart designedly, first, through sympathy for him; and second, because he wished that if Vinicius had to die, he should die beautiful, — not with a face deformed and black from pain and watching.

"To-day I will speak more or less thus to Augusta," said he: " 'Save Lygia for Vinicius, I will save Rufius for thee.' And I will think of that seriously.

One word spoken to Ahenobarbus at the right moment may save or ruin any one. In the worst case, we will gain time."

"Thanks to thee," repeated Vinicius.

"Thou wilt thank me best if thou eat and sleep. By Athene! In the greatest straits Odysseus had sleep and food in mind. Thou hast spent the whole night in prison, of course?"

"No," answered Vinicius; "I wished to visit the prison to-day, but there is an order to admit no one. Learn, O Petronius, if the order is for to-day alone, or till the day of the games."

"I will discover this evening, and to-morrow morning will tell thee for what time and why the order was issued. But now, even were Helios to go to Cimmerian regions from sorrow, I shall sleep, and do thou follow my example."

They separated; but Vinicius went to the library and wrote a letter to Lygia. When he had finished, he took it himself to the Christian centurion, who carried it at once to the prison. After a while he returned with a greeting from Lygia, and promised to deliver her answer that day.

Vinicius did not wish to return home, but sat on a stone and waited for Lygia's letter. The sun had risen high in the heavens, and crowds of people flowed in, as usual, through the Clivus Argentarius to the Forum. Hucksters called out their wares, soothsayers offered their services to passers-by, citizens walked with deliberate steps toward the rostra to hear orators of the day, or tell the latest news to one another. As the heat increased, crowds of idlers betook themselves to the porticos of the temples, from under which flew from moment to moment, with great rustle of wings, flocks of doves, whose white feathers glistened in the sunlight and in the blue of the sky.

From excess of light and the influence of bustle, heat, and great weariness, the eyes of Vinicius began to close. The monotonous calls of boys playing mora, and the measured tread of soldiers, lulled him to sleep. He raised his head still a number of times, and took in the prison with his eyes; then he leaned against a stone, sighed like a child drowsy after long weeping, and dropped asleep.

Soon dreams came. It seemed to him that he was carrying Lygia in his arms at night through a strange vineyard. Before him was Pomponia Græcina lighting the way with a lamp. A voice, as it were of Petronius called from afar to him, "Turn back!" but he did not mind the call, and followed Pomponia till they reached a cottage; at the threshold of the cottage stood Peter. He showed Peter Lygia, and said, "We are coming from the arena, lord, but we cannot wake her; wake her thou." "Christ himself will come to wake her," answered the Apostle.

Then the pictures began to change. Through the dream he saw Nero, and Poppæa holding in her arms little Rufius with bleeding head, which Petronius was washing; and he saw Tigellinus sprinkling ashes on tables covered with costly dishes, and Vitelius devouring those dishes, while a multitude of other Augustians were sitting at the feast. He himself was resting near Lygia; but between the tables walked lions from out whose yellow manes trickled blood. Lygia begged him to take her away, but so terrible a weakness had seized him that he could not even move. Then still greater disorder involved his visions, and finally all fell into perfect darkness.

He was roused from deep sleep at last by the heat of the sun, and shouts given forth right there around the place where he was sitting. Vinicius rubbed his eyes. The street was swarming with people; but two runners, wearing yellow tunics, pushed aside the throng with long staffs, crying and making room for a splendid litter which was carried by four stalwart Egyptian slaves.

In the litter sat a man in white robes, whose face was not easily seen, for he held close to his eyes a roll of papyrus and was reading something diligently.

"Make way for the noble Augustian!" cried the runners.

But the street was so crowded that the litter had to wait awhile. The Augustian put down his roll of papyrus and bent his head, crying, —

"Push aside those wretches! Make haste!"

Seeing Vinicius suddenly, he drew back his head and raised the papyrus quickly.

Vinicius drew his hand across his forehead, thinking that he was dreaming yet.

In the litter was sitting Chilo.

Meanwhile the runners had opened the way, and the Egyptians were ready to move, when the young tribune, who in one moment understood many things which till then had been incomprehensible, approached the litter.

"A greeting to thee, O Chilo!" said he.

"Young man," answered the Greek, with pride and importance, endeavoring to give his face an expression of calmness which was not in his soul, "be greeted, but detain me not, for I am hastening to my friend, the noble Tigellinus."

Vinicius, grasping the edge of the litter and looking him straight in the eyes, said with a lowered voice, —

"Didst thou betray Lygia?"

"Colossus of Memnon!" cried Chilo, with fear.

But there was no threat in the eyes of Vinicius; hence the old Greek's alarm vanished quickly. He remembered that he was under the protection of Tigellinus and of Cæsar himself, — that is, of a power before which everything trembled, — that he was surrounded by sturdy slaves, and that Vinicius stood before him unarmed, with an emaciated face and body bent by suffering.

At this thought his insolence returned to him. He fixed on Vinicius his eyes, which were surrounded by red lids, and whispered in answer, —

"But thou, when I was dying of hunger, didst give command to flog me."

For a moment both were silent; then the dull voice of Vinicius was heard, —

"I wronged thee, Chilo."

The Greek raised his head, and, snapping his fingers which in Rome was a mark of slight and contempt, said so loudly that all could hear him, —

"Friend, if thou hast a petition to present, come to my house on the Esquiline in the morning hour, when I receive guests and clients after my bath."

And he waved his hand; at that sign the Egyptians raised the litter, and the slaves, dressed in yellow tunics, began to cry as they brandished their staffs, —

"Make way for the litter of the noble Chilo Chilonides! Make way, make way!"

CHAPTER LIV

LYGIA, in a long letter written hurriedly, took farewell to Vinicius forever. She knew that no one was permitted to enter the prison, and that she could see Vinicius only from the arena. She begged him therefore to discover when the turn of the Mamertine prisoners would come, and to be at the games, for she wished to see him once more in life. No fear was evident in her letter. She wrote that she and the others were longing for the arena, where they would find liberation from imprisonment. She hoped for the coming of Pomponia and Aulus; she entreated that they too be present. Every word of her showed ecstasy, and that separation from life in which all the prisoners lived, and at the same time an unshaken faith that all promises would be fulfilled beyond the grave.

"Whether Christ," wrote she, "frees me in this life or after death, He has promised me to thee by the lips of the Apostle; therefore I am thine." She implored him not to grieve for her, and not to let himself be overcome by suffering. For her death was not a dissolution of marriage. With the confidence of a child she assured Vinicius that immediately after her suffering in the arena she would tell Christ that her betrothed Marcus had remained in Rome, that he was longing for her with his whole heart. And she thought that Christ would permit her soul, perhaps, to return to him for a moment, to tell him that she was living, that she did not remember her torments, and that she was happy. Her whole letter breathed happiness and immense hope. There was only one request in it connected with affairs of earth, — that Vinicius should take her body from the spoliarium and bury it as that of his wife in the tomb in which he himself would rest sometime.

He read this letter with a suffering spirit, but at the same time it seemed to him impossible that Lygia should perish under the claws of wild beasts, and that Christ would not take compassion on her. But just in that were hidden hope and trust. When he returned home, he wrote that he would come every day to the walls of the Tullianum to wait till Christ crushed the walls and restored her. He commanded her to believe that Christ could give her to him, even in the Circus; that the great Apostle was imploring Him to do so, and that the hour of liberation was near. The converted centurion was to bear this letter to her on the morrow.

But when Vinicius came to the prison next morning, the centurion left the rank, approached him first, and said, —

"Listen to me, lord. Christ, who enlightened thee, has shown thee favor. Last night Cæsar's freedman and those of the prefect came to select Christian maidens for disgrace; they inquired for thy betrothed, but our Lord sent her a fever, of which prisoners are dying in the Tullianum, and they left her. Last evening she was unconscious, and blessed be the name of the Redeemer, for the sickness which has saved her from shame may save her from death."

Vinicius placed his hand on the soldier's shoulder to guard himself from falling; but the other continued, —

"Thank the mercy of the Lord! They took and tortured Linus, but, seeing that he was dying, they surrendered him. They may give her now to thee, and Christ will give back health to her."

The young tribune stood some time with drooping head; then raised it and said in a whisper, —

"True, centurion. Christ, who saved her from shame, will save her from death." And sitting at the wall of the prison till evening, he returned home to send people for Linus and have him taken to one of his suburban villas.

But when Petronius had heard everything, he determined to act also. He had visited the Augusta; now he went to her a second time. He found her at the bed of little Rufius. The child with broken head was struggling in a fever; his mother, with despair and terror in her heart, was trying to save him, thinking, however, that if she did save him it might be only to perish soon by a more dreadful death.

Occupied exclusively with her own suffering, she would not even hear of Vinicius and Lygia; but Petronius terrified her.

"Thou hast offended," said he to her, "a new, unknown divinity. Thou, Augusta, art a worshipper, it seems, of the Hebrew Jehovah; but the Christians maintain that Chrestos is his son. Reflect, then, if the anger of the father is not pursuing thee. Who knows but it is their vengeance which has struck thee? Who knows but the life of Rufius depends on this, — how thou wilt act?"

"What dost thou wish me to do?" asked Poppæa, with terror.

"Mollify the offended deities."

"How?"

"Lygia is sick; influence Cæsar or Tigellinus to give her to Vinicius."

"Dost thou think that I can do that?" asked she, in despair.

"Thou canst do something else. If Lygia recovers, she must die. Go thou to the temple of Vesta, and ask the virgo magna to happen near the Tullianum at the moment when they are leading prisoners out to death, and give command to free that maiden. The chief vestal will not refuse thee."

"But if Lygia dies of the fever?"

"The Christians say that Christ is vengeful, but just; maybe thou wilt soften Him by thy wish alone."

"Let Him give me some sign that will heal Rufius."

Petronius shrugged his shoulders.

"I have not come as His envoy; O divinity, I merely say to thee, Be on better terms with all the gods, Roman and foreign."

"I will go!" said Poppæa, with a broken voice.

Petronius drew a deep breath. "At last I have done something," thought he, and returning to Vinicius he said to him, —

"Implore thy God that Lygia die not of the fever, for should she survive, the chief vestal will give command to free her. The Augusta herself will ask her to do so."

"Christ will free her," said Vinicius, looking at him with eyes in which fever was glittering.

Poppæa, who for the recovery of Rufius was willing to burn hecatombs to all the gods of the world, went that same evening through the Forum to the vestals, leaving care over the sick child to her faithful nurse, Silvia, by whom she herself had been reared.

But on the Palatine sentence had been issued against the child already; for barely had Poppæa's litter vanished behind the great gate when two freedmen entered the chamber in which her son was resting. One of these threw himself on old Silvia and gagged her; the other, seizing a bronze statue of the Sphinx, stunned the old woman with the first blow.

Then they approached Rufius. The little boy, tormented with fever and insensible, not knowing what was passing around him, smiled at them, and blinked with his beautiful eyes, as if trying to recognize the men. Stripping from the nurse her girdle, they put it around his neck and pulled it. The child called once for his mother, and died easily. Then they wound him in a sheet, and sitting on horses which were waiting, hurried to Ostia, where they threw the body into the sea.

Poppæa, not finding the virgo magna, who with other vestals was at the house of Vatinius, returned soon to the Palatine. Seeing the empty bed and the cold body of Silvia, she fainted, and when they restored her she began to scream; her wild cries were heard all that night and the day following.

But Cæsar commanded her to appear at a feast on the third day; so, arraying herself in an amethyst-colored tunic, she came and sat with stony face, golden-haired, silent, wonderful, and as ominous as an angel of death.

CHAPTER LV

BEFORE the Flavii had reared the Colosseum, amphitheatres in Rome were built of wood mainly; for that reason nearly all of them had burned during the fire. But Nero, for the celebration of the promised games, had given command to build several, and among them a gigantic one, for which they began, immediately after the fire was extinguished, to bring by sea and the Tiber great trunks of trees cut on the slopes of Atlas; for the games were to surpass all previous ones in splendor and the number of victims.

Large spaces were given therefore for people and for animals. Thousands of mechanics worked at the structure night and day. They built and ornamented without rest. Wonders were told concerning pillars inlaid with bronze, amber, ivory, mother of pearl, and transmarine tortoise-shells. Canals filled with ice-cold water from the mountains and running along the seats were to keep an agreeable coolness in the building, even during the greatest heat. A gigantic purple velarium gave shelter from the rays of the sun. Among the rows of seats were disposed vessels for the burning of Arabian perfumes; above them were fixed instruments to sprinkle the spectators with dew of saffron and verbena. The renowned builders Severus and Celer put forth all their skill to construct an amphitheatre at once incomparable and fitted for such a number of the curious as none of those known before had been able to accommodate.

Hence, the day when the ludus matutinus was to begin, throngs of the populace were awaiting from daylight the opening of the gates, listening with delight to the roars of lions, the hoarse growls of panthers, and the howls of dogs. The beasts had not been fed for two days, but pieces of bloody flesh had been pushed before them to rouse their rage and hunger all the more. At times such a storm of wild voices was raised that people standing before the Circus could not converse, and the most sensitive grew pale from fear.

With the rising of the sun were intoned in the enclosure of the Circus hymns resonant but calm. The people heard these with amazement, and said one to another, "The Christians! the Christians!" In fact, many detachments of Christians had been brought to the amphitheatre that night, and not from one place, as planned at first, but a few from each prison. It was known in the crowd that the spectacles would continue through weeks and months, but they doubted that it would be possible to finish in a single day those Christians who had been intended for that one occasion. The voices of men, women, and children singing the morning hymn were so numerous that spectators of experience asserted that even if one or two hundred persons were sent out at once, the beasts would grow tired, become sated, and not tear all to pieces before evening. Others declared that an excessive number of victims in the arena would divert attention, and not give a chance to enjoy the spectacle properly.

As the moment drew near for opening the vomitoria, or passages which led to the interior, people grew animated and joyous; they discussed and disputed about various things touching the spectacle. Parties were formed praising the greater efficiency of lions or tigers in tearing. Here and there bets were made. Others however talked about gladiators who were to appear in the arena earlier than the Christians; and again there were parties, some in favor of Samnites, others of Gauls, others of Mirmillons, others of Thracians, others of the retiarii.

Early in the morning larger or smaller detachments of gladiators began to arrive at the amphitheatre under the lead of masters, called lanistæ. Not wishing to be wearied too soon, they entered unarmed, often entirely naked, often with green boughs in their hands, or crowned with flowers, young, beautiful, in the light of morning, and full of life. Their bodies, shining from olive oil, were strong as if chiselled from marble; they roused to delight people who loved shapely forms. Many were known personally, and from moment to moment were heard: "A greeting, Furnius! A greeting, Leo! A greeting, Maximus! A greeting, Diomed!" Young maidens raised to them eyes full of admiration; they, selecting the maiden most beautiful, answered with jests, as if no care weighed on them, sending kisses, or exclaiming, "Embrace me before death does!" Then they vanished in the gates, through which many of them were never to come forth again.

New arrivals drew away the attention of the throngs. Behind the gladiators came mastigophori; that is, men armed with scourges, whose office it was to lash and urge forward combatants. Next mules drew, in the direction of the spoliarium, whole rows of vehicles on which were piled wooden coffins. People were diverted at sight of this, inferring from the number of coffins the greatness of the spectacle. Now marched in men who were to kill the wounded; these were dressed so that each resembled Charon or Mercury. Next came those who looked after order in the Circus, and assigned places; after that slaves to bear around food and refreshments; finally, pretorians, whom every Cæsar had always at hand in the amphitheatre.

At last the vomitoria were opened, and crowds rushed to the centre. But such was the number of those assembled that they flowed in and flowed in for hours, till it was a marvel that the Circus could hold such a countless multitude. The roars of wild beasts, catching the exhalations of people, grew louder. While taking their places, the spectators made an uproar like the sea in time of storm.

Finally, the prefect of the city came, surrounded by guards; and after him, in unbroken line, appeared the litters of senators, consuls, pretors, ediles, officials of the government and the palace, of pretorian officers, patricians, and exquisite ladies. Some litters were preceded by lictors bearing maces in bundles of rods; others by crowds of slaves. In the sun gleamed the gilding of the litters, the white and varied colored stuffs, feathers, earrings, jewels, steel of the maces. From the Circus came shouts with which the people greeted great dignitaries. Small divisions of pretorians arrived from time to time.

The priests of various temples came somewhat later; only after them were brought in the sacred virgins of Vesta, preceded by lictors.

To begin the spectacle, they were waiting now only for Cæsar, who, unwilling to expose the people to over-long waiting, and wishing to win them by promptness, came soon, in company with the Augusta and Augustians.

Petronius arrived among the Augustians, having Vinicius in his litter. The latter knew that Lygia was sick and unconscious; but as access to the prison had been forbidden most strictly during the preceding days, and as the former guards had been replaced by new ones who were not permitted to speak with the jailers or even to communicate the least information to those who came to inquire about prisoners, he was not even sure that she was not among the victims intended for the first day of spectacles. They might send out even a sick woman for the lions, though she were unconscious. But since the victims were to be sewed up in skins of wild beasts and sent to the arena in crowds, no spectator could be certain that one more or less might not be among them, and no man could recognize any one. The jailers and all the servants of the amphitheatre had been bribed, and a bargain made with the beast-keepers to hide Lygia in some dark corner, and give her at night into the hands of a confidant of Vinicius, who would take her at once to the Alban Hills. Petronius, admitted to the secret, advised Vinicius to go with him openly to the amphitheatre, and after he had entered to disappear in the throng and hurry to the vaults, where, to avoid possible mistake, he was to point out Lygia to the guards personally.

The guards admitted him through a small door by which they came out themselves. One of these, named Cyrus, led him at once to the Christians. On the way he said, —

"I know not, lord, that thou wilt find what thou art seeking. We inquired for a maiden named Lygia, but no one gave us answer; it may be, though, that they do not trust us."

"Are there many?" asked Vinicius.

"Many, lord, had to wait till to-morrow."

"Are there sick ones among them?"

"There were none who could not stand."

Cyrus opened a door and entered as it were an enormous chamber, but low and dark, for the light came in only through grated openings which separated it from the arena. At first Vinicius could see nothing; he heard only the murmur of voices in the room, and the shouts of people in the amphitheatre. But after a time, when his eyes had grown used to the gloom, he saw crowds of strange beings, resembling wolves and bears. Those were Christians sewed up in skins of beasts. Some of them were standing; others were kneeling in prayer. Here and there one might divine by the long hair flowing over the skin that the victim was a woman. Women, looking like wolves, carried in their arms children sewed up in equally shaggy coverings. But from beneath the skins appeared bright faces and eyes which in the darkness gleamed with delight and feverishness. It was evident that the greater number of those people were mastered by one thought, exclusive and beyond the earth, — a thought which during life made them indifferent to everything which happened around them and which could meet them. Some, when asked by Vinicius about Lygia, looked at him with eyes as if roused from sleep, without answering his questions; others smiled at him, placing a finger on their lips or pointing to the iron grating through which bright streaks of light entered. But here and there children were crying, frightened by the roaring of beasts, the howling of dogs, the uproar of people, and the forms of their own parents who looked like wild beasts. Vinicius as he walked by the side of Cyrus looked into faces, searched, inquired, at times stumbled against bodies of people who had fainted from the crowd, the stifling air, the heat, and pushed farther into the dark depth of the room, which seemed to be as spacious as a whole amphitheatre.

But he stopped on a sudden, for he seemed to hear near the grating a voice known to him. He listened for a while, turned, and, pushing through the crowd, went near. Light fell on the face of the speaker, and Vinicius recognized under the skin of a wolf the emaciated and implacable countenance of Crispus.

"Mourn for your sins!" exclaimed Crispus, "for the moment is near. But whoso thinks by death itself to redeem his sins commits a fresh sin, and will be hurled into endless fire. With every sin committed in life ye have renewed the Lord's suffering; how dare ye think that that life which awaits you will redeem this one? To-day the just and the sinner will die the same death; but the Lord will find His own. Woe to you, the claws of the lions will rend your bodies; but not your sins, nor your reckoning with God. The Lord showed mercy sufficient when He let Himself be nailed to the cross; but thenceforth He will be only the judge, who will leave no fault unpunished. Whoso among you has thought to extinguish his sins by suffering, has blasphemed against God's justice, and will sink all the deeper. Mercy is at an end, and the hour of God's wrath has come. Soon ye will stand before the awful Judge in whose presence the good will hardly be justified. Bewail your sins, for the jaws of hell are open; woe to you, husbands and wives; woe to you, parents and children."

And stretching forth his bony hands, he shook them above the bent heads; he was unterrified and implacable even in the presence of death, to which in a while all those doomed people were to go. After his words, were heard voices: "We bewail our sins!" Then came silence, and only the cry of children was audible, and the beating of hands against breasts.

The blood of Vinicius stiffened in his veins. He, who had placed all his hope in the mercy of Christ, heard now that the day of wrath had come, and that even death in the arena would not obtain mercy. Through his head shot, it is true, the thought, clear and swift as lightning, that Peter would have spoken otherwise to those about to die. Still those terrible words of Crispus filled with fanaticism that dark chamber with its grating, beyond which was the field of torture. The nearness of that torture, and the throng of victims arrayed for death already, filled his soul with fear and terror. All this seemed to him dreadful, and a hundred times more ghastly than the bloodiest battle in which he had ever taken part. The odor and heat began to stifle him; cold sweat came out on his forehead. He was seized by fear that he would faint like those against whose bodies he had stumbled while searching in the depth of the apartment; so when he remembered that they might open the grating any moment, he began to call Lygia and Ursus aloud, in the hope that, if not they, some one knowing them would answer.

In fact, some man, clothed as a bear, pulled his toga, and said, —

"Lord, they remained in prison. I was the last one brought out; I saw her sick on the couch."

"Who art thou?" inquired Vinicius.

"The quarryman in whose hut the Apostle baptized thee, lord. They imprisoned me three days ago, and to-day I die."

Vinicius was relieved. When entering, he had wished to find Lygia; now he was ready to thank Christ that she was not there, and to see in that a sign of mercy. Meanwhile the quarryman pulled his toga again, and said, —

"Dost remember, lord, that I conducted thee to the vineyard of Cornelius, when the Apostle discoursed in the shed?"

"I remember."

"I saw him later, the day before they imprisoned me. He blessed me, and said that he would come to the amphitheatre to bless the perishing. If I could look at him in the moment of death and see the sign of the cross, it would be easier for me to die. If thou know where he is, lord, inform me."

Vinicius lowered his voice, and said, —

"He is among the people of Petronius, disguised as a slave. I know not where they chose their places, but I will return to the Circus and see. Look thou at me when ye enter the arena. I will rise and turn my face toward them; then thou wilt find him with thy eyes."

"Thanks to thee, lord, and peace be with thee."

"May the Redeemer be merciful to thee."

"Amen."

Vinicius went out of the cuniculum, and betook himself to the amphitheatre, where he had a place near Petronius among the other Augustians.

"Is she there?" inquired Petronius.

"No; she remained in prison."

"Hear what has occurred to me, but while listening look at Nigidia for example, so that we may seem to talk of her hair-dressing. Tigellinus and Chilo are looking at us now. Listen then. Let them put Lygia in a coffin at night and carry her out of the prison as a corpse; thou divinest the rest?"

"Yes," answered Vinicius.

Their further conversation was interrupted by Tullius Senecio, who, bending toward them, asked, —

"Do ye know whether they will give weapons to the Christians?"

"We do not," answered Petronius.

"I should prefer that arms were given," said Tullius; "if not, the arena will become like butcher's shambles too early. But what a splendid amphitheatre!"

The sight was, in truth, magnificent. The lower seats, crowded with togas, were as white as snow. In the gilded podium sat Cæsar, wearing a diamond collar and a golden crown on his head; next to him sat the beautiful and gloomy Augusta, and on both sides were vestal virgins, great officials, senators with embroidered togas, officers of the army with glittering weapons, — in a word, all that was powerful, brilliant, and wealthy in Rome. In the farther rows sat knights; and higher up darkened in rows a sea of common heads, above which from pillar to pillar hung festoons of roses, lilies, ivy, and grape-vines.

People conversed aloud, called to one another, sang; at times they broke into laughter at some witty word which was sent from row to row, and they stamped with impatience to hasten the spectacle.

At last the stamping became like thunder, and unbroken. Then the prefect of the city, who rode around the arena with a brilliant retinue, gave a signal with a handkerchief, which was answered throughout the amphitheatre by "A-a-a!" from thousands of breasts.

Usually a spectacle was begun by hunts of wild beasts, in which various Northern and Southern barbarians excelled; but this time they had too many beasts, so they began with andabates, — that is, men wearing helmets without an opening for the eyes, hence fighting blindfold. A number of these came into the arena together, and slashed at random with their swords; the scourg-ers with long forks pushed some toward others to make them meet. The more select of the audience looked with contempt and indifference at this spectacle; but the crowd were amused by the awkward motions of the swordsmen. When it happened that they met with their shoulders, they burst out in loud laughter. "To the right!" "To the left!" cried they, misleading the opponents frequently by design. A number of pairs closed, however, and the struggle began to be bloody. The determined combatants cast aside their shields, and giving their left hands to each other, so as not to part again, struggled to the death with their right. Whoever fell raised his fingers, begging mercy by that sign; but in the beginning of a spectacle the audience demanded death usually for the wounded, especially in the case of men who had their faces covered and were unknown. Gradually the number of combatants decreased; and when at last only two remained, these were pushed together; both fell on the sand, and stabbed each other mutually. Then, amid cries of "Peractum est!" servants carried out the bodies, youths raked away the bloody traces on the sand and sprinkled it with leaves of saffron.

Now a more important contest was to come, — rousing interest not only in the herd, but in exquisites; during this contest young patricians made enor-mous bets at times, often losing all they owned. Straightway from hand to hand went tablets on which were written names of favorites, and also the num-ber of sestertia which each man wagered on his favorite. "Spectati" — that is, champions who had appeared already on the arena and gained victories — found most partisans; but among betters were also those who risked con-siderably on gladiators who were new and quite unknown, hoping to win immense sums should these conquer. Cæsar himself bet; priests, vestals, senators, knights bet; the populace bet. People of the crowd, when money failed them, bet their own freedom frequently. They waited with heart-beating and even with fear for the combatants, and more than one made audible vows to the gods to gain their protection for a favorite.

In fact, when the shrill sound of trumpets was heard, there was a stillness of expectation in the amphitheatre. Thousands of eyes were turned to the great bolts, which a man approached dressed like Charon, and amid the universal silence struck three times with a hammer, as if summoning to death those who were hidden behind them. Then both halves of the gate opened slowly, showing a black gully, out of which gladiators began to appear in the bright arena. They came in divisions of twenty-five, Thracians, Mirmillons, Samnites, Gauls, each nation separately, all heavily armed; and last the retiarii, holding in one hand a net, in the other a trident. At sight of them, here and there on the benches rose applause, which soon turned into one immense and unbroken storm. From above to below were seen excited faces, clapping hands, and open mouths, from which shouts burst forth. The gladiators encircled the whole arena with even and springy tread, gleaming with their weapons and rich outfit; they halted before Cæsar's podium, proud, calm, and brilliant. The shrill sound of a horn stopped the applause; the combatants stretched their right hands upward, raised their eyes and heads toward Cæsar, and began to cry or rather to chant with drawling voice, —

"Ave, Cæsar imperator!
Morituri te salutant!"

Then they pushed apart quickly, occupying their places on the arena. They were to attack one another in whole detachments; but first it was permitted the most famous fencers to have a series of single combats, in which the strength, dexterity, and courage of opponents were best exhibited. In fact, from among the Gauls appeared a champion, well known to lovers of the amphitheatre under the name of Lanio, a victor in many games. With a great helmet on his head, and in mail which formed a ridge in front of his powerful breast and behind, he looked in the gleam of the golden arena like a giant beetle. The no less famous retiarius Calendio came out against him.

Among the spectators people began to bet.

"Five hundred sestertia on the Gaul!"

"Five hundred on Calendio!"

"By Hercules, one thousand!"

"Two thousand!"

Meanwhile the Gaul, reaching the centre of the arena, began to withdraw with pointed sword, and, lowering his head, watched his opponent carefully through the opening of his visor; the light retiarius, stately, statuesque, wholly naked save a belt around his loins, circled quickly about his heavy antagonist, waving the net with graceful movement, lowering or raising his trident, and singing the usual song of the retiarius, —

"Non te peto, piscem peto;
Quid me fugis, Galle?" [1]

But the Gaul was not fleeing, for after a while he stopped, and standing in one place began to turn with barely a slight movement, so as to have his enemy always in front. In his form and monstrously large head there was now something terrible. The spectators understood perfectly that that heavy body encased in bronze was preparing for a sudden throw to decide the battle. The retiarius meanwhile sprang up to him, then sprang away, making with his three-toothed fork motions so quick that the eye hardly followed them. The sound of the teeth on the shield was heard repeatedly; but the Gaul did not quiver, giving proof by this of his gigantic strength. All his attention seemed fixed, not on the trident, but the net which was circling above his head, like a bird of ill omen. The spectators held the breath in their breasts, and followed the masterly play of the gladiators. The Gaul waited, chose the moment, and rushed at last on his enemy; the latter with equal quickness shot past under his sword, straightened himself with raised arm, and threw the net.

The Gaul, turning where he stood, caught it on his shield; then both sprang apart. In the amphitheatre shouts of "Macte!" thundered; in the lower rows they began to make new bets. Cæsar himself, who at first had been talking with Rubria, and so far had not paid much attention to the spectacle, turned his head toward the arena.

They began to struggle again, so regularly and with such precision in their movements, that sometimes it seemed that with them it was not a question of life or death, but of exhibiting skill. The Gaul escaping twice more from the net, pushed toward the edge of the arena; those who held bets against him, not wishing the champion to rest, began to cry, "Bear on!" The Gaul obeyed, and attacked. The arm of the retiarius was covered on a sudden with blood, and his net dropped. The Gaul summoned his strength, and sprang forward to give the final blow. That instant Calendio, who feigned inability to wield the net, sprang aside, escaped the thrust, ran the trident between the knees of his opponent, and brought him to the earth.

The Gaul tried to rise, but in a twinkle he was covered by the fatal meshes, in which he was entangled more and more by every movement of his feet and hands. Meanwhile stabs of the trident fixed him time after time to the earth. He made one more effort, rested on his arm, and tried to rise; in vain! He raised to his head his falling hand which could hold the sword no longer, and fell on his back. Calendio pressed his neck to the ground with the trident, and, resting both hands on the handle of it, turned toward Cæsar's box.

The whole Circus was trembling from plaudits and the roar of people. For those who had bet on Calendio he was at that moment greater than Cæsar; but for this very reason animosity against the Gaul vanished from their hearts. At the cost of his blood he had filled their purses. The voices of the audience were divided. On the upper seats half the signs were for death, and

[1] "I seek not thee, I seek a fish;
Why flee from me, O Gaul?"

half for mercy; but the retiarius looked only at the box of Cæsar and the vestals, waiting for what they would decide.

To the misfortune of the fallen gladiator, Nero did not like him, for at the last games before the fire he had bet against the Gaul, and had lost considerable sums to Licinus; hence he thrust his hand out of the podium, and turned his thumb toward the earth.

The vestals supported the sign at once. Calendio knelt on the breast of the Gaul, drew a short knife from his belt, pushed apart the armor around the neck of his opponent, and drove the three-edged blade into his throat to the handle.

"Peractum est!" sounded voices in the amphitheatre.

The Gaul quivered a time, like a stabbed bullock, dug the sand with his heels, stretched, and was motionless.

Mercury had no need to try with heated iron if he were living yet. He was hidden away quickly, and other pairs appeared. After them came a battle of whole detachments. The audience took part in it with soul, heart, and eyes. They howled, roared, whistled, applauded, laughed, urged on the combatants, grew wild. The gladiators on the arena, divided into two legions, fought with the rage of wild beasts; breast struck breast, bodies were intertwined in a death grapple, strong limbs cracked in their joints, swords were buried in breasts and in stomachs, pale lips threw blood on to the sand. Toward the end such terrible fear seized some novices that, tearing themselves from the turmoil, they fled; but the scourgers drove them back again quickly to the battle with lashes tipped with lead. On the sand great dark spots were formed; more and more naked and armed bodies lay stretched like grain sheaves. The living fought on the corpses; they struck against armor and shields, cut their feet against broken weapons, and fell. The audience lost self-command from delight; and intoxicated with death breathed it, sated their eyes with the sight of it, and drew into their lungs the exhalations of it with ecstasy.

The conquered lay dead, almost every man. Barely a few wounded knelt in the middle of the arena, and trembling stretched their hands to the audience with a prayer for mercy. To the victors were given rewards, — crowns, olive wreaths. And a moment of rest came, which, at command of the all-powerful Cæsar, was turned into a feast. Perfumes were burned in vases. Sprinklers scattered saffron and violet rain on the people. Cooling drinks were served, roasted meats, sweet cakes, wine, olives, and fruits. The people devoured, talked, and shouted in honor of Cæsar, to incline him to greater bounteousness. When hunger and thirst had been satisfied, hundreds of slaves bore around baskets full of gifts, from which boys, dressed as Cupids, took various objects and threw them with both hands among the seats. When lottery tickets were distributed, a battle began. People crowded, threw, trampled one another; cried for rescue, sprang over rows of seats, stifled one another in the terrible crush, since whoever got a lucky number might win possibly a house with a garden, a slave, a splendid dress, or a wild beast which he could sell to the amphitheatre afterward. For this reason there were such disorders that frequently the pretorians had to interfere; and after every distribution they carried out people with broken arms or legs, and some were even trampled to death in the throng.

But the more wealthy took no part in the fight for tesseræ. The Augustians amused themselves now with the spectacle of Chilo, and with making sport of his vain efforts to show that he could look at fighting and blood-spilling as well as any man. But in vain did the unfortunate Greek wrinkle his brow, gnaw his lips, and squeeze his fists till the nails entered his palms. His Greek nature and his personal cowardice were unable to endure such sights. His face grew pale, his forehead was dotted with drops of sweat, his lips were blue, his eyes turned in, his teeth began to chatter, and a trembling seized his body. At the end of the battle he recovered somewhat; but when they attacked him with tongues, sudden anger seized him, and he defended himself desperately.

"Ha, Greek! the sight of torn skin on a man is beyond thy strength!" said Vatinius, taking him by the beard.

Chilo bared his last two yellow teeth at him and answered, —

"My father was not a cobbler, so I cannot mend it."

"Macte! habet (Good! he has caught it!)!" called a number of voices; but others jeered on.

"He is not to blame that instead of a heart he has a piece of cheese in his breast," said Senecio.

"Thou art not to blame that instead of a head thou hast a bladder," retorted Chilo.

"Maybe thou wilt become a gladiator! thou wouldst look well with a net on the arena."

"If I should catch thee in it, I should catch a stinking hoopoe."

"And how will it be with the Christians?" asked Festus, from Liguria. "Wouldst thou not like to be a dog and bite them?"

"I should not like to be thy brother."

"Thou Mæotian copper-nose!"

"Thou Ligurian mule!"

"Thy skin is itching, evidently, but I don't advise thee to ask me to scratch it."

"Scratch thyself. If thou scratch thy own pimple, thou wilt destroy what is best in thee."

And in this manner they attacked him. He defended himself venomously, amid universal laughter. Cæsar, clapping his hands, repeated, "Macte!" and urged them on. After a while Petronius approached, and, touching the Greek's shoulder with his carved ivory cane, said coldly, —

"This is well, philosopher; but in one thing thou hast blundered: the gods created thee a pickpocket, and thou hast become a demon. That is why thou canst not endure."

The old man looked at him with his red eyes, but this time somehow he did not find a ready insult. He was silent for a moment; then answered, as if with a certain effort, —

"I shall endure."

Meanwhile the trumpets announced the end of the interval. People began to leave the passages where they had assembled to straighten their legs and converse. A general movement set in with the usual dispute about seats occupied previously. Senators and patricians hastened to their places. The uproar ceased after a time, and the amphitheatre returned to order. On the arena a crowd of people appeared whose work was to dig out here and there lumps of sand formed with stiffened blood.

The turn of the Christians was at hand. But since that was a new spectacle for people, and no one knew how the Christians would bear themselves, all waited with a certain curiosity. The disposition of the audience was attentive but unfriendly; they were waiting for uncommon scenes. Those people who were to appear had burned Rome and its ancient treasures. They had drunk the blood of infants, and poisoned water; they had cursed the whole human race, and committed the vilest crimes. The harshest punishment did not suffice the roused hatred; and if any fear possessed people's hearts, it was this: that the torture of the Christians would not equal the guilt of those ominous criminals.

Meanwhile the sun had risen high; its rays, passing through the purple velarium, had filled the amphitheatre with blood-colored light. The sand assumed a fiery hue, and in those gleams, in the faces of people, as well as in the empty arena, which after a time was to be filled with the torture of people and the rage of savage beasts, there was something terrible. Death and terror seemed hovering in the air. The throng, usually gladsome, became moody under the influence of hate and silence. Faces had a sullen expression.

Now the prefect gave a sign. The same old man appeared, dressed as Charon, who had called the gladiators to death, and, passing with slow step across the arena amid silence, he struck three times again on the door.

Throughout the amphitheatre was heard the deep murmur, —

"The Christians! the Christians!"

The iron gratings creaked; through the dark openings were heard the usual cries of the scourgers, "To the sand!" and in one moment the arena was peopled with crowds as it were of satyrs covered with skins. All ran quickly, somewhat feverishly, and, reaching the middle of the circle, they knelt one by another with raised heads. The spectators, judging this to be a prayer for pity, and enraged by such cowardice, began to stamp, whistle, throw empty wine-vessels, bones from which the flesh had been eaten, and shout, "The beasts! the beasts!" But all at once something unexpected took place. From out the shaggy assembly singing voices were raised, and then sounded that hymn heard for the first time in a Roman amphitheatre, "Christus regnat!" [1]

Astonishment seized the spectators. The condemned sang with eyes raised to the velarium. The audience saw faces pale, but as it were inspired. All understood that those people were not asking for mercy, and that they seemed not to see the Circus, the audience, the Senate, or Cæsar. "Christus regnat!" rose ever louder, and in the seats, far up to the highest, among the rows of

[1] "Christ reigns!"

spectators, more than one asked himself the question, "What is happening, and who is that Christus who reigns in the mouths of those people who are about to die?" But meanwhile a new grating was opened, and into the arena rushed, with mad speed and barking, whole packs of dogs, — gigantic, yellow Molossians from the Peloponnesus, pied dogs from the Pyrenees, and wolf-like hounds from Hibernia, purposely famished; their sides lank, and their eyes bloodshot. Their howls and whines filled the amphitheatre. When the Christians had finished their hymn, they remained kneeling, motionless, as if petrified, merely repeating in one groaning chorus, "Pro Christo! Pro Christo!" The dogs, catching the odor of people under the skins of beasts, and surprised by their silence, did not rush on them at once. Some stood against the walls of the boxes, as if wishing to go among the spectators; others ran around barking furiously, as though chasing some unseen beast. The people were angry. A thousand voices began to call; some howled like wild beasts; some barked like dogs; others urged them on in every language. The amphitheatre was trembling from uproar. The excited dogs began to run to the kneeling people, then to draw back, snapping their teeth, till at last one of the Molossians drove his teeth into the shoulder of a woman kneeling in front, and dragged her under him.

Tens of dogs rushed into the crowd now, as if to break through it. The audience ceased to howl, so as to look with greater attention. Amidst the howling and whining were heard yet plaintive voices of men and women: "Pro Christo! Pro Christo!" but on the arena were formed quivering masses of the bodies of dogs and people. Blood flowed in streams from the torn bodies. Dogs dragged from each other the bloody limbs of people. The odor of blood and torn entrails was stronger than Arabian perfumes, and filled the whole Circus.

At last only here and there were visible single kneeling forms, which were soon covered by moving squirming masses.

Vinicius, who at the moment when the Christians ran in, stood up and turned so as to indicate to the quarryman, as he had promised, the direction in which the Apostle was hidden among the people of Petronius, sat down again, and with the face of a dead man continued to look with glassy eyes on the ghastly spectacle. At first fear that the quarryman might have been mistaken, and that perchance Lygia was among the victims, benumbed him completely; but when he heard the voices, "Pro Christo!" when he saw the torture of so many victims who, in dying, confessed their faith and their God, another feeling possessed him, piercing him like the most dreadful pain, but irresistible. That feeling was this, — if Christ Himself died in torment, if thousands are perishing for Him now, if a sea of blood is poured forth, one drop more signifies nothing, and it is a sin even to ask for mercy. That thought came to him from the arena, penetrated him with the groans of the dying, with the odor of their blood. But still he prayed and repeated with parched lips, "O Christ! O Christ! and Thy Apostle prayed for her!" Then he forgot himself, lost consciousness of where he was. It seemed to him that blood on the arena was rising and rising, that it was coming up and flowing out of the Circus over all Rome. For the rest he heard nothing, neither the howling of dogs nor the uproar of the people nor the voices of the Augustians, who began all at once to cry, —

"Chilo has fainted!"

"Chilo has fainted!" said Petronius, turning toward the Greek.

And he had fainted really; he sat there white as linen, his head fallen back, his mouth wide open, like that of a corpse.

At that same moment they were urging into the arena new victims, sewed up in skins.

These knelt immediately, like those who had gone before; but the weary dogs would not rend them. Barely a few threw themselves on to those kneeling nearest; but others lay down, and, raising their bloody jaws, began to scratch their sides and yawn heavily.

Then the audience, disturbed in spirit, but drunk with blood and wild, began to cry with hoarse voices, —

"The lions! the lions! Let out the lions!"

The lions were to be kept for the next day; but in the amphitheatres the people imposed their will on every one, even on Cæsar. Caligula alone, insolent and changeable in his wishes, dared to oppose them, and there were cases when he gave command to beat the people with clubs; but even he yielded most frequently. Nero, to whom plaudits were dearer than all else in the world, never resisted. All the more did he not resist now, when it was a question of mollifying the populace, excited after the conflagration, and a question of the Christians, on whom he wished to cast the blame of the catastrophe.

He gave the sign therefore to open the cuniculum, seeing which, the people were calmed in a moment. They heard the creaking of the doors behind which were the lions. At sight of the lions the dogs gathered with low whines, on the opposite side of the arena. The lions walked into the arena one after another, immense, tawny, with great shaggy heads. Cæsar himself turned his wearied face toward them, and placed the emerald to his eye to see better. The Augustians greeted them with applause; the crowd counted them on their fingers, and followed eagerly the impression which the sight of them would make on the Christians kneeling in the centre, who again had begun to repeat the words, without meaning for many, though annoying to all, "Pro Christo! Pro Christo!"

But the lions, though hungry, did not hasten to their victims. The ruddy light in the arena dazzled them and they half closed their eyes as if dazed. Some stretched their yellowish bodies lazily; some, opening their jaws, yawned, — one might have said that they wanted to show their terrible teeth to the audience. But later the odor of blood and torn bodies, many of which were lying on the sand, began to act on them. Soon their movements became restless, their manes rose, their nostrils drew in the air with hoarse sound. One fell suddenly on the body of a woman with a torn face, and, lying with his fore paws on the body, licked with a rough tongue the stiffened blood: another approached a man who was holding in his arms a child sewed up in a fawn's skin.

The child, trembling from crying, and weeping, clung convulsively to the neck of its father; he, to prolong its life even for a moment, tried to pull it from his neck, so as to hand it to those kneeling farther on. But the cry and the movement irritated the lion. All at once he gave out a short, broken roar, killed the child with one blow of his paw, and seizing the head of the father in his jaws, crushed it in a twinkle.

At sight of this all the other lions fell upon the crowd of Christians. Some women could not restrain cries of terror; but the audience drowned these with plaudits, which soon ceased, however, for the wish to see gained the mastery. They beheld terrible things then: heads disappearing entirely in open jaws, breasts torn apart with one blow, hearts and lungs swept away; the crushing of bones under the teeth of lions. Some lions, seizing victims by the ribs or loins, ran with mad springs through the arena, as if seeking hidden places in which to devour them; others fought, rose on their hind legs, grappled one another like wrestlers, and filled the amphitheatre with thunder. People rose from their places. Some left their seats, went down lower through the passages to see better, and crowded one another mortally. It seemed that the excited multitude would throw itself at last into the arena, and rend the Christians in company with the lions. At moments an unearthly noise was heard; at moments applause; at moments roaring, rumbling, the clashing of teeth, the howling of Molossian dogs; at times only groans.

Cæsar, holding the emerald to his eye, looked now with attention. The face of Petronius assumed an expression of contempt and disgust. Chilo had been borne out of the Circus.

But from the cuniculum new victims were driven forth continually.

From the highest row in the amphitheatre the Apostle Peter looked at them. No one saw him, for all heads were turned to the arena; so he rose and as formerly in the vineyard of Cornelius he had blessed for death and eternity those who were intended for imprisonment, so now he blessed with the cross those who were perishing under the teeth of wild beasts. He blessed their blood, their torture, their dead bodies turned into shapeless masses, and their souls flying away from the bloody sand. Some raised their eyes to him, and their faces grew radiant; they smiled when they saw high above them the sign of the cross. But his heart was rent, and he said, "O Lord! let Thy will be done. These my sheep perish to Thy glory in testimony of the truth. Thou didst command me to feed them; hence I give them to Thee, and do Thou count them, Lord, take them, heal their wounds, soften their pain, give them happiness greater than the torments which they suffered here."

And he blessed them one after another, crowd after crowd, with as much love as if they had been his children whom he was giving directly into the hands of Christ. Then Cæsar, whether from madness, or the wish that the exhibition should surpass everything seen in Rome so far, whispered a few words to the prefect of the city. He left the podium and went at once to the cuniculum. Even the populace were astonished when, after a while, they saw the gratings open again. Beasts of all kinds were let out this time, — tigers from the Euphrates, Numidian panthers, bears, wolves, hyenas, and jackals. The whole arena was covered as with a moving sea of striped, yellow, flax-colored, dark-brown, and spotted skins. There rose a chaos in which the eye could distinguish nothing save a terrible turning and twisting of the backs of wild beasts. The spectacle lost the appearance of reality, and became as it were an orgy of blood, a dreadful dream, a gigantic kaleidoscope of mad fancy. The measure was surpassed. Amidst roars, howls, whines, here and there on the seats of the spectators were heard the terrified and spasmodic laughter of women, whose strength had given way at last. The people were terrified. Faces grew dark. Various voices began to cry, "Enough! enough!"

But it was easier to let the beasts in than drive them back again. Cæsar, however, found a means of clearing the arena, and a new amusement for the people. In all the passages between the seats appeared detachments of Numidians, black and stately, in feathers and earrings, with bows in their hands. The people divined what was coming, and greeted the archers with a shout of delight. The Numidians approached the railing, and, putting their arrows to the strings, began to shoot from their bows into the crowd of beasts. That was a new spectacle truly. Their bodies, shapely as if cut from dark marble, bent backward, stretched the flexible bows, and sent bolt after bolt. The whizzing of the strings and the whistling of the feathered missiles were mingled with the howling of beasts and cries of wonder from the audience. Wolves, bears, panthers, and people yet alive fell side by side. Here and there a lion, feeling a shaft in his ribs, turned with sudden movement, his jaws wrinkled from rage, to seize and break the arrow. Others groaned from pain. The small beasts, falling into a panic, ran around the arena at random, or thrust their heads into the grating; meanwhile the arrows whizzed and whizzed on, till all that was living had lain down in the final quiver of death.

Hundreds of slaves rushed into the arena armed with spades, shovels, brooms, wheelbarrows, baskets for carrying out entrails, and bags of sand. They came, crowd after crowd, and over the whole circle there seethed up a feverish activity. The space was soon cleared of bodies, blood, and mire, dug over, made smooth, and sprinkled with a thick layer of fresh sand. That done, Cupids ran in, scattering leaves of roses, lilies, and the greatest variety of flowers. The censers were ignited again, and the velarium was removed, for the sun had sunk now considerably. But people looked at one another with amazement, and inquired what kind of new spectacle was waiting for them on that day.

Indeed, such a spectacle was waiting as no one had looked for. Cæsar, who had left the podium some time before, appeared all at once on the flowery arena, wearing a purple mantle, and a crown of gold. Twelve choristers holding citharæ followed him. He had a silver lute, and advanced with solemn tread to the middle, bowed a number of times to the spectators, raised his eyes, and stood as if waiting for inspiration.

Then he struck the strings and began to sing, —

> "O radiant son of Leto,
> Ruler of Tenedos, Chios, Chrysos,
> Art thou he who, having in his care
> The sacred city of Ilion,
> Could yield it to Argive anger,
> And suffer sacred altars,
> Which blazed unceasingly to his honor,
> To be stained with Trojan blood?
> Aged men raised trembling hands to thee,
> O thou of the far-shooting silver bow,
> Mothers from the depth of their breasts
> Raised tearful cries to thee,
> Imploring pity on their offspring.
> Those complaints might have moved a stone,
> But to the suffering of people
> Thou, O Smintheus, wert less feeling than a stone!"

The song passed gradually into an elegy, plaintive and full of pain. In the Circus there was silence. After a while Cæsar, himself affected, sang on, —

> "With the sound of thy heavenly lyre
> Thou couldst drown the wailing,
> The lament of hearts.
> At the sad sound of this song
> The eye to-day is filled with tears,
> As a flower is filled with dew,
> But who can raise from dust and ashes
> That day of fire, disaster, ruin?
> O Smintheus, where wert thou then?"

Here his voice quivered and his eyes grew moist. Tears appeared on the lids of the vestals; the people listened in silence before they burst into a long unbroken storm of applause.

Meanwhile from outside through the vomitoria came the sound of creaking vehicles on which were placed the bloody remnants of Christians, men, women, and children, to be taken to the pits called "puticuli."

But the Apostle Peter seized his trembling white head with his hands, and cried in spirit, —

"O Lord, O Lord! to whom hast Thou given rule over the earth, and why wilt Thou found in this place Thy capital?"

CHAPTER LVI

THE sun had lowered toward its setting, and seemed to dissolve in the red of the evening. The spectacle was finished. Crowds were leaving the amphitheatre and pouring out to the city through the passages called vomitoria. Only Augustians delayed; they were waiting for the stream of people to pass. They had all left their seats and assembled at the podium, in which Cæsar appeared again to hear praises. Though the spectators had not spared plaudits at the end of the song, Nero was not satisfied; he had looked for enthusiasm touching on frenzy. In vain did hymns of praise sound in his ears; in vain did vestals kiss his "divine" hand, and while doing so Rubria bent till her reddish hair touched his breast. Nero was not satisfied, and could not hide the fact. He was astonished and also disturbed because Petronius was silent. Some flattering and pointed word from his mouth would have been a great consolation at that moment. Unable at last to restrain himself, Cæsar beckoned to the arbiter.

"Speak," said he, when Petronius entered the podium.

"I am silent," answered Petronius, coldly, "for I cannot find words. Thou hast surpassed thyself."

"So it seemed to me too; but still this people — "

"Canst thou expect mongrels to appreciate poetry?"

"But thou too hast noticed that they have not thanked me as I deserve."

"Because thou hast chosen a bad moment."

"How?"

"When men's brains are filled with the odor of blood, they cannot listen attentively."

"Ah, those Christians!" replied Nero, clenching his fists. "They burned Rome, and injure me now in addition. What new punishment shall I invent for them?"

Petronius saw that he had taken the wrong road, that his words had produced an effect the very opposite of what he intended; so, to turn Cæsar's mind in another direction, he bent toward him and whispered, —

"Thy song is marvellous, but I will make one remark: in the fourth line of the third strophe the metre leaves something to be desired."

Nero, blushing with shame, as if caught in a disgraceful deed, had fear in his look, and answered in a whisper also, —

"Thou seest everything. I know. I will re-write that. But no one else noticed it, I think. And do thou, for the love of the gods, mention it to no one, — if life is dear to thee."

To this Petronius answered, as if in an outburst of vexation and anger, —

"Condemn me to death, O divinity, if I deceive thee; but thou wilt not terrify me, for the gods know best of all if I fear death."

And while speaking he looked straight into Cæsar's eyes, who answered after a while, —

"Be not angry; thou knowest that I love thee."

"A bad sign!" thought Petronius.

"I wanted to invite thee to-day to a feast," continued Nero, "but I prefer to shut myself in and polish that cursed line in the third strophe. Besides thee Seneca may have noticed it, and perhaps Secundus Carinas did; but I will rid myself of them quickly."

Then he summoned Seneca, and declared that with Acratus and Secundus Carinas, he sent him to the Italian and all other provinces for money, which he commanded him to obtain from cities, villages, famous temples, — in a word, from every place where it was possible to find money, or from which they could force it. But Seneca, who saw that Cæsar was confiding to him a work of plunder, sacrilege, and robbery, refused straightway.

"I must go to the country, lord," said he, "and await death, for I am old and my nerves are sick."

Seneca's Iberian nerves were stronger than Chilo's; they were not sick, perhaps, but in general his health was bad, for he seemed like a shadow, and recently his hair had grown white altogether.

Nero, too, when he looked at him, thought that he would not have to wait long for the man's death, and answered, —

"I will not expose thee to a journey if thou art ill, but through affection I wish to keep thee near me. Instead of going to the country, then, thou wilt stay in thy own house, and not leave it."

Then he laughed, and said, "If I send Acratus and Carinas by themselves, it will be like sending wolves for sheep. Whom shall I set above them?"

"Me, lord," said Domitius Afer.

"No! I have no wish to draw on Rome the wrath of Mercury, whom ye would put to shame with your villainy. I need some stoic like Seneca, or like my new friend, the philosopher Chilo."

Then he looked around, and asked, —

"But what has happened to Chilo?"

Chilo, who had recovered in the open air and returned to the amphitheatre for Cæsar's song, pushed up, and said, —

"I am here, O Radiant Offspring of the sun and moon. I was ill, but thy song has restored me."

"I will send thee to Achæa," said Nero. "Thou must know to a copper how much there is in each temple there."

"Do so, O Zeus, and the gods will give thee such tribute as they have never given any one."

"I would, but I do not like to prevent thee from seeing the games."

"Baal!" said Chilo.

The Augustians, delighted that Cæsar had regained humor, fell to laughing, and exclaimed, —

"No, lord, deprive not this valiant Greek of a sight of the games."

"But preserve me, O lord, from the sight of these noisy geese of the Capitol, whose brains put together would not fill a nutshell," retorted Chilo. "O first-born of Apollo, I am writing a Greek hymn in thy honor, and I wish to spend a few days in the temple of the Muses to implore inspiration."

"Oh, no!" exclaimed Nero. "It is thy wish to escape future games. Nothing will come of that!"

"I swear to thee, lord, that I am writing a hymn."

"Then thou wilt write it at night. Beg inspiration of Diana, who, by the way, is a sister of Apollo."

Chilo dropped his head and looked with malice on those present, who began to laugh again. Cæsar, turning to Senecio and Suilius Nerulinus, said, —

"Imagine, of the Christians appointed for to-day we have been able to finish hardly half!"

At this old Aquilus Regulus, who had great knowledge of everything touching the amphitheatre, thought a while, and said, —

"Spectacles in which people appear *sine armis et sine arte* last almost as long and are less entertaining."

"I will command to give them weapons," answered Nero.

But the superstitious Vestinius was roused from meditation at once, and asked in a mysterious voice, —

"Have ye noticed that when dying they see something? They look up, and die as it were without pain. I am sure that they see something."

He raised his eyes then to the opening of the amphitheatre, over which night had begun to extend its velarium dotted with stars. But others answered with laughter and jesting suppositions as to what the Christians could see at the moment of death. Meanwhile Cæsar gave a signal to the slave torch-bearers, and left the Circus; after him followed vestals, senators, dignitaries, and Augustians.

The night was clear and warm. Before the Circus were moving throngs of people, curious to witness the departure of Cæsar; but in some way they were gloomy and silent. Here and there applause was heard, but it ceased quickly. From the spoliarium creaking carts bore away the bloody remnants of Christians.

Petronius and Vinicius passed over their road in silence. Only when near his villa did Petronius inquire, —

"Hast thou thought of what I told thee?"

"I have," answered Vinicius.

"Dost believe that for me too this is a question of the highest importance? I must liberate her in spite of Cæsar and Tigellinus. This is a kind of battle in which I have undertaken to conquer, a kind of play in which I wish to win, even at the cost of my life. This day has confirmed me still more in my plan."

"May Christ reward thee."

"Thou wilt see."

Thus conversing, they stopped at the door of the villa and descended from the litter. At that moment a dark figure approached them, and asked, —

"Is the noble Vinicius here?"

"He is," answered the tribune. "What is thy wish?"

"I am Nazarius, the son of Miriam. I come from the prison, and bring tidings of Lygia."

Vinicius placed his hand on the young man's shoulder and looked into his eyes by the torchlight, without power to speak a word, but Nazarius divined the question which was dying on his lips, and replied, —

"She is living yet. Ursus sent me to say that she prays in her fever, and repeats thy name."

"Praise be to Christ, who has power to restore her to me," said Vinicius.

He conducted Nazarius to the library, and after a while Petronius came in to hear their conversation.

"Sickness saved her from shame, for executioners are timid," said the youth. "Ursus and Glaucus the physician watch over her night and day."

"Are the guards the same?"

"They are, and she is in their chamber. All the prisoners in the lower dungeon died of fever, or were stifled from foul air."

"Who art thou?" inquired Petronius.

"The noble Vinicius knows me. I am the son of that widow with whom Lygia lodged."

"And a Christian?"

The youth looked with inquiring glance at Vinicius, but, seeing him in prayer, he raised his head, and answered, —

"I am."

"How canst thou enter the prison freely?"

"I hired myself to carry out corpses; I did so to assist my brethren and bring them news from the city."

Petronius looked more attentively at the comely face of the youth, his blue eyes, and dark, abundant hair.

"From what country art thou, youth?" asked he.

"I am a Galilean, lord."

"Wouldst thou like to see Lygia free?"

The youth raised his eyes. "Yes, even had I to die afterwards."

Then Vinicius ceased to pray, and said, —

"Tell the guards to place her in a coffin as if she were dead. Thou wilt find assistants to bear her out in the night with thee. Near the 'Putrid Pits' will be people with a litter waiting for you; to them ye will give the coffin. Promise the guards from me as much gold as each can carry in his mantle."

While speaking, his face lost its usual torpor, and in him was roused the soldier to whom hope had restored his former energy.

Nazarius was flushed with delight, and, raising his hands, he exclaimed, —

"May Christ give her health, for she will be free."

"Dost thou think that the guards will consent?" inquired Petronius.

"They, lord? Yes, if they know that punishment and torture will not touch them."

"The guards would consent to her flight; all the more will they let us bear her out as a corpse," said Vinicius.

"There is a man, it is true," said Nazarius, "who burns with red-hot iron to see if the bodies which we carry out are dead. But he will take even a few sestertia not to touch the face of the dead with iron. For one aureus he will touch the coffin, not the body."

"Tell him that he will get a cap full of aurei," said Petronius. "But canst thou find reliable assistants?"

"I can find men who would sell their own wives and children for money."

"Where wilt thou find them?"

"In the prison itself or in the city. Once the guards are paid, they will admit whomever I like."

"In that case take me as a hired servant," said Vinicius.

But Petronius opposed this most earnestly. "The pretorians might recognize thee even in disguise, and all would be lost. Go neither to the prison nor the 'Putrid Pits.' All, including Cæsar and Tigellinus, should be convinced that she died; otherwise they will order immediate pursuit. We can lull suspicion only in this way: When she is taken to the Alban Hills or farther, to Sicily, we shall be in Rome. A week or two later thou wilt fall ill, and summon Nero's physician; he will tell thee to go to the mountains. Thou and she will meet, and afterward — "

Here he thought a while; then, waving his hand, he said, —

"Other times may come."

"May Christ have mercy on her," said Vinicius. "Thou art speaking of Sicily, while she is sick and may die."

"Let us keep her nearer Rome at first. The air alone will restore her, if only we snatch her from the dungeon. Hast thou no manager in the mountains whom thou canst trust?"

"I have," replied Vinicius, hurriedly. "Near Corioli is a reliable man who carried me in his arms when I was a child, and who loves me yet."

"Write to him to come to-morrow," said Petronius, handing Vinicius tablets. "I will send a courier at once."

He called the chief of the atrium then, and gave the needful orders. A few minutes later, a mounted slave was coursing in the night toward Corioli.

"It would please me were Ursus to accompany her," said Vinicius. "I should be more at rest."

"Lord," said Nazarius, "that is a man of superhuman strength; he can break gratings and follow her. There is one window above a steep, high rock where no guard is placed. I will take Ursus a rope; the rest he will do himself."

"By Hercules!" said Petronius, "let him tear himself out as he pleases, but not at the same time with her, and not two or three days later, for they would follow him and discover her hiding-place. By Hercules! do ye wish to destroy yourselves and her? I forbid you to name Corioli to him, or I wash my hands."

Both recognized the justice of these words, and were silent. Nazarius took leave, promising to come the next morning at daybreak.

He hoped to finish that night with the guards, but wished first to run in to see his mother, who in that uncertain and dreadful time had no rest for a moment thinking of her son. After some thought he had determined not to seek an assistant in the city, but to find and bribe one from among his fellow corpse-bearers. When going, he stopped, and, taking Vinicius aside, whispered, —

"I will not mention our plan to any one, not even to my mother, but the Apostle Peter promised to come from the amphitheatre to our house; I will tell him everything."

"Here thou canst speak openly," replied Vinicius. "The Apostle was in the amphitheatre with the people of Petronius. But I will go with you myself."

He gave command to bring him a slave's mantle, and they passed out. Petronius sighed deeply.

"I wished her to die of that fever," thought he, "since that would have been less terrible for Vinicius. But now I am ready to offer a golden tripod to Esculapius for her health. Ah! Ahenobarbus, thou hast the wish to turn a lover's pain into a spectacle; thou, Augusta, wert jealous of the maiden's beauty, and wouldst devour her alive because thy Rufius has perished. Thou, Tigellinus, wouldst destroy her to spite me! We shall see. I tell you that your eyes will not behold her on the arena, for she will either die her own death, or I shall wrest her from you as from the jaws of dogs, and wrest her in such fashion that ye shall not know it; and as often afterward as I look at you I shall think, These are the fools whom Caius Petronius outwitted."

And, self-satisfied, he passed to the triclinium, where he sat down to supper with Eunice. During the meal a lector read to them the Idyls of Theocritus. Out of doors the wind brought clouds from the direction of Soracte, and a sudden storm broke the silence of the calm summer night. From time to time thunder reverberated on the seven hills, while they, reclining near each other at the table, listened to the bucolic poet, who in the singing Doric dialect celebrated the loves of shepherds. Later on, with minds at rest, they prepared for sweet slumber.

But before this Vinicius returned. Petronius heard of his coming, and went to meet him.

"Well? Have ye fixed anything new?" inquired he. "Has Nazarius gone to the prison?"

"He has," answered the young man, arranging his hair, wet from the rain. "Nazarius went to arrange with the guards, and I have seen Peter, who commanded me to pray and believe."

"That is well. If all goes favorably, we can bear her away to-morrow night."

"My manager must be here at daybreak with men."

"The road is a short one. Now go to rest."

But Vinicius knelt in his cubiculum and prayed.

At sunrise Niger, the manager, arrived from Corioli, bringing with him, at the order of Vinicius, mules, a litter, and four trusty men selected among slaves from Britain, whom, to save appearances, he had left at an inn in the

Subura. Vinicius, who had watched all night, went to meet him. Niger, moved at sight of his youthful master, kissed his hands and eyes, saying, —

"My dear, thou art ill, or else suffering has sucked the blood from thy face, for hardly did I know thee at first."

Vinicius took him to the interior colonnade, and there admitted him to the secret. Niger listened with fixed attention, and on his dry, sunburnt face great emotion was evident; this he did not even try to master.

"Then she is a Christian?" exclaimed Niger; and he looked inquiringly into the face of Vinicius, who divined evidently what the gaze of the countryman was asking, since he answered, —

"I too am a Christian."

Tears glistened in Niger's eyes that moment. He was silent for a while; then, raising his hands, he said, —

"I thank Thee, O Christ, for having taken the beam from eyes which are the dearest on earth to me."

Then he embraced the head of Vinicius, and, weeping from happiness, fell to kissing his forehead. A moment later, Petronius appeared, bringing Nazarius.

"Good news!" cried he, while still at a distance.

Indeed, the news was good. First, Glaucus the physician guaranteed Lygia's life, though she had the same prison fever of which, in the Tullianum and other dungeons, hundreds of people were dying daily. As to the guards and the man who tried corpses with red-hot iron, there was not the least difficulty. Attys, the assistant, was satisfied also.

"We made openings in the coffin to let the sick woman breathe," said Nazarius. "The only danger is that she may groan or speak as we pass the pretorians. But she is very weak, and is lying with closed eyes since early morning. Besides, Glaucus will give her a sleeping draught prepared by himself from drugs brought by me purposely from the city. The cover will not be nailed to the coffin; ye will raise it easily and take the patient to the litter. We will place in the coffin a long bag of sand, which ye will provide."

Vinicius, while hearing these words, was as pale as linen; but he listened with such attention that he seemed to divine at a glance what Nazarius had to say.

"Will they carry out other bodies from the prison?" inquired Petronius.

"About twenty died last night, and before evening more will be dead," said the youth. "We must go with a whole company, but we will delay and drop into the rear. At the first corner my comrade will get lame purposely. In that way we shall remain behind the others considerably. Ye will wait for us at the small temple of Libitina. May God give a night as dark as possible!"

"He will," said Niger. "Last evening was bright, and then a sudden storm came. To-day the sky is clear, but since morning it is sultry. Every night now there will be wind and rain."

"Will ye go without torches?" inquired Vinicius.

"The torches are carried only in advance. In every event, be near the tem-

ple of Libitina at dark, though usually we carry out the corpses only just before midnight."

They stopped. Nothing was to be heard save the hurried breathing of
Vinicius. Petronius turned to him, —

"I said yesterday that it would be best were we both to stay at home, but
now I see that I could not stay. Were it a question of flight, there would be
need of the greatest caution; but since she will be borne out as a corpse, it
seems that not the least suspicion will enter the head of any one."

"True, true!" answered Vinicius. "I must be there. I will take her from the
coffin myself."

"Once she is in my house at Corioli, I answer for her," said Niger.

Conversation stopped here. Niger returned to his men at the inn. Nazarius
took a purse of gold under his tunic and went to the prison. For Vinicius
began a day filled with alarm, excitement, disquiet, and hope.

"The undertaking ought to succeed, for it is well planned," said Petronius.
"It was impossible to plan better. Thou must feign suffering, and wear a dark
toga. Do not desert the amphitheatre. Let people see thee. All is so fixed that
there cannot be failure. But — art thou perfectly sure of thy manager?"

"He is a Christian," replied Vinicius.

Petronius looked at him with amazement, then shrugged his shoulders, and
said, as if in soliloquy, —

"By Pollux! how it spreads, and commands people's souls. Under such terror as the present, men would renounce straightway all the gods of Rome,
Greece, and Egypt. Still, this is wonderful! By Pollux! if I believed that anything depended on our gods, I would sacrifice six white bullocks to each of
them, and twelve to Capitoline Jove. Spare no promises to thy Christ."

"I have given Him my soul," said Vinicius.

And they parted. Petronius returned to his cubiculum; but Vinicius went
to look from a distance at the prison, and thence betook himself to the slope
of the Vatican hill, — to that hut of the quarryman where he had received
baptism from the hands of the Apostle. It seemed to him that Christ would
hear him more readily there than in any other place; so when he found it, he
threw himself on the ground and exerted all the strength of his suffering
soul in prayer for mercy, and so forgot himself that he remembered not where
he was or what he was doing. In the afternoon he was roused by the sound
of trumpets which came from the direction of Nero's Circus. He went out of
the hut, and gazed around with eyes which were as if just opened from sleep.

It was hot; the stillness was broken at intervals by the sound of brass and
continually by the ceaseless noise of grasshoppers. The air had become sultry,
the sky was still clear over the city, but near the Sabine Hills dark clouds were
gathering at the edge of the horizon.

Vinicius went home. Petronius was waiting for him in the atrium.

"I have been on the Palatine," said he. "I showed myself there purposely,
and even sat down at dice. There is a feast at the house of Anicius this evening; I promised to go, but only after midnight, saying that I must sleep

before that hour. In fact I shall be there, and it would be well wert thou to go also."

"Are there no tidings from Niger or Nazarius?" inquired Vinicius.

"No; we shall see them only at midnight. Hast noticed that a storm is threatening?"

"Yes."

"To-morrow there is to be an exhibition of crucified Christians, but perhaps rain will prevent it."

Then he drew nearer and said, touching his nephew's shoulder, —

"But thou wilt not see her on the cross; thou wilt see her only in Corioli. By Castor! I would not give the moment in which we free her for all the gems in Rome. The evening is near."

In truth the evening was near, and darkness began to encircle the city earlier than usual because clouds covered the whole horizon. With the coming of night heavy rain fell, which turned into steam on the stones warmed by the heat of the day, and filled the streets of the city with mist. After that came a lull, then brief violent showers.

"Let us hurry!" said Vinicius at last; "they may carry bodies from the prison earlier because of the storm."

"It is time!" said Petronius.

And taking Gallic mantles with hoods, they passed through the garden door to the street. Petronius had armed himself with a short Roman knife called *sicca*, which he took always during night trips.

The city was empty because of the storm. From time to time lightning rent the clouds, illuminating with its glare the fresh walls of houses newly built or in process of building and the wet flag-stones with which the streets were paved. At last a flash came, when they saw, after a rather long road, the mound on which stood the small temple of Libitina, and at the foot of the mound a group of mules and horses.

"Niger!" called Vinicius, in a low voice.

"I am here, lord," said a voice in the rain.

"Is everything ready?"

"It is. We were here at dark. But hide yourselves under the rampart, or ye will be drenched. What a storm! Hail will fall, I think."

In fact Niger's fear was justified, for soon hail began to fall, at first fine, then larger and more frequent. The air grew cold at once. While standing under the rampart, sheltered from the wind and icy missiles, they conversed in low voices.

"Even should some one see us," said Niger, "there will be no suspicion; we look like people waiting for the storm to pass. But I fear that they may not bring the bodies out till morning."

"The hail-storm will not last," said Petronius. "We must wait even till daybreak."

They waited, listening to hear the sound of the procession. The hail-storm passed, but immediately after a shower began to roar. At times the wind rose, and brought from the "Putrid Pits" a dreadful odor of decaying bodies, buried near the surface and carelessly.

"I see a light through the mist," said Niger, — "one, two, three, — those are torches. See that the mules do not snort," said he, turning to the men.

"They are coming!" said Petronius.

The lights were growing more and more distinct. After a time it was possible to see torches under the quivering flames.

Niger made the sign of the cross, and began to pray. Meanwhile the gloomy procession drew nearer, and halted at last in front of the temple of Libitina. Petronius, Vinicius, and Niger pressed up to the rampart in silence, not knowing why the halt was made. But the men had stopped only to cover their mouths and faces with cloths to ward off the stifling stench which at the edge of the "Putrid Pits" was simply unendurable; then they raised the biers with coffins and moved on. Only one coffin stopped before the temple. Vinicius sprang toward it, and after him Petronius, Niger, and two British slaves with the litter.

But before they had reached it in the darkness, the voice of Nazarius was heard, full of pain, —

"Lord, they took her with Ursus to the Esquiline prison. We are carrying another body! They removed her before midnight."

Petronius, when he had returned home, was gloomy as a storm, and did not even try to console Vinicius. He understood that to free Lygia from the Esquiline dungeons was not to be dreamed of. He divined that very likely she had been taken from the Tullianum so as not to die of fever and escape the amphitheatre assigned to her. But for this very reason she was watched and guarded more carefully than others. From the bottom of his soul Petronius was sorry for her and Vinicius, but he was wounded also by the thought that for the first time in life he had not succeeded, and for the first time was beaten in a struggle.

"Fortune seems to desert me," said he to himself, "but the gods are mistaken if they think that I will accept such a life as his, for example."

Here he turned toward Vinicius, who looked at him with staring eyes.

"What is the matter? Thou hast a fever," said Petronius.

But Vinicius answered with a certain strange, broken, halting voice, like that of a sick child, —

"But I believe that He — can restore her to me."

Above the city the last thunders of the storm had ceased.

CHAPTER LVII

THREE days' rain, an exceptional phenomenon in Rome during summer, and hail falling in opposition to the natural order, not only in the day, but even at night, interrupted the spectacles. People were growing alarmed. A failure of grapes was predicted, and when on a certain afternoon a thunderbolt melted the bronze statue of Ceres on the Capitol, sacrifices were ordered in the temple of Jupiter Salvator. The priests of Ceres spread a report that the anger of the gods was turned on the city because of the too hasty punishment of Christians; hence crowds began to insist that the spectacles be given without reference to weather. Delight seized all Rome when the announcement was made at last that the ludus would begin again after three days' interval.

Meanwhile beautiful weather returned. The amphitheatre was filled at daybreak with thousands of people. Cæsar came early with the vestals and the court. The spectacle was to begin with a battle among the Christians, who to this end were arrayed as gladiators and furnished with all kinds of weapons which served gladiators by profession in offensive and defensive struggles. But here came disappointment. The Christians threw nets, darts, tridents, and swords on the arena, embraced and encouraged one another to endurance in view of torture and death. At this deep indignation and resentment seized the hearts of the multitude. Some reproached the Christians with cowardice and pusillanimity; others asserted that they refused to fight through hatred of the people, so as to deprive them of that pleasure which the sight of bravery produces. Finally, at command of Cæsar, real gladiators were let out, who despatched in one twinkle the kneeling and defenceless victims.

When these bodies were removed, the spectacle was a series of mythologic pictures, — Cæsar's own idea. The audience saw Hercules blazing in living fire on Mount Oeta. Vinicius had trembled at the thought that the rôle of Hercules might be intended for Ursus; but evidently the turn of Lygia's faithful servant had not come, for on the pile some other Christian was burning, — a man quite unknown to Vinicius. In the next picture Chilo, whom Cæsar would not excuse from attendance, saw acquaintances. The death of Dædalus was represented, and also that of Icarus. In the rôle of Dædalus appeared Euricius, that old man who had given Chilo the sign of the fish; the rôle of Icarus was taken by his son, Quartus. Both were raised aloft with cunning machinery, and then hurled suddenly from an immense height to the arena. Young Quartus fell so near Cæsar's podium that he spattered with blood not only the external ornaments but the purple covering spread over the front of the podium. Chilo did not see the fall, for he closed his eyes; but he heard the dull thump of the body, and when after a time he saw blood there close to him, he came near fainting a second time.

The pictures changed quickly. The shameful torments of maidens violated before death by gladiators dressed as wild beasts, delighted the hearts of the rabble. They saw priestesses of Cybele and Ceres, they saw the Danaides, they saw Dirce and Pasiphaë; finally they saw young girls, not mature yet, torn asunder by wild horses. Every moment the crowd applauded new ideas of Nero, who, proud of them, and made happy by plaudits, did not take the emerald from his eye for one instant while looking at white bodies torn with iron, and the convulsive quivering of victims.

Pictures were given also from the history of the city. After the maidens they saw Mucius Scævola, whose hand fastened over a fire to a tripod filled the amphitheatre with the odor of burnt flesh; but this man, like the real Scævola, remained without a groan, his eyes raised and the murmur of prayer on his blackening lips. When he had expired and his body was dragged to the spoliarium, the usual midday interlude followed. Cæsar with the vestals and the Augustians left the amphitheatre, and withdrew to an immense scarlet tent erected purposely; in this was prepared for him and the guests a magnificent prandium. The spectators for the greater part followed his example, and, streaming out, disposed themselves in picturesque groups around the tent, to rest their limbs wearied from long sitting, and enjoy the food which, through Cæsar's favor, was served by slaves to them. Only the most curious descended to the arena itself, and, touching with their fingers lumps of sand held together by blood, conversed, as specialists and amateurs, of that which had happened and of that which was to follow. Soon even these went away, lest they might be late for the feast; only those few were left who stayed not through curiosity, but sympathy for the coming victims. Those concealed themselves behind seats or in the lower places.

Meanwhile the arena was levelled, and slaves began to dig holes one near the other in rows throughout the whole circuit from side to side, so that the last row was but a few paces distant from Cæsar's podium. From outside came the murmur of people, shouts and plaudits, while within they were preparing in hot haste for new tortures. The cunicula were opened simultaneously, and in all passages leading to the arena were urged forward crowds of Christians naked and carrying crosses on their shoulders. The whole arena was filled with them. Old men, bending under the weight of wooden beams, ran forward; at the side of these went men in the prime of life, women with loosened hair behind which they strove to hide their nakedness, small boys, and little children. The crosses, for the greater part, as well as the victims, were wreathed with flowers. The servants of the amphitheatre beat the unfortunates with clubs, forcing them to lay down their crosses near the holes prepared, and stand themselves there in rows. Thus were to perish those whom executioners had had no chance to drive out as food for dogs and wild beasts the first day of the games. Black slaves seized the victims, laid them face upward on the wood, and fell to nailing their hands hurriedly and quickly to the arms of the crosses, so that people returning after the interlude might find all the crosses standing. The whole amphitheatre resounded with the noise of hammers which echoed through all the rows, went out to the space surrounding the amphitheatre, and into the tent where Cæsar was entertaining his suite and the vestals. There he drank wine, bantered with Chilo, and whispered strange words in the ears of the priestesses of Vesta; but on the arena the work was seething, — nails were going into the hands and feet of the Christians; shovels moved quickly, filling the holes in which the crosses had been planted.

Among the new victims whose turn was to come soon was Crispus. The lions had not had time to rend him; hence he was appointed to the cross. He, ready at all times for death, was delighted with the thought that his hour was approaching. He seemed another man, for his emaciated body was wholly naked, — only a girdle of ivy encircled his hips, on his head was a garland of roses. But in his eyes gleamed always that same exhaustless energy; that same fanatical stern face gazed from beneath the crown of roses. Neither had his heart changed; for, as once in the cuniculum he had threatened with the wrath of God his brethren sewed up in the skins of wild beasts, so to-day he thundered in place of consoling them.

"Thank the Redeemer," said Crispus, "that He permits you to die the same death that He Himself died. Maybe a part of your sins will be remitted for this cause; but tremble, since justice must be satisfied, and there cannot be one reward for the just and the wicked."

His words were accompanied by the sound of the hammers nailing the hands and feet of victims. Every moment more crosses were raised on the arena; but he, turning to the crowd standing each man by his own cross, continued, —

"I see heaven open, but I see also the yawning abyss. I know not what account of my life to give the Lord, though I have believed, and hated evil. I fear, not death, but resurrection; I fear, not torture, but judgment, for the day of wrath is at hand."

At that moment was heard from between the nearest rows some voice, calm and solemn, —

"Not the day of wrath, but of mercy, the day of salvation and happiness; for I say that Christ will gather you in, will comfort you and seat you at His right hand. Be confident, for heaven is opening before you."

At these words all eyes were turned to the benches; even those who were hanging on the crosses raised their pale, tortured faces, and looked toward the man who was speaking.

But he went to the barrier surrounding the arena, and blessed them with the sign of the cross.

Crispus stretched out his arm as if to thunder at him; but when he saw the man's face, he dropped his arm, the knees bent under him, and his lips whispered, "Paul the Apostle!"

To the great astonishment of the servants of the Circus, all of those who were not nailed to the crosses yet knelt down. Paul turned to Crispus and said, —

"Threaten them not, Crispus, for this day they will be with thee in paradise. It is thy thought that they may be condemned. But who will condemn?

Will God, who gave His Son for them? Will Christ, who died for their salvation, condemn when they die for His name? And how is it possible that He who loves can condemn? Who will accuse the chosen of God? Who will say of this blood, 'It is cursed'?"

"I have hated evil," said the old priest.

"Christ's command to love men was higher than that to hate evil, for His religion is not hatred, but love."

"I have sinned in the hour of death," answered Crispus, beating his breast.

The manager of the seats approached the Apostle, and inquired, —

"Who art thou, speaking to the condemned?"

"A Roman citizen," answered Paul, calmly. Then, turning to Crispus, he said: "Be confident, for to-day is a day of grace; die in peace, O servant of God."

The black men approached Crispus at that moment to place him on the cross; but he looked around once again, and cried, —

"My brethren, pray for me!"

His face had lost its usual sternness; his stony features had taken an expression of peace and sweetness. He stretched his arms himself along the arms of the cross, to make the work easier, and, looking directly into heaven, began to pray earnestly. He seemed to feel nothing; for when the nails entered his hands, not the least quiver shook his body, nor on his face did there appear any wrinkle of pain. He prayed when they raised the cross and trampled the earth around it. Only when crowds began to fill the amphitheatre with shouts and laughter did his brows frown somewhat, as if in anger that a pagan people were disturbing the calm and peace of a sweet death.

But all the crosses had been raised, so that in the arena there stood as it were a forest, with people hanging on the trees. On the arms of the crosses and on the heads of the martyrs fell the gleam of the sun; but on the arena was a deep shadow, forming a kind of black involved grating through which glittered the golden sand. That was a spectacle in which the whole delight of the audience consisted in looking at a lingering death. Never before had men seen such a density of crosses. The arena was packed so closely that the servants squeezed between them only with effort. On the edges were women especially; but Crispus, as a leader, was raised almost in front of Cæsar's podium, on an immense cross, wreathed below with honeysuckle. None of the victims had died yet, but some of those fastened earlier had fainted. No one groaned; no one called for mercy. Some were hanging with head inclined on one arm, or dropped on the breast, as if seized by sleep; some were as if in meditation; some, looking toward heaven, were moving their lips quietly. In this terrible forest of crosses, among those crucified bodies, in that silence of victims there was something ominous. The people who, filled by the feast and gladsome, had returned to the Circus with shouts, became silent, not knowing on which body to rest their eyes, or what to think of the spectacle. The nakedness of strained female forms roused no feeling. They did not make the usual bets as to who would die first, — a thing done generally when there was even the smallest number of criminals on the arena. It seemed that Cæsar himself was bored, for he turned lazily and with drowsy expression to arrange his necklace.

At that moment Crispus, who was hanging opposite, and who, like a man in a faint or dying, had kept his eyes closed, opened them and looked at Cæsar. His face assumed an expression so pitiless, and his eyes flashed with such fire, that the Augustians whispered to one another, pointing at him with their fingers, and at last Cæsar himself turned to that cross, and placed the emerald to his eye sluggishly.

Perfect silence followed. The eyes of the spectators were fixed on Crispus, who strove to move his right hand, as if to tear it from the tree.

After a while his breast rose, his ribs were visible, and he cried: "Matricide! woe to thee!"

The Augustians, hearing this mortal insult flung at the lord of the world in presence of thousands, did not dare to breathe. Chilo was half dead. Cæsar trembled, and dropped the emerald from his fingers. The people, too, held the breath in their breasts. The voice of Crispus was heard, as it rose in power, throughout the amphitheatre, —

"Woe to thee, murderer of wife and brother! woe to thee, Antichrist. The abyss is opening beneath thee, death is stretching its hands to thee, the grave is waiting for thee. Woe, living corpse, for in terror shalt thou die and be damned to eternity!"

Unable to tear his hand from the cross, Crispus strained awfully. He was terrible,—a living skeleton; unbending as predestination, he shook his white beard over Nero's podium, scattering, as he nodded, rose leaves from the garland on his head.

"Woe to thee, murderer! Thy measure is surpassed, and thy hour is at hand!"

Here he made one more effort. It seemed for a moment that he would free his hand from the cross and hold it in menace above Cæsar; but all at once his emaciated arms extended still more, his body settled down, his head fell on his breast, and he died.

In that forest of crosses the weakest began also the sleep of eternity.

CHAPTER LVIII

"Lord," said Chilo, "the sea is like olive oil, the waves seem to sleep. Let us go to Achæa. There the glory of Apollo is awaiting thee, crowns and triumph are awaiting thee, the people will deify thee, the gods will receive thee as a guest, their own equal; but here, O lord — "

And he stopped, for his lower lip began to quiver so violently that his words passed into meaningless sounds.

"We will go when the games are over," replied Nero. "I know that even now some call the Christians *innoxia corpora*. If I were to go, all would repeat this. What dost thou fear?"

Then he frowned, but looked with inquiring glance at Chilo, as if expecting an answer, for he only feigned cool blood. At the last exhibition he himself feared the words of Crispus; and when he had returned to the Palatine, he could not sleep from rage and shame, but also from fear.

Then Vestinius, who heard their conversation in silence, looked around, and said in a mysterious voice, —

"Listen, lord, to this old man. There is something strange in those Christians. Their deity gives them an easy death, but he may be vengeful."

"It was not I who arranged the games, but Tigellinus," replied Nero, quickly.

"True! it was I," added Tigellinus, who heard Cæsar's answer, "and I jeer at all Christian gods. Vestinius is a bladder full of prejudices, and this valiant Greek is ready to die of terror at sight of a hen with feathers up in defence of her chickens."

"True!" said Nero; "but henceforth give command to cut the tongues out of Christians and stop their mouths."

"Fire will stop them, O divinity."

"Woe is me!" groaned Chilo.

But Cæsar, to whom the insolent confidence of Tigellinus gave courage, began to laugh, and said, pointing to the old Greek, —

"See how the descendant of Achilles looks!"

Indeed Chilo looked terribly. The remnant of hair on his head had grown white; on his face was fixed an expression of some immense dread, alarm, and oppression. He seemed at times, too, as if stunned and only half conscious. Often he gave no answer to questions; then again he fell into anger, and became so insolent that the Augustians preferred not to attack him. Such a moment had come to him then.

"Do what ye like with me, but I will not go to the games!" cried he, in desperation.

Nero looked at him for a while, and, turning to Tigellinus, said, —

"Have a care that this Stoic is near me in the gardens. I want to see what impression our torches will make on him."

Chilo was afraid of the threat which quivered in Cæsar's voice. "O lord," said he, "I shall see nothing, for I cannot see in the night-time."

"The night will be as bright as day," replied Cæsar, with a threatening laugh.

Turning then to the Augustians, Nero talked about races which he intended to have when the games were over.

Petronius approached Chilo, and asked, pushing him on the shoulder, —

"Have I not said that thou wouldst not hold out?"

"I wish to drink," said Chilo, stretching his trembling hand toward a goblet of wine; but he was unable to raise it to his lips. Seeing this, Vestinius took the vessel; but later he drew near, and inquired with curious and frightened face, —

"Are the Furies pursuing thee?"

The old man looked at him a certain time with open lips, as if not understanding what he said. But Vestinius repeated, —

"Are the Furies pursuing thee?"

"No," answered Chilo; "but night is before me."

"How, night? May the gods have mercy on thee. How night?"

"Night, ghastly and impenetrable, in which something is moving, something coming toward me; but I know not what it is, and I am terrified."

"I have always been sure that there are witches. Dost thou not dream of something?"

"No, for I do not sleep. I did not think that they would be punished thus."

"Art thou sorry for them?"

"Why do ye shed so much blood? Hast heard what that one said from the cross? Woe to us!"

"I heard," answered Vestinius, in a low voice. "But they are incendiaries."

"Not true!"

"And enemies of the human race."

"Not true!"

"And poisoners of water."

"Not true!"

"And murderers of children."

"Not true!"

"How?" inquired Vestinius, with astonishment. "Thou hast said so thyself, and given them into the hands of Tigellinus."

"Therefore night has surrounded me, and death is coming toward me. At times it seems to me that I am dead already, and ye also."

"No! it is they who are dying; we are alive. But tell me, what do they see when they are dying?"

"Christ."

"That is their god. Is he a mighty god?"

But Chilo answered with a question, —

"What kind of torches are to burn in the gardens? Hast thou heard what Cæsar said?"

"I heard, and I know. Those torches are called Sarmentitii and Semaxii. They are made by arraying men in painful tunics, steeped in pitch, and binding them to pillars, to which fire is set afterward. May their god not send misfortune on the city. Semaxii! that is a dreadful punishment!"

"I would rather see it, for there will not be blood," answered Chilo. "Command a slave to hold the goblet to my mouth. I wish to drink, but I spill the wine; my hand trembles from age."

Others also were speaking of the Christians. Old Domitius Afer reviled them.

"There is such a multitude of them," said he, "that they might raise a civil war; and, remember, there were fears lest they might arm. But they die like sheep."

"Let them try to die otherwise!" said Tigellinus.

To this Petronius answered, "Ye deceive yourselves. They are arming."

"With what?"

"With patience."

"That is a new kind of weapon."

"True. But can ye say that they die like common criminals? No! They die as if the criminals were those who condemned them to death, — that is, we and the whole Roman people."

"What raving!" said Tigellinus.

"Hic Abdera!" [1] answered Petronius.

But others, struck by the justice of his remark, began to look at one another with astonishment, and repeat, —

"True! there is something peculiar and strange in their death."

"I tell you that they see their divinity!" cried Vestinius, from one side.

Thereupon a number of Augustians turned to Chilo, —

"Hai, old man, thou knowest them well; tell us what they see."

The Greek spat out wine on his tunic, and answered, —

"The resurrection." And he began to tremble so that the guests sitting nearer burst into loud laughter.

---

[1] A proverbial expression meaning "the dullest of the dull" — *Note by the Author.*

CHAPTER LIX

For some time Vinicius had spent his nights away from home. It occurred to Petronius that perhaps he had formed a new plan, and was working to liberate Lygia from the Esquiline dungeon; he did not wish, however, to inquire about anything, lest he might bring misfortune to the work. This sceptical exquisite had become in a certain sense superstitious. He had failed to snatch Lygia from the Mamertine prison, hence had ceased to believe in his own star.

Besides, he did not count this time on a favorable outcome for the efforts of Vinicius. The Esquiline prison, formed in a hurry from the cellars of houses thrown down to stop the fire, was not, it is true, so terrible as the old Tullianum near the Capitol, but it was a hundred times better guarded. Petronius understood perfectly that Lygia had been taken there only to escape death and not escape the amphitheatre. He could understand at once that for this very reason they were guarding her as a man guards the eye in his head.

"Evidently," said he to himself, "Cæsar and Tigellinus have reserved her for some special spectacle, more dreadful than all others, and Vinicius is more likely to perish than rescue her."

Vinicius, too, had lost hope of being able to free Lygia. Christ alone could do that. The young tribune now thought only of seeing her in prison.

For some time the knowledge that Nazarius had penetrated the Mamertine prison as a corpse-bearer had given him no peace; hence he resolved to try that method also.

The overseer of the "Putrid Pits," who had been bribed for an immense sum of money, admitted him at last among servants whom he sent nightly to prisons for corpses. The danger that Vinicius might be recognized was really small. He was preserved from it by night, the dress of a slave, and the defective illumination of the prison. Besides, into whose head could it enter that a patrician, the grandson of one consul, the son of another, could be found among servants, corpse-bearers, exposed to the miasma of prisons and the "Putrid Pits"? And he began work to which men were forced only by slavery or the direst need.

When the desired evening came, he girded his loins gladly, covered his head with a cloth steeped in turpentine, and with throbbing heart betook himself, with a crowd of others, to the Esquiline.

The pretorian guards made no trouble, for all had brought proper tesseræ, which the centurion examined by the light of a lantern. After a while the great iron doors opened before them, and they entered.

Vinicius saw an extensive vaulted cellar, from which they passed to a series of others. Dim tapers illuminated the interior of each, which was filled with people. Some of these were lying at the walls sunk in sleep, or dead, perhaps. Others surrounded large vessels of water, standing in the middle, out of which they drank as people tormented with fever; others were sitting on the grounds, their elbows on their knees, their heads on their palms; here and there children were sleeping, nestled up to their mothers. Groans, loud hurried breathing of the sick, weeping, whispered prayers, hymns in an undertone, the curses of overseers were heard round about it. In this dungeon was the odor of crowds and corpses. In its gloomy depth dark figures were swarming; nearer, close to flickering lights, were visible faces, pale, terrified, hungry, and cadaverous, with eyes dim, or else flaming with fever, with lips blue, with streams of sweat on their foreheads, and with clammy hair. In corners the sick were moaning loudly; some begged for water; others, to be led to death. And still that prison was less terrible than the old Tullianum. The legs bent under Vinicius when he saw all this, and breath was failing in his breast. At the thought that Lygia was in the midst of this misery and misfortune, the hair rose on his head, and he stifled a cry of despair. The amphitheatre, the teeth of wild beasts, the cross, — anything was better than those dreadful dungeons filled with the odor of corpses, places in which imploring voices called from every corner, —

"Lead us to death!"

Vinicius pressed his nails into his palms, for he felt that he was growing weak, and that presence of mind was deserting him. All that he had felt till then, all his love and pain, changed in him to one desire for death.

Just then near his side was heard the overseer of the "Putrid Pits," —

"How many corpses have ye to-day?"

"About a dozen," answered the guardian of the prison, "but there will be more before morning; some are in agony at the walls."

And he fell to complaining of women who concealed dead children so as to keep them near and not yield them to the "Putrid Pits." "We must discover corpses first by the odor; through this the air, so terrible already, is spoiled still more. I would rather be a slave in some rural prison than guard these dogs rotting here while alive — "

The overseer of the pits comforted him, saying that his own service was no easier. By this time the sense of reality had returned to Vinicius. He began to search the dungeon; but sought in vain for Lygia, fearing meanwhile that he would never see her alive. A number of cellars were connected by newly made passages; the corpse-bearers entered only those from which corpses were to be carried. Fear seized Vinicius lest that privilege which had cost so much trouble might serve no purpose. Luckily his patron aided him.

"Infection spreads most through corpses," said he. "Ye must carry out the bodies at once, or die yourselves, together with the prisoners."

"There are only ten of us for all the cellars," said the guardian, "and we must sleep."

"I will leave four men of mine, who will go through the cellars at night to see if these are dead."

"We will drink to-morrow if thou do that. Everybody must be taken to the test; for an order has come to pierce the neck of each corpse, and then to the 'Putrid Pits' at once with it."

"Very well, but we will drink," said the overseer.

Four men were selected, and among them Vinicius; the others he took to put the corpses on the biers.

Vinicius was at rest; he was certain now at least of finding Lygia. The young tribune began by examining the first dungeon carefully; he looked into all the dark corners hardly reached by the light of his torch; he examined figures sleeping at the walls under coarse cloths; he saw that the most grievously ill were drawn into a corner apart. But Lygia he found in no place. In a second and third dungeon his search was equally fruitless.

Meanwhile the hour had grown late; all corpses had been carried out. The guards, disposing themselves in the corridors between cellars, were asleep; the children, wearied with crying, were silent; nothing was heard save the breathing of troubled breasts, and here and there the murmur of prayer.

Vinicius went with his torch to the fourth dungeon, which was considerably smaller. Raising the light, he began to examine it, and trembled all at once, for it seemed to him that he saw, near a latticed opening in the wall, the gigantic form of Ursus. Then, blowing out the light, he approached him, and asked, —

"Ursus, art thou here?"

"Who art thou?" asked the giant, turning his head.

"Dost not know me?"

"Thou hast quenched the torch; how could I know thee?"

But at that moment Vinicius saw Lygia lying on a cloak near the wall; so, without speaking further, he knelt near her. Ursus recognized him, and said, —

"Praise be to Christ! but do not wake her, lord."

Vinicius, kneeling down, gazed at her through his tears. In spite of the darkness he could distinguish her face, which seemed to him as pale as alabaster, and her emaciated arms. At that sight he was seized by a love which was like a rending pain, a love which shook his soul to its uttermost depth, and which at the same time was so full of pity, respect, and homage that he fell on his face, and pressed to his lips the hem of the cloak on which rested that head dearer to him than all else on earth.

Ursus looked at Vinicius for a long time in silence, but at last he pulled his tunic.

"Lord," asked he, "how didst thou come, and hast thou come here to save her?"

Vinicius rose, and struggled for a time with his emotion. "Show me the means," replied he.

"I thought that thou wouldst find them, lord. Only one method came to my head — "

Here he turned toward the grating in the wall, as if in answer to himself, and said, —

"In that way — but there are soldiers outside — "

"A hundred pretorians."

"Then we cannot pass?"

"No!"

The Lygian rubbed his forehead, and asked again, —

"How didst thou enter?"

"I have a tessera from the overseer of the 'Putrid Pits.'" Then Vinicius stopped suddenly, as if some idea had flashed through his head.

"By the Passion of the Redeemer," said he, in a hurried voice, "I will stay here. Let her take my tessera; she can wrap her head in a cloth, cover her shoulders with a mantle, and pass out. Among the slaves who carry out corpses there are several youths not full grown; hence the pretorians will not notice her, and once at the house of Petronius she is safe."

But the Lygian dropped his head on his breast, and said, —

"She would not consent, for she loves thee; besides, she is sick, and unable to stand alone. If thou and the noble Petronius cannot save her from prison, who can?" said he, after a while.

"Christ alone."

Then both were silent.

"Christ could save all Christians," thought the Lygian, in his simple heart; "but since He does not save them, it is clear that the hour of torture and death has come."

He accepted it for himself, but was grieved to the depth of his soul for that child who had grown up in his arms, and whom he loved beyond life.

Vinicius knelt again near Lygia. Through the grating in the wall moonbeams came in, and gave better light than the one candle burning yet over the entrance. Lygia opened her eyes now, and said, placing her feverish hand on the arm of Vinicius,—

"I see thee; I knew that thou wouldst come."

He seized her hands, pressed them to his forehead and his heart, raised her somewhat, and held her to his breast.

"I have come, dearest. May Christ guard and free thee, beloved Lygia!"

He could say no more, for the heart began to whine in his breast from pain and love, and he would not show pain in her presence.

"I am sick, Marcus," said Lygia, "and I must die either on the arena or here in prison — I have prayed to see thee before death; thou hast come, — Christ has heard me."

Unable to utter a word yet, he pressed her to his bosom, and she continued, —

"I saw thee through the window in the Tullianum. I saw that thou hadst the wish to come to me. Now the Redeemer has given me a moment of consciousness, so that we may take farewell of each other. I am going to Him, Marcus, but I love thee, and shall love always."

Vinicius conquered himself; he stifled his pain and began to speak in a voice which he tried to make calm, —

"No, dear Lygia, thou wilt not die. The Apostle commanded me to believe, and he promised to pray for thee; he knew Christ, — Christ loved him and will not refuse him. Hadst thou to die, Peter would not have commanded me to be confident; but he said, 'Have confidence!' — No, Lygia! Christ will have mercy. He does not wish thy death. He will not permit it. I swear to thee by the name of the Redeemer that Peter is praying for thee."

Silence followed. The one candle hanging above the entrance went out. but moonlight entered through the whole opening. In the opposite corner of the cellar a child whined and was silent. From outside came the voices of pretorians, who, after watching their turn out, were playing under the wall at *scriptæ duodecim.*

"O Marcus," said Lygia, "Christ Himself called to the Father, 'Remove this bitter cup from Me'; still He drank it. Christ Himself died on the cross, and thousands are perishing for His sake. Why, then, should He spare me alone? Who am I, Marcus? I have heard Peter say that he too would die in torture. Who am I, compared with Peter? When the pretorians came to us, I dreaded death and torture, but I dread them no longer. See what a terrible prison this is, but I am going to heaven. Think of it: Cæsar is here, but there the Redeemer, kind and merciful. And there is no death there. Thou lovest me; think, then, how happy I shall be. Oh, dear Marcus, think that thou wilt come to me there."

Here she stopped to get breath in her sick breast, and then raised his hand to her lips, —

"Marcus?"

"What, dear one?"

"Do not weep for me, and remember this, — thou wilt come to me. I have lived a short time, but God gave thy soul to me; hence I shall tell Christ that though I died, and thou wert looking at my death, though thou wert left in grief, thou didst not blaspheme against His will, and that thou lovest Him always. Thou wilt love Him, and endure my death patiently? For then He will unite us. I love thee and I wish to be with thee."

Breath failed her then, and in a barely audible voice she finished, —

"Promise me this, Marcus!"

Vinicius embraced her with trembling arms, and said, —

"By thy sacred head! I promise."

Her pale face became radiant in the sad light of the moon, and once more she raised his hand to her lips, and whispered, —

"I am thy wife!"

Beyond the wall the pretorians playing *scriptæ duodecim* raised a loudet dispute; but Vinicius and Lygia forgot the prison, the guards, the world, and, feeling within them the souls of angels, they began to pray.

CHAPTER LX

For three days, or rather three nights, nothing disturbed their peace. When the usual prison work was finished, which consisted in separating the dead from the living and the grievously sick from those in better health, when the wearied guards had lain down to sleep in the corridors, Vinicius entered Lygia's dungeon and remained there till daylight. She put her head on his breast, and they talked in low voices of love and of death. In thought and speech, in desires and hopes even, both were removed unconsciously more and more from life, and they lost the sense of it. Both were like people who, having sailed from land in a ship, saw the shore no more, and were sinking gradually into infinity. Both changed by degrees into sad souls in love with each other and with Christ, and ready to fly away. Only at times did pain start up in the heart of Vinicius like a whirlwind, at times there flashed in him like lightning, hope, born of love and faith in the crucified God; but he tore himself away more and more each day from the earth, and yielded to death. In the morning, when he went from the prison, he looked on the world, on the city, on acquaintances, on vital interests, as through a dream. Everything seemed to him strange, distant, vain, fleeting. Even torture ceased to terrify, since one might pass through it while sunk in thought and with eyes fixed on another thing. It seemed to both that eternity had begun to receive them. They conversed of how they would love and live together, but beyond the grave; and if their thoughts returned to the earth at intervals, these were thoughts of people who, setting out on a long journey, speak of preparations for the road. Moreover they were surrounded by such silence as in some desert surrounds two columns far away and forgotten. Their only care was that Christ should not separate them; and as each moment strengthened their conviction that He would not, they loved Him as a link uniting them in endless happiness and peace. While still on earth, the dust of earth fell from them. The soul of each was as pure as a tear. Under terror of death, amid misery and suffering, in that prison den, heaven had begun, for she had taken him by the hand, and, as if saved and a saint, had led him to the source of endless life.

Petronius was astonished at seeing in the face of Vinicius increasing peace and a certain wonderful serenity which he had not noted before. At times even he supposed that Vinicius had found some mode of rescue, and he was piqued because his nephew had not confided his hopes to him. At last, unable to restrain himself, he said, —

"Now thou hast another look; do not keep from me secrets, for I wish and am able to aid thee. Hast thou arranged anything?"

"I have," said Vinicius; "but thou canst not help me. After her death I will confess that I am a Christian and follow her."

"Then thou hast no hope?"

"On the contrary, I have. Christ will give her to me, and I shall never be separated from her."

Petronius began to walk in the atrium; disillusion and impatience were evident on his face.

"Thy Christ is not needed for this, — our Thanatos[1] can render the same service."

Vinicius smiled sadly, and said, —

"No, my dear, thou art unwilling to understand."

"I am unwilling and unable. It is not the time for discussion, but remember what I said when we failed to free her from the Tullianum. I lost all hope, and on the way home thou didst say, 'But I believe that Christ can restore her to me.' Let Him restore her. If I throw a costly goblet into the sea, no god of ours can give it back to me; if yours is no better, I know not why I should honor Him beyond the old ones."

"But He will restore her to me."

Petronius shrugged his shoulders. "Dost know," inquired he, "that Christians are to illuminate Cæsar's gardens to-morrow?"

"To-morrow?" repeated Vinicius.

And in view of the near and dreadful reality his heart trembled with pain and fear. "This is the last night, perhaps, which I can pass with Lygia," thought he. So bidding farewell to Petronius, he went hurriedly to the overseer of the "Putrid Pits" for his tessera. But disappointment was in waiting, — the overseer would not give the tessera.

"Pardon me," said he, "I have done what I could for thee, but I cannot risk my life. To-night they are to conduct the Christians to Cæsar's gardens. The prisons will be full of soldiers and officials. Shouldst thou be recognized, I and my children would be lost."

Vinicius understood that it would be vain to insist. The hope gleamed in him, however, that the soldiers who had seen him before would admit him even without a tessera; so, with the coming of night, he disguised himself as usual in the tunic of a corpse-bearer, and, winding a cloth around his head, betook himself to the prison.

But that day the tesseræ were verified with greater care than usual; and what was more, the centurion Scevinus, a strict soldier, devoted soul and body to Cæsar, recognized Vinicius. But evidently in his iron-clad breast there glimmered yet some spark of pity for misfortunes. Instead of striking his spear in token of alarm, he led Vinicius aside and said, —

"Return to thy house, lord. I recognize thee; but not wishing thy ruin, I am silent. I cannot admit thee; go thy way, and may the gods send thee solace."

"Thou canst not admit me," said Vinicius, "but let me stand here and look at those who are led forth."

"My order does not forbid that," said Scevinus.

[1] Death.

Vinicius stood before the gate and waited. About midnight the prison gate was opened widely, and whole ranks of prisoners appeared, — men, women, and children, surrounded by armed pretorians. The night was very bright; hence it was possible to distinguish not only the forms, but the faces of the unfortunates. They went two abreast, in a long, gloomy train, amid stillness broken only by the clatter of weapons. So many were led out that all the dungeons must be empty, as it seemed. In the rear of the line Vinicius saw Glaucus the physician distinctly, but Lygia and Ursus were not among the condemned.

CHAPTER LXI

DARKNESS had not come when the first waves of people began to flow into Cæsar's gardens. The crowds, in holiday costume, crowned with flowers, joyous, singing, and some of them drunk, were going to look at the new, magnificent spectacle. Shouts of "Semaxii! Sarmentitii!" were heard on the Via Tecta, on the bridge of Æmilius, and from the other side of the Tiber, on the Triumphal Way, around the Circus of Nero, and off towards the Vatican Hill. In Rome people had been seen burnt on pillars before, but never had any one seen such a number of victims.

Cæsar and Tigellinus, wishing to finish at once with the Christians and also to avoid infection, which from the prisons was spreading more and more through the city, had given command to empty all dungeons, so that there remained in them barely a few tens of people intended for the close of the spectacles. So, when the crowds had passed the gates, they were dumb with amazement. All the main and side alleys, which lay through dense groves and along lawns, thickets, ponds, fields, and squares filled with flowers, were packed with pillars smeared with pitch, to which Christians were fastened. In higher places, where the view was not hindered by trees, one could see whole rows of pillars and bodies decked with flowers, myrtle, and ivy, extending into the distance on high and low places, so far that, though the nearest were like masts of ships, the farthest seemed colored darts, or staffs thrust into the earth. The number of them surpassed the expectation of the multitude. One might suppose that a whole nation had been lashed to pillars for Rome's amusement and for Cæsar's. The throng of spectators stopped before single masts when their curiosity was roused by the form or the sex of the victim; they looked at the faces, the crowns, the garlands of ivy; then they went farther and farther, asking themselves with amazement, "Could there have been so many criminals, or how could children barely able to walk have set fire to Rome?" and astonishment passed by degrees into fear.

Meanwhile darkness came, and the first stars twinkled in the sky. Near each condemned person a slave took his place, torch in hand; when the sound of trumpets was heard in various parts of the gardens, in sign that the spectacle was to begin, each slave put his torch to the foot of a pillar. The straw, hidden under the flowers and steeped in pitch, burned at once with a bright flame which, increasing every instant, withered the ivy, and rising embraced the feet of the victims. The people were silent; the gardens resounded with one immense groan and with cries of pain. Some victims, however, raising their faces toward the starry sky, began to sing, praising Christ. The people listened. But the hardest hearts were filled with terror when, on smaller pillars, children cried with shrill voices, "Mamma! Mamma!" A shiver ran through even spectators who were drunk when they saw little heads and innocent faces distorted with pain, or children fainting in the smoke which began to stifle them. But the flames rose, and seized new crowns of roses and ivy every instant. The main and side alleys were illuminated; the groups of trees, the lawns, and the flowery squares were illuminated; the water in pools and ponds was gleaming, the trembling leaves on the trees had grown rose-colored, and all was as visible as in daylight. When the odor of burnt bodies filled the gardens, slaves sprinkled between the pillars myrrh and aloes prepared purposely. In the crowds were heard here and there shouts, — whether of sympathy or delight and joy, it was unknown; and they increased every moment with the fire, which embraced the pillars, climbed to the breasts of the victims, shrivelled with burning breath the hair on their heads, threw veils over their blackened faces, and then shot up higher, as if showing the victory and triumph of that power which had given command to rouse it.

At the very beginning of the spectacle Cæsar had appeared among the people in a magnificent quadriga of the Circus, drawn by four white steeds. He was dressed as a charioteer in the color of the Greens, — the court party and his. After him followed other chariots filled with courtiers in brilliant array, senators, priests, bacchantes, naked and crowned, holding pitchers of wine, and partly drunk, uttering wild shouts. At the side of these were musicians dressed as fauns and satyrs, who played on citharas, formingas, flutes, and horns. In other chariots advanced matrons and maidens of Rome, drunk also and half naked. Around the quadriga ran men who shook thyrses ornamented with ribbons; others beat drums; others scattered flowers.

All that brilliant throng moved forward, shouting, "Evoe!" on the widest road of the garden, amidst smoke and processions of people. Cæsar, keeping near him Tigellinus and also Chilo, in whose terror he sought to find amusement, drove the steeds himself, and, advancing at a walk, looked at the burning bodies, and heard the shouts of the multitude. Standing on the lofty gilded chariot, surrounded by a sea of people who bent to his feet, in the glitter of the fire, in the golden crown of a circus-victor, he was a head above the courtiers and the crowd. He seemed a giant. His immense arms, stretched forward to hold the reins, seemed to bless the multitude. There was a smile on his face and in his blinking eyes; he shone above the throng as a sun or a deity, terrible but commanding and mighty.

At times he stopped to look with more care at some maiden whose bosom had begun to shrink in the flames, or at the face of a child distorted by convulsions; and again he drove on, leading behind him a wild, excited retinue. At times he bowed to the people, then again he bent backward, drew in the golden reins, and spoke to Tigellinus. At last, when he had reached the great fountain in the middle of two crossing streets, he stepped from the quadriga, and, nodding to his attendants, mingled with the throng.

He was greeted with shouts and plaudits. The bacchantes, the nymphs, the senators and Augustians, the priests, the fauns, satyrs, and soldiers surrounded him at once in an excited circle; but he, with Tigellinus on one side and Chilo on the other, walked around the fountain, about which were burning some tens of torches; stopping before each one, he made remarks on the victims, or jeered at the old Greek, on whose face boundless despair was depicted.

At last he stood before a lofty mast decked with myrtle and ivy. The red tongues of fire had risen only to the knees of the victim; but it was impossible to see his face, for the green burning twigs had covered it with smoke. After a while, however, the light breeze of night turned away the smoke and uncovered the head of a man with gray beard falling on his breast.

At sight of him Chilo was twisted into a lump like a wounded snake, and from his mouth came a cry more like cawing than a human voice.

"Glaucus! Glaucus!"

In fact, Glaucus the physician looked down from the burning pillar at him.

Glaucus was alive yet. His face expressed pain, and was inclined forward, as if to look closely for the last time at his executioner, at the man who had betrayed him, robbed him of wife and children, set a murderer on him, and who, when all this had been forgiven in the name of Christ, had delivered him to executioners. Never had one person inflicted more dreadful or bloody wrongs on another. Now the victim was burning on the pitched pillar, and the executioner was standing at his feet. The eyes of Glaucus did not leave the face of the Greek. At moments they were hidden by smoke; but when the breeze blew this away, Chilo saw again those eyes fixed on him. He rose and tried to flee, but had not strength. All at once his legs seemed of lead; an invisible hand seemed to hold him at that pillar with superhuman force. He was petrified. He felt that something was overflowing in him, something giving way; he felt that he had had a surfeit of blood and torture, that the end of his life was approaching, that everything was vanishing, Cæsar, the court, the multitude, and around him was only a kind of bottomless, dreadful black vacuum with no visible thing in it, save those eyes of a martyr which were summoning him to judgment. But Glaucus, bending his head lower down, looked at him fixedly. Those present divined that something was taking place between those two men. Laughter died on their lips, however, for in Chilo's face there was something terrible: such pain and fear had distorted it as if those tongues of fire were burning his body. On a sudden he staggered, and, stretching his arms upward, cried in a terrible and piercing voice, —

"Glaucus! in Christ's name! forgive me!"

It grew silent round about, a quiver ran through the spectators, and all eyes were raised involuntarily.

The head of the martyr moved slightly, and from the top of the mast was heard a voice like a groan, —

"I forgive!"

Chilo threw himself on his face, and howled like a wild beast; grasping earth in both hands, he sprinkled it on his head. Meanwhile the flames shot up, seizing the breast and face of Glaucus; they unbound the myrtle crown on his head, and seized the ribbons on the top of the pillar, the whole of which shone with great blazing.

Chilo stood up after a while with face so changed that to the Augustians he seemed another man. His eyes flashed with a light new to him, ecstasy issued from his wrinkled forehead; the Greek, incompetent a short time before, looked now like some priest visited by a divinity and ready to reveal unknown truths.

"What is the matter? Has he gone mad?" asked a number of voices.

But he turned to the multitude, and, raising his right hand, cried, or rather shouted, in a voice so piercing that not only the Augustians but the multitude heard him, —

"Roman people! I swear by my death, that innocent persons are perishing here. That is the incendiary!"

And he pointed his finger at Nero.

Then came a moment of silence. The courtiers were benumbed. Chilo continued to stand with outstretched, trembling arm, and with finger pointed at Nero. All at once a tumult arose. The people, like a wave, urged by a sudden whirlwind, rushed toward the old man to look at him more closely. Here and there were heard cries, "Hold!" In another place, "Woe to us!" In the throng a hissing and uproar began. "Ahenobarbus! Matricide! Incendiary!" Disorder increased every instant. The bacchantes screamed in heaven-piercing voices, and began to hide in the chariots. Then some pillars which were burned through, fell, scattered sparks, and increased the confusion. A blind dense wave of people swept away Chilo, and bore him to the depth of the garden.

The pillars began to burn through in every direction and fall across the streets, filling alleys with smoke, sparks, the odor of burnt wood and burnt flesh. The nearer lights died. The gardens began to grow dark. The crowds, alarmed, gloomy, and disturbed, pressed toward the gates. News of what had happened passed from mouth to mouth, distorted and increased. Some said that Cæsar had fainted; others that he had confessed, saying that he had given command to burn Rome; others that he had fallen seriously ill; and still others that he had been borne out, as if dead, in the chariot. Here and there were heard voices of sympathy for the Christians: "If they had not burned Rome, why so much blood, torture, and injustice? Will not the gods avenge the innocent, and what *piacula* can mollify them now?" The words *innoxia corpora* were repeated oftener and oftener. Women expressed aloud their pity for children thrown in such numbers to wild beasts, nailed to crosses, or burned in those cursed gardens! And finally pity was turned into abuse of Cæsar and Tigellinus. There were persons, too, who, stopping suddenly, asked themselves or others the question, "What kind of divinity is that which gives such strength to meet torture and death?" And they returned home in meditation.

But Chilo was wandering about in the gardens, not knowing where to go or where to turn. Again he felt himself a weak, helpless, sick old man.

Now he stumbled against partly burnt bodies; now he struck a torch, which sent a shower of sparks after him; now he sat down, and looked around with vacant stare. The gardens had become almost dark. The pale moon moving among the trees shone with uncertain light on the alleys, the dark pillars lying across them, and the partly burnt victims turned into shapeless lumps. But the old Greek thought that in the moon he saw the face of Glaucus, whose eyes were looking at him yet persistently, and he hid before the light. At last he went out of the shadow, in spite of himself; as if pushed by some hidden power, he turned toward the fountain where Glaucus had yielded up the spirit.

Then some hand touched his shoulder. He turned, and saw an unknown person before him.

"Who art thou?" exclaimed he, with terror.

"Paul of Tarsus."

"I am accursed! — What dost thou wish?"

"I wish to save thee," answered the Apostle.

Chilo supported himself against a tree. His legs bent under him, and his arms hung parallel with his body.

"For me there is no salvation," said he, gloomily.

"Hast thou heard how God forgave the thief on the cross who pitied Him?" inquired Paul.

"Dost thou know what I have done?"

"I saw thy suffering, and heard thy testimony to the truth."

"O Lord!"

"And if a servant of Christ forgave thee in the hour of torture and death, why should Christ not forgive thee?"

Chilo seized his head with both hands, as if in bewilderment.

"Forgiveness! for me, forgiveness!"

"Our God is a God of mercy," said Paul.

"For me?" repeated Chilo; and he began to groan like a man who lacks strength to control his pain and suffering.

"Lean on me," said Paul, "and go with me."

And taking him he went to the crossing of the streets, guided by the voice of the fountain, which seemed to weep in the night stillness over the bodies of those who had died in torture.

"Our God is a God of mercy," repeated the Apostle. "Wert thou to stand at the sea and cast in pebbles, couldst thou fill its depth with them? I tell thee that the mercy of Christ is as the sea, and that the sins and faults of men sink in it as pebbles in the abyss; I tell thee that it is like the sky which covers mountains, lands, and seas, for it is everywhere and has neither end nor limit. Thou hast suffered at the pillar of Glaucus. Christ saw thy suffering. Without reference to what may meet thee to-morrow, thou didst say, 'That is the incendiary,' and Christ remembers thy words. Thy malice and falsehood are gone; in thy heart is left only boundless sorrow. Follow me and listen to what I say. I am he who hated Christ and persecuted His chosen ones. I did not want Him, I did not believe in Him till He manifested Himself and called me. Since then He is, for me, mercy. He has visited thee with compunction, with alarm, and with pain, to call thee to Himself. Thou didst hate Him, but He loved thee. Thou didst deliver His confessors to torture, but He wishes to forgive and save thee."

Immense sobbing shook the breast of the wretched man, sobbing by which the soul in him was rent to its depths; but Paul took possession of him, mastered him, led him away, as a soldier leads a captive.

After a while the Apostle began again to speak: —

"Come with me; I will lead thee to Him. For why else have I come to thee? Christ commanded me to gather in souls in the name of love; hence I perform His service. Thou thinkest thyself accursed, but I say: Believe in Him, and salvation awaits thee. Thou thinkest that thou art hated, but I repeat that He loves thee. Look at me. Before I had Him I had nothing save malice, which dwelt in my heart, and now His love suffices me instead of father and mother, wealth and power. In Him alone is refuge. He alone will see thy sorrow, believe in thy misery, remove thy alarm, and raise thee to Himself."

Thus speaking, he led him to the fountain, the silver stream of which gleamed from afar in the moonlight. Round about was silence; the gardens were empty, for slaves had removed the charred pillars and the bodies of the martyrs.

Chilo threw himself on his knees with a groan, and hiding his face in his hands remained motionless. Paul raised his face to the stars. "O Lord," prayed he, "look on this wretched man, on his sorrow, his tears, and his suffering! O God of mercy, who hast shed Thy blood for our sins, forgive him, through Thy torment, Thy death and resurrection!"

Then he was silent; but for a long time he looked toward the stars, and prayed.

Meanwhile from under his feet was heard a cry which resembled a groan, —

"O Christ! O Christ! forgive me!"

Paul approached the fountain then, and, taking water in his hand, turned to the kneeling wretch, —

"Chilo! — I baptize thee in the name of the Father, Son, and Spirit. Amen!"

Chilo raised his head, opened his arms, and remained in that posture. The moon shone with full light on his white hair and on his equally white face, which was as motionless as if dead or cut out of stone. The moments passed one after another. From the great aviaries in the gardens of Domitian came the crowing of cocks; but Chilo remained kneeling, like a statue on a monument. At last he recovered, spoke to the Apostle, and asked, —

"What am I to do before death?"

Paul was roused also from meditation on the measureless power which even such spirits as that of this Greek could not resist, and answered, —

"Have faith, and bear witness to the truth."

They went out together. At the gate the Apostle blessed the old man again, and they parted. Chilo himself insisted on this, for after what had happened he knew that Cæsar and Tigellinus would give command to pursue him.

Indeed he was not mistaken. When he returned home, he found the house surrounded by pretorians, who led him away, and took him under direction of Scevinus to the Palatine.

Cæsar had gone to rest, but Tigellinus was waiting. When he saw the unfortunate Greek, he greeted him with a calm but ominous face.

"Thou hast committed the crime of treason," said he, "and punishment will not pass thee; but if to-morrow thou testify in the amphitheatre that thou wert drunk and mad, and that the authors of the conflagration are Christians, thy punishment will be limited to stripes and exile."

"I cannot do that," answered Chilo, calmly.

Tigellinus approached him with slow step, and with a voice also low but terrible, —

"How is that?" asked he. "Thou canst not, Greek dog? Wert thou not drunk, and dost thou not understand what is waiting for thee? Look there!" and he pointed to a corner of the atrium in which, near a long wooden bench, stood four Thracian slaves in the shade with ropes, and with pincers in their hands.

But Chilo answered, —

"I cannot!"

Rage seized Tigellinus, but he restrained himself yet.

"Hast thou seen," inquired he, "how Christians die? Dost wish to die in that way?"

The old man raised his pale face; for a time his lips moved in silence, and he answered, —

"I too believe in Christ."

Tigellinus looked at him with amazement.

"Dog, thou hast gone mad in fact!"

And suddenly the rage in his breast broke its bounds. Springing at Chilo, he caught him by the beard with both hands, hurled him to the floor, trampled him, repeating, with foam on his lips, —

"Thou wilt retract! thou wilt!"

"I cannot!" answered Chilo from the floor.

"To the tortures with him!"

At this command the Thracians seized the old man, and placed him on the bench; then, fastening him with ropes to it, they began to squeeze his thin shanks with pincers. But when they were tying him he kissed their hands with humility; then he closed his eyes, and seemed dead.

He was alive, though; for when Tigellinus bent over him and inquired once again, "Wilt thou retract?" his white lips moved slightly, and from them came the barely audible whisper, —

"I cannot."

Tigellinus gave command to stop the torture, and began to walk up and down in the atrium with a face distorted by anger, but helpless. At last a new idea came to his head, for he turned to the Thracians and said, —

"Tear out his tongue!"

CHAPTER LXII

THE drama "Aureolus" was given usually in theatres or amphitheatres, so arranged that they could open and present as it were two separate stages. But after the spectacle in the gardens of Cæsar the usual method was omitted; for in this case the problem was to let the greatest number of people look at a slave who, in the drama, is devoured by a bear. In the theatres the rôle of the bear is played by an actor sewed up in a skin, but this time the representation was to be real. This was a new idea of Tigellinus. At first Cæsar refused to come, but changed his mind at persuasion of the favorite. Tigellinus explained that after what had happened in the gardens it was all the more his duty to appear before the people, and he guaranteed that the crucified slave would not insult him as had Crispus. The people were somewhat sated and tired of blood-spilling; hence a new distribution of lottery tickets and gifts was promised, as well as a feast, for the spectacle was to be in the evening, in a brilliantly lighted amphitheatre.

About dusk the whole amphitheatre was packed; the Augustians, with Tigellinus at the head of them, came to a man, — not only for the spectacle itself, but to show their devotion to Cæsar and their opinion of Chilo, of whom all Rome was then talking.

They whispered to one another that Cæsar, when returning from the gardens, had fallen into a frenzy and could not sleep, that terrors and wonderful visions had attacked him; therefore he had announced on the following morning his early journey to Achæa. But others denied this, declaring that he would be all the more pitiless to the Christians. Cowards, however, were not lacking, who foresaw that the accusation which Chilo had thrown into Cæsar's face might have the worst result possible. In conclusion, there were those who through humanity begged Tigellinus to stop persecution.

"See whither ye are going," said Barcus Soranus. "Ye wished to allay people's anger and convince them that punishment was falling on the guilty; the result is just the opposite."

"True!" added Antistius Verus, "all whisper to one another now that the Christians were innocent. If that be cleverness, Chilo was right when he said that your brains could be held in a nut-shell."

Tigellinus turned to them and said: "Barcus Soranus, people whisper also to one another that thy daughter Servilia secreted her Christian slaves from Cæsar's justice; they say the same also of thy wife, Antistius."

"That is not true!" exclaimed Barcus, with alarm.

"Your divorced women wished to ruin my wife, whose virtue they envy," said Antistius Verus, with no less alarm.

But others spoke of Chilo.

"What has happened to him?" asked Eprius Marcellus. "He delivered them himself into the hands of Tigellinus; from a beggar he became rich; it was possible for him to live out his days in peace, have a splendid funeral, and a tomb: but, no! All at once he preferred to lose everything and destroy himself; he must, in truth, be a maniac."

"Not a maniac, but he has become a Christian," said Tigellinus.

"Impossible!" said Vitelius.

"Have I not said," put in Vestinius, " 'Kill Christians if ye like; but believe me ye cannot war with their divinity. With it there is no jesting'? See what is taking place. I have not burned Rome; but if Cæsar permitted I would give a hecatomb at once to their divinity. And all should do the same, for I repeat: With it there is no jesting! Remember my words to you."

"And I said something else," added Petronius. "Tigellinus laughed when I said that they were arming, but I say more, — they are conquering."

"How is that? how is that?" inquired a number of voices.

"By Pollux, they are! For if such a man as Chilo could not resist them, who can? If ye think that after every spectacle the Christians do not increase, become coppersmiths, or go to shaving beards, for then ye will know better what people think, and what is happening in the city."

"He speaks pure truth, by the sacred peplus of Diana," cried Vestinius.

But Barcus turned to Petronius.

"What is thy conclusion?"

"I conclude where ye began, — there has been enough of bloodshed."

Tigellinus looked at him jeeringly, —

"Ei! — a little more!"

"If thy head is not sufficient, thou hast another on thy cane," said Petronius.

Further conversation was interrupted by the coming of Cæsar, who occupied his place in company with Pythagoras. Immediately after began the representation of "Aureolus," to which not much attention was paid, for the minds of the audience were fixed on Chilo. The spectators, familiar with blood and torture, were bored; they hissed, gave out shouts uncomplimentary to the court, and demanded the bear scene, which for them was the only thing of interest. Had it not been for gifts and the hope of seeing Chilo, the spectacle would not have held the audience.

At last the looked-for moment came. Servants of the Circus brought in first a wooden cross, so low that a bear standing on his hind feet might reach the martyr's breast; then two men brought, or rather dragged in, Chilo, for as the bones in his legs were broken, he was unable to walk alone. They laid him down and nailed him to the wood so quickly that the curious Augustians had not even a good look at him, and only after the cross had been fixed in the place prepared for it did all eyes turn to the victim. But it was a rare person who could recognize in that naked man the former Chilo. After the tortures which Tigellinus had commanded, there was not one drop of blood in his face, and only on his white beard was evident a red trace left by blood after they had torn his tongue out. Through the transparent skin it was quite possible to see his bones. He seemed far older also, almost decrepit, Formerly his eyes cast glances ever filled with disquiet and ill-will, his watchful face reflected constant alarm and uncertainty; now his face had an expression of pain, but it was as mild and calm as faces of the sleeping or the dead. Perhaps remembrance of that thief on the cross whom Christ had forgiven lent him confidence; perhaps, also, he said in his soul to the merciful God, —

"O Lord, I bit like a venomous worm; but all my life I was unfortunate. I was famishing from hunger, people trampled on me, beat me, jeered at me. I was poor and very unhappy, and now they put me to torture and nail me to a cross; but Thou, O Merciful, wilt not reject me in this hour!" Peace descended evidently into his crushed heart. No one laughed, for there was in that crucified man something so calm, he seemed so old, so defenceless, so weak, calling so much for pity with his lowliness, that each one asked himself unconsciously how it was possible to torture and nail to crosses men who would die soon in any case. The crowd was silent. Among the Augustians Vestinius, bending to right and left, whispered in a terrified voice, "See how they die!" Others were looking for the bear, wishing the spectacle to end at the earliest.

The bear came into the arena at last, and, swaying from side to side a head which hung low, he looked around from beneath his forehead, as if thinking of something or seeking something. At last he saw the cross and the naked body. He approached it, and stood on his hind legs; but after a moment he dropped again on his fore-paws, and sitting under the cross began to growl, as if in his heart of a beast pity for that remnant of a man had made itself heard.

Cries were heard from Circus slaves urging on the bear, but the people were silent.

Meanwhile Chilo raised his head with slow motion, and for a time moved his eyes over the audience. At last his glance rested somewhere on the highest rows of the amphitheatre; his breast moved with more life, and something happened which caused wonder and astonishment. That face became bright with a smile; a ray of light, as it were, encircled that forehead; his eyes were uplifted before death, and after a while two great tears which had risen between the lids flowed slowly down his face.

And he died.

At that same moment a resonant manly voice high up under the velarium exclaimed, —

"Peace to the martyrs!"

Deep silence reigned in the amphitheatre.

CHAPTER LXIII

AFTER the spectacle in Cæsar's gardens the prisons were emptied considerably. It is true that victims suspected of the Oriental superstition were seized yet and imprisoned, but pursuit brought in fewer and fewer persons, — barely enough for coming exhibitions, which were to follow quickly. People were sated with blood; they showed growing weariness, and increasing alarm because of the unparalleled conduct of the condemned. Fears like those of the superstitious Vestinius seized thousands of people. Among the crowds tales more and more wonderful were related of the vengefulness of the Christian God. Prison typhus, which had spread through the city, increased the general dread. The number of funerals was evident, and it was repeated from ear to ear that fresh piacula were needed to mollify the unknown god. Offerings were made in the temples to Jove and Libitina. At last, in spite of every effort of Tigellinus and his assistants, the opinion kept spreading that the city had been burned at command of Cæsar, and that the Christians were suffering innocently.

But for this very reason Nero and Tigellinus were untiring in persecution. To calm the multitude, fresh orders were issued to distribute wheat, wine, and olives. To relieve owners, new rules were published to facilitate the building of houses; and others touching width of streets and materials to be used in building so as to avoid fires in future. Cæsar himself attended sessions of the Senate, and counselled with the "fathers" on the good of the people and the city; but not a shadow of favor fell on the doomed. The ruler of the world was anxious, above all, to fix in people's minds a conviction that such merciless punishments could strike only the guilty. In the Senate no voice was heard on behalf of the Christians, for no one wished to offend Cæsar; and besides, those who looked farther into the future insisted that the foundations of Roman rule could not stand against the new faith.

The dead and the dying were given to their relatives, as Roman law took no vengeance on the dead. Vinicius received a certain solace from the thought that if Lygia died he would bury her in his family tomb, and rest near her. At that time he had no hope of rescuing her; half separated from life, he was himself wholly absorbed in Christ, and dreamed no longer of any union except an eternal one. His faith had become simply boundless; for it eternity seemed something incomparably truer and more real than the fleeting life which he had lived up to that time. His heart was overflowing with concentrated enthusiasm. Though yet alive, he had changed into a being almost immaterial, which desiring complete liberation for itself desired it also for another. He imagined that when free he and Lygia would each take the other's hand and go to heaven, where Christ would bless them, and let them live in light as peaceful and boundless as the light of dawn. He merely implored Christ to spare Lygia the torments of the Circus, and let her fall asleep calmly in prison; he felt with perfect certainty that he himself would die at the same time. In view of the sea of blood which had been shed, he did not even think it permitted to hope that she alone would be spared. He had heard from Peter and Paul that they, too, must die as martyrs. The sight of Chilo on the cross had convinced him that even a martyr's death could be sweet; hence he wished it for Lygia and himself as the change of an evil, sad, and oppressive fate for a better.

At times he had a foretaste of life beyond the grave. That sadness which hung over the souls of both was losing its former burning bitterness, and changing gradually into a kind of trans-terrestrial, calm abandon to the will of God. Vinicius, who formerly had toiled against the current, had struggled and tortured himself, yielded now to the stream, believing that it would bear him to eternal calm. He divined, too, that Lygia, as well as he, was preparing for death, — that, in spite of the prison walls separating them, they were advancing together; and he smiled at that thought as at happiness.

In fact, they were advancing with as much agreement as if they had exchanged thoughts every day for a long time. Neither had Lygia any desire, any hope, save the hope of a life beyond the grave. Death was presented to her not only as a liberation from the terrible walls of the prison, from the hands of Cæsar and Tigellinus, — not only as liberation, but as the hour of her marriage to Vinicius. In view of this unshaken certainty, all else lost importance. After death would come her happiness, which was even earthly, so that she waited for it also as a betrothed waits for the wedding-day.

And that immense current of faith, which swept away from life and bore beyond the grave thousands of those first confessors, bore away Ursus also. Neither had he in his heart been resigned to Lygia's death; but when day after day through the prison walls came news of what was happening in the amphitheatres and the gardens, when death seemed the common, inevitable lot of all Christians and also their good, higher than all mortal conceptions of happiness, he did not dare to pray to Christ to deprive Lygia of that happiness or to delay it for long years. In his simple barbarian soul he thought, besides, that more of those heavenly delights would belong to the daughter of the Lygian chief, that she would have more of them than would a whole crowd of simple ones to whom he himself belonged, and that in eternal glory she would sit nearer to the "Lamb" than would others. He had heard, it is true, that before God men are equal; but a conviction was lingering at the bottom of his soul that the daughter of a leader, and besides of a leader of all the Lygians, was not the same as the first slave one might meet. He hoped also that Christ would let him continue to serve her. His one secret wish was to die on a cross as the "Lamb" died. But this seemed a happiness so great that he hardly dared to pray for it, though he knew that in Rome even the worst criminals were crucified. He thought that surely he would be condemned to die under the teeth of wild beasts; and this was his one sorrow. From childhood he had lived in impassable forests, amid continual hunts, in which, thanks to his superhuman strength, he was famous among the Lygians even before he had grown to manhood. This occupation had become for him so agreeable that later, when in Rome, and forced to live without hunting, he went to vivaria and amphitheatres just to look at beasts known and unknown to him. The sight of these always roused in the man an irresistible desire for struggle and killing; so now he feared in his soul that on meeting them in the amphitheatre he would be attacked by thoughts unworthy of a Christian, whose duty it was to die piously and patiently. But in this he committed himself to Christ, and found other and more agreeable thoughts to comfort him. Hearing that the "Lamb" had declared war against the powers of hell and evil spirits with which the Christian faith connected all pagan divinities, he thought that in this war he might serve the "Lamb" greatly, and serve better than others, for he could not help believing that his soul was stronger than the souls of other martyrs. Finally, he prayed whole days, rendered service to prisoners, helped overseers, and comforted his queen, who complained at times that in her short life she had not been able to do so many good deeds as the renowned Tabitha of whom Peter the Apostle had told her. Even the prison guards, who feared the terrible strength of this giant, since neither bars nor chains could restrain it, came to love him at last for his mildness. Amazed at his good temper, they asked more than once what its cause was. He spoke with such firm certainty of the life waiting after death for him, that they listened with surprise, seeing for the first time that happiness might penetrate a dungeon which sunlight could not reach. And when he urged them to believe in the "Lamb," it occurred to more than one of those people that his own service was the service of a slave, his own life the life of an unfortunate; and he fell to thinking over his evil fate, the only end to which was death.

But death brought new fear, and promised nothing beyond; while that giant and that maiden, who was like a flower cast on the straw of the prison, went toward it with delight, as toward the gates of happiness.

CHAPTER LXIV

ONE evening Scevinus, a Senator, visited Petronius and began a long conversation, touching the grievous times in which they were living, and also touching Cæsar. He spoke so openly that Petronius, though his friend, began to be cautious. Scevinus complained that the world was living madly and unjustly, that all must end in some catastrophe more dreadful still than the burning of Rome. He said that even Augustians were dissatisfied; that Fenius Rufus, second prefect of the pretorians, endured with the greatest effort the vile orders of Tigellinus; and that all Seneca's relatives were driven to extremes by Cæsar's conduct as well toward his old master as toward Lucan. Finally, he began to hint of the dissatisfaction of the people, and even of the pretorians, the greater part of whom had been won by Fenius Rufus.

"Why dost thou say this?" inquired Petronius.

"Out of care for Cæsar," said Scevinus. "I have a distant relative among the pretorians, also Scevinus; through him I know what takes place in the camp. Disaffection is growing there also; Caligula, knowest thou, was mad too, and see what happened. Cassius Chærea appeared. That was a dreadful deed, and surely there is no one among us to praise it; still Chærea freed the world of a monster."

"Is thy meaning as follows: 'I do not praise Chærea, but he was a perfect man, and would that the gods had given us as many such as possible'?" inquired Petronius.

But Scevinus changed the conversation, and began all at once to praise Piso, exalting his family, his nobility of mind, his attachment to his wife, and, finally, his intellect, his calmness, and his wonderful gift of winning people.

"Cæsar is childless," said he, "and all see his successor in Piso. Doubtless, too, every man would help him with whole soul to gain power. Fenius Rufus loves him; the relatives of Annæus are devoted to him altogether. Plautius Lateranus and Tullius Senecio would spring into fire for him; as would Natalis, and Subrius Flavius, and Sulpicius Asper, and Afranius Quinetianus, and even Vestinius."

"From this last man not much will result to Piso," replied Petronius. "Vestinius is afraid of his own shadow."

"Vestinius fears dreams and spirits," answered Scevinus, "but he is a practical man, whom people wish wisely to make consul. That in his soul he is opposed to persecuting Christians, thou shouldst not take ill of him, for it concerns thee too that this madness should cease."

"Not me, but Vinicius," answered Petronius. "Out of concern for Vinicius,

I should like to save a certain maiden; but I cannot, for I have fallen out of favor with Ahenobarbus."

"How is that? Dost thou not notice that Cæsar is approaching thee again, and beginning to talk with thee? And I will tell thee why. He is preparing again for Achæa, where he is to sing songs in Greek of his own composition. He is burning for that journey; but also he trembles at thought of the cynical genius of the Greeks. He imagines that either the greatest triumph may meet him or the greatest failure. He needs good counsel, and he knows that no one can give it better than thou. This is why thou art returning to favor."

"Lucan might take my place."

"Bronzebeard hates Lucan, and in his soul has written down death for the poet. He is merely seeking a pretext, for he seeks pretexts always."

"By Castor!" said Petronius, "that may be. But I might have still another way for a quick return to favor."

"What?"

"To repeat to Bronzebeard what thou hast told me just now."

"I have said nothing!" cried Scevinus, with alarm.

Petronius placed his hand upon the Senator's shoulder. "Thou hast called Cæsar a madman, thou hast foreseen the heirship of Piso, and hast said, 'Lucan understands that there is need to hasten.' What wouldst thou hasten, carissime?"

Scevinus grew pale, and for a moment each looked into the eyes of the other.

"Thou wilt not repeat!"

"By the hips of Kypris, I will not! How well thou knowest me! No; I will not repeat. I have heard nothing, and, moreover, I wish to hear nothing. Dost understand? Life is too short to make any undertaking worth the while. I beg thee only to visit Tigellinus to-day, and talk with him as long as thou hast with me of whatever may please thee."

"Why?"

"So that should Tigellinus ever say to me, 'Scevinus was with thee,' I might answer, 'He was with thee, too, that very day.'"

Scevinus, when he heard this, broke the ivory cane which he had in his hand, and said, —

"May the evil fall on this stick! I shall be with Tigellinus to-day, and later at Nerva's feast. Thou, too, wilt be there? In every case till we meet in the amphitheatre, where the last of the Christians will appear the day after to-morrow. Till we meet!"

"After to-morrow!" repeated Petronius, when alone. "There is no time to lose. Ahenobarbus will need me really in Achæa; hence he may count with me."

And he determined to try the last means.

In fact, at Nerva's feast Cæsar himself asked that Petronius recline opposite, for he wished to speak with the arbiter about Achæa and the cities in which he might appear with hopes of the greatest success. He cared most for the Athenians, whom he feared. Other Augustians listened to this conversation with attention, so as to seize crumbs of the arbiter's opinions, and give them out later on as their own.

"It seems to me that I have not lived up to this time," said Nero, "and that my birth will come only in Greece."

"Thou wilt be born to new glory and immortality," answered Petronius.

"I trust that this is true, and that Apollo will not seem jealous. If I return in triumph, I will offer him such a hecatomb as no god has had so far."

Scevinus fell to repeating the lines of Horace: —

> "Sic te diva potens Cypri,
> Sic fratres Helenæ, lucida sidera,
> Ventorumque regat Pater — "

"The vessel is ready at Naples," said Cæsar. "I should like to go even to-morrow."

At this Petronius rose, and, looking straight into Nero's eyes, said, —

"Permit me, O divinity, to celebrate a wedding-feast, to which I shall invite thee before others."

"A wedding-feast! What wedding-feast?" inquired Nero.

"That of Vinicius with thy hostage the daughter of the Lygian king. She is in prison at present, it is true; but as a hostage she is not subject to imprisonment, and, secondly, thou thyself hast permitted Vinicius to marry her; and as thy sentences, like those of Zeus, are unchangeable, thou wilt give command to free her from prison, and I will give her to thy favorite."

The cool blood and calm self-possession with which Petronius spoke disturbed Nero, who was disturbed whenever any one spoke in that fashion to him.

"I know," said he, dropping his eyes. "I have thought of her and of that giant who killed Croton."

"In that case both are saved," answered Petronius, calmly.

But Tigellinus came to the aid of his master: "She is in prison by the will of Cæsar; thou thyself hast said, O Petronius, that his sentences are unchangeable."

All present, knowing the history of Vinicius and Lygia, understood perfectly what the question was; hence they were silent, curious as to the end of the conversation.

"She is in prison against the will of Cæsar and through thy error, through thy ignorance of the law of nations," said Petronius, with emphasis. "Thou art a naïve man, Tigellinus; but even thou wilt not assert that she burnt Rome, and if thou wert to do so, Cæsar would not believe thee."

But Nero had recovered and begun to half close his near-sighted eyes with an expression of indescribable malice.

"Petronius is right," said he, after a while.

Tigellinus looked at him with amazement.

"Petronius is right," repeated Nero; "to-morrow the gates of the prison will be open to her, and of the marriage feast we will speak the day after at the amphitheatre."

"I have lost again," thought Petronius.

When he had returned home, he was so certain that the end of Lygia's life had come that he sent a trusty freedman to the amphitheatre to bargain with the chief of the spoliarium for the delivery of her body, since he wished to give it to Vinicius.

CHAPTER LXV

EVENING exhibitions, rare up to that period and given only exceptionally, became common in Nero's time, both in the Circus and amphitheatre. The Augustians liked them, frequently because they were followed by feasts and drinking-bouts which lasted till daylight. Though the people were sated already with blood-spilling, still, when the news went forth that the end of the games was approaching, and that the last of the Christians were to die at an evening spectacle, a countless audience assembled in the amphitheatre. The Augustians came to a man, for they understood that it would not be a common spectacle; they knew that Cæsar had determined to make for himself a tragedy out of the suffering of Vinicius. Tigellinus had kept secret the kind of punishment intended for the betrothed of the young tribune; but that merely roused general curiosity. Those who had seen Lygia at the house of Plautius told wonders of her beauty. Others were occupied above all with the question, would they see her really on the arena that day; for many of those who had heard the answer given Petronius and Nerva by Cæsar explained it in two ways: some supposed simply that Nero would give or perhaps had given the maiden to Vinicius; they remembered that she was a hostage, hence free to worship whatever divinities she liked, and that the law of nations did not permit her punishment.

Uncertainty, waiting, and curiosity had mastered all spectators. Cæsar arrived earlier than usual; and immediately at his coming people whispered that something uncommon would happen, for besides Tigellinus and Vatinius, Cæsar had with him Cassius, a centurion of enormous size and gigantic strength, whom he summoned only when he wished to have a defender at his side, — for example, when he desired night expeditions to the Subura, where he arranged the amusement called "sagatio," which consisted in tossing on a soldier's mantle maidens met on the way. It was noted also that certain precautions had been taken in the amphitheatre itself. The pretorian guards were increased; command over them was held, not by a centurion, but by the tribune Subrius Flavius, known hitherto for blind attachment to Nero. It was understood, then, that Cæsar wished in every case to guard himself against an outburst of despair from Vinicius, and curiosity rose all the more.

Every eye was turned with strained gaze to the place where the unfortunate lover was sitting. He was exceedingly pale, and his forehead was covered with drops of sweat; he was in as much doubt as were other spectators, but alarmed to the lowest depth of his soul. Petronius knew not what would happen; he was silent, except that, while turning from Nerva, he asked Vinicius whether he was ready for everything, and next, whether he would remain at the spectacle. To both questions Vinicius answered "Yes," but a shudder passed through his whole body; he divined that Petronius did not ask without reason. For some time he had lived with only half his life,—he had sunk in death, and reconciled himself to Lygia's death, since for both it was to be liberation and marriage; but he learned now that it was one thing to think of the last moment when it was distant as of a quiet dropping asleep, and another to look at the torment of a person dearer to one than life. All sufferings endured formerly rose in him anew. Despair, which had been set at rest, began again to cry in his soul; the former desire to save Lygia at any price seized him anew. Beginning with the morning, he had tried to go to the cunicula to be sure that she was there; but the pretorians watched every entrance, and orders were so strict that the soldiers, even those whom he knew, would not be softened by prayers or gold. It seemed to the tribune that uncertainty would kill him before he should see the spectacle. Somewhere at the bottom of his heart the hope was still throbbing, that perhaps Lygia was not in the amphitheatre, that his fears were groundless. At times he seized on this hope with all his strength. He said in his soul that Christ might take her to Himself out of the prison, but could not permit her torture in the Circus. Formerly he was resigned to the divine will in everything; now, when repulsed from the doors of the cunicula, he returned to his place in the amphitheatre, and when he learned, from the curious glances turned on him, that the most dreadful suppositions might be true, he began to implore in his soul with passionateness almost approaching a threat. "Thou canst!" repeated he, clenching his fists convulsively, "Thou canst!" Hitherto he had not supposed that that moment when present would be so terrible. Now, without clear consciousness of what was happening in his mind, he had the feeling that if he should see Lygia tortured, his love for God would be turned to hatred, and his faith to despair. But he was amazed at the feeling, for he feared to offend Christ, whom he was imploring for mercy and miracles. He implored no longer for her life; he wished merely that she should die before they brought her to the arena, and from the abyss of his pain he repeated in spirit: "Do not refuse even this, and I will love Thee still more than hitherto." And then his thoughts raged as a sea torn by a whirlwind. A desire for blood and vengeance was roused in him. He was seized by a mad wish to rush at Nero and stifle him there in presence of all the spectators; but he felt that desire to be a new offence against Christ, and a breach of His command. To his head flew at times flashes of hope that everything before which his soul was trembling would be turned aside by an almighty and merciful hand; but they were quenched at once, as if in measureless sorrow that He who could destroy that Circus with one word and save Lygia had abandoned her, though she trusted in Him and loved Him with all the strength of her pure heart. And he thought, moreover, that she was lying there in that dark place, weak, defenceless, deserted, abandoned to the whim or disfavor of brutal guards, drawing her last breath, perhaps, while he had to wait, helpless, in that dreadful amphitheatre, without knowing what torture was prepared for her, or what he would witness in a moment. Finally, as a man falling over a precipice grasps at everything which grows on the edge of it, so did he grasp with both hands at the thought that faith of itself could save her. That one method remained! Peter had said that faith could move the earth to its foundations.

Hence he rallied; he crushed doubt in himself, he compressed his whole being into the sentence, "I believe," and he looked for a miracle.

But as an overdrawn cord may break, so exertion broke him. The pallor of death covered his face, and his body relaxed. He thought then that his prayer had been heard, for he was dying. It seemed to him that Lygia must surely die too, and that Christ would take them to Himself in that way. The arena, the white togas, the countless spectators, the light of thousands of lamps and torches, all vanished from his vision.

But his weakness did not last long. After a while he roused himself, or rather the stamping of the impatient multitude roused him.

"Thou art ill," said Petronius; "give command to bear thee home."

And without regard to what Cæsar would say, he rose to support Vinicius and go out with him. His heart was filled with pity, and, moreover, he was irritated beyond endurance because Cæsar was looking through the emerald at Vinicius, studying his pain with satisfaction, to describe it afterwards, perhaps, in pathetic strophes, and win the applause of hearers.

Vinicius shook his head. He might die in that amphitheatre, but he could not go out of it. Moreover the spectacle might begin any moment.

In fact, at that very instant almost, the prefect of the city waved a red handkerchief, the hinges opposite Cæsar's podium creaked, and out of the dark gully came Ursus into the brightly lighted arena.

The giant blinked, dazed evidently by the glitter of the arena; then he pushed into the centre, gazing around as if to see what he had to meet. It was known to all the Augustians and to most of the spectators that he was the man who had stifled Croton; hence at sight of him a murmur passed along every bench. In Rome there was no lack of gladiators larger by far than the common measure of man, but Roman eyes had never seen the like of Ursus. Cassius, standing in Cæsar's podium, seemed puny compared with that Lygian. Senators, vestals, Cæsar, the Augustians, and the people gazed with the delight of experts at his mighty limbs as large as tree-trunks, at his breast as large as two shields joined together, and his arms of a Hercules. The murmur rose every instant. For those multitudes there could be no higher pleasure than to look at those muscles in play in the exertion of a struggle. The murmur rose to shouts, and eager questions were put: "Where do the people live who can produce such a giant?" He stood there, in the middle of the amphitheatre, naked, more like a stone colossus than a man, with a collected expression, and at the same time the sad look of a barbarian; and while surveying the empty arena, he gazed wonderingly with his blue childlike eyes, now at the spectators, now at Cæsar, now at the grating of the cunicula, whence, as he thought, his executioners would come.

At the moment when he stepped into the arena his simple heart was beating for the last time with the hope that perhaps a cross was waiting for him, but when he saw neither the cross nor the hole in which it might be put, he thought that he was unworthy of such favor, — that he would find death in another way, and surely from wild beasts. He was unarmed, and had determined to die as became a confessor of the "Lamb," peacefully and patiently. Meanwhile he wished to pray once more to the Saviour; so he knelt on the arena, joined his hands, and raised his eyes toward the stars which were glittering in the lofty opening of the amphitheatre.

That act displeased the crowds. They had had enough of those Christians who died like sheep. They understood that if the giant would not defend himself the spectacle would be a failure. Here and there hisses were heard. Some began to cry for scourgers, whose office it was to lash combatants unwilling to fight. But soon all had grown silent, for no one knew what was waiting for the giant, nor whether he would not be ready to struggle when he met death eye to eye.

In fact, they had not long to wait. Suddenly the shrill sound of brazen trumpets was heard, and at that signal a grating opposite Cæsar's podium was opened, and into the arena rushed, amid shouts of beast-keepers, an enormous German aurochs, bearing on his head the naked body of a woman.

"Lygia! Lygia!" cried Vinicius.

Then he seized his hair near the temples, squirmed like a man who feels a sharp dart in his body, and began to repeat in hoarse accents, —

"I believe! I believe! O Christ, a miracle!"

And he did not even feel that Petronius covered his head that moment with the toga. It seemed to him that death or pain had closed his eyes. He did not look, he did not see. The feeling of some awful emptiness possessed him. In his head there remained not a thought; his lips merely repeated, as if in madness, —

"I believe! I believe! I believe!"

This time the amphitheatre was silent. The Augustians rose in their places, as one man, for in the arena something uncommon had happened. That Lygian, obedient and ready to die, when he saw his queen on the horns of the wild beast, sprang up, as if touched by living fire, and bending forward he ran at the raging animal.

From all breasts a sudden cry of amazement was heard, after which came deep silence.

The Lygian fell on the raging bull in a twinkle, and seized him by the horns.

"Look!" cried Petronius, snatching the toga from the head of Vinicius.

The latter rose and bent back his head; his face was as pale as linen, and he looked into the arena with a glassy, vacant stare.

All breasts ceased to breathe. In the amphitheatre a fly might be heard on the wing. People could not believe their own eyes. Since Rome was Rome, no one had seen such a spectacle.

The Lygian held the wild beast by the horns. The man's feet sank in the sand to his ankles, his back was bent like a drawn bow, his head was hidden between his shoulders, on his arms the muscles came out so that the skin almost burst from their pressure; but he had stopped the bull in his tracks. And the man and the beast remained so still that the spectators thought themselves looking at a picture showing a deed of Hercules or Theseus, or a group hewn from stone. But in that apparent repose there was a tremendous exertion of two struggling forces. The bull sank his feet as well as did the man in the sand, and his dark, shaggy body was curved so that it seemed a gigantic ball. Which of the two would fail first, which would fall first, — that was the question for those spectators enamoured of such struggles; a question which at that moment meant more for them than their own fate, than all Rome and its lordship over the world. That Lygian was in their eyes then a demigod worthy of honor and statues. Cæsar himself stood up as well as others. He and Tigellinus, hearing of the man's strength, had arranged this spectacle purposely, and said to each other with a jeer, "Let that slayer of Croton kill the bull which we choose for him"; so they looked now with amazement at that picture, as if not believing that it could be real.

In the amphitheatre were men who had raised their arms and remained in that posture. Sweat covered the faces of others, as if they themselves were struggling with the beast. In the Circus nothing was heard save the sound of flame in the lamps, and the crackle of bits of coal as they dropped from the torches. Their voices died on the lips of the spectators, but their hearts were beating in their breasts as if to split them. It seemed to all that the struggle was lasting for ages. But the man and the beast continued on in their monstrous exertion; one might have said that they were planted in the earth.

Meanwhile a dull roar resembling a groan was heard from the arena, after which a brief shout was wrested from every breast, and again there was silence. People thought themselves dreaming till the enormous head of the bull began to turn in the iron hands of the barbarian. The face, neck, and arms of the Lygian grew purple; his back bent still more. It was clear that he was rallying the remnant of his superhuman strength, but that he could not last long.

Duller and duller, hoarser and hoarser, more and more painful grew the groan of the bull as it mingled with the whistling breath from the breast of the giant. The head of the beast turned more and more, and from his jaws crept forth a long, foaming tongue.

A moment more, and to the ears of spectators sitting nearer came as it were the crack of breaking bones; then the beast rolled on the earth with his neck twisted in death.

The giant removed in a twinkle the ropes from the horns of the bull and, raising the maiden, began to breathe hurriedly. His face became pale, his hair stuck together from sweat, his shoulders and arms seemed flooded with water. For a moment he stood as if only half conscious; then he raised his eyes and looked at the spectators.

The amphitheatre had gone wild.

The walls of the building were trembling from the roar of tens of thousands of people. Since the beginning of spectacles there was no memory of such excitement. Those who were sitting on the highest rows came down, crowding in the passages between benches to look more nearly at the strong man. Everywhere were heard cries for mercy, passionate and persistent, which soon turned into one unbroken thunder. That giant had become dear to those people enamoured of physical strength; he was the first personage in Rome.

He understood that the multitude were striving to grant him his life and restore him his freedom, but clearly his thought was not on himself alone. He looked around a while; then approached Cæsar's podium, and, holding the body of the maiden on his outstretched arms, raised his eyes with entreaty, as if to say, —

"Have mercy on her! Save the maiden. I did that for her sake!"

The spectators understood perfectly what he wanted. At sight of the unconscious maiden, who near the enormous Lygian seemed a child, emotion seized the multitude of knights and senators. Her slender form, as white as if chiselled from alabaster, her fainting, the dreadful danger from which the giant had freed her, and finally her beauty and attachment had moved every heart. Some thought the man a father begging mercy for his child. Pity burst forth suddenly, like a flame. They had had blood, death, and torture in sufficiency. Voices choked with tears began to entreat mercy for both.

Meanwhile Ursus, holding the girl in his arms, moved around the arena, and with his eyes and with motions begged her life for her. Now Vinicius started up from his seat, sprang over the barrier which separated the front places from the arena, and, running to Lygia, covered her naked body with his toga.

Then he tore apart the tunic on his breast, laid bare the scars left by wounds received in the Armenian war, and stretched out his hands to the audience.

At this the enthusiasm of the multitude passed everything seen in a circus before. The crowd stamped and howled. Voices calling for mercy grew simply terrible. People not only took the part of the athlete, but rose in defense of the soldier, the maiden, their love. Thousands of spectators turned to Cæsar with flashes of anger in their eyes and with clinched fists.

But Cæsar halted and hesitated. Against Vinicius he had no hatred indeed, and the death of Lygia did not concern him; but he preferred to see the body of the maiden rent by the horns of the bull or torn by the claws of beasts. His cruelty, his deformed imagination, and deformed desires found a kind of delight in such spectacles. And now the people wanted to rob him. Hence anger appeared on his bloated face. Self-love also would not let him yield to the wish of the multitude, and still he did not dare to oppose it, through his inborn cowardice.

So he gazed around to see if among the Augustians at least, he could not find fingers turned down in sign of death. But Petronius held up his hand, and looked into Nero's face almost challengingly. Vestinius, superstitious but inclined to enthusiasm, a man who feared ghosts but not the living, gave a sign for mercy also. So did Scevinus, the Senator; so did Nerva, so did Tullius Senecio, so did the famous leader Ostorius Scapula, and Antistius, and Piso, and Vetus, and Crispinus, and Minucius Thermus, and Pontius Telesinus, and the most important of all, one honored by the people, Thrasea.

In view of this, Cæsar took the emerald from his eye with an expression of contempt and offence; when Tigellinus, whose desire was to spite Petronius, turned to him and said, —

"Yield not, divinity; we have the pretorians."

Then Nero turned to the place where command over the pretorians was held by the stern Subrius Flavius, hitherto devoted with whole soul to him, and saw something unusual. The face of the old tribune was stern, but covered with tears, and he was holding his hand up in sign of mercy.

Now rage began to possess the multitude. Dust rose from beneath the stamping feet, and filled the amphitheatre. In the midst of shouts were heard cries: "Ahenobarbus! matricide! incendiary!"

Nero was alarmed. Romans were absolute lords in the Circus. Former Cæsars, and especially Caligula, had permitted themselves sometimes to act against the will of the people; this, however, called forth disturbance always, going sometimes to bloodshed. But Nero was in a different position. First, as a comedian and a singer he needed the people's favor; second, he wanted it on his side against the Senate and the patricians, and especially after the burning of Rome he strove by all means to win it, and turn their anger against the Christians. He understood, besides, that to oppose longer was simply dangerous. A disturbance begun in the Circus might seize the whole city, and have results incalculable.

He looked once more at Subrius Flavius, at Scevinus the centurion, a relative of the senator, at the soldiers; and seeing everywhere frowning brows, excited faces, and eyes fixed on him, he gave the sign for mercy.

Then a thunder of applause was heard from the highest seats to the lowest. The people were sure of the lives of the condemned, for from that moment they went under their protection, and even Cæsar would not have dared to pursue them any longer with his vengeance.

CHAPTER LXVI

FOUR Bithynians carried Lygia carefully to the house of Petronius. Vinicius and Ursus walked at her side, hurrying so as to give her into the hands of the Greek physician as quickly as possible. They walked in silence, for after the events of the day they had not power to speak. Vinicius so far was as if half conscious. He kept repeating to himself that Lygia was saved; that she was threatened no longer by imprisonment, or death in the Circus; that their misfortunes had ended once and forever; that he would take her home and not separate again from her. This appeared to him the beginning of some other life rather than reality. From moment to moment he bent over the open litter to look on the beloved face, which in the moonlight seemed sleeping, and he repeated mentally, "This is she! Christ has saved her!" He remembered also that while he and Ursus were carrying her from the spoliarium an unknown physician had assured him that she was living and would recover. At this thought delight so filled his breast that at moments he grew weak, and being unable to walk with his own strength leaned on the arm of Ursus. Ursus meanwhile was looking into the sky filled with stars, and was praying.

They advanced hurriedly along streets where newly erected white buildings shone brightly in the moonlight. The city was empty, save here and there where crowds of people crowned with ivy, sang and danced before porticos to the sound of flutes, thus taking advantage of the wonderful night and the festive season, unbroken from the beginning of the games. Only when they were near the house did Ursus stop praying, and say in a low voice, as if he feared to waken Lygia, —

"Lord, it was the Saviour who rescued her from death. When I saw her on the horns of the aurochs, I heard a voice in my soul saying, 'Defend her!' and that was the voice of the Lamb. The prison took strength from me, but He gave it back in that moment, and inspired that cruel people to take her part. Let His will be done!"

And Vinicius answered, —

"Magnified be His name!"

He had not power to continue, for all at once he felt that a mighty weeping was swelling his breast. He was seized by an overpowering wish to throw himself on the earth and thank the Saviour for His miracles and His mercy.

Meanwhile they had come to the house; the servants, informed by a slave despatched in advance, crowded out to meet them. Paul of Tarsus had sent back from Antium the greater part of those people. The misfortune of Vinicius was known to them perfectly; therefore their delight at seeing those victims which had been snatched from the malice of Nero was immense, and increased still more when the physician Theocles declared that Lygia had not suffered serious injury, and that when the weakness caused by prison fever had passed, she would regain health.

Consciousness returned to her that night. Waking in the splendid chamber lighted by Corinthian lamps, amidst the odor of verbena and nard, she knew not where she was, or what was taking place with her. She remembered the moment in which she had been lashed to the horns of the chained bull; and now, seeing above her the face of Vinicius, lighted by the mild rays of the lamp, she supposed herself no longer on earth. The thoughts were confused in her weakened head; it seemed to her natural to be detained somewhere on the way to heaven, because of her tortures and weakness. Feeling no pain, however, she smiled at Vinicius, and wanted to ask where they were; but from her lips came merely a low whisper in which he could barely detect his own name.

Then he knelt near her, and, placing his hand on her forehead lightly, he said, —

"Christ saved thee, and returned thee to me!"

Her lips moved again with a meaningless whisper; her lids closed after a moment, her breast rose with a light sigh, and she fell into a deep sleep, for which the physician had been waiting, and after which she would return to health, he said.

Vinicius remained kneeling near her, however, sunk in prayer. His soul was melting with a love so immense that he forgot himself utterly. Theocles returned often to the chamber, and the golden-haired Eunice appeared behind the raised curtain a number of times; finally cranes, reared in the gardens, began to call, heralding the coming day, but Vinicius was still embracing in his mind the feet of Christ, neither seeing nor hearing what was passing around him, with a heart turned into a thanksgiving, sacrificial flame, sunk in ecstasy, and though alive, half seized into heaven.

CHAPTER LXVII

PETRONIUS, after the liberation of Lygia, not wishing to irritate Cæsar, went to the Palatine with other Augustians. He wanted to hear what they were saying, and especially to learn if Tigellinus was devising something new to destroy Lygia. Both she and Ursus had passed under the protection of the people, it is true, and no one could place a hand on them without raising a riot; still Petronius, knowing the hatred toward him of the all-powerful pretorian prefect, considered that very likely Tigellinus, while unable to strike him directly, would strive to find some means of revenge against his nephew.

Nero was angry and irritated, since the spectacle had ended quite differently from what he had planned. At first he did not wish even to look at Petronius; but the latter, without losing cool blood, approached him, with all the freedom of the "arbiter elegantiarum," and said, —

"Dost thou know, divinity, what occurs to me? Write a poem on the maiden who, at command of the lord of the world, was freed from the horns of the wild bull and given to her lover. The Greeks are sensitive, and I am sure that the poem will enchant them."

This thought pleased Nero in spite of all his irritation, and it pleased him doubly, first, as a subject for a poem, and second, because in it he could glorify himself as the magnanimous lord of the earth; hence he looked for a time at Petronius, and then said, —

"Yes! perhaps thou art right. But does it become me to celebrate my own goodness?"

"There is no need to give names. In Rome all will know who is meant, and from Rome reports go through the whole world."

"But art thou sure that this will please the people in Achæa?"

"By Pollux, it will!" said Petronius.

And he went away satisfied, for he felt certain that Nero, whose whole life was an arrangement of reality to literary plans, would not spoil the subject, and by this alone he would tie the hands of Tigellinus. This, however, did not change his plan of sending Vinicius out of Rome as soon as Lygia's health should permit. So when he saw him next day, he said, —

"Take her to Sicily. As things have happened, on Cæsar's part thou art threatened by nothing; but Tigellinus is ready to use even poison, — if not out of hatred to you both, out of hatred to me."

Vinicius smiled at him, and said: "She was on the horns of the wild bull; still Christ saved her."

"Then honor Him with a hecatomb," replied Petronius, with an accent of impatience, "but do not beg Him to save her a second time. Dost remember how Eolus received Ulysses when he returned to ask a second time for favoring winds? Deities do not like to repeat themselves."

"When her health returns, I will take her to Pomponia Græcina," said Vinicius.

"And thou wilt do that all the better since Pomponia is ill; Antistius, a relative of Aulus, told me so. Meanwhile things will happen here to make people forget thee, and in these times the forgotten are the happiest. May Fortune be thy sun in winter, and thy shade in summer."

Then he left Vinicius to his happiness, but went himself to inquire of Theocles touching the life and health of Lygia.

Danger threatened her no longer. Emaciated as she was in the dungeon after prison fever, foul air and discomfort would have killed her; but now she had the most tender care, and not only plenty, but luxury. At command of Theocles they took her to the gardens of the villa after two days; in these gardens she remained for hours. Vinicius decked her litter with anemones, and especially with irises, to remind her of the atrium of the house of Aulus. More than once, hidden in the shade of spreading trees, they spoke of past sufferings and fears, each holding the other's hand. Lygia said that Christ had conducted him through suffering purposely to change his soul and raise it to Himself. Vinicius felt that this was true, and that there was in him nothing of the former patrician, who knew no law but his own desire. In those memories there was nothing bitter, however. It seemed to both that whole years had gone over their heads, and that the dreadful past lay far behind. At the same time such a calmness possessed them as they had never known before. A new life of immense happiness had come and taken them into itself. In Rome Cæsar might rage and fill the world with terror — they felt above them a guardianship a hundred times mightier than his power, and had no further fear of his rage or his malice, just as if for them he had ceased to be the lord of life or death. Once, about sunset, the roar of lions and other beasts reached them from distant vivaria. Formerly those sounds filled Vinicius with fear because they were ominous; now he and Lygia merely looked at each other and raised their eyes to the evening twilight. At times Lygia, still very weak and unable to walk alone, fell asleep in the quiet of the garden; he watched over her, and, looking at her sleeping face, thought involuntarily that she was not that Lygia whom he had met at the house of Aulus. In fact, imprisonment and disease had to some extent quenched her beauty. When he saw her at the house of Aulus, and later, when he went to Miriam's house to seize her, she was as wonderful as a statue and also as a flower; now her face had become almost transparent, her hands thin, her body reduced by disease, her lips pale, and even her eyes seemed less blue than formerly. The golden-haired Eunice who brought her flowers and rich stuffs to cover her feet was a divinity of Cyprus in comparison. Petronius tried in vain to find the former charms in her, and, shrugging his shoulders, thought that that shadow from Elysian fields was not worth those struggles, those pains, and those tortures which had almost sucked the life out of Vinicius. But Vinicius, in love now with her spirit, loved it all the more; and when he was watching over her while asleep, it seemed to him that he was watching over the whole world.

CHAPTER LXVIII

News of the miraculous rescue of Lygia was circulated quickly among those scattered Christians who had escaped destruction. Confessors came to look at her to whom Christ's favor had been shown clearly. First came Nazarius and Miriam, with whom Peter the Apostle was hiding thus far; after them came others. All, as well as Vinicius, Lygia, and the Christian slaves of Petronius, listened with attention to the narrative of Ursus about the voice which he had heard in his soul, and which commanded him to struggle with the wild bull. All went away consoled, hoping that Christ would not let His followers be exterminated on earth before His coming at the day of judgment. And hope sustained their hearts, for persecution had not ceased yet. Whoever was declared a Christian by public report was thrown into prison at once by the city watches. It is true that the victims were fewer, for the majority of confessors had been seized and tortured to death. The Christians who remained had either left Rome to wait out the storm in distant provinces, or had hidden most carefully, not daring to assemble in common prayer, unless in sand-pits outside the city. They were persecuted yet, however, and though the games were at an end, the newly arrested were reserved for future games or punished specially. Though it was believed in Rome no longer that Christians had caused the conflagration, they were declared enemies of humanity and the State, and the edict against them remained in former force.

The Apostle Peter did not venture for a long time to appear in the house of Petronius, but at last on a certain evening Nazarius announced his arrival. Lygia, who was able to walk alone now, and Vinicius ran out to meet him, and fell to embracing his feet. He greeted them with emotion all the greater that not many sheep in that flock over which Christ had given him authority, and over the fate of which his great heart was weeping, remained to him. So when Vinicius said, "Lord, because of thee the Redeemer returned her to me," he answered: "He returned her because of thy faith, and so that not all the lips which profess His name should grow silent." And evidently he was thinking then of those thousands of his children torn by wild beasts, of those crosses with which the arena had been filled, and those fiery pillars in the gardens of the "Beast"; for he spoke with great sadness. Vinicius and Lygia noticed also that his hair had grown entirely white, that his whole form was bent, and that in his face there was as much sadness and suffering as if he had passed through all those pains and torments which the victims of Nero's rage and madness had endured. But both understood that since Christ had given Himself to torture and to death, no one was permitted to avoid it. Still their hearts were cut at sight of the Apostle, bent by years, toil, and pain. So Vinicius, who intended to take Lygia soon to Naples, where they would meet Pomponia and go to Sicily, implored him to leave Rome in their company.

But the Apostle placed his hand on the tribune's head and answered, —

"In my soul I hear these words of the Lord, which He spoke to me on the Lake of Tiberias: 'When thou wert young, thou didst gird thyself, and walk whither thou wouldst; but when thou shalt be old, thou shalt stretch forth thy hands, and another shall gird thee, and carry thee whither thou wouldst not.' Therefore it is proper that I follow my flock."

And when they were silent, not knowing the sense of his speech, he added, —

"My toil is nearing its end; I shall find entertainment and rest only in the house of the Lord."

Then he turned to them saying: "Remember me, for I have loved you as a father loves his children; and whatever ye do in life, do it for the glory of God."

Thus speaking, he raised his aged, trembling hands and blessed them; they nestled up to him, feeling that to be the last blessing, perhaps, which they should receive from him.

It was destined them, however, to see him once more. A few days later Petronius brought terrible news from the Palatine. It had been discovered there that one of Cæsar's freedmen was a Christian; and on this man were found letters of the Apostles Peter and Paul, with letters of James, John, and Judas. Peter's presence in Rome was known formerly to Tigellinus, but he thought that the Apostle had perished with thousands of other confessors. Now it transpired that the two leaders of the new faith were alive and in the capital. It was determined, therefore, to seize them at all costs, for it was hoped that with their death the last root of the hated sect would be plucked out. Petronius heard from Vestinius that Cæsar himself had issued an order to put Peter and Paul in the Mamertine prison within three days, and that whole detachments of pretorians had been sent to search every house in the Trans-Tiber.

When he heard this, Vinicius resolved to warn the Apostle. In the evening he and Ursus put on Gallic mantles and went to the house of Miriam, where Peter was living. The house was at the very edge of the Trans-Tiber division of the city, at the foot of the Janiculum. On the road they saw houses surrounded by soldiers, who were guided by certain unknown persons. This division of the city was alarmed, and in places crowds of curious people had assembled. Here and there centurions interrogated prisoners touching Simon Peter and Paul of Tarsus.

Ursus and Vinicius were in advance of the soldiers, and went safely to Miriam's house, in which they found Peter surrounded by a handful of the faithful. Timothy, Paul's assistant, and Linus were at the side of the Apostle.

At news of the approaching danger, Nazarius led all by a hidden passage to the garden gate, and then to deserted stone quarries, a few hundred yards distant from the Janiculum Gate. Ursus had to carry Linus, whose bones, broken by torture, had not grown together yet. But once in the quarry, they felt safe; and by the light of a torch ignited by Nazarius they began to consult, in a low voice, how to save the life of the Apostle who was so dear to them.

"Lord," said Vinicius, "let Nazarius guide thee at daybreak to the Alban Hills. There I will find thee, and we will take thee to Antium, where a ship is ready to take us to Naples and Sicily. Blessed will the day and the hour be in which thou shalt enter my house, and thou wilt bless my hearth."

The others heard this with delight, and pressed the Apostle, saying, —

"Hide thyself, sacred leader; remain not in Rome. Preserve the living truth, so that it perish not with us and thee. Hear us, who entreat thee as a father."

"Do this in Christ's name!" cried others, grasping at his robes.

"My children," answered Peter, "who knows the time when the Lord will mark the end of his life?"

But he did not say that he would not leave Rome, and he hesitated what to do; for uncertainty, and even fear, had been creeping into his soul for some time. His flock was scattered; the work was wrecked; that church, which before the burning of the city had been flourishing like a splendid tree, was turned into dust by the power of the "Beast." Nothing remained save tears, nothing save memories of torture and death. The sowing had yielded rich fruit, but Satan had trampled it into the earth. Legions of angels had not come to aid the perishing, — and Nero was extending in glory over the earth, terrible, mightier than ever, the lord of all seas and all lands. More than once had that fisherman of the Lord stretched his hands heavenward in loneliness and asked: "Lord, what must I do? How must I act? And how am I, a feeble old man, to fight with this invincible power of Evil, which Thou hast permitted to rule, and have victory?"

And he called out thus in the depth of his immense pain, repeating in spirit: "Those sheep which Thou didst command me to feed are no more, Thy church is no more; loneliness and mourning are in Thy capital; what dost Thou command me to do now? Am I to stay here, or lead forth the remnant of the flock to glorify Thy name in secret somewhere beyond the sea?"

And he hesitated. He believed that the living truth would not perish, that it must conquer; but at moments he thought that the hour had not come yet, that it would come only when the Lord should descend to the earth in the day of judgment in glory and power a hundred times greater than the might of Nero.

Frequently it seemed to him that if he left Rome, the faithful would follow; that he would lead them then far away to the shady groves of Galilee, to the quiet surface of the Lake of Tiberias, to shepherds as peaceful as doves, or as sheep, who feed there among thyme and pepperwort. And an increasing desire for peace and rest, an increasing yearning for the lake and Galilee, seized the heart of the fisherman; tears came more frequently to the old man's eyes.

But at the moment when he made the choice, sudden alarm and fear came on him. How was he to leave that city, in which so much martyrs' blood had sunk into the earth, and where so many lips had given the true testimony of the dying? Was he alone to yield? And what would he answer the Lord on hearing the words, "These have died for the faith, but thou didst flee"?

Nights and days passed for him in anxiety and suffering. Others, who had been torn by lions, who had been fastened to crosses, who had been burnt in the gardens of Cæsar, had fallen asleep in the Lord after moments of torture; but he could not sleep, and he felt greater tortures than any of those invented by executioners for victims. Often was the dawn whitening the roofs of houses while he was still crying from the depth of his mourning heart: "Lord, why didst Thou command me to come hither and found Thy capital in the den of the 'Beast'?"

For thirty-three years after the death of his Master he knew no rest. Staff in hand, he had gone through the world and declared the "good tidings." His strength had been exhausted in journeys and toil, till at last, when in that city, which was the head of the world, he had established the work of his Master, one bloody breath of wrath had burned it, and he saw that there was need to take up the struggle anew. And what a struggle! On one side Cæsar, the Senate, the people, the legions holding the world with a circle of iron, countless cities, countless lands, — power such as the eye of man had not seen; on the other side he, so bent with age and toil that his trembling hand was hardly able to carry his staff.

At times, therefore, he said to himself that it was not for him to measure with the Cæsar of Rome, — that Christ alone could do that.

All these thoughts were passing through his care-filled head, when he heard the prayers of the last handful of the faithful. They, surrounding him in an ever narrowing circle, repeated with voices of entreaty, —

"Hide thyself, Rabbi, and lead us away from the power of the 'Beast.'"

Finally Linus also bowed his tortured head before him.

"O lord," said he, "the Redeemer commanded thee to feed His sheep, but they are here no longer, or to-morrow they will not be here; go, therefore, where thou mayst find them yet. The word of God is living still in Jerusalem, in Antioch, in Ephesus, and in other cities. What wilt thou do by remaining in Rome? If thou fall, thou wilt merely swell the triumph of the 'Beast.' The Lord has not designated the limit of John's life; Paul is a Roman citizen, they cannot condemn him without trial; but if the power of hell rise up against thee, O teacher, those whose hearts are dejected will ask, 'Who is above Nero?' Thou art the rock on which the church of God is founded. Let us die, but permit not the victory of Antichrist over the vicegerent of God, and return not hither till the Lord has crushed him who shed innocent blood."

"Look at our tears!" repeated all who were present.

Tears flowed over Peter's face too. After a while he rose, and, stretching his hands over the kneeling figures, said, —

"May the name of the Lord be magnified, and may His will be done!"

CHAPTER LXIX

ABOUT dawn of the following day two dark figures were moving along the Appian Way toward the Campania.

One of them was Nazarius; the other the Apostle Peter, who was leaving Rome and his martyred co-religionists.

The sky in the east was assuming a light tinge of green, bordered gradually and more distinctly on the lower edge with saffron color. Silver-leafed trees, the white marble of villas, and the arches of aqueducts, stretching through the plain toward the city, were emerging from shade. The greenness of the sky was clearing gradually, and becoming permeated with gold. Then the east began to grow rosy and illuminate the Alban Hills, which seemed marvellously beautiful, lily-colored, as if formed of rays of light alone.

The light was reflected in trembling leaves of trees, in the dew-drops. The haze grew thinner, opening wider and wider views on the plain, on the houses dotting it, on the cemeteries, on the towns, and on groups of trees, among which stood white columns of temples.

The road was empty. The villagers who took vegetables to the city had not succeeded yet, evidently, in harnessing beasts to their vehicles. From the stone blocks with which the road was paved as far as the mountains, there came a low sound from the bark shoes on the feet of the two travellers.

Then the sun appeared over the line of hills; but at once a wonderful vision struck the Apostle's eyes. It seemed to him that the golden circle, instead of rising in the sky, moved down from the heights and was advancing on the road. Peter stopped, and asked, —

"Seest thou that brightness approaching us?"

"I see nothing," replied Nazarius.

But Peter shaded his eyes with his hand, and said after a while, —

"Some figure is coming in the gleam of the sun."

But not the slightest sound of steps reached their ears. It was perfectly still all around. Nazarius saw only that the trees were quivering in the distance, as if some one were shaking them, and the light was spreading more broadly over the plain. He looked with wonder at the Apostle.

"Rabbi! what ails thee?" cried he, with alarm.

The pilgrim's staff fell from Peter's hands to the earth; his eyes were looking forward, motionless; his mouth was open; on his face were depicted astonishment, delight, rapture.

Then he threw himself on his knees, his arms stretched forward; and this cry left his lips, —

"O Christ! O Christ!"

He fell with his face to the earth, as if kissing some one's feet.

The silence continued long; then were heard the words of the aged man, broken by sobs, —

"*Quo vadis, Domine?*"

Nazarius did not hear the answer; but to Peter's ears came a sad and sweet voice, which said, —

"If thou desert my people, I am going to Rome to be crucified a second time."

The Apostle lay on the ground, his face in the dust, without motion or speech. It seemed to Nazarius that he had fainted or was dead; but he rose at last, seized the staff with trembling hands, and turned without a word toward the seven hills of the city.

The boy, seeing this, repeated as an echo, —

"*Quo vadis, Domine?*"

"To Rome," said the Apostle, in a low voice.

And he returned.

Paul, John, Linus, and all the faithful received him with amazement; and the alarm was the greater, since at daybreak, just after his departure, pretorians had surrounded Miriam's house and searched it for the Apostle. But to every question he answered only with delight and peace, —

"I have seen the Lord!"

And that same evening he went to the Ostian cemetery to teach and baptize those who wished to bathe in the water of life.

And thenceforward he went there daily, and after him went increasing numbers. It seemed that out of every tear of a martyr new confessors were born, and that every groan on the arena found an echo in thousands of breasts. Cæsar was swimming in blood, Rome and the whole pagan world was mad. But those who had had enough of transgression and madness, those who were trampled upon, those whose lives were misery and oppression, all the weighed down, all the sad, all the unfortunate, came to hear the wonderful tidings of God, who out of love for men had given Himself to be crucified and redeem their sins.

When they found a God whom they could love, they had found that which the society of the time could not give any one, — happiness and love.

And Peter understood that neither Cæsar nor all his legions could overcome the living truth, — that they could not overwhelm it with tears or blood, and that now its victory was beginning. He understood with equal force why the Lord had turned him back on the road. That city of pride, crime, wickedness, and power was beginning to be His city, and the double capital, from which would flow out upon the world government of souls and bodies.

CHAPTER LXX

At last the hour was accomplished for both Apostles. But, as if to complete his service, it was given to the fisherman of the Lord to win two souls even in confinement. The soldiers, Processus and Martinianus, who guarded him in the Mamertine prison, received baptism. Then came the hour of torture. Nero was not in Rome at that time. Sentence was passed by Helius and Polythetes, two freedmen to whom Cæsar had confided the government of Rome during his absence.

On the aged Apostle had been inflicted the stripes prescribed by law; and next day he was led forth beyond the walls of the city, toward the Vatican Hill, where he was to suffer the punishment of the cross assigned to him. Soldiers were astonished by the crowd which had gathered before the prison, for in their minds the death of a common man, and besides a foreigner, should not rouse such interest; they did not understand that that retinue was composed not of sightseers, but confessors, anxious to escort the great Apostle to the place of execution. In the afternoon the gates of the prison were thrown open at last, and Peter appeared in the midst of a detachment of pretorians. The sun had inclined somewhat toward Ostia already; the day was clear and calm. Because of his advanced age, Peter was not required to carry the cross; it was supposed that he could not carry it; they had not put the fork on his neck, either, so as not to retard his pace. He walked without hindrance, and the faithful could see him perfectly.

At moments when his white head showed itself among the iron helmets of the soldiers, weeping was heard in the crowd; but it was restrained immediately, for the face of the old man had in it so much calmness, and was so bright with joy, that all understood him to be not a victim going to destruction, but a victor celebrating his triumph.

And thus it was really. The fisherman, usually humble and stooping, walked now erect, taller than the soldiers, full of dignity. Never had men seen such majesty in his bearing. It might have seemed that he was a monarch attended by people and military. From every side voices were raised, —

"There is Peter going to the Lord!"

All forgot, as it were, that torture and death were waiting for him. He walked with solemn attention, but with calmness, feeling that since the death on Golgotha nothing equally important had happened, and that as the first death had redeemed the whole world, this was to redeem the city.

Along the road people halted from wonder at sight of that old man; but believers, laying hands on their shoulders, said with calm voices, —

"See how a just man goes to death, — one who knew Christ and proclaimed love to the world."

These became thoughtful, and walked away, saying to themselves, "He cannot, indeed, be unjust!"

Along the road noise was hushed, and the cries of the street. The retinue moved on before houses newly reared, before white columns of temples, over whose summits hung the deep sky, calm and blue. They went in quiet; only at times the weapons of the soldiers clattered, or the murmur of prayer rose. Peter heard the last, and his face grew bright with increasing joy, for his glance could hardly take in those thousands of confessors. He felt that he had done his work, and he knew now that that truth which he had been declaring all his life would overwhelm everything, like a sea, and that nothing would have power to restrain it. And thus thinking, he raised his eyes, and said: "O Lord, Thou didst command me to conquer this world-ruling city; hence I have conquered it. Thou hast commanded me to found here Thy capital; hence I have founded it. This is Thy city now, O Lord, and I go to Thee, for I have toiled greatly."

As he passed before temples, he said to them, "Ye will be temples of Christ." Looking at throngs of people moving before his eyes, he said to them, "Your children will be servants of Christ"; and he advanced with the feeling that he had conquered, conscious of his service, conscious of his strength, solaced, — great. The soldiers conducted him over the Pons Triumphalis, as if giving involuntary testimony to his triumph, and they led him farther toward the Naumachia and the Circus. The faithful from beyond the Tiber joined the procession; and such a throng of people was formed that the centurion commanding the pretorians understood at last that he was leading a high-priest surrounded by believers, and grew alarmed because of the small number of soldiers. But no cry of indignation or rage was given out in the throng. Men's faces were penetrated with the greatness of the moment, solemn and full of expectation. Some believers, remembering that when the Lord died the earth opened from fright and the dead rose from their graves, thought that now some evident signs would appear, after which the death of the Apostle would not be forgotten for ages. Others said to themselves, "Perhaps the Lord will select the hour of Peter's death to come from heaven as He promised, and judge the world." With this idea they recommended themselves to the mercy of the Redeemer.

But round about there was calm. The hills seemed to be warming themselves, and resting in the sun. The procession stopped at last between the Circus and the Vatican Hill. Soldiers began now to dig a hole; others placed on the ground the cross, hammers, and nails, waiting till all preparations were finished. The crowd, continuing quiet and attentive, knelt round about.

The Apostle, with his head in the sun-rays and golden light, turned for the last time toward the city. At a distance lower down was seen the gleaming Tiber; beyond was the Campus Martius; higher up, the Mausoleum of Augustus; below that, the gigantic baths just begun by Nero; still lower, Pompey's theatre; and beyond them were visible in places, and in places hidden by other buildings, the Septa Julia, a multitude of porticos, temples, columns, great edifices; and, finally, far in the distance, hills covered with houses, a gigantic resort of people, the borders of which vanished in the blue haze, — an abode of crime, but of power; of madness, but of order, — which had become the head of the world, its oppressor, but its law and its peace, almighty, invincible, eternal.

But Peter, surrounded by soldiers, looked at the city as a ruler and king looks at his inheritance. And he said to it, "Thou art redeemed and mine!" And no one, not merely among the soldiers digging the hole in which to plant the cross, but even among believers, could divine that standing there among them was the true ruler of that moving life; that Cæsars would pass away, waves of barbarians go by, and ages vanish, but that old man would be lord there unbrokenly.

The sun had sunk still more toward Ostia, and had become large and red. The whole western side of the sky had begun to glow with immense brightness. The soldiers approached Peter to strip him.

But he, while praying, straightened himself all at once, and stretched his right hand high. The executioners stopped, as if made timid by his posture; the faithful held the breath in their breasts, thinking that he wished to say something, and silence unbroken followed.

But he, standing on the height, with his extended right hand made the sign of the cross, blessing in the hour of death,—

Urbi et orbi! (the city and the world).

In that same wonderful evening another detachment of soldiers conducted along the Ostian Way Paul of Tarsus toward a place called Aquæ Salviæ. And behind him also advanced a crowd of the faithful whom he had converted; but when he recognized near acquaintances, he halted and conversed with them, for, being a Roman citizen, the guard showed more respect to him. Beyond the gate called Tergemina he met Plautilla, the daughter of the prefect Flavius Sabinus, and, seeing her youthful face covered with tears, he said: "Plautilla, daughter of Eternal Salvation, depart in peace. Only give me a veil with which to bind my eyes when I am going to the Lord." And taking it, he advanced with a face as full of delight as that of a laborer who when he has toiled the whole day successfully is returning home. His thoughts, like those of Peter, were as calm and quiet as that evening sky. His eyes gazed with thoughtfulness upon the plain which stretched out before him, and to the Alban Hills, immersed in light. He remembered his journeys, his toils, his labor, the struggles in which he had conquered, the churches which he had founded in all lands and beyond all seas; and he thought that he had earned his rest honestly, that he had finished his work. He felt now that the seed which he had planted would not be blown away by the wind of malice. He was leaving this life with the certainty that in the battle which his truth had declared against the world it would conquer; and a mighty peace settled down on his soul.

The road to the place of execution was long, and evening was coming. The mountains became purple, and the bases of them went gradually into the shade. Flocks were returning home. Here and there groups of slaves were walking with the tools of labor on their shoulders. Children, playing on the road before houses, looked with curiosity at the passing soldiers. But in that evening, in that transparent golden air, there were not only peace and lovingness, but a certain harmony, which seemed to lift from earth to heaven. Paul felt this; and his heart was filled with delight at the thought that to that harmony of the world he had added one note which had not been in it hitherto, but without which the whole earth was like sounding brass or a tinkling cymbal.

He remembered how he had taught people love, — how he had told them that though they were to give their property to the poor, though they knew all languages, all secrets, and all sciences, they would be nothing without love, which is kind, enduring, which does not return evil, which does not desire honor, suffers all things, believes all things, hopes all things, is patient of all things.

And so his life had passed in teaching people this truth. And now he said in spirit: What power can equal it, what can conquer it? Could Cæsar stop it, though he had twice as many legions and twice as many cities, seas, lands, and nations?

And he went to his reward like a conqueror.

The detachment left the main road at last, and turned toward the east on a narrow path leading to the Aquæ Salviæ. The red sun was lying now on the heather. The centurion stopped the soldiers at the fountain, for the moment had come.

Paul placed Plautilla's veil on his arm, intending to bind his eyes with it; for the last time he raised those eyes, full of unspeakable peace, toward the eternal light of the evening, and prayed. Yes, the moment had come; but he saw before him a great road in the light, leading to heaven; and in his soul he repeated the same words which formerly he had written in the feeling of his own finished service and his near end, —

"I have fought a good fight, I have finished my course, I have kept the faith. Henceforth there is laid up for me a crown of righteousness."

CHAPTER LXXI

ROME had gone mad for a long time, so that the world-conquering city seemed ready at last to tear itself to pieces for want of leadership. Even before the last hour of the Apostles had struck, Piso's conspiracy appeared; and then such merciless reaping of Rome's highest heads, that even to those who saw divinity in Nero, he seemed at last a divinity of death. Mourning fell on the city, terror took its lodgment in houses and in hearts, but porticos were crowned with ivy and flowers, for it was not permitted to show sorrow for the dead. People waking in the morning asked themselves whose turn would come next. The retinue of ghosts following Cæsar increased every day.

Piso paid for the conspiracy with his head; after him followed Seneca, and Lucan, Fenius Rufus, and Plautius Lateranus, and Flavius Scevinus, and Afranius Quinetianus, and the dissolute companion of Cæsar's madnesses, Tullius Senecio, and Proculus, and Araricus, and Tugurinus, and Gratus, and Silanus, and Proximus, — once devoted with his whole soul to Nero, — and Sulpicius Asper. Some were destroyed by their own insignificance, some by fear, some by wealth, others by bravery. Cæsar, astonished at the very number of the conspirators, covered the walls with soldiery and held the city as if by siege, sending out daily centurions with sentences of death to suspected houses. The condemned humiliated themselves in letters filled with flattery, thanking Cæsar for his sentences, and leaving him a part of their property, so as to save the rest for their children. It seemed, at last, that Nero was exceeding every measure on purpose to convince himself of the degree in which men had grown abject, and how long they would endure bloody rule. After the conspirators, their relatives were executed; then their friends, and even simple acquaintances. Dwellers in lordly mansions built after the fire, when they went out on the street, felt sure of seeing a whole row of funerals. Pompeius, Cornelius, Martialis, Flavius Nepos, and Statius Domitius died because accused of lack of love for Cæsar; Novius Priscus, as a friend of Seneca. Rufius Crispus was deprived of the right of fire and water because on a time he had been the husband of Poppæa. The great Thrasea was ruined by his virtue; many paid with their lives for noble origin; even Poppæa fell a victim to the momentary rage of Nero.

The Senate crouched before the dreadful ruler; it raised a temple in his honor, made an offering in favor of his voice, crowned his statues, appointed priests to him as to a divinity. Senators, trembling in their souls, went to the Palatine to magnify the song of the "Periodonices," and go wild with him amid orgies of naked bodies, wine, and flowers.

But meanwhile from below, in the field soaked in blood and tears, rose the sowing of Peter, stronger and stronger every moment.

CHAPTER LXXII

"We know, carissime, most of what is happening in Rome, and what we do not know is told us in thy letters. When one casts a stone in the water, the wave goes farther and farther in a circle; so the wave of madness and malice has come from the Palatine to us. On the road to Greece, Carinas was sent hither by Cæsar, who plundered cities and temples to fill the empty treasury. At the price of the sweat and tears of people, he is building the 'golden house' in Rome. It is possible that the world has not seen such a house, but it has not seen such injustice. Thou knowest Carinas. Chilo was like him till he redeemed his life with death. But to the towns lying nearer us his men have not come yet, perhaps because there are no temples or treasures in them. Thou askest if we are out of danger. I answer that we are out of mind, and let that suffice for an answer. At this moment, from the portico under which I write, I see our calm bay, and on it Ursus in a boat, letting down a net in the clear water. My wife is spinning red wool near me, and in the gardens, under the shade of almond-trees, our slaves are singing. Oh, what calm, carissime, and what a forgetfulness of former fear and suffering! But it is not the Parcæ, as thou writest, who spin out our lives so agreeably; it is Christ who is blessing us, our beloved God and Saviour. We know tears and sorrow, for our religion teaches us to weep over the misfortunes of others; but in these tears is a consolation unknown to thee; for whenever the time of our life is ended, we shall find all those dear ones who perished and who are perishing yet for God's truth. For us Peter and Paul are not dead; they are merely born into glory. Our souls see them, and when our eyes weep our hearts are glad with their joy. Oh, yes, my dear friend, we are happy with a happiness which nothing can destroy, since death, which for thee is the end of everything, is for us only a passage into superior rest.

"And so days and months pass here in calmness of heart. Our servants and slaves believe, as we do, in Christ, and that He enjoins love; hence we love one another. Frequently, when the sun has gone down, or when the moon is shining in the water, Lygia and I talk of past times, which seem a dream to us; but when I think how that dear head was near torture and death, I magnify my Lord with my whole soul, for out of those hands He alone could wrest her, save her from the arena, and return her to me forever. O Petronius, thou hast seen what endurance and comfort that religion gives in misfortune, how much patience and courage before death; so come and see how much happiness it gives in ordinary, common days of life. People thus far did not know a God whom man could love, hence they did not love one another; and from that came their misfortune, for as light comes from the sun, so does happiness come from love. Neither lawgivers nor philosophers taught this truth, and it did not exist in Greece or Rome; and when I say, not in Rome, that means the whole world. The dry and cold teaching of the Stoics, to which virtuous people rally, tempers the heart as a sword is tempered, but it makes it indifferent rather than better. Though why do I write this to thee, who hast learned more, and hast more understanding than I have? Thou wert acquainted with Paul of Tarsus, and more than once didst converse long with him; hence thou knowest better if in comparison with the truth which he taught all the teachings of philosophers and rhetors are not a vain and empty jingle of words without meaning. Thou rememberest the question which he put thee: 'But if Cæsar were a Christian, would ye not all feel safer, surer of possessing that which ye possess, free of alarm, and sure of to-morrow?' Thou didst say to me that our teaching was an enemy of life; and I answer thee now, that, if from the beginning of this letter I had been repeating only the three words, 'I am happy!' I could not have expressed my happiness to thee. To this thou wilt answer, that my happiness is Lygia. True, my friend. Because I love her immortal soul, and because we both love each other in Christ; for such love there is no separation, no deceit, no change, no old age, no death. For, when youth and beauty pass, when our bodies wither and death comes, love will remain, for the spirit remains. Before my eyes were open to the light I was ready to burn my own house even, for Lygia's sake; but now I tell thee that I did not love her, for it was Christ who first taught me to love. In Him is the source of peace and happiness. It is not I who say this, but reality itself. Compare thy own luxury, my friend, lined with alarm, thy delights, not sure of a morrow, thy orgies, with the lives of Christians, and thou wilt find a ready answer. But, to compare better, come to our mountains with the odor of thyme, to our shady olive groves on our shores lined with ivy. A peace is waiting for thee, such as thou hast not known for a long time, and hearts that love thee sincerely. Thou, having a noble soul and a good one, shouldst be happy. Thy quick mind can recognize the truth, and knowing it thou wilt love it. To be its enemy, like Cæsar and Tigellinus, is possible, but indifferent to it no one can be. O my Petronius, Lygia and I are comforting ourselves with the hope of seeing thee soon. Be well, be happy, and come to us."

Petronius received this letter in Cumæ, whither he had gone with other Augustians who were following Cæsar. His struggle of long years with Tigellinus was nearing its end. Petronius knew already that he must fall in that struggle, and he understood why. As Cæsar fell lower daily to the rôle of a comedian, a buffoon, and a charioteer; as he sank deeper in a sickly, foul, and coarse dissipation, — the exquisite arbiter became a mere burden to him. Even when Petronius was silent, Nero saw blame in his silence; when the arbiter praised, he saw ridicule. The brilliant patrician annoyed his self-love and roused his envy. His wealth and splendid works of art had become an object of desire both to the ruler and the all-powerful minister. Petronius was spared so far in view of the journey to Achæa, in which his taste, his knowledge of everything Greek, might be useful. But gradually Tigellinus explained to Cæsar that Carinas surpassed him in taste and knowledge, and would be better able to arrange in Achæa games, receptions, and triumphs. From that moment Petronius was lost. There was not courage to send him his sentence in Rome. Cæsar and Tigellinus remembered that that apparently effeminate and æsthetic person, who made "day out of night," and was occupied only in luxury, art, and feasts, had shown amazing industry and energy, when proconsul in Bithynia and later when consul in the capital. They considered him capable of anything, and it was known that in Rome he possessed not only the love of the people, but even of the pretorians. None of Cæsar's confidants could foresee how Petronius might act in a given case; it seemed wiser, therefore, to entice him out of the city, and reach him in a province.

With this object he received an invitation to go to Cumæ with other Augustians. He went, though suspecting the ambush, perhaps so as not to appear in open opposition, perhaps to show once more a joyful face devoid of every care to Cæsar and the Augustians, and to gain a last victory before death over Tigellinus.

Meanwhile the latter accused him of friendship with the Senator Scevinus, who was the soul of Piso's conspiracy. The people of Petronius, left in Rome, were imprisoned; his house was surrounded by pretorian guards. When he learned this, he showed neither alarm nor concern, and with a smile said to Augustians whom he received in his own splendid villa in Cumæ, —

"Ahenobarbus does not like direct questions; hence ye will see his confusion when I ask him if it was he who gave command to imprison my 'familia' in the capital."

Then he invited them to a feast "before the longer journey," and he had just made preparations for it when the letter from Vinicius came.

When he received this letter, Petronius grew somewhat thoughtful, but after a time his face regained its usual composure, and that same evening he answered as follows: —

"I rejoice at your happiness and admire your hearts, for I had not thought that two lovers could remember a third person who was far away. Ye have not only not forgotten me, but ye wish to persuade me to go to Sicily, so that ye may share with me your bread and your Christ, who, as thou writest, has given you happiness so bountifully.

"If that be true, honor Him. To my thinking, however, Ursus had something to do with saving Lygia, and the Roman people also had a little to do with it. But since thy belief is that Christ did the work, I will not contradict. Spare no offerings to Him. Prometheus also sacrificed himself for man; but, alas! Prometheus is an invention of the poets apparently, while people worthy of credit have told me that they saw Christ with their own eyes. I agree with thee that He is the most worthy of the gods.

"I remember the question by Paul of Tarsus, and I think that if Ahenobarbus lived according to Christ's teaching I might have time to visit you in Sicily. In that case we could converse, in the shade of trees and near fountains, of all the gods and all the truths discussed by Greek philosophers at any time. To-day I must give thee a brief answer.

"I care for two philosophers only: Pyrrho and Anacreon. I am ready to sell the rest to thee cheaply, with all the Greek and Roman Stoics. Truth, Vinicius, dwells somewhere so high that the gods themselves cannot see it from the top of Olympus. To thee, carissime, thy Olympus seems higher still, and, standing there, thou callest to me, 'Come, thou wilt see such sights as thou hast not seen yet!' I might. But I answer, 'I have not feet for the journey.' And if thou read this letter to the end, thou wilt acknowledge, I think, that I am right.

"No, happy husband of the Aurora princess! thy religion is not for me. Am I to love the Bithynians who carry my litter, the Egyptians who heat my bath? Am I to love Ahenobarbus and Tigellinus? I swear by the white knees of the Graces, that even if I wished to love them I could not. In Rome there are a hundred thousand persons at least who have either crooked shoulders, or big knees, or thin thighs, or staring eyes, or heads that are too large. Dost thou command me to love these too? Where am I to find the love, since it is not in my heart? And if thy God desires me to love such persons, why in His all might did He not give them the forms of Niobe's children, for example, which thou hast seen on the Palatine? Whoso loves beauty is unable for that very reason to love deformity. One may not believe in our gods, but it is possible to love them, as Phidias, Praxiteles, Miron, Skopas, and Lysias loved.

"Should I wish to go whither thou wouldst lead me, I could not. But since I do not wish, I am doubly unable. Thou believest, like Paul of Tarsus, that on the other side of the Styx thou wilt see thy Christ in certain Elysian fields. Let Him tell thee then Himself whether He would receive me with my gems, my Myrrhene vase, my books published by Sozius, and my golden-haired Eunice. I laugh at this thought; for Paul of Tarsus told me that for Christ's sake one must give up wreaths of roses, feasts, and luxury. It is true that he promised me other happiness, but I answered that I was too old for new happiness, that my eyes would be delighted always with roses, and that the odor of violets is dearer to me than stench from my foul neighbor of the Subura.

"These are reasons why thy happiness is not for me. But there is one reason more, which I have reserved for the last: Thanatos summons me. For thee the light of life is beginning; but my sun has set, and twilight is embracing my head. In other words, I must die, carissime.

"It is not worth while to talk long of this. It had to end thus. Thou, who knowest Ahenobarbus, wilt understand the position easily. Tigellinus has conquered, or rather my victories have touched their end. I have lived as I wished, and I will die as pleases me.

"Do not take this to heart. No God has promised me immortality; hence no surprise meets me. At the same time thou art mistaken, Vinicius, in asserting that only thy God teaches man to die calmly. No. Our world knew, before thou wert born, that when the last cup was drained, it was time to go, — time to rest, — and it knows yet how to do that with calmness. Plato declares that virtue is music, that the life of a sage is harmony. If that be true, I shall die as I have lived, — virtuously.

"I should like to take farewell of thy godlike wife in the words with which on a time I greeted her in the house of Aulus, 'Very many persons have I seen, but thy equal I know not.'

"If the soul is more than what Pyrrho thinks, mine will fly to thee and Lygia, on its way to the edge of the ocean, and will alight at your house in the form of a butterfly or, as the Egyptians believe, in the form of a sparrow-hawk. Otherwise I cannot come.

"Meanwhile let Sicily replace for you the gardens of Hesperides; may the goddesses of the fields, woods, and fountains scatter flowers on your path, and may white doves build their nests on every acanthus of the columns of your house."

CHAPTER LXXIII

Petronius was not mistaken. Two days later young Nerva, who had always been friendly and devoted, sent his freedman to Cumæ with news of what was happening at the court of Cæsar.

The death of Petronius had been determined. On the morning of the following day they intended to send him a centurion, with the order to stop at Cumæ, and wait there for further instructions; the next messenger, to follow a few days later, was to bring the death sentence.

Petronius heard the news with unruffled calmness.

"Thou wilt take to thy lord," said he, "one of my vases; say from me that I thank him with my whole soul, for now I am able to anticipate the sentence."

And all at once he began to laugh, like a man who has come upon a perfect thought, and rejoices in advance at its fulfilment.

That same afternoon his slaves rushed about, inviting the Augustians, who were staying in Cumæ, and all the ladies, to a magnificent banquet at the villa of the arbiter.

He wrote that afternoon in the library; next he took a bath, after which he commanded the vestiplicæ to arrange his dress. Brilliant and stately as one of the gods, he went to the triclinium, to cast the eye of a critic on the preparations, and then to the gardens, where youths and Grecian maidens from the islands were weaving wreaths of roses for the evening.

Not the least care was visible on his face. The servants only knew that the feast would be something uncommon, for he had issued a command to give unusual rewards to those with whom he was satisfied, and some slight blows to all whose work should not please him, or who had deserved blame or punishment earlier. To the cithara players and the singers he had ordered beforehand liberal pay. At last, sitting in the garden under a beech, through whose leaves the sun-rays marked the earth with bright spots, he called Eunice.

She came, dressed in white, with a sprig of myrtle in her hair, beautiful as one of the Graces. He seated her at his side, and, touching her temple gently with his fingers, he gazed at her with that admiration with which a critic gazes at a statue from the chisel of a master.

"Eunice," asked he, "dost thou know that thou art not a slave this long time?"

She raised to him her calm eyes, as blue as the sky, and denied with a motion of her head.

"I am thine always," said she.

"But perhaps thou knowest not," continued Petronius, "that the villa, and those slaves twining wreaths here, and all which is in the villa, with the fields and the herds, are thine henceforward."

Eunice, when she heard this, drew away from him quickly, and asked in a voice filled with sudden fear, —

"Why dost thou tell me this?"

Then she approached again, and looked at him, blinking with amazement. After a while her face became as pale as linen. He smiled, and said only one word, —

"So!"

A moment of silence followed; merely a slight breeze moved the leaves of the beech.

Petronius might have thought that before him was a statue cut from white marble.

"Eunice," said he, "I wish to die calmly."

And the maiden, looking at him with a heart-rending smile, whispered, — "I hear thee."

In the evening the guests, who had been at feasts given by Petronius previously, and knew that in comparison with them even Cæsar's banquets seemed tiresome and barbarous, began to arrive in numbers. To no one did it occur, even, that that was to be the last "symposium." Many knew, it is true, that the clouds of Cæsar's anger were hanging over the exquisite arbiter; but that had happened so often, and Petronius had been able so often to scatter them by some dexterous act or by a single bold word, that no one thought really that serious danger threatened him. His glad face and usual smile, free of care, confirmed all, to the last man, in that opinion. The beautiful Eunice, to whom he had declared his wish to die calmly, and for whom every word of his was like an utterance of fate, had in her features a perfect calmness, and in her eyes a kind of wonderful radiance, which might have been considered delight. At the door of the triclinium, youths with hair in golden nets put wreaths of roses on the heads of the guests, warning them, as the custom was, to pass the threshold right foot foremost. In the hall there was a slight odor of violets; the lamps burned in Alexandrian glass of various colors. At the couches stood Grecian maidens, whose office it was to moisten the feet of guests with perfumes. At the walls cithara players and Athenian choristers were waiting for the signal of their leader.

The table service gleamed with splendor, but that splendor did not offend or oppress; it seemed a natural development. Joyousness and freedom spread through the hall with the odor of violets. The guests as they entered felt that neither threat nor constraint was hanging over them, as in Cæsar's house, where a man might forfeit his life for praises not sufficiently great or sufficiently apposite. At sight of the lamps, the goblets entwined with ivy, the wine cooling on banks of snow, and the exquisite dishes, the hearts of the guests became joyous. Conversation of various kinds began to buzz, as bees buzz on an apple-tree in blossom. At moments it was interrupted by an outburst of glad laughter, at moments by murmurs of applause, at moments by a kiss placed too loudly on some white shoulder.

The guests, while drinking wine, spilled from their goblets a few drops to the immortal gods, to gain their protection, and their favor for the host. It mattered not that many of them had no belief in the gods. Custom and superstition prescribed it. Petronius, inclining near Eunice, talked of Rome, of the latest divorces, of love affairs, of the races, of Spiculus, who had become famous recently in the arena, and of the latest books in the shops of Atractus and the Sozii. When he spilled wine, he said that he spilled it only in honor of the Lady of Cyprus, the most ancient divinity and the greatest, the only immortal, enduring, and ruling one.

His conversation was like sunlight which lights up some new object every instant, or like the summer breeze which stirs flowers in a garden. At last he gave a signal to the leader of the music, and at that signal the citharæ began to sound lightly, and youthful voices accompanied. Then maidens from Kos, the birthplace of Eunice, danced, and showed their rosy forms through robes of gauze. Finally, an Egyptian soothsayer told the guests their future from the movement of rainbow colors in a vessel of crystal.

When they had enough of these amusements, Petronius rose somewhat on his Syrian cushion, and said with hesitation, —

"Pardon me, friends, for asking a favor at a feast. Will each man accept as a gift that goblet from which he first shook wine in honor of the gods and to my prosperity?"

The goblets of Petronius were gleaming in gold, precious stones, and the carving of artists; hence, though giftgiving was common in Rome, delight filled every heart. Some thanked him loudly: others said that Jove had never honored gods with such gifts in Olympus; finally, there were some who refused to accept, since the gifts surpassed common estimate.

But he raised aloft the Myrrhene vase, which resembled a rainbow in brilliancy, and was simply beyond price.

"This," said he, "is the one out of which I poured in honor of the Lady of Cyprus. The lips of no man may touch it henceforth, and no hand may ever pour from it in honor of another divinity."

He cast the precious vessel to the pavement, which was covered with lily-colored saffron flowers; and when it was broken into small pieces, he said, seeing around him astonished faces, —

"My dear friends, be glad and not astonished. Old age and weakness are sad attendants in the last years of life. But I will give you a good example and good advice: Ye have the power, as ye see, not to wait for old age; ye can depart before it comes, as I do."

"What dost thou wish?" asked a number of voices, with alarm.

"I wish to rejoice, to drink wine, to hear music, to look on those divine forms which ye see around me, and fall asleep with a garlanded head. I have taken farewell of Cæsar, and do ye wish to hear what I wrote him at parting?"

He took from beneath the purple cushion a paper, and read as follows: —

"I know, O Cæsar, that thou art awaiting my arrival with impatience, that thy true heart of a friend is yearning day and night for me. I know that thou art ready to cover me with gifts, make me prefect of the pretorian guards, and command Tigellinus to be that which the gods made him, a mule-driver in those lands which thou didst inherit after poisoning Domitius. Pardon me, however, for I swear to thee by Hades, and by the shades of thy mother, thy wife, thy brother, and Seneca, that I cannot go to thee. Life is a great treasure. I have taken the most precious jewels from that treasure, but in life there are many things which I cannot endure any longer. Do not suppose, I pray, that I am offended because thou didst kill thy mother, thy wife, and thy brother; that thou didst burn Rome and send to Erebus all the honest men in thy dominions. No, grandson of Chronos. Death is the inheritance of man; from thee other deeds could not have been expected. But to destroy one's ear for whole years with thy poetry, to see thy belly of a Domitius on slim legs whirled about in Pyrrhic dance; to hear thy music, thy declamation, thy doggerel verses, wretched poet of the suburbs, — is a thing surpassing my power, and it has roused in me the wish to die. Rome stuffs its ears when it hears thee; the world reviles thee. I can blush for thee no longer, and I have no wish to do so. The howls of Cerberus, though resembling thy music, will be less offensive to me, for I have never been the friend of Cerberus, and I need not be ashamed of his howling. Farewell, but make no music; commit murder, but write no verses; poison people, but dance not; be an incendiary, but play not on a cithara. This is the wish and the last friendly counsel sent thee by the — Arbiter Elegantiæ."

The guests were terrified, for they knew that the loss of dominion would have been less cruel to Nero than this blow. They understood, too, that the man who had written that paper must die; and at the same time pale fear flew over them because they had heard such a paper.

But Petronius laughed with sincere and gladsome joy, as if it were a question of the most innocent joke; then he cast his eyes on all present, and said, —

"Be joyous, and drive away fear. No one need boast that he heard this letter. I will boast of it only to Charon when I am crossing in the boat with him."

He beckoned then to the Greek physician, and stretched out his arm. The skilled Greek in the twinkle of an eye opened the vein at the bend of the arm. Blood spurted on the cushion, and covered Eunice, who, supporting the head of Petronius, bent over him and said, —

"Didst thou think that I would leave thee? If the gods gave me immortality, and Cæsar gave me power over the earth, I would follow thee still."

Petronius smiled, raised himself a little, touched her lips with his, and said, —
"Come with me."

She stretched her rosy arm to the physician, and after a while her blood began to mingle and be lost in his blood.

Then he gave a signal to the leader of the music, and again the voices and citharæ were heard. They sang "Harmodius"; next the song of Anacreon resounded, — that song in which he complained that on a time he had found Aphrodite's boy chilled and weeping under trees; that he brought him in, warmed him, dried his wings, and the ungrateful child pierced his heart with an arrow, — from that moment peace had deserted the poet.

Petronius and Eunice, resting against each other, beautiful as two divinities, listened, smiling and growing pale. At the end of the song Petronius gave directions to serve more wine and food; then he conversed with the guests sitting near him of trifling but pleasant things, such as are mentioned usually at feasts. Finally, he called to the Greek to bind his arm for a moment; for he said that sleep was tormenting him, and he wanted to yield himself to Hypnos before Thanatos put him to sleep forever.

In fact, he fell asleep. When he woke, the head of Eunice was lying on his breast like a white flower. He placed it on the pillow to look at it once more. After that his veins were opened again.

At his signal the singers raised the song of Anacreon anew, and the citharæ accompanied them so softly as not to drown a word. Petronius grew paler and paler; but when the last sound had ceased, he turned to his guests again and said, —

"Friends, confess that with us perishes — "

But he had not power to finish; his arm with its last movement embraced Eunice, his head fell on the pillow, and he died.

The guests looking at those two white forms, which resembled two wonderful statues, understood well that with them perished all that was left to their world at that time, — poetry and beauty.

EPILOGUE

AT first the revolt of the Gallic legions under Vindex did not seem very serious. Cæsar was only in his thirty-first year, and no one was bold enough to hope that the world could be freed so soon from the nightmare which was stifling it. Men remembered that revolts had occurred more than once among the legions, — they had occurred in previous reigns, — revolts, however, which passed without involving a change of government; as during the reign of Tiberius, Drusus put down the revolt of the Pannonian legions. "Who," said the people, "can take the government after Nero, since all the descendants of the divine Augustus have perished?" Others, looking at the Colossus, imagined him a Hercules, and thought that no force could break such power. There were those even who since he went to Achæa were sorry for him, because Helius and Polythetes, to whom he left the government of Rome and Italy, governed more murderously than he had.

No one was sure of life or property. Law ceased to protect. Human dignity and virtue had perished, family bonds existed no longer, and degraded hearts did not even dare to admit hope. From Greece came accounts of the incomparable triumphs of Cæsar, of the thousands of crowns which he had won, the thousands of competitors whom he had vanquished. The world seemed to be one orgy of buffoonery and blood; but at the same time the opinion was fixed that virtue and deeds of dignity had ceased, that the time of dancing and music, of profligacy, of blood, had come, and that life must flow on for the future in that way. Cæsar himself, to whom rebellion opened the road to new robberies, was not concerned much about the revolt of the legions and Vindex; he even expressed his delight on that subject frequently. He did not wish to leave Achæa even; and only when Helius informed him that further delay might cause the loss of dominion did he move to Naples.

There he played and sang, neglecting news of events of growing danger. In vain did Tigellinus explain to him that former rebellions of legions had no leaders, while at the head of affairs this time was a man descended from the ancient kings of Gaul and Aquitania, a famous and tried soldier. "Here," answered Nero, "the Greeks listen to me, — the Greeks, who alone know how to listen, and who alone are worthy of my song." He said that his first duty was art and glory. But when at last the news came that Vindex had proclaimed him a wretched artist, he sprang up and moved toward Rome. The wounds inflicted by Petronius, and healed by his stay in Greece, opened in his heart anew, and he wished to seek retribution from the Senate for such unheard-of injustice.

On the road he saw a group cast in bronze, representing a Gallic warrior as overcome by a Roman knight; he considered that a good omen, and thenceforward, if he mentioned the rebellious legions and Vindex, it was only to ridicule them. His entrance to the city surpassed all that had been witnessed earlier. He entered in the chariot used by Augustus in his triumph. One arch of the Circus was destroyed to give a road to the procession. The Senate, knights, and innumerable throngs of people went forth to meet him. The walls trembled from shouts of "Hail, Augustus! Hail, Hercules! Hail, divinity, the incomparable, the Olympian, the Pythian, the immortal!" Behind him were borne the crowns, the names of cities in which he had triumphed; and on tablets were inscribed the names of the masters whom he had vanquished. Nero himself was intoxicated with delight, and with emotion he asked the Augustians who stood around him, "What was the triumph of Julius compared with this?" The idea that any mortal should dare to raise a hand on such a demigod did not enter his head. He felt himself really Olympian, and therefore safe. The excitement and the madness of the crowd roused his own madness. In fact, it might seem in the day of that triumph that not merely Cæsar and the city, but the world, had lost its senses.

Through the flowers and the piles of wreaths no one could see the precipice. Still that same evening columns and walls of temples were covered with inscriptions, describing Nero's crimes, threatening him with coming vengeance, and ridiculing him as an artist. From mouth to mouth went the phrase, "He sang till he roused the Gauls." Alarming news made the rounds of the city, and reached enormous measures. Alarm seized the Augustians. People, uncertain of the future, dared not express hopes or wishes; they hardly dared to feel or think.

But he went on living only in the theatre and music. Instruments newly invented occupied him, and a new water-organ, of which trials were made on the Palatine. With childish mind, incapable of plan or action, he imagined that he could ward off danger by promises of spectacles and theatrical exhibitions reaching far into the future. Persons nearest him, seeing that instead of providing means and an army, he was merely searching for expressions to depict the danger graphically, began to lose their heads. Others thought that he was simply deafening himself and others with quotations, while in his soul he was alarmed and terrified. In fact, his acts became feverish. Every day a thousand new plans flew through his head. At times he sprang up to rush out against danger; gave command to pack up his lutes and citharæ, to arm the young slave women as Amazons, and lead the legions to the East. Again he thought to finish the rebellion of the Gallic legions, not with war, but with song; and his soul laughed at the spectacle which was to follow his conquest of the soldiers by song. The legionaries would surround him with tears in their eyes; he would sing to them an epinicium, after which the golden epoch would begin for him and for Rome. At one time he called for blood; at another he declared that he would be satisfied with governing in Egypt. He recalled the prediction which promised him lordship in Jerusalem, and he was moved by the thought that as a wandering minstrel he would earn his daily bread, — that cities and countries would honor in him, not Cæsar, the lord of the earth, but a poet whose like the world had not produced before.

And so he struggled, raged, played, sang, changed his plan, changed his quotations, changed his life and the world into a dream absurd, fantastic, dreadful, into an uproarious hunt composed of unnatural expressions, bad verses, groans, tears, and blood; but meanwhile the cloud in the west was increasing and thickening every day. The measure was exceeded; the insane comedy was nearing its end.

When news that Galba and Spain had joined the uprising came to his ears, he fell into rage and madness. He broke goblets, overturned the table at a feast, and issued orders which neither Helius nor Tigellinus himself dared to execute. To kill Gauls resident in Rome, fire the city a second time, let out the wild beasts, and transfer the capital to Alexandria seemed to him great, astonishing, and easy. But the days of his dominion had passed, and even those who shared in his former crimes began to look on him as a madman.

The death of Vindex, and disagreement in the revolting legions seemed, however, to turn the scale to his side. Again new feasts, new triumphs, and new sentences were issued in Rome, till a certain night when a messenger rushed up on a foaming horse, with the news that in the city itself the soldiers had raised the standard of revolt, and proclaimed Galba Cæsar.

Nero was asleep when the messenger came; but when he woke he called in vain for the night-guard, which watched at the entrance to his chambers. The palace was empty. Slaves were plundering in the most distant corners that which could be taken most quickly. But the sight of Nero frightened them; he wandered alone through the palace, filling it with cries of despair and fear.

At last his freedmen, Phaon, Sporus, and Epaphroditus, came to his rescue. They wished him to flee, and said that there was no time to be lost; but he deceived himself still. If he should dress in mourning and speak to the Senate, would it resist his prayers and eloquence? If he should use all his eloquence, his rhetoric and skill of an actor, would any one on earth have power to resist him? Would they not give him even the prefecture of Egypt?

The freedmen, accustomed to flatter, had not the boldness yet to refuse him directly; they only warned him that before he could reach the Forum the people would tear him to pieces, and declared that if he did not mount his horse immediately, they too would desert him.

Phaon offered refuge in his villa outside the Nomentan Gate. After a while they mounted horses, and, covering Nero's head with a mantle, they galloped off toward the edge of the city. The night was growing pale. But on the streets there was a movement which showed the exceptional nature of the time. Soldiers, now singly and now in small groups, were scattered through the city. Not far from the camp Cæsar's horse sprang aside suddenly at sight of a corpse. The mantle slipped from his head; a soldier recognized Nero, and, confused by the unexpected meeting, gave the military salute. While passing the pretorian camp, they heard thundering shouts in honor of Galba. Nero understood at last that the hour of death was near. Terror and reproaches of conscience seized him. He declared that he saw darkness in front of him in the form of a black cloud. From that cloud came forth faces in which he saw his mother, his wife, and his brother. His teeth were chattering from fright; still his soul of a comedian found a kind of charm in the horror of the moment. To be absolute lord of the earth and lose all things, seemed to him the height of tragedy; and faithful to himself, he played the first rôle to the end. A fever for quotations took possession of him, and a passionate wish that those present should preserve them for posterity. At moments he said that he wished to die, and called for Spiculus, the most skilled of all gladiators in killing. At moments he declaimed, "Mother, wife, father, call me to death!" Flashes of hope rose in him, however, from time to time, — hope vain and childish. He knew that he was going to death, and still he did not believe it.

They found the Nomentan Gate open. Going farther, they passed near Ostrianum, where Peter had taught and baptized. At daybreak they reached Phaon's villa.

There the freedmen hid from him no longer the fact that it was time to die. He gave command then to dig a grave, and lay on the ground so that they might take accurate measurement. At sight of the earth thrown up, however, terror seized him. His fat face became pale, and on his forehead sweat stood like drops of dew in the morning. He delayed. In a voice at once abject and theatrical, he declared that the hour had not come yet; then he began again to quote. At last he begged them to burn his body. "What an artist is perishing!" repeated he, as if in amazement.

Meanwhile Phaon's messenger arrived with the announcement that the Senate had issued the sentence that the "parricide" was to be punished according to ancient custom.

"What is the ancient custom?" asked Nero, with whitened lips.

"They will fix thy neck in a fork, flog thee to death, and hurl thy body into the Tiber," answered Epaphroditus, abruptly.

Nero drew aside the robe from his breast.

"It is time, then!" said he, looking into the sky. And he repeated once more, "What an artist is perishing!"

At that moment the tramp of a horse was heard. That was the centurion coming with soldiers for the head of Ahenobarbus.

"Hurry!" cried the freedmen.

Nero placed the knife to his neck, but pushed it only timidly. It was clear that he would never have courage to thrust it in. Epaphroditus pushed his hand suddenly, — the knife sank to the handle. Nero's eyes turned in his head, terrible, immense, frightened.

"I bring thee life!" cried the centurion, entering.

"Too late!" said Nero, with a hoarse voice; then he added, —

"Here is faithfulness!"

In a twinkle death seized his head. Blood from his heavy neck gushed in a dark stream on the flowers of the garden. His legs kicked the ground, and he died.

On the morrow the faithful Acte wrapped his body in costly stuffs, and burned him on a pile filled with perfumes.

And so Nero passed, as a whirlwind, as a storm, as a fire, as war or death passes; but the basilica of Peter rules till now, from the Vatican heights, the city, and the world.

Near the ancient Porta Capena stands to this day a little chapel with the inscription, somewhat worn: *Quo Vadis, Domine?*